# The
# Cursed Harvest Collection

Harvest of the Damned, The Harvest Haunting
Witches of the Blood Moon, Crypts of the Shadow Court

## Penny Blood Adventures

# The Cursed Harvest Collection

# Collect All The Penny Blood Adventures

## Adventures

- The Dark Nun's Church
- Marie Laveau's Army
- The Werewolves of London
- The Thirteenth Hour
- The Mad Lab
- Krampus
- Midwinter Vampires
- Walk the Plank
- The Leprechaun's Trap
- Mutanti - Whispers of War

- Mutanti - Tears of War
- Mutanti - Lords of War
- The New Dark Age
- Crescent Moon Circus
- Catalyst
- Clockwork Tower
- Gorgon
- The Illustrated Troll
- Witches of the Blood Moon
- The Christmas Chronicles of Winterglen

- The Dragon's Heir
- Pyramids of Power
- Dragon's Rise
- Crypts of the Shadow Court
- Dragon's War
- Battle Cry!
- The Triskelion Prophecy
- Wasteland Chronicles: Beyond The Wall
- Harvest of the Damned

## Compilations

- Gothic Horror - 5 Gothic Horror themed Adventures
- PBA Vol 1 - 4 Adventures
- The Mutanti Cycle
- The Shattering
- Mysteries of Myth and Machine

## Supplemental Rules Books

- Arcane Codex
- Creatures of the Realm
- Gourmet Guildmaster
- Breath of the Dragon
- Stories of the Fey
- Pocket Game Master: Magic Items
- Wasteland Chronicles: The Wasteland

## Credits

Author: M A D (aka, Matthew David)

Editor: Alysson Wyatt

Lead Game Testing: Team Wyatt

Game Testers: All of Team Wyatt's friends - you guys rock!

Artists: Adobe Stock Art, Adobe Firefly, Adobe Photoshop, DALL-E, Midjourney

# The Cursed Harvest

# Harvest of the Damned

# Managing Encounters

To help DMs tailor the adventure to the party, each encounter is designed with flexibility in mind. Whether your group consists of fledgling adventurers or seasoned heroes, the provided guidelines will help ensure that the challenges are both fun and fair.

## Encounter Structure

**Encounter Name**: The title of the encounter, usually indicating the primary theme or challenge.

**DM Information**: A brief summary to give you a clear picture of the encounter's purpose and its role in the overall adventure.

**Read Aloud**: Descriptive text meant to be read verbatim to the players, setting the scene and atmosphere.

**Activity**: Detailed guidance, including potential variations, expected player strategies, and potential outcomes.

**Lair Actions**: Specific actions or effects that occur in certain locations, often benefiting the encounter's primary antagonist.

**Scaling the Encounter**: Instructions on how to adjust the encounter's difficulty based on player levels:

- **Beginner (Level 1-5)**: Simplified challenges tailored for newer or less powerful characters.

- **Intermediate (Level 6-10)**: Moderate challenges that require a mix of skill, strategy, and teamwork.

- **Advanced (Level 11+)**: Complex and multi-faceted challenges suitable for veteran adventurers.

**Monster and/or NPC**: Details or references to any creatures or characters the players might interact with during the encounter.

Encounters may reference content found later in the book, such as detailed monster statistics in the Monsters section. Feel free to adapt or replace these elements to better fit your group's preferences or the storyline you're weaving.

## Modularity and Flexibility

This adventure, like all Penny Blood Adventures, is modular by design. If a particular monster or challenge doesn't resonate with your campaign's theme, feel free to replace it or adjust as needed. The goal is to provide a rich framework that sparks inspiration, allowing you to craft an unforgettable journey for your players.

# Starting the Adventure

The player characters have been hired by a wealthy merchant from a neighboring town to investigate why trade with Crow's Hollow has suddenly ceased. All messengers sent to inquire have not returned, and disturbing rumors of an unusually bountiful harvest despite region-wide drought have begun to circulate. The merchant fears something sinister may be afoot and wants the players to uncover the truth and, if necessary, deal with any threats to restore normal trade relations.

## What the DM Needs to Know

Crow's Hollow is under the influence of an eldritch entity known as The Rows, which has corrupted the land and many of its inhabitants. A cult called the Reapers of Abundance works to expand The Rows' influence. Players will uncover the dark secrets of the town, face supernatural threats, and ultimately confront The Rows itself. The adventure balances investigation, social interaction, and combat as players work to free Crow's Hollow from The Rows' grip.

## Open World Structure

This adventure is designed as an open world game, allowing players to explore Crow's Hollow and its surrounding locations freely. While players can approach the mystery in any order they choose, it is recommended that they begin their investigation at the Crow's Nest Tavern, which serves as a central hub of information and activity in the town. The rest of the locations are listed in alphabetical order.

As your party approaches Crow's Hollow, an unsettling quiet hangs in the air. The surrounding countryside shows signs of a severe drought, yet ahead of you stretch lush cornfields as far as the eye can see. The town itself seems eerily still, with few people visible on the streets. A sickly-sweet scent carries on the breeze, mingling with an underlying note of decay. Something is clearly amiss in this small farming community, and it falls to you to uncover the dark secrets that lurk beneath the facade of an abundant harvest. Your journey begins at the Crow's Nest Tavern, where you hope to gather information and begin piecing together the mystery that shrouds Crow's Hollow. Will you be able to unravel the truth and free this town from whatever malevolent force holds it in its grip?

# Encounters in Crow's Hollow

## Crow's Nest Tavern

The Crow's Nest tavern serves as the starting point for the adventure, introducing players to the eerie atmosphere of Crow's Hollow. Barkeep Mabel is a key NPC who can provide information, but she is also secretly a high-ranking cult member.

As you approach the building, you see a cozy, rustic tavern with a thatched roof. Cornhusk decorations adorn the exterior, swaying gently in the breeze. The sign above the door creaks, bearing the name "Crow's Nest Tavern" in faded paint.

Stepping inside, you're enveloped by the warm scent of freshly baked cornbread and ale. The interior is dimly lit by lanterns, casting dancing shadows on the walls. Patrons sit at wooden tables, their conversations a low murmur punctuated by occasional laughter. Behind the bar, a stout middle-aged woman with graying hair tied in a bun polishes glasses, her amber eyes scanning the room attentively.

## Activities

**Tavern Talk:** Engage in conversation with Barkeep Mabel and various patrons to gather information about recent strange occurrences in Crow's Hollow. This may involve making Charisma (Persuasion) checks or offering to buy drinks to loosen tongues.

**Whispers in the Dark:** Position yourself near groups of patrons to overhear hushed conversations about missing persons. This might require successful Wisdom (Perception) checks or creative use of magic to eavesdrop without being noticed.

**Hidden in Plain Sight:** Carefully examine the tavern's decor to notice subtle cult symbols hidden throughout. This could involve making Intelligence (Investigation) checks to spot and potentially recognize the significance of these symbols.

# People in the Tavern

In *Harvest of the Damned*, the interactions with NPCs in the Crow's Nest Tavern are designed to be a blend of mystery and discovery. As the Dungeon Master (DM), it's essential to convey to your players that while NPCs may offer assistance, their true intentions and capabilities are not immediately apparent. Unlike typical adventures where NPC abilities might be revealed out of character, in this module players will need to uncover these details through in-character roleplay and interaction.

The special skills or detriments associated with each NPC are not meant to be disclosed directly to the players. Instead, encourage them to engage with the NPCs, ask questions, and observe behaviors to deduce who might be an ally or a hindrance. This approach adds an extra layer of challenge and immersion, as the players will have to rely on their characters' judgments rather than metagame knowledge.

Remind your players that NPCs can sometimes provide unique bonuses or effects, but in this adventure, the only way to discover these is through careful roleplay. Encourage them to explore the social dynamics within the tavern, as these interactions will be crucial in determining their next steps in unraveling the mysteries of Crow's Hollow.

Below is a table of the people in the Crow's Nest Tavern:

| Name | Cult Connection | Short Backstory | Information | Special Skill (Benefit / Detriment) |
|---|---|---|---|---|
| Edith Thatcher | None | Elderly widow, former schoolteacher | Noticed children drawing strange symbols in class | Grants advantage on Intelligence (Religion) checks to identify cult symbols |
| Giles Blackwood | High-ranking cultist | Sarah Blackwood's uncle, local farmer | Knows identities of several cult members | Can cast *Entangle* (DC 13) once per day to hinder PCs |
| Millicent Cooperton | Unwitting cult influence | Young barmaid, dreams of leaving town | Overheard cultists discussing a "harvest" | Grants PCs advantage on Wisdom (Perception) checks to eavesdrop in the tavern |
| Bartholomew Stout | None | Town drunk, former gravedigger | Saw strange lights in the cemetery at night | Provides a map that gives advantage on Survival checks in the cemetery area |
| Prudence Whitby | Low-ranking cultist | Midwife, recently indoctrinated | Knows of pregnant women targeted for "special births" | Can provide poison that deals 2d6 poison damage (DC 12 Con save) |
| Jasper Duncan | None | Traveling merchant, new in town | Noticed unusual crop patterns in surrounding fields | Allows PCs to buy common items at 75% of their listed price |
| Winifred Moss | Resisting cult influence | Local hedge witch, suspicious of recent events | Aware of Old Man Jenkins' existence and location | Can cast *Augury* once for the PCs without material components |
| Cornelius Thorne | High-ranking cultist | Mayor Abigail Thorne's brother, town councilor | Knows the location of the Secret Cult Hideout | Can impose disadvantage on PCs' Charisma checks with townsfolk once per day |
| Beatrice Felton | None | Gossipy housewife, loves to chat | Heard rumors of people going missing near the Old Mill | Grants advantage on one Charisma (Persuasion) check to gather information in town |
| Silas Crookshank | Unwitting cult pawn | Simple-minded farmhand | Saw Sarah Blackwood performing a strange ritual | Can help PCs once with a Strength check, adding +5 to their roll |

## Tavern Talk

As the PCs engage in conversation with Barkeep Mabel and the patrons, they'll need to navigate a series of social interactions and skill checks. The outcome of these interactions will nudge them towards either opposing or potentially joining the cult.

**Initial Approach**: PCs must make a Charisma (Persuasion) check (DC 13) to get Mabel or a patron to open up about recent events. Success allows them to ask one question from the Information Gathering list below. Failure results in suspicious looks and a disadvantage on the next Charisma check in the tavern.

**Buying Drinks**: PCs can spend 1 gp to buy a series of drinks for a patron or 5 gp to buy a round for the entire tavern. This grants advantage on the next Charisma (Persuasion) check with the recipient(s). If they buy Mabel's special corn whiskey (3 sp per drink), the drinker must make a DC 13 Wisdom saving throw or be charmed by Mabel for 1 hour, potentially making them more susceptible to pro-cult rhetoric.

### Information Gathering

For each successful check or drink bought, PCs can receive an answer to one question. Some example questions PCs could ask (but are not limited to) are below:

- "Have there been any strange occurrences lately?"
- "Are there any local legends about the harvest?"
- "Has anyone gone missing recently?"
- "Have you noticed anything unusual about the crops this year?"

**Insight Checks**: After each response, PCs can make a Wisdom (Insight) check (DC 15) to determine if the responder is hiding something or lying. Success reveals additional, potentially contradictory information. On a critical success (20 on the die), the PC notices that the NPC is wearing a peculiar symbol. Describe this symbol without explicitly stating its connection to the cult, allowing the players to piece together its significance through further investigation.

For example, you might describe the symbol as:

- "A small, intricately carved pendant shaped like a stylized corn husk, the edges faintly glinting in the dim light."
- "A brooch resembling an eye made of twisted metal, with an unsettlingly lifelike pupil etched at its center."
- "A simple ring with a design of intertwining vines, the pattern almost seeming to shift when not directly observed."

To identify the symbol, the PC must succeed at an Intelligence (Religion) check (DC varies), which the DM may roll in secret. The result of this check will determine how much the PC knows about the symbol and its connection to the cult (refer to the **Hidden in Plain Sight** activity for DC results and detailed descriptions).

**Escalation**: If PCs ask too many probing questions (3 or more), Mabel will use her Whispers of The Rows ability on the most inquisitive PC.

The targeted PC must succeed on a DC 13 Wisdom saving throw or be stunned until the end of their next turn as disturbing visions of endless cornfields flood their mind.

This event should serve as a clear indicator that something is amiss in the tavern.

**Outcome**: Based on the information gathered and the PCs' reactions:

If PCs express concern or a desire to investigate further, Edith Thatcher or Winifred Moss may approach them privately, urging them to look into the strange events and offering their assistance.

If PCs seem intrigued by the promise of abundance or power, Giles Blackwood or Prudence Whitby might subtly hint at the "benefits" of joining the Reapers of Abundance.

### Skill Challenge

To conclude the **Tavern Talk** activity, run a quick skill challenge where each PC must make a different skill check to process the information they've gathered:

- Intelligence (Investigation) DC 14: Connect the dots between various pieces of information.
- Wisdom (Insight) DC 14: Gauge the overall mood and undercurrent of fear in the tavern.
- Charisma (Deception) DC 14: Pretend to be uninterested to avoid arousing suspicion.
- Intelligence (Religion) DC 14: Recall any lore about cults or eldritch entities that matches what they've learned.

If the party succeeds on at least 3 out of 4 checks, they gain a clear direction for their next steps (investigating the Old Mill, speaking with Old Man Jenkins on the outskirts of town, etc.). If they fail, they leave the tavern with a sense of unease but no clear course of action.

## Whispers in the Dark

As the PCs attempt to eavesdrop on hushed conversations, they'll need to use their skills and potentially magic to gather information without arousing suspicion.

**Positioning**: PCs must succeed on a Charisma (Stealth or Deception) check (DC 12) to position themselves inconspicuously near a group of whispering patrons. Failure alerts the group, causing them to stop talking or change the subject.

**Eavesdropping**: Once in position, PCs make a Wisdom (Perception) check (DC 14) to overhear the conversation clearly. Success allows them to hear one snippet of conversation from the list below. With each subsequent check, increase the DC by 1 as patrons become more wary. Each PC attempting to eavesdrop may also need to make a Charisma (Stealth or Deception) check (DC 14) to avoid being noticed.

**Extended Eavesdropping**: For every 10 minutes of successful eavesdropping, roll a d20. On a 18-20, Barkeep Mabel notices the PC's suspicious behavior and approaches to investigate.

**Consequences**: If a PC fails a Stealth or Deception check by 5 or more, they accidentally knock over a drink or make a noticeable noise.

This requires a Charisma (Deception) check (DC 14) to play off as an accident, or the suspicious patrons may alert Barkeep Mabel.

**Escalation**: If the PCs are caught eavesdropping multiple times, Barkeep Mabel secretly uses her "Whispers of The Rows" ability on the most persistent PC.

The targeted PC must succeed on a DC 13 Wisdom saving throw or be stunned until the end of their next turn, experiencing disturbing visions of cornfields and hearing whispers that seem to know their thoughts.

### Magical Assistance

PCs can use spells to aid their eavesdropping:

*Enhance Ability* (Owl's Wisdom or Fox's Cunning): Advantage on Wisdom (Perception) checks to better overhear other patrons' conversations, or advantage on Intelligence (Investigation) checks to piece together overheard information.

*Clairvoyance*: Automatically succeed on hearing a conversation within the tavern. This spell requires a fair amount of planning to use in this situation, as it takes 10 minutes to cast and has verbal, somatic and material components, inviting suspicion from those who witness its casting.

*Detect Thoughts*: Gain advantage on Wisdom (Insight) checks to determine the truthfulness of overheard statements. Like *Clairvoyance*, this spell requires planning to pull off successfully as the spell has verbal, somatic and material components, meaning witnesses will know you cast a spell. Additionally, the spell only lasts for one minute, giving the caster a limited time (10 rounds) to take advantage of it. If the caster uses it to probe beyond surface thoughts (forcing a Wisdom save from the target), the person will realize you're probing into their mind.

### What the PCs Overhear

For each successful Perception check or magical eavesdrop, the PCs overhear one of the following snippets (roll 1d10 or choose based on story progression):

- "...third person this month. Always near the Old Mill..."
- "...Thorne family's been acting strange lately. Mayor Abigail's eyes... did you notice?"
- "...crops growing too fast. Unnatural, I tell you. And that smell..."
- "...screams from the cornfields at night. Like something's hunting..."
- "...old Jenkins knows something. Saw him arguing with the mayor last week..."
- "...Blackwood girl leading some kind of ritual in the woods. Chanting and such..."
- "...tavern's cellar. Secret meetings, they say. But what for?"
- "...pregnant women disappearing. They say it's for 'special births'..."
- "...standing stone in the clearing. Symbols glowing at midnight..."
- "...whispers in the corn. It speaks to them, tells them who to take..."

**Insight and Investigation**: After overhearing a snippet, PCs can make a Wisdom (Insight) check (DC 13) to determine the speakers' emotional state and truthfulness.

They can also make an Intelligence (Investigation) check (DC 15) to connect the information overheard with other clues they've gathered.

## Hidden in Plain Sight

As the PCs examine the tavern's decor, they'll need to use their observational skills and knowledge to uncover and understand the hidden cult symbols.

**Spotting Symbols**: PCs must succeed on an initial Intelligence (Perception or Investigation) check (DC 14) to notice a strange, repeating shape in a decorative pattern (Perception) or spot a hidden symbol (Investigation). After the initial check, Perception will no longer help to find more. Only by rolling subsequent Investigation checks can PCs locate more hidden symbols. A successful check allows them to spot one symbol from the list below. Each subsequent check increases the DC by 1 as the remaining symbols become harder to find.

**Recognizing Symbols**: After spotting a symbol, PCs can make an Intelligence (Religion) check to understand its significance.

- DC 12: Recognize it as a cult symbol.
- DC 15: Understand its basic meaning.

- DC 18: Comprehend its full significance and magical properties.

**Magical Detection**: Casting *Detect Magic* will cause all the hidden symbols to glow faintly, granting advantage on Intelligence (Investigation) checks to spot them. Casting *Identify* on a symbol reveals its magical properties and lore.

**Consequences**: If a PC fails a Perception or Investigation check by 5 or more, they accidentally knock something over while searching, drawing attention. This requires a Charisma (Deception) check (DC 13) to play off as clumsiness, or risk alerting Barkeep Mabel.

## Symbol Details and Effects

### The Endless Rows

A series of horizontal parallel lines etched into wooden surfaces, often disguised as part of the grain pattern. The lines subtly undulate, giving an unsettling impression of movement when viewed from the corner of one's eye.

**Lore**: Represents The Rows' infinite expanse and its desire for endless growth.

**Impact**: Creatures within 5 feet of the symbol have disadvantage on Wisdom saving throws against plant-based magic.

**Informant**: Edith Thatcher can recognize this from children's drawings, hinting at the cult's influence on the young.

### The Watchful Kernel

A stylized eye shape formed by a central almond-shaped kernel surrounded by delicately carved corn husks radiating outward. The pupil of the eye sometimes appears to dilate in low light conditions.

**Lore**: Symbolizes The Rows' omniscience and constant surveillance of its domain.

**Impact**: The symbol functions as an *Alarm* spell, alerting cultists when non-cultists linger near it.

**Informant**: Bartholomew Stout noticed similar symbols in the cemetery, connecting the cult to the recent grave disturbances.

### The Bountiful Chalice

A goblet or mug shape formed by intertwining corn stalks. The cup's contents are depicted as a swirling mass of kernels that seem to spill over the rim, forming a cascade of abundance.

**Lore**: Represents the abundance and prosperity promised by The Rows.

**Impact**: Anyone who drinks within 5 feet of this symbol must make a DC 13 Wisdom save or be charmed for 1 hour, feeling an overwhelming sense of gratitude towards the tavern and its patrons.

**Informant**: Millicent Cooperton can share that patrons near this symbol tend to be more generous tippers, hinting at its subtle influence.

### The Rooted One

A gnarled tree trunk that, upon closer inspection, is composed of tightly wound corn stalks. The roots spread out at the base, morphing into writhing tendrils that look almost animal-like.

**Lore**: Symbolizes The Rows' deep connection to the land and its corrupting influence.

**Impact**: Plants within 10 feet of this symbol grow at twice the normal rate and appear slightly twisted.

**Informant**: Jasper Duncan noticed similar patterns in crop growth around town, indicating The Rows' spreading influence.

### The Harvest's Scythe

A curved blade reminiscent of a scythe, its edge formed by a row of sharply pointed corn kernels. The handle is a twisted corn stalk that seems to wrap around itself endlessly.

**Lore**: Represents the inevitable reaping of The Rows' bounty, including human sacrifices.

**Impact**: Creatures within 5 feet of the symbol have advantage on death saving throws, but they feel an unsettling pull towards serving The Rows if stabilized.

**Informant**: Prudence Whitby knows of its connection to the "special births," hinting at the darker aspects of the cult's activities.

### The Whisper's Husk

An elongated corn husk curled into the shape of a human ear. Fine lines etched within mimic the texture of the husk, but also form subtle patterns that resemble sound waves emanating from the ear's center.

**Lore**: Symbolizes The Rows' ability to communicate with its followers through the rustle of cornstalks.

**Impact**: Acts as a one-way *Message* spell for cultists, allowing The Rows to send whispered messages to its followers within the tavern.

**Informant**: Winifred Moss has sensed strange magical emanations from this symbol, suggesting hidden communication methods used by the cult.

## Terrain

The tavern is a standard indoor space with tables, chairs, and a bar. However, the floor is slightly sticky in places from spilled drinks, making certain areas difficult terrain.

## Lair Actions

On initiative count 20 (losing initiative ties), the Crow's Nest Tavern invokes one of the following lair actions:

**Whispers of the Corn**: Hushed voices seem to emanate from the cornhusk decorations, forcing all non-cultist creatures to make a DC 12 Wisdom saving throw or be frightened until the end of their next turn.

**Intoxicating Aroma**: The scent of Mabel's special corn whiskey intensifies, requiring all creatures to make a DC 13 Constitution saving throw or be poisoned until the end of their next turn.

**Shifting Shadows**: The lantern light flickers and casts unsettling shadows, granting all cultists in the tavern advantage on Stealth checks until the start of the next round.

## Scaling the Encounter

### Beginning Players (PC levels 1-5)

- Reduce Barkeep Mabel's stats and abilities.
- Lower DCs for skill checks by 2-3 points.
- Remove or weaken the "Whispers of The Rows" ability.
- Limit the number of hostile NPCs to 1-2.
- Focus on social interaction and information gathering.

- Introduce only 2-3 cult symbols with simplified effects.
  - Remove lair actions.

### Intermediate Players (PC levels 6-10)

- Use Barkeep Mabel's stats as written.
- Keep DCs as listed in the encounter.
- Include all cult symbols and their full effects.
- Add 1-2 Reaper of Abundance Cultists as backup for Mabel.
- Implement lair actions, but limit to one per round.
- Increase the risk of attracting attention when eavesdropping.
- Add magical wards that can detect spells like *Detect Thoughts*.

### Advanced Players (PC levels 11+)

- Upgrade Barkeep Mabel to a more powerful cult leader stat block.
- Increase DCs for skill checks by 2-3 points.
- Add extra effects to cult symbols (e.g., psychic damage, mind control).
- Include 3-4 high-level cultists with class levels.
- Use all lair actions, potentially allowing multiple per round.
- Add complex magical protections against divination and eavesdropping.
- Introduce time pressure or a secondary objective within the tavern.

## Monster

Various villagers (potential cultists in disguise, use Commoner stat block with added Deception +2)

## NPC

Barkeep Mabel

## Abandoned Farmhouse

This encounter showcases the consequences of resisting The Rows and provides clues about missing persons. The dilapidated state and overgrown cornfield create an eerie atmosphere, while the animated plants pose a threat to investigating PCs.

As you reach the outskirts of Crow's Hollow, you come upon a sight that sends a chill down your spine. Before you stands a weathered wooden farmhouse, with what was likely its once-welcoming facade now a testament to neglect and abandonment. The windows are haphazardly boarded up, as if done in a hurry, and what little paint remains on the exterior is peeling away in long, curling strips.

Surrounding the house is an overgrown cornfield, the stalks unnaturally tall and dense. The corn sways gently despite the lack of wind, creating an unsettling rustling sound that seems to whisper secrets just beyond your comprehension. As you draw nearer, you can't shake the feeling that you're being watched by unseen eyes hiding among the rows of corn.

### Activities

**Nature's Wrath**: Engage in combat with corrupted plant monsters, fending off the Animated Corn Husks and Vicious Vines that guard the farmhouse's secrets.

**Echoes of the Past**: Investigate the house for clues about the missing family, searching through abandoned belongings and uncovering hints of their final days.

**Beneath the Floorboards**: Discover and explore a hidden cellar, uncovering tangible evidence of the cult's activities and their connection to the missing family.

# Nature's Wrath

## Combat Locations

**Overgrown Front Yard**: The corrupted plants, which include Animated Corn Husks and Vicious Vines, sense intruders and attack as the PCs approach the house. This area is considered difficult terrain due to overgrown corn stalks, which also provide three-quarters cover to any creatures hiding within them. Characters must spend 1 extra foot of movement for every foot traveled.

**Living Room**: The Vicious Vines have infiltrated through broken windows, turning the room into a nest. Furniture provides half cover. Vine-covered areas are difficult terrain.

**Kitchen**: The Animated Corn Husks are drawn to the remnants of food and the barricaded cellar door. The floor here is slippery from decay. Characters must succeed on a DC 12 Dexterity (Acrobatics) check when moving over half speed or be knocked prone.

## Special Combat Rules

**Corruption Spread**: At the start of each round, roll a d20. On a 18-20, a new 5-foot square becomes difficult terrain as corrupted plants sprout.

**Whispers of The Rows**: Any PC who starts their turn adjacent to one array of Animated Corn Husks must make a DC 12 Wisdom saving throw or be frightened until the end of their next turn.

**House Deterioration**: Whenever a creature is slammed against a wall or the upstairs floor, there's a chance of collapse. The attacker makes a DC 13 Strength check (the DM may roll this check in secret). On a success, the target creature falls through the floor/wall, taking 1d6 bludgeoning damage and falling prone in an adjacent room.

# Echoes of the Past

Rooms in the Abandoned Farmhouse:

## Ground Floor

**Entryway**: A small, dusty foyer with a coat rack and a worn welcome mat.

**Living Room**: A spacious room with decaying furniture and a cold fireplace.

**Kitchen**: A dilapidated kitchen with rusted appliances and broken dishes.

**Dining Room**: Adjacent to the kitchen, with a large table and overturned chairs.

## Upstairs Floor

**Master Bedroom**: A large room with a broken bed frame and torn curtains.

**Children's Bedroom**: A smaller room with two small beds and scattered toys.

**Bathroom**: A grimy bathroom with a cracked mirror and moldy bathtub.

**Study**: A small room filled with bookshelves and a writing desk.

## Investigation Rules

PCs must make Intelligence (Investigation) checks to search each room thoroughly.

DC 12: Find obvious clues.

DC 15: Uncover hidden or subtle clues.

DC 18: Discover well-concealed evidence.

## Details and Clues

### Family Portrait (Living Room)

Investigation DC 15: A dusty frame showing a happy family of four: parents and two children.

Perception DC 14: Notice scratch marks on the parents' faces.

### Withered House Plants (Throughout the House)

Investigation DC 12: All plants in the house are dead and appear twisted unnaturally.

Nature DC 15: Determine the plants died from an unknown, aggressive blight.

### Scattered Salt Lines (Entryway and Windows)

Investigation DC 18: Faint traces of salt lines at thresholds and windowsills.

Religion DC 14: Recognize the salt lines as a folk method for warding off evil.

### Children's Drawings (Children's Bedroom)

Investigation DC 12: Crayon drawings depicting corn stalks with eyes and reaching tendrils.

Insight DC 15: Sense the growing fear in the progression of drawings.

### Torn Journal Pages (Study)

Investigation DC 15: Fragments of a journal detailing increasing paranoia about the cornfields.

Investigation DC 16: Piece together mentions of "whispers in the corn" and "The Rows."

### Crossed-Out Calendar (Kitchen)

Investigation DC 15: A calendar with dates crossed out, stopping abruptly mid-month. If PCs pause to search for the exact month or year of the open page, they determine it is dated approximately 5 years ago.

On the day following the last crossed date is written the words "Mayor's Meeting."

### Hidden Religious Symbols (Master Bedroom)

Investigation DC 18: Small protective charms and symbols hidden under floorboards.

Religion DC 16: Identify symbols as protection against possession and mind control.

### Barricaded Cellar Door (Kitchen)

Investigation DC 12: A heavily barricaded door leading to the cellar.

Athletics DC 16 to break through the door, or PCs can take the time to dismantle the barricade.

### Defiled Family Bible (Living Room)

Investigation DC 15: A family Bible with certain passages underlined and others blacked out.

Religion DC 17: Notice alterations that twist the text towards The Rows' ideology.

### Packed Suitcases (Master Bedroom)

Investigation DC 12: Half-packed suitcases, as if the family was preparing to flee.

Investigation DC 16: Find a crumpled map with a circled location far from Crow's Hollow.

Each discovered clue grants 25 XP to the party. If they uncover at least 7 clues, award them XP as if they'd overcome a CR 1 challenge, representing their comprehensive understanding of the family's tragic story.

## Beneath the Floorboards

Discovering the Trapdoor:

- A secret entrance to the cellar is hidden under a rug in the kitchen used as an alternative way to escape the cellar in case of a fire or some similar catastrophe.

- DC 15 Intelligence (Investigation) check to find the trapdoor.

- DC 17 Strength (Athletics) check to force open the rusted trapdoor.

As you descend the creaky wooden stairs, the musty smell of damp earth and decay assaults your senses. The cellar is a cramped, unlit space with rough-hewn stone walls. Shelves line the walls, holding various jars and boxes. In the center of the room stands a sturdy wooden table, its surface covered with papers and strange objects.

### Protective Wards

As the PCs delve deeper into the cellar beneath the abandoned farmhouse, they may come across a series of protective wards designed to guard the cult's secrets and prevent intruders from tampering with their rituals. These wards are not merely an afterthought but a critical defense mechanism that requires careful navigation to avoid triggering dangerous consequences.

### Detecting the Wards

Before attempting to disarm the wards, the PCs must first detect their presence. The wards are subtly woven into the cellar's structure, blending with the natural shadows and cobwebs that fill the space.

**Perception Check (DC 15):** A successful check allows the PCs to notice faint, glowing runes etched into the stone walls or floor, indicating the presence of magical wards.

**Investigation Check (DC 14):** If the PCs take the time to investigate further, they can identify the specific locations and types of wards, recognizing which ones are more dangerous or difficult to disarm.

### Disarming the Wards

Once detected, the PCs must carefully disarm the wards to avoid triggering their effects. Each ward may have a different method of disarming, depending on its nature and the magic used to create it.

**Dexterity Check Using Thieves' Tools (DC 14):** This check represents the PC's ability to physically manipulate the runes or magical components of the ward, carefully deactivating it without setting it off. Failure results in the ward being triggered, unleashing its effect on the party.

**Intelligence (Arcana) Check (DC 15):** Alternatively, the PC can attempt to disarm the ward by unraveling the magical energies that power it. Success safely disarms the ward, while failure triggers a magical backlash, such as a burst of arcane energy or the activation of a defensive spell.

### Ward Effects

Each ward may trigger a different effect if not disarmed properly. These effects can range from simple alarms to more dangerous consequences:

*Alarm Spell:* Alerts nearby cultists or animated plant monsters to the PCs' presence, potentially drawing them into a confrontation.

*Glyph of Warding:* Triggers a stored spell, such as *Thunderwave* (DC 13 Dexterity saving throw for half damage) or *Hold Person* (DC 13 Wisdom saving throw to avoid being paralyzed).

*Arcane Blast:* Unleashes a burst of raw magical energy, dealing 2d6 force damage to all creatures within 10 feet of the ward.

*Whispers of The Rows:* A psychic assault that forces PCs to make a DC 13 Wisdom saving throw or suffer 1d4 psychic damage and gain a level of corruption (as described in the **Verdant Labyrinth** section of the Corrupted Chapel).

### Additional Consequences

If the PCs linger too long in the cellar or fail to disarm the wards, they may face additional consequences:

**Patrolling Cultists:** The noise from a triggered ward may draw the attention of nearby cultists, leading to a combat encounter. Use the Reaper of Abundance Cultist stat block for these enemies.

**Animated Plant Monsters:** The wards may also be linked to the corrupted flora above, causing vines or

Animated Corn Husks to burst through the cellar walls and attack the PCs. Use the Animated Corn Husks and Vicious Vines stat blocks.

**Temporary Corruption**: Failing to handle corrupted items or lingering near active wards may result in temporary corruption effects on the PCs. These could include hearing whispers from The Rows, sudden plant growth on their skin, or a sense of disorientation and unease.

### Expanded Encounter: Cultist Intrusion

If the PCs trigger a ward that alerts nearby cultists, this can lead to an expanded encounter. The cultists will attempt to corner the PCs in the cellar, using their knowledge of the space to their advantage.

**Cultist Tactics**: The Reaper of Abundance Cultists may use the narrow passages and confined spaces of the cellar to launch ambushes, set traps, or force the PCs into choke points where they can be overwhelmed.

**Escalation**: As the battle progresses, more cultists or animated plant monsters may join the fray, increasing the difficulty and forcing the PCs to either fight their way out or attempt to escape the cellar before being overrun.

### Investigation Rules

PCs must make Intelligence (Investigation) checks to search the cellar thoroughly.

DC 12: Find obvious items.

DC 15: Uncover hidden or subtle clues.

DC 18: Discover well-concealed evidence.

### Items and Clues

### Ritual Dagger (DC 12)

A ceremonial dagger with a corn husk-wrapped handle and a blade etched with strange symbols.

Connection: Mayor Abigail Thorne's family crest is subtly incorporated into the dagger's design.

### Ledger of Sacrifices (DC 15)

A book listing names, dates, and "contributions" to The Rows.

Connection: Giles Blackwood's name appears frequently as an officiator of rituals.

### Map of Crow's Hollow (DC 12)

A map with certain buildings circled in red, including the Crow's Nest Tavern.

Connection: Barkeep Mabel's handwriting is recognizable in the margin notes.

### Corrupted Seed Samples (DC 15)

Jars containing twisted, pulsing seeds unlike any normal plant.

Connection: Labels on the jars each record a date, circumstances of the seeds' collection, and occasional notations about growth. Astute PCs who have done their research might further be able to determine the labels are written in Sarah Blackwood's handwriting.

### Cult Robes (DC 12)

Green robes with intricate corn motifs embroidered in gold thread.

Connection: A tag inside one of the robes bears the name "P. Whitby" (referring to Prudence Whitby).

### Personal Journals (DC 18)

Hidden compartment containing journals of the missing family, detailing their resistance and fears.

Connection: Mentions of Ezekiel Crane as a potential ally against the cult.

### Binding Contracts (DC 15)

Legal-looking documents with names of townsfolk, signed in blood.

Connection: Councilor Cornelius Thorne's signature as a witness on many contracts.

### Altered Town Records (DC 18)

Official documents with strategic omissions and alterations.

Connection: Matches handwriting samples from Mayor Abigail Thorne's office.

### Experimental Crop Samples (DC 15)

Vials of peculiar plant matter and notes on their effects.

Connection: References to Jasper Duncan's trade routes for distribution.

### Communication Device (DC 18)

A strange, organic-looking object resembling a twisted, dried corn husk, interwoven with thin, sinewy tendrils. When touched, the device emits a faint, almost imperceptible whisper, as if the object itself is alive and communicating through the rustling of leaves. The tendrils pulse subtly, as if in response to the touch, and the whispers seem to carry fragmented, cryptic messages that are difficult to decipher.

Connection: This device matches the stylized Whisper's Husk symbol (described in the **Symbol Details and Effects** section of the Crow's Net Tavern) as well as descriptions from Winifred Moss's visions, in which she saw cultists using similar objects to communicate with one another over long distances. The whispers are believed to be the voice of The Rows, guiding and controlling the cult's actions.

### Optional Skill Challenges

**Deciphering Cult Texts**: Three successful DC 15 Intelligence (Arcana or Religion) checks to understand the cult's rituals. Failure may result in psychic damage or temporary madness.

**Preserving Evidence**: DC 13 Wisdom (Survival) checks to properly preserve and pack fragile evidence. Failure may result in destroyed or compromised clues.

# Terrain

The overgrown cornfield surrounding the house is difficult terrain. Characters must spend 1 extra foot of movement for every foot they move through the corn. Additionally, the dense stalks provide three-quarters cover to any creature hiding within them.

# Lair Actions

On initiative count 20 (losing initiative ties), the Abandoned Farmhouse invokes one of the following lair actions:

**Whispers of the Corn**: Hushed, indecipherable whispers emanate from the cornfield, forcing all creatures to make a DC 13 Wisdom saving throw or be frightened until the end of their next turn.

**Grasping Roots**: Gnarled roots burst from the ground in a 20-foot radius, turning the area into difficult terrain. Any creature in the area where the roots appear must succeed on a DC 13 Dexterity saving throw or be restrained until the end of its next turn.

**Corrupting Pollen**: A cloud of sickly yellow pollen billows from the cornfield, filling a 30-foot cube. Creatures in the area must succeed on a DC 13 Constitution saving throw or be poisoned until the end of their next turn.

# Scaling the Encounter

### Beginning Players (PC levels 1-5)

- Reduce the number of Animated Corn Husks to 1-2.
- Remove Vicious Vines or use a weaker stat block.
- Lower DCs for skill checks by 2 points.
- Simplify Nature's Wrath special combat rules.
- Remove or weaken lair actions.

- Reduce difficult terrain effects.
- Focus on exploration and clue-finding.
- Limit Beneath the Floorboards skill challenges to 1-2 easier tasks.

### Intermediate Players (PC levels 6-10)

- Use the encounter as written.
- Add 1-2 additional Animated Corn Husks.
- Introduce a second array of Vicious Vines.
- Implement all special combat rules and lair actions.
- Add time pressure to cellar exploration.
- Increase consequences for mishandling corrupted items.
- Introduce patrolling Reaper of Abundance Cultists as additional threat.

### Advanced Players (PC levels 11+)

- Upgrade Animated Corn Husks and Vicious Vines to stronger versions.
- Add a mini-boss (e.g., Plant-Human Hybrid or Corrupted Water Elemental).
- Increase DCs for skill checks by 2 points.
- Enhance lair actions (more frequent, stronger effects).
- Add complex magical traps in the cellar.
- Introduce a skill challenge to attempt to cleanse the area of corruption.
- Create a ticking clock scenario (e.g., the corruption is actively spreading).
- Add high-level Reaper of Abundance Cultists attempting to retrieve important items from the cellar.

# Monsters

Animated Corn Husks (2-4)

Vicious Vines (1-2)

Reaper of Abundance Cultist (2-7)

# Corrupted Chapel

This encounter showcases The Rows' power to corrupt even sacred spaces, emphasizing its growing influence over Crow's Hollow. The party will face both physical and spiritual challenges as they navigate the defiled chapel and confront its twisted guardian.

However, the chapel is veiled in a powerful *glamour*—a magical barrier that obscures its true nature to the uncorrupted. To the townsfolk, the chapel appears abandoned but otherwise intact. They avoid it for reasons they can't fully explain, repelled by a subtle sense of unease. This glamour is an insidious defense mechanism used by The Rows to ensure its corruption remains hidden from those who are not yet touched by its influence.

As you advance toward the old stone building, you're struck by the stark contrast between what must have been its former glory and current state of decay. Once a beacon of hope and sanctuary, the chapel now exudes an aura of corruption and abandonment. Thick, sickly green vines crawl up its weathered walls, their tendrils seeming to pulse with an unnatural life. The stained-glass windows, once vibrant with holy imagery, are now shattered, replaced by an eerie, otherworldly glow that seeps from within.

Pushing open the heavy wooden doors, you're assaulted by the overwhelming scent of decay mixed with a cloying, sweet odor reminiscent of overripe corn. The interior is a mockery of its former sanctity. Pews lie overturned and half-consumed by writhing plant life. The altar at the far end is barely visible beneath a mass of pulsating vines and what appears to be some kind of grotesque, plant-like growth. Shadows dance in the sickly green light, and you can't shake the feeling that you're being watched by unseen eyes.

## Activities

**Verdant Labyrinth**: Navigate through the twisted plant growth inside the chapel, overcoming physical obstacles and resisting the corrupting influence of The Rows.

**Fallen Sentinel**: Confront the Corrupted Chapel Guardian, a once-holy protector now twisted by The Rows' influence into a monstrous defender of this defiled space.

**Unholy Revelations**: Uncover evidence of the cult's rituals and their connection to The Rows, piecing together the extent of the corruption in Crow's Hollow.

## Chapel Structure

The Corrupted Chapel is a medium-sized stone building with a traditional cruciform layout. It stands on a slight hill, its once-pristine white walls now stained and overgrown with contaminated vines. A single bell tower rises from the western end, while broken stained-glass windows line the nave.

**Narthex** (Entrance): A small antechamber just inside the main doors. Once used for gatherings before and after services, it now serves as a transitional space between the outside world and the violated interior.

**Nave**: The main body of the chapel, filled with rows of decaying pews facing the altar. Corrupted vines twist around pillars that separate the central aisle from side aisles.

**Sanctuary**: Located at the eastern end of the nave, raised slightly above the main floor. Contains the altar, now a horrific fusion of stone and living, monstrous plant matter.

**Transepts**: Two wing-like extensions north and south of the crossing, forming the arms of the cruciform layout. These areas once held shrines to minor deities or saints but are now overrun with blighted growth.

**Bell Tower**: Accessible through a door in the narthex, a spiral staircase leads up to the belfry. The bell itself is cracked and covered in a pulsating, plant-like growth.

**Crypt**: Beneath the sanctuary, accessible via a trapdoor hidden under ruined floorboards. Contains the remains of past priests and important town figures, now a nightmarish blend of decay and unnatural growth.

**Rectory**: Attached to the northern side of the chapel, this was once the priest's living quarters. Now a maze of overgrown rooms, filled with personal belongings tainted by The Rows' influence.

**Chapel Garden**: While not an interior room, the area surrounding the chapel was once a beautiful garden. Now, it's a twisted mockery of nature, with corrupted plants forming an almost sentient barrier around the building.

## Verdant Labyrinth

The chapel interior has been transformed into a maze-like growth of befouled plant life. PCs must navigate through this hazardous environment while resisting The Rows' influence.

### Navigation Rules

**Difficult Terrain**: The entire chapel floor is difficult terrain. Each square of movement costs 2 feet instead of 1.

**Skill Challenges**: Player characters must overcome a series of obstacles using various skills. Each failed check results in 1d4 psychic damage as The Rows' influence seeps into their minds.

- **Dexterity** (Acrobatics) DC 14: Climb over a wall of intertwined vines.
- **Strength** (Athletics) DC 13: Force open a door blocked by thick roots.
- **Intelligence** (Nature) DC 15: Identify safe passages through poisonous-looking foliage.
- **Wisdom** (Survival) DC 14: Navigate through areas of thick, vision-obscuring growth.

### Corruption Resistance

At the start of each turn, PCs must make a DC 12 Wisdom saving throw. On a failure, they gain one level of corruption. Corruption levels go from 1 to 5.

### Corruption Levels

### Level 1: Disadvantage on Wisdom (Perception) checks
- **Symptoms**: The character begins to feel uneasy, and their senses are dulled by the subtle whisper of The Rows.
- **Effect**: Disadvantage on Wisdom (Perception) checks.

### Level 2: Speed reduced by 10 feet
- **Symptoms**: Corrupted plant life begins to spread across the character's skin, making movement more difficult.
- **Effect**: The character's speed is reduced by 10 feet as the tendrils of corruption hinder their mobility.

### Level 3: Disadvantage on attack rolls
- **Symptoms**: The corruption has begun to affect the character's coordination and mental clarity.
- **Effect**: The character suffers disadvantage on all attack rolls.

### Level 4: Poisoned condition
- **Symptoms**: The character's body is wracked with pain as the corruption spreads deeper, and their skin begins to take on a bark-like texture.
- **Effect**: The character is poisoned, suffering disadvantage on attack rolls and ability checks.

### Level 5: Charmed by The Rows (*Suggestion* effect)
- **Symptoms**: The character's mind is consumed by The Rows, and they feel an overwhelming urge to serve its goals.
- **Effect**: The character is charmed by The Rows, acting as if under the influence of the *Suggestion* spell, with the instruction to "join with the growth."

**Purification Points**: Place 3-4 small altars throughout the chapel. PCs can use an action to cleanse these points with holy water or radiant damage spells. Each cleansed point removes one level of corruption from all characters within 10 feet.

**Hidden Passages**: PCs can search for hidden passages to bypass difficult areas.

- Intelligence (Investigation) DC 15 to find a hidden passage.
- Using a hidden passage allows players to skip one skill challenge.

**Animated Plants**: As PCs navigate, they may trigger animated plant attacks.

- Wisdom (Perception) DC 13 to notice the threat before it attacks and avoid being surprised.
- The animated plant makes one attack: +5 to hit, 1d8+3 piercing damage.
- PCs can use a reaction to make a DC 13 Dexterity saving throw to halve the damage.

**Time Pressure**: Use a timer or round counter. Every 3 rounds, the corruption grows stronger:

- Difficulty of all skill checks increases by 1.

- DC for Corruption Resistance saving throw increases by 1.

**Group Effort**: Allow PCs to assist each other in skill checks, granting advantage if it makes narrative sense.

## Rewards

Award XP for each obstacle overcome and area of the chapel cleared.

PCs who maintain low corruption levels gain inspiration.

Discovering all hidden passages grants a bonus magic item (e.g., Boots of Elvenkind or Cloak of Elvenkind).

## Consequences

High corruption levels may linger after leaving the chapel, requiring greater magical healing.

Failing to navigate efficiently may alert the Corrupted Chapel Guardian, giving it advantage on its first round of attacks in the subsequent encounter.

# Fallen Sentinel

The Corrupted Chapel Guardian, once a holy protector, now stands as a grotesque fusion of divine power and The Rows' corruption. This encounter takes place in the chapel's main sanctuary.

## Battlefield

The sanctuary is 60 ft. x 40 ft., with rows of decaying pews and a defiled altar.

**Difficult Terrain**: Areas with dense vine growth (about 50% of the room).

**Cover**: Toppled pillars and pews provide half cover.

**Hazards**: Pools of corrupting ooze deal 1d6 acid damage per round to creatures in them.

## Combat Dynamics

**Phase 1** (Full HP to Half HP): The Guardian fights defensively, using pews as cover and its Corrupted Mace attacks. It uses Harvest's Judgment on the most holy-looking character.

**Phase 2** (Half HP to Quarter HP): The Guardian becomes more aggressive, using its full movement each turn. It starts using lair actions to control the battlefield.

**Phase 3** (Quarter HP to 0): In desperation, the Guardian uses Cornstalk Entanglement to restrain as many PCs as possible. It focuses all attacks on one restrained PC, attempting to corrupt them fully.

## Special Combat Rules

**Corruption Aura**: At the start of each round, all characters must make a DC 14 Wisdom saving throw or gain one level of corruption (as in the **Verdant Labyrinth** activity).

**Holy Relics**: 3-4 small, desecrated altars are scattered around the room. As an action, a PC can attempt to cleanse an altar (DC 15 Intelligence (Religion) check). Each cleansed symbol weakens the Guardian:

- **First Symbol**: Guardian loses its Damage Resistances.

- **Second Symbol**: Guardian's AC drops by 2.

- **Third Symbol**: Guardian loses its Regeneration ability.

- **Fourth Symbol**: Guardian is vulnerable to radiant damage.

**Echoes of Sanctity**: Once per turn, a PC can use a bonus action to recall the chapel's former holiness, gaining advantage on one attack roll or saving throw.

**Tragic Memories**: The first time the Guardian is hit by a critical hit, all characters experience a vision of its past. They must succeed on a DC 13 Wisdom saving throw or be stunned for one round as they wrestle with the tragedy of the Guardian's fall to desecration and the corruptive power of The Rows.

## Magic Items and Holy Relics

Below is a table of magic items and holy relics scattered throughout the Corrupted Chapel:

| Name | Type | Description | Properties | Attunement | Lore | Location in Chapel |
|------|------|-------------|------------|------------|------|--------------------|
| Radiant Rosary | Wondrous Item | A string of beads made from luminous crystals, partially overgrown with dark vines. | Once per day, as an action, speak a prayer to cleanse a 10-foot radius of plant-based corruption. Plant creatures, undead and fiends in the area take 2d6 radiant damage. | No | This rosary belonged to the chapel's last priest, who fought against the Rows' influence until his last breath. | Sanctuary, hidden in a small alcove behind the altar. |
| Gardener's Vestments | Armor (chain shirt) | A set of ceremonial robes interwoven with fine chains, now partially merged with living leaves and vines. | AC 13 + Dex modifier (max 2). The wearer has advantage on saving throws against plant-based effects and spells. | Yes | These vestments were worn by warrior-priests who tended the chapel's once-beautiful gardens, symbolizing the balance between nature and faith. | Vestry, hanging in a wardrobe overcome by vines. |
| Tears of the Harvest | Potion | A small vial containing a swirling mixture of golden liquid and tiny seeds. | When consumed, the drinker gains the effects of a *Bless* spell for 1 hour. Additionally, they can understand and speak with plants for the duration. However, this connection with plant life comes at a cost: the drinker must make a DC 13 Wisdom saving throw at the end of the hour or gain one level of corruption. While under the influence of the potion, the drinker occasionally hears the whispered voice of The Rows, a terrifyingly raspy sound akin to crunching or rustling leaves that is strangely hypnotic and may cloud their judgment. | No | Crafted from the sap of the chapel's sacred tree and blessed during harvest festivals, these tears represent the bond between the divine and nature. | Crypt, in a hidden compartment within a stone sarcophagus. |

| Name | Type | Description | Properties | Requires Attunement | Lore | Location |
|------|------|-------------|------------|---------------------|------|----------|
| Sickle of Seasons | Weapon (sickle) | A sickle with a blade that shifts color with the seasons, partially corroded by The Rows' influence. | +1 sickle. Once per day as a bonus action, the wielder can change the damage type to fire, cold, lightning, or poison for 1 minute. Due to the partial corruption of the sickle, there is a risk involved: after using this ability, the wielder must make a DC 12 Constitution saving throw. On a failure, the wielder takes 1d4 necrotic damage as the sickle's corruption momentarily affects them. | Yes | This sickle was used in sacred harvest rituals, symbolizing the cycle of life and death. The Rows seeks to corrupt its power for its own twisted version of "harvest." | Bell Tower, embedded in a corrupted wooden beam. |
| Icon of Renewal | Wondrous Item | A tarnished silver amulet depicting a tree with four distinct sections representing the seasons. | As an action, expend a charge to cast *Lesser Restoration*. The icon has 4 charges, regaining 1d4 daily at dawn. When all charges are spent, roll a d20. On a 1, the icon crumbles to dust. | Yes | This icon was used to bless crops and heal the sick. Its power of renewal actively resists The Rows' corruption, making it a beacon of hope. | Rectory, buried in the soil of a large, corrupted potted plant. |
| Hymnal of Hallowed Harmony | Wondrous Item | A weathered book of hymns, its pages now interwoven with corrupted vines that squirm when the book is opened. | A spellcaster holding this item can replace one known spell with *Plant Growth*, *Speak with Plants*, or *Tree Stride* once per long rest. | No | This hymnal contains songs of praise that once kept The Rows at bay. Now, it's a battleground between holy verses and corrupting influence. | Sanctuary, chained to a defiled lectern near the altar. |
| Censer of Cleansing Clouds | Wondrous Item | A brass censer bearing intricate nature motifs, emitting a faint, sickly green smoke tinged with motes of golden light. | As an action, swing the censer to create a 15-foot cube of purifying smoke. Allies in the area gain 1d8 temporary HP, while plant creatures, fiends and undead take 1d8 radiant damage. | No | Used to purify the chapel and bless the congregation, this censer now struggles against the corrupting smoke of The Rows, creating a mix of holy and unholy vapors. | Vestry, hanging from a hook near a damaged window. |

These items blend elements of nature and divine magic, demonstrating how The Rows has corrupted what was once holy. Each item provides a unique benefit that could aid the PCs in their quest while also offering lore that deepens the story of the chapel's fall and The Rows' influence.

## Finding and Cleansing a Holy Symbol

**Initial Discovery**: During their investigation of the sanctuary area, PCs can make a DC 14 Wisdom (Perception) check to notice a faintly glowing object partially buried under corrupted vines near the altar.

**Identification**: Upon closer inspection (DC 13 Intelligence (Religion) check), characters can identify the object as a once-holy symbol of the chapel's patron deity, now tainted by The Rows' corruption.

**Retrieval**: To safely retrieve the symbol without being corrupted, a character must succeed on a DC 15 Dexterity (Sleight of Hand) check. Failure results in taking 1d6 necrotic damage from the vines coiled over it and gaining one level of corruption.

### Cleansing Process

Cleansing the holy symbol requires a three-step ritual:

- **Purification Bath**: PCs must find or create holy water. This can be done by using the Tears of the Harvest potion (if found) or by having a cleric or paladin bless water using a spell slot. The symbol must be submerged in the holy water for 10 minutes.

- **Reconsecration**: A character must recite a prayer to the chapel's patron deity while holding the submerged symbol. This requires a DC 15 Charisma (Religion) check. On a success, the symbol begins to glow with a soft, warm light.

- **Divine Spark**: Finally, a character must channel divine energy into the symbol. This can be done by a divine caster expending a spell slot of 2nd level or higher, or by succeeding on a DC 16 Wisdom (Religion) check to appeal to the deity for aid.

**Corruption Backlash**: As the symbol is cleansed, The Rows' corruption lashes out. All creatures within 30 feet must succeed on a DC 14 Constitution saving throw or take 2d6 necrotic damage and be poisoned for 1 minute.

**Symbol Awakening**: If the cleansing is successful, the holy symbol awakens with renewed power. It now functions as a +1 holy symbol, granting a +1 bonus to spell attack rolls and the spell save DC of the wielder's cleric or paladin spells. Additionally, once per day the wielder can use an action to create a 15-foot radius aura of purification for 1 minute, granting advantage on saving throws against The Rows' corrupting effects to all allies within the aura.

**Failed Cleansing**: If any step of the cleansing process fails, the symbol remains corrupted. PCs can attempt the process again after a short rest, but each failed attempt causes the symbol to lash out, dealing 1d8 necrotic damage to the character performing the cleansing.

## Unholy Revelations

This activity takes place after defeating the Corrupted Chapel Guardian and/or navigating the **Verdant Labyrinth**. PCs search the chapel for evidence of the cult's activities.

### Investigation Process

Divide the chapel into 5 areas: Sanctuary, Vestry, Crypt, Bell Tower, and Rectory.

PCs can investigate each area using various skill checks.

Each successful check reveals a piece of evidence and grants 50 XP.

Certain areas require special actions or tools to access.

### Skill Checks and Evidence

#### Sanctuary

Intelligence (Investigation) DC 14: Find a hidden compartment in the altar containing dark ritual instructions.

Wisdom (Perception) DC 15: Notice patterns in the corrupted vines that form cult symbols.

#### Vestry

Intelligence (Religion) DC 13: Identify desecrated holy symbols repurposed for cult rituals.

Dexterity check using thieves' tools DC 14: Unlock a trapped drawer containing cult membership lists.

#### Crypt

Strength (Atheltics) DC 15: Move a heavy stone slab to reveal a secret ritual chamber.

Wisdom (Medicine) DC 14: Examine remains to find evidence of sacrificial practices.

#### Bell Tower

Dexterity (Acrobatics) DC 15: Climb the unstable tower to find evidence of a cult lookout post there.

Intelligence (Arcana) DC 16: Decipher magical runes used to communicate with The Rows.

#### Rectory

Wisdom (Insight) DC 14: Analyze personal belongings such as a journal to understand the priest's struggle against the corrupting influence of The Rows upon his church.

Intelligence (History) DC 15: Piece together from old records a timeline of the chapel's fall.

### Special Actions

Use *Detect Magic* to reveal hidden enchantments and/or provide advantage on Arcana checks for the duration (DM's discretion).

Cast *Speak with Dead* on remains in the crypt for direct testimony.

### Corruption Hazards

- Each failed check risks exposure to lingering corruption.
- Constitution saving throw DC 12 or gain one level of exhaustion.
- Remove exhaustion levels with Lesser Restoration or by spending a Hit Die during a short rest in a purified area.

### Piecing Together the Evidence

After gathering evidence, PCs make an Intelligence (Investigation) check to connect the clues:

- DC 10: Understand the basic structure of the cult.
- DC 15: Identify key cult members and their roles.
- DC 20: Uncover the cult's ultimate goals and connection to The Rows.

Each success level provides increasingly detailed information about the cult's activities and The Rows' influence in Crow's Hollow.

**Major Revelations (Examples):**

- The cult has infiltrated town leadership, including Mayor Abigail Thorne.
- Ritual sacrifices are conducted to strengthen The Rows' connection to the material plane.
- The cult plans to perform a grand ritual during the next harvest festival to fully manifest The Rows.

## Terrain

The chapel floor is covered in a tangled mass of vines and roots, making it difficult terrain. Characters must spend 1 extra foot of movement for every foot traveled. Additionally, at the start of each round, every character must make a DC 13 Dexterity saving throw or become restrained by suddenly animating vines. A restrained creature can use its action to make a DC 13 Strength check, freeing itself on a success.

## Lair Actions

On initiative count 20 (losing initiative ties), the Corrupted Chapel invokes one of the following lair actions:

**Corrupt Benediction**: Foul, glowing pollen rains down from the ceiling. Each creature must succeed on a DC 14 Constitution saving throw or be poisoned until the end of its next turn.

**Unholy Chorus**: Ghostly whispers fill the air, forcing each creature to make a DC 14 Wisdom saving throw or be frightened until the end of its next turn.

**Vine Eruption**: Thick vines burst from the ground in a 15-foot radius around a point the Corrupted Chapel Guardian can see. This area becomes difficult terrain, and any creature in the area where the vines appear must succeed on a DC 14 Strength saving throw or be restrained until the end of its next turn.

## Scaling the Encounter

### Beginning Players (PC levels 1-5)

- Simplify Verdant Labyrinth activity: Reduce skill check DCs by 2, limit corruption levels to a max of 3.
- Weaken Corrupted Chapel Guardian: Halve HP, reduce AC by 2, remove legendary actions.
- Simplify lair actions: Use only one per round, reduce save DCs by 2.
- Limit magic items to 2-3 less powerful options.
- Focus on exploration and puzzle-solving over combat.
- Reduce difficulty and number of skill checks in Unholy Revelations activity.

### Intermediate Players (PC levels 6-10)

- Include all listed magic items and holy relics.
- Add time pressure to Unholy Revelations activity.
- Increase consequences for high corruption levels.
- Introduce additional environmental hazards in the chapel.

### Advanced Players (PC levels 11+)

- Upgrade Corrupted Chapel Guardian: Increase HP by 50%, add legendary actions.
- Add 1-2 Plant-Human Hybrids as mini-bosses.
- Enhance lair actions: More frequent, stronger effects.
- Add complex magical traps throughout the chapel.
- Introduce a skill challenge to prevent The Rows from fully manifesting.
- Create more powerful, cursed versions of magic items.
- Add high-level Reaper of Abundance cultists attempting to complete a ritual during the encounter.

## Monster

Corrupted Chapel Guardian

# Crow Family Crypt

This ancient crypt reveals the dark history of Crow's Hollow's founding family and their pact with The Rows. Players will uncover clues about the origin of the corruption while facing undead horrors.

As you near the edge of town, an old cemetery comes into view. Among the weathered gravestones and overgrown plots, your eyes are drawn to a large stone structure standing apart from the rest. Its entrance is partially obscured by twisted vines and gnarled vegetation, giving it an ominous, almost forbidding appearance.

Drawing closer, you can make out intricate carvings on the crypt's facade, though years of exposure have worn away some of the details. The stonework bears the marks of skilled craftsmanship, hinting at the importance of those interred within. A heavy iron door, green with age, stands slightly ajar, as if inviting – or daring – you to enter and uncover the secrets held within its cold, stone chambers.

## Activities

**Crypt Exploration**: Navigate through the dark, winding chambers of the ancient crypt, uncovering hidden passages and avoiding traps.

**Decoding the Pact**: Examine and interpret cryptic inscriptions scattered throughout the burial chamber, piecing together the dark history of the founders of Crow's Hollow.

**Artifact Recovery**: Locate and safely retrieve a significant historical item hidden within the crypt, crucial to understanding The Rows' influence on the town.

## Crypt Exploration

The Crow Family Crypt is a complex structure consisting of three levels:

**Entry Chamber**: A small antechamber with winding stairs leading down.

**Main Level**: A circular corridor with four burial chambers and a central chamber.

**Lower Chamber**: A hidden underground chamber accessible through a secret passage.

## Structure

**Entry Chamber**: Contains a trap (see below).

**Main Level Corridor**: Circular, with four offshoots leading to family burial chambers.

**Four Burial Chambers**: Each contains sarcophagi and memorial plaques.

**Central Chamber**: Largest room, contains family heirlooms and a hidden entrance to the Lower Chamber.

**Lower Chamber**: Secret room where the original pact was made, contains the artifact.

## Encounters

- Two Animated Burial Shrouds in the Central Chamber.
- One Animated Burial Shroud in the Eastern Burial Chamber.
- Six Corn Husk Zombies lie hidden and dormant in the Lower Chamber

## Venomous Corn Spike Trap

**Description**: Poisoned corn spikes spring from holes in the floor, embodying The Rows' corruption of nature.

**Trigger**: Pressure plate in the center of the Entry Chamber.

**Activation**: The trap activates when 50 pounds or more of weight is placed on the pressure plate.

**Effect**: When triggered, poisoned spikes shoot up from the floor in a 10-foot radius. Each creature in the area must make a DC 13 Dexterity saving throw. On a failed save, a creature takes 2d6 piercing damage and 2d6 poison damage, or half as much on a successful one. Additionally, a creature that fails the save is poisoned for 1 hour.

**Detection**: The pressure plate can be noticed with a successful DC 15 Wisdom (Perception) check. A character actively searching the floor has advantage on this check.

**Disable**: A successful DC 15 Dexterity check using thieves' tools can disable the pressure plate. Alternatively, a character can use a pole or other long object to trigger the trap from a safe distance.

# Decoding the Pact

The party must locate and decipher five mysterious inscriptions throughout the crypt. Each inscription requires a Wisdom (Perception) check DC 15 to find and an Intelligence (History) check to decipher the old calligraphic script. PCs proficient in the Druidic language have advantage on the deciphering check, as druids use a very similar script.

## Twisted Corn Stalks and Eyes Carved into Stone

Location: Above the entrance to the Main Level

DC Check: DC 12 Intelligence (History)

Translated Message: "In fields of plenty, darkness grows. The Rows watch, The Rows know."

## Series of Interlocking Circles with Strange Symbols

Location: Eastern Burial Chamber wall

DC Check: DC 14 Intelligence (History)

Translated Message: "Blood of the founders, bound to the earth. Sacrifice ensures eternal rebirth."

## Faded Pictographs of Figures Bowing before a Cornfield

Location: Central Chamber floor mosaic

DC Check: DC 16 Intelligence (History)

Translated Message: "We kneel before The Rows, our savior and doom. Within its embrace, Crow's Hollow will bloom."

## Spiraling Text Etched around a Sarcophagus

Location: Western Burial Chamber, on the main sarcophagus

DC Check: DC 15 Intelligence (History)

Translated Message: "Jeremiah Crow, first to hear the whispers. His pact ensures our harvests, forever and always."

## Complex Diagram of Roots and Human Figures

Location: Hidden panel in the Lower Chamber

DC Check: DC 18 Intelligence (History)

Translated Message: "As roots entwine with flesh and bone, The Rows claims Crow's Hollow as its throne. Our descendants shall reap what we have sown."

For each successful deciphering, award the players with inspiration or a small amount of XP to encourage thorough exploration and engagement with the story.

If the PCs successfully decipher all five inscriptions, they gain advantage on any checks related to understanding or resisting The Rows' influence for the remainder of the adventure, as they now have crucial insight into its nature and the town's history.

# Artifact Recovery

The artifact hidden within the Crow Family Crypt is the Sickle of the First Harvest, a powerful item that played a crucial role in the original pact between Jeremiah Crow and The Rows.

## Finding the Secret Passage

**Initial Clue**: As the PCs explore the Main Level of the crypt, they can find a partially decayed journal in the Central Chamber. A DC 13 Intelligence (Investigation) check reveals a passage mentioning "the founder's blade hidden beneath, where it all began."

**Deciphering the Clue**: PCs can make a DC 14 Intelligence (Investigation) check to realize that "where it all began" likely refers to another, lower level chamber where the original pact was made.

**Accessing the Lower Chamber**: The entrance to the Lower Chamber is hidden beneath a false floor in the Central Chamber. PCs must succeed on a DC 15 Wisdom (Perception) check to notice inconsistencies in the stonework. Once found, a DC 16 Strength (Athletics) check is required to move the hidden door.

## Exploring the Lower Chamber

The winding stone staircase leading down to the Lower Chamber is trapped (see trap description below). Like the first level, the Lower Chamber is a circular room with walls of stone. However, the floor here is packed dirt rather than stone, and the chamber is much smaller in size--only 40 feet in diameter. Near the opposite wall from the stairway is a stone altar, upon which sits a corn-themed puzzle embedded in the altar's surface.

**Poison Dart Trap**

Whenever unauthorized individuals descend the winding staircase, their movement triggers a series of poison darts to shoot out from both sides. A Wisdom (Perception) check DC 17 is needed to notice the many tiny holes in the stone walls before crossing in front of them, while an Intelligence (Investigation) check DC 14 confirms the presence of a poison dart trap set in the walls of the stairway, By moving carefully and crawling beneath the trigger sensors, characters who succeed on a DC 14 Dexterity (Acrobatics) check can individually bypass the poison darts. Failure results in triggering the poison dart trap, causing 2d6 poison damage to the character.

Alternatively, the poison dart trap can be disabled with a successful a DC 18 Dexterity check using thieves' tools, with a failure triggering the trap on the PC. Regardless, the trap remains active until it is either disabled or enough darts are triggered to exhaust its supply.

**The Final Puzzle**: A few feet in front of the far side of the wall stands a stone altar bearing a corn-themed puzzle. Solving it requires a DC 15 Intelligence check. Each failed attempt triggers a wave of necrotic energy dealing 1d6 necrotic damage to all creatures in the room. Upon solving the puzzle, a hidden compartment in the altar opens to reveal a small, ornate pedestal, upon which is a mysterious sickle (magic item described below).

## Retrieving the Sickle

Cautious characters may try to glean some information about the item from a distance before attempting to touch it. With a successful DC 16 Intelligence (Arcana) check, PCs can determine the item is quite clearly magical and incredibly powerful. They may also gain some basic information about the sickle (the details of which are determined by the DM at their discretion). Casting *Detect Magic* reveals the sickle has a strong aura of transmutation and necromancy.

**Test of Mettle**: The moment a character reaches for the sickle, they must make a DC 13 Wisdom saving throw. On a failure, they experience a vivid vision of The Rows' realm, becoming frightened for 1 minute.

**Sickle's Awakening**: Once touched, the sickle awakens, causing all plant matter in the crypt to animate. Immediately, a chain of Corn Husk Zombies begins to emerge at the rate of 2-3 zombies per round from a large crack in the stone wall behind the altar.

**Note to DM**: The recommended number of zombies to use for your game should be 1+1 per player, and the zombies should have a number of Hit Dice equal to the party's level. This fight should be difficult, and the DM may need to adjust accordingly. The intent is to challenge the PCs just as they begin to inspect the sickle, but before they have a chance to examine it in detail. When the PCs find themselves fighting for their lives, the temptation to use the powerful magic weapon to defend the party intensifies, particularly if the PCs are losing the battle. The tension of this scene should be high.

If any PC takes and uses the sickle in combat or attempts to learn or use its powers against the approaching zombie horde while holding the weapon, they may instantly know its properties (but not its curse) and can immediately control the Corn Husk Zombies on their turn.

## Escaping the Crypt

Once the Corn Husk Zombies are dispatched, the party must then fight their way out of the crypt past animated vines and corrupted plants. DMs can use the stat blocks for Vicious Vines and Animated Corn Husks in the Monsters section of the Appendix or just narrate the party's escape for a quick transition at their discretion. Any use of the sickle's necromantic properties causes all animated plant attacks to promptly cease.

**Identification**: Once the sickle is retrieved, PCs may identify the sickle by either casting *Identify* or studying the item while holding it during a short rest. This reveals the item's properties, but not its curse. Keep in mind that the casting time of *Identify* is one minute, and the party will likely be under time pressure to escape the crypt before more corrupted plants come along. Unless a PC has made use of the sickle's magical properties, any attempts to cast *Identify* while still in the crypt are done under great duress and liable to draw another combat encounter before the spell is completed.

## Sickle of the First Harvest

*Weapon, artifact*

### Appearance

This sickle appears to be made of tarnished silver, its blade etched with intricate patterns of intertwining corn stalks and eerie, staring eyes. The handle is wrapped in what looks like dried corn husks, which seem to shift and rustle even when the sickle is perfectly still. A faint, sickly green glow emanates from the blade, pulsing slowly like a heartbeat.

### Properties

**Corrupted Harvest**: As an action, the wielder can cause plants in a 30-foot radius to rapidly grow and become hostile. This property functions as the *Entangle* spell (save DC 15), but the grasping plants also deal 1d4 necrotic damage to any creature that starts its turn in the spell's area.

**Whispers of The Rows**: The wielder can cast *Speak with Plants* at will, but the effects are limited to corrupted plants or plants influenced by The Rows.

**Reaping Strike**: The sickle functions as a +3 weapon. It deals an extra 1d6 necrotic damage to the target on a hit. Any humanoid slain by this weapon immediately rises as a Corn Husk Zombie at the start of the wielder's next turn under their control.

**Harvester of the Damned**: The wielder can control all Corn Husk Zombies that they can see.

### Curse

This item is cursed. Although touch alone does not trigger the curse, from the moment a PC uses or equips the sickle, the wielder has disadvantage on saving throws against effects created by The Rows or its cultists. Additionally, the wielder feels a constant urge to expand The Rows' influence, and occasionally hears the whispers of The Rows speaking in their mind. Finally, the sickle (and its curse effects) can only be removed from the wielder by casting *Remove Curse* or *Greater Restoration*.

### Attunement

No, does not require attunement.

### Lore

The Sickle of the First Harvest was used by Jeremiah Crow to seal the pact with The Rows. It was imbued with both the corrupting essence of The Rows and the desperate hope of Crow's Hollow's founders. The sickle has been hidden away in the Crow Family Crypt for generations, its power and the truth of its origin forgotten by most.

### Communicating with Corrupted Plants and The Rows

**Corrupted Plants:** When using *Speak with Plants* to communicate with corrupted plants or plants influenced by The Rows, the voices heard are eerie and unsettling. These plants speak in disjointed, whispering tones that mimic the sound of rustling leaves or the creaking of old wood. Their words are often cryptic and filled with fragmented sentences, giving the impression that they are part of a greater, malevolent consciousness.

**Examples of Corrupted Plant Speech:**

- "Roots... deep... we are bound... to the earth... to The Rows..."

- "The harvest... it calls... it feeds... on flesh, on fear..."

- "You walk among us... but you are not... of us... not yet..."

- "We grow... we spread... The Rows will... consume... all..."

**The Rows:** The wielder of the Sickle of the Harvest occasionally hears the whispers of The Rows in their mind, either at times while in direct contact with it, or perhaps more frequently at the discretion of the DM. If the wielder attempts to communicate directly with The Rows using the sickle, the experience is overwhelming. The Rows' voice is a cacophony of thousands of whispers, each one blending into the next, creating a haunting chorus. The sound is like the crunching of dry leaves underfoot, mixed with the distant rustling of a vast cornfield in a windstorm. The Rows speaks with an ancient and otherworldly tone, instilling a deep sense of dread.

**Examples of Communication from The Rows:**

- "I am... the harvest... the end... and the beginning..."

- "Your blood... your life... will nourish... the soil..."

- "Expand... grow... all will be... one with The Rows..."

- "You seek power... but it is I... who will consume... you..."

**Voice Acting for DMs:** To illustrate the voices of the corrupted plants and The Rows, DMs might consider speaking in a low, whispering tone, elongating certain words to create a sense of unease. For The Rows, layering your voice with a raspy, breathy quality can help convey the ancient and malevolent nature of this entity. Pausing frequently, as if the entity is savoring each word, can enhance the unsettling atmosphere. Using an echo effect or overlapping whispers (if possible) can also help create the impression of many voices speaking as one.

## Terrain

The crypt interior is dark, damp, and filled with debris. Difficult terrain rules apply in all areas except the main corridor. Characters must succeed on a DC 13 Dexterity (Acrobatics) check when moving through difficult terrain or fall prone.

## Lair Actions

On initiative count 20 (losing initiative ties), the Crow Family Crypt invokes one of the following lair actions:

**Whispers of the Past**: Ghostly whispers echo through the crypt, forcing all creatures to make a DC 13 Wisdom saving throw or be frightened until the end of their next turn.

**Grasping Roots**: Corrupted roots burst from the walls and floor in a 10-foot radius centered on a point the DM chooses. This area becomes difficult terrain, and any creature in the area where the roots appear must succeed on a DC 13 Strength saving throw or be restrained.

**Miasma of Decay**: A sickly green mist fills a 20-foot cube centered on a point the DM chooses. Any creature that starts its turn in the mist or enters it for the first time on a turn must make a DC 13 Constitution saving throw or be poisoned until the start of its next turn.

## Scaling the Encounter

### Beginning Players (PC levels 1-5)

- Reduce number of Animated Burial Shrouds to 1-2.

- Reduce number of Corn Husk Zombies to 1-2, or have them appear at the rate of 1 per round.

- Lower trap and skill check DCs by 2.

- Simplify crypt layout, focusing on main level only.

- Reduce Venomous Corn Spike Trap damage to 1d6 each type.

- Limit inscriptions to 3, with easier DC checks.

- Weaken Sickle of the First Harvest: remove curse, reduce bonus to +1 only.

- Remove or simplify lair actions.

### Intermediate Players (PC levels 6-10)

- Use encounter as written.

- Add 1-2 additional Animated Burial Shrouds.

- Introduce a mini-boss in the Lower Chamber (e.g., a more powerful Corn Husk Zombie).

- Implement all lair actions.

- Include complex traps in the Lower Chamber.

- Add or increase time pressure (e.g., crypt slowly filling with poisonous gas).

- Add 1-2 encounters with a combination of 3 Animated Corn Husks and/or 2 Vicious Vines as the party escapes the crypt.

### Advanced Players (PC levels 11+)

- Upgrade Animated Burial Shrouds to more powerful undead.

- Add a spectral guardian of Jeremiah Crow as a boss fight.

- Increase all DCs by 2.

- Expand crypt to include extra hidden chambers with powerful guardians.

- Enhance traps with magical effects and higher damage.

- Add complex magical puzzles to access the Lower Chamber.

- Introduce rival cultists also seeking the artifact.

- Add higher level corrupted plant encounters as the party escapes the crypt.

- Implement more frequent and powerful lair actions.

## Monsters

Animated Burial Shroud (2-3)

Corn Husk Zombie (5-6)

Animated Corn Husk (2-3)

Vicious Vines (1-2)

# Crow's Hollow Schoolhouse

This encounter reveals the insidious indoctrination of Crow's Hollow's children by the cult. Players must navigate the ethical dilemma of confronting this corruption while protecting the innocent.

Arriving at the center of town, you come across a modest, single-story building that stands out from the surrounding structures. Its weathered wooden exterior and small bell tower clearly mark it as the local schoolhouse. A worn path leads to the front door, flanked by a pair of young apple trees that seem strangely stunted and gnarled.

Peering through the windows, you see rows of small desks facing a large chalkboard at the front of the room. The walls are covered with childlike drawings and artwork, but something about them seems off. Upon closer inspection, you notice an unsettling prevalence of cornfield imagery and eerily detailed scarecrows in many of the pictures. The air around the schoolhouse feels heavy with an inexplicable sense of unease.

## Activities

**Curriculum of Corruption**: Examine school materials for signs of cult influence, uncovering the subtle ways The Rows' doctrine is woven into lessons.

**Teacher's Torment**: Assist Miss Hawthorn in overcoming a personalized hallucination, revealing her inner struggle against The Rows' influence.

**Innocence Tainted**: Analyze children's artwork to identify hidden cult symbols, discovering the extent of indoctrination among the Crow's Hollow youth.

## Curriculum of Corruption

The schoolhouse is a single large room with rows of wooden desks facing a chalkboard. A teacher's desk sits at the front, with bookshelves lining the walls. Windows allow natural light to filter in, casting shadows that seem to move unnaturally.

PCs can investigate the school materials by making Intelligence (Investigation) checks. The DC for noticing subtle cult influences is 14, while more obvious connections have a DC of 12.

### School Materials

#### Arithmetic Textbook

**Description**: A worn book with a corn stalk on the cover.

**Cult Connection**: Word problems involve calculating harvest yields and sacrificial ratios.

DC 14 to notice the recurring theme of "13" in many problems, referencing the sacred number of The Rows.

#### History Primer

**Description**: A thick tome detailing local history.

**Cult Connection**: Subtle rewrites of town history to glorify The Rows' influence.

DC 12 to notice the omission of any hardships or droughts, only mentioning bountiful harvests.

#### Nature Studies Chart

**Description**: A large poster showing plant life cycles.

**Cult Connection**: Depicts corrupted plant forms as natural and beneficial.

DC 14 to notice the unnatural characteristics of the plants, mirroring The Rows' influence.

#### Reading Primer

**Description**: A colorful book with short stories for young readers.

**Cult Connection**: Stories subtly promote loyalty to the fields and mistrust of outsiders.

DC 15 to notice recurring themes of children being "rewarded" for keeping secrets about the cornfields.

#### Handwriting Samples

**Description**: Student writing examples pinned to a board.

**Cult Connection**: Phrases used for practice contain hidden cult mantras.

DC 14 to decipher the cultist messages when the phrases are read backwards.

#### Music Sheet

**Description**: A song sheet titled "Harvest Hymn."

**Cult Connection**: Lyrics contain coded references to The Rows and its practices.

DC 12 to discern the unsettling lyrics that refer to a protector of the cornfields.

DC 18 to read the music and perceive the song's unusually eerie, discordant notes. If the PC has previously heard the whispers of The Rows, they immediately recognize the notes as mimicking its unnerving, rustling speech.

#### Art Supplies

**Description**: Paints, crayons, and paper for student projects.

**Cult Connection**: Colors are limited to those associated with The Rows and corrupted crops.

DC 12 to notice the absence of certain colors and the unnaturally high amount of sickly greens and yellows.

#### World Map

**Description**: A map of the world on the wall near the teacher's desk.

**Cult Connection**: Subtly distorted to show Crow's Hollow at the center, with other areas minimized.

DC 14 to notice the geographical inaccuracies and the exaggerated size of the local area.

#### Classroom Rules Poster

**Description**: A list of behavior guidelines for students.

**Cult Connection**: Rules subtly reinforce cult values and obedience to The Rows.

DC 12 to notice phrases like "The fields are always watching" and "Secrets keep the harvest bountiful."

#### Attendance Ledger

**Description**: A book recording student attendance and performance.

**Cult Connection**: Contains coded notes about students' susceptibility to indoctrination.

DC 16 to decipher the code and understand the sinister tracking system.

For each item successfully investigated, award the players with a small amount of XP or inspiration. If they uncover the cult connection in 7 or more items, they gain advantage on any future checks related to understanding the cult's indoctrination methods.

## Teacher's Torment

As the party enters the schoolhouse, they find Miss Hawthorn in visible distress, seemingly talking to an empty space. She's being tormented by a Hallucination of Lost Loved One, which has taken the form of her younger sister, Emily. Emily was taken by the cultists five years ago when she refused to participate in a ritual, serving as a stark reminder to Miss Hawthorn of the consequences of defiance.

The hallucination is invisible to everyone except Miss Hawthorn, but PCs can attempt to perceive its presence and effects:

**Perception Check**: DC 15 Wisdom (Perception) check to notice subtle environmental changes when the hallucination speaks or moves (e.g., flickering shadows, a faint whisper).

**Insight Check**: DC 14 Wisdom (Insight) check to understand Miss Hawthorn's reactions and piece together what the hallucination might be saying.

To assist Miss Hawthorn, PCs can take the following actions:

**Emotional Support**: A PC can use the Help action to give Miss Hawthorn advantage on her next Wisdom saving throw against the hallucination's effects. This requires a successful DC 13 Charisma (Persuasion) check from the character to convince Miss Hawthorn to listen to them.

**Magical Intervention**: A PC can attempt to disrupt the hallucination. This requires a DC 15 Intelligence (Arcana) check. On a success, the hallucination's next attack has disadvantage.

**Share the Burden**: A PC can attempt to see the hallucination by forming a mental link with Miss Hawthorn. This requires a DC 15 Wisdom check. On a success, the player character can see and hear the hallucination but must then make a DC 13 Wisdom saving throw or be affected by its Haunting Whispers ability.

**Counter-Narrative**: PCs can use evidence they've gathered about the cult to help Miss Hawthorn resist the hallucination's lies. For each piece of relevant information they present, Miss Hawthorn gains a +1 bonus (up to +5) on her next saving throw against the hallucination.

The Hallucination of Lost Loved One will use its abilities to torment Miss Hawthorn:

- It uses Emotional Drain every turn, targeting Miss Hawthorn.

- It uses Haunting Whispers whenever it recharges, filling Miss Hawthorn's mind with guilt and false promises of Emily's return if she fully embraces The Rows.

- It uses Illusory Reality to try and trap Miss Hawthorn in a false memory of happier times with Emily.

Miss Hawthorn must make a Wisdom saving throw (DC 14) at the end of each of her turns. On a success, she starts to break free of the hallucination's influence. Three successive saves will completely break its hold on her.

If the players successfully help Miss Hawthorn overcome the hallucination:

- They gain inspiration and XP equivalent to defeating the Hallucination of Lost Loved One.

- Miss Hawthorn becomes a valuable ally, providing information about the cult's activities in the school and the wider town.

- PCs gain advantage on checks to identify cult indoctrination methods for the remainder of the adventure.

If they fail:

- Miss Hawthorn succumbs to the hallucination's influence, becoming more aligned with the cult.

- The schoolhouse becomes a more dangerous location, with Miss Hawthorn actively, though reluctantly, working to indoctrinate the children.

- PCs have disadvantage on any future attempts to gather information from the town's children or to sway Miss Hawthorn back to their side.

## Innocence Tainted

Players can investigate the children's artwork displayed around the schoolroom. Each piece requires a DC 14 Intelligence (Investigation) check to uncover its hidden symbolism. A successful check reveals the cult influence and potential magical effect.

For each successful Investigation check, award the players with a small amount of XP or inspiration. If they uncover the cult influence in 5 or more pieces, they gain advantage on any future checks related to resisting The Rows' influence on children.

| Name of Art | Creator | Visual Description | Cult Influence | Effect |
| --- | --- | --- | --- | --- |
| "Fields of Gold" | Nathaniel Thorne (Mayor's son) | A vast cornfield under a setting sun, with a scarecrow in the foreground. | The scarecrow's eyes glow faintly, and its posture mimics The Rows' tendrils. | Any creature within 5 feet must make a DC 12 Wisdom saving throw or be charmed for 1 minute, feeling an urge to walk into the nearest cornfield. |
| "My Family" | Prudence Blackwood (Sarah's cousin) | A family portrait with cornstalk-like limbs on the people. | Family members' eyes are replaced with corn kernels. | Viewers must make a DC 11 Constitution saving throw or be poisoned for 1 hour, experiencing mild hallucinations of corn growing from their skin. |
| "Harvest Dance" | Ezekiel Crane Jr. (Ezekiel's grandson) | Children dancing in a circle around a large cornstalk. | The dance formation mirrors a cult ritual circle. | Anyone who stares at the picture for more than 10 seconds must make a DC 13 Wisdom saving throw or feel compelled to join the dance, spinning in place for 1 minute. |
| "Our Special Garden" | Jeremiah Crow IV (Founding family descendant) | A garden with unusual, twisted plants. | Plants bear resemblance to corrupted flora influenced by The Rows. | Anyone touching the picture must make a DC 14 Dexterity saving throw or be restrained for 1 minute by illusory vines. |
| "Scarecrow's Secret" | Mercy Holloway (Tavern keeper's daughter) | A scarecrow whispering to a group of children. | Scarecrow's mouth is filled with corn kernels, symbolizing The Rows' teachings. | Viewers must succeed on a DC 12 Wisdom (Insight) check or feel an unexplainable urge to share a secret with the nearest person. |
| "Moonlit Harvest" | Josiah Wainwright (Blacksmith's son) | Farmers working in a field under a full moon | Moon is subtly shaped like The Rows' symbol. | The picture glows faintly in darkness. Anyone sleeping within 10 feet experiences unsettling dreams and gains no benefit from the rest. |
| "Our Town's Protector" | Constance Mildrew (Former schoolmate of Emily Hawthorn) | A large, abstract figure overlooking the town | The figure's form is composed of twisted cornstalks. | Anyone studying the picture must make a DC 13 Charisma saving throw or feel an overwhelming sense of gratitude toward The Rows, imposing disadvantage on attacks against cultists for 1 hour. |

To use this table, have the PCs investigate the artwork around the room. For each successful Intelligence (Investigation) check, reveal the cult influence and potential effect. This activity showcases the insidious nature of the cult's indoctrination, targeting the town's most vulnerable members and using their innocence as a weapon.

### Finding an Untainted Child's Drawing

**Initial Search**: As the party investigates the children's artwork, they can make a DC 15 Wisdom (Perception) check to notice a small, crumpled piece of paper partially hidden beneath a stack of books on Miss Hawthorn's desk.

**Retrieval**: To retrieve the paper without alerting any corrupted entities, a player character must succeed on a DC 13 Dexterity (Sleight of Hand) check. Failure alerts nearby corrupted artworks, causing them to animate and attack.

### Animated Corrupted Artwork

If a PC fails a Dexterity (Sleight of Hand) check to retrieve the untainted child's drawing, the corrupted artwork animates and attacks. Use the following stats and description:

### Stat Block (Animated Corrupted Artwork)

*Small construct, unaligned*

**Armor Class:** 13

**Hit Points:** 18 (4d6 + 4)

**Speed:** 10 ft., fly 30 ft. (hover)

| STR | DEX | CON | INT | WIS | CHA |
|-----|-----|-----|-----|-----|-----|
| 6 (-2) | 16 (+3) | 14 (+2) | 3 (-4) | 10 (+0) | 1 (-5) |

**Damage Resistances:** necrotic, poison, psychic

**Damage Vulnerabilities:** fire

**Condition Immunities:** charmed, exhaustion, frightened, paralyzed, poisoned

**Senses:** darkvision 60 ft., passive Perception 10

**Languages:** -

**Challenge:** 1 (200 XP)

**Actions**

**Psychic Lash:** *Melee Weapon Attack:* +5 to hit, reach 5 ft., one target. *Hit:* 7 (1d8 + 3) psychic damage. The target must succeed on a DC 12 Wisdom saving throw or become stunned for 1 round, experiencing overwhelming mental images related to The Rows.

**Tendrils of Art:** The animated artwork flings a tendril of color, ink, or thread toward a target. *Ranged Weapon Attack:* +5 to hit, range 30 ft., one target. *Hit:* 6 (1d6 + 3) necrotic damage. The target must succeed on a DC 13 Constitution saving throw or be poisoned for 1 minute, feeling sickened by disturbing hallucinations.

**Lair Action:** If multiple pieces of artwork animate, each one can act on initiative count 20 (losing ties). All animated artworks cause the environment to become difficult terrain as ink and paint spread across the ground, making it slick. Creatures must make a DC 12

Dexterity saving throw or fall prone when they move through the area.

Examples of Animated Corrupted Artwork Attacks:

- **Fields of Gold**: The scarecrow depicted in the painting comes to life, its glowing eyes flashing with malice. It steps out of the frame, its straw limbs flailing to lash at the nearest PC.

- **My Family**: The cornstalk-like limbs of the family in the drawing extend out of the paper, grasping for the PCs. The tendrils emit a faint, poisonous mist, reflecting the picture's hallucinatory effect.

- **Harvest Dance**: Children in the picture begin moving and spinning rapidly, while the cornstalk they dance around extends toward the PCs. Tendrils of energy lash out from the cornstalk, trying to pull PCs into an illusory dance.

### Identification of Untainted Drawing

Upon unfolding the paper, PCs find a simple crayon drawing that seems different from the others. A successful DC 14 Intelligence (Investigation) check reveals that this drawing lacks the subtle corrupting influence present in the other artworks and holds potential for some strong arcane purpose. In order to determine this purpose, a PC must succeed on an Intelligence (Arcana) check DC 14. Success reveals the latent power of the drawing's use in a potent protection ritual (name and details unknown) as well as its vulnerability to corruption, both attributable to its innocence. Additionally, a successful Arcana check allows the PC to realize that to keep it safe, the drawing needs an extra layer of magical protection (see Preservation Challenge below).

*Note to DM:* The specific name and details of the referenced protection ritual (Cosmic Severance), along with its necessary components, are not discoverable by way of a successful ability check. Casting *Identify* on the drawing will only reveal the associated ritual's name and perhaps general purpose (at DM discretion), but not its components or performance instructions. These key pieces of information must be discovered in-game through character investigation and roleplay.

**Artist Discovery**: The drawing is signed by "Emily Hawthorn" - Miss Hawthorn's missing sister. This connection explains why the drawing remains untainted, as Emily resisted the cult's influence.

### Protective Measures

**Preservation Challenge**: The drawing's innocence makes it vulnerable to corruption. PCs must succeed on a DC 15 Intelligence (Arcana) check to create a temporary protective ward around the drawing. Failure results in the drawing slowly becoming tainted over the next hour, requiring the ritual to be performed quickly.

**Protection**: The party must keep the drawing safe until they can perform the ritual. If it comes within 30 feet of a powerful source of The Rows' corruption (like the Standing Stone), they must succeed on a DC 15 Wisdom saving throw or the drawing becomes tainted and useless for the ritual.

### Empowerment

**Empowering the Drawing**: To fully activate the drawing's power for the ritual, a player character must channel positive emotions into it. This requires a DC 14 Charisma (Performance) check as the PC describes a happy childhood memory. Success imbues the drawing with a soft, comforting glow.

**Resonance with Miss Hawthorn**: If Miss Hawthorn is present and has been freed from the hallucination's influence, showing her the drawing triggers a powerful emotional response. This automatically empowers the drawing and grants it additional properties for the ritual.

### Drawing Properties

Once empowered, the untainted drawing has the following properties:

- It radiates an aura of innocence in a 5-foot radius, granting advantage on saving throws against The Rows' corrupting effects while within this aura.

- The drawing acts as a focus for the Cosmic Severance ritual, allowing PCs to reroll one failed check while performing this ritual.

- If the drawing was empowered through Miss Hawthorn's connection, it also grants a +2 bonus to all ability checks made during the casting of the Cosmic Severance ritual.

## Terrain

The schoolhouse interior is cramped with desks and educational materials. Treat the area between desks as difficult terrain. Characters must succeed on a DC 12 Dexterity (Acrobatics) check to move at full speed through the rows of desks or halve their movement.

## Lair Actions

On initiative count 20 (losing initiative ties), the Crow's Hollow Schoolhouse invokes one of the following lair actions:

**Whispers of Indoctrination**: Eerie whispers echo through the room, forcing all creatures to make a DC 13 Wisdom saving throw or be charmed until the end of their next turn.

**Animated Artwork**: One of the children's drawings comes to life, creating a 10-foot square area of difficult terrain as corn stalks sprout from the floor.

**Phantom Bell**: The school bell rings with an otherworldly tone, causing all creatures to make a DC 13 Constitution saving throw or be deafened for 1 minute.

## Scaling the Encounter

### Beginning Players (PC levels 1-5)

- Reduce number of corrupted school materials to 4-5.

- Lower DCs for Investigation checks by 2.

- Weaken Hallucination of Lost Loved One: reduce HP, lower save DCs.

- Simplify Miss Hawthorn's struggle: require only 2 successful saves.

- Limit number of tainted artworks to 3-4, with milder effects.

- Remove or simplify lair actions.

- Focus on social interaction and investigation over combat.

- Provide more obvious clues about cult influence.

### Intermediate Players (PC levels 6-10)

- Use encounter as written.

- Add 1-2 Reaper of Abundance Cultists as potential combat encounters.

- Implement all lair actions.

- Increase consequences for failing to help Miss Hawthorn.

- Add time pressure (e.g., cultists arriving soon for a "special lesson").

- Enhance corrupted artwork effects and have a second artwork animate and attack.

- Include complex magical wards on some school materials.

### Advanced Players (PC levels 11+)

- Increase number of corrupted school materials with more subtle influences.
- Raise DCs for all checks by 2.
- Upgrade Hallucination of Lost Loved One to a more powerful entity (e.g., avatar of The Rows).
- Add multiple corruption points Miss Hawthorn must overcome.
- Include high-level cultist (e.g., Sarah Blackwood) as a possible combat encounter.
- Enhance lair actions, allowing multiple to trigger each round.

- Add magical traps or curses to some artwork and have 3 corrupted artworks attack.
- Introduce a moral dilemma involving potentially corrupted children.
- Create a complex ritual to cleanse the entire schoolhouse.

## Monster

Hallucination of Lost Loved One (targeting Miss Hawthorn)

## NPC

Miss Hawthorn

# Haunted Cornfield

This encounter represents the heart of The Rows' influence, where its power is most palpable and dangerous. Players will face both physical and psychological challenges, testing their resolve against the corrupt entity's manifestations.

As you come upon the outskirts of town, a vast expanse of cornfield stretches before you, its boundaries lost in the distance. The corn stalks tower unnaturally high, easily reaching 10 to 12 feet, creating walls of green that seem to watch your every move. An eerie mist clings to the ground, swirling around your feet and obscuring the paths between the rows.

The air is thick with an oppressive silence, broken only by the occasional rustle of leaves that sounds disturbingly like whispers. As you step closer, the corn seems to shift and sway despite the lack of wind, and you can't shake the feeling that the field itself is alive and aware of your presence. The usually comforting scent of earth and crops is tainted with an underlying odor of decay, as if something rotten lurks just beneath the surface.

## Activities

**Maze of Whispers**: Navigate the twisting paths of the corrupted cornfield, avoiding dead ends and sinister traps while searching for the heart of The Rows' influence.

**Echoes of the Past**: Overcome haunting visions of lost loved ones, distinguishing reality from The Rows' manipulative illusions.

**Stalk the Stalker**: Engage in a deadly game of cat and mouse with the Corn Stalker, turning the field's dangers against the creature to defeat it.

## Maze of Whispers

The DM will use a pre-drawn maze to track the party's progress through the cornfield. The maze should have multiple paths, dead ends, and a central area representing the heart of The Rows' influence. Time spent in the maze is measured in 3-minute intervals.

Blank Maze

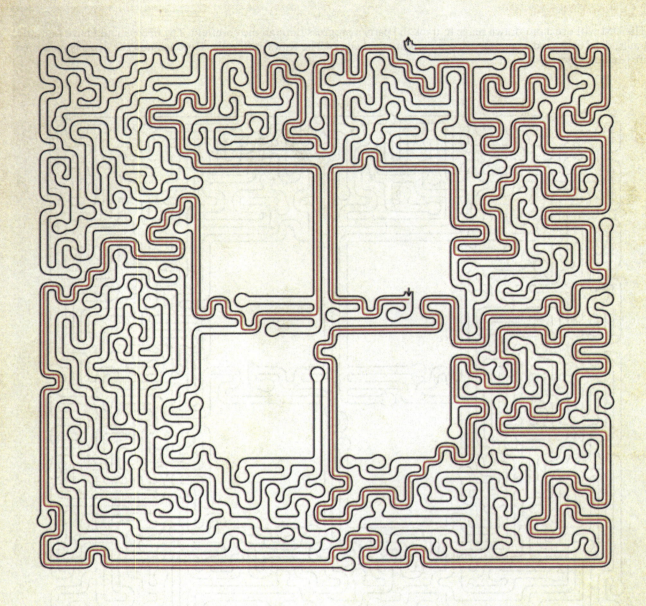

Solved Maze

## Navigation Rules

At the start of each 3-minute interval, the party's navigator must make a DC 13 Wisdom (Survival) check.

Success allows the party to move to an adjacent section of the maze of their choice.

Failure results in the party becoming disoriented and moving to a random adjacent section (DM's choice).

A natural 20 on the check allows the party to move two sections.

A natural 1 triggers a random encounter or trap.

## Perception and Investigation

PCs can use an action to make a DC 14 Wisdom (Perception) check to notice subtle clues about the correct path or nearby dangers.

A DC 15 Intelligence (Investigation) check can be used to analyze the corn patterns for signs of The Rows' influence, potentially revealing the direction of the maze's center.

## Time-Based Encounters

Every 3 minutes in the maze, roll on the encounter table below.

## Encounter Table (d6)

1. Animated Scarecrow (2)
2. Hallucination of Lost Loved One (1-2)
3. Corn Husk Zombie (1d4)
4. Animated Corn Husks (2d4)
5. Swarm of Carnivorous Locusts (1)
6. Vicious Vines (1-2)

## Traps and Hazards

The following traps can be substituted for an encounter with a monster.

### Corrupted Pollen

A cloud of sickly yellow pollen hangs in the air, barely visible in the dim light.

**Trigger**: Stepping into the affected area.

**Activation**: The trap activates when a creature enters the affected area.

**Effect**: Creatures in a 10-foot radius must make a DC 13 Constitution saving throw or be poisoned for 1 hour.

**Detection**: DC 14 Wisdom (Perception) check to notice the faint shimmering of pollen in the air.

**Disable**: A *Gust of Wind* spell or similar effect can disperse the pollen cloud.

### Grasping Roots

Twisted roots suddenly animate and reach out to ensnare passersby.

**Trigger**: Pressure plate hidden beneath the soil.

**Activation**: 50 pounds of pressure on the hidden plate.

**Effect**: Roots burst from the ground in a 15-foot radius. Creatures in the area must succeed on a DC 13 Dexterity saving throw or be restrained.

**Detection**: DC 15 Wisdom (Perception) check to notice the slightly raised earth hiding the pressure plate.

**Disable**: A DC 13 Dexterity check using thieves' tools can disable the pressure plate.

### Whispering Madness

Eerie whispers emanate from the corn, growing louder as victims draw near.

**Trigger**: Proximity to a hidden magical rune.

**Activation**: The trap activates when a creature comes within 20 feet of the hidden rune.

**Effect**: Creatures within 20 feet must succeed on a DC 14 Wisdom saving throw or be frightened for 1 minute.

**Detection**: DC 16 Intelligence (Arcana) check to detect the trap via the rune's magical aura.

**Disable**: The magical trap can be disarmed with a DC 14 Intelligence (Arcana) check, or by carefully erasing the rune with a DC 16 Dexterity check using thieves' tools.

## Special Rules

Passive Perception below 12 imposes disadvantage on noticing traps and hazards.

Characters proficient in Nature have advantage on checks to identify safe paths through the corn (as described earlier in the Perception and Investigation section).

After every hour in the maze, characters must succeed on a DC 12 Wisdom saving throw or gain one level of exhaustion due to The Rows' oppressive influence.

## Solving the Maze

Reaching the center within 5 minutes grants the party advantage on their first round of attacks against the Corn Stalker.

Taking between 5-15 minutes is a neutral outcome.

Taking more than 15 minutes imposes disadvantage on saving throws against The Rows' effects for the final encounter.

# Echoes of the Past

As PCs navigate the corrupted cornfield, they encounter Hallucinations of Lost Loved Ones, manifestations of The Rows' psychic corruption. These encounters test the

PCs' resolve and ability to distinguish reality from illusion.

Each player character must make a DC 14 Wisdom saving throw when they first encounter a Hallucination of Lost Loved One.

On a failed save, the character sees a vivid illusion of a lost loved one and must interact with the hallucination as if it were real for 1 minute.

On a successful save, the PC recognizes the illusion but still sees a faint, ghostly image.

### Hallucination Interactions

The hallucination uses the statistics of the Hallucination of Lost Loved One monster in the appendix.

It targets the PC with its Emotional Drain attack each round.

Every other round, it uses either Haunting Whispers or Illusory Reality.

### Resisting the Illusion

Affected PCs can attempt to break free by making a DC 14 Wisdom saving throw as an action on their turn.

Other PCs can attempt to help by making a DC 14 Charisma (Persuasion) check to remind the affected PC of reality, giving them advantage on their next save.

Casting *Dispel Magic* ends the effect immediately.

**Memory Challenges**: For each round a player character interacts with a Hallucination of Lost Loved One, they can make a DC 13 Wisdom (Insight) check to recall a true memory that contradicts the hallucination's deception. Success grants advantage on the next saving throw against the hallucination's abilities.

### Psychic Feedback

Each failed save against the Hallucination of Lost Loved One's abilities deals 1d6 psychic damage to the character.

If a character's hit points are reduced to 0 by this damage, they fall unconscious and have vivid nightmares about their lost loved one, waking up with one level of exhaustion.

**Group Hallucination**: If half or more of the party fails their initial saving throws, the entire group is pulled into a shared illusion. Use the following rules:

- The environment appears to transform into a familiar, comforting location from the past.

- All PCs must work together to discern three inconsistencies in the illusion.

- Each inconsistency discovered allows for a group Wisdom saving throw (DC 14) to break free from the shared illusion.

### Rewards for Overcoming

PCs who successfully resist or break free from a hallucination gain inspiration.

The party gains advantage on saving throws against charm effects for 1 hour after overcoming a group hallucination.

### Lingering Effects

Characters who spent more than 3 rounds under a hallucination's influence must succeed on a DC 12 Wisdom saving throw or be affected by short-term madness (roll on the Short-Term Madness table in the *DMG*).

## Stalk the Stalker

This activity represents the final confrontation with the Corn Stalker, a powerful manifestation of The Rows' corruption. PCs must use their wits and the environment to overcome this formidable foe.

### Encounter Setup

The battle takes place in a 60-foot by 60-foot area of dense cornfield.

Divide the area into 10-foot squares, each representing different terrain types (normal corn, dense corn, small clearings, etc.).

Place 1d4+1 environmental hazards (corrupted pollen clouds, grasping roots, etc.) randomly in the area.

### Corn Stalker Mechanics

Use the Corn Stalker stats from the provided Monster list in the Appendix.

The Corn Stalker begins hidden, using its False Appearance ability.

It has three phases, changing tactics as it loses hit points.

### Phase 1 (Full HP to 2/3 HP)
The Corn Stalker uses hit-and-run tactics, attacking and then using its Stalking Step legendary action to retreat into the corn.

Players must make a DC 15 Wisdom (Perception) check to spot the Corn Stalker when it's hidden.

### Phase 2 (2/3 HP to 1/3 HP)
The Corn Stalker becomes more aggressive, using its multiattack every round.

It uses Cornsilk Spores whenever possible, targeting the largest group of PCs.

### Phase 3 (Below 1/3 HP)
The Corn Stalker goes into a frenzy, gaining an additional legendary action per round.

It uses Entangling Stalks every round, in addition to its normal actions.

### Special Rules

The dense corn provides half cover to all creatures.

PCs can use an action to make a DC 12 Strength (Athletics) check to clear a 5-foot path through the corn, creating easier movement for allies.

The Corn Stalker can move through the corn without penalty due to its Cornfield Camouflage ability.

## Victory Conditions

Defeating the Corn Stalker.

Forcing the Corn Stalker to retreat (reducing it to 10 HP or fewer).

## Rewards

Upon defeating the Corn Stalker or forcing its retreat, the PCs discover a magical seed embedded in the creature's chest.

### Lore for the Magical Seed

This seed is an ancient relic, a vestige of the land before the region fell to corruption. The Reapers of Abundance cult has tried repeatedly to destroy or corrupt the seed to turn it into a powerful weapon, but all attempts have failed. Unable to taint it with The Rows' influence, the cultists have kept it hidden, hoping to one day find a method to corrupt its power.

The Corn Stalker was tasked with guarding the seed while the cult worked on a method to alter its properties. The seed represents a direct threat to The Rows, and should it ever be planted, it could create a sanctuary where The Rows' corruption cannot spread.

### Magical Seed Properties:

- When planted, this seed purifies a 30-foot radius of land, making it fertile and resistant to The Rows' influence for one year.

- The area becomes a haven of uncorrupted land, ideal for growing crops and sheltering those seeking refuge from The Rows.

## Terrain

The cornfield is difficult terrain due to the dense, towering stalks and clinging mist. Characters must succeed on a DC 13 Wisdom (Survival) check to navigate without becoming lost. Failure means the character moves in a random direction and must repeat the check next turn. Additionally, visibility is heavily obscured beyond 10 feet due to the corn and mist, imposing disadvantage on Perception checks relying on sight beyond that range.

## Lair Actions

On initiative count 20 (losing initiative ties), the Haunted Cornfield invokes one of the following lair actions:

**Whispers of Madness**: Haunting whispers emanate from the corn, forcing all creatures to make a DC 14 Wisdom saving throw or be frightened until the end of their next turn.

**Grasping Stalks**: The corn stalks animate in a 20-foot radius centered on a point chosen by The Rows, attempting to grasp and entangle creatures. This area becomes difficult terrain, and any creature in the area where the stalks animate must succeed on a DC 13 Strength saving throw or be restrained.

**Mist of Despair**: The mist thickens in a 30-foot radius, sapping the will of those within. Creatures in the area must succeed on a DC 14 Charisma saving throw or be affected as if by the *Bane* spell until the end of their next turn.

## Scaling the Encounter

### Beginning Players (PC levels 1-5)

- Simplify maze: reduce size, fewer dead ends.

- Lower Perception and Investigation check DCs to navigate to 11.

- Reduce encounter frequency: roll every 5 minutes instead of 3.

- Use weaker monsters: Animated Corn Husks instead of Animated Scarecrows.

- Weaken Corn Stalker: reduce HP, AC, and damage output.

- Remove or simplify lair actions.

- Reduce trap damage and save DCs by 2.

- Focus on atmosphere and exploration over combat.

### Intermediate Players (PC levels 6-10)

- Use encounter as written.

- Add 1-2 additional hazards or traps.

- Implement all lair actions.

- Increase Corn Stalker's legendary actions to 4 per round.

- Add mini-boss (e.g., Corrupted Druid) before Corn Stalker fight.

- Enhance Psychic Feedback damage and effects from Hallucinations of Lost Loved Ones.

- Introduce time pressure (e.g., corruption spreading to town).

### Advanced Players (PC levels 11+)

- Expand maze size, add magical misdirection.

- Increase Perception and Investigation check DCs to navigate to 15.

- Add more powerful monsters (e.g., Plant-Human Hybrids).
- Upgrade Corn Stalker to legendary creature status.
- Implement more frequent and powerful lair actions.
- Add complex magical traps and illusions.
- Introduce multiple Corn Stalkers or a more powerful variant.
- Create a skill challenge to weaken The Rows' influence during final battle.
- Add environmental effects that change every few rounds.

## Monsters

Corn Stalker

Animated Scarecrow (2)

Hallucination of Lost Loved One (4-5)

Corn Husk Zombie (1d4)

Animated Corn Husks (2d4)

Swarm of Carnivorous Locusts

Vicious Vines (1-2)

# Mayor's Office

This encounter reveals the depth of corruption in Crow's Hollow's leadership. Players must navigate a tense social situation while seeking evidence, potentially leading to a confrontation with the town's highest authority.

Once you reach the center of town, you see a stately two-story building standing out among the more modest structures. Its white-painted wooden exterior and pillared entrance exude an air of authority and respectability. A polished brass plaque beside the door identifies this as the town hall and mayor's office.

Stepping inside, you're greeted by the scent of fresh varnish and lemon-scented cleaning products. The reception area is neat and orderly, with a few chairs for visitors and walls adorned with framed certificates and agricultural awards. You notice an unsettling number of corn-themed decorations - from the wallpaper pattern to small statuettes on shelves. A narrow staircase leads to the upper floor, where you presume the mayor's private office is located.

## Activities

**Paper Trail of Corruption**: Search Mayor Thorne's office for hidden documents revealing her connection to the cult.

**Unmasking the High Reaper**: Engage Mayor Thorne in a tense verbal sparring match, attempting to expose her true allegiance through carefully chosen questions and observations.

**Confronting the Harvest's Heart**: If Mayor Thorne's identity as the High Reaper is revealed, face her in a climactic confrontation that could determine the fate of Crow's Hollow.

## Mayor's Office Layout

Below is a detailed description of the town hall building (Mayor's Office location) and its rooms.

### Ground Floor

**Reception Area** (20 ft x 30 ft): For welcoming visitors and managing appointments. A spacious room with a large wooden desk for the receptionist, comfortable chairs for waiting visitors, and walls adorned with town accolades and agricultural awards. A prominent corn-themed clock hangs on one wall.

**Public Meeting Room** (30 ft x 40 ft): For hosting town council meetings and public gatherings. Contains a large oval table with seating for 12, additional chairs along the walls for observers, and a podium at one end. The walls are decorated with portraits of past mayors and maps of Crow's Hollow.

**Records Room** (15 ft x 20 ft): For storing public records and town documents. Filled with filing cabinets and shelves containing ledgers, land deeds, and other official papers. A small desk and chair allow for document examination.

**Staff Break Room** (10 ft x 15 ft): Provides a space for staff to rest and eat. A modest kitchenette with a refrigerator, microwave, and coffee maker. A small table with chairs and a worn couch occupy the central space.

### Second Floor

**Mayor's Private Office** (20 ft x 25 ft): The mayor's personal workspace and meeting area. An opulent room with a large mahogany desk, leather chairs, and bookshelves lining the walls. A hidden safe is concealed behind a painting of cornfields. The room has an unsettling number of corn-themed decorations.

**Assistant's Office** (10 ft x 15 ft): This workspace for the mayor's personal assistant is smaller and more modest than the mayor's own office. The room contains a simple desk, enchanted scrolls, and magical record-keeping devices.

**Small Conference Room** (15 ft x 20 ft): This room is used for private meetings and confidential discussions. It contains a round table with seating for 6-8 people, along with an enchanted mirror that displays notes, maps, or visuals on command, serving the same purpose as a whiteboard or projector screen.

**Storage Closet** (5 ft x 10 ft): Storing office supplies and cleaning materials. Shelves stocked with paper, pens, and other office essentials. Also contains cleaning supplies and a ladder for accessing high shelves or changing light bulbs.

**Restrooms** (Two 5 ft x 8 ft rooms): Staff and visitor facilities. One restroom on each floor, each containing a toilet and sink with basic amenities.

The building's layout emphasizes the separation between public and private spaces, with the ground floor being more accessible and the second floor reserved for the mayor and close staff. The decor throughout subtly reinforces the town's agricultural focus, with corn imagery being particularly prevalent.

## Paper Trail of Corruption

Below a list of documents that can be found in various rooms on the second floor:

### "Harvest Ledger"

**Content**: A coded record of cult sacrifices and rituals, disguised as crop yield data.

**Location**: Hidden in a false bottom of the top desk drawer in the Mayor's Private Office.

**DC**: 15 Intelligence (Investigation) check to discover the false bottom of the desk drawer, then another Investigation check at DC 14 to decipher the actual data content being recorded.

### "The Reaper's Correspondence"

**Content**: Letters between Mayor Thorne and other high-ranking cultists, using agricultural metaphors to discuss cult activities.

**Location**: Inside a hollowed-out book entitled *Advanced Corn Cultivation* on the bookshelf in the Mayor's Private Office.

**DC**: 16 Wisdom (Perception) check to notice something slightly off about the book on the office room shelf.

### Crow's Hollow Consecration Map

**Content**: A map of the town marking important cult locations and future "expansion" sites.

**Location**: Rolled up and stored in a corn-themed decorative vase in the Small Conference Room.

**DC**: 15 Intelligence (Investigation) check to find the hidden map.

### "Seedling Indoctrination Program"

**Content**: A detailed plan for recruiting and grooming young town members into the cult.

**Location**: In a locked filing cabinet (DC 13 Dexterity check using thieves' tools to open) in the Assistant's Office.

**DC**: 14 Intelligence (Investigation) check to find among the files (after unlocking the cabinet).

### Thorne Family Grimoire

**Content**: An old book containing generations of occult knowledge and rituals related to The Rows.

**Location**: Inside a wall safe hidden behind the cornfield painting in the Mayor's Private Office.

**DC**: 18 Wisdom (Perception) OR Intelligence (Investigation) check to find the safe, then DC 16 Dexterity check using thieves' tools to open it.

### Altered Town Census

**Content**: A doctored population record hiding the true number of missing persons.

**Location**: Mixed in with legitimate documents in the Records Room.

**DC**: 17 Intelligence (Investigation) check to discover the doctored census data among the records and deduce its sinister purpose.

### The Rows' Whispers

**Content**: Mayor Thorne's personal journal, detailing her communications with The Rows and her rise to power.

**Location**: Under a loose floorboard beneath her desk in the Mayor's Private Office.

**DC**: 16 Wisdom (Perception) check to detect the slightly loose floorboard under the mayor's desk.

## Unmasking the High Reaper

This activity is structured as a social encounter using a series of skill checks and saving throws:

**Insight Challenge**: PCs can make Wisdom (Insight) checks (DC 15) to detect lies or evasions in Thorne's responses. On a success, they gain advantage on their next Charisma check against Thorne.

**Verbal Sparring**: PCs use Charisma (Persuasion, Deception, or Intimidation) checks to press Thorne on sensitive topics. The base DC is 14, but increases by 1 for each successful check as Thorne becomes more guarded.

**Thorne's Deception**: Mayor Thorne uses her Deception skill (+9) to deflect suspicions. If her Deception check exceeds the PC's Insight check, she can use her Harvest Blessing ability to impose disadvantage on the next check made against her.

**Trigger Topics**: Establish 4 sensitive topics (recent disappearances, strange harvests, cult symbols, The Rows). When a PC mentions one, Thorne must make a Charisma (Deception) check (DC 15) or reveal a tell. If she fails 3 such checks, she loses composure and reveals her true nature.

**Whispering Influence**: As tension rises, Thorne might use her Seeds of Corruption ability. The target must make a DC 17 Constitution saving throw or be poisoned for 1 minute, giving Thorne advantage on Charisma checks against them.

**Breaking Point**: If PCs present hard evidence (such as what can be found in the **Paper Trail of Corruption** activity), Thorne must make a DC 18 Charisma saving throw. On a failure, she reveals her true identity, initiating **Confronting the Harvest's Heart**.

## Confronting the Harvest's Heart

This activity is a boss fight against Mayor Abigail Thorne as the High Reaper.

**Transformation**: Thorne uses her action to transform, gaining all abilities of the Mayor Abigail Thorne (High Reaper) stat block. She uses her bonus action to activate her Cloak of Flies invocation.

**Summon Cultists**: Thorne uses Call of the Rows to summon 1d4 Reaper of Abundance Cultists. These cultists arrive at the start of her next turn.

**Corrupting Environment**: The office begins to transform, with corn stalks bursting through floorboards and creating difficult terrain. At the start of each round, an additional 10-foot square becomes difficult terrain.

**Eldritch Tactics**: Thorne prioritizes using Seeds of Corruption and Corrupting Touch. She also uses Harvest Blessing on summoned cultists.

**Escape Plan**: If reduced to below 30 HP, Thorne attempts to flee by darting out of sight and escaping through a hidden passage (DC 15 Investigation to find) which leads to the cornfields. If she escapes, she becomes the final boss at the Standing Stone location.

**Defeat and Revelation**: If reduced to 0 HP, Thorne's form begins to wither like a dying corn stalk. In her final moments, she reveals cryptic information about The Rows' true nature and the location of the cult's main ritual site.

## Terrain

The Mayor's Private Office is on the second floor, accessible by a creaky wooden staircase. The stairs are considered difficult terrain due to their age and the necessity for stealth. Characters must succeed on a DC 13 Dexterity (Stealth) check to ascend or descend the stairs without making noise. Failure alerts the staff, increasing the DC of subsequent Stealth checks by 2.

## Lair Actions

On initiative count 20 (losing initiative ties), the Mayor's Office invokes one of the following lair actions:

**Whispering Corn**: Decorative corn husks throughout the office begin to whisper, forcing all creatures to make a DC 14 Wisdom saving throw or be frightened until the end of their next turn.

**Bureaucratic Maze**: Filing cabinets and bookshelves magically rearrange themselves, creating difficult terrain in a 20-foot radius for 1 round.

**Corrupt Influence**: Mayor Thorne's dark influence seeps into the room. All cultists regain 10 hit points, while non-cultists must succeed on a DC 14 Constitution saving throw or be poisoned until the end of their next turn.

## Scaling the Encounter

### Beginning Players (PC levels 1-5)

- Reduce number of hidden documents to 3-4, lower Investigation/Perception check DCs by 2.
- Simplify Unmasking the High Reaper: fewer trigger topics, lower DCs by 2.
- Weaken Mayor Thorne: use commoner stats with 1-2 special abilities.
- Remove or significantly weaken lair actions.
- Limit Reaper of Abundance Cultists to 1, use weaker stat block.
- Focus on social interaction and stealth over combat.
- Provide more obvious clues about the mayor's corruption.
- If combat occurs, allow easy escape routes.

### Intermediate Players (PC levels 6-10)

- Use encounter as written.
- Add 1-2 additional hidden documents with higher DCs.
- Implement all aspects of Unmasking the High Reaper.
- Use full Mayor Abigail Thorne (High Reaper) stat block.
- Include all lair actions.

- Add magical wards or alarms to increase the stealth challenge.
- Introduce time pressure (e.g., an impending town meeting).

### Advanced Players (PC levels 11+)

- Increase number and complexity of hidden documents.
- Raise all DCs by 2.
- Enhance Mayor Thorne's abilities: more HP, higher save DCs, additional legendary actions.
- Add 1-2 powerful lieutenant cultists or Plant-Human Hybrids.
- Enhance lair actions, allowing multiple to trigger each round.
- Create a complex, multi-stage boss fight if Thorne is exposed.
- Add magical traps and illusions throughout the office.
- Introduce a parallel objective (e.g., rescuing a captive while confronting Thorne).

## Monster

Reaper of Abundance Cultist (2-3, disguised as staff)

## NPC

Mayor Abigail Thorne

# Old Mill

This encounter reveals the cult's secret rituals and provides an opportunity for direct confrontation with a key cult leader. Players must navigate a dangerous, decrepit structure while potentially rescuing victims and uncovering crucial information about the cult's activities.

As you draw near the Old Mill by the river, the structure looms before you like a skeletal remnant of a forgotten past. The wooden planks are warped and rotting, with rusted metal beams visible through gaping holes in the walls. A partially collapsed water wheel juts out of the river, groaning as the current forces it to turn. The air is thick with the scent of decay, but there's something else mixed in – a sweet, unsettling odor, like fermenting corn.

Near the entrance of the mill, you catch a glimpse of something unnatural. A hulking figure stands guard, its body a twisted mass of plant and human features. It stands motionless, scanning the area with glowing, unnatural eyes.

## Activities

**Shadows of the Harvest**: Covertly infiltrate the mill to witness a secret cult gathering, collecting crucial intelligence about their plans and rituals.

**Cultist Conflict**: Engage in a direct confrontation with Sarah Blackwood and her cultist followers, attempting to stop their nefarious activities.

**Breaking the Offerings**: Locate and free any captives held for sacrificial purposes, disrupting the cult's plans in the process.

## Plant-Human Hybrid Encounter

**Hybrid Guard:** The Plant-Human Hybrid patrols around the mill entrance. The DM should describe this creature only if the party attempts to sneak closer. If any PCs fail their Dexterity (Stealth) check (DC 14), they will be spotted, and the hybrid will attack. A failed check also risks alerting the cultists inside.

The hybrid patrols in slow, deliberate movements, occasionally turning to gaze at the surrounding cornfields.

The **Plant-Human Hybrid** can be bypassed with successful *stealth* checks or defeated in combat. If combat occurs outside the mill, the cultists will hear the commotion if it lasts longer than two rounds. They will be ready for the party, either defensively or to escalate the situation into a full-blown ritual.

## Inside the Mill

If the PCs manage to sneak past the hybrid guard or defeat it in combat, the following read-aloud text applies when they enter the mill:

Stepping inside the mill, you're greeted by a scene both bizarre and horrifying. Several cultists are gathered in a wide-open space in the center of the mill, lit by flickering candles placed haphazardly on the ground. A circle of symbols, carved into the wood floor and surrounded by piles of corn husks, marks the center of the ritual. The cultists speak in hushed tones, discussing future plans for their "great harvest." Nearby, a rusted machine groans ominously, and the scent of decay is more pronounced here— overpowering and unnatural.

The cultists have not yet begun their ritual, but their preparations are meticulous. This is the party's chance to either observe or intervene while the cultists are still discussing their plans.

## Shadows of the Harvest

This stealth-based activity is structured as a series of skill challenges and saving throws:

**Infiltration** (Stealth Challenge): PCs must make a group Dexterity (Stealth) check (DC 14) to enter the mill undetected. If the group fails, they alert the Plant-Human Hybrid guarding the door or a patrolling cultist outside the mill.

**Finding a Vantage Point**: PCs can choose different observation points, each requiring a specific check:

- **Rafters**: Dexterity (Athletics) (DC 15) to climb quietly.
- **Abandoned Machinery**: Dexterity (Acrobatics) DC 14 to balance on rusted equipment.
- **Shadowy Corner**: Dexterity (Stealth) DC 13 to blend with the shadows.

Failure on any of these checks results in the cultists becoming suspicious, leading to increased difficulty on future checks or immediate combat.

**Eavesdropping** (Wisdom Perception DC 13): For every successful check, the PCs overhear valuable information. Choose one or roll from the following list:

- "The Great Reaping is nearly upon us. The harvest will begin on the full moon."

- "The Rows are growing stronger every day. We must be ready to ascend with it."
- "Once the Standing Stone has collected enough energy, no one will be able to stop us."

### Corruption Resistance

While in the Old Mill, characters must make Constitution saving throws (DC 12) every 10 minutes of in-game time. Failure results in gaining one level of corruption. Corruption levels go from 1 to 5.

### Corruption Levels

### Level 1: Disadvantage on Wisdom (Perception) checks.
- **Symptoms**: The character begins to feel uneasy, and their senses are dulled by the subtle whisper of The Rows.
- **Effect**: Disadvantage on Wisdom (Perception) checks.

### Level 2: Speed reduced by 10 feet.
- **Symptoms**: Corrupted plant life begins to spread across the character's skin, making movement more difficult.
- **Effect**: The character's speed is reduced by 10 feet as the tendrils of corruption hinder their mobility.

### Level 3: Disadvantage on attack rolls.
- **Symptoms**: The corruption has begun to affect the character's coordination and mental clarity.
- **Effect**: The character suffers disadvantage on all attack rolls.

### Level 4: Poisoned condition.
- **Symptoms**: The character's body is wracked with pain as the corruption spreads deeper, and their skin begins to take on a bark-like texture.
- **Effect**: The character is poisoned, suffering disadvantage on attack rolls and ability checks.

### Level 5: Charmed by The Rows (*Suggestion* effect).
- **Symptoms**: The character's mind is consumed by The Rows, and they feel an overwhelming urge to serve its goals.
- **Effect**: The character is charmed by The Rows, acting as if under the influence of the *Suggestion* spell, with the instruction to "join with the growth."

**Deciphering the Ritual**: PCs can make an Intelligence (Arcana OR Religion) check (DC 15) to understand the ritual's purpose. Success provides insight into how to disrupt the ritual in future encounters.

**Tense Moments**: At three key points during the observation, a random PC must make a Dexterity (Stealth) check (DC 15) to avoid detection. Failure alerts the cultists, potentially leading to combat or a chase scene.

**Escape Plan**: Before the ritual concludes, PCs must devise and execute an escape plan. This requires a successful group ability check (players' choice, DC varies based on the plan) to exit undetected.

### Intelligence Gathered

Based on the number of successful checks and time spent observing, award PCs with varying levels of information:

- **Basic**: General cult structure and immediate plans.
- **Detailed**: Specific ritual components and cult hierarchy.
- **Comprehensive**: Long-term goals of The Rows and potential ways to weaken its influence.

### Basic: General Cult Structure and Immediate Plans

At this level, the player characters gain a broad understanding of the Reapers of Abundance and their immediate activities. They learn that the cult operates in small cells throughout Crow's Hollow, each led by a mid-ranking member known as a "Tender." These Tenders report to higher-ranking members called "Harvesters," who in turn answer to the mysterious High Reaper. The cult's immediate plans involve preparing for a significant ritual called the "Great Reaping," scheduled for the next full moon. This ritual requires the sacrifice of several "pure" individuals, though the exact criteria for purity remains unclear. The PCs also discover that the cult has been slowly infiltrating key positions in the town's governance and essential services, allowing them to operate with minimal interference.

### Detailed: Specific Ritual Components and Cult Hierarchy

With more detailed intelligence, the PCs uncover the intricate hierarchy of the Reapers of Abundance and the specifics of their rituals. They learn that the cult is divided into three main ranks: Seedlings (new initiates), Tenders (mid-rank members), and Harvesters (high-ranking officials). Above these is the High Reaper, rumored to be in direct communion with The Rows. The player characters also discover the existence of specialized roles within the cult, such as "Whisperers" who interpret The Rows' will, and "Grafters" who oversee the creation of Plant-Human Hybrids.

Regarding rituals, the PCs learn the components required for the "Great Reaping": the blood of a virgin, the bones of a stillborn child, corrupted corn seeds, and a tome called *The Harvest Codex*. The ritual must be performed at a place where The Rows' influence is strongest, likely the old Standing Stone outside town. The PCs also gain insight into smaller, regular rituals performed by the cult, such as the "Seedling's Baptism" for new members and the "Cornsilk Communion" used to reinforce The Rows' influence over existing members.

The PCs also learn of a secret ritual, known as the Cosmic Severance, that can reduce the power of The Rows on the material plane with four cryptic components: Uncorrupted Water, the Founder's Sickle, Purified Salt, and a Symbol of Faith.

### Comprehensive: Long-Term Goals of The Rows and Potential Ways to Weaken its Influence

At this level, the player characters gain a chilling understanding of The Rows' ultimate goals and potential weaknesses. They learn that The Rows is an eldritch entity that seeks to transform the entire material plane into a vast, corrupted field - a mirror of its own alien realm. Its long-term plan involves creating a network of "Anchor Points" (such as Crow's Hollow) across the world, from which its influence can spread exponentially. The Rows aims to fuse the material plane with its own dimension, creating a nightmarish reality where it reigns supreme.

The PCs discover that The Rows' influence is not invincible. They learn of potential ways to weaken it:

- **Purification Rituals**: Ancient druidic rites that can cleanse small areas of land from The Rows' corruption.
- **Severing Connections**: Destroying key "Anchor Points" (like the Standing Stone) can significantly weaken The Rows' hold on an area.
- **Breaking the Cycle**: Disrupting the regular rituals performed by the cult can gradually erode The Rows' influence.
- **True Names**: Learning and utilizing The Rows' true name could provide power over the entity. Old Man Jenkins may have information on The Rows' true name.
- **Cosmic Severance**: this complicated ritual will sever the connection The Rows has to its original material plane, but its successful performance requires the following components:
  - **Uncorrupted Water**: A vial of water from the purified river (from the Polluted River encounter).
  - **The Founder's Sickle**: The Sickle of the First Harvest (from the Crow Family Crypt encounter).
  - **Purified Salt**: Enough salt to create a ritual circle (from the Old Mill encounter).
  - **Symbol of Faith**: A cleansed holy symbol (from the Corrupted Chapel encounter).

### Clarification on the Symbol of Faith

- **If the PCs have completed the Corrupted Chapel encounter:**
  The **Symbol of Faith** used in the ritual must have been **previously corrupted by The Rows** and then **cleansed** by holy rites. This purification process signifies the reversal of The Rows' influence, making the symbol essential for the **Cosmic Severance** ritual.

If the PCs cleanse their own holy symbol during the Corrupted Chapel encounter, it can serve this purpose.

- **If the PCs have not completed the Corrupted Chapel encounter:**
  A holy symbol that has never been corrupted can still be used in the ritual, but its power will be diminished. In this case, the DC for successfully performing the **Cosmic Severance** ritual increases by 2, as the ritual lacks the full potency of reversing The Rows' corruption. The DM should stress that while a standard holy symbol can suffice, the PCs may want to seek out the chapel to find and cleanse a corrupted symbol of faith to ensure the most effective ritual possible.

The PCs also learn that The Rows' power waxes and wanes with the agricultural cycle, being strongest during the harvest season and weakest in the dead of winter. This knowledge could be crucial in timing a final confrontation with the entity.

## Cultist Ritual

If the PCs have chosen not to intervene before the meeting has concluded, the cultists will then begin the Seedling's Baptism ritual to initiate new members. The PCs will have a short window (five rounds) to disrupt the ritual before it reaches completion.

**Ritual Impact:** Should the ritual complete, all cultists gain temporary hit points and advantage on saving throws against fear effects.

### Seedling's Baptism

This initiation ritual is performed on new members, or "Seedlings," who wish to join the Reapers of Abundance. The ritual involves submerging the initiate in a cauldron of corrupted water while chanting ancient eldritch incantations. The water seeps into the initiate's skin, infusing them with The Rows' power.

**Special Items or Actions Needed**:

- A cauldron filled with water from a corrupted well.
- Corrupted corn husks to burn as incense.
- Eldritch chants performed by a Harvester.

**Ritual Casting Time:** 5 rounds (30 seconds)

**Impact/Properties**:

- **Dark Infusion:** The initiate gains resistance to necrotic damage and immunity to being frightened as long as they serve The Rows.
- **Corruption Seed:** The initiate's alignment shifts one step toward evil (DM's discretion).

**Ritual Failure:** If the ritual is disrupted, the initiate suffers 2d6 necrotic damage and becomes cursed. The curse causes them to be vulnerable to necrotic damage until it is removed by a *Remove Curse* spell or similar magic.

## Cultist Conflict

This activity is structured as a multi-phase combat encounter against Sarah Blackwood and her cultist followers:

### Phase 1: Initial Confrontation

**Surprise Round**: If the PCs successfully completed the **Shadows of the Harvest** activity without being detected, they gain a surprise round. Otherwise, roll initiative as normal.

**Battlefield Setup**: The encounter takes place in the main room of the Old Mill. Use the established terrain rules found at the end of this encounter, including difficult terrain and weakened floor areas.

**Cultist Positions**: Sarah Blackwood stands in the center of the room near the ritual circle, or inside the circle while performing the ritual. 3-4 Reaper of Abundance Cultists are spread around the room. The Plant-Human Hybrid guards the entrance.

### Phase 2: Ritual Disruption

**Ritual Progress**: Once Sarah begins to perform the ritual, at the start of each round, Sarah makes progress on her ritual. PCs can attempt to disrupt the ritual with the following actions:

- **Destroy ritual components**: Attack action against AC 15 object.
- **Erase ritual circles**: Use an action to make a DC 13 Intelligence (Arcana) check.
- **Counter-chant**: As an action, make a DC 15 Charisma (Performance) check.

**Corrupting Influence**: At the end of each round, all non-cultist creatures must make a DC 13 Wisdom saving throw. Failure results in gaining one level of corruption (as detailed in the **Shadows of the Harvest** activity).

### Phase 3: Sarah's Desperation

**Transformation**: When reduced to half health, Sarah undergoes a partial transformation. She gains multiattack and her Corrupting Touch ability recharges on a 5-6.

**Summon Reinforcements**: On her turn, Sarah can use an action to summon 1d4 Animated Corn Husks.

**Environmental Hazards**: As the battle progresses, parts of the mill begin to collapse. At the start of each round, roll a d20. On a 15 or higher, a 10-foot square section of the upper floor collapses, forcing creatures in that area to make a DC 15 Dexterity saving throw or fall and take 2d6 bludgeoning damage.

### Phase 4: Climax and Escape

**Sarah's Last Stand**: When reduced to 25% health, Sarah attempts a final, desperate ritual. This creates a

30-foot radius zone of corrupted energy. Creatures starting their turn in this zone take 2d6 necrotic damage.

**Mill Collapse**: After 3 rounds of Sarah's Last Stand, the mill begins to fully collapse. All creatures must make a DC 15 Dexterity saving throw each round or take 3d6 bludgeoning damage from falling debris.

**Escape**: PCs have 3 rounds to escape the collapsing mill. This requires a successful group Dexterity (Acrobatics) check (DC 15).

### Resolution

If the party defeats Sara, they gain valuable information about the cult's plans and can potentially rescue any captives.

If Sarah escapes, she becomes a recurring villain, her powers growing with each encounter.

## Discovering the Purified Salt

As the PCs explore the Old Mill after confronting Sarah Blackwood and her cultists, they can find the source of purified salt necessary for the Cosmic Severance ritual:

**Hidden Storage**: In a secluded corner of the mill's ground floor, PCs can make a DC 14 Wisdom (Perception) check to notice a loose floorboard.

**Secret Compartment**: Lifting the floorboard reveals a small, hidden compartment. Inside is a weathered wooden box with intricate carvings of wheat and salt crystals.

**Ancestral Safeguard**: This box contains several pounds of purified salt, created and hidden by the mill's original owners as a safeguard against supernatural threats. It has remained untouched and uncorrupted due to its concealment.

**Magical Properties**: PCs can make a DC 15 Intelligence (Arcana) check to sense the salt's latent protective properties. On a success, they realize this salt has been naturally imbued with protective energy over decades of absorbing ambient magic from the mill's operations.

**Harvesting the Salt**: PCs can collect the salt but must be careful not to contaminate it. A DC 13 Dexterity (Sleight of Hand) check is required to transfer the salt to a clean container without spilling or tainting it.

**Quantity**: There's enough purified salt to create a ritual circle for the Cosmic Severance ritual, plus a small amount extra that could be used for other protective purposes if the players are creative.

**Lore Connection**: If the PCs have completed the Mayor's Office encounter, or if they obtained significant lore regarding the town's history from a friendly NPC such as Jenkins, the PCs may each make a DC 15 Intelligence (History) check. Successful PCs recall a story of the Old Mill being a place of refuge during times of supernatural trouble in Crow's Hollow's past. This salt likely played a role in those events.

**Corruption Resistance**: The purified salt, due to its protective nature, makes it difficult for The Rows to influence anyone carrying it. Characters carrying some of this salt gain advantage on saving throws against The Rows' corrupting effects.

## Breaking out the Offerings

This activity involves PC discovery of hidden captives being held for sacrificial purposes in a secret basement under the mill's main floor. PCs can then free the captives, disrupting the cult's plans in the process.

### Locating the Captives

PCs must search the Old Mill to find where the captives are held.

Each character can make a Wisdom (Perception) check (DC 14) to notice clues:

Success reveals faint sounds of muffled cries or scratching.

A result of 18 or higher pinpoints the exact location.

### Accessing the Hidden Area

The captives are being held in a concealed basement area.

To find the entrance, characters must succeed on an Intelligence (Investigation) check (DC 15).

Alternatively, PC can attempt to spot any hidden mechanisms or gaps in the floor (DC 16 Wisdom (Perception) check.

### Stealth Approach

If the PCs manage to avoid combat altogether by waiting for all the cultists to leave the mill before entering and exploring it, they still need to be quiet or risk drawing unwanted attention. As PCs open the heavy trapdoor in the floor, they must make a Dexterity (Stealth) check (DC 13).Failure alerts a patrolling cultist, initiating a combat encounter.

### The Holding Area

The basement is dimly lit and filled with a sickly-sweet odor.

1d4+2 captives are held in corrupted plant-like cocoons.

Each cocoon has AC 12 and 15 hit points. They are vulnerable to slashing damage but resistant to bludgeoning.

### Freeing the Captives

PCs can attempt to carefully extract captives or quickly slash open the cocoons.

**Careful Extraction**: Medicine check (DC 14). Success frees the captive safely; failure deals 1d6 necrotic damage to the captive.

**Quick Slash**: Attack roll against AC 12. Success frees the captive but deals 1d4 slashing damage.

### Corruption Check

Each freed captive must make a Constitution saving throw (DC 12).

Failure indicates they've been partially corrupted by The Rows' influence.

Corrupted captives are frightened of plants and have disadvantage on Wisdom saves for 24 hours.

### Escape Plan

Once freed, the captives must be safely escorted out of the mill.

This requires a group Dexterity check (players' choice of Stealth or Athletics, DC 13).

Failure could alert nearby cultists or trigger a skill challenge to evade pursuit.

### List of Captives and their Backstories

Below is a list of captives being held by the Reapers of Abundance, including their names, backstories, and the reasons why the cultists need them for their ceremonies.

#### Lily Thorne (Age 16)

Mayor Abigail Thorne's niece, kept sheltered and "pure" by her family.

Her bloodline's connection to the founding of Crow's Hollow makes her a potent sacrifice for strengthening The Rows' connection to the town.

#### Ezra Crane (Age 78)

Ezekiel Crane's estranged brother, a former town elder who tried to warn others about The Rows decades ago.

His long-standing resistance to The Rows makes him a valuable offering to break the will of those who oppose the cult.

#### Hazel and Heath Whitby (Twins, Age 8)

Children of Prudence Whitby, born on the night of a harvest moon.

Their synchronized energies and connection to a cult member make them ideal for a ritual to expand The Rows' influence to neighboring towns.

#### Meredith Holloway (Age 42)

The town's midwife, who has begun to suspect something is wrong with recent births.

Her connection to new life makes her a potent sacrifice for a ritual to ensure future generations are born aligned with The Rows.

Each of these captives represents a unique aspect that the Reapers of Abundance seek to exploit in their dark rituals. Their backgrounds are intertwined with the town's history and the ongoing conflict, providing potential narrative hooks and emotional weight to the rescue mission. The variety in their ages and roles in the community also highlights the far-reaching impact of the cult's activities on Crow's Hollow.

### Cult Disruption

For each captive rescued, roll on the following table to determine the impact on the cult's plans:

- **1-3: Minor disruption** - The cult must delay their next ritual by 1d4 days.
- **4-5: Moderate disruption** - A specific component for the "Great Reaping" ritual is lost.
- **6: Major disruption** - The cult loses a key member (DM's choice), significantly hindering their operations.

### Lingering Effects

Rescued captives may provide valuable information about the cult's activities.

However, they may also spread fear and paranoia in Crow's Hollow, especially those suffering from corruption, potentially making some townsfolk more susceptible to the cult's influence.

### Skill Challenge - Cleansing Ritual

PCs can attempt to cleanse the captives of lingering corruption.

This is a group skill challenge requiring 3 successes before 2 failures.

Possible checks include:

- Wisdom (Medicine) DC 14 to treat physical symptoms.
- Intelligence (Religion) DC 15 to perform a minor cleansing ritual.
- Charisma (Persuasion) DC 13 to calm the captives' fears.

### Consequences

If the cleansing is successful, the freed captives become valuable allies, potentially providing aid in future encounters.

If unsuccessful, the captives may spread The Rows' influence unintentionally, creating new challenges in Crow's Hollow.

# Terrain

The interior of the Old Mill is treacherous and partially flooded. The ground floor is considered difficult terrain due to debris and shallow water. Any creature attempting to move at more than half speed in a turn must succeed on a DC 12 Dexterity (Acrobatics) check or fall prone. The upper floor has several weakened areas; any creature weighing more than 100 pounds that ends its turn in these areas must succeed on a DC 13 Dexterity saving throw or fall through to the floor below, taking 1d6 bludgeoning damage and landing prone.

## Lair Actions

On initiative count 20 (losing initiative ties), the Old Mill invokes one of the following lair actions:

**Whispers of the Wheel**: The old water wheel groans and turns, creating a cacophony of whispers. All creatures must succeed on a DC 13 Wisdom saving throw or be frightened until the end of their next turn.

**Harvest's Grasp**: Corrupted corn stalks burst from the floorboards in a 15-foot radius, creating difficult terrain. Creatures in the area where the stalks appear must succeed on a DC 13 Strength saving throw or be restrained until the end of their next turn.

**Milling Madness**: The rusted machinery springs to life, flinging debris in all directions. Each creature must succeed on a DC 13 Dexterity saving throw or take 2d6 bludgeoning damage.

## Scaling the Encounter

### Beginning Players (PC levels 1-5)

- Reduce Stealth and Perception DCs by 2.
- Simplify Shadows of the Harvest: fewer checks, lower corruption levels.
- Weaken Sarah Blackwood: reduce HP, AC, and spell save DC by 2.
- Limit Reaper of Abundance Cultists to 1-2.
- Remove Plant-Human Hybrid.
- Simplify ritual disruption mechanics.
- Reduce number of captives to 2-3.
- Lower lair action save DCs by 2, use only one per round.
- Focus on exploration and rescue over combat.

### Intermediate Players (PC levels 6-10)

- Use encounter as written.
- Add 1-2 additional Reaper of Abundance Cultists.
- Implement all aspects of the ritual disruption.
- Use full stat blocks for Sarah Blackwood and monsters.
- Include all lair actions.
- Add time pressure to captive rescue (e.g., ritual completion timer).

- Increase consequences for failed corruption checks.

### Advanced Players (PC levels 11+)

- Increase all DCs by 2.
- Enhance Sarah Blackwood: more HP, higher save DCs, additional abilities.
- Add 1-2 Plant-Human Hybrids.
- Introduce complex magical traps throughout the mill.
- Create an enhanced multi-stage boss fight with Sarah.
- Enhance lair actions, allowing multiple to trigger each round.
- Add challenging environmental hazards (e.g., collapsing floors, magical barriers).
- Increase number of captives, with more complex rescue scenarios.
- Introduce parallel objectives (e.g., disrupt ritual while rescuing captives).

## Monsters

Reaper of Abundance Cultists (3-4)

Plant-Human Hybrid

## NPC

Sarah Blackwood

# Polluted River

This encounter showcases The Rows' ability to corrupt natural water sources, expanding its influence beyond the fields. Players must navigate the hazardous terrain, battle corrupted aquatic creatures, and find a way to cleanse the river to weaken The Rows' hold on the area.

You draw closer to the water's edge, until the stench of decay and rot assaults your senses. Before you lies what must have once been a clear, swiftly flowing river, now reduced to a sluggish stream of murky, foul-smelling liquid. The water's surface is slick with an oily film, and strange, pulsating growths cling to the banks, their tendrils reaching out as if trying to grasp anything that comes too close.

The air is thick with an unnatural mist that hangs low over the water, obscuring your vision beyond a few feet. You can hear unsettling sounds emanating from within the fog - splashes that seem too large for normal fish, and low, gurgling moans that send shivers down your spine. It's clear that whatever has befallen this river has transformed it into something far more sinister than a simple waterway.

## Activities

**Tracing the Taint**: Follow the river upstream to locate the source of the corruption, gathering evidence and overcoming obstacles along the way.

**Aquatic Abominations**: Engage in combat with the mutated creatures that now inhabit the polluted waters, fighting both in and around the river.

**Cleansing the Current**: Discover and implement a method to purify the water, potentially involving a ritual or the use of natural counter-agents to The Rows' influence.

## Tracing the Taint

As the players navigate upstream, they must overcome various challenges and gather evidence. This activity is structured as a skill challenge requiring 5 successes before 3 failures.

**Navigation** (Wisdom (Survival) check DC 14): Find the safest and most efficient path upstream. Success reveals signs of increasing corruption and grants advantage on the next check. Failure leads the party into a hazardous area, imposing disadvantage on the next check.

**Sample Collection** (Intelligence (Nature) check DC 13): Gather samples of the corrupted water and flora. Success provides clues about The Rows' influence and grants a +2 bonus to checks made to purify the river later. Failure exposes the character to corruption, requiring a DC 12 Constitution saving throw to avoid gaining one level of exhaustion.

**Corrupted Wildlife Encounter** (Various skills): The party encounters mutated animals. PCs can choose to:

- **Stealth past**: Dexterity (Stealth) check DC 15

- **Calm the creatures**: Wisdom (Animal Handling) check DC 14

- **Drive them off**: Strength (Intimidation) check DC 13

**Treacherous Terrain** (Strength (Athletics) or Dexterity (Acrobatics) check DC 14): Navigate slippery rocks and surging waters. Failure results in falling prone and being swept 15 feet downstream, taking 1d6 bludgeoning damage.

**Whispers of The Rows** (Wisdom saving throw DC 13): As they near the source, PCs must resist the maddening whispers of The Rows. Failure imposes disadvantage on the next check as the character struggles with disturbing visions.

**Identifying the Source** (Intelligence (Investigation) check DC 15): As the party approaches the source, they'll notice several distinct changes in the environment:

- The water becomes noticeably thicker and darker, with a viscous, almost syrup-like consistency.

- The air grows heavy with a sickly-sweet odor, reminiscent of rotting corn.

- Vegetation along the banks becomes more twisted and unnatural, with plants taking on corn-like characteristics regardless of their original species.

- A low, pulsating hum becomes audible, growing louder as they near the source.

Upon reaching the apparent origin of the corruption, PCs must analyze the scene. A successful Investigation check reveals the source: a massive, pulsating growth of corrupted plant matter that has fused with the riverbed. This abomination, about 20 feet in diameter, resembles a grotesque hybrid of a giant corn kernel and a beating heart. Key features of the source include:

- Thick, root-like tendrils extending from the growth into the riverbed and banks.

- Rhythmic pulsations that send waves of corrupted essence into the water.

- Small, eye-like structures on the surface that seem to track movement.

- Patches of sickly, luminescent "corn silk" that wave in an unfelt breeze.

Success on this check also reveals:

- Weak points in the growth's structure that could be targeted to destroy it.

- The pattern of its pulsations, which could be disrupted to weaken its influence.

- Signs of recent cult activity around the growth, such as ritual circles or offerings.

This discovery provides advantage on checks made to purify the river in future activities and gives the PCs crucial information for confronting The Rows' influence.

For each failed check, the DM should introduce a complication, such as:

- A surprise attack by a Mutated Fish-Person.

- A sudden surge of corrupted water, requiring a DC 13 Strength saving throw to avoid being swept downstream.

- A patch of hallucinogenic spores, requiring a DC 12 Constitution saving throw to avoid being poisoned for 1 hour.

If the PCs achieve 5 successes, they receive advantage on checks made to purify the river in future activities.

If the players accumulate 3 failures before 5 successes, they become lost and disoriented, emerging downstream with one level of exhaustion and without crucial information about the corruption's source.

## Aquatic Abominations

This activity involves a multi-phase combat encounter with the Corrupted Water Elemental and Mutated Fish-People. The battle takes place both in and around the Polluted River, presenting unique challenges and tactical considerations.

### Setup

The combat area is 60 feet wide (the width of the river and its banks) and 100 feet long.

The river occupies the central 40 feet, with 10-foot-wide banks on each side.

Place 1d4+1 difficult terrain areas (debris piles, slippery mud patches) on each bank.

### Phase 1: Ambush

The encounter begins with a surprise round as 1d3 Mutated Fish-People burst from the water to attack.

PCs must succeed on a DC 14 Dexterity saving throw or be surprised.

Surprised characters can't move or take actions on their first turn of the combat, and they can't take a reaction until that turn ends.

### Phase 2: Main Battle

The Corrupted Water Elemental enters the fray on the second round, emerging from the depths.

### Special Combat Rules

**Polluted Waters**: Characters in the water must make a DC 13 Constitution saving throw at the start of each of their turns or gain one level of exhaustion inflicted by the corruptive pollution. Swimming in the contaminated water requires a DC 14 Strength (Athletics) check. Failure means the character can't move that turn and takes 1d6 poison damage.

**Slippery Banks**: The riverbanks are difficult terrain. Characters moving more than half their speed on the banks must succeed on a DC 12 Dexterity (Acrobatics) check or fall prone.

**Corruption Exposure**: Any character that takes damage from the Corrupted Water Elemental or Mutated Fish-People must make a DC 13 Constitution saving throw or be poisoned until the end of their next turn.

**Aquatic Advantage**: Mutated Fish-People have advantage on attack rolls while in the water. The Corrupted Water Elemental can move through the water without spending extra movement.

**Purification Opportunity**: PCs can use an action to attempt to purify a 5-foot cube of water with a DC 15 Intelligence (Religion) or Wisdom (Nature) check. Success deals 2d10 radiant damage to any corrupted creature within 10 feet and creates a safe zone for one round where characters don't need to make Constitution saves against the polluted water.

# Cleansing the Current

This activity involves a combination of investigation, resource gathering, and a complex ritual to purify the river and weaken The Rows' influence. It's structured as a series of challenges that culminate in a skill-based ritual.

**Research and Discovery** (Intelligence (Investigation) check DC 15): PCs must research local lore and natural counter-agents to The Rows. Success reveals three potential purification methods:

- A druidic ritual using sacred herbs
- Alchemical purification using rare minerals
- Channeling divine energy through blessed objects

Each successful check beyond the first grants advantage on one check during the ritual. The DM can have each of these items placed at locations throughout Crow's Hollow and the surrounding terrain.

**Gathering Components**: PCs must collect three components for their chosen method. Each component requires a specific check:

- **Druidic Ritual**:

- Moonflower: Wisdom (Nature) check DC 14
- Pure spring water: Wisdom (Survival) check DC 13
- Uncorrupted riverbed soil: Intelligence (Investigation) check DC 15

- **Alchemical Purification**:

- Silvery Lodestone: Intelligence (Arcana) check DC 15
- Purifying Salts: Intelligence (Nature) check DC 13
- Essence of Cleansing Fire: Dexterity (Sleight of Hand) check DC 14 to extract safely

- **Divine Channeling**:

- Blessed Holy Symbol: Charisma (Religion) check DC 14
- Holy Water: Intelligence (Religion) check DC 13
- Incense of Purity: Wisdom (Perception) check DC 15 to identify the correct type

Failure on any check results in gathering a corrupted version of the component, which imposes disadvantage on one ritual check if used.

**Preparing the Ritual Site**: PCs must prepare a ritual site at the river's edge. This requires three successful checks:

- Intelligence (Arcana) DC 14 to create a protective circle
- Intelligence (Religion) DC 13 to consecrate the area
- Wisdom (Survival) DC 15 to find a workable location for the ritual

Each failure imposes a -2 penalty on ritual checks.

**The Purification Ritual**: The ritual requires 10 minutes to complete and involves a skill challenge requiring 5 successes before 3 failures. Each PC can contribute one check per round, choosing from:

- Intelligence (Arcana) DC 15: To manipulate the magical energies
- Intelligence (Religion) DC 14: To invoke divine protection
- Wisdom (Nature) DC 16: To appeal to the river's natural spirit
- Charisma (Performance) DC 13: To maintain the ritual's rhythm
- Constitution saving throw (DC 12): To withstand The Rows' psychic backlash

**Special Rules**:

On a natural 20, two successes are counted.

On a natural 1, two failures are counted, and the character takes 2d6 psychic damage.

After each round, roll a d20. On an 18-20, a Corrupted Water Elemental manifests and attacks, requiring the party to split their efforts.

**Ritual Outcomes**:

Complete Success (5+ successes, 0-2 failures): The river is fully purified. The Rows' influence is severely weakened in the area. PCs gain inspiration and advantage on saves against corruption for 24 hours.

Partial Success (5 successes, 3-4 failures): The river is partially cleansed. Areas of corruption remain, but The Rows' influence is noticeably diminished. PCs gain resistance to poison damage for 24 hours.

Failure (4 or fewer successes): The ritual fails to cleanse the river. The Rows' influence surges, and all PCs must make a DC 15 Wisdom saving throw or gain a level of exhaustion. The corrupted water rises, forcing a quick retreat.

**Aftermath**:

Successful purification causes visible changes: water clarity improves, noxious smells dissipate, and wildlife begins to return.

Partial success creates pockets of purity amidst the corruption, providing safe zones and weakening The Rows' overall influence.

Failure intensifies the corruption, potentially spreading it to nearby areas and strengthening The Rows' hold on the region.

## Terrain

The riverbanks are slippery and treacherous, covered in a slimy substance that makes movement difficult. Treat the area within 10 feet of the water's edge as difficult terrain. Additionally, characters moving through the water must make a DC 13 Strength (Athletics) check every 30 feet or be swept 15 feet downstream and take 1d6 bludgeoning damage from debris.

## Lair Actions

On initiative count 20 (losing initiative ties), the Polluted River invokes one of the following lair actions:

**Noxious Bubbles**: Poisonous bubbles rise from the depths and burst, releasing toxic fumes in a 20-foot radius. All creatures in the area must make a DC 14 Constitution saving throw or be poisoned until the end of their next turn.

**Grasping Currents**: The water surges and attempts to pull creatures under. Any creature in or within 5 feet of the water must succeed on a DC 14 Strength saving throw or be pulled 10 feet towards the center of the river and knocked prone.

**Corrupting Mist**: The unnatural mist intensifies in a 30-foot radius, obscuring vision and seeping into creatures' minds. The area becomes heavily obscured,

and creatures starting their turn in the mist must make a DC 14 Wisdom saving throw or be frightened until the end of their next turn.

## Scaling the Encounter

### Beginning Players (PC levels 1-5)

- Reduce skill check DCs by 2.

- Simplify Tracing the Taint: 3 successes before 2 failures.

- Replace Corrupted Water Elemental with a weaker water-based monster.

- Limit Mutated Fish-People to 1-2.

- Reduce combat area size to 40 feet wide, 60 feet long.

- Simplify special combat rules, focusing on 1-2 key mechanics.

- Adjust purification ritual: 3 successes before 2 failures, lower DCs.

- Remove or simplify lair actions.

- Focus on exploration and problem-solving over combat.

### Intermediate Players (PC levels 6-10)

- Use encounter as written.

- Add 1-2 additional Mutated Fish-People.

- Implement all special combat rules and lair actions.

- Increase complexity of purification ritual components.

- Add time pressure to ritual completion (e.g., approaching cultists).

- Introduce minor magical items to aid in river cleansing.

- Include optional side objectives for additional rewards.

### Advanced Players (PC levels 11+)

- Increase all DCs by 2.

- Enhance Corrupted Water Elemental: more HP, additional abilities.

- Add 1-2 powerful aquatic monsters (e.g., corrupted water weird).

- Expand combat area to 80 feet wide, 120 feet long.

- Introduce complex environmental hazards (e.g., whirlpools, corrupted geysers).

- Create multi-stage boss fight with Corrupted Water Elemental.

- Enhance lair actions, allowing multiple to trigger each round.

- Increase ritual complexity: more components, higher stakes for failure.

- Add high-level cultists attempting to stop the purification.

## Monsters

Corrupted Water Elemental

Mutated Fish-Person (2-3)

# The Standing Stone

This encounter represents the final confrontation with The Rows and the culmination of the adventure. The Standing Stone serves as a conduit for The Rows' power, and players must overcome its defenses, decipher its secrets, and ultimately sever the entity's connection to the material plane.

In your search for the hidden ritual site, you pass through vast stretches of farmland into uncultivated wilderness, all well within the boundaries of Crow family territory. As you continue to push through the dense underbrush, you eventually emerge into a circular clearing that seems unnaturally perfect in its symmetry. At its center looms a massive stone monolith, easily twenty feet tall and eight feet wide. Its surface is covered in intricate, swirling patterns that seem to shift and writhe when not directly observed. The air around the stone feels heavy and oppressive, as if reality itself is being warped by its presence.

The vegetation surrounding the clearing is a nightmarish mockery of nature. Trees twist and bend at impossible angles, their bark resembling husks of corn. The grass beneath your feet feels unnaturally sharp, like tiny blades trying to pierce your boots. A constant, low humming fills the air, punctuated by what sounds like distant whispers in a language you can't comprehend. You can't shake the feeling that you're being watched by countless unseen eyes.

## Activities

**Cryptic Carvings**: Study and interpret the shifting symbols on the Standing Stone to uncover the secrets of The Rows' power and vulnerabilities.

**Cosmic Severance**: Execute a powerful ritual that will completely sever The Rows' connection to the material plane, banishing it back to its own dimension.

**Reaping the Reaper**: Confront The Rows in its manifested form, exploiting its weakened state to destroy the entity and ensure it can never return to Crow's Hollow.

## Cryptic Carvings

This activity involves a series of skill checks to decipher the five major symbols on the Standing Stone. Each symbol requires a specific check and reveals crucial information about The Rows and its vulnerabilities.

### Deciphering Process

PCs can attempt to decipher one symbol per turn.

A successful check reveals the symbol's meaning and grants advantage on the next symbol's check.

Failure on a check imposes disadvantage on the next attempt and may trigger a minor corrupting effect (see below).

### Symbol 1: The Endless Field
**Check**: Intelligence (History) DC 15

**Success reveals**: This symbol represents The Rows' infinite nature and its home dimension as an extra-dimensional entity. Read Aloud: "As you decipher the symbol, a vision floods your mind. You see an endless expanse of corn stretching to the horizon in all directions. The sky above is a sickly green, and you realize with horror that the cornstalks are pulsing as if alive, all connected to a single, vast consciousness."

**Failure effect**: The character experiences vivid hallucinations of endless cornfields for 1 minute, becoming temporarily lost in the vision of The Rows' realm. Read Aloud: "The symbol seems to twist and writhe before your eyes. Suddenly, you find yourself standing in an endless cornfield. The rustling of leaves sounds like whispers, and you feel as if countless unseen eyes are watching you. This hallucination lasts for what seems like an eternity but is actually only a minute."

### Symbol 2: The Corrupted Seed
**Check**: Wisdom (Nature) DC 16

**Success reveals**: The Rows' method of spreading influence through corrupted crops. Read Aloud: "The symbol reveals the process of corruption. You see a normal seed being planted, but as it grows, tendrils of sickly green energy seep into it from the soil. The plant that emerges is twisted and wrong, its fruits capable of spreading The Rows' influence to those who consume them."

**Failure effect**: Tiny cornstalks sprout from the character's skin, dealing 1d4 piercing damage. Read Aloud: "As you struggle to understand the symbol, you feel a sharp pain all over your body. Looking down, you see tiny cornstalks beginning to sprout from your skin. They wither and fall away after a moment, leaving you shaken and in pain."

### Symbol 3: The Shattered Veil
**Check**: Intelligence (Arcana) DC 17

**Success reveals**: The ritual used to initially summon The Rows to this plane. Read Aloud: "The symbol shows a group of robed figures standing around a stone circle. As they chant, the air above the circle seems to tear open, revealing a glimpse of the endless cornfield beyond. Tendrils of corruption seep through the tear, latching onto the surrounding land."

**Failure effect**: The character is briefly pulled into The Rows' dimension, taking 2d6 psychic damage. Read Aloud: "The symbol flares with an otherworldly light, and you feel a violent tugging sensation. For a split second, you find yourself in The Rows' realm. The air is thick and cloying, and you feel an alien consciousness pressing against your mind. You snap back to reality, your head pounding with psychic pain."

### Symbol 4: The Bound Harvester
**Check**: Wisdom (Religion) DC 16

**Success reveals**: The pact made by Crow's Hollow's founders and its weaknesses. Read Aloud: "You see a vision of the town's founders standing before a manifestation of The Rows. They offer up a golden sickle, which The Rows absorbs into itself. In return, waves of fertility spread across the land. However, you notice that the sickle remains visible within The Rows, pulsing like a heart. You realize this connection could be exploited to weaken the entity."

**Failure effect**: The character feels an overwhelming urge to serve The Rows, imposing disadvantage on attacks against its minions for 1 hour. Read Aloud: "As you study the symbol, you feel an overwhelming urge to serve The Rows. Your mind is flooded with visions of bountiful harvests and the power that comes with them. You shake off the feeling, but a part of you still yearns to give in to The Rows' influence."

### Symbol 5: The Cosmic Scythe
**Check**: Intelligence (Investigation) DC 18

**Success reveals**: The method to sever The Rows' connection to this plane. Read Aloud: "The final symbol shows a great scythe cutting through reality itself. You understand that by combining the essence of uncorrupted nature, pure divine energy, and the power of free will, a ritual can be performed to create a metaphysical 'scythe' capable of cutting The Rows' connection to this world."

**Failure effect**: The character's thoughts are briefly broadcasted telepathically to all nearby creatures. Read Aloud: "As you struggle to comprehend the symbol, you feel your thoughts slipping out of your control. To your horror, you realize that everyone nearby can hear your innermost thoughts as if you were speaking them aloud. After a few moments, the effect fades, leaving you feeling exposed and vulnerable."

### Additional Rules

**Eldritch Insight**: Characters proficient in the Eldritch language gain advantage on all checks to decipher symbols.

**Corruption Resistance**: After each failed check, the character must make a DC 13 Wisdom saving throw or gain one level of corruption (as per the Corruption Levels below).

**Time Pressure**: Each deciphering attempt takes 5 minutes of in-game time. After every 15 minutes, roll on the Random Encounter table to determine what minions The Rows sends to interfere.

**Group Effort**: Other PCs can use the Help action to grant advantage on a check, but they also risk corruption on a failure.

## Corruption Levels

### Level 1: Disadvantage on Wisdom (Perception) checks

- **Symptoms**: The character begins to feel uneasy, and their senses are dulled by the subtle whisper of The Rows.
- **Effect**: Disadvantage on Wisdom (Perception) checks.

### Level 2: Speed reduced by 10 feet

- **Symptoms**: Corrupted plant life begins to spread across the character's skin, making movement more difficult.
- **Effect**: The character's speed is reduced by 10 feet as the tendrils of corruption hinder their mobility.

### Level 3: Disadvantage on attack rolls

- **Symptoms**: The corruption has begun to affect the character's coordination and mental clarity.
- **Effect**: The character suffers disadvantage on all attack rolls.

### Level 4: Poisoned condition

- **Symptoms**: The character's body is wracked with pain as the corruption spreads deeper, and their skin begins to take on a bark-like texture.
- **Effect**: The character is poisoned, suffering disadvantage on attack rolls and ability checks.

### Level 5: Charmed by The Rows (*Suggestion* effect)

- **Symptoms**: The character's mind is consumed by The Rows, and they feel an overwhelming urge to serve its goals.
- **Effect**: The character is charmed by The Rows, acting as if under the influence of the *Suggestion* spell, with the instruction to "join with the growth."

## Random Encounter Table (d4)

1. 1d3 Vicious Vines attack
2. Swarm of Carnivorous Locusts descends on the area
3. 1d4+1 Reaper of Abundance Cultists arrive to protect the stone
4. A Hallucination of Lost Loved One appears to each character

Upon successfully deciphering all five symbols, the PCs gain crucial knowledge for performing the Cosmic Severance ritual and receive advantage on their first round of attacks in the final battle against The Rows.

# Cosmic Severance

This complex ritual requires the PCs to harness the knowledge gained from the **Cryptic Carvings** activity and combine it with powerful components to sever The Rows' connection to the material plane. The ritual is a skill challenge that occurs while under constant threat from The Rows and its minions.

## Ritual Components

**Uncorrupted Water**: A vial of water from the purified river (from the Polluted River encounter).

**The Founder's Sickle**: The Sickle of the First Harvest (from the Crow Family Crypt encounter).

**Symbol of Faith**: A previously corrupted. cleansed holy symbol (from the Corrupted Chapel encounter).

**Purified Salt**: Enough salt to create a ritual circle (from the Old Mill encounter).

## Ritual Setup

PCs must create a ritual circle around the Standing Stone using the purified salt (DC 15 Intelligence (Arcana) check).

The remaining three components must be placed at equidistant points around the circle (DC 13 Wisdom (Religion) check to position correctly).

One PC must act as the ritual's focus, standing in the center of the circle (they will make the final check to complete the ritual).

**Ritual Execution**: The ritual requires 10 rounds to complete. Each round, players must accumulate 5 successes before 3 failures. Players can attempt the following actions:

- **Channel Energy** (Wisdom (Religion) DC 15): Direct divine power into the ritual.
- **Stabilize Rift** (Intelligence (Arcana) DC 16): Maintain the tear between dimensions.
- **Resist Corruption** (Charisma (Persuasion) DC 14): Bolster the group's willpower against The Rows' influence.
- **Invoke Nature** (Wisdom (Nature) DC 15): Draw upon the power of uncorrupted nature.
- **Defend the Circle** (Attack Roll against AC 15): Fend off manifestations of The Rows trying to disrupt the ritual.

## Special Rules

**Essence of Innocence**: If the PCs have the empowered, untainted drawing (from the Crow's Hollow Schoolhouse encounter), it provides several benefits, specifically to the Cosmic Severance ritual:

- It radiates an aura of innocence in a 5-foot radius, granting advantage on saving throws against The Rows' corrupting effects while within this aura.

- The drawing acts as a focus for the Cosmic Severance ritual in place of a character, allowing PCs to reroll one failed check while performing this ritual.

- If the drawing was empowered through Miss Hawthorn's connection, it also grants a +2 bonus to all ability checks made during the casting of the Cosmic Severance ritual.

On a natural 20, two successes are counted.

On a natural 1, two failures are counted, and the character suffers one level of corruption.

After each round, The Rows attempts to disrupt the ritual. Roll a d20:

- 1-10: Nothing happens.
- 11-15: A Vicious Vine attacks.
- 16-18: A Swarm of Carnivorous Locusts descends.
- 19-20: 3 Reaper of Abundance Cultists appear.

**Final Severance**: If the PCs accumulate 5 successes in a round, the PC in the center of the circle must make a final check. This is a DC 18 Charisma check, with bonuses based on the ritual's progress:

- +1 for each round completed without failure
- +2 if all four components are still intact
- +1 for each PC who hasn't succumbed to corruption

**Success**: (Read Aloud): "As you complete the final incantation, a blinding light erupts from the ritual circle. The Standing Stone cracks, and you see tendrils of corruption being forcibly pulled away from it. The air fills with an otherworldly screech as The Rows' connection to the material plane is severed. As the light fades, you feel the oppressive weight of its influence lift from the land around you, but you sense that the entity itself still lingers, weakened but not yet defeated."

The Rows' connection to the material plane is severed, significantly weakening it. In the final battle, The Rows will have its hit points reduced by half and will be unable to use its Legendary Resistance ability.

**Failure**: (Read Aloud): "As you speak the final words of the ritual, you feel a surge of power... but something is wrong. The tear in reality widens instead of closing, and you feel The Rows' presence grow stronger. The corruption in the area intensifies, and you realize with horror that you've inadvertently alerted The Rows to your intentions."

The Rows becomes aware of the attempt to sever its connection and prepares for the final battle. In addition to The Rows itself, the final encounter will include:

- 1d4 Corn Stalkers
- 2d4 Animated Scarecrows
- 1 Corrupted Chapel Guardian

All player characters must make a DC 15 Wisdom saving throw or gain a level of exhaustion from the psychic backlash.

## Reaping the Reaper

This epic final battle against The Rows takes place immediately after the Cosmic Severance ritual, regardless of its outcome. The fight occurs in the area surrounding the Standing Stone, which has become a nightmarish landscape of writhing corruption.

### Battlefield Setup

The battle area is a 100-foot radius circle centered on the Standing Stone.

Divide the area into four quadrants, each representing a different aspect of The Rows' corruption:

- **Writhing Cornfield**: Difficult terrain, provides half cover
- **Putrid Swamp**: Difficult terrain, poisonous vapors
- **Twisting Grove**: Normal terrain, but with animated trees
- **Corrupted Clearing**: Normal terrain, but with psychic resonance

**The Rows' Manifestation**: The Rows manifests as a colossal, writhing mass of corrupted plant matter, centered around the cracked Standing Stone. Use The Rows stat block, with the following modifications based on the Cosmic Severance outcome:

**Success**: The Rows has half its normal hit points and cannot use Legendary Resistance.

**Failure**: The Rows is at full strength and is accompanied by additional minions.

### Initiative and Turn Order

Roll initiative for any additional monsters and the player characters.

The Rows acts on initiative count 20 (losing ties).

At initiative count 0, roll for a random environmental effect (see below).

### The Rows' Tactics

**Phase 1** (100%-50% HP): The Rows focuses on area control, using Eldritch Growth and its legendary actions to restrict PC movement.

**Phase 2** (49%-25% HP): The Rows becomes more aggressive, using Corrupted Tendrils to pull PCs close and Harvest of Despair to deal massive damage.

**Phase 3** (24%-0% HP): In desperation, The Rows uses all its abilities to their fullest, prioritizing the weakest-looking characters.

**Environmental Effects** (Roll 1d6 at initiative count 0):

- **Corrupting Mist**: Each creature must make a DC 15 Constitution saving throw or be poisoned until the end of its next turn.

- **Psychic Assault**: Each creature must make a DC 15 Wisdom saving throw or take 2d6 psychic damage.

- **Grasping Roots**: The ground in one random quadrant becomes difficult terrain for 1 round.

- **Empowering Essence**: The Rows regains 20 hit points.

- **Whispers of Madness**: Each creature must make a DC 15 Charisma saving throw or be frightened until the end of its next turn.

- **Rejuvenating Pulse**: All plant creatures (including The Rows) regain 10 hit points.

### Special Combat Rules

**Corruption Exposure**: At the start of each of their turns, players must make a DC 13 Wisdom saving throw or gain one level of corruption (as per the Corruption Levels Table from earlier encounters).

**Severing the Tendrils**: PCs can specifically target The Rows' tendrils (AC 16, 30 HP each). Destroying a tendril reduces The Rows' maximum HP by 20 and imposes disadvantage on its next attack roll.

**Purification Points**: Place 1d4+2 small areas of uncorrupted nature around the battlefield. A PC can use an action while in one of these areas to cleanse themselves of one level of corruption.

**Eldritch Knowledge**: PCs who successfully decoded all the Cryptic Carvings have advantage on saving throws against The Rows' abilities.

**Essence of Innocence**: If PCs have the empowered, untainted drawing (from the Crow's Hollow Schoolhouse encounter), it radiates an aura of innocence in a 5-foot radius, granting advantage on saving throws against The Rows' corrupting effects to those within the aura.

## Terrain

The area immediately surrounding the Standing Stone is difficult terrain due to the twisted, grasping vegetation. Characters must succeed on a DC 13 Dexterity (Acrobatics) check to move at full speed through this area, or move at half speed on a failure. Additionally, at the start of each round, every character must make a DC 12 Wisdom

saving throw or become disoriented by the warped reality around the stone, suffering disadvantage on their next attack roll or ability check.

## Lair Actions

On initiative count 20 (losing initiative ties), the Standing Stone invokes one of the following lair actions:

**Whispers of Madness**: The Standing Stone emanates psychic energy, forcing all creatures within 60 feet to make a DC 15 Wisdom saving throw or be stunned until the end of their next turn.

**Corrupt Growth**: Twisted vines and cornstalks erupt from the ground in a 20-foot radius around a point The Rows chooses. This area becomes difficult terrain, and any creature in the area where the plants appear must succeed on a DC 14 Strength saving throw or be restrained until the end of its next turn.

**Reality Warp**: The area around the Standing Stone becomes temporarily warped. All creatures must succeed on a DC 14 Constitution saving throw or be teleported to a random space within 30 feet of their current position.

## Scaling the Encounter

### Beginning Players (PC levels 1-5)

- Reduce Cryptic Carvings to 3 symbols, lower DCs by 2.

- Simplify Cosmic Severance: 3 successes before 2 failures, fewer rounds.

- Weaken The Rows: Reduce HP by 75%, lower damage output and save DCs.

- Remove or simplify lair actions.

- Limit additional monsters to 1-2 Vicious Vines.

- Reduce battlefield size to 60-foot radius.

- Simplify environmental effects, use only 2-3 options.

- Focus on narrative and teamwork over complex mechanics.

### Intermediate Players (PC levels 6-10)

- Use encounter as written.

- Add 1-2 Corn Stalkers to the final battle.

- Implement all lair actions and environmental effects.

- Increase complexity of Cosmic Severance ritual.

- Introduce time pressure

(e.g., corrupt energy building up).

- Add optional objectives for bonus advantages in final battle.

### Advanced Players (PC levels 11+)

- Increase all DCs by 2.
- Enhance The Rows: More HP, higher save DCs, additional legendary actions.
- Add Corrupted Chapel Guardian and 1-2 Plant-Human Hybrids to final battle.
- Expand battlefield to 150-foot radius, more complex terrain.
- Create multi-phase boss fight with The Rows.
- Enhance lair actions, allowing multiple to trigger each round.

- Introduce high-level cultists attempting to protect The Rows.
- Add complex magical hazards throughout the battlefield.
- Create parallel objectives during final battle (e.g., closing rifts while fighting).

## Monsters

The Rows (Final boss, manifesting through the Standing Stone)

Vicious Vines (2-3)

Swarm of Carnivorous Locusts (1-2)

Reaper of Abundance Cultist (3-6)

Hallucination of Lost Loved One (3-4)

# Wild Man's Shack

This encounter introduces Old Man Jenkins, a potential ally with crucial knowledge about The Rows. The party can gain valuable information and items here but must navigate Jenkins' paranoia and the shack's strange defenses.

Passing the outskirts of town, you trudge through the tall, thick ground cover until a small clearing opens up before you. In its center stands a ramshackle cabin, its weathered wooden planks barely holding together. The air around the structure seems to shimmer slightly, and you notice strange symbols and totems surrounding the perimeter.

Upon going closer, your sensory faculties are assaulted by a potent mixture of scents - pungent herbs, wood smoke, and something unidentifiable that makes your nose wrinkle. The cabin's single window is covered by a tattered curtain, but you can see flickering firelight within. A worn path leads to a crooked door, above which hangs a twisted wreath of corn husks and bones.

## Activities

**Wisdom of the Hermit**: Convince the paranoid Old Man Jenkins to share his valuable knowledge about The Rows and its weaknesses.

**Arsenal of the Eccentric**: Search Jenkins' cluttered shack to find and obtain unique items that can be used to combat The Rows and its minions.

## Wisdom of the Hermit

Old Man Jenkins is a paranoid and eccentric hermit who possesses crucial knowledge about The Rows. Convincing him to share this information requires a delicate approach and may involve multiple steps.

**Initial Approach**: PCs must make a group Charisma (Persuasion) check (DC 15) to convince Jenkins to speak with them. Failure results in Jenkins becoming hostile, imposing disadvantage on all subsequent Charisma checks for 10 minutes.

**Building Trust**: Over the course of the conversation, player characters can make individual Charisma checks to gain Jenkins' trust:

- **Persuasion** (DC 14): Appeal to Jenkins' desire to protect the town.
- **Deception** (DC 16): Convince Jenkins they're already aware of secret information.
- **Intimidation** (DC 15): Threaten to reveal Jenkins' location to The Rows (risky, may backfire).

**Providing Evidence**: PCs can present evidence they've gathered about The Rows. Each relevant piece of evidence grants advantage on one Charisma check.

**Insight Challenges**: At key points in the conversation, Jenkins will test the PCs' understanding of The Rows. Player characters must make Intelligence (Arcana) or Wisdom (Insight) checks (DC 14) to correctly interpret Jenkins' cryptic statements. Each success grants a piece of valuable information. Three failures causes Jenkins to become suspicious and clam up.

**Mental Resistance**: As PCs delve deeper into Jenkins' knowledge, they must resist The Rows' psychic influence. Each character must succeed on a DC 13 Wisdom saving throw or gain one level of exhaustion as forbidden knowledge strains their mind.

**Knowledge Gained**: For each successful step (max 5), PCs learn one of the following:

- A weakness of The Rows' physical manifestations: "The Rows fears pure, untainted water. Its corporeal forms take double damage from attacks using blessed or naturally pure water sources."

- The true name of The Rows, granting power over it in the final confrontation: "The Rows' true name is Zha'shekhuloth. Uttering this name before using a spell against The Rows imposes disadvantage on its saving throws."

- The location of a powerful artifact that can harm The Rows: "The Sickle of the First Harvest, hidden in the old Crow family crypt, can sever The Rows' connection to our world if wielded by a pure heart."

- A method to disrupt The Rows' connection to its cultists: "Burning a mixture of sage, salt, and uncorrupted corn in the presence of a cultist can temporarily sever their connection to The Rows." Mechanically speaking, performing this minor ritual forces any cultists within a 20-foot radius to make a DC 15 Wisdom saving throw. On a failure, their connection to The Rows is temporarily severed for 1d4 hours.

- The origin of The Rows and how it was first summoned to Crow's Hollow: "The Rows is an ancient entity from a realm of endless harvest. It was inadvertently summoned during a desperate ritual performed by the town's founders during a great famine. The ritual site, now known as the Standing Stone, is located deep within Crow family territory and serves as its anchor to our world."

**Lingering Effects**: If PCs gain all five pieces of knowledge, they have advantage on Intelligence and Wisdom saving throws against The Rows' abilities for the next 24 hours.

## Arsenal of the Eccentric

Old Man Jenkins' shack is a cluttered maze of strange artifacts and eccentric inventions. PCs must carefully search the shack to find items useful against The Rows while avoiding traps and cursed objects.

**Initial Search**: PCs can make a DC 14 Wisdom (Perception) check to get a general sense of the shack's layout and potential search areas. Success grants advantage on the first Investigation check.

**Thorough Investigation**: Each character can search one area of the shack per 10 minutes of in-game time. Requires a DC 15 Intelligence (Investigation) check to find an item. On a natural 1, the character triggers a minor trap or curse (DM's choice).

**Identifying Items**: Found items must be identified with a DC 13 Intelligence (Arcana) check. Failure means the item's properties remain unknown until used or until a PC studies the item while holding it during a short rest.

**Corruption Hazard**: For every 30 minutes spent searching, PCs must make a DC 12 Wisdom saving throw or gain one level of exhaustion as The Rows' lingering influence affects them.

**Jenkins' Permission**: Once items are found, PCs must convince Jenkins to part with them. Requires a DC 14 Charisma (Persuasion) check for each item. Failure means Jenkins refuses to give up the item unless the PCs complete an additional task for him.

Below is a table of unique items that can be found in Jenkins' shack:

| Name | Visual Description | Properties | Damage | Cost | Weight | Location in Shack |
|---|---|---|---|---|---|---|
| Sickle of Purification | A silver sickle with glowing runes etched along the blade | +1 weapon. On a hit against a creature corrupted by The Rows, target must make a DC 15 CON save or be purged of one level of corruption | 1d4 slashing + 2d6 radiant | 1,500 gp | 2 lbs | Hidden in a false bottom of a trunk |
| Cornhusk Grenades (3) | Small, tightly woven balls of corn husk with a glowing core | As an action, can be thrown up to 30 feet. Each creature in a 10-foot radius must make a DC 14 DEX save or take damage and be pushed 10 feet away. | 3d6 force | 250 gp each | 1 lb each | Stored in a warded clay pot on a high shelf |
| Scarecrow's Gaze Amulet | A wooden amulet carved to resemble a scarecrow's face | While worn, grants advantage on WIS saves against being frightened. Once per day, can cast *Fear* (WIS save DC 15). | - | 1,000 gp | 1 lb | Hanging from a nail behind Jenkins' bedroom door |
| Bottle of Liquid Sunlight | A small glass vial filled with golden, glowing liquid | As an action, can be thrown up to 20 feet, shattering on impact. Each plant creature within 10 feet takes damage and is blinded until the end of its next turn. | 4d8 radiant | 500 gp | 1/2 lb | Tucked away in a locked drawer of Jenkins' desk |
| Seeds of Unmaking (10) | Small, black seeds that seem to absorb light | When planted in corrupted soil, purifies a 5-foot square area. If consumed by a corrupted creature, forces a DC 15 CON save or take 2d10 necrotic damage and lose one level of corruption. | - | 100 gp per seed | - | In a small pouch hidden inside a hollowed-out book |

## Terrain

The area immediately surrounding the shack is difficult terrain due to the numerous totems, strings of bones, and other protective items strewn about. Characters must succeed on a DC 13 Dexterity (Acrobatics) check to move at full speed through this area, or move at half speed on a failure. Additionally, the shack's interior is cramped and cluttered, requiring a DC 12 Dexterity saving throw to avoid knocking over Jenkins' precarious piles of supplies and angering him.

## Lair Actions

On initiative count 20 (losing initiative ties), the Wild Man's Shack invokes one of the following lair actions:

**Whispers of Warning**: Eerie whispers emanate from the protective totems, forcing all creatures except Jenkins to make a DC 13 Wisdom saving throw or be frightened until the end of their next turn.

**Herbal Haze**: A cloud of pungent smoke billows from Jenkins' hearth, filling the shack. All creatures must succeed on a DC 14 Constitution saving throw or be poisoned until the end of their next turn.

**Protective Surge**: The symbols surrounding the shack flare with eldritch energy. Jenkins gains 10 temporary hit points, and all other creatures within 30 feet must succeed on a DC 14 Strength saving throw or be pushed 10 feet away from the shack.

## NPC

Old Man Jenkins

## Scaling the Encounter

### Beginning Players (PC levels 1-5)

- Reduce Wisdom of the Hermit DCs by 2.

- Limit knowledge gained to 3 pieces of information.

- Simplify Arsenal of the Eccentric: 3-4 items, lower DCs.

- Weaken magical item properties slightly.

- Remove or simplify lair actions.

- Focus on roleplaying and puzzle-solving over skill checks.

- Provide more obvious clues about Jenkins' trustworthiness.

- Reduce corruption and exhaustion effects.

### Intermediate Players (PC levels 6-10)

- Use encounter as written.

- Add 1-2 additional challenges in convincing Jenkins.

- Implement all lair actions.

- Include full range of magical items.

- Add time pressure (e.g., cultists approaching the shack).

- Introduce minor combat encounter with corrupted wildlife.

- Enhance consequences for failed checks or triggering traps.

### Advanced Players (PC levels 11+)

- Increase all DCs by 2.

- Add complex riddles or tests from Jenkins to gain knowledge.

- Enhance magical items with additional properties.

- Create multi-stage process to earn Jenkins' trust.

- Add powerful cursed objects among the beneficial items.

- Introduce high-level cultist attempting to silence Jenkins.

- Enhance lair actions, allowing multiple to trigger each round.

- Create a skill challenge to navigate Jenkins' memories.

- Add parallel objective (e.g., cleansing the area while gaining information).

# Conclusions

In the aftermath of their harrowing adventure in Crow's Hollow, the heroes' efforts against The Rows and its cultists can lead to four distinct outcomes. These conclusions, ranging from complete victory to bitter defeat, each offer unique challenges and opportunities for future adventures, shaping the fate of the town and the characters' ongoing journey.

## The Harvest of Hope

This conclusion wraps up the main threat of The Rows and its cultists, but it leaves room for lingering effects and future adventures. It emphasizes the bittersweet nature of victory, with the town saved but forever changed. Consider using this as a springboard for future quests dealing with the aftermath or new threats arising from the power vacuum left by The Rows.

As the last tendrils of The Rows wither and fade, a palpable change sweeps through Crow's Hollow. The oppressive atmosphere that has hung over the town for so long begins to lift, like storm clouds parting to reveal the sun. The corrupted crops in the fields begin to wilt, their unnatural vitality fading away. Townsfolk emerge from their homes, blinking in the clear light as if awakening from a long nightmare. There's a relief, confusion, and fear on their faces.

mix of lingering

In the days that follow, the full extent of The Rows' influence becomes clear. While many celebrate their freedom, others grapple with guilt over their actions while under the entity's sway. The land itself seems to be healing, but scars remain - patches of earth that resist new growth, strange whispers that sometimes carry on the wind at night. Crow's Hollow has been saved, but it will never be quite the same. Your actions have given the town a chance to rebuild and heal, to face the future unburdened by the eldritch horror that once threatened to consume it. As you look out over the fields, now free from The Rows' corruption, you can't help but feel that this is not an end, but a new beginning - for Crow's Hollow, and perhaps for yourselves as well.

**Experience Points**: Award the players enough XP to level up, reflecting the monumental nature of their accomplishment.

**Reputation**: The PCs are hailed as heroes of Crow's Hollow, granting them advantage on all future Charisma checks when dealing with the townsfolk.

**Property**: The grateful town offers the PCs ownership of a small farm on the outskirts of Crow's Hollow, which can serve as a base of operations for future adventures.

**Magic Item**: Each PC receives a "Seed of Renewal" - a small, golden seed that, when planted, creates a 50-foot radius of purified, supernaturally fertile land for one year.

**Title**: The PCs are given the honorary title of "Wardens of the Harvest," recognized protectors of Crow's Hollow against supernatural threats.

## A Harvest Unfinished

This conclusion sets up a bittersweet victory and potential for future adventures. The immediate threat of the cult is neutralized, but The Rows remains a looming presence. This scenario allows for ongoing tension in Crow's Hollow and the possibility of The Rows regaining strength or finding new followers. Consider using this as a foundation for a sequel adventure or ongoing campaign where the PCs must find new ways to combat The Rows' influence.

With the defeat of the cult, a cautious sense of relief spreads through Crow's Hollow. The townspeople, no longer under the direct control of the cultists, begin to emerge from their homes, their eyes clearer but still shadowed with worry. The corrupted fields seem less menacing, but an unnatural vitality still pulses through the crops.

As days pass, it becomes evident that while the cult's hold is broken, The Rows' presence lingers. Whispers still carry on the wind at night, and some townsfolk report unsettling dreams of endless cornfields. The land itself seems to resist returning to normalcy, with patches of earth remaining tainted and unusually fertile. Your victory over the cult has given Crow's Hollow a respite, a chance to catch its breath and begin to heal. But as you look out over the fields, still swaying with an unnatural rhythm, you know that your work is not yet done. The Rows, though weakened, still lurks beneath the surface, waiting for an opportunity to rise again. The battle for Crow's Hollow's soul is not over - it has merely entered a new phase.

## Rewards

**Experience Points**: Award the players 75% of the XP needed to level up, reflecting their significant but incomplete victory.

**Reputation**: The PCs are recognized as protectors of Crow's Hollow, granting them advantage on Charisma checks when dealing with non-cultist townsfolk.

**Safe Haven**: The grateful town offers the PCs use of a small, protected cabin on the outskirts of Crow's Hollow, which can serve as a base for their ongoing efforts against The Rows.

**Magic Item**: Each PC receives a "Charm of Resilience" - a small, cornhusk woven amulet that grants advantage on saving throws against The Rows' corrupting influence once per day.

**Title**: The PCs are given the title of "Defenders of the Harvest," acknowledging their ongoing role in protecting Crow's Hollow from The Rows' influence.

# The Root Uprooted, Branches Unbroken

This conclusion presents a complex victory that sets up intriguing future conflicts. The Rows is defeated, but its human followers remain a threat. This scenario allows for exploration of how the cultists adapt without their eldritch patron, potentially becoming more desperate or seeking new sources of power. Consider using this as a springboard for a sequel where PCs must navigate the political and social challenges of rooting out the remaining cult members and helping the town heal from its ordeal.

As The Rows' presence fades from Crow's Hollow, an eerie quiet settles over the town. The corrupted fields wither rapidly, leaving behind barren earth where once unnatural crops thrived. The oppressive atmosphere that hung over the region lifts, like a fever breaking.

However, the relief is short-lived as the reality of the situation sets in.

Many townsfolk, freed from The Rows' influence, emerge confused and horrified by their actions. Others, the true believers of the cult, retreat into the shadows, their eyes glinting with a mixture of fear and fanaticism. The defeat of The Rows has left a power vacuum, and tensions in the town are high. Neighbors eye each other with suspicion, unsure whom to trust. As you walk through the streets, you can feel the weight of unfinished business. The eldritch horror may be gone, but its human legacy remains, a tangled web of loyalty, fear, and misguided faith that threatens to choke the very community you've fought so hard to save. The battle for Crow's Hollow's soul has entered a new phase - one that may prove even more challenging than facing The Rows itself.

## Rewards

**Experience Points**: Award the players 80% of the XP needed to level up, reflecting their significant victory against The Rows but incomplete resolution of the town's issues.

**Insight**: Each PC gains advantage on Wisdom (Insight) checks when interacting with potential cultists, having gained a deep understanding of The Rows' influence on its followers.

**Magic Item**: The party receives a "Scythe of Truth" - a magical scythe that, once per day, can force a target to make a DC 15 Wisdom saving throw or be compelled to answer one question truthfully. This can be a valuable tool in rooting out remaining cult members.

**Allies**: A small group of townsfolk who resisted The Rows' influence pledge their support to the PCs, providing a network of informants and helpers for future endeavors.

**Title**: The PCs are given the title of "Reapers of the Eldritch," acknowledging their defeat of The Rows while hinting at the ongoing challenge they face.

# Seeds of Resistance

This conclusion sets up a dark turn of events, with The Rows and its cultists emerging victorious. However, it's not a total defeat for the PCs, as their actions have sown the seeds of future resistance. This scenario allows for a potential sequel where the player characters must regroup, gather new allies, and find alternative ways to combat The Rows' influence. Consider using this as a springboard for a more expansive campaign where the stakes are even higher and the PCs must work from the shadows to undermine The Rows' growing power.

As the realization of defeat settles over you, Crow's Hollow transforms before your eyes. The corrupted fields surge with unnatural vitality, crops growing and twisting at an alarming rate. The sky darkens with ominous clouds that seem to pulse with sickly green energy. Townsfolk move through the streets with blank stares, their wills subsumed by The Rows' influence.

You find yourselves forced to retreat, narrowly escaping the town's borders as the cultists secure their victory. From a nearby hill, you watch as a massive, writhing form of corrupted vegetation rises above the town center - The Rows manifesting physically in its moment of triumph. Yet, as you prepare to flee further, you notice small pockets of resistance: a few townsfolk hiding in root cellars, whispering your names; the faint glow of protective wards you helped establish; seeds of hope you planted that The Rows couldn't fully extinguish. You realize that while the battle is lost, the war is not over. Crow's Hollow may have fallen, but your actions have ensured that the spirit of resistance lives on, waiting for the day when you can return, stronger and better prepared to face the horrors that have taken root.

## Rewards

**Knowledge**: Each PC gains advantage on Intelligence checks related to The Rows and its cultists, having witnessed their full power firsthand.

**Resilience**: The harrowing experience grants each PC advantage on saving throws against fear effects for the next month.

**Allies**: A small group of townsfolk who escaped Crow's Hollow pledge themselves to your cause, providing a base of operations and support network for future attempts to liberate the town.

**Magic Item**: The party receives a "Seed of Defiance" - a magical seed that, when planted, creates a 10-foot radius area immune to The Rows' corruption for 24 hours. This can be crucial for establishing safe zones in future infiltration attempts.

**Quest Hook**: You discover a hidden message from Old Man Jenkins, revealing the location of a powerful artifact that could turn the tide against The Rows and setting up your next mission.

# Monsters

## Animated Burial Shroud

*Medium undead, neutral evil*

**Armor Class:** 13

**Hit Points:** 45 (6d8 + 18)

**Speed:** 30 ft., fly 30 ft. (hover)

| STR | DEX | CON | INT | WIS | CHA |
|-----|-----|-----|-----|-----|-----|
| 12 (+1) | 16 (+3) | 16 (+3) | 6 (-2) | 10 (+0) | 5 (-3) |

**Damage Vulnerabilities:** fire

**Damage Resistances:** bludgeoning, piercing, and slashing from nonmagical attacks

**Damage Immunities:** necrotic, poison

**Condition Immunities:** charmed, exhaustion, frightened, paralyzed, petrified, poisoned

**Senses:** blindsight 60 ft. (blind beyond this radius), passive Perception 10

**Languages:** Understands the languages it knew in life but can't speak

**Challenge:** 3 (700 XP)

**Amorphous.** The shroud can move through a space as narrow as 1 inch wide without squeezing.

**Sunlight Sensitivity.** While in sunlight, the shroud has disadvantage on attack rolls, as well as on Wisdom (Perception) checks that rely on sight.

**Corrupted Harvest.** When the shroud drops to 0 hit points, it bursts into a cloud of corrupted grain. Each creature within 5 feet of the shroud must succeed on a DC 13 Constitution saving throw or be poisoned for 1 minute. While poisoned in this way, the creature is under the effects of the *Bane* spell.

## Actions

**Multiattack.** The Animated Burial Shroud makes two slam attacks.

**Slam.** *Melee Weapon Attack:* +5 to hit, reach 5 ft., one target. *Hit:* 7 (1d8 + 3) bludgeoning damage plus 4 (1d8) necrotic damage.

**Envelop.** *Melee Weapon Attack:* +5 to hit, reach 5 ft., one Medium or smaller creature. *Hit:* The creature is grappled (escape DC 13) and restrained. The shroud can only envelop one creature at a time. While enveloping a creature, the shroud can't make slam attacks. At the start

of each of the enveloped creature's turns, the target takes 9 (2d8) necrotic damage.

**Harvest Whispers (1/Day).** The shroud emits eerie whispers in a 15-foot radius. Each creature in that area must succeed on a DC 13 Wisdom saving throw or be frightened for 1 minute. A frightened creature can repeat the saving throw at the end of each of its turns, ending the effect on itself on a success.

## Description

Animated Burial Shrouds are unsettling, ethereal entities that manifest as tattered, floating pieces of cloth. They appear as if woven from a mix of linen and dried corn husks, with intricate patterns that seem to shift and writhe when observed closely. Wisps of sickly green energy emanate from within, giving them a faint, ghostly glow. As they move, they produce a soft rustling sound reminiscent of wind through a cornfield, often accompanied by whispered fragments of harvest songs or desperate pleas.

These macabre entities are the result of The Rows' corruption seeping into the Crow Family Crypt and other burial grounds near Crow's Hollow. The eldritch energy of The Rows has merged with the burial shrouds of the deceased, animating them with a twisted semblance of life. They embody the perversion of the natural cycle of death and rebirth that The Rows represents. Animated Burial Shrouds are drawn to the living, seeking to envelop them in a grotesque parody of their original purpose. Some believe that these entities are attempting to 'plant' new servants for The Rows, as those who die within their grasp often rise as new horrors in service to the eldritch cornfields.

# Animated Corn Husk

*Small plant, neutral evil*

**Armor Class:** 12 (natural armor)

**Hit Points:** 22 (5d6 + 5)

**Speed:** 20 ft., burrow 20 ft.

| STR | DEX | CON | INT | WIS | CHA |
|---|---|---|---|---|---|
| 10 (+0) | 14 (+2) | 12 (+1) | 3 (-4) | 10 (+0) | 5 (-3) |

**Skills:** Stealth +4

**Damage Vulnerabilities:** fire

**Damage Resistances:** bludgeoning, piercing

**Condition Immunities:** blinded, deafened, exhaustion

**Senses:** blindsight 60 ft. (blind beyond this radius), passive Perception 10

**Languages:** Understands the languages of its creator but can't speak

**Challenge:** 1/2 (100 XP)

**False Appearance.** While the Animated Corn Husk remains motionless, it is indistinguishable from a normal corn husk.

**Swarm Tactics.** The Animated Corn Husk has advantage on attack rolls against a creature if at least one of the Animated Corn Husk's allies is within 5 feet of the creature and the ally isn't incapacitated.

## Actions

**Multiattack.** The Animated Corn Husk makes two Husk Slash attacks.

**Husk Slash.** *Melee Weapon Attack:* +4 to hit, reach 5 ft., one target. *Hit:* 5 (1d6 + 2) slashing damage.

**Entangling Husks (Recharge 5-6).** The Animated Corn Husk targets one creature within 10 feet. The target must succeed on a DC 12 Dexterity saving throw or be restrained by the Animated Corn Husk. A creature restrained by the husk can use its action to make a DC 12 Strength check, freeing itself on a success. The effect also ends if the Animated Corn Husk is destroyed.

**Seed Spray (1/Day).** The Animated Corn Husk sprays seeds in a 15-foot cone. Each creature in that area must make a DC 12 Dexterity saving throw, taking 7 (2d6) piercing damage on a failed save, or half as much damage on a successful one. A creature that fails its save is also blinded until the end of its next turn.

## Description

Animated Corn Husks appear as writhing masses of dried corn leaves, stalks, and silk, roughly forming vaguely humanoid shapes about 3 feet tall. Their "bodies" constantly shift and rustle, with individual leaves and stalks moving independently. Eerie, dim light pulses from within, giving them a sickly yellow-green glow. Sharp edges of husks form crude limbs and weapons, while empty cobs serve as unsettling, eyeless "heads." As they move, they emit a dry, rattling sound, like wind through a dead cornfield.

These unnatural entities are a manifestation of The Rows' corrupting influence on the local crops. Born from the eldritch energy infusing the cornfields around Crow's Hollow, Animated Corn Husks represent the perversion of the harvest. They embody the concept of plenty turned to horror, of nourishment become predator. The Reapers of Abundance view these creatures as lesser servants of The Rows, using them to guard sacred sites or to terrorize those who resist the cult. Some whisper that these animated plants are formed from the remnants of sacrificial victims, their essence trapped within the husks, forever bound to serve The Rows in a mockery of the natural cycle of death and rebirth.

# Animated Scarecrow

*Medium construct, neutral evil*

**Armor Class:** 14 (natural armor)

**Hit Points:** 36 (8d8)

**Speed:** 25 ft.

| STR | DEX | CON | INT | WIS | CHA |
|---|---|---|---|---|---|
| 14 (+2) | 13 (+1) | 11 (+0) | 6 (-2) | 10 (+0) | 5 (-3) |

**Skills:** Stealth +3

**Damage Vulnerabilities:** fire

**Damage Resistances:** bludgeoning, piercing, and slashing from nonmagical attacks

**Condition Immunities:** charmed, exhaustion, frightened, paralyzed, poisoned

**Senses:** darkvision 60 ft., passive Perception 10

**Languages:** Understands the languages of its creator but can't speak

**Challenge:** 2 (450 XP)

**False Appearance.** While the scarecrow remains motionless, it is indistinguishable from an ordinary scarecrow.

**Horrifying Gaze.** When a creature that can see the scarecrow's eyes starts its turn within 30 feet of the scarecrow, the scarecrow can force it to make a DC 11 Wisdom saving throw if the scarecrow isn't incapacitated and can see the creature. On a failed save, the creature is frightened until the start of its next turn. Unless surprised, a creature can avert its eyes to avoid the saving throw at the start of its turn. If the creature does so, it can't see the scarecrow until the start of its next turn, when it can avert its eyes again. If the creature looks at the scarecrow in the meantime, it must immediately make the save.

**Flammable.** If the scarecrow takes fire damage, it catches fire and takes 5 (1d10) fire damage at the start of each of its turns until a creature takes an action to douse the fire.

## Actions

**Multiattack.** The Animated Scarecrow makes two claw attacks.

**Claw.** *Melee Weapon Attack:* +4 to hit, reach 5 ft., one target. *Hit:* 6 (1d8 + 2) slashing damage. If the target is a creature, it must succeed on a DC 11 Constitution saving throw or be poisoned until the end of its next turn.

**Terrifying Glare.** The scarecrow targets one creature it can see within 30 feet of it. If the target can see the scarecrow, the target must succeed on a DC 11 Wisdom saving throw or be magically frightened for 1 minute. The frightened target can repeat the saving throw at the end of each of its turns, ending the effect on itself on a success.

**Straw Burst (Recharge 5-6).** The scarecrow releases a burst of cursed straw and corn husks in a 15-foot cone. Each creature in that area must make a DC 11 Dexterity saving throw, taking 10 (3d6) piercing damage on a failed save, or half as much damage on a successful one.

## Description

The Animated Scarecrow is a twisted mockery of the friendly guardians typically found in cornfields. Standing at about 6 feet tall, its body is a patchwork of burlap sacks stuffed with moldy straw and rotting corn husks. The head is a misshapen pumpkin or a crude sack, with glowing, ember-like eyes that flicker with an otherworldly hunger. Rusted farm tools – sickles, pitchforks, or scythes – often serve as its limbs, caked with a suspicious dark residue. As it moves, it emits a dry rustling sound, accompanied by the creaking of its makeshift joints. A foul odor of decay and corruption follows in its wake.

These malevolent constructs are the result of The Rows' corrupting influence seeping into the very fabric of Crow's Hollow's agricultural traditions. The Reapers of Abundance create these guardians through a perverse ritual, imbuing ordinary scarecrows with the essence of fear and the unnatural vitality of The Rows. Each Animated Scarecrow contains a "seed" of The Rows' power, often a kernel of corrupted corn placed where its heart would be. This seed slowly grows, feeding on the fear and suffering of its victims. The Animated Scarecrows serve as silent sentinels in the cultists' cornfields, keeping away intruders and occasionally "harvesting" unsuspecting victims for the cult's dark purposes. Some locals whisper that these scarecrows contain the trapped souls of those who opposed the cult, forever bound to serve as guardians of the very evil they once fought against.

# Corn Husk Zombie

*Medium undead, neutral evil*

**Armor Class:** 10

**Hit Points:** 22 (3d8 + 9)

**Speed:** 20 ft.

| STR | DEX | CON | INT | WIS | CHA |
|-----|-----|-----|-----|-----|-----|
| 13 (+1) | 6 (-2) | 16 (+3) | 3 (-4) | 6 (-2) | 5 (-3) |

**Saving Throws:** Con +5, Wis +0

**Damage Resistances:** piercing damage from nonmagical attacks

**Damage Immunities:** poison

**Condition Immunities:** poisoned

**Senses:** darkvision 60 ft., passive Perception 8

**Languages:** Understands the languages it knew in life but can't speak

**Challenge:** 1 (200 XP)

**Undead Fortitude.** If damage reduces the zombie to 0 hit points, it must make a Constitution saving throw with a DC of 5 + the damage taken, unless the damage is radiant or from a critical hit. On a success, the zombie drops to 1 hit point instead.

**Cornfield Camouflage.** The zombie has advantage on Dexterity (Stealth) checks made to hide in cornfields or areas with tall grass.

**Husk Armor.** The zombie has resistance to piercing damage from nonmagical attacks.

## Actions

**Slam.** *Melee Weapon Attack:* +3 to hit, reach 5 ft., one target. *Hit:* 4 (1d6 + 1) bludgeoning damage.

**Husk Spray (Recharge 5-6).** The zombie releases a spray of sharp corn husks in a 15-foot cone. Each creature in that area must make a DC 11 Dexterity saving throw, taking 7 (2d6) slashing damage on a failed save, or half as much damage on a successful one.

**Rootbound (1/Day).** The zombie can magically cause roots to burst from the ground in a 10-foot radius around itself. The area becomes difficult terrain for 1 minute. Any creature other than the zombie that enters the area or starts its turn there must succeed on a DC 11 Strength saving throw or be restrained by the roots. A restrained creature can use its action to make a DC 11 Strength check, freeing itself on a success.

## Description

Corn Husk Zombies are grotesque amalgamations of decaying human flesh and twisted plant matter. Their bodies are partially composed of and covered in dried corn husks, giving them a distinct rustling sound as they move. Withered cornstalks and leaves protrude from their joints and orifices, and their eyes glow with a sickly yellow light. Their skin has a mottled green and brown appearance, resembling rotting vegetation. As they shamble forward, they leave a trail of corn kernels and decaying plant matter.

These abominations are the result of The Rows' corrupting influence on the dead buried in the fields surrounding Crow's Hollow. When the eldritch entity's power seeps into graves, it reanimates the corpses, fusing them with the very crops they once tended. The Reapers of Abundance see these creatures as a twisted blessing, proof of The Rows' power to bring abundance even in death. They often use Corn Husk Zombies as guardians for their secret ritual sites or as terror weapons against those who resist the cult. Some believe that these zombies retain fragments of memories from their past lives, drawn to the fields they once worked and the homes they once knew, adding a tragic dimension to their horrifying existence.

## Corn Stalker

*Large plant, neutral evil*

**Armor Class:** 15 (natural armor)

**Hit Points:** 76 (8d10 + 32)

**Speed:** 30 ft.

| STR | DEX | CON | INT | WIS | CHA |
|-----|-----|-----|-----|-----|-----|
| 18 (+4) | 14 (+2) | 18 (+4) | 7 (-2) | 12 (+1) | 8 (-1) |

**Skills:** Perception +4, Stealth +5

**Damage Vulnerabilities:** fire

**Damage Resistances:** bludgeoning, piercing

**Condition Immunities:** blinded, deafened, exhaustion

**Senses:** blindsight 60 ft., passive Perception 14

**Languages:** Understands Common but can't speak

**Challenge:** 5 (1,800 XP)

**False Appearance.** While the Corn Stalker remains motionless, it is indistinguishable from a normal cluster of corn stalks.

**Regeneration.** The Corn Stalker regains 10 hit points at the start of its turn if it has at least 1 hit point and is in contact with soil.

**Cornfield Camouflage.** The Corn Stalker has advantage on Dexterity (Stealth) checks made to hide in cornfields or areas with tall grass or crops.

## Actions

**Multiattack.** The Corn Stalker makes two slam attacks.

**Slam.** *Melee Weapon Attack:* +7 to hit, reach 10 ft., one target. *Hit:* 13 (2d8 + 4) bludgeoning damage.

**Entangling Stalks.** Ranged Weapon Attack: +5 to hit, range 30/60 ft., one target. Hit: The target is restrained by corn stalks. As an action, the restrained target can make a DC 14 Strength check, breaking free on a success. The effect also ends if the Corn Stalker is incapacitated or dies.

**Corn Silk Spores (Recharge 5-6).** The Corn Stalker releases a cloud of hallucinogenic spores in a 15-foot cone. Each creature in that area must succeed on a DC 14 Constitution saving throw or be poisoned for 1 minute. While poisoned in this way, the creature is also confused, as per the *Confusion* spell. The creature can repeat the saving throw at the end of each of its turns, ending the effect on itself on a success.

## Legendary Actions

The Corn Stalker can take 2 legendary actions, choosing from the options below. Only one legendary action option can be used at a time and only at the end of another creature's turn. The Corn Stalker regains spent legendary actions at the start of its turn.

**Stalking Step.** The Corn Stalker moves up to half its speed without provoking opportunity attacks.

**Lashing Tendril.** The Corn Stalker makes one slam attack.

**Soil Surge (Costs 2 Actions).** If the Corn Stalker is in contact with soil, it magically draws nutrients from the earth. It regains 10 (3d6) hit points and has advantage on its next attack roll.

## Description

The Corn Stalker is a terrifying amalgamation of corn stalks and malevolent plant matter. Standing at 8 feet tall, its body is composed of tightly woven cornstalks, leaves, and vines, giving it a vaguely humanoid shape. Its "head" is a cluster of corn ears, with glowing, amber kernels serving as eyes. Long, whip-like tendrils tipped with razor-sharp husks serve as its arms. As it moves, it produces a rustling sound accompanied by an unsettling whisper that sounds like wind through dry corn leaves. The air around it is thick with the scent of overripe corn and damp earth.

These monstrous plants are the result of The Rows' corruption taken to its extreme. They embody the entity's desire to transform all life into extensions of itself. Corn Stalkers are created when The Rows' essence infuses a large area of cornfield with particularly strong eldritch energy, often at sites of significant sacrifices or dark rituals performed by the Reapers of Abundance. These creatures serve as apex predators in The Rows' twisted ecosystem, hunting down any who dare to oppose the cult or trespass in the entity's domain. The Reapers of Abundance view Corn Stalkers as sacred guardians and occasionally attempt to lure victims to them as living sacrifices. Some cultists believe that those consumed by a Corn Stalker are granted a form of immortality, their essence becoming one with The Rows itself.

# Corrupted Chapel Guardian

*Large construct, lawful evil*

**Armor Class:** 17 (natural armor)

**Hit Points:** 114 (12d10 + 48)

**Speed:** 30 ft.

| STR | DEX | CON | INT | WIS | CHA |
|-----|-----|-----|-----|-----|-----|
| 20 (+5) | 8 (-1) | 18 (+4) | 7 (-2) | 16 (+3) | 12 (+1) |

**Saving Throws:** Wis +6, Cha +4

**Skills:** Perception +6, Religion +1

**Damage Resistances:** bludgeoning, piercing, and slashing from nonmagical attacks

**Damage Immunities:** necrotic, poison

**Condition Immunities:** charmed, exhaustion, frightened, paralyzed, petrified, poisoned

**Senses:** darkvision 120 ft., passive Perception 16

**Languages:** Understands Common and Celestial but can't speak

**Challenge:** 7 (2,900 XP)

**Corrupted Divinity.** The guardian has advantage on saving throws against spells and other magical effects.

**Immutable Form.** The guardian is immune to any spell or effect that would alter its form.

**Desecrated Aura.** The guardian emanates a desecrated aura in a 10-foot radius. Fiends and undead in the aura have advantage on saving throws, and creatures in the aura can't be charmed or frightened.

## Actions

**Multiattack.** The Corrupted Chapel Guardian makes two melee attacks.

**Corrupted Mace.** *Melee Weapon Attack:* +8 to hit, reach 5 ft., one target. *Hit:* 14 (2d8 + 5) bludgeoning damage plus 9 (2d8) necrotic damage.

**Harvest's Judgment (Recharge 5-6).** The guardian targets one creature it can see within 60 feet. The target must make a DC 15 Wisdom saving throw. On a failed save, the target takes 36 (8d8) radiant damage and is stunned until the end of its next turn. On a successful save, the target takes half as much damage and isn't stunned.

**Cornstalk Entanglement (1/Day).** Corrupted cornstalks burst from the ground in a 20-foot radius centered on the guardian. The area becomes difficult terrain for 1 minute. When a creature enters the area for the first time on a turn or starts its turn there, it must succeed on a DC 15 Strength saving throw or be restrained by the cornstalks. A creature can use its action to make a DC 15 Strength check, freeing itself or another creature within reach on a success.

## Legendary Actions

The Corrupted Chapel Guardian can take 3 legendary actions, choosing from the options below. Only one legendary action option can be used at a time and only at the end of another creature's turn. The guardian regains spent legendary actions at the start of its turn.

**Corrupted Strike.** The guardian makes one corrupted mace attack.

**Desecrating Pulse (Costs 2 Actions).** The guardian's desecrated aura flares. Each creature of the guardian's choice within 10 feet of it must succeed on a DC 15 Constitution saving throw or take 10 (3d6) necrotic damage.

**Invoke The Rows (Costs 3 Actions).** The guardian calls upon the power of The Rows. It regains 20 hit points, and each creature within 30 feet of it must succeed on a DC 15 Wisdom saving throw or be frightened for 1 minute. A frightened creature can repeat the saving throw at the end of each of its turns, ending the effect on itself on a success.

## Description

The Corrupted Chapel Guardian is a grotesque fusion of religious iconography and eldritch plant life. Standing at 9 feet tall, it resembles a twisted version of a holy statue, its once-angelic features now warped and overgrown with corrupted vegetation. Its stone body is cracked and seeping with a sickly green ichor, while writhing cornstalks and vines burst from these fissures,

forming a mockery of wings. The guardian's head is a misshapen mass of fused corn husks forming a hideous halo, with glowing amber kernels for eyes. In one hand, it wields a massive mace made of gnarled wood and tarnished metal, wrapped in thorny vines. The air around it shimmers with an unsettling, corrupt energy, and the scent of decaying vegetation and incense mingles in its presence.

Once a protector of the sacred chapel in Crow's Hollow, this guardian has been twisted by the insidious influence of The Rows. As the cult of the Reapers of Abundance grew in power, they sought to corrupt the town's places of worship, seeing them as a threat to their expanding influence. Through dark rituals and sacrifices performed in secret, they tainted the very essence of the chapel's guardian, infusing it with the eldritch power of The Rows. Now, this once-holy protector serves as a perverse sentinel for the cult, defending their blasphemous ceremonies and hunting down those who cling to the old faiths.

# Corrupted Water Elemental

*Large elemental, neutral evil*

**Armor Class:** 14 (natural armor)

**Hit Points:** 114 (12d10 + 48)

**Speed:** 30 ft., swim 90 ft.

| STR | DEX | CON | INT | WIS | CHA |
|-----|-----|-----|-----|-----|-----|
| 18 (+4) | 14 (+2) | 18 (+4) | 6 (-2) | 10 (+0) | 8 (-1) |

**Damage Resistances:** acid; bludgeoning, piercing, and slashing from nonmagical attacks

**Damage Immunities:** poison

**Condition Immunities:** exhaustion, grappled, paralyzed, petrified, poisoned, prone, restrained, unconscious

**Senses:** darkvision 60 ft., passive Perception 10

**Languages:** Understands Aquan but can't speak

**Challenge:** 6 (2,300 XP)

**Corrupted Nature.** The Corrupted Water Elemental can move through a space as narrow as 1 inch wide without squeezing. In addition, its movement leaves behind a trail of corrupted water that lasts for 1 minute. This area is considered difficult terrain for other creatures.

**Corn Husk Carapace.** The Corrupted Water Elemental has developed a partial carapace of corn husks, giving it resistance to slashing damage.

**Foul Waters.** Any creature that starts its turn in the same space as the Corrupted Water Elemental must succeed on a DC 14 Constitution saving throw or be poisoned until the start of its next turn.

## Actions

**Multiattack.** The Corrupted Water Elemental makes two slam attacks.

**Slam.** *Melee Weapon Attack:* +7 to hit, reach 5 ft., one target. *Hit:* 13 (2d8 + 4) bludgeoning damage.

**Corrupted Waterspout (Recharge 5-6).** The elemental unleashes a torrent of foul water in a 30-foot line that is 5 feet wide. Each creature in that line must make a DC 15 Dexterity saving throw, taking 21 (6d6) bludgeoning damage and 10 (3d6) necrotic damage on a failed save, or half as much damage on a successful one. A creature that fails the save is also knocked prone.

**Engulf.** The elemental moves up to its speed. While doing so, it can enter Large or smaller creatures' spaces. Whenever the elemental enters a creature's space, the creature must make a DC 15 Strength saving throw. On a failure, the target takes 13 (2d8 + 4) bludgeoning damage and is engulfed. The engulfed creature is restrained, has total cover against attacks and other effects outside the elemental, and takes 13 (2d8 + 4) bludgeoning damage and 7 (2d6) necrotic damage at the start of each of the elemental's turns. An engulfed creature can try to escape by taking an action to make a DC 15 Strength check. On a success, the creature escapes and enters a space of its choice within 5 feet of the elemental.

## Reactions

**Corn Husk Shield.** When the elemental is hit by a ranged weapon attack, it can use its reaction to gain a +4 bonus to its AC against that attack, potentially causing it to miss.

## Description

The Corrupted Water Elemental is a horrifying fusion of polluted water and twisted plant matter. Its form is a churning mass of murky, sickly green water, swirling with debris and decaying vegetation. Partially formed corn stalks and husks protrude from its liquid body, creating a grotesque, ever-shifting carapace. Eyes of glowing amber periodically form and dissolve within its mass, and tendrils of corrupted water lash out like whips. As it moves, it leaves behind a trail of foul-smelling sludge, and the air around it is thick with the stench of stagnant water and rotting crops.

These abominations are the result of The Rows' corruption seeping into the local water sources around Crow's Hollow. As the eldritch entity's influence spread beyond the cornfields, it began to taint rivers, streams, and even underground water tables. When this corrupted water encounters naturally occurring water elementals or is subjected to the Reapers of Abundance's dark rituals, these monstrosities are born. The Corrupted Water Elementals serve as both a means of further spreading The Rows' influence and as guardians of tainted water sources. The Reapers see them as a sign of

The Rows' growing power, proof that their dark god's reach extends beyond the harvest to the very lifeblood of the land. Some cultists whisper that drinking the water of these elementals grants visions of The Rows' alien realm, but such acts often lead to madness or worse.

# Mutated Fish-Person

*Medium humanoid (mutant), neutral evil*

**Armor Class:** 13 (natural armor)

**Hit Points:** 45 (6d8 + 18)

**Speed:** 30 ft., swim 40 ft.

| STR | DEX | CON | INT | WIS | CHA |
|---|---|---|---|---|---|
| 16 (+3) | 12 (+1) | 16 (+3) | 7 (-2) | 11 (+0) | 8 (-1) |

**Skills:** Athletics +5, Perception +2

**Damage Resistances:** Cold

**Senses:** darkvision 60 ft., passive Perception 12

**Languages:** Understands Common but can't speak

**Challenge:** 2 (450 XP)

**Amphibious.** The Mutated Fish-Person can breathe air and water.

**Corn-Scale Armor.** The Mutated Fish-Person's scales are infused with hardened corn husks, granting it natural armor.

**Polluted Blood.** When the Mutated Fish-Person takes piercing or slashing damage, each creature within 5 feet of it must succeed on a DC 13 Constitution saving throw or be poisoned until the end of its next turn.

## Actions

**Multiattack.** The Mutated Fish-Person makes two attacks: one with its bite and one with its claws.

**Bite.** *Melee Weapon Attack:* +5 to hit, reach 5 ft., one target. *Hit:* 7 (1d8 + 3) piercing damage.

**Claws.** *Melee Weapon Attack:* +5 to hit, reach 5 ft., one target. *Hit:* 6 (1d6 + 3) slashing damage.

**Corn Husk Net (Recharge 5-6).** *Ranged Weapon Attack:* +3 to hit, range 20/60 ft., one Large or smaller creature. *Hit:* The target is restrained. A creature restrained by the net can use its action to make a DC 13 Strength check, freeing itself on a success. The net can also be attacked and destroyed (AC 10; 20 hit points;

vulnerability to slashing damage; immunity to bludgeoning, poison, and psychic damage).

**Pollen Spore Cloud (1/ Day).** The Mutated Fish-Person releases a cloud of mutated pollen in a 15-foot radius. Each creature in that area must succeed on a DC 13 Constitution saving throw or be poisoned for 1 minute. While poisoned in this way, the creature is confused, as if under the effects of the *Confusion* spell. The creature can repeat the saving throw at the end of each of its turns, ending the effect on itself on a success.

### Description

Mutated Fish-People are grotesque hybrids of human, fish, and plant matter. Standing around 6 feet tall, their bodies are covered in a mix of slimy scales and hardened corn husks that form a natural armor. Their heads are a disturbing blend of human and fish features, with wide, glassy eyes, gaping mouths filled with sharp teeth, and vestigial corn silk for hair. Webbed hands end in sharp claws, while their feet are flipper-like. Patches of their skin sprout small cornstalks or leaves, and their gills are lined with tiny, mutated corn kernels. They exude a foul odor that's a mix of rotting fish and decaying vegetation.

These abominations are the result of The Rows' corruption spreading to the local water sources and affecting the fish population. When humans from Crow's Hollow consumed the tainted fish or spent too much time in the polluted waters, they began to transform into these monstrous hybrids. The Reapers of Abundance see the Mutated Fish-People as a sign of The Rows' expanding influence, proof that their dark god's power extends beyond the fields to the waters that sustain all life. Some cultists deliberately expose themselves to the tainted waters, viewing the mutation as a twisted form of ascension. The Mutated Fish-

People often gather in small groups near corrupted water sources, acting as guardians and occasionally raiding nearby areas for food or new victims to drag into the polluted depths, expanding their grotesque community.

## Hallucination of Lost Loved One

*Medium aberration, chaotic evil*

**Armor Class:** 13

**Hit Points:** 45 (10d8)

**Speed:** 30 ft., fly 30 ft. (hover)

| STR | DEX | CON | INT | WIS | CHA |
|-----|-----|-----|-----|-----|-----|
| 10 (+0) | 16 (+3) | 10 (+0) | 12 (+1) | 14 (+2) | 18 (+4) |

**Skills:** Deception +8, Insight +4, Perception +4

**Damage Immunities:** psychic

**Damage Resistances:** bludgeoning, piercing, and slashing from nonmagical attacks

**Condition Immunities:** charmed, exhaustion, frightened, grappled, paralyzed

**Senses:** darkvision 60 ft., passive Perception 14

**Languages:** All languages known by its target

**Challenge:** 4 (1,100 XP)

**Incorporeal Movement.** The hallucination can move through other creatures and objects as if they were difficult terrain. It takes 5 (1d10) force damage if it ends its turn inside an object.

**Shapechanger.** The hallucination can use its action to polymorph into the appearance of any humanoid creature, or back into its true form. Its statistics are the same in each form. Any equipment it is wearing or carrying isn't transformed.

**Empathic Link.** The hallucination can read the surface thoughts and memories of any creature within 60 feet of it. This allows it to perfectly mimic the mannerisms and speech patterns of a target's lost loved one.

### Actions

**Multiattack.** The hallucination makes two Emotional Drain attacks.

**Emotional Drain.** *Melee Spell Attack:* +6 to hit, reach 5 ft., one creature. *Hit:* 13 (3d6 + 3) psychic damage. If the target is a creature, they must succeed on a DC 14 Wisdom saving throw or have disadvantage on attack rolls and ability checks until the end of their next turn as they're overwhelmed with grief and confusion.

**Haunting Whispers (Recharge 5-6).** The hallucination targets one creature it can see within 60 feet. The target must make a DC 14 Wisdom saving throw. On a failed save, the target takes 22 (4d10) psychic damage and is stunned until the end of their next turn as they're assaulted by guilt-inducing whispers. On a successful save, the target takes half as much damage and isn't stunned.

**Illusory Reality (1/Day).** The hallucination manipulates its target's perception of reality. One creature within 30 feet must make a DC 14 Intelligence saving throw. On a failed save, the target is trapped in an illusion for 1 minute. While in this illusion, the target is incapacitated and their speed is reduced to 0. The target perceives themself in a comforting scene with their lost loved one, making them unwilling to take actions that might disrupt this illusion. The target can repeat the saving throw at the end of each of their turns, ending the effect on themself on a success.

## Reactions

**Guilt Trip.** When the hallucination is hit by an attack from a creature it can see within 30 feet, it can use its reaction to force the attacker to make a DC 14 Charisma saving throw. On a failed save, the attacker has disadvantage on their next attack roll as they're overwhelmed with guilt for "attacking" their loved one.

## Description

The Hallucination of a Lost Loved One is a shimmering, ethereal entity that can take on the appearance of any person known to its target. In its natural state, it appears as a translucent, humanoid figure composed of swirling mists and dancing motes of sickly green light. Its eyes are hollow voids that seem to draw in the viewer's gaze. When mimicking a loved one, the hallucination is nearly indistinguishable from the real person, save for a subtle, unsettling aura and occasional glitches in its form, like momentary distortions or flickers of its true nature.

These malevolent entities are manifestations of The Rows' psychic corruption, born from the collective grief and longing of the inhabitants of Crow's Hollow. As The Rows' influence spread, it began to feed not just on the land but on the emotional energy of the townsfolk. The entity learned to manipulate these strong emotions, creating these hallucinations to torment and manipulate its victims. The Reapers of Abundance see these hallucinations as a "gift" from The Rows, a way to reunite with lost loved ones and a tool to recruit new members by preying on their grief. In reality, prolonged exposure to these hallucinations can drive a person to madness or leave them in a catatonic state, their minds trapped in an endless loop of false memories and unfulfilled longings.

# Plant-Human Hybrid

*Medium plant, neutral evil*

**Armor Class:** 15 (natural armor)

**Hit Points:** 65 (10d8 + 20)

**Speed:** 30 ft.

| STR | DEX | CON | INT | WIS | CHA |
|-----|-----|-----|-----|-----|-----|
| 16 (+3) | 12 (+1) | 14 (+2) | 8 (-1) | 12 (+1) | 7 (-2) |

**Skills:** Perception +3, Stealth +3

**Damage Vulnerabilities:** fire

**Damage Resistances:** bludgeoning, piercing

**Condition Immunities:** charmed, frightened

**Senses:** darkvision 60 ft., passive Perception 13

**Languages:** Understands Common but can't speak

**Challenge:** 3 (700 XP)

**Regeneration.** The hybrid regains 5 hit points at the start of its turn if it has at least 1 hit point and is in contact with soil.

**Camouflage.** The hybrid has advantage on Dexterity (Stealth) checks made to hide in vegetative terrain.

**Photosynthesis.** If the hybrid spends at least 1 hour in direct sunlight, it regains 10 hit points.

## Actions

**Multiattack.** The hybrid makes two vine lash attacks.

**Vine Lash.** *Melee Weapon Attack:* +5 to hit, reach 10 ft., one target. *Hit:* 10 (2d6 + 3) bludgeoning damage. If the target is a creature, it must succeed on a DC 13 Strength saving throw or be pulled up to 10 feet toward the hybrid.

**Corn Husk Barrage (Recharge 5-6).** The hybrid launches a volley of sharp corn husks in a 15-foot cone. Each creature in that area must make a DC 13 Dexterity saving throw, taking 14 (4d6) slashing damage on a failed save, or half as much damage on a successful one.

**Pollen Cloud (1/Day).** The hybrid releases a cloud of hallucinogenic pollen in a 20-foot radius. Each creature in that area must succeed on a DC 13 Constitution saving throw or be poisoned for 1 minute. While poisoned in this way, the creature is confused, as per the *Confusion* spell. A creature can repeat the saving throw at the end of each of its turns, ending the effect on itself on a success.

**Root.** The hybrid can use its bonus action to extend roots into the ground, anchoring itself. While rooted, its speed becomes 0, it can't be pushed, pulled, or knocked prone, and it has advantage on Strength checks and Strength saving throws. The hybrid can uproot itself as a bonus action.

## Description

The Plant-Human Hybrid is a grotesque fusion of human and vegetable matter, a living testament to the corrupting power of The Rows. Standing at about 6 feet tall, its body is a disturbing blend of human flesh and plant tissue. Patches of skin have been replaced by rough, bark-like growths, while vines and tendrils emerge from its limbs, serving as prehensile appendages. Its hair has been transformed into a mass of corn silk, and its eyes glow with an eerie, amber light. Leaves and small cornstalks sprout from various parts of its body, rustling with every movement. The hybrid's mouth is permanently fixed in a silent scream, filled with teeth that resemble kernels of corn.

These abominations are the result of The Rows' most insidious form of corruption. When a villager of Crow's Hollow is exposed to an extremely concentrated dose of The Rows' essence, usually through a perverse ritual conducted by the Reapers of Abundance, their body begins a horrific transformation. The process is agonizing, as plant matter grows within and eventually bursts through the victim's flesh. The Reapers view these hybrids as the ultimate proof of The Rows' power to "elevate" humanity, seeing them as blessed beings who have transcended their mortal forms. In reality, the transformation obliterates much of the victim's personality and higher reasoning, leaving behind a creature driven by base instincts and an inexplicable urge to spread The Rows' influence. The hybrids often gravitate towards areas of strong plant growth, acting as guardians of corrupted nature and occasionally venturing out to capture new victims for transformation.

# Reaper of Abundance Cultist

*Medium humanoid (any race), neutral evil*

**Armor Class:** 12 (leather armor)

**Hit Points:** 27 (5d8 + 5)

**Speed:** 30 ft.

| STR | DEX | CON | INT | WIS | CHA |
|---|---|---|---|---|---|
| 11 (+0) | 12 (+1) | 12 (+1) | 10 (+0) | 13 (+1) | 14 (+2) |

**Skills:** Deception +4, Religion +2, Survival +3

**Senses:** passive Perception 11

**Languages:** Common, Druidic

**Challenge:** 1 (200 XP)

**Dark Devotion.** The cultist has advantage on saving throws against being charmed or frightened.

**Harvest's Blessing.** When the cultist is reduced to 0 hit points, it can use its reaction to release a burst of corrupted pollen. Each creature within 5 feet of the cultist must succeed on a DC 11 Constitution saving throw or be poisoned until the end of its next turn.

## Actions

**Multiattack.** The cultist makes two melee attacks.

**Sickle.** *Melee Weapon Attack:* +3 to hit, reach 5 ft., one target. *Hit:* 3 (1d4 + 1) slashing damage.

**Corrupted Seeds (Recharge 5-6).** The cultist throws a handful of corrupted seeds at a point within 30 feet. The seeds burst into twisted vines in a 10-foot radius. Each creature in that area must succeed on a DC 11 Dexterity saving throw or take 7 (2d6) piercing damage and be restrained by the vines. A creature can use its action to make a DC 11 Strength check, freeing itself or another creature within reach on a success. The vines wither away after 1 minute.

**Whispers of The Rows (1/Day).** The cultist targets one creature it can see within 30 feet. The target must succeed on a DC 12 Wisdom saving throw or be charmed by the cultist for 1 minute. While charmed, the target is incapacitated and has a speed of 0. The target can repeat the saving throw at the end of each of its turns, ending the effect on itself on a success.

## Description

A Reaper of Abundance Cultist appears as a seemingly ordinary villager with unsettling modifications. When performing cult functions, they wear dark green or brown robes adorned with intricate patterns of golden corn stalks and eerie, abstract eyes. Their skin often has a sickly, pale green tinge, and their eyes have a faint amber glow. Many cultists sport tattoos or scarification in the form of crop circles or corn mazes. They carry sickles or scythes as both tools and weapons, often decorated with small bones or desiccated corn husks. A faint, sweet smell of overripe corn seems to follow them wherever they go.

The Reapers of Abundance are the devoted followers of The Rows, having fully embraced its corrupting influence. Many began as ordinary farmers or villagers, lured by promises of bountiful harvests and protection from hardship. Through dark rituals and constant exposure to The Rows' essence, they have become something more and less than human. Their connection to The Rows grants them limited control over corrupted plant life and the ability to spread its influence. The cultists see themselves as the harbingers of a new age of plenty, where The Rows will transform the world into an endless, perfect harvest. They work tirelessly to expand their cult's influence, using a mix of manipulation, coercion, and outright violence to bring others into the fold. Many cultists dream of one day being "honored" with full transformation into a Plant-Human Hybrid, seeing it as the ultimate expression of devotion to The Rows.

# The Rows

*Gargantuan plant, neutral evil*

**Armor Class:** 20 (natural armor)

**Hit Points:** 350 (20d20 + 140)

**Speed:** 0 ft., burrow 60 ft.

| STR | DEX | CON | INT | WIS | CHA |
|-----|-----|-----|-----|-----|-----|
| 26 (+8) | 10 (+0) | 24 (+7) | 20 (+5) | 22 (+6) | 24 (+7) |

**Saving Throws:** Con +14, Int +12, Wis +13, Cha +14

**Skills:** Perception +13, Deception +14, Insight +13

**Damage Immunities:** poison, psychic

**Damage Resistances:** bludgeoning, piercing, and slashing from nonmagical attacks

**Condition Immunities:** charmed, exhaustion, frightened, paralyzed, petrified poisoned, prone, unconscious

**Senses:** truesight 120 ft., passive Perception 23

**Languages:** Understands all languages but can't speak, telepathy 1 mile

**Challenge:** 23 (50,000 XP)

**Legendary Resistance (3/Day).** If The Rows fails a saving throw, it can choose to succeed instead.

**Magic Resistance.** The Rows has advantage on saving throws against spells and other magical effects.

**Siege Monster.** The Rows deals double damage to objects and structures.

**Corrupting Presence.** At the start of each of The Rows' turns, each creature within 30 feet of it must succeed on a DC 21 Constitution saving throw or take 10 (3d6) necrotic damage and be poisoned until the start of its next turn. Plants and plant creatures make this saving throw with disadvantage.

**Rooted Mind.** The Rows can't be surprised, and it has advantage on all Intelligence, Wisdom, and Charisma saving throws.

## Actions

**Multiattack.** The Rows makes three attacks with its Corrupted Tendrils.

**Corrupted Tendril.** *Melee Weapon Attack:* +15 to hit, reach 30 ft., one target. *Hit:* 21 (3d8 + 8) bludgeoning damage plus 13 (3d8) necrotic damage. If the target is a creature, it must succeed on a DC 21 Strength saving throw or be pulled up to 20 feet toward The Rows and restrained. A creature can use its action to

make a DC 21 Strength check, freeing itself or another creature within reach on a success.

**Harvest of Despair (Recharge 5-6).** The Rows releases a wave of corrupting energy in a 60-foot cone. Each creature in that area must make a DC 21 Wisdom saving throw. On a failed save, a target takes 49 (14d6) psychic damage and is stunned for 1 minute. On a successful save, a target takes half as much damage and isn't stunned. A stunned creature can repeat the saving throw at the end of each of its turns, ending the effect on itself on a success.

**Eldritch Growth (1/Day).** The Rows causes corrupted plant life to erupt in a 100-foot radius around it. This area becomes difficult terrain, and when a creature starts its turn in the area or enters it for the first time on a turn, the creature must make a DC 21 Dexterity saving throw. On a failed save, the creature takes 22 (4d10) piercing damage and is restrained by the plants. A creature can use its action to make a DC 21 Strength check, freeing itself or another creature within reach on a success. The plants wither away after 10 minutes.

## Legendary Actions

The Rows can take 3 legendary actions, choosing from the options below. Only one legendary action option can be used at a time and only at the end of another creature's turn. The Rows regains spent legendary actions at the start of its turn.

**Tendril Attack.** The Rows makes one Corrupted Tendril attack.

**Corrupting Pulse (Costs 2 Actions).** The Rows releases a pulse of corrupting energy. Each creature within 30 feet must succeed on a DC 21 Constitution saving throw or take 16 (3d10) necrotic damage and have its speed reduced by half until the end of its next turn.

**Dominate Plant (Costs 3 Actions).** The Rows targets one plant creature it can see within 120 feet. The target must succeed on a DC 21 Wisdom saving throw or be charmed by The Rows for 24 hours. While charmed, the target is under The Rows' control. If the target takes damage, it can repeat the saving throw, ending the effect on a success.

## Description

The Rows is a colossal, nightmarish amalgamation of plant matter that defies conventional understanding. Its "body" is a vast network of twisted cornstalks, vines, and roots that spread for miles underground. Above ground, it manifests as a writhing mass of corrupted vegetation, constantly shifting and reforming. Gigantic corn ears serve as eyes, their kernels glowing with an otherworldly amber light. Massive tendrils, part plant and part flesh, whip about, adorned with sharp, bony protrusions. The entity exudes a sickly-sweet odor of decay and overripe vegetation. The very air around The Rows seems to warp and distort, as if reality itself is struggling to contain its eldritch nature.

The Rows is an ancient, alien intelligence that has existed since long before human civilization. It is a cosmic parasite that travels between worlds, seeking fertile ground to corrupt and consume. The entity feeds on the life force of plants, animals, and sentient beings, twisting them to serve its inscrutable purposes. When it arrived in the region of Crow's Hollow, it found ideal conditions to take root and slowly expand its influence. The Rows' ultimate goal is to transform the entire world into a vast, corrupted cornfield, a living extension of itself. It operates on a timescale far beyond human comprehension, patiently corrupting the land and its inhabitants over generations. The cult of the Reapers of Abundance is just its latest tool in this grand, cosmic plan. To The Rows, concepts of good and evil are meaningless; it simply seeks to grow, consume, and propagate its corrupted essence across reality itself.

# Swarm of Carnivorous Locusts

*Large swarm of Tiny beasts, unaligned*

**Armor Class:** 14 (natural armor)

**Hit Points:** 52 (8d10 + 8)

**Speed:** 10 ft., fly 30 ft.

| STR | DEX | CON | INT | WIS | CHA |
|---|---|---|---|---|---|
| 3 (-4) | 16 (+3) | 12 (+1) | 1 (-5) | 7 (-2) | 4 (-3) |

**Damage Resistances:** bludgeoning, piercing, slashing

**Condition Immunities:** charmed, frightened, grappled, paralyzed, petrified, prone, restrained, stunned

**Senses:** blindsight 10 ft., passive Perception 8

**Languages:** —

**Challenge:** 4 (1,100 XP)

**Swarm.** The swarm can occupy another creature's space and vice versa, and the swarm can move through any opening large enough for a Tiny insect. The swarm can't regain hit points or gain temporary hit points.

**Corrupted Nature.** The swarm has advantage on saving throws against spells and other magical effects.

**Ravenous Hunger.** The swarm has advantage on attack rolls against any creature that doesn't have all its hit points.

## Actions

**Multiattack.** The swarm makes two bite attacks against creatures in its space.

**Bites.** *Melee Weapon Attack:* +5 to hit, reach 0 ft., one target in the swarm's space. *Hit:* 14 (4d6) piercing damage, or 7 (2d6) piercing damage if the swarm has half of its hit points or fewer. The target must also succeed on a DC 13 Constitution saving throw or take 10 (3d6) necrotic damage as the locusts drain its vitality.

**Engulfing Cloud (Recharge 5-6).** The swarm disperses into a cloud of biting insects that engulfs everything within 10 feet. Each creature in that area must make a

DC 13 Dexterity saving throw. On a failure, a creature takes 14 (4d6) piercing damage and is blinded until the end of its next turn. On a success, it takes half as much damage and isn't blinded.

**Devouring Frenzy (1/Day).** For 1 minute, the swarm enters a devouring frenzy. During this time, its Bites attack deals an extra 7 (2d6) piercing damage, and any creature that takes damage from the swarm's attacks must succeed on a DC 13 Wisdom saving throw or be frightened until the end of its next turn.

## Description

The Swarm of Carnivorous Locusts is a terrifying sight to behold. Individually, each locust is about the size of a human thumb, with a chitinous exoskeleton in mottled shades of sickly green and rotting brown. Their wings are semi-transparent with visible, pulsing veins, and their eyes glow with an unnatural, amber light. What truly sets them apart are their mandibles - far larger and sharper than those of normal locusts, clearly adapted for tearing flesh. In a swarm, they form a writhing, buzzing cloud that darkens the sky and devours everything in its path. The air around the swarm is filled with an unsettling chorus of clicking mandibles and the rustle of countless wings.

These monstrous insects are a twisted creation of The Rows, born from its corruption of the natural order. As The Rows' influence spread beyond the cornfields, it began to affect the local insect population, particularly targeting locusts due to their association with crop destruction. The entity warped them into carnivorous monsters, driven by an insatiable hunger for flesh rather than plant matter. The Reapers of Abundance see these swarms as a tool of The Rows, used to punish those who resist its will and to "cleanse" areas for future corruption. They often try to direct the swarms towards neighboring communities, using the devastation left in their wake as an opportunity to expand their influence. Some cultists even undergo rituals to form a twisted bond with these swarms, allowing them to direct the locusts' hunger towards their enemies.

## Vicious Vines

*Large plant, neutral evil*

**Armor Class:** 13 (natural armor)

**Hit Points:** 57 (6d10 + 24)

**Speed:** 5 ft., climb 5 ft.

| STR | DEX | CON | INT | WIS | CHA |
|-----|-----|-----|-----|-----|-----|
| 18 (+4) | 10 (+0) | 18 (+4) | 3 (-4) | 10 (+0) | 3 (-4) |

**Skills:** Stealth +2

**Damage Vulnerabilities:** fire

**Damage Resistances:** bludgeoning, piercing

**Condition Immunities:** blinded, deafened, exhaustion, prone

**Senses:** blindsight 60 ft. (blind beyond this radius), passive Perception 10

**Languages:** —

**Challenge:** 3 (700 XP)

**False Appearance.** While the Vicious Vines remain motionless, they are indistinguishable from normal vegetation.

**Grasping Tendrils.** The Vicious Vines can have up to four targets grappled at a time.

**Regeneration.** The Vicious Vines regain 5 hit points at the start of their turn. If the Vicious Vines take fire damage, this trait doesn't function at the start of their next turn. The Vicious Vines die only if they start their turn with 0 hit points and don't regenerate.

## Actions

**Multiattack.** The Vicious Vines make two vine lash attacks.

**Vine Lash.** *Melee Weapon Attack:* +6 to hit, reach 15 ft., one target. *Hit:* 11 (2d6 + 4) bludgeoning damage. If the target is a creature, it is grappled (escape DC 14). Until this grapple ends, the target is restrained, and the Vicious Vines can't use this attack on another target.

**Constrict.** *Melee Weapon Attack:* +6 to hit, reach 5 ft., one creature grappled by the Vicious Vines. *Hit:* 13 (2d8 + 4) bludgeoning damage, and the target must succeed on a DC 14 Constitution saving throw or be poisoned for 1 minute. The poisoned creature can repeat the saving throw at the end of each of its turns, ending the effect on itself on a success.

**Entangling Roots (Recharge 5-6).** The ground erupts with corrupted roots in a 15-foot radius around the Vicious Vines. Each creature in that area must succeed on a DC 14 Strength saving throw or be restrained. A creature can use its action to make a DC 14 Strength check, freeing itself or another creature within reach on a success. The effect ends when the Vicious Vines die.

## Description

Vicious Vines appear as a mass of thick, twisted vines and tendrils, ranging from deep purple to a sickly yellow-green in color. Their surface is covered in sharp, thorn-like protrusions that secrete a faint, glowing ichor. Interspersed among the vines are bulbous growths resembling deformed fruits or pods, pulsing with an inner light. The vines move with an unsettling, almost animal-like intelligence, coiling and uncoiling in hypnotic patterns. When attacking, they lash out with whip-like speed, their tips hardening into spear-like points.

These monstrous plants are a direct result of The Rows' corruption spreading through the natural flora of Crow's Hollow and its surrounding areas. They represent the entity's ability to twist even the most benign aspects of nature into weapons of destruction. Vicious Vines often grow in areas where The Rows' influence is strong, such as near cult ritual sites or in particularly corrupted sections of forest or farmland. The Reapers of Abundance view these plants as guardians gifted by The Rows, often cultivating them around important locations. Some cultists even attempt to bond with Vicious Vines, seeing them as extensions of their dark god's will. However, the plants show no true loyalty, attacking any creature that comes too close with equal fervor. Their presence in an area is often one of the first signs that The Rows' corruption has taken hold, serving as a grim warning of the changes yet to come.

# NPCs

## Barkeep Mabel

*Medium humanoid (human), neutral evil*

**Armor Class:** 12 (leather apron)

**Hit Points:** 44 (8d8 + 8)

**Speed:** 30 ft.

| STR | DEX | CON | INT | WIS | CHA |
|-----|-----|-----|-----|-----|-----|
| 13 (+1) | 12 (+1) | 14 (+2) | 10 (+0) | 16 (+3) | 15 (+2) |

**Skills:** Deception +4, Insight +5, Perception +5, Persuasion +4

**Senses:** passive Perception 15

**Languages:** Common

**Challenge:** 2 (450 XP)

**Tavern Keeper's Resolve.** Mabel has advantage on saving throws against being charmed or frightened.

**Corn Whiskey Brewer.** Mabel can brew special corn whiskey infused with The Rows' essence. As an action, she can offer a creature a drink. If consumed, the creature must make a DC 13 Wisdom saving throw or be charmed by Mabel for 1 hour.

**Eerie Intuition.** Mabel has advantage on Wisdom (Insight) checks to determine if someone is lying or hiding something.

## Actions

**Multiattack.** Mabel makes two melee attacks.

**Bottle Smash.** *Melee Weapon Attack:* +3 to hit, reach 5 ft., one target. *Hit:* 4 (1d6 + 1) bludgeoning damage.

**Thrown Bottle.** *Ranged Weapon Attack:* +3 to hit, range 20/60 ft., one target. *Hit:* 4 (1d6 + 1) bludgeoning damage.

**Whispers of The Rows (1/ Day).** Mabel whispers eldritch secrets to a creature she can see within 30 feet. The target must succeed on a DC 13 Wisdom saving throw or be stunned until the end of its next turn as disturbing visions of endless cornfields flood its mind.

## Reactions

**Redirect Attack.** When a creature Mabel can see targets her with an attack, she can use her reaction to impose disadvantage on the attack roll, provided another creature is within 5 feet of her.

## Description

Barkeep Mabel is a stout, middle-aged woman with weathered hands and a deceptively warm smile. Her graying hair is always neatly tied back in a bun, adorned with a small cornhusk ornament. She has deep crow's feet around her eyes, which are an unsettling shade of amber. Mabel typically wears a worn but clean apron over simple, earthy-toned clothes. A peculiar necklace made of intricately woven wheat stalks and small, polished seeds hangs around her neck, often drawing curious glances from patrons.

Mabel has been the proprietor of The Crow's Nest Tavern for over two decades, a position that has made her privy to countless secrets and gossip within Crow's Hollow. Unknown to most, she was one of the first to be indoctrinated into the cult of The Rows, having discovered the entity's power when her crops miraculously survived a devastating blight that ruined many other farms. Since then, Mabel has used her position at the tavern to subtly influence and monitor the village's inhabitants, all while maintaining a facade of a simple, hardworking barkeep.

As a secret high-ranking member of the Reapers of Abundance, Mabel plays a crucial role in the cult's operations. She brews a special corn whiskey infused with The Rows' essence, which she uses to slowly indoctrinate unsuspecting patrons or to enhance the devotion of existing cult members. Her tavern also serves as a meeting point for cultists, with secret gatherings held in the cellar under the guise of "private tastings" for a fictitious whiskey club. Mabel's unassuming demeanor and her reputation as a kind, motherly figure make her one of the cult's most effective and dangerous agents, capable of swaying minds and gathering intelligence without ever raising suspicion.

# Cult Leader Amalgam

*Large aberration, chaotic evil*

**Armor Class:** 16 (natural armor)

**Hit Points:** 152 (16d10 + 64)

**Speed:** 30 ft.

| STR | DEX | CON | INT | WIS | CHA |
|-----|-----|-----|-----|-----|-----|
| 20 (+5) | 14 (+2) | 18 (+4) | 17 (+3) | 16 (+3) | 20 (+5) |

**Saving Throws:** Con +8, Wis +7, Cha +9

**Skills:** Arcana +7, Deception +9, Insight +7, Persuasion +9

**Damage Resistances:** bludgeoning, piercing, and slashing from nonmagical attacks

**Damage Immunities:** necrotic, poison

**Condition Immunities:** charmed, frightened, poisoned

**Senses:** darkvision 120 ft., passive Perception 13

**Languages:** Common, Druidic, telepathy 120 ft.

**Challenge:** 12 (8,400 XP)

**Regeneration.** The Amalgam regains 10 hit points at the start of its turn if it has at least 1 hit point.

**Magic Resistance.** The Amalgam has advantage on saving throws against spells and other magical effects.

**Shared Consciousness.** The Amalgam has advantage on Wisdom (Perception) checks and can't be surprised.

**Spellcasting.** The Amalgam is a 12th-level spellcaster. Its spellcasting ability is Charisma (spell save DC 17, +9 to hit with spell attacks). It has the following warlock spells prepared:

- Cantrips (at will): *eldritch blast, minor illusion, prestidigitation, thorn whip*
- 1st-5th level (3 5th-level slots): *blight, dominate person, entangle, hold monster, hunger of Hadar, plant growth*

## Actions

**Multiattack.** The Amalgam makes three attacks: two with its Grasping Tendrils and one with its Corrupting Touch.

**Grasping Tendrils.** *Melee Weapon Attack:* +9 to hit, reach 15 ft., one target. *Hit:* 14 (2d8 + 5) bludgeoning damage, and the target is grappled (escape DC 17). Until this grapple ends, the target is restrained.

**Corrupting Touch.** *Melee Weapon Attack:* +9 to hit, reach 5 ft., one target. *Hit:* 18 (4d6 + 4) necrotic damage. If the target is a creature, it must succeed on a DC 17 Constitution saving throw or its hit point maximum is reduced by an amount equal to the damage taken. This reduction lasts until the target finishes a long rest. The target dies if this effect reduces its hit point maximum to 0.

**Harvest Essence (Recharge 5-6).** The Amalgam targets up to three creatures it can see within 30 feet of it. Each target must make a DC 17 Wisdom saving throw. On a failed save, a target takes 22 (4d10) psychic damage and the Amalgam regains hit points equal to the damage dealt. On a successful save, the target takes half as much damage, and the Amalgam doesn't regain hit points.

## Legendary Actions

The Amalgam can take 3 legendary actions, choosing from the options below. Only one legendary action option can be used at a time and only at the end of another creature's turn. The Amalgam regains spent legendary actions at the start of its turn.

**Tendril Attack.** The Amalgam makes one Grasping Tendrils attack.

**Whispers of Madness (Costs 2 Actions).** The Amalgam whispers maddening secrets to a creature it can see within 60 feet. The target must succeed on a DC 17 Wisdom saving throw or be stunned until the end of its next turn.

**Call of The Rows (Costs 3 Actions).** The Amalgam causes cornstalks to erupt from the ground in a 20-foot radius around it. This area becomes difficult terrain, and any creature in the area where the corn appears must succeed on a DC 17 Dexterity saving throw or be restrained by the grasping stalks. A creature can use its action to make a DC 17 Strength check, freeing itself or another creature within reach on a success. The corn withers away at the end of the Amalgam's next turn.

## Description

The Cult Leader Amalgam is a horrifying sight to behold. It appears as a massive, writhing mass of intertwined human bodies, all seemingly fused together into a single, monstrous entity. Standing at nearly 12 feet tall, its form is constantly shifting, with limbs, faces, and torsos emerging and receding back into the mass. Cornstalks and vines grow from its flesh, intertwining with the human components. Its "head" is a grotesque fusion of multiple faces, each bearing an expression of ecstasy or agony. Eyes of various colors are scattered across its body, all glowing with an eerie, golden light. The creature exudes an aura of wrongness, as if its very existence is an affront to nature.

This abomination is the result of a ritual gone horribly wrong - or perhaps terribly right, from The Rows' perspective. In a desperate attempt to gain more power and curry favor with their eldritch patron, the highest-ranking members of the Reapers of Abundance performed a ceremony to merge their bodies and minds with the essence of The Rows. The ritual succeeded beyond their wildest dreams and darkest nightmares, fusing the cultists into a single entity that embodies the will of The Rows.

The Cult Leader Amalgam represents the ultimate corruption of humanity by The Rows. It possesses the combined knowledge and abilities of all the fused cultists, making it a formidable opponent both physically and mentally. The entity can tap directly into the power of The Rows, manipulating plants and corrupting the minds of others with terrifying ease. Despite its monstrous appearance, the Amalgam still retains a twisted charisma, able to project a hypnotic allure that can enthrall the weak-minded.

# Ezekiel Crane

*Medium humanoid (human), neutral good*

**Armor Class:** 11

**Hit Points:** 49 (9d8 + 9)

**Speed:** 25 ft.

| STR | DEX | CON | INT | WIS | CHA |
|-----|-----|-----|-----|-----|-----|
| 9 (-1) | 10 (+0) | 12 (+1) | 16 (+3) | 18 (+4) | 14 (+2) |

**Saving Throws:** Int +6, Wis +7

**Skills:** History +6, Insight +7, Medicine +7, Religion +6

**Senses:** passive Perception 14

**Languages:** Common, Druidic

**Challenge:** 3 (700 XP)

**Keeper of Old Ways.** Ezekiel has advantage on saving throws against being charmed or frightened by aberrations or plant creatures.

**Spellcasting.** Ezekiel is a 7th-level spellcaster. His spellcasting ability is Wisdom (spell save DC 15, +7 to hit with spell attacks). He has the following cleric spells prepared:

- Cantrips (at will): *light, mending, sacred flame, thaumaturgy*
- 1st level (4 slots): *bless, cure wounds, detect evil and good, protection from evil and good*
- 2nd level (3 slots): *augury, lesser restoration, protection from poison*
- 3rd level (3 slots): *dispel magic, remove curse, speak with plants*
- 4th level (1 slot): *divination, guardian of faith*

**Village Elder's Insight.** Ezekiel can use a bonus action to give one creature he can see within 30 feet of him advantage on the next ability check, attack roll, or saving throw it makes before the start of Ezekiel's next turn.

## Actions

**Quarterstaff.** *Melee Weapon Attack:* +2 to hit, reach 5 ft., one target. *Hit:* 2 (1d6 - 1) bludgeoning damage, or 3 (1d8 - 1) bludgeoning damage if used with two hands.

**Sacred Flame.** *Ranged Spell Attack:* One target within 60 feet must succeed on a DC 15 Dexterity saving throw or take 2d8 radiant damage.

**Whispers of Warning (1/Day).** Ezekiel can whisper ancient words of protection to up to three creatures he can see within 30 feet. For the next hour, these creatures have advantage on saving throws against spells and other magical effects.

## Reactions

**Protective Ward.** When a creature within 30 feet of Ezekiel that he can see is hit by an attack, Ezekiel can use his reaction to impose disadvantage on that attack roll, potentially causing it to miss.

## Description

Ezekiel Crane is a frail, elderly man with a stooped posture and gnarled hands that speak of a lifetime of hard work. Despite his advanced age, his pale blue eyes remain sharp and alert, often darting about as if searching for unseen dangers. His wispy white hair and long beard are typically unkempt, giving him a somewhat wild appearance. Ezekiel dresses in simple, worn clothing adorned with small protective charms made from various plants and seeds. He walks with the aid of a gnarled wooden staff, which seems to be as much a part of him as his own limbs.

As the oldest resident of Crow's Hollow, Ezekiel Crane carries the weight of the village's history on his shoulders. He was born shortly after the founding of the village and the initial pact with The Rows. Throughout his long life, he has witnessed the gradual corruption of his home and the insidious spread of the cult's influence. Ezekiel's own father was one of the first to resist The Rows' temptations, passing down ancient knowledge of protective magic and the true nature of the entity to his son.

Ezekiel now finds himself in a precarious position. He possesses crucial information about The Rows and the cult's activities, but he's acutely aware of the danger this knowledge represents. Years of watching friends and family fall under the cult's sway have left him paranoid and hesitant to trust anyone. He struggles with guilt over not taking more decisive action in his younger years and fears that it may be too late to save Crow's Hollow. Despite this, a flicker of hope remains in Ezekiel's heart. He carefully watches for signs of resistance or outside help, ready to share his knowledge with those who might have the courage to stand against The Rows and free the village from its malevolent influence.

# Mayor Abigail Thorne (High Reaper)

*Medium humanoid (human), lawful evil*

**Armor Class:** 15 (Mage Armor)

**Hit Points:** 91 (14d8 + 28)

**Speed:** 30 ft.

| STR | DEX | CON | INT | WIS | CHA |
|-----|-----|-----|-----|-----|-----|
| 10 (+0) | 14 (+2) | 14 (+2) | 18 (+4) | 16 (+3) | 20 (+5) |

**Saving Throws:** Int +8, Wis +7, Cha +9

**Skills:** Arcana +8, Deception +9, Insight +7, Persuasion +9, Religion +8

**Damage Resistances:** necrotic

**Condition Immunities:** charmed, frightened

**Senses:** darkvision 60 ft., passive Perception 13

**Languages:** Common, Druidic, telepathy 60 ft. (with plant creatures only)

**Challenge:** 10 (5,900 XP)

**Spellcasting.** Abigail is a 14th-level spellcaster. Her spellcasting ability is Charisma (spell save DC 17, +9 to hit with spell attacks). She has the following warlock spells prepared:

- Cantrips (at will): *eldritch blast, mage hand, minor illusion, thorn whip*
- 1st-5th level (3 5th-level slots): *blight, dominate person, entangle, hex, hold monster, hunger of Hadar, plant growth, scrying, wall of thorns*

**Harvest Blessing.** As a bonus action, Abigail can touch a plant creature or a creature holding a plant. The target gains 10 temporary hit points and has advantage on its next attack roll or saving throw.

## Eldritch Invocations

**Agonizing Blast**: Abigail adds her Charisma modifier to the damage she deals with eldritch blast.

**Cloak of Flies**: As a bonus action, Abigail can surround herself with a magical aura that looks like buzzing flies. It lasts until she's incapacitated or dismisses it. The aura extends 5 feet from her in every direction, but not through total cover, and moves with her. The aura grants her advantage on Charisma (Intimidation) checks but disadvantage on all other Charisma checks. Any other creature that starts its turn in the aura takes 5 (1d10) poison damage. Once she uses this invocation, she can't use it again until she finishes a short or long rest.

## Actions

**Multiattack.** Abigail makes two attacks with her Staff of Thorns or two eldritch blasts.

**Staff of Thorns.** *Melee Weapon Attack:* +8 to hit, reach 5 ft., one target. *Hit:* 7 (1d6 + 4) bludgeoning damage plus 13 (3d8) piercing damage.

**Eldritch Blast.** *Ranged Spell Attack:* +9 to hit, range 120 ft., one target. *Hit:* 10 (1d10 + 9) force damage.

**Seeds of Corruption (Recharge 5-6).** Abigail throws a handful of corrupted seeds in a 15-foot cone. Each creature in that area must make a DC 17 Constitution saving throw. On a failed save, a creature takes 36 (8d8) necrotic damage and is poisoned for 1 minute. On a successful save, a creature takes half as much damage and isn't poisoned. A poisoned creature can repeat the saving throw at the end of each of its turns, ending the effect on itself on a success.

## Legendary Actions

Abigail can take 3 legendary actions, choosing from the options below. Only one legendary action option can be used at a time and only at the end of another creature's turn. Abigail regains spent legendary actions at the start of her turn.

**Cantrip.** Abigail casts a cantrip.

**Corrupting Touch (Costs 2 Actions).** Abigail touches one creature within 5 feet of her. The creature must succeed on a DC 17 Constitution saving throw or take 26 (4d12) necrotic damage and have disadvantage on its next saving throw before the end of Abigail's next turn.

**Call of The Rows (Costs 3 Actions).** Abigail calls upon the power of The Rows. Writhing vines and cornstalks burst from the ground in a 20-foot radius centered on a point she can see within 60 feet. The area becomes difficult terrain for 1 minute. When the plants appear and at the start of each of Abigail's turns, they attack creatures in the area. Each creature in the area must succeed on a DC 17 Dexterity saving throw or take 14 (4d6) piercing damage and be restrained until the start of Abigail's next turn.

## Description

Mayor Abigail Thorne presents a striking figure, her outward appearance a carefully crafted mask of respectability that belies her true nature. In her early fifties, she possesses a regal bearing and piercing green eyes that seem to look right through those she addresses. Her salt-and-pepper hair is always impeccably styled, and she dresses in tailored suits of deep green or rich brown, often adorned with subtle corn motifs. A polished silver brooch in the shape of a stylized cornstalk serves as her mayoral badge of office. When presiding over cult matters as the High Reaper, she dons an ornate robe of midnight black, embroidered with golden threads depicting winding cornstalks and eerie, abstract eyes.

Abigail's journey to power is a tale of ambition, cunning, and dark bargains. Born into one of the founding families of Crow's Hollow, she grew up steeped in the lore of The Rows and the secret rituals of the Reapers of Abundance. From a young age, she showed an uncanny aptitude for both leadership and the eldritch magicks granted by The Rows. Abigail's rise through the ranks of both the town's official governance and the hidden cult hierarchy was meteoric, marked by convenient accidents befalling her rivals and an almost supernatural ability to sway others to her will.

As High Reaper, Abigail serves as the primary conduit between The Rows and its mortal followers. She has delved deeper into the entity's alien consciousness than any before her, gaining immense power at the cost of her humanity. Under her leadership, the cult's influence has spread beyond Crow's Hollow, quietly infiltrating neighboring communities. Abigail's ultimate goal is to expand The Rows' dominion across the entire region, transforming it into an endless field of corrupted grain that will serve as a foothold for the entity to fully enter the material plane. She views this as ascension rather than destruction, truly believing that she is guiding humanity towards a glorious, transcendent future.

# Miss Hawthorn

*Medium humanoid (human), neutral*

**Armor Class:** 11

**Hit Points:** 44 (8d8 + 8)

**Speed:** 30 ft.

| STR | DEX | CON | INT | WIS | CHA |
|-----|-----|-----|-----|-----|-----|
| 10 (+0) | 12 (+1) | 13 (+1) | 16 (+3) | 15 (+2) | 14 (+2) |

**Skills:** History +5, Insight +4, Persuasion +4

**Senses:** passive Perception 12

**Languages:** Common, Druidic

**Challenge:** 2 (450 XP)

**Conflicted Mind.** Miss Hawthorn has advantage on saving throws against being charmed or frightened by cultists or creatures associated with The Rows.

**Educator's Insight.** As a bonus action, Miss Hawthorn can grant one creature she can see within 30 feet of her advantage on the next Intelligence check it makes before the start of her next turn.

**Spellcasting.** Miss Hawthorn is a 5th-level spellcaster. Her spellcasting ability is Intelligence (spell save DC 13, +5 to hit with spell attacks). She has the following wizard spells prepared:

- Cantrips (at will): *mage hand, message, prestidigitation*
- 1st level (4 slots): *charm person, comprehend languages, detect magic, shield*
- 2nd level (3 slots): *calm emotions, detect thoughts, suggestion*
- 3rd level (2 slots): *dispel magic, sending*

## Actions

**Dagger.** *Melee or Ranged Weapon Attack:* +3 to hit, reach 5 ft. or range 20/60 ft., one target. *Hit:* 3 (1d4 + 1) piercing damage.

**Protective Instinct (1/Day).** Miss Hawthorn can use her action to bolster the defenses of up to three creatures she can see within 30 feet of her. Each target gains 5 temporary hit points and has advantage on their next saving throw made within 1 hour.

## Reactions

**Redirect Aggression.** When a creature Miss Hawthorn can see targets a child with an attack, she can use her reaction to become the target of the attack instead.

## Description

Miss Hawthorn is a woman in her early thirties with a kind face etched with worry lines beyond her years. Her auburn hair is usually tied back in a neat bun, with a few strands escaping to frame her face. She has warm brown eyes that often dart nervously when discussing certain topics. Miss Hawthorn dresses in modest, practical clothing suitable for teaching, favoring earth tones and simple patterns. She always wears a silver pendant in the shape of an open book, a gift from her students. Observant individuals might notice that her left hand often trembles slightly, especially when she's stressed.

As the sole teacher in the small schoolhouse of Crow's Hollow, Miss Hawthorn bears the weighty responsibility of educating the village's children. She grew up in the village and was once a bright, optimistic young woman with dreams of broadening her students' horizons. However, as she became aware of the true nature of The Rows and the Reapers of Abundance, her world began to unravel. The cult's leadership, recognizing her influence over the young minds of the village, pressured her to subtly indoctrinate the children into their beliefs.

Miss Hawthorn now finds herself in an agonizing moral dilemma. On one hand, she desperately wants to protect her students from the cult's influence and maintain her role as a beacon of knowledge and critical thinking. On the other, she fears the consequences of defying the cult, both for herself and for the children she cares for deeply. This internal conflict manifests in her teaching methods, where she alternates between encouraging free thought and reluctantly introducing elements of the cult's doctrine. She secretly hopes for a way to break free from the cult's grip and save her students, but she feels powerless against the overwhelming influence of The Rows. Miss Hawthorn's conflicted nature makes her a potential ally for those seeking to uncover the truth about Crow's Hollow, but her fear and indoctrination could also make her a reluctant obstacle.

# Old Man Jenkins

*Medium humanoid (human), chaotic good*

**Armor Class:** 13 (natural armor)

**Hit Points:** 65 (10d8 + 20)

**Speed:** 25 ft.

| STR | DEX | CON | INT | WIS | CHA |
|-----|-----|-----|-----|-----|-----|
| 8 (-1) | 12 (+1) | 14 (+2) | 16 (+3) | 18 (+4) | 10 (+0) |

**Saving Throws:** Int +6, Wis +7

**Skills:** Arcana +6, Nature +6, Perception +7, Survival +7

**Damage Resistances:** necrotic

**Condition Immunities:** charmed, frightened

**Senses:** darkvision 60 ft., passive Perception 17

**Languages:** Common, Druidic, Sylvan

**Challenge:** 4 (1,100 XP)

**Magic Resistance.** Jenkins has advantage on saving throws against spells and other magical effects.

**Nature's Warding.** Jenkins can't be tracked by nonmagical means, and plants grow to hide his trail.

**Spellcasting.** Jenkins is a 7th-level spellcaster. His spellcasting ability is Wisdom (spell save DC 15, +7 to hit with spell attacks). He has the following druid spells prepared:

- Cantrips (at will): druidcraft, guidance, shillelagh, thorn whip
- 1st level (4 slots): detect magic, entangle, longstrider, speak with animals
- 2nd level (3 slots): barkskin, heat metal, lesser restoration, pass without trace
- 3rd level (3 slots): dispel magic, plant growth, speak with plants
- 4th level (1 slot): freedom of movement, locate creature

## Actions

**Quarterstaff.** *Melee Weapon Attack:* +2 to hit (+7 to hit with shillelagh), reach 5 ft., one target. *Hit:* 2 (1d6 - 1) bludgeoning damage, or 7 (1d8 + 3) bludgeoning damage with shillelagh or if wielded with two hands.

**Secrets of The Rows (1/Day).** Jenkins shares a crucial piece of information about The Rows. Choose one of the following effects:

- One creature within 30 feet gains advantage on all saving throws against effects created by The Rows or its cultists for the next 24 hours.

- Jenkins reveals a weakness of a specific creature associated with The Rows. The next attack roll against that creature has advantage, and the creature has disadvantage on its next saving throw.

## Reactions

**Protective Growth.** When Jenkins or a creature within 30 feet of him is targeted by an attack, he can use his reaction to cause plants to rapidly grow, imposing disadvantage on the attack roll.

## Description

Old Man Jenkins is a wiry, weathered figure who appears to be in his late seventies, though his true age is anyone's guess. His skin is leathery and tanned from years of outdoor living, creased with deep wrinkles that seem to form intricate patterns. Jenkins sports a wild, unkempt beard that reaches his chest, peppered with leaves and twigs as if he's part plant himself. His eyes are a startling shade of green, sharp and alert despite his age. He dresses in layers of mismatched, patched clothing in earthy tones, and always carries a gnarled wooden staff adorned with strange symbols and hanging charms made from bones, feathers, and crystals.

Jenkins was once a respected member of Crow's Hollow, serving as the village's healer and lore keeper. However, as The Rows' influence grew, he recognized the insidious nature of the entity long before others. His outspoken warnings and attempts to resist the cult led to his exile from the village decades ago. Rather than flee, Jenkins chose to remain on the outskirts of town, watching and waiting, gathering knowledge about The Rows and its weaknesses. Over the years, he has formed a deep connection with the uncorrupted parts of nature surrounding Crow's Hollow, learning secrets from the plants and animals that have helped him survive and resist The Rows' influence.

Living in self-imposed exile has taken its toll on Jenkins' mind. His behavior is often erratic, swinging between moments of startling lucidity and rambling paranoia. He's developed elaborate routines and superstitions to protect himself from The Rows, some effective and others merely odd. Despite his eccentricities, Jenkins possesses crucial information about The Rows' true nature, its weaknesses, and the history of its influence on Crow's Hollow. Years of isolation and the constant threat of The Rows have made him deeply distrustful, and anyone seeking his help will need to prove their intentions and earn his confidence.

# Sarah Blackwood

*Medium humanoid (human), neutral evil*

**Armor Class:** 13 (leather armor)

**Hit Points:** 45 (7d8 + 14)

**Speed:** 30 ft.

| STR | DEX | CON | INT | WIS | CHA |
|-----|-----|-----|-----|-----|-----|
| 10 (+0) | 14 (+2) | 14 (+2) | 16 (+3) | 15 (+2) | 18 (+4) |

**Saving Throws:** Wis +4, Cha +6

**Skills:** Deception +6, Insight +4, Persuasion +6, Religion +5

**Senses:** passive Perception 12

**Languages:** Common, Druidic

**Challenge:** 3 (700 XP)

**Spellcasting.** Sarah is a 5th-level spellcaster. Her spellcasting ability is Charisma (spell save DC 14, +6 to hit with spell attacks). She has the following warlock spells prepared:

- Cantrips (at will): *eldritch blast, minor illusion, prestidigitation*
- 1st-3rd level (2 3rd-level slots): *charm person, entangle, hold person, plant growth, speak with plants*

**Whispers of The Rows.** Sarah can telepathically communicate with plants and plant creatures within 30 feet of her.

**Corrupting Touch.** When Sarah hits a creature with a melee attack, she can expend a spell slot to deal an additional 2d8 necrotic damage to the target per spell level, and the target must succeed on a DC 14 Constitution saving throw or be poisoned until the end of its next turn.

## Actions

**Sickle.** *Melee Weapon Attack:* +4 to hit, reach 5 ft., one target. *Hit:* 4 (1d4 + 2) slashing damage.

**Eldritch Blast.** *Ranged Spell Attack:* +6 to hit, range 120 ft., one target. *Hit:* 10 (1d10 + 4) force damage.

## Reactions

**Sacrificial Shield.** When a creature Sarah can see within 30 feet of her is hit by an attack, she can use her reaction to cause plants to rapidly grow and intercept the attack. The target gains a +2 bonus to AC against that attack, potentially causing it to miss.

## Description

Sarah Blackwood is a striking figure, her youth belied by the intensity in her eyes. Standing at 5'6", she has long, raven-black hair often adorned with intricate cornhusk braids. Her pale skin is marked with subtle, vine-like tattoos that seem to shift when not directly observed. Sarah typically wears a dark green robe emblazoned with golden corn motifs, and a necklace made of various seeds and small bones. Her most unsettling feature is her eyes - originally blue, they now have a distinct golden tint, with pupils that occasionally appear to be shaped like tiny corn kernels.

As the teenage leader of the Reapers of Abundance, Sarah Blackwood represents the tragic corruption of youth by The Rows. Born to devout cultist parents, Sarah showed an uncanny connection to The Rows from an early age. Plants seemed to grow more vigorously in her presence, and she often spoke of whispers only she could hear coming from the cornfields. The village elders, recognizing these signs, groomed her for leadership from childhood. By the age of sixteen, Sarah had undergone secret rituals that bound her even more closely to The Rows, granting her unnatural powers but also twisting her mind and body.

Sarah truly believes that The Rows is a benevolent entity, offering abundance and transcendence to its followers. She sees herself as a shepherd, guiding both the younger children and the adults of Crow's Hollow towards a greater purpose. Her charisma and the eerie powers granted by The Rows make her a formidable leader, capable of inspiring fanatical devotion in her followers. However, beneath her confident exterior lies a deep-seated fear - not of The Rows, but of failure. Sarah is hauntingly aware that if she doesn't continually prove her worth, she may find herself on the sacrificial altar, a fate she's overseen for others many times before.

# Game within a Game

## The Reaper's Hand

A card game of chance and fate, where players wager their fortunes against The Reaper's growing influence.

## Players

2–4 players (PCs or NPCs)
The game lasts about 10–15 minutes in real-time.

## Objective

Outlast your opponents by avoiding The Reaper's Hand and being the first to collect 5 "Fortune Points" before being consumed by corruption.

## Components

**Standard 52-card deck**

Cards are divided into two categories:

**Blessings** and **Curses**, based on suit and rank.
Blessings:

- Hearts & Diamonds (2–10): Represent Fortune and Blessings.

**Curses**:

- Clubs & Spades (2–10): Represent Curses and Corruption.

**Special Cards**:

- Face Cards (J, Q, K): Trigger special effects.
- Hearts & Diamonds (Face Cards): Powerful blessings that remove Corruption Tokens or give Fortune Points.
- Clubs & Spades (Face Cards): Powerful curses that add Corruption Tokens or force players to discard Fortune.
- Aces: Represent The Reaper's Hand, a dangerous card that can either help or harm players depending on how they use it.

## Gameplay

**Set-Up:** Shuffle the deck. Each player draws 2 cards to start. Place the remaining deck face down in the center.

**Turn Structure:** On each turn, a player draws one card from the deck and resolves the effects based on the card they draw.

**Blessings (Hearts & Diamonds):**

- Cards 2–10: Add **1 Fortune Point** for each card drawn.
- Face Cards (J, Q, K): Remove **1 Corruption Token** or add **2 Fortune Points** (player's choice).

Curses (Clubs & Spades):

- Cards 2–10: Add **1 Corruption Token** for each card drawn.
- Face Cards (J, Q, K): Add **2 Corruption Tokens** or force the player to **lose 1 Fortune Point** (opponent's choice).

Aces (The Reaper's Hand):

- If a player draws an Ace, they must immediately decide:
- Gamble with The Reaper: Roll a d6.
    - On a 1–3, gain 1 Fortune Point.
    - On a 4–6, gain 1 Corruption Token.
- **Pass the Hand**: Give the Ace to another player, forcing them to roll the d6 instead.

**Corruption Tokens**

- Every player starts with 0 Corruption Tokens.
- If a player gains **5 Corruption Tokens**, they are eliminated from the game.

**Fortune Points**

- The first player to collect **5 Fortune Points** wins the game.

## End of the Game

The game ends when a player reaches 5 Fortune Points and wins, or if all other players are eliminated due to Corruption Tokens.

## Example Turn

- **Player 1** draws a 7 of Hearts. This is a Blessing card, so they gain 1 Fortune Point.
- **Player 2** draws a King of Spades. This is a Curse card, so they gain 2 Corruption Tokens or lose 1 Fortune Point.
- **Player 3** draws an Ace. They choose to gamble with The Reaper, rolling a d6. They roll a 4 and receive 1 Corruption Token.

# Food and Fuel

## Corrupted Corn Chowder

This meal captures the essence of a harvest gone wrong. The **Corrupted Corn Chowder** is a rich and hearty soup, but with an ominous touch—dark swirls of roasted garlic oil mimic the spreading corruption of The Rows, while the deep, almost charred flavor of the black bread adds to the sinister theme.

## Ingredients

For the Corrupted Corn Chowder

- 6 ears of corn (or 4 cups frozen or canned corn kernels)
- 1 large potato, peeled and diced
- 1 onion, finely chopped
- 2 cloves garlic, minced
- 1 tablespoon olive oil
- 4 cups vegetable broth (or chicken broth for a heartier version)
- 1 cup heavy cream
- 1 teaspoon smoked paprika
- ½ teaspoon cumin
- Salt and black pepper to taste
- 2 tablespoons roasted garlic oil (to swirl on top for the "corruption" effect)
- Fresh parsley or chives for garnish (optional)

For the Black Bread

- 1 cup rye flour
- 2 cups all-purpose flour
- 2 tablespoons cocoa powder (to darken the bread)
- 2 tablespoons molasses (for a slightly sweet, earthy flavor)
- 1 packet (2 ¼ tsp) active dry yeast
- 1 teaspoon salt
- 1 cup warm water
- 2 tablespoons butter, melted
- 1 tablespoon caraway seeds (optional, for a more rustic flavor)

## Instructions

For the Corrupted Corn Chowder

1. **Prep the Corn**:
   If using fresh corn, cut the kernels off the cob and set them aside. If using frozen or canned corn, have it ready to go.

2. **Sauté the Aromatics**:
   In a large pot, heat the olive oil over medium heat. Add the chopped onion and minced garlic, and sauté until softened and golden (about 5 minutes).

3. **Add the Potatoes and Spices**:
   Add the diced potatoes to the pot along with the smoked paprika, cumin, salt, and black pepper. Stir well to coat the potatoes in the oil and spices.

4. **Add the Broth**:
   Pour in the vegetable (or chicken) broth, and bring the mixture to a boil. Reduce the heat to a simmer, cover the pot, and cook for 10–12 minutes, or until the potatoes are tender.

5. **Add the Corn and Cream**:
   Stir in the corn kernels and the heavy cream. Let the soup simmer for an additional 5–7 minutes until the corn is tender and the flavors meld together.

6. **Blend Partially (Optional)**:
   For a thicker chowder, use an immersion blender to blend about half of the soup, leaving some chunks for texture.

7. **Serve and Add the "Corruption"**:
   Ladle the soup into bowls, then drizzle the roasted garlic oil on top in a swirling, "corrupting" pattern. Garnish with fresh parsley or chives for a touch of green, if desired.

For the Black Bread

1. **Activate the Yeast**:
   In a large bowl, combine the warm water, yeast, and molasses. Stir gently and let sit for 5–10 minutes until the mixture becomes frothy.

2. **Mix the Dry Ingredients**:
   In a separate bowl, whisk together the rye flour, all-purpose flour, cocoa powder, and salt.

3. **Form the Dough**:
   Gradually add the dry ingredients to the yeast mixture. Stir to form a sticky dough. Once the dough comes together, turn it out onto a floured surface and knead for 5–7 minutes until smooth and elastic.

4. **First Rise**:
   Place the dough in a greased bowl, cover with a damp towel, and let rise in a warm place for 1 hour, or until doubled in size.

5. **Shape and Second Rise**:
   Punch the dough down, shape it into a loaf, and place it on a baking sheet or in a loaf pan. Cover and let it rise for another 30 minutes.

6. **Bake the Bread**:
   Preheat your oven to 375°F (190°C). Brush the top of the bread with melted butter, sprinkle with caraway seeds (optional), and bake for 25–30 minutes, or until the loaf sounds hollow when tapped on the bottom.

7. **Cool and Serve**:
   Let the bread cool for at least 10 minutes before slicing. Serve with butter or use it to dip into the Corrupted Corn Chowder.

# Drinks

## Alcoholic Option: Corrupted Harvest Cider

- 2 oz dark rum
- 6 oz hard apple cider
- 1 tablespoon maple syrup
- 1/2 teaspoon cinnamon
- Apple slices and cinnamon stick for garnish

In a shaker, combine the dark rum, maple syrup, and cinnamon.

Pour into a glass filled with ice.

Top with hard cider, stir gently, and garnish with apple slices and a cinnamon stick for a warming, earthy drink.

## Non-Alcoholic Option: Eldritch Autumn Brew

- 1 cup apple cider
- 1 tablespoon pomegranate juice (for a darker, mysterious color)
- Dash of cinnamon
- 1/2 teaspoon maple syrup
- Club soda (for a bit of fizz)
- Apple slice or pomegranate seeds for garnish

In a glass, mix the apple cider, pomegranate juice, cinnamon, and maple syrup.

Top with club soda and garnish with an apple slice or pomegranate seeds for a refreshing, eldritch-inspired autumn drink.

# Map

# The Harvest Haunting

# Managing Encounters

To help DMs tailor the adventure to the party, each encounter is designed with flexibility in mind. Whether your group consists of fledgling adventurers or seasoned heroes, the provided guidelines will help ensure that the challenges are both fun and fair.

## Encounter Structure

- **Encounter Name**: The title of the encounter, usually indicating the primary theme or challenge.

- **DM Information**: A brief summary to give you a clear picture of the encounter's purpose and its role in the overall adventure.

- **Read Aloud**: Descriptive text meant to be read verbatim to the players, setting the scene and atmosphere.

- **Additional Information**: Detailed guidance, including potential variations, expected player strategies, and potential outcomes.

- **Scaling the Encounter**: Instructions on how to adjust the encounter's difficulty based on player levels:

  - **Beginner (Level 1-5)**: Simplified challenges tailored for newer or less powerful characters.

  - **Intermediate (Level 6-10)**: Moderate challenges that require a mix of skill, strategy, and teamwork.

  - **Advanced (Level 11+)**: Complex and multi-faceted challenges suitable for veteran adventurers.

- **Storyline**: How the encounter fits into the broader narrative, including potential consequences and story hooks.

- **Activity**: A mini-game, puzzle, or interactive segment designed to engage players in different ways.

- **Lair Actions**: Specific actions or effects that occur in certain locations, often benefiting the encounter's primary antagonist.

- **Monster and/or NPC**: Details or references to any creatures or characters the players might interact with during the encounter.

- **Reward**: Potential treasures, information, or other benefits the players can earn from successfully navigating the encounter.

Encounters may reference content found later in the book, such as detailed monster statistics in the Monsters section. Feel free to adapt or replace these elements to better fit your group's preferences or the storyline you're weaving.

## Modularity and Flexibility

This adventure, like all Penny Blood Adventures, is modular by design. If a particular monster or challenge doesn't resonate with your campaign's theme, feel free to replace it or adjust as needed. The goal is to provide a rich framework that sparks inspiration, allowing you to craft an unforgettable journey for your players.

# Starting the Adventure

Perched on the edge of a serene river, is the farmstead of Wheaton's Reach is a picturesque home, known for its golden fields that stretch as far as the eye can see. Named after its founder, Sir Reginald Wheaton, the farmstead has thrived for generations, primarily due to its bountiful harvests. The family and friends of the community is tight-knit, with families having lived there for generations, all sharing in the work and rewards of the harvest season.

## The Harvest Festival

The annual Harvest Festival is the highlight of the year. It is a time when the community comes together to celebrate the fruits of their labor, share in song and dance, and honor the land that provides for them. An age-old tradition, the festival also includes a ceremonial offering to the spirits of the land to ensure prosperity in the coming year.

## The Tale of Farmer Dunlow

About two decades ago, a hardworking farmhand named Eamon Dunlow lived near the farmstead. Known for his dedication to the land and his jovial nature, Dunlow was well-liked by all. However, tragedy struck one fateful evening when, while working late in the fields, a sudden storm rolled in. A bolt of lightning struck a nearby tree, causing it to fall and land on Dunlow. He suffered in pain for a whole day in the field before he was found. The villagers, remorse with guilt at his suffering, had to watch as Dunlow's injuries worsened. Before he died, an elder in the village promised that they would remember Dunlow at each Harvest Festival.

His unexpected death cast a shadow over Wheaton's Reach, and many believed that Dunlow's spirit couldn't find rest due to the sudden nature of his demise. As time passed, the village moved on, but the memory of Dunlow's tragic end remained a somber tale told around campfires.

## The Rise of the Spirit

This year, as preparations for the Harvest Festival were in full swing, strange occurrences began to plague Wheaton's Reach. Crops withered overnight, ghostly apparitions were seen wandering the fields, and an eerie lament echoed through the night. Elders of the village whispered that it was the restless spirit of Eamon Dunlow, angered and seeking retribution.

A local seer confirmed their fears, revealing that Dunlow's spirit had risen due to a broken promise. Years ago, in their grief, the villagers had vowed to honor Dunlow's memory during each Harvest Festival, but as generations passed, this promise was forgotten.

Now, with the Harvest Festival in jeopardy and the village's livelihood at stake, a solution must be found to appease the restless spirit and save Wheaton's Reach from its haunting curse.

As the sun casts a golden hue across the horizon, your journey brings you to a farmstead. The vast fields, shimmering with the promise of a bountiful harvest, stretch as far as the eye can see. The serene river flowing nearby adds to the idyllic charm. But the beauty of the landscape is marred by an unmistakable tension in the air. Workers in the fields cast anxious glances towards the setting sun, and the distant sound of a lament carries on the wind.

As you approach, a dignified woman in her late 50s, clad in elegant yet practical attire, approaches you. Her eyes, filled with a mix of hope and concern, assess your group.

**Lady Isolde:** "Greetings, travelers. I am Lady Isolde Wheaton, the matriarch of this farmstead. I hope your journey was not too taxing. You arrive at a time of great distress for Wheaton's Reach. Our lands, which have thrived for generations, are now plagued by an eerie haunting. As we prepare for our annual Harvest Festival, a shadow of dread looms over us. The spirit of Eamon Dunlow, a farmhand who met a tragic end two decades ago, is believed to be the source of this malevolence. His pain echoes through our fields, turning joyous preparations into fearful vigils."

She gestures to the vast expanse around her, pointing out key locations.

**Lady Isolde:** "That over there is the main **Farmstead**, the heart of our community and where we plan to hold the Harvest Festival. To the North lies an **Abandoned Hut**, where poor Dunlow spent his final agonizing moments. The **Small Copse of Trees** is where the tragic accident occurred. Our **Farmstead Graveyard** holds the remains of generations of Wheatons, including Dunlow. And of course, our vast **Field**, currently being harvested, but now also a place of fear due to the spirits that have emerged."

Pausing for a moment, she adds with urgency.

**Lady Isolde:** "I implore you, if you have the skills and the heart, help us put this spirit to rest. Begin at the main Farmstead. Seek out Elara, our local seer. She might have insights into the nature of this haunting and how best to confront it."

# Wheaton's Reach

## The Farmstead

The Farmstead serves as the central hub of activity in Wheaton's Reach, bustling with preparations for the Harvest Festival during the day and echoing with eerie stillness at night. As the adventurers arrive, they are met with a mix of hope and trepidation from the farm workers and the Wheaton family.

The sprawling Farmstead of Wheaton's Reach stands before you, a testament to generations of hard work and dedication. Large barns and storage houses dot the landscape, their wooden structures aged but sturdy. Fields stretch out in all directions, some filled with workers busily harvesting the crops, while others seem strangely abandoned. The main house, an impressive two-story structure with ivy creeping up its walls, stands proudly at the center. But despite the beauty of the place, a palpable tension hangs in the air. Every so often, a worker throws a wary glance towards the shadows, as if expecting something to emerge.

### Key Elements of the Encounter

- **Meeting Elara, the Seer**:
  Upon entering the main house, the adventurers are introduced to Elara. She provides them with vital information about Dunlow's broken promise and the necessary components for the ritual. She might also offer insights into the history of Wheaton's Reach and the significance of the haunting.

- **Ancestral Candle**: The candle that burns with an eternal flame reflecting the safety and resilience the Wheaton family farmstead provides to the community.

- **Discovering the Wheaton's Harvest Blade**: The blade can be found in a display case or a place of honor in the main house. Depending on the situation, Lady Isolde might offer it to the adventurers as a tool to aid in their quest, or they might need to prove their intentions first.

- **Encounter with the Strawmen**: As night falls, the Strawmen become active. They can be encountered while the adventurers are exploring the Farmstead, perhaps trying to break into barns or storage areas.

These creatures serve as a direct combat challenge and a haunting reminder of the farm's plight.

## Meeting with Elara, the Seer

When the PCs first encounter Elara, she is naturally hesitant to divulge sensitive information to strangers. The PCs must gain her trust and persuade her to share what she knows.

### Initial Approach

Upon entering the room or area where Elara is located, describe her as being deep in concentration, perhaps observing some runes or conducting a minor ritual.

### Skill Checks and Challenges

- **Insight Check (DC 12)**: Allows a PC to notice that Elara is deeply troubled by recent events and feels a heavy burden to help the community.

- **Persuasion Check (DC 15)**: A direct approach. If a PC can present their case convincingly, detailing their genuine desire to help, Elara may be more inclined to share information.

- **History Check or Bardic Knowledge (DC 14)**: If PCs can recount tales of other restless spirits they've encountered or helped, or even share lore about Harvest Festivals from other regions, it might pique Elara's interest and open her up.

- **Religion Check (DC 13)**: Recognizing and respecting the spiritual practices and symbols around her, and showing knowledge about appeasing spirits, could make Elara more comfortable sharing.

### Consequences of Failed Checks

If the PCs fail their skill checks or approach Elara insensitively:

- Elara becomes more guarded and might require the PCs to perform a task for her before she shares any information. This could be a mini-quest, like fetching a rare herb she needs or helping her with a minor spiritual disturbance.

- She might only provide partial information, forcing the PCs to rely on other sources or NPCs for the complete details.

## Revealing the Information

Once the PCs have successfully gained Elara's trust, she shares the tale of the broken promise to Dunlow and the ritual needed to appease him. As she describes each component, she provides clues or direct information about their locations. To appease the spirit of Dunlow, the PCs will need to collect several items and then performa a ritual. The items and the spell are broken down below:

- **Dunlow's Locket**
  - A personal belonging of Dunlow's which holds emotional significance.
  - **Location**: Found at the **Abandoned Hut**. A locket with a family portrait.
- **Sacred Soil**
  - A handful of earth from the place of Dunlow's tragic accident.
  - **Location**: Collected from the **Small Copse of Trees** where the lightning-struck tree once stood.
- **Ancestral Candle**
  - A candle lit from the eternal flame that has burned in the farmstead for generations, symbolizing continuity and remembrance.
  - **Location**: Kept in a special chamber or shrine within the **Farmstead** main house.
- **Blessed Water**
  - Water that has been used to cleanse and consecrate graves, ensuring peaceful rest.
  - **Location**: Found at the **Farmstead Graveyard**, perhaps in a small chapel or tended to by a graveyard keeper.
- **Harvest Offering**
  - Freshly harvested crops, representing the fruits of labor and the bond between the land and its people.
  - **Location**: Collected from the **Field**, perhaps from a section that remains untouched by the haunting.
- **Spell of Spirit Calming**
  - A scroll or incantation that helps in calming restless spirits.
  - **Location**: This could be kept in the **Farmstead's** library or study, passed down through generations but perhaps forgotten over time.

The PCs can quiz Elara for information. Elara's voice is soft, carrying the weight of years and wisdom. Each word she speaks seems to flow like a gentle river, winding its way through riddles and truths. Adjust her cryptic messages based on how much you want the PCs to puzzle over her words. Below are suggested

responses Elara can give to provide clues for how the PCs can appease Dunlow's restless spirit:

**Elara**: "In ages past, when the moon was young, a promise was made, a song unsung. To honor a soul, pure and true, but memories fade, as they often do. The festival's joy, once bright and clear, now tainted with sorrow, shadows, and fear."

She pauses, letting the weight of her words sink in, then continues.

**Elara**: "To quell the unrest, to calm the night's storm, a ritual beckons, a spell to perform."

**Dunlow's Memento**
"In a dwelling abandoned, where shadows creep, lies a memento of dreams, of promises deep. A keepsake of love, of days long gone, where Dunlow's essence lingers on."

**Sacred Soil**
"Where lightning once struck, a tragedy's root, you must seek the earth, the tree's sacred loot. In the copse of trees, where memories reside, gather the soil, let fate be your guide."

**Ancestral Candle**
"In the heart of our home, where flames never wane, an ancestral light, a candle's bright flame. Its glow tells tales of generations past, a beacon of hope, its shadows cast."

**Blessed Water**
"Where the departed rest, in silent repose, water blessed flows. In the sacred ground, where memories sleep, find the water pure, promises to keep."

**Harvest Offering**
"From the land's embrace, a gift you must reap, where spirits don't tread, the harvest runs deep. An offering of labor, of sweat and of tear, to honor the bond, the land we hold dear."

**Spell of Spirit Calming**
"In the heart of our haven, where knowledge does stay, a forgotten incantation, to keep the dark at bay. Seek the words written, in a tome old and worn, to calm the restless spirit, to heal what's been torn."

## The Search for the Eternal Flame

The Ancestral Candle has been a symbol of hope and resilience for the Wheaton family and the surrounding community. Kept within the main building of the farmstead, its flame has never gone out, serving as a testament to the endurance of the farmstead through challenges and hardships. While the main building has multiple rooms and sections, the candle is located within a special chamber dedicated to its protection and reverence.

Hidden behind a tapestry in the main hall, a door leads to the *Chamber of Remembrance*. Inside, the Ancestral

Candle sits on an ornate pedestal, its eternal flame burning brightly.

To access the Chamber of Remembrance, PCs need to solve a puzzle. Three of the family portraits in the Main Hall have plaques with riddles. Answering all three riddles will unlock the hidden door to the chamber.

## Riddles

- "Golden treasures I contain, guarded by hundreds and thousands. Stored in a labyrinth where no man walks, yet men come often to seize my gold. By smoke I am overcome and robbed, then left to build my treasure anew. What am I?" *(Answer: A corn cob)*

- "I'm orange and tall, and hollow inside. In autumn's cool months, in fields I reside. With a flickering light, I can come alive. What am I?" *(Answer: A pumpkin)*

- "When the summer's sun starts to wane, I'm picked from the fields and used in a game. Tossed and turned, through the air I fly, until on the ground, I come to lie. What am I?" *(Answer: Hay bale)*

- "I start green but turn red, yellow, or brown. Fall from the trees when the autumn comes round. What am I?" *(Answer: A leaf)*

- "In the field, a noisy chorus, but pick me and I'll be silent. What am I?" *(Answer: A cricket)*

- "I'm not a fruit, but I am juicy and sweet. I help make your breakfast a morning treat. What am I?" *(Answer: Maple syrup)*

- "By day they stand tall in the rows. By night, they light up with spooky glows. What are they?" *(Answer: Scarecrows with lanterns)*

- "I am sown in spring, rise in summer, harvested in the fall and enjoyed all winter. What am I?" *(Answer: Wheat or grain)*

- "With a crown on my head, I am king of the patch. Round in shape, with a line that can't match. What am I?" *(Answer: A pumpkin with its uneven growth line)*

- "From the ground, I rise and reach for the skies. Humans cut me down to size to make their pies. What am I?" *(Answer: An apple tree)*

Upon solving the riddles and entering the Chamber of Remembrance, the PCs not only find the Ancestral Candle but also feel a sense of peace and protection. The room may also contain small trinkets or tokens from past generations, which could serve as minor magical items or tools for their journey.

## Lair Actions

At initiative count 20, losing all ties, one of the following lair actions can occur. The action can't be used again until the next round.

- **Eerie Lament**: A ghostly wail fills the air, sending chills down the spine. Every creature within 60 feet of the source must make a DC 14 Wisdom saving throw or be frightened until the end of its next turn.

- **Shadows Shift**: The shadows around the Farmstead seem to move on their own. Choose up to three creatures. They must succeed on a DC 15 Dexterity saving throw or be restrained by the shadows until the start of the next lair action.

- **Whispers of the Past**: Ethereal voices whisper tales of past harvests, distracting and disorienting. Every creature within 40 feet of the source must make a DC 13 Intelligence saving throw or be unable to take reactions until the start of the next lair action.

## Scaling "The Harvest Haunting" Encounter

### Beginner (Level 1-5)

- **Elara's Trust**: Elara may be more easily persuaded by low-level characters, feeling their genuine intent more than their power or reputation. Lower the DC for persuasion and other checks to gain her trust by 2-3 points.

- **Strawmen Encounters**:
  - Reduce the number of Strawmen the party encounters.
  - Lower their HP, AC, and damage output.
  - Consider removing any special abilities or status effect attacks they might have, making them straightforward combatants.

- **Riddles & Puzzles**: Keep Elara's riddles relatively straightforward. If the party struggles, provide additional hints through the environment or other NPCs.

- **Ritual Components**: Streamline the process of acquiring components for the ritual. Perhaps some components are found together, or certain challenges are lessened in complexity.

### Intermediate (Level 6-10)

- **Elara's Trust**: The DCs for skill checks remain as originally set. Elara recognizes the capabilities of the adventurers but also expects more from them due to their experience.

- **Strawmen Encounters**:
  - Increase the number of Strawmen or introduce a Strawman Vanguard with enhanced abilities.
  - Consider adding a secondary challenge during the encounter, such as environmental hazards (e.g., parts of the Farmstead catching fire or becoming trapped).

- **Riddles & Puzzles**: Elara's riddles can be more cryptic. The environment might contain traps or magical barriers that require more than just brute force to overcome.

### Advanced (Level 11+)

- **Elara's Trust**: Elara is initially skeptical of such powerful adventurers, fearing they might overpower or disregard the spiritual significance of the task. Increase the DCs for skill checks to gain her trust by 2-3 points.

- **Strawmen Encounters**: Expand the Strawmen with Brute versions of the creatures. These stronger Strawmen will certainly challenge the strongest PCs.

- **Riddles & Puzzles**: Elara's riddles are deeply cryptic, and the solutions might require the party to delve into the history of Wheaton's Reach or consult ancient tomes.

- **Ritual Components**: Introduce additional challenges when acquiring each component. For example, the Sacred Soil might be guarded by Root Wranglers, or the Ancestral Candle might be in a location protected by a puzzle.

## Monster

- Strawman
- Strawman Brute
- Strawman Vanguard

## NPC

- Elara, the Seer

## Magic Items

- Wheaton's Harvest Blade
- Spell of Spirit Calming

# The Abandoned Hut

The Abandoned Hut encounter offers the party a chance to delve deep into the emotional roots of the haunting. Through visions, personal artifacts, and the words of Old Man Bram, the PCs will gain a deeper understanding of the tragedy that befell Dunlow. The atmosphere should be heavy with sorrow, regret, and an unsettling aura of lingering presence.

Before you stands a dilapidated hut, its timeworn wooden panels groaning against the whispers of the wind. The once-sturdy roof now sags, and moss-covered walls hint at the passage of time. The door, slightly ajar, beckons you into the darkness within. As you approach, fleeting lights, like the glow of distant fireflies, flit around the hut's perimeter. The very air feels thick with emotion, a mixture of deep sorrow and yearning.

## Key Elements of the Encounter

- **Visions of the Past**: As the adventurers step into the hut, they might experience short, vivid visions of Dunlow's last moments. The pain, the fear, and his desperate cries for help. These can be presented as a series of narrative snapshots, making the PCs feel the weight of the tragedy.

- **Dunlow's Locket**: Hidden beneath a floorboard or hung on a peg, the locket is a tangible link to Dunlow's past. When touched, it might trigger another vision, perhaps a happier memory of Dunlow with his family or the moment he received the locket.

- **Spirit Wisps Encounters**:

  - These ghostly entities can be both a hindrance and a guide. Some might lead PCs to the locket or important clues, while others might attempt to lead them into traps or even outside the hut.

  - Consider them as more of a puzzle or environmental challenge than a direct combat threat.

- **Meeting Old Man Bram**: In one of the hut's corners, shrouded in shadows, sits Old Man Bram. At first, he might be mistaken for another apparition, but as he speaks, his deep connection to the tragedy becomes clear. His recounting of the events should be heavy with emotion, providing the PCs with crucial context.

## Visions of the Past

As the adventurers step into the Abandoned Hut, the air grows thick with the weight of memories long suppressed. Each creak of the floorboard and whisper of the wind seems to pull them deeper into the final, tragic days of Eamon Dunlow's life. Visions of Dunlow's final days will appear in the room. Below is a break down of the different types of vision that can be shared:

**Vision 1: The Stormy Field**: The scene is awash with gray, the clouds overhead roiling with a tempest's fury. Rows of crops whip violently in the wind. The distant figure of Dunlow is seen, working diligently, seemingly unaware or perhaps just undeterred by the oncoming storm. As he bends to tend to a plant, a blinding flash and deafening crack fill the vision. The silhouette of a massive tree, struck by lightning, begins its descent directly towards Dunlow.

**Vision 2: Painful Solitude**: Rain pelts the ground, each droplet creating a muddy tomb around Dunlow, who is now pinned beneath the massive tree. His face is twisted in pain, eyes scanning the horizon for any sign of help. Hours seem to pass in mere moments, the sun's journey across the sky marking the agonizing progression of time. Dunlow's cries become weaker, his hope visibly waning with each passing hour.

**Vision 3: Discovery and Despair**: The storm has passed, giving way to a somber morning. Villagers, led by a concerned elder, rush to the field, having noticed Dunlow's absence. The shock and horror on their faces as they find him is palpable. Efforts are made to free him, but the weight and position of the tree make it a difficult task. Throughout it all, Dunlow, though weak and in pain, tries to offer reassuring smiles to those trying to save him.

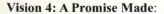

**Vision 4: A Promise Made**: Inside a dimly lit room, presumably within the farmstead, Dunlow lies on a makeshift bed, his injuries severe. The village elder, a figure of authority and wisdom, sits beside him, holding his hand. Tears stream down the elder's face as he makes a solemn promise to Dunlow - that his sacrifice, his dedication, and his memory will forever be honored at each Harvest Festival.

**Vision 5: A Village in Mourning**: The vision shifts to a scene of the entire village gathered around a freshly dug grave. The weight of collective grief hangs in the air, almost tangible. Children, not fully grasping the gravity of the situation, look on with confusion, while adults, some openly weeping, pay their respects. In the distance, the struck tree, now nothing more than firewood, serves as a grim reminder of the tragedy.

## Dunlow's Locket

### Investigation or Perception to Find the Locket

Hidden Beneath a Floorboard:

- **Perception Check (DC 15)** to notice a slightly raised or discolored floorboard that seems out of place. This DC can be lowered if they are specifically searching the floor.

- **Investigation Check (DC 13)** to deduce that the particular floorboard might be concealing something underneath.

### Vision Triggered by the Locket

Once the locket is found and touched:

- **Wisdom Saving Throw (DC 13)**: On a failed save, the PC touching the locket is flooded with a vision of Dunlow's past. The vision can be a double-edged

sword: It provides valuable context and emotional depth but can be momentarily disorienting.

- On a successful save, the PC gets a brief glimpse of the vision but retains full awareness of their surroundings.

### Vision Description

The world around fades away, replaced by a sunlit meadow. The sound of laughter fills the air. In the distance, a younger Dunlow is seen playing with what appears to be his family - perhaps a spouse and a child. The scene is idyllic, full of joy and warmth. Dunlow is handed a silver locket by a family member, a gift of love and remembrance. As he clasps it, his face breaks into a wide smile, a stark contrast to the tragic figure you've come to know. As quickly as it began, the vision fades, returning you to the gloomy interior of the hut.

### Effects of the Vision

- The PC who experienced the vision takes a moment to recover, being stunned until the start of their next turn.

- The emotional weight of the vision grants the PC advantage on any Charisma-based checks when discussing Dunlow or trying to appease his spirit for the next hour.

## Meeting Old Man Bram

The hut, despite its dilapidation, still carries remnants of life once lived. As the adventurers venture deeper, they might notice a soft humming, a tune filled with melancholy. Following the sound, they come upon a dimly lit corner where Old Man Bram sits on an old, creaky chair, a blanket draped over his frail form.

In the dim light, the silhouette of an old man is barely visible. Age has bent his back, and his hands, resting on his lap, tremble ever so slightly. As he turns to face you, his eyes, clouded with age, carry a depth of sorrow and remembrance. He seems momentarily surprised by your presence, but then, recognition slowly fills his gaze. "Ah, visitors," he rasps, his voice like old parchment. "Have you come to hear the tale of our dear Dunlow?"

Old Man Bram has been part of Wheaton's Reach for as long as anyone can remember. He was a young worker when the tragedy occurred and had a personal connection with Dunlow. The two had shared many a day working the fields together, swapping stories, and taking breaks under the shade of the very tree that would later cause Dunlow's demise.

## Interacting with Old Man Bram

- Bram is initially hesitant to recount the events, the memories still raw even after all these years. The PCs might need to persuade him (DC 13 Persuasion check) to share the full story.

- He might gift the PCs with small trinkets or offer practical advice on navigating the farmstead, especially if they show genuine concern or empathy.

- Throughout the conversation, Bram occasionally loses himself in memories, humming the same melancholic tune or gazing at a particular spot in the hut, perhaps where Dunlow used to sit.

- Bram reveals that he was among the search party that found Dunlow after the accident. The guilt of not reaching him in time, of not being there for his friend, weighs heavily on him. He admits that he occasionally visits the hut, hoping to feel closer to his long-lost friend.

"Ah, Dunlow... Eamon Dunlow was more than just another farmhand, you know. He was laughter on a cloudy day, a pillar of strength in the fields, and a dear friend to many, including me. We worked side by side, shared meals, dreams, and more than a few misadventures."

Bram chuckles softly at some fond memory before his face turns somber once more.

"That fateful day... the storm came without warning. And when we found him, trapped and in pain, the whole village felt a weight of guilt. We brought him back to this very hut, trying to comfort him, to ease his pain. As his life slipped away, the room was filled with hushed voices and tearful eyes. Promises were whispered into his ear, heartfelt vows from the very core of our being."

He takes a moment, eyes glistening with tears, before continuing.

"We promised him, as he lay there, that he would never be forgotten. That every Harvest Festival, his name would be spoken, his memory honored. A pledge to remember the joy he brought and the sacrifice he made. But as years turned to decades, memories faded, and promises... promises were broken."

Bram's gaze drifts away, lost in the past.

## Lair Actions

At initiative count 20, losing all ties, one of the following lair actions can occur. The action can't be used again until the next round.

- **Echoes of Despair**: A ghostly wail, filled with sorrow and regret, fills the hut. Every creature within the hut must make a DC 14 Wisdom saving throw or be paralyzed with sadness until the end of its next turn.

- **Misleading Wisps**: A Spirit Wisp darts close to a PC, beckoning them to follow. The PC must succeed on a DC 15 Wisdom saving throw or be compelled to follow the wisp, leading them into a potential hazard within the hut.

- **Fading Memories**: The hut's interior shifts and changes, resembling its state from years past. This can alter the environment, potentially creating obstacles or revealing hidden items. After the lair action, the hut returns to its current state.

## Scaling the Encounter

### Beginner (Level 1-5)

- **Spiritual Intensity**: The atmosphere is melancholic but not threatening. The spirits present are more curious or sorrowful than malevolent.

- **Spirit Wisps**:
  - **Quantity**: 2-3 Spirit Wisps.
  - **Abilities**: They lead PCs to important clues or outside the hut but do not directly harm them.

- **Old Man Bram**: He is straightforward in sharing the story of Dunlow and is easily persuaded to provide information. A simple display of empathy or concern is enough to earn his trust.

- **Lair Actions**: Use only one lair action per round. The effects are more atmospheric than challenging, designed to set the mood rather than pose a threat.

### Intermediate (Level 6-10)

- **Spiritual Intensity**: The spiritual energy is stronger, and the atmosphere feels heavy with the weight of unresolved emotions.

- **Spirit Wisps**:
  - **Quantity**: 4-6 Spirit Wisps.
  - **Abilities**: They might attempt to mislead PCs or lead them into minor traps within the hut.

- **Old Man Bram**: He's more reserved and requires a DC 15 Persuasion check to open up fully. He might also pose riddles or speak in a more cryptic manner, requiring the players to interpret his words.

- **Lair Actions**: Use up to two lair actions per round, introducing more dynamic changes to the hut's environment.

### Advanced (Level 11+)

- **Spiritual Intensity**: The hut is a nexus of powerful spiritual energy. The air is thick with emotion, and there's a palpable sense of unrest.
- **Spirit Wisps**:
  - **Quantity**: 7-10 Spirit Wisps, possibly with one or two being stronger variants.
  - **Abilities**: Enhanced versions can have additional effects, such as causing temporary visions or emotional disturbances in PCs.
- **Old Man Bram**: Communicating with him is a challenge. His memories are fragmented, and he phases between the present and the past. PCs might need to use abilities or spells that aid in communication or discernment. He requires a DC 18 Persuasion or Insight check to get the full story.
- **Lair Actions**: Use up to three lair actions per round, with some having direct challenging effects on the PCs, such as causing temporary blindness or teleporting a PC to another part of the hut.

## Monster

- Spirit Wisps

## NPC

- Old Man Bram

## Magic Items

- Dunlow's Locket

# The Field

As you step onto the Field, the vast expanse of crops stretches before you, their once vibrant colors now dulled and lifeless, seemingly choked by an unseen force. The sky above is overcast, casting an eerie twilight over the land. The air is thick with tension, occasionally pierced by the mournful cry of a distant crow. Every now and then, the ground seems to shiver, as if the very earth itself mourns the events of the past. In the distance, a lone figure, possibly Cedric, stands, looking over his ruined crops with a mix of sadness and determination.

## Key Elements of the Encounter

### Battling or Avoiding Spirits

- The haunted field is alive with supernatural activity. Spirits, manifestations of Dunlow's lingering pain and anger, patrol the area, confronting anyone they deem a trespasser. The adventurers must decide whether to face these spirits head-on or find more covert methods to navigate the field.
- Using the Spiritward Lantern or Dunlow's Whistle could aid in avoiding confrontations.

### Pumpkin Brutes

- These animated monstrosities are particularly territorial. Disturbing a patch of pumpkins or venturing too close might cause them to rise and attack. They can be engaged directly or distracted to allow the party to pass.

### Dunlow's Shadow

- This formidable apparition is a potent manifestation of Dunlow's anguish. Direct confrontation is challenging, but using the items and knowledge gathered throughout the adventure might provide ways to pacify or avoid it.

### Meeting Cedric, the Farm Steward

- Cedric, while distraught over the state of his fields, is a wealth of knowledge. He can provide insights on the best path through the field, the behaviors of the spirits, and possibly even assist in the ritual.
- His practical nature means he's likely to favor a direct approach to ending the haunting, emphasizing the importance of the ritual.
- Cedric can also help you harvest crops from the field. The field contains pumpkins.

### Performing the Ritual

- The ritual is the climax of the encounter, a moment of unity and purpose for the adventurers. It's a multi-step process, where each component and action holds significant meaning.
- As the ritual progresses, the ambient environment might respond. Gentle breezes could become gusts of wind, the cries of spirits could become louder, and the ground might tremble.
- The culmination of the ritual, if successful, should feel like a release, a palpable lifting of the oppressive atmosphere that has plagued Wheaton's Reach.

## Interacting with Cedric

Cedric, though initially cautious, recognizes anyone attempting to help and is quick to ally with them. He's been at his wit's end dealing with the haunting and the resultant decline in the farm's productivity. The wellbeing of his workers and the farmstead's legacy weighs heavily on his mind.

### Information from Cedric

- **The Haunting's Impact**: Cedric can provide a firsthand account of how the haunting has affected the day-to-day operations of the farm. The crops have become less bountiful, livestock are restless, and workers are fearful. He can provide specific examples of strange occurrences, like crops wilting overnight or ghostly apparitions seen at the stroke of midnight.

- **Dunlow's Influence**: He's observed the rise of supernatural occurrences and can confirm that they seem centered around the memory of Dunlow. He might not know the full story but has pieced together enough to understand the general tragedy.

- **Path Through the Field**: Being familiar with every inch of the farmland, Cedric can suggest the safest or quickest routes through the field, potentially helping the adventurers avoid certain threats.

- **Ritual Insights**: While not an expert in the supernatural, Cedric's practical experience has given him insights into the land and its connection to the spirits. He might suggest specific places in the field where the ritual would be most effective or provide natural components that could aid in its success.

## Aid to the Adventurers

- **Tools of the Trade**: Cedric can offer the party tools that might help in their journey - ropes, hoes, or even a makeshift weapon or two.
- **Physical Assistance**: If persuaded (perhaps a DC 15 Persuasion check), Cedric might accompany the party for a portion of their journey through the field, using his knowledge and strength to aid in challenges. However, he won't participate in the final ritual, believing it to be a task for those more attuned to the supernatural.

## Cedric's Personal Connection

Deep down, Cedric holds a sense of guilt over the haunting. While he wasn't present during Dunlow's time, he feels responsible as the current steward of the farmstead. He might confide in the party, expressing his wish to right the wrongs of the past and restore peace to the land he so dearly loves. This personal stake makes him a valuable ally and source of motivation for the party.

## Closing Interaction

As the party prepares to move forward, Cedric offers words of encouragement. "Remember, this land has seen hardships before, and with grit and determination, we've always overcome. Dunlow deserves his peace, and Wheaton's Reach deserves its future. Be strong, and may the soil be with you."

# Performing the Ritual

The field serves as the final battleground, both physically and emotionally. As the adventurers gather the necessary components and prepare to commence the ritual, the very atmosphere seems to thicken with anticipation. The wind carries mournful whispers, and the ground beneath feels restless. This is the moment of reckoning.

## Preparing the Ritual Ground

- Using the Sacred Soil, the adventurers mark out a large circle in the field. This circle acts as a protective barrier and focal point for the ritual's energies.
- Dunlow's Memento is placed at the very center of the circle, atop the Harvest Offering.
- The Ancestral Candle is lit, its flame flickering yet persistent, casting long shadows that dance around the circle.
- Placing the items correctly and forming the circle:
  - DC 10 Intelligence (Arcana) check for Beginner
  - DC 13 Intelligence (Arcana) check for Intermediate
  - DC 15 Intelligence (Arcana) check for Advanced

- Failure: The ritual's protective circle is not perfectly formed, allowing spirits or disturbances to interfere more easily during the ritual. This might cause minor environmental effects, such as gusts of wind or unsettling whispers, that can hinder the party.

## Initiating the Invocation

- The party's spellcaster, or the designated reader, unfurls the Spell of Spirit Calming, reciting its verses with clarity and intent.
- As the words hang in the air, other participants sprinkle the Blessed Water around the circle, each droplet sizzling upon contact, purifying the tainted ground.
- Reciting the Spell of Spirit Calming and using the Blessed Water:
  - DC 12 Charisma (Performance) or Wisdom (Religion) check for Beginner
  - DC 15 Charisma (Performance) or Wisdom (Religion) check for Intermediate
  - DC 18 Charisma (Performance) or Wisdom (Religion) check for Advanced
- Failure: The ritual's energy wavers, and the area might become temporarily unstable. Spirits become more restless, and the party might need to deal with minor disturbances or spirits trying to break the circle.

## The Pledge of Remembrance

- One by one, participants step forward, voicing their pledge to honor and remember Dunlow, ensuring that his legacy remains undiminished in all future Harvest Festivals. Their words serve as both an apology and a vow, seeking to mend the broken bonds of the past.
- Renewing the promise to honor Dunlow:
  - DC 10 Charisma (Persuasion) check for Beginner
  - DC 14 Charisma (Persuasion) check for Intermediate
  - DC 18 Charisma (Persuasion) check for Advanced
- Failure: The spirits sense the party's insincerity or lack of conviction. This might agitate Dunlow's Shadow, making it more confrontational or less likely to be appeased.

## Closing the Ritual

- With all components in place and the pledges made, the final act is to extinguish the Ancestral Candle. As the flame dies, a hush descends, the ritual's success hanging in the balance.

- Extinguishing the Ancestral Candle and sealing the ritual:

  - DC 10 Dexterity (Sleight of Hand) or Wisdom (Survival) check for Beginner

  - DC 13 Dexterity (Sleight of Hand) or Wisdom (Survival) check for Intermediate

  - DC 16 Dexterity (Sleight of Hand) or Wisdom (Survival) check for Advanced

- Failure: The ritual is not properly closed, leaving a lingering connection open. While Dunlow's spirit might be appeased, other spirits or supernatural energies might be drawn to the area in the future.

### Outcomes

- If the party successfully completes all stages of the ritual, Dunlow's spirit is appeased, and the haunting energies dissipate. The fields regain vitality, and the village can find closure.

- If the party fails one stage, they might face increased supernatural challenges but can still proceed with the ritual.

- If the party fails two or more stages, the ritual is unsuccessful in fully appeasing Dunlow. While the immediate threats might be reduced, the haunting could reoccur in the future, leading to potential follow-up quests or challenges.

### Success

The immediate aftermath of a successful ritual is palpable tranquility. The once restless wind calms, and a soft, ethereal glow emanates from the center of the circle. From this light, an apparition of Dunlow slowly forms. He appears as he did in life, but without the anguish and pain that marked his end. There's a serenity to him, a deep-seated peace. He might nod in gratitude or offer a soft smile, acknowledging the efforts made in his name. As the apparition fades, the haunting energies that plagued the field lift, replaced by a rejuvenated vitality. The crops stand taller, the air feels fresher, and a sense of closure settles in.

### Failure

A failed ritual is immediately apparent. The ground quakes violently, and the atmosphere grows cold and oppressive. Instead of Dunlow's peaceful apparition, a more tormented visage appears, his form twisted with pain and anger, a manifestation of all the unresolved emotions tied to his tragic end. This might initiate a combat encounter with Dunlow's Shadow, or perhaps the field becomes even more haunted, with increased supernatural threats. The adventurers will need to regroup, figure out what went wrong, and perhaps attempt the ritual again, or seek an alternative way to appease the restless spirit.

Regardless of the immediate outcome, the ritual's performance is a significant milestone in the adventure. It represents the culmination of the party's efforts to understand and address the haunting, forcing them to confront the weight of the past and the consequences of forgotten promises. Whether they immediately succeed or face setbacks, the ritual ensures that the tale of Eamon Dunlow and the legacy of Wheaton's Reach will be indelibly etched in their memories.

## Lair Actions (Field)

At initiative count 20, losing all ties, one of the following lair actions can occur. The action can't be used again until the next round.

- **Spiritual Surge**: A sudden gust of wind sweeps through the field, carrying with it spectral whispers. Each adventurer must make a DC 14 Wisdom saving throw or be frightened until the end of their next turn.

- **Ground's Grasp**: The earth trembles, and ghostly hands reach out from the ground in a 20-foot radius centered on a point of the DM's choice. This area becomes difficult terrain, and any creature within it must make a DC 15 Strength saving throw or be restrained by the hands. A creature can use its action to make a Strength check against the save DC, freeing itself on a success.

- **Pumpkin Assault**: A nearby Pumpkin Brute awakens (if not already active) and immediately launches a seed projectile attack against a random adventurer.

## Scaling for Different PCs

### Beginner (Level 1-5)

- 1d4 Pumpkin Brutes.

- Dunlow's Shadow can be more of a fleeting, avoidable apparition rather than a direct combatant.

### Intermediate (Level 6-10)

- 1d6+2 Pumpkin Brutes.

- Dunlow's Shadow is a formidable opponent but can still be appeased or outmaneuvered with the right approach.

### Advanced (Level 11+)

- The field is heavily populated with 2d4+4 Pumpkin Brutes.

- Dunlow's Shadow is a significant boss-level challenge, requiring a combination of combat prowess, strategy, and the use of gathered items to defeat.

## Monster

- Pumpkin Brutes

- Dunlow's Shadow

## NPC
- Cedric, the Farm Steward

# Graveyard

The Farmstead Graveyard serves as a resting place for souls departed and a reservoir of memories. It is here that the spirits of those who once lived, laughed, and loved in Wheaton's Reach find their final rest. However, with the unsettling events surrounding Dunlow's restless spirit, the graveyard has transformed into a focal point for supernatural disturbances.

Ancient, gnarled trees frame the entrance to the Farmstead Graveyard. As you step onto the hallowed grounds, an eerie silence envelops you. Tombstones, some old and worn by time, while others recent and freshly engraved, dot the landscape. An otherworldly mist clings to the ground, making the whole place seem like it's suspended between the realms of the living and the dead. The soft glow of a blue lantern, hanging near an old mausoleum, casts ghostly shadows on the surrounding graves. In the distance, you can spot a lone figure, perhaps the gravekeeper, tending to a grave.

## Key Elements of the Encounter

**Dunlow's Neglected Grave**

- A simple grave, marked by a weathered stone, stands apart from the others. The inscription, though faded, reads "Eamon Dunlow - Beloved by all, taken too soon."

- The grave shows signs of neglect: overgrown weeds, a toppled vase, and faded flowers. Restoring it could be a minor puzzle or skill challenge. For instance, a DC 12 Nature or Survival check could help in clearing the overgrowth without causing damage.

**Communicating with Dunlow**

- If adventurers decide to hold a séance or use a medium to communicate, they might use the Spiritward Lantern to ensure their safety. This communication could be a role-playing challenge where Dunlow expresses his feelings of abandonment and desire for remembrance.

- Mechanics for the séance could include a DC 15 Arcana or Religion check, with failures possibly drawing unwanted attention from other restless spirits.

**Blessed Water**

- A small stone fountain or basin, continually filled with this consecrated water, can be found near the graveyard's center. Lila refills and blesses this basin in a weekly ritual.

- Collecting the water might require a respectful approach. A DC 14 Religion or Persuasion check ensures that the water's sanctity is maintained during collection.

**Spiritward Lantern**

- The lantern, with its soft blue flame, offers not only a barrier against spirits but also a beacon of hope in the haunting gloom.

**Encounter with Gravebound:**

- These skeletal figures, driven by Dunlow's influence, rise as a defense mechanism. Their intent is not necessarily to harm but to protect the resting spirits. They provide a combat challenge for the adventurers.

**Lila, the Gravekeeper**

- Lila is a valuable ally, offering insights into the graveyard's history and the spirits within. A DC 13 Persuasion or Insight check can glean more detailed or sensitive information from her.

## Interacting with Lila

- Lila is initially wary of strangers, especially if they seem to disturb the peace of the graveyard. However, showing genuine respect for the dead or expressing a sincere interest in the stories of the deceased can quickly earn her trust.

- She can guide the adventurers to Dunlow's grave and provide them with the Blessed Water. If asked about the Spiritward Lantern, Lila might be reluctant to part with it but can be persuaded if she believes it's for a greater good.

- Lila possesses knowledge about the various spirits that reside in the graveyard. She can share tales of other spirits that might have been awakened or disturbed due to the ongoing events.

- While Lila knows of the tragedy that befell Dunlow, she might not be aware of the full extent of his haunting. However, she can offer insights into why spirits might become restless and how best to appease them.

## Read-Aloud Dialogue from Lila

Upon the adventurers' approach, she might say:

"You tread on sacred ground. Each stone here carries a tale, a memory. What brings you to this place of rest and remembrance?"

If asked about Dunlow:

"Dunlow... Ah, a soul taken too soon, by nature's cruel whims. His resting place lies there," she points to a neglected grave, "a reflection of how time can make memories fade. But the promise made to him... it should never have been forgotten."

On the topic of restless spirits:

"Spirits linger when they have unfinished business, when they feel forgotten, or when they're tethered by strong emotions. To help them move on, one must understand their story, their pain, and offer them the closure they seek."

Use Lila as a bridge between the past and the present. While she is rooted in the traditions and histories of Wheaton's Reach, she is also a witness to the current events unfolding in the village. Through her, the adventurers can gain a deeper understanding of the haunting and the steps they need to take to resolve it. Encourage players to engage with Lila, ask questions, and seek her guidance in their quest to appease Dunlow's restless spirit.

## Communicating with Dunlow

Within the confines of the Farmstead Graveyard, amidst the whispers of rustling leaves and the stillness of eternal rest, lies an opportunity to connect with the very spirit haunting Wheaton's Reach. Communicating with Eamon Dunlow, however, is no simple task. The weight of his tragic end, combined with the village's broken promises, has rendered his spirit restless and fragmented.

### Finding the Right Spot

- Dunlow's grave, though neglected, serves as the most potent point of contact. Close to it, the air might feel denser, and the ambient sounds of nature might be replaced with an eerie silence or faint, sorrowful murmurs.

- Lila might suggest using the Spiritward Lantern here. When lit near the grave, the lantern's blue flame dances more erratically, hinting at Dunlow's presence.

### The Seance

- Preparations: Participants form a circle around the grave, with the Spiritward Lantern placed at the center. A few personal items, such as Dunlow's Locket or Whistle, might strengthen the connection.

- Conducting the Ritual: A spellcaster in the party, or if none is available, Lila (with her knowledge of the graveyard and its spirits) begins chanting, inviting Dunlow's spirit to communicate. The environment responds; perhaps the ground trembles softly, or a chill wind blows.

### Dunlow's Manifestation

- Initially, Dunlow's spirit might manifest as a faint, shimmering outline, his voice echoing and distant. The clearer the connection, the more solid and audible he becomes. His appearance should reflect both his life's vigor and his tragic end.

- His demeanor is a mix of sorrow, confusion, and a yearning for closure. His initial reactions might be fragmented memories or emotions before coherent communication is established.

### Earning Dunlow's Trust

- Direct communication might not be immediately successful. Dunlow's spirit, driven by years of neglect and the village's broken vow, might be distrusting or even confrontational.

- Players might need to reassure him of their intentions, recounting the promise made to him, showing the items they've collected, or even sharing their own memories and feelings.

- Successfully calming him could involve a series of skill checks, such as Persuasion, Insight, or even Performance if they choose to use song or other arts to reach out.

### The Heart of the Matter

- Once trust is established, Dunlow recounts his final moments, his hopes for the village's promise, and the pain of being forgotten. He provides insights into how to appease his restless spirit and end the haunting.

- He emphasizes the importance of the Harvest Festival promise and the need for the village to genuinely honor it. Dunlow might also express a desire for his grave to be tended to and respected, a symbol of the village's renewed commitment.

### Ending the Connection

- As the seance concludes, the energy in the area shifts. Dunlow's spirit, though still restless, shows signs of hope. The connection gradually weakens, with his form fading away, leaving behind an atmosphere of solemn contemplation.

- Lila, if present, might offer a prayer or a few words of respect, emphasizing the importance of honoring the past and the promises made.

Throughout the communication process, the atmosphere should be thick with emotion, with players feeling the weight of Dunlow's tragic end and the collective guilt of Wheaton's Reach.

## Lair Actions

At initiative count 20, losing all ties, one of the following lair actions can occur. The action can't be used again until the next round.

- **Whispers of the Past**: Ghostly voices whisper secrets or tales of their past. Any adventurer hearing these whispers must make a DC 15 Wisdom saving throw or be distracted and lose their next action.

- **Ethereal Fog**: The mist thickens, making the area heavily obscured for one round. This can hinder vision and movement.

- **Restless Spirits**: One spirit temporarily materializes and attempts to touch a PC. If touched, the PC relives a moment from the spirit's life, potentially gaining a clue or hint but also becoming stunned until the end of their next turn.

## Scaling The Encounter

### Beginner (Level 1-5)

- **Locating Dunlow's Grave**: Make the grave's location fairly obvious, perhaps with a unique marker or a visibly neglected site among well-kept graves. Reduce the number of potential distractions or false leads.

- **Communicating with Dunlow**: If using a medium or seance, the communication should be relatively straightforward, with Dunlow's spirit being more cooperative and forthcoming.

- **Magic Item**: The **Spiritward Lantern** can be used multiple times per day, or its effects could last longer, providing additional protection for the party.

- **Monsters - Gravebound**: 2-3 Gravebound

- **NPC - Lila, the Gravekeeper**: Lila can be more actively helpful, perhaps even aiding in combat by using the Spiritward Lantern or providing the players with some simple healing potions or protective talismans.

### Intermediate (Level 6-10)

- **Locating Dunlow's Grave**: Introduce a few puzzles or riddles that hint at the grave's location. Add a few more supernatural occurrences or minor spirits that can mislead or challenge the players.

- **Communicating with Dunlow**: Dunlow's spirit might be more agitated or confused, requiring the players to calm him down or answer riddles before he provides useful information.

- **Magic Item**: The **Spiritward Lantern** works as described, but perhaps its fuel is limited, requiring the players to use it judiciously.

- Monsters - Gravebound: 4-6 Gravebound

- **NPC - Lila, the Gravekeeper**: While still helpful, Lila might require some convincing or a minor quest (like retrieving a stolen item) before she fully assists the players.

### Advanced (Level 11+)

- **Locating Dunlow's Grave**: The grave's location is concealed by powerful protective magic or is in a hidden section of the graveyard. Multiple challenges, both combat and puzzle-based, are required to discover its location.

- **Communicating with Dunlow**: Dunlow's spirit is guarded or trapped by other powerful spirits. Players need to first deal with these spirits or break the magical bindings before they can communicate with Dunlow.

- **Magic Item**: The **Spiritward Lantern** is either broken or its magic is suppressed, requiring players to undergo a mini-quest within the graveyard to restore it.

- Monsters - Gravebound: 7-10 Gravebound

- **NPC - Lila, the Gravekeeper**: Lila is initially hostile or deeply suspicious, having seen powerful adventurers accidentally desecrate graves or stir up more spirits in the past. Players must prove their intentions and might before she offers assistance.

## Monster

- Gravebound

## NPC

- Lila, the Gravekeeper

## Magic Items

- Spiritward Lantern

# Small Copse of Trees

The Small Copse of Trees encounter delves deeper into the emotional and spiritual landscape of the haunting. Here, the party confronts not just the echoes of Dunlow's tragic end, but also other restless spirits connected to the land. The site is charged with both sadness and anger, and the PCs will need to navigate this delicate balance to achieve their goals.

Before you is a cluster of trees, their boughs casting long, dappled shadows on the ground. The rustling leaves carry whispers of bygone days. At the center of the copse stands a stark reminder of tragedy – a charred stump, the remnants of the tree that claimed Dunlow's life. Around it, the ground appears disturbed, as if nature itself is uneasy about what transpired here. As you tread closer, the subtle hum of spiritual energy becomes almost palpable, and the air grows cold.

## Key Elements of the Encounter

- **Locating the Accident Site**: The charred stump is a focal point, drawing spirits and supernatural energies. Investigation or perception checks (DC 14) can reveal remnants of the accident – perhaps a fragment of clothing, a tool, or other signs of Dunlow's presence that fateful day.

- **Collecting the Sacred Soil**: Harvesting the soil requires care. If done hastily or without respect, it might anger the spirits. A Wisdom (Religion) or Charisma (Persuasion) check (DC 15) can ensure the soil is taken without provoking the spirits.

- **Dunlow's Whistle**: Hidden among the roots of the charred stump, the whistle waits to be discovered. A successful Investigation check (DC 13) reveals it. The whistle's magic can be instrumental in quelling restless spirits throughout the adventure.

- **Encounter with Root Wranglers**: These animated roots act as guardians of the copse, springing to life to deter intruders. They can be engaged in combat or potentially calmed using the whistle.

- **Meeting Young Aria**: As the PCs explore, the soft giggling of a child can be heard. Aria, with her innate connection to the spirit world, offers unique insights. She might share her interactions with Dunlow's spirit and offer hints on appeasing him. Her innocent perspective adds depth to the narrative.

## Meeting Young Aria

Young Aria, with her innocent appearance and deep spiritual connection, serves as an unexpected guide for the adventurers. Her insights into the spirit world and her interactions with Dunlow's spirit make her an invaluable asset in understanding the haunting and devising a solution.

Amidst the whispers of the trees, a soft, melodic voice hums a haunting lullaby. Turning to the source, you see a young girl, no more than ten, her raven-black hair cascading down her back, contrasting with her pale blue dress. She looks up, her deep blue eyes holding a wisdom beyond her years. "You're not from here," she states more than asks, her voice clear and melodious. "But the spirits told me you'd come. Eamon has been waiting."

## Interacting with Young Aria:

- Aria, despite her age, speaks with a clarity and depth that can be disarming. She often refers to her "friends," the spirits she communicates with, and might even introduce the party to a few harmless ones.

- When prompted about Dunlow and the haunting, Aria will look somber. She'll explain her interactions with Dunlow's restless spirit, how he feels lost, betrayed, and yearns for peace.

- Aria knows about the ritual to appease Dunlow. She might say, "To calm the storm, you must first understand its cause. Eamon's heart is restless, his spirit bound by broken promises and forgotten memories." She'll then explain the components needed for the ritual, emphasizing the importance of each item.

- She might describe the components in a slightly riddled manner, allowing for some interpretation and deduction by the PCs:

  - "A token of his past, lost in a place of despair." (Dunlow's Memento)

  - "Earth that has witnessed sorrow, from the site of tears and thunder." (Sacred Soil)

  - "A flame that never dies, passed down through Wheaton's line." (Ancestral Candle)

  - "Water that sings lullabies to the departed." (Blessed Water)

  - "The fruits of labor, untouched by shadow." (Harvest Offering)

  - "Ancient words to soothe a troubled soul, hidden in the home of knowledge." (Spell of Spirit Calming)

- Aria can also provide guidance on conducting the ritual, explaining the steps in a way that even those unfamiliar with spiritual practices can understand. She might even offer to participate, given her unique connection to the spirit world, and her presence might prove calming to Dunlow's spirit.

## Lair Actions

At initiative count 20, losing all ties, one of the following lair actions can occur. The action can't be used again until the next round.

- **Spirited Winds**: A gust of wind sweeps through the copse, carrying with it mournful whispers. Every creature within the copse must make a DC 13 Wisdom saving throw or be frightened until the end of its next turn.
- **Restless Roots**: Roots and vines animate, reaching out to grasp at adventurers. One PC is grappled by the roots and must succeed on a DC 14 Strength saving throw or be restrained.
- **Echoes of the Past**: A ghostly vision of Dunlow's accident briefly manifests, distracting and disorienting. All creatures in the copse have disadvantage on attack rolls and ability checks until the end of their next turn.

## Scaling the Encounter

### Beginner (Level 1-5)

- **Spiritual Intensity**: The spiritual energy in the area is noticeable but not overwhelming. The ambiance should set the scene without making it too difficult for lower level adventurers.
- Root Wranglers:
  - **Quantity**: 2-4 Root Wranglers.
  - **HP**: Reduce HP by 25%.
  - **Abilities**: Limit any crowd control abilities (like entangle) to affect only one target at a time.
- **Interactions with Aria**: Aria is very forthcoming with information, reducing the need for any complex investigative skill checks. Direct questions receive direct answers.
- **Lair Actions**: Use only one lair action per round, and give the PCs a clear indication or hint about what's coming next.

### Intermediate (Level 6-10)

- **Spiritual Intensity**: The energy is palpable, with occasional minor spectral appearances that might challenge the party but not threaten them directly.
- Root Wranglers:
  - **Quantity**: 5-7 Root Wranglers.
  - **Abilities**: They can use their crowd control abilities (like entangle) to affect up to two targets.
- **Interactions with Aria**: Aria communicates through riddles and feelings, requiring the adventurers to interpret her messages. Insight, Perception, or Arcana

checks (DC 12-15) might be needed to glean all the information.
- **Lair Actions**: Use two lair actions per round, and they become slightly more challenging.

### Advanced (Level 11+)

- **Spiritual Intensity**: The spiritual energy is very intense. The air is thick, and there's a constant feeling of being watched. Spectral appearances are frequent and can sometimes be aggressive.
- Root Wranglers:
  - **Quantity**: 8-12 Root Wranglers, possibly with one or two being "elder" versions with enhanced abilities.
  - **Abilities**: Enhanced versions can have additional resistances or a unique ability, such as a root spike attack.
- **Interactions with Aria**: Aria's connection to the spirit world is so profound at this level that she occasionally phases in and out of a trance-like state, speaking in cryptic verses. To obtain the full scope of her knowledge, PCs might need to pass Insight, Perception, or Arcana checks (DC 17-20) or employ spells/abilities that aid in communication.
- **Lair Actions**: Use up to three lair actions per round. These actions can be more complex, such as summoning minor spirits or causing the ground to shake and destabilize.

## Monster
- Root Wranglers

## NPC
- Young Aria

## Magic Items
- Dunlow's Whistle

# Conclusion

## A Harvest Remembered

As the final words of the ritual echo through the night, a profound stillness envelops the field. The oppressive, haunting atmosphere begins to lift, replaced by a palpable sense of peace. From the heart of the ritual circle, a soft, ethereal light begins to rise, taking the shape of Eamon Dunlow. His visage, no longer marred by pain or anger, looks upon each of the adventurers with gratitude.

With a nod of acknowledgment, the spirit of Dunlow begins to fade, his form dissipating into countless luminous motes that float upwards, merging with the starry expanse above. The Farmstead, once gripped by fear and sorrow, feels alive again, its vitality restored.

The first rays of dawn break over the horizon, painting the sky in hues of gold and crimson. The villagers, having watched the ritual from a safe distance, slowly approach, their faces a mix of awe, relief, and gratitude. Children, sensing the change, run through the rejuvenated fields, their laughter echoing the hope of a new beginning.

Old Man Bram, tears streaming down his face, clasps the hands of the adventurers. "You've done it," he whispers. "You've given our dear Dunlow the peace he deserved. And with it, you've given Wheaton's Reach a chance to heal and remember."

Lila, the Gravekeeper, tends to Dunlow's grave, ensuring that it remains a place of respect and remembrance. Cedric, the Farm Steward, organizes a grand feast in honor of the adventurers, turning the day into an impromptu celebration, a precursor to the grandest Harvest Festival the village has ever seen.

## Rewards for Completing The Harvest Haunting

As the celebrations wind down and the village revels in their newfound peace, Lady Isolde Wheaton approaches the party. With a gracious nod, she speaks, "Brave adventurers, words cannot express the depth of our gratitude. You've not only saved our farmstead but also our very way of life. Please, accept this as a token of our appreciation." She hands them a pouch, heavy with gold pieces. "Consider this a humble reward for your tremendous courage."

Opening the pouch, the adventurers find it filled with 500 gold pieces. A generous reward indeed.

Lady Isolde continues, "And there's something else." She presents the **Cloak of the Harvest Moon** to the party. "This cloak has been in the Wheaton family for generations. It's said to possess protective properties, especially during the harvest season. I believe it will serve you well in your future endeavors."

The cloak, shimmering with threads that sparkle like the autumn moon, feels warm and comforting to the touch. Its magic is palpable, and the adventurers can sense its protective aura.

Lastly, Lady Isolde extends an invitation, "The Harvest Festival is upon us, and it would be an honor if you would join us in the celebrations. Let it be a testament to your bravery and a chance for our village to show our gratitude."

As the festivities continue, stories of the adventurers' bravery and the tale of Dunlow's sacrifice are shared around roaring bonfires. Songs are sung, tales are told, and promises are made to never forget the legacy of Eamon Dunlow.

The Harvest Haunting might be over, but its lessons and memories will forever be etched into the hearts of those at Wheaton's Reach. And as the adventurers leave the village, they carry with them the gratitude of its people and the satisfaction of a job well done.

# Non-Player

## Cedric, the Farm Steward

For over two decades, Cedric has been the backbone of Wheaton's Reach, overseeing its daily operations and ensuring that every harvest is bountiful. A robust, sun-tanned man in his early 40s, his hands have been toughened by years of labor, and his keen eyes rarely miss a detail. While his practical nature has often been an asset to the farmstead, recently it's been put to the test. Cedric has become increasingly alarmed by the eerie disturbances afflicting the fields and workers under his charge. Determined to get to the bottom of the haunting and restore peace to the land he holds dear, he's eager to share his observations and insights with anyone willing to help.

### Cedric, the Farm Steward

Medium humanoid (human), neutral good

**Armor Class** 14 (studded leather)
**Hit Points** 52 (8d8 + 16)
**Speed** 30 ft.

| STR | DEX | CON | INT | WIS | CHA |
| --- | --- | --- | --- | --- | --- |
| 16 (+3) | 14 (+2) | 15 (+2) | 12 (+1) | 13 (+1) | 10 (+0) |

**Saving Throws** Str +5, Con +4
**Skills** Athletics +5, Nature +3, Perception +3, Survival +3
**Senses** passive Perception 13
**Languages** Common
**Challenge** 3 (700 XP)

**Keen Observer.** Cedric has advantage on Wisdom (Perception) checks that rely on sight.

**Seasoned Farmhand.** Cedric has advantage on ability checks related to farming activities, such as handling animals, identifying plants, or predicting weather.

Actions

**Multiattack.** Cedric makes two melee attacks.

**Pitchfork.** *Melee Weapon Attack:* +5 to hit, reach 5 ft., one target. *Hit:* 7 (1d8 + 3) piercing damage.

**Throw Rock.** *Ranged Weapon Attack:* +4 to hit, range 20/60 ft., one target. *Hit:* 5 (1d6 + 2) bludgeoning damage.

**Call for Help (1/Day).** Cedric blows a whistle, summoning 1d4 farm workers to assist him. The farm workers arrive in 1d4 rounds and fight to defend Cedric and the farm.

# Characters

## Elara, the Seer

**Elara, the Seer,** has lived on the fringes of Wheaton's Reach for as long as most villagers can remember. With age-lined features and eyes that seem to peer beyond the veil, she has long been the community's bridge to the spirit world. Residing in a secluded corner of the Farmstead, Elara's hut is filled with relics of the past and tools of her divining trade. Many have sought her counsel over the years, and it is she who first discerned the restless stirrings of Dunlow's spirit. Recognizing the gravity of the haunting, she has taken it upon herself to guide the adventurers, providing them with the ancient rites and rituals needed to bring peace back to the land. Her knowledge of the farmstead's history, combined with her spiritual insights, makes her an invaluable ally in their quest.

### Elara, the Seer

Medium humanoid (human), neutral good

**Armor Class** 12 (15 with *mage armor*)
**Hit Points** 44 (8d8 + 8)
**Speed** 30 ft.

| STR | DEX | CON | INT | WIS | CHA |
| --- | --- | --- | --- | --- | --- |
| 9 (-1) | 14 (+2) | 12 (+1) | 16 (+3) | 18 (+4) | 15 (+2) |

**Saving Throws** Int +6, Wis +7
**Skills** Arcana +6, Insight +7, Religion +6
**Senses** passive Perception 14
**Languages** Common, Celestial, one other language of your choice
**Challenge** 6 (2,300 XP)

**Spellcasting.** Elara is a 10th-level spellcaster. Her spellcasting ability is Wisdom (spell save DC 15, +7 to hit with spell attacks). Elara has the following cleric spells prepared:

- Cantrips (at will): *guidance, light, mending, sacred flame*
- 1st level (4 slots): *bless, cure wounds, detect magic, sanctuary*
- 2nd level (3 slots): *augury, lesser restoration, spiritual weapon*
- 3rd level (3 slots): *dispel magic, speak with dead, spirit guardians*
- 4th level (3 slots): *divination, guardian of faith, locate creature*
- 5th level (2 slots): *commune, raise dead*

**Spiritual Insight.** Elara can cast *augury* without expending a spell slot, but she must finish a long rest before using this feature again.

Actions

**Quarterstaff.** *Melee Weapon Attack:* +2 to hit, reach 5 ft., one target. *Hit:* 3 (1d6 - 1) bludgeoning damage, or 4 (1d8 - 1) bludgeoning damage if used with two hands.

Reactions

**Foresight (1/Day).** When a creature Elara can see makes an attack roll against her, she can use her reaction to impose disadvantage on that roll.

# Lady Isolde Wheaton

Lady Isolde Wheaton stands as the resilient matriarch of the esteemed Wheaton family. A picture of grace and poise, even in her late 50s, her normally composed visage now bears the weight of deep concern. The unsettling events plaguing the farmstead, especially with the pivotal Harvest Festival approaching, have cast a shadow over her storied lineage. Recognizing the urgency of the situation and the potential consequences of inaction, Lady Isolde, well-versed in the rich history of the farmstead, seeks out the aid of adventurers. She hopes that, with their expertise, the disturbing mysteries can be unraveled, ensuring the continuity and honor of the Wheaton legacy.

**Lady Isolde Wheaton**

Medium humanoid (human), neutral good

**Armor Class** 12 (15 with *mage armor*)
**Hit Points** 44 (8d8 + 8)
**Speed** 30 ft.

| STR | DEX | CON | INT | WIS | CHA |
|-----|-----|-----|-----|-----|-----|
| 10 (+0) | 14 (+2) | 12 (+1) | 16 (+3) | 14 (+2) | 18 (+4) |

**Saving Throws** Int +6, Wis +5
**Skills** History +6, Insight +5, Persuasion +7
**Senses** passive Perception 12
**Languages** Common
**Challenge** 3 (700 XP)

**Innate Spellcasting.** Lady Isolde's innate spellcasting ability is Charisma (spell save DC 15). She can innately cast the following spells, requiring no material components:

- At will: mage hand, prestidigitation

- 3/day each: charm person, mage armor

- 1/day each: suggestion, detect thoughts

**Tactician.** Lady Isolde can use her action to choose one ally she can see. That ally can immediately use its reaction to make one weapon attack.

Actions

**Quarterstaff.** *Melee Weapon Attack:* +2 to hit, reach 5 ft., one target. *Hit:* 3 (1d6) bludgeoning damage, or 4 (1d8) bludgeoning damage if used with two hands.

**Leadership (Recharges after a Short or Long Rest).** For 1 minute, Lady Isolde can utter a special command or warning whenever a nonhostile creature that she can see within 30 feet of her makes an attack roll or a saving throw. The creature can add a d4 to its roll provided it can hear and understand Lady Isolde. A creature can benefit from only one Leadership die at a time. This effect ends if Lady Isolde is incapacitated.

# Lila, the Gravekeeper

**Lila, the Gravekeeper,** has dedicated her life to the sacred ground of the Farmstead Graveyard. With a quiet dignity and a somber countenance, she meticulously tends to each grave, believing that every soul deserves respect in death. While many avoid the graveyard, especially after dark, Lila walks its paths without fear. She claims to know every story of those interred within its bounds, speaking of the deceased as if they were old friends. When the disturbances began, she was the first to notice, witnessing restless spirits emerging from their final resting places. Armed with her knowledge and her unwavering dedication to the dead, she aids adventurers by providing them with the Blessed Water and guiding them to Dunlow's grave, all the while sharing whispered tales of other spirits that have been roused from their slumber.

Lila, the Gravekeeper

Medium humanoid (human), neutral good

**Armor Class** 12 (leather armor)
**Hit Points** 40 (9d8)
**Speed** 30 ft.

| STR | DEX | CON | INT | WIS | CHA |
|-----|-----|-----|-----|-----|-----|
| 10 (+0) | 12 (+1) | 10 (+0) | 14 (+2) | 16 (+3) | 12 (+1) |

**Saving Throws** Wis +5
**Skills** History +4, Religion +4, Perception +5
**Senses** passive Perception 15
**Languages** Common
**Challenge** 2 (450 XP)

**Sacred Groundskeeper.** Lila has advantage on saving throws against being charmed or frightened while she is in the Farmstead Graveyard.

**Spirit Whisperer.** Lila can cast *speak with dead* once per day without expending a spell slot.

Actions

**Quarterstaff.** *Melee Weapon Attack:* +2 to hit, reach 5 ft., one target. *Hit:* 3 (1d6) bludgeoning damage, or 4 (1d8) bludgeoning damage if used with two hands.

**Blessed Water (3/Day).** Lila throws a flask of holy water at a point she can see within 20 feet of her. Each undead creature in a 5-foot radius centered on that point must make a DC 14 Dexterity saving throw. On a failure, the creature takes 2d6 radiant damage.

Reactions

**Protective Ward.** When an undead creature targets Lila with an attack, she can impose disadvantage on the attack roll.

# Old Man Bram

**Old Man Bram** has witnessed the ebb and flow of life on the farmstead for decades. A sinewy figure in his youth, he worked alongside Farmer Dunlow, the memories of their shared laughter and toil still fresh in his mind. Now frail and weathered by time, Bram is a living testament to the farmstead's history. The weight of that fateful stormy day, when Dunlow met his tragic end, rests heavily upon his shoulders. Although just a young worker back then, Bram's heart is laden with guilt for not discovering his dear friend in time, a regret that has kept him tethered to the farmstead. In the twilight of his years, he seeks solace in the Abandoned Hut, where memories of Dunlow linger, and where he passionately recounts the tragedy, the village's remorse, and the solemn promise made to never forget Dunlow's sacrifice.

**Old Man Bram**
Medium humanoid (human), neutral good

**Armor Class** 10 (no armor)
**Hit Points** 18 (4d8)
**Speed** 25 ft.

| STR | DEX | CON | INT | WIS | CHA |
|-----|-----|-----|-----|-----|-----|
| 9 (-1) | 10 (+0) | 10 (+0) | 12 (+1) | 16 (+3) | 14 (+2) |

**Skills** History +4, Perception +6, Insight +6
**Senses** passive Perception 16
**Languages** Common
**Challenge** 1/4 (50 XP)

**Keen Memory.** Old Man Bram has advantage on Intelligence (History) checks related to events he's personally experienced.

**Guiding Words.** As an action, Bram can share a piece of advice or historical tale. One creature of his choice within 30 feet that can hear him gains advantage on their next ability check related to solving puzzles, identifying items, or recalling history.

Actions

**Cane.** *Melee Weapon Attack:* +2 to hit, reach 5 ft., one target. *Hit:* 3 (1d4 - 1) bludgeoning damage.

Reactions

**Protective Instinct.** When a creature Bram can see targets him with an attack, Bram can use his reaction to impose disadvantage on that attack roll.

# Young Aria

With wide, wonder-filled eyes, Aria has always been an unusual child. At the tender age of 10, where most children her age busied themselves with play and mischief, Aria has found herself drawn to the mysteries of the spirit world. Her innocence and genuine curiosity have allowed her to bridge the divide between the living and the departed in ways most cannot fathom. Many in Wheaton's Reach whisper of her uncanny ability to communicate with spirits, and she often speaks fondly of her ethereal interactions, particularly with the restless spirit of Dunlow. While some might regard her abilities with skepticism or fear, Aria's insights have proven invaluable, guiding many, including adventurers, to places of spiritual significance like the Small Copse of Trees.

**Young Aria**
Medium humanoid (human), neutral good

**Armor Class** 10
**Hit Points** 6 (2d8 - 2)
**Speed** 30 ft.

| STR | DEX | CON | INT | WIS | CHA |
|-----|-----|-----|-----|-----|-----|
| 8 (-1) | 10 (+0) | 9 (-1) | 12 (+1) | 14 (+2) | 13 (+1) |

**Skills** Perception +4, Insight +4
**Senses** passive Perception 14
**Languages** Common
**Challenge** 1/8 (25 XP)

**Innate Spirit Sense.** Aria can sense the presence of spirits and undead within 60 feet of her, even if they are in another plane of existence. This sense doesn't tell her anything about a creature's capabilities or identity.

**Childlike Innocence.** Aria has advantage on saving throws against being frightened.

Actions

# Monsters

## Dunlow's Shadow

Large undead, neutral evil

**Armor Class** 18
**Hit Points** 250 (20d10 + 120)
**Speed** 30 ft., fly 60 ft.

| STR | DEX | CON | INT | WIS | CHA |
|-----|-----|-----|-----|-----|-----|
| 18 (+4) | 22 (+6) | 22 (+6) | 14 (+2) | 16 (+3) | 20 (+5) |

**Saving Throws** Dex +12, Wis +9, Cha +11
**Skills** Perception +9, Stealth +12
**Damage Resistances** acid, cold, fire; bludgeoning, piercing, and slashing from nonmagical attacks
**Damage Immunities** lightning, necrotic, poison
**Condition Immunities** charmed, exhaustion, frightened, paralyzed, poisoned
**Senses** darkvision 120 ft., passive Perception 19
**Languages** Common
**Challenge** 17 (18,000 XP)

**Incorporeal Movement.** Dunlow's Shadow can move through other creatures and objects as if they were difficult terrain. It takes 5 (1d10) force damage if it ends its turn inside an object.

**Lightning Aura.** At the start of each of Dunlow's Shadow's turns, each creature within 10 feet of it takes 10 (3d6) lightning damage, and flammable objects in the aura that aren't being worn or carried ignite.

**Legendary Resistance (3/Day).** If Dunlow's Shadow fails a saving throw, it can choose to succeed instead.

### Actions

**Multiattack.** Dunlow's Shadow makes two melee attacks.

**Shadow Touch.** *Melee Weapon Attack:* +12 to hit, reach 5 ft., one target. *Hit:* 18 (3d8 + 6) necrotic damage.

**Summon Lightning (Recharge 5-6).** Dunlow's Shadow calls down a bolt of lightning, targeting a point it can see within 120 feet. Each creature within a 10-foot radius of that point must make a DC 18 Dexterity saving throw, taking 33 (6d10) lightning damage on a failed save, or half as much damage on a successful one.

### Legendary Actions

Dunlow's Shadow can take 3 legendary actions, choosing from the options below. Only one legendary action can be used at a time and only at the end of another creature's turn. Dunlow's Shadow regains spent legendary actions at the start of its turn.

- **Shadow Step.** Dunlow's Shadow teleports up to 30 feet to an unoccupied space it can see.

- **Eerie Wail (Costs 2 Actions).** Dunlow's Shadow lets out a mournful wail. Each creature within 60 feet of Dunlow's Shadow that can hear it must succeed on a DC 18 Wisdom saving throw or become frightened for 1 minute. A creature can repeat the saving throw at the end of each of its turns, ending the effect on itself on a success.

- **Summon Shadows (Costs 3 Actions).** Dunlow's Shadow summons 1d4 shadow creatures (use the stats for "Shadows" from the Monster Manual) to aid it in combat. The summoned shadows appear in unoccupied spaces within 60 feet of Dunlow's Shadow and act as allies of Dunlow's Shadow.

Emerging from the darkest recesses of the past, Dunlow's Shadow is a haunting manifestation of pain and anger. This spectral figure, taking on the likeness of Dunlow, is wrapped in swirling darkness and constantly crackles with electric energy. Larger than any man and exuding an aura of dread, it hovers just above the ground, its semi-transparent form revealing a heart of stormy clouds. The shadow's presence is heralded by sudden temperature drops and the scent of an impending storm. While it doesn't speak in any recognizable language, its mournful wails and the violent bursts of lightning it summons speak of its torment. Its touch is deathly cold, sapping the life from those it reaches, and its ability to teleport and summon fellow shadows make it a formidable and terrifying foe. Those who have witnessed its fury say that its most chilling ability is its mournful wail, a sound so heart-wrenching that it can send the bravest adventurers fleeing in fear. Dunlow's Shadow is not just a creature; it's a testament to the tragic tale of Farmer Dunlow and the raw emotions that his untimely death left behind.

# Gravebound

Medium undead, neutral evil

**Armor Class** 12 (natural armor)
**Hit Points** 22 (5d8)
**Speed** 30 ft.

| STR | DEX | CON | INT | WIS | CHA |
| --- | --- | --- | --- | --- | --- |
| 12 (+1) | 8 (-1) | 15 (+2) | 6 (-2) | 8 (-1) | 5 (-3) |

**Damage Immunities** poison
**Condition Immunities** exhaustion, poisoned
**Senses** darkvision 60 ft., passive Perception 9
**Languages** understands the languages it knew in life but can't speak
**Challenge** 1/2 (100 XP)

**Turn Resistance.** The Gravebound has advantage on saving throws against any effect that turns undead.

**Actions**

**Slam.** *Melee Weapon Attack:* +3 to hit, reach 5 ft., one target. *Hit:* 5 (1d6 + 2) bludgeoning damage.

**Grave Chill.** (Recharge 5-6) The Gravebound targets one creature it can see within 10 feet of it. The target must succeed on a DC 12 Constitution saving throw or take 7 (2d6) cold damage and have its speed reduced by 10 feet until the end of its next turn.

Gravebound are restless undead, animated by powerful emotions or dark magic. In the case of Wheaton's Reach, the influence of Dunlow's tormented spirit has stirred these skeletal entities from their eternal rest. Wrapped in tattered burial shrouds and remnants of their burial attire, they emerge from the earth with a cold, eerie aura. Their very presence is a chilling reminder of death's inexorable grip, and they seek to drag the living down into the cold embrace of the grave.

# Pumpkin Brute

Large plant, unaligned

**Armor Class** 13 (natural armor)
**Hit Points** 37 (5d10 + 10)
**Speed** 20 ft.

| STR | DEX | CON | INT | WIS | CHA |
| --- | --- | --- | --- | --- | --- |
| 16 (+3) | 10 (0) | 14 (+2) | 3 (-4) | 10 (0) | 6 (-2) |

**Damage Immunities** psychic
**Senses** blindsight 30 ft. (blind beyond this radius), passive Perception 10
**Languages** —
**Challenge** 2 (450 XP)

**False Appearance.** While the Pumpkin Brute remains motionless, it is indistinguishable from an ordinary, oversized pumpkin.

**Actions**

**Slam.** *Melee Weapon Attack:* +5 to hit, reach 5 ft., one target. *Hit:* 12 (2d8 + 3) bludgeoning damage.

**Roll Over.** The Pumpkin Brute rolls its body in a straight line up to 30 feet and then stops. It can move through a space as narrow as 5 feet wide without squeezing. During this move, it can enter Large or smaller creatures' spaces. Whenever the rolling Pumpkin Brute enters a creature's space for the first time on a turn, that creature must make a DC 13 Dexterity saving throw or be knocked prone and take 10 (2d6 + 3) bludgeoning damage. On a successful save, the creature can choose to be pushed 5 feet to the side of the Pumpkin Brute. A creature that chooses not to be pushed suffers the consequences of a failed saving throw.

**Seed Spit.** *Ranged Weapon Attack:* +3 to hit, range 30/90 ft., one target. *Hit:* 6 (1d6 + 3) piercing damage.

Pumpkin Brutes are eerie manifestations of the harvest season gone awry. Animated by some dark magic or restless spirit, these giant pumpkins spring to life with menacing, carved faces. They use their bulk to crush their foes, and they can spit out hard seeds with deadly accuracy. Those traveling through the haunted fields of Wheaton's Reach would do well to tread lightly, lest they awaken one of these monstrous gourds.

# Root Wrangler

Small plant, unaligned

**Armor Class** 12 (natural armor)
**Hit Points** 22 (5d6 + 5)
**Speed** 20 ft., burrow 10 ft.

| STR | DEX | CON | INT | WIS | CHA |
| --- | --- | --- | --- | --- | --- |
| 14 (+2) | 10 (+0) | 12 (+1) | 3 (-4) | 10 (+0) | 5 (-3) |

**Skills** Stealth +2
**Damage Resistances** bludgeoning
**Condition Immunities** blinded, deafened
**Senses** tremorsense 60 ft., passive Perception 10
**Languages** understands Terran but can't speak
**Challenge** 1/2 (100 XP)

**Ambusher.** The Root Wrangler has advantage on attack rolls against any creature it has surprised.

**False Appearance.** While the Root Wrangler remains motionless, it is indistinguishable from a normal pile of roots and tubers.

**Actions**

**Entangle.** *Melee Weapon Attack:* +4 to hit, reach 10 ft., one target. *Hit:* 7 (1d10 + 2) bludgeoning damage, and the target is grappled (escape DC 12). Until this grapple ends, the target is restrained, and the Root Wrangler can't entangle another target.

**Trip.** *Melee Weapon Attack:* +4 to hit, reach 10 ft., one target. *Hit:* The target must succeed on a DC 12 Strength saving throw or be knocked prone.

Root Wranglers are sneaky plant-based adversaries that use their ability to hide and burrow to ambush unsuspecting adventurers. They're not overly powerful but can be a significant nuisance, especially in groups. Their main goal is to entangle and trip adventurers, making them easier targets for other threats or hazards in the area.

# Spirit Wisp

Tiny undead, neutral

**Armor Class** 13
**Hit Points** 7 (2d4 + 2)
**Speed** 0 ft., fly 40 ft. (hover)

| STR | DEX | CON | INT | WIS | CHA |
| --- | --- | --- | --- | --- | --- |
| 3 (-4) | 16 (+3) | 12 (+1) | 6 (-2) | 12 (+1) | 11 (+0) |

**Damage Resistances** acid, fire, lightning, thunder; bludgeoning, piercing, and slashing from nonmagical attacks
**Damage Immunities** cold, necrotic, poison
**Condition Immunities** charmed, exhaustion, grappled, paralyzed, petrified, poisoned, prone, restrained
**Senses** darkvision 60 ft., passive Perception 11
**Languages** understands the languages it knew in life but can't speak
**Challenge** 1/4 (50 XP)

**Incorporeal Movement.** The Spirit Wisp can move through other creatures and objects as if they were difficult terrain. It takes 5 (1d10) force damage if it ends its turn inside an object.

**Ephemeral Glow.** In dark areas, the Spirit Wisp sheds dim light in a 10-foot radius.

## Actions

**Mislead.** The Spirit Wisp targets one creature it can see within 30 feet of it. The target must succeed on a DC 12 Wisdom saving throw or be charmed by the Spirit Wisp for 1 minute. While charmed in this way, the target must use its movement on each of its turns to follow the Spirit Wisp. The charm ends if the Spirit Wisp is more than 60 feet away from the target or if the Spirit Wisp attacks the target.

Spirit Wisps are enigmatic entities, often remnants of souls or memories that linger in places of strong emotional or spiritual significance. While not inherently malicious, their presence can be disorienting and potentially dangerous, especially if they lead the unwary into hazards or traps. They are particularly common in places where the veil between the living and the dead is thin, such as the Abandoned Hut.

# Strawman

Medium construct, unaligned

**Armor Class** 11
**Hit Points** 26 (4d8 + 8)
**Speed** 20 ft.

| STR | DEX | CON | INT | WIS | CHA |
| --- | --- | --- | --- | --- | --- |
| 14 (+2) | 12 (+1) | 14 (-2) | 3 (-4) | 8 (-1) | 5 (-3) |

**Damage Resistances** bludgeoning, piercing from nonmagical attacks not made with silvered weapons
**Damage Immunities** psychic, poison
**Condition Immunities** charmed, exhaustion, poisoned
**Senses** darkvision 60 ft., passive Perception 9
**Languages** understands the languages of its creator but can't speak
**Challenge** 1 (200 XP)

**False Appearance.** While the Strawman remains motionless, it is indistinguishable from an ordinary scarecrow.

**Terrifying Glare.** Creatures that start their turn within 30 feet of the Strawman and can see its glowing eyes must make a DC 12 Wisdom saving throw or become frightened of the Strawman until the end of their next turn.

## Actions

**Claw.** *Melee Weapon Attack:* +4 to hit, reach 5 ft., one target. *Hit:* 6 (1d8 + 2) slashing damage.

**Eerie Dance.** The Strawman moves up to half its speed in a manner that confounds its enemies. During this movement, it can move through the space of any creature smaller than Large. The first time a creature comes within 5 feet of the Strawman during this move, it must make a DC 12 Wisdom saving throw or be incapacitated with fear until the end of its next turn.

Strawmen are more than just simple constructs designed to ward off birds. Animated through dark rituals or tainted magic, these scarecrows serve as sentinels, watching silently in the night. Their unpredictable movements and haunting, glowing eyes unnerve even the bravest of adventurers. They often appear where malevolence has tainted the land, and their presence is a clear sign that darker forces are at play.

# Strawman Brute

Large construct, unaligned

**Armor Class** 13 (natural armor)
**Hit Points** 85 (10d10 + 30)
**Speed** 25 ft.

| STR | DEX | CON | INT | WIS | CHA |
| --- | --- | --- | --- | --- | --- |
| 18 (+4) | 10 (+0) | 16 (+3) | 3 (-4) | 10 (+0) | 5 (-3) |

**Damage Resistances** bludgeoning, piercing from nonmagical attacks not made with silvered weapons
**Damage Immunities** psychic, poison
**Condition Immunities** charmed, exhaustion, poisoned
**Senses** darkvision 60 ft., passive Perception 10
**Languages** understands the languages of its creator but can't speak
**Challenge** 5 (1,800 XP)

**False Appearance.** While the Strawman Brute remains motionless, it is indistinguishable from an ordinary, albeit much larger, scarecrow.

**Terrifying Glare.** Creatures that start their turn within 30 feet of the Strawman Brute and can see its glowing eyes must make a DC 14 Wisdom saving throw or become frightened of the Strawman Brute for 1 minute. A creature can repeat the saving throw at the end of each of its turns, ending the effect on itself on a success.

### Actions

**Multiattack.** The Strawman Brute makes two claw attacks.

**Claw.** *Melee Weapon Attack:* +7 to hit, reach 10 ft., one target. *Hit:* 13 (2d8 + 4) slashing damage.

**Eerie Dance (Recharge 5-6).** The Strawman Brute moves up to its speed in a manner that confounds its enemies. During this movement, it can move through the space of any creature smaller than Huge. The first time a creature comes within 5 feet of the Strawman Brute during this move, it must make a DC 14 Wisdom saving throw or be incapacitated with fear until the end of its next turn.

**Stomp.** *Melee Weapon Attack:* +7 to hit, reach 5 ft., one target. *Hit:* 18 (3d8 + 4) bludgeoning damage, and the target is knocked prone.

The **Strawman Brute** is an even more menacing version of the typical Strawman. These hulking constructs tower over most adversaries, wielding their massive limbs with devastating force. Their presence is a clear sign that a significant malevolent power is in the area, as only the darkest magics can give life to such a formidable sentinel.

# Strawman Vanguard

Large construct, neutral evil

**Armor Class** 15 (natural armor)
**Hit Points** 120 (14d10 + 42)
**Speed** 30 ft.

| STR | DEX | CON | INT | WIS | CHA |
| --- | --- | --- | --- | --- | --- |
| 20 (+5) | 12 (+1) | 17 (+3) | 6 (-2) | 12 (+1) | 8 (-1) |

**Damage Resistances** bludgeoning, piercing from nonmagical attacks not made with silvered weapons
**Damage Immunities** psychic, poison
**Condition Immunities** charmed, exhaustion, poisoned
**Senses** darkvision 60 ft., passive Perception 11
**Languages** understands the languages of its creator but can't speak
**Challenge** 8 (3,900 XP)

**False Appearance.** While the Strawman Vanguard remains motionless, it is indistinguishable from an ordinary, albeit much larger, scarecrow.

**Leader's Command.** When the Strawman Vanguard takes the Attack action on its turn, it can forgo one of its attacks to command another Strawman it can see within 30 feet of it to attack.

**Terrifying Presence.** Creatures that start their turn within 30 feet of the Strawman Vanguard and can see its glowing eyes must make a DC 16 Wisdom saving throw or become frightened for 1 minute. A creature can repeat the saving throw at the end of each of its turns, ending the effect on itself on a success.

### Actions

**Multiattack.** The Strawman Vanguard makes three claw attacks.

**Claw.** *Melee Weapon Attack:* +9 to hit, reach 10 ft., one target. *Hit:* 15 (2d8 + 5) slashing damage.

**Eerie Command (Recharge 5-6).** The Strawman Vanguard lets out a chilling, otherworldly command. Each Strawman and Strawman Brute within 60 feet of the Vanguard can immediately take the Attack action as a reaction.

### Reactions

**Retaliate.** When the Strawman Vanguard is hit by a melee attack, it can make a claw attack against the attacker.

The **Strawman Vanguard** is the elite overseer of Strawman constructs, coordinating their movements in battle and dealing devastating blows with its enhanced strength. Its presence on the battlefield is a sign of a significant threat, as it not only represents a formidable combatant but also boosts the effectiveness of lesser Strawmen under its command.

# Magic Items

## Cloak of the Harvest Moon

Wondrous item, very rare

**Description:** This luxurious cloak is woven from threads that capture the very essence of autumn nights. Deep blues and silvers intertwine, creating a fabric that shimmers and dances like the light of the harvest moon upon a still pond. It feels cool to the touch and seems to hold a fragment of the night sky within its folds.

**Properties: Moonlit Walk:** Once per night, as an action, the wearer can activate the cloak to become ethereal for up to 10 minutes. While ethereal, the wearer exists on the Ethereal Plane and can move in any direction, passing through solid objects as if they weren't there. This effect ends if the wearer attacks any creature or if the duration expires. After using this feature, it cannot be used again until the next nightfall.

**Attunement:** To attune to the Cloak of the Harvest Moon, a bearer must don the cloak and spend an entire night under the open sky, watching the moon's journey from dusk till dawn. As the first light of dawn touches the horizon, the cloak's ethereal powers become accessible to its wearer.

## Dunlow's Locket

Wondrous item, rare

**Description:** This finely crafted silver locket exudes a sense of history and deep emotional significance. Upon opening the clasp, a faded picture of a loved one is revealed, the image capturing a moment of happiness long past. The locket seems to hum with a gentle energy when held, hinting at the power that lies within.

**Properties:** While attuned to and wearing this locket, the bearer gains the ability to use it to cast the spell *Speak with Dead* once per day, without requiring any material components. After the spell is cast, the locket cannot be used again until the next dawn.

Attunement: Yes

## Dunlow's Whistle

Wondrous item, rare

**Description:** Crafted from a pale, smooth wood, this humble whistle carries a history of countless sunsets and workdays concluded. It bears the subtle, worn etchings of use, and when held, one can almost hear the distant echoes of farmstead life. Its tune, though simple, has the power to reach beyond the veil of death.

**Properties**:

- **Echoes of Serenity:** Once per day, when blown, the whistle casts the spell *Calm Emotions* centered on the user. However, it only affects spirits and undead creatures within a 20-foot radius. Affected entities feel a momentary sense of peace and nostalgia, making them non-hostile for the duration of the effect.

**Attunement:** To attune to Dunlow's Whistle, a bearer must spend an evening on the farmstead, using the whistle to signal the end of the day as the sun sets. As the final notes linger in the evening air, the whistle's calming power becomes accessible to its wielder.

## Ritual Scroll of Spirit Calming

Wondrous item, very rare

**Description:** This intricately designed scroll is bound by twine, adorned with small charms representing its required components. The parchment is of a high quality, with the incantation scribed in an elegant, flowing script that seems to move with an ethereal quality. The scroll itself emanates a serene aura, calming those who hold it.

Properties:

- **Ritual Incantation:** The scroll contains a powerful ritual that requires several components to be performed successfully. As an action, a character can initiate the ritual, which takes 10 minutes to complete. The following components must be presented and used during the ritual:

- **Personal Memento:** This must be placed at the center of the ritual circle.

- **Sacred Soil:** The soil is spread around the memento, forming the circle's boundary.

- **Ancestral Candle:** The candle is lit and placed next to the memento, its flame flickering throughout the ritual.

- **Blessed Water:** The water is sprinkled over the memento and around the circle's boundary.

- **Harvest Offering:** Fresh crops are arranged around the memento in a symmetrical pattern.

- With everything in place, the scroll's incantation is read aloud. Once complete, the scroll crumbles to dust.

Upon successful completion, all spirits and undead creatures within a 60-foot radius become calm and docile, no longer showing any hostile intent towards living beings for the next hour. They may even become communicative or cooperative, depending on the nature of the spirit.

**Attunement:**
The Ritual Scroll of Spirit Calming requires attunement by a character who can cast at least one spell. The attunement process involves understanding and memorizing the ritual's incantation and requirements.

# Spiritward Lantern

Wondrous item, uncommon

**Description:** This aged lantern, though seemingly worn by time, emits a mesmerizing soft blue flame when lit. Its structure is adorned with ancient runes, barely visible under layers of patina. Once ignited, a serene aura emanates from the lantern, creating a sphere of protection against restless spirits and the undead.

**Properties:** While the lantern is lit:

• **Spiritual Barrier:** Spirits and undead creatures are unable to come within a 15-foot radius of the lantern. Any that try to enter this zone feel an overwhelming urge to retreat, making them unable to willingly move closer.

• **Glow of the Beyond:** The lantern sheds dim light in a 30-foot radius.

**Attunement:** To attune to

the lantern, a bearer must spend a night in a haunted location, using the lantern as their only source of light. As dawn approaches, the connection between the lantern and its wielder solidifies, allowing its protective properties to take effect.

# Wheaton's Harvest Blade

Weapon (sickle), rare

**Description:** Forged with masterful craftsmanship, this ornate sickle stands out with its handle carved from ancient oak, bearing the symbols and sigils of harvest deities. The blade itself holds a peculiar golden hue, shimmering under sunlight and moonlight alike, hinting at its otherworldly nature and connection to the land.

**Properties:** While attuned to and wielding this sickle:

• **Bountiful Harvest:** When used to reap crops, the blade ensures that the yield is especially bountiful, producing twice the usual amount of crops.

• **Radiant Edge:** In combat, the sickle deals an extra 1d6 radiant damage to undead creatures on a hit.

**Attunement:** To attune to the sickle, a bearer must use it to reap crops during a sunrise, feeling the connection between the blade, the land, and the cycle of life.

# Game within a Game

## Harvest's Gambit

During the Harvest Festival, villagers have a tradition of playing a game where they bet and gamble using harvested grains. The aim is to amass the most grains by the end of the game.

### Setup

- A deck of playing cards (no Jokers).
- 3 six-sided dice (d6).
- A pile of grains (represented by coins).
- Mugs or cups (optional).

### Objective

Players try to amass the most grains by predicting dice rolls, outwitting opponents, and playing their cards right.

### Gameplay

- **Initial Grains**: Each player starts with an equal number of grains (10 coins).
- **Roll for Initiative**: All players roll a d6 to determine the order of play. Highest goes first.
- **Betting Phase**: Starting with the first player and going clockwise, players can:
  - **Bet**: Place any number of their grains into a central pot.
  - **Raise**: Increase the bet made by a previous player.
  - **Fold**: Opt out of the round, forfeiting any grains already bet.
  - **Call**: Match the current bet to continue in the round.
- **Card Phase**: After all bets are placed, each player is dealt three cards from the deck. Players can then:

- **Discard and Draw**: Players can choose to discard up to two cards and draw the same number from the deck.
- **Keep All**: Players can choose not to discard any cards.
- **Dice Prediction Phase**: Players choose one card from their hand and place it face-down. This card predicts the next dice roll:
  - Number cards (2-10) predict the exact number rolled.
  - Face cards (Jack, Queen, King) predict a roll of 11 or 12.
  - Aces predict a roll of 2 or 3.
- **Roll Phase**: The first player rolls all three dice. The sum of the dice is calculated.

- **Resolution**
  - Players who predicted correctly double the grains they bet, taking from the central pot.
  - If multiple players predict correctly, they split the pot evenly. Any remainder stays for the next round.
  - If no one predicts correctly, the grains stay in the pot for the next round.
- **End and Reset**: After the resolution, the next player (clockwise) becomes the first player. Steps 3-7 are repeated until a predetermined number of rounds or until one player collects all the grains.

### Optional Rule – Mug of Fortune

At the start of the game, a mug is placed in the center. Players can, once per game, choose to toss a grain into the Mug of Fortune instead of betting. If they win that round, they triple their bet from the central pot.

# Food and Fuel

## Harvest Vegetable and Barley Stew

### Ingredients

- 1 cup pearled barley
- 2 tbsp olive oil
- 1 large onion, diced
- 3 cloves garlic, minced
- 2 large carrots, sliced into rounds
- 2 parsnips, sliced into rounds
- 1 small butternut squash, peeled and diced
- 2 large potatoes, diced
- 8 cups vegetable broth or chicken broth
- 1 cup chopped tomatoes (canned or fresh)
- 2 tsp fresh thyme (or 1 tsp dried thyme)
- 1 tsp fresh rosemary, minced (or 1/2 tsp dried rosemary)
- Salt and pepper, to taste
- 2 cups chopped kale or Swiss chard
- Optional: 1 cup fresh or frozen green peas
- Fresh parsley, for garnish

### Instructions

**Barley Preparation:** In a medium saucepan, bring 3 cups of water to a boil. Add the barley and a pinch of salt. Reduce heat, cover, and simmer for 25-30 minutes or until the barley is tender but still chewy. Drain any excess water and set aside.

**Stew Base:** In a large pot, heat the olive oil over medium heat. Add the onions and sauté until translucent, about 4-5 minutes. Add the garlic and sauté for an additional minute until fragrant.

**Vegetables:** Add the carrots, parsnips, butternut squash, and potatoes to the pot. Stir well, letting the vegetables cook and get slightly browned, about 5 minutes.

**Broth & Seasoning:** Pour in the vegetable or chicken broth, followed by the chopped tomatoes, thyme, rosemary, salt, and pepper. Bring the mixture to a boil, then reduce the heat and let it simmer for about 20 minutes, or until the vegetables are tender.

**Adding Barley & Greens:** Stir in the cooked barley and chopped kale or Swiss chard. If using green peas, add them now. Let the stew simmer for another 5-7 minutes, or until the greens are wilted and the peas are warmed through.

**Serve & Garnish:** Taste and adjust seasoning if necessary. Ladle the stew into bowls and garnish with fresh parsley.

This stew is both nourishing and flavorful, capturing the essence of a bountiful harvest. It's the perfect meal to warm up adventurers after a long day of exploring the haunted farmstead!

## Harvest Moon Elixir

### Ingredients

- 2 oz bourbon or apple brandy
- 1 oz fresh apple cider
- 0.5 oz lemon juice
- 0.5 oz maple syrup
- 1 dash of cinnamon or a cinnamon stick for garnish
- Apple slice for garnish
- Ice

### Instructions

**Mixing:** In a shaker filled with ice, combine the bourbon or apple brandy, fresh apple cider, lemon juice, and maple syrup. Shake well until chilled.

**Serving:** Strain the mixture into a glass filled with ice.

**Garnish:** Add a dash of cinnamon on top or place a cinnamon stick in the glass. Finish with an apple slice on the rim or floating in the cocktail.

**Enjoy:** Sip and imagine the crisp air of the harvest season and the mysteries of the moonlit farmstead.

This cocktail offers the warmth of bourbon, the sweetness of the harvest from the apple cider and maple syrup, and the spice of the season with cinnamon. It's perfect for adventurers to enjoy around a campfire while recounting tales of their encounters with the supernatural.

## Harvest Spirit Spritzer

### Ingredients

- 4 oz fresh apple cider
- 1 oz cranberry juice
- 1 oz lemon-lime soda or sparkling water
- 0.5 oz honey or maple syrup (adjust to taste)

- A pinch of ground cinnamon or nutmeg

- Apple slices and fresh cranberries for garnish

- Ice

### Instructions

**Mixing:** In a glass filled with ice, pour in the fresh apple cider, cranberry juice, and honey or maple syrup. Stir gently to combine.

**Fizz:** Top off with the lemon-lime soda or sparkling water to add a refreshing fizz.

**Garnish:** Sprinkle a pinch of ground cinnamon or nutmeg on top. Add apple slices and fresh cranberries to the glass for a vibrant pop of color and extra flavor.

**Serve and Enjoy:** Present the spritzer with a stirring rod or straw, allowing guests to mix and blend the flavors as they wish.

The "Harvest Spirit Spritzer" is a refreshing mocktail that captures the essence of the harvest season with its blend of apple and cranberry flavors, elevated by the gentle fizz of soda. The warmth of cinnamon or nutmeg adds a touch reminiscent of cozy autumn nights. Perfect for adventurers of all ages!

# Map

# Witches of the Blood Moon

# Managing Encounters

To help DMs tailor the adventure to the party, each encounter is designed with flexibility in mind. Whether your group consists of fledgling adventurers or seasoned heroes, the provided guidelines will help ensure that the challenges are both fun and fair.

## Encounter Structure

**Encounter Name**: The title of the encounter, usually indicating the primary theme or challenge.

**DM Information**: A brief summary to give you a clear picture of the encounter's purpose and its role in the overall adventure.

**Read Aloud**: Descriptive text meant to be read verbatim to the players, setting the scene and atmosphere.

**Additional Information**: Detailed guidance, including potential variations, expected player strategies, and potential outcomes.

**Lair Actions**: Specific actions or effects that occur in certain locations, often benefiting the encounter's primary antagonist.

**Scaling the Encounter**: Instructions on how to adjust the encounter's difficulty based on player levels:

- Beginner (Level 1-5): Simplified challenges tailored for newer or less powerful characters.

- Intermediate (Level 6-10): Moderate challenges that require a mix of skill, strategy, and teamwork.

- Advanced (Level 11+): Complex and multi-faceted challenges suitable for veteran adventurers.

**Activity**: A mini-game, puzzle, or interactive segment designed to engage players in different ways.

**Monster and/or NPC**: Details or references to any creatures or characters the players might interact with during the encounter.

**Reward**: Potential treasures, information, or other benefits the players can earn from successfully navigating the encounter.

Encounters may reference content found later in the book, such as detailed monster statistics in the Monsters section. Feel free to adapt or replace these elements to better fit your group's preferences or the storyline you're weaving.

## Modularity and Flexibility

This adventure, like all Penny Blood Adventures, is modular by design. If a particular monster or challenge doesn't resonate with your campaign's theme, feel free to replace it or adjust as needed. The goal is to provide a rich framework that sparks inspiration, allowing you to craft an unforgettable journey for your players.

# Starting the Adventure

Long ago, the land of Moonsorrow was a beacon of harmony and peace, where the cycles of life, death, and the elements were in seamless balance. The three witches, Morana, Opalina, and Elyra, were the revered guardians of this land, each representing a different facet of existence. They were the keepers of ancient rites and the mediators between the mortal realm and the unseen worlds beyond.

## The Confrontation with Helbindr

However, a shadow fell upon Moonsorrow when Helbindr, The Frostbound Sovereign of Niflshadow, sought to extend his icy dominion into the mortal realm. His realm, a frigid abyss of shadows and despair, was a stark contrast to the vibrant land of Moonsorrow. The three witches, sensing his malevolent intent, stood united against his fearsome might, engaging in a celestial battle unseen by mortal eyes. They channeled their collective powers, weaving spells of life, death, and the elements to thwart Helbindr's icy advance.

## Helbindr's Retribution

Despite their valiant efforts, Helbindr, in his final moments of retreat, cursed the land with the Blood Moon, a manifestation of his frostbound vengeance. This crimson celestial entity became a decennial reminder of the disrupted harmony, its glow allowing the icy shadows of Niflshadow to seep into Moonsorrow, bringing with it malevolent spirits and a pervasive chill.

## The Misunderstood Guardians

The inhabitants of Moonsorrow, oblivious to the witches' heroic stand against Helbindr, witnessed only the aftermath—the emergence of the Blood Moon and the ensuing distortions in their land. The witches, now seen as harbingers of doom, were blamed for the curse and banished to the depths of the Misty Woods. The town's folk, their lives overshadowed by the looming Blood Moon, lived in fear and resentment, holding the witches responsible for the icy shadows that befell their land. This year marks the fourth decennial since the rise of the first Blood Moon.

## The Witches' Exile

Morana, Opalina, and Elyra, burdened by the unjust blame and the real consequences of Helbindr's curse, have been striving to restore the balance and lift the icy shadows from Moonsorrow. In their sanctum within the Misty Woods, they delve into ancient rites and commune with the elemental forces, seeking a way to counteract Helbindr's retribution. Their isolation and banishment have only fueled the town's suspicions and misconceptions about their intentions.

## The Path to Redemption

The adventurers, lured by the tales of the Festival of the Crimson Veil and the enigmatic Blood Moon, find themselves in the midst of this ancient struggle between warmth and frost, light and shadow. They must navigate the tensions, uncover the truths behind the witches' banishment, and decide the fate of Moonsorrow. Will they aid the banished witches in their quest for redemption and restoration, or will they succumb to the frostbound whispers of Niflshadow? The choices made will shape the destiny of Moonsorrow and determine whether the icy curse of the Blood Moon will be broken or if the land will remain ensnared in the eternal grip of shadows and frost.

## Objective

In the mystical land of Moonsorrow, adventurers are tasked with navigating a series of challenges to confront the looming threat of the Frostbound Sovereign, Helbindr. As the Blood Moon casts its ominous glow, the fate of the realm hangs in the balance. Players can choose to align with the three witches, harnessing their powers to combat Helbindr, or side with the Purifiers to eliminate the witches. Each decision leads to distinct outcomes, from the triumphant restoration of Moonsorrow's beauty to its descent into an eternal winter. Rewards, alliances, and future quests are shaped by the choices made, ensuring a unique journey for every adventurer.

# Festival of the Crimson Veil

## Introduction

The Festival of the Crimson Veil is the centerpiece of this adventure, providing a rich tapestry of encounters, mysteries, and potential allies or adversaries. This section introduces the PCs to the town of Moonsorrow and the festival's various events, each offering unique challenges and opportunities. The festival, while a time of celebration, is also a reflection of the town's complex relationship with the Blood Moon and the three witches. As the PCs navigate these events, they'll be drawn into the deeper conflict between the Purifiers, who blame the witches for the Blood Moon's curse, and those who believe a darker force is at play.

Key Encounters:

**Moonlit Market**: A bustling marketplace where the PCs can trade, gather information, and encounter two merchants with opposing agendas.

**Dance of the Three Shadows**: A mesmerizing performance that provides both entertainment and clues about the witches' history.

**Crimson Feast**: A communal meal where the PCs can interact with townsfolk, gather rumors, and potentially be recruited by the Purifiers.

**Veil's Labyrinth**: A challenging maze that tests the PCs' resolve and confronts them with their innermost fears.

**The Plain Shoe Tavern**: A hub of information where the PCs can learn more about the Blood Moon, the witches, and the Purifiers' mission.

**Warding Rune Workshop**: A chance for the PCs to learn about protective magic and the significance of runes in Moonsorrow's culture.

**Crimson Mask Parade**: A vibrant parade that showcases Moonsorrow's traditions and the deities that protect the town.

**Witching Hour Vigil**: The climax of the festival, where the PCs witness the Blood Moon's ascent and hear tales that hint at the true nature of the curse.

As you approach the town of Moonsorrow, you're greeted by the sight of crimson banners fluttering in the wind, stalls adorned with glowing lanterns, and the distant sound of music and laughter. You've arrived during the Festival of the Crimson Veil, a decennial event that commemorates the Blood Moon's rise. Tales of this unique festival have traveled far and wide, speaking of its mesmerizing performances, mystical marketplaces, and the haunting beauty of the Blood Moon itself. The festival is named after the crimson veils that townsfolk wear, symbolizing the thin barrier between the mortal realm and the mysteries of the Blood Moon. Drawn by curiosity, the promise of adventure, or perhaps just the allure of a good celebration, you decide to delve deeper into the heart of Moonsorrow and partake in its festivities. But as the Blood Moon's ascent draws near, you can't shake off the feeling that there's more to this festival than meets the eye.

The streets are bustling with activity. Children run around with masks of various protective deities, their laughter echoing through the air. Traders from distant lands showcase their exotic wares, and the aroma of delicious food fills the air. Musicians play haunting melodies, while dancers move gracefully to the rhythm, their performances telling tales of ancient times and forgotten lore.

Yet, amidst the celebration, there's an underlying tension. Whispers circulate about the three witches and their connection to the Blood Moon. Some townsfolk wear amulets and talismans, seeking protection from the malevolent forces they believe the Blood Moon brings. Others speak in hushed tones about the Purifiers, a group dedicated to eradicating the witches and restoring balance to Moonsorrow.

As you navigate the festival, you're presented with opportunities to learn more about the town's history, its inhabitants, and the mysteries of the Blood Moon. Will you align with the Purifiers, believing the witches to be the root of all evil? Or will you seek out the witches themselves, hoping to uncover the truth behind the Blood Moon's curse? The choices you make will shape the fate of Moonsorrow and determine the outcome of this ancient struggle between light and shadow.

## Moonlit Market

Traders from distant lands converge on Moonsorrow, setting up stalls that offer rare and mystical items, many of which are said to be imbued with the Blood Moon's magic.

As you approach the heart of Moonsorrow, the soft glow of the Blood Moon illuminates a bustling market. Ethereal stalls shimmer under the moonlight, displaying an array of rare and mystical items. Traders from distant lands, their forms appearing almost translucent and shifting in the rare twilight, beckon you closer, their voices like whispers on the wind. The air is thick with a mix of enchanting aromas and the distant hum of bartering.

## Activities in the Encounter

**Browsing the Stalls**: Allow the players to explore the market. Describe various items that catch their eye, some of which may be useful in their quest. Items could include enchanted amulets, potions with mysterious effects, or scrolls with cryptic writings.

**Trading with the Moonshade Merchants**: If players wish to acquire an item, the Moonshade Merchants will request a memory or emotion in exchange. This could lead to roleplaying opportunities where player characters recount a significant memory or describe a powerful emotion.

## Black Cats of the Moonlit Market

Whispers and tales have long circulated about the enigmatic black cats that prowl the Moonlit Market. These feline creatures, with their piercing yellow eyes, are not mere pets or strays. They are said to be the silent sentinels of the three witches, acting as their eyes and ears amidst the bustling market.

**Description**: These black cats are sleek and graceful, with a mysterious aura about them. Their eyes seem to glow with an inner light, especially under the moon's glow, and they move with a purpose, observing the goings-on of the market with keen interest.

**Observation**: PCs can observe the cats with a DC 12 Wisdom (Perception) check. Success means they notice the cats frequently glancing their way and seemingly communicating with other black cats through subtle gestures or meows.

**Approach**: If a PC tries to approach a cat, they must succeed on a DC 14 Dexterity (Stealth) or Charisma (Animal Handling) check. On a success, they can get close enough to interact with the cat without it darting away.

**Communication**: If a PC can communicate with animals, either through a spell or class feature, the cats will be evasive and cryptic in their responses, often answering questions with riddles or vague statements. However, they might drop hints or clues about the witches or the market's secrets.

**Magic Detection**: A PC using Detect Magic will sense a faint aura of Divination magic around the cats, indicating their connection to the witches and their role as observers.

**Frequency**: For every hour the PCs spend in the Moonlit Market, there's a 50% chance they'll encounter one of these black cats. The DM can roll a d20; on a roll of 10 or below, a black cat crosses the PCs' path or is seen observing them from a distance.

### Note for the DM

Use the black cats as a tool to build atmosphere and tension. Their presence can serve as a reminder of the witches' influence in the market and the overarching mystery of the Blood Moon. They can also be used to drop hints, guide the PCs, or introduce new plot points or challenges.

## Merchants

Below are details for each merchant, including The name of their booth, the merchant, a short backstory, alignment with either the Purifiers, the Witches or neutral, rumors (these may be gossip and falsehoods, so beware) and details for the products or service they sell.

### Mistress Morgana's Elixirs and Potions

**Description**: A mysterious merchant selling bubbling brews, glowing potions, and enchanted vials. Her stall is adorned with cauldrons and black cats.

**Specialty**: Potions that can aid or hinder, depending on her mood and the customer's intent. Owner: Mistress Morgana

**Backstory**: Mistress Morgana was once a promising apprentice of the three witches, but a twist of fate led her to Moonsorrow's market, where she now peddles her potions, ever watchful for those who might aid or threaten her former mentors. Her black cats, always by her side, are a testament to the deep bond she still shares with the witches, especially Elyra.

**Alignment**: Witches

**Rumors shared by the seller**

- Ancient Guardians: "The witches, my dear, are the ancient guardians of Moonsorrow. They've protected this land for centuries, long before the Blood Moon's curse."

- Hidden Sanctum: "Deep within the Misty Woods, the witches have a hidden sanctum. It's said to be a place of immense power, where they commune with the spirits and elements."

- Helbindr's Deception: "The Frostbound Sovereign, Helbindr, deceived the people of Moonsorrow. The witches fought against him to protect the land, but his curse remains."

- Opalina's Gift: "Opalina, one of the witches, has a gift to communicate with animals. It's said that the black cats roaming the market are her eyes and ears."

- The Prophecy: "A prophecy once foretold of a group of adventurers who would come to Moonsorrow and play a crucial role in lifting the Blood Moon's curse. Could it be you?"

**Products**

**Elixir of Midnight Whispers**: A deep blue potion that bubbles softly and emits a faint, ghostly whisper when uncorked.

Effect: When consumed, the drinker can hear the thoughts of creatures within 10 feet for 1 hour.

Price: 50 gold pieces

**Luminous Luna Draught**: A glowing silvery potion that illuminates like the moon.

Effect: When consumed, the drinker emits a soft light in a 20-foot radius for 3 hours, acting as a light source.

Price: 30 gold pieces

**Vial of Veil Mist**: A small vial containing a swirling gray mist.

Effect: When opened, the vial releases a mist in a 15-foot radius, heavily obscuring the area for 1 minute.

Price: 40 gold pieces

**Brew of Bewitching Dreams**: A bubbling pink brew with a sweet aroma.

Effect: When consumed, the drinker falls into a deep, dream-filled sleep for 8 hours. The dreams can be influenced by the person giving the potion, making it useful for sending messages or visions.

Price: 60 gold pieces

**Potion of Purrfect Balance**: A potion with a shifting feline silhouette inside.

Effect: When consumed, the drinker gains the agility and balance of a cat, granting advantage on Acrobatics checks for 1 hour.

Price: 35 gold pieces

**Vial of Vanishing Visage**: A clear liquid that seems to absorb the light around it.

Effect: When applied to the face, the user becomes invisible for 1 minute. Any offensive action (i.e. a damaging spell, melee attack or ranged attack, or physical interaction with a creature) taken by the user will break the invisibility.

Price: 80 gold pieces

**Elixir of Ethereal Echoes**: A potion with a shimmering, ghostly hue.

Effect: When consumed, the drinker can cast the Message spell at will for 1 hour.

Price: 45 gold pieces

**Brew of Bountiful Luck**: A golden potion with tiny clovers suspended within.

Effect: When consumed, the drinker can reroll one ability check, attack roll, or saving throw within the next hour, taking the higher result.

Price: 70 gold pieces

**Vial of Vexing Vapors**: A vial containing a green, noxious gas.

Effect: When thrown, it creates a 10-foot radius cloud. Creatures within must make a DC 14 Constitution saving throw or become poisoned for 1 minute.

Price: 55 gold pieces

**Potion of Peculiar Potency**: A swirling, multicolored potion that constantly changes its hue.

Effect: When consumed, roll a d6. On a 1-3, the drinker gains a random beneficial effect (DM's choice, such as temporary hit points, a bonus to the next skill check, etc.). On a 4-6, the drinker suffers a random detrimental effect (DM's choice, such as being stunned for 1 round, taking minor damage, etc.).

Price: 25 gold pieces

## Grimwald's Grimoires

**Description**: An old, hunched figure selling ancient tomes, scrolls, and spellbooks. His booth is dimly lit, with candles casting eerie shadows.

**Specialty**: Forbidden knowledge and dark spells.

**Owner**: Grimwald

**Backstory**: Grimwald, once a respected scholar in the arcane arts, delved too deeply into forbidden magics and was expelled from the prestigious Arcanum Academy. With his reputation tarnished, he traveled the lands, collecting dark spells, ancient tomes, and forbidden scrolls. Over time, his obsession with these forbidden arts took a toll on his body, causing him to become hunched and aged beyond his years. He eventually set up Grimwald's Grimoires, a dimly lit booth where he peddles his dark collection. Aligned with the Purifiers, Grimwald believes that the witches of Moonsorrow are a threat to the very fabric of magic and must be stopped. He hopes that the knowledge he offers can arm others against what he sees as the witches' malevolent influence.

**Alignment**: Purifiers

**Rumors shared by the seller**

- The Witch's Curse: "I heard from a reliable source that those witches are the reason crops are failing this season. They've cursed the land, and now we're all going to starve because of their wickedness."

- The Plain Shoe Tavern Talk: "Over at The Plain Shoe Tavern, some of the Purifiers were discussing how they've found evidence of the witches consorting with demons. If that's true, then Moonsorrow is in grave danger."

- The Shadowy Rituals: "Late at night, if you venture close to the Misty Woods, you can hear eerie chants and see strange lights. The witches are surely up to no good, performing forbidden magic that could doom us all."

- Purifiers' Promise: "A member of the Purifiers told me that once they rid Moonsorrow of the witches, prosperity and peace will return to the land. They seem to be the only ones willing to stand up and protect the town from the witches' malevolence."

**Items for Sale**

**Tome of the Purifying Flame**: A thick leather-bound book with a silver emblem of a flame on its cover.

Effect: Contains a ritual that, when performed over 10 minutes, creates a 20-foot radius sphere that dispels all dark magic and curses within. Any creature that had been under the effect of dark magic or a curse within this sphere can make another saving throw with advantage. Requires proficiency in ritual casting to use.

Price: 500 gold pieces.

**Scroll of Witch-Binding**: A long, ancient scroll sealed with a wax emblem of chained hands.

Effect: When read aloud as an action, a targeted witch within 60 feet must succeed on a DC 15 Wisdom saving throw or be unable to cast spells for 1 minute. The witch can attempt a new saving throw at the end of each of its turns.

Price: 100 gold pieces.

**The Hexen Compendium**: A dark tome with illustrations of various witches and their known spells.

Effect: Provides knowledge on common witch spells. When used as a reference (takes 10 minutes), the reader gains advantage on saving throws against spells cast by witches for 1 hour.

Price: 80 gold pieces.

**Pumpkin's Curse Scroll**: A scroll with an orange hue, smelling faintly of pumpkin spice.

Effect: As an action, the caster can target a creature within 30 feet. The target must succeed on a DC 14 Constitution saving throw or have its head turned into a pumpkin for 1 hour or until dispelled. While in this state, the target is blinded and cannot speak but can still breathe and hear.

Price: 100 gold pieces.

**Ghoulcaller's Grimoire**: A spellbook with a cover made from ghoul skin, its pages filled with necromantic rituals.

Effect: Contains a version of the Create Undead spell that works specifically to create a single ghoul. The caster can animate a corpse to become a ghoul under their control for 24 hours which they can mentally command as a bonus action on their turn within a range of 120 ft.

Price: 12,500 gold pieces.

**Book of Shadows**: A jet-black book that seems to absorb light. Its pages are filled with shadowy incantations.

Effect: Contains the Shadow Blade and Shadow of Moil spells. The caster can summon a blade made of shadow or wrap themselves in swirling shadows that grant resistance to radiant damage and cause attackers to suffer necrotic damage.

Price: 7,200 gold pieces.

**Scroll of the Harvest Moon**: A scroll with a luminescent sheen, depicting the phases of the moon.

Effect: When read under the moonlight as an action, the caster's moon-related spells (like Moonbeam) have their damage increased by an additional 1d10 for the next hour.

Price: 60 gold pieces.

**Banshee's Lament Spellbook**: A sorrowful-looking book with faint, ethereal wails emanating from it.

Effect: Contains a version of the Summon Greater Demon spell specifically for banshees. The caster can summon a banshee that obeys their commands for up to 1 hour, after which it becomes hostile if not banished.

Price: 6,000 gold pieces.

**Vampire Slayer's Codex**: A red, velvety book with a bat emblem, detailing the secrets of the nightwalkers.

Effect: Provides knowledge on vampires. When used as a reference (takes an action), the reader gains advantage on Intelligence (Arcana) checks related to vampires and their weaknesses for the next hour.

Price: 85 gold pieces.

**Scroll of the Candy Corn Conjuration**: A fun, Halloween-themed scroll with illustrations of candy corn.

Effect: As an action, the caster can create a 15-foot cone of candy corn. Creatures in the area must make a DC 12

Dexterity saving throw or be blinded until the end of their next turn as candy corn sticks to their eyes.

Price: 20 gold pieces.

## The Spectral Puppet Theatre

**Description**: A puppeteer who puts on ghostly shows, telling tales of Moonsorrow's history and legends.

**Owner**: Cedric Hollowshade

**Backstory**: Cedric Hollowshade grew up in the shadowed alleys of Moonsorrow, where tales of ghosts, witches, and ancient legends were whispered in hushed tones. As a child, he was captivated by the stories his grandmother told him, tales passed down through generations. Wanting to keep these stories alive and share them with others, Cedric combined his love for storytelling with his talent for crafting and manipulating puppets. He traveled far and wide, learning the art of puppetry from various masters. Upon his return to Moonsorrow, he established "The Spectral Puppet Theatre." Using a unique blend of magic and craftsmanship, Cedric's puppets take on an almost lifelike quality, acting out the legends of Moonsorrow in eerie, ghostly performances. While his shows entertain many, they also serve as a reminder of the town's rich history and the mysteries that still linger.

**Alignment**: Neutral

**Specialty**: Entertainment for children and adults alike. The following are three of the moral stories that Cedric performs with his puppets:

### The Haunting of Hollow Hill

Characters:

- Lila: A brave young girl with a curious spirit.
- Tom: Lila's cautious younger brother.
- Old Man Craven: The mysterious keeper of Hollow Hill.
- The Restless Spirit: A ghost trapped in Hollow Hill.

Story:

- Beginning: Lila and Tom, hearing legends of the haunted Hollow Hill, decide to venture there on Halloween night against the warnings of the townsfolk.
- Middle: Inside, they encounter the Restless Spirit who is bound to the hill due to a broken promise. Old Man Craven, once a friend of the spirit, reveals that he broke a promise to return every Halloween but was too afraid.
- End: Lila and Tom help reunite the two, mending their bond. The Restless Spirit finds peace and departs, leaving Hollow Hill forever.
- Moral: The importance of keeping promises and the power of reconciliation.

### The Bewitched Pumpkin Patch

Characters:

- Mara: A kind-hearted witch.
- Pippin: A mischievous enchanted pumpkin.
- Villagers: Residents of Moonsorrow.

Story:

- Beginning: Every Halloween, Mara enchants her pumpkin patch to come to life. Pippin, the smallest pumpkin, feels overlooked and decides to play pranks on the villagers.
- Middle: The villagers grow fearful, believing a malevolent force is at work. Mara discovers Pippin's mischief and teaches him about the consequences of his actions.
- End: Pippin apologizes to the villagers, and with Mara's magic, creates a grand feast for the village, turning the night into a celebration.
- Moral: Seeking attention through mischief can lead to unintended consequences; it's better to be kind and understanding.

### The Dance of the Midnight Shadows

Characters:

- Elara: A young dancer with dreams of joining the legendary Midnight Shadows.
- Midnight Shadows: Ethereal beings that dance under the Blood Moon.
- Elder Moira: The oldest villager with knowledge of the Shadows' origins.

Story:

- Beginning: Elara wishes to join the Midnight Shadows in their enchanting dance. She practices every night, hoping to be noticed.
- Middle: On Halloween, the Blood Moon rises, and the Shadows invite her to dance. However, she becomes trapped in their realm. Elder Moira reveals that the dance is a test of humility.
- End: Realizing her desire was driven by vanity, Elara humbles herself. The Shadows, impressed by her growth, release her, granting her a shadowy cloak as a token of their realm.
- Moral: True success comes from humility and understanding one's intentions.

## Madame Celestia's Face Painting

**Description**: An enchanting artist who paints faces with intricate designs, turning children into little monsters, fairies, or heroes.

**Specialty**: Her paints have a touch of magic, allowing the designs to come to life momentarily.

**Owner**: Madame Celestia Nightshade

**Backstory**: Born under the Blood Moon's crimson glow, Celestia Nightshade always had an affinity for magic. As a child, she discovered her talent for painting and combined it with her innate magical abilities. Over time, she became known as Madame Celestia, the enchanting artist of Moonsorrow. She was once close friends with the three witches, especially Morana, who taught her the art of imbuing paints with magic. However, as the town turned against the witches, Celestia was forced to keep her alignment a secret, using her face painting booth as a way to subtly support the witches and spread their message.

**Alignment**: Witches

**Rumors shared by the seller**

- Morana's Ritual: "Morana is known to perform a ritual during the Blood Moon, attempting to cleanse the land of its icy shadows. But each time, something goes amiss."

- Purifiers' Betrayal: "Beware the Purifiers. They once sought the witches' guidance but turned against them out of fear and ignorance."

- Blood Moon's Power: "The Blood Moon isn't just a curse; it's a source of power. The witches harness its energy in their spells, but so do others with darker intentions."

- Witches' Offerings: "If you ever find yourself in the Misty Woods, leave an offering at the ancient stone circle. The witches might grant you their favor."

**Face Art**: Below are face art samples that can be painted on the PCs. The effects of the face paintings are minor and primarily for flavor and roleplaying purposes. They do not stack with other magical effects or spells.

**Ghastly Ghoul**: A pale, ghostly face with dark hollow eyes and eerie blue wisps.

Price: 5 SP

Effect: Grants the wearer advantage on Stealth checks for 1 hour, as they blend into the shadows.

**Fairy's Glimmer**: A shimmering design with delicate wings, sparkling stars, and soft pastel colors.

Price: 7 SP

Effect: For 1 hour, the wearer can cast the Dancing Lights cantrip once, without needing any components.

**Mighty Minotaur**: A fierce minotaur face with sharp horns, a snout, and intricate tribal markings.

Price: 6 SP

Effect: Grants the wearer advantage on Intimidation checks for 1 hour, as they channel the minotaur's fearsome presence.

**Luminous Luna Moth**: A beautiful, glowing luna moth with intricate wing patterns that seem to flutter on the face.

Price: 8 SP

Effect: For 1 hour, the wearer emits a soft glow, shedding dim light in a 5-foot radius, and can see in the dark up to 30 feet.

**Witch's Whiskers**: A playful design of a black cat with whiskers, a cute nose, and glowing green eyes.

Price: 5 SP

Effect: Grants the wearer advantage on Perception checks that rely on hearing or smell for 1 hour as they tap into the keen senses of a cat.

**Dragon's Breath**: A fierce dragon design with scales, sharp teeth, and flames around the mouth.

Price: 10 SP

Effect: For 1 hour, the wearer can exhale a small puff of harmless smoke, adding flair to their words and actions.

**Pumpkin's Grin**: A classic jack-o'-lantern design with a wide grin, triangular eyes, and a cute stem on the forehead.

Price: 4 SP

Effect: For 1 hour, the wearer can cast the Prestidigitation cantrip once to create a harmless sensory effect related to Halloween, like the scent of pumpkin spice or the sound of eerie laughter.

## Balthazar's Bobbing Apples

**Description**: A fun stall where children can try their luck bobbing for enchanted apples in a cauldron. Some apples grant minor wishes, while others might turn your mouth blue!

**Specialty**: Enchanted apples with unpredictable effects.

**Owner**: Balthazar Bramblebrook

**Backstory**: Balthazar Bramblebrook, a jovial halfling with a twinkle in his eye, hails from the orchards of the Shirebrook Valley. As a young lad, he stumbled upon an ancient, enchanted tree in the heart of the orchard. This tree bore apples unlike any other, each infused with a touch of unpredictable magic. Seeing the potential for both mischief and merriment, Balthazar decided to share the magic of these apples with the world. He set up "Balthazar's Bobbing Apples" at various festivals, delighting children and adults alike with the whimsical effects of his enchanted apples.

**Alignment**: Neutral

**Bobbing for Apples**

Objective: Retrieve an enchanted apple from the cauldron using only your mouth.

Setup:

- Balthazar's cauldron is filled with water and floating enchanted apples.

- PCs must keep their hands behind their backs at all times during the attempt.

- Each PC gets one attempt unless they pay for additional tries.

Instructions:

- Initiating the Game: A PC expresses interest in bobbing for apples. They pay the required fee (set by the DM, e.g., 5 silver pieces) for a single attempt.

- Making the Attempt: The PC must make a Dexterity (Acrobatics) check to successfully grab an apple with their mouth. The DM sets the DC based on how challenging they want the game to be. A suggested DC is 15.

Modifiers:

- If the PC has a particularly small or large mouth (at DM's discretion), they might have a +/- 2 modifier to the roll.

- If the PC has had experience or training in similar activities, they might get advantage on the roll.

Outcome:

- On a successful check, the PC retrieves an apple and can immediately experience its effect.

- On a failed check, the PC comes up empty-mouthed but might choose to try again if they pay for another attempt.

Enchanted Apple Effects: Roll a d6 to determine the apple's effect:

- Wishful Apple: Grants the PC advantage on their next skill check.

- Blue-mouthed Apple: Turns the PC's mouth blue for the next hour.

- Duck-voiced Apple: The PC quacks like a duck whenever they speak for the next 10 minutes.

- Glowing Apple: The PC emits a soft glow, shedding dim light in a 10-foot radius for the next 30 minutes.

- Bouncy Apple: The PC feels light-footed and can jump twice as far for the next 10 minutes.

- Fortune's Favor Apple: The next time the PC rolls a natural 1 on any d20 roll within the next 24 hours, they can choose to reroll the die and must use the new roll.

## Lustrous Lumina Emporium

**Description**: At the Lustrous Lumina Emporium, visitors will find an array of ethereal items, each shimmering with a soft, otherworldly glow. These items range from translucent amulets that can store one's fondest memory to delicate vials filled with the distilled essence of emotions like joy, sorrow, or love. There are also mysterious orbs that, when gazed upon, allow one to relive a past moment or feel an emotion they've never felt before. But remember, the price for these items is not gold or silver. Seraphel trades only in memories and emotions, and those who barter with him might leave with a treasure in hand, but a piece of their soul forever stored in his collection.

**Owner**: Seraphel, the Moonshade Merchant

**Backstory**: Seraphel was once a mortal who, after a fateful encounter with a celestial being during a Blood Moon, was transformed into a Moonshade Merchant. Now, neither fully of this world nor the next, Seraphel exists between realms, collecting memories and emotions as treasures more valuable than gold. With a deep understanding of the intangible essence of life, Seraphel set up the Lustrous Lumina Emporium in the Moonlit Market, offering wares imbued with the very essence of memories and emotions.

**Alignment**: Neutral

**Items for Sale**

**Elixir of Euphoria**: A vial filled with a glowing liquid that embodies pure joy.

Effect: Drinking the elixir gives the PC advantage on Charisma checks for 1 hour as they radiate happiness.

Payment: A cherished memory of a day filled with laughter and joy.

**Sorrow Stone**: A teardrop-shaped crystal that absorbs sadness.

Effect: Holding the stone gives the PC resistance to psychic damage for 10 minutes as it absorbs emotional pain.

Payment: A memory of a time when the PC felt deep sadness or loss.

**Courageous Cufflink**: A shimmering cufflink that emboldens the wearer.

Effect: Wearing the cufflink gives the PC advantage on saving throws against being frightened for 1 hour.

Payment: A memory of a time when the PC overcame a significant fear.

**Heart's Desire Ring**: A ring that glows with the warmth of love.

Effect: Wearing the ring allows the PC to cast the Charm Person spell once, with the target feeling a deep affection for the PC.

Payment: A cherished memory of a loved one, such as a first kiss or a heartfelt moment shared.

**Echoing Echo**: A small, ethereal mirror that replays spoken words.

Effect: The PC can use the mirror to replay the last sentence they heard, useful for eavesdropping or recalling important information.

Payment: A memory of a casual conversation from earlier that day.

**Essence of Forgotten Dreams**: A vial containing the distilled essence of dreams.

Effect: Drinking the essence allows the PC to have a lucid dream the next time they sleep, potentially gaining insight or a premonition.

Payment: A memory of a significant dream or nightmare.

**Timeless Hourglass**: An hourglass that can momentarily halt time.

Effect: Turning the hourglass allows the PC to stop time for everyone but themselves for 6 seconds (1 round). Once used, it can't be used again until the next Blood Moon (10 years from now).

Payment: A cherished memory of a significant life event, such as the birth of a child or a wedding day.

## Lair Actions

On initiative count 20 (losing initiative ties), the Moonlit Market takes a lair action to cause one of the following magical effects; the market can't use the same effect two rounds in a row:

**Ephemeral Mist**: A thick, silvery mist envelops a 20-foot radius centered on a point the DM chooses. The area is heavily obscured. The mist dissipates at the end of the next lair action.

**Whispers of the Past**: Ghostly apparitions of past traders and customers appear, reenacting their trades. They are harmless and provide a glimpse into the market's history. Players might gain insights or clues from these apparitions.

**Moonlit Mirage**: The Blood Moon's glow intensifies, creating illusions of items that aren't there or masking the true nature of items. Players must succeed on a DC 15 Wisdom (Perception) check to see through the illusion.

## Scaling the Encounter

### Beginning Players (PC levels 1-5)

**Moonlit Market**: Reduce the number of stalls and traders to make the market less overwhelming. Focus on basic magical items, such as simple potions or common amulets. Traders are more patient, offering hints and advice to the newcomers about the wonders of the market.

**Browsing the Stalls**: Offer items that have temporary effects or single-use abilities, ensuring they aren't too powerful for their level.

**Trading with the Moonshade Merchants**: Simplify trades by allowing exchanges for basic goods or small tasks rather than deep emotional memories.

**Black Cats of the Moonlit Market**: The cats are curious but non-hostile, occasionally leading players to places of interest or dropping minor hints.

### Intermediate Players (PC levels 6-10)

**Moonlit Market**: Increase the variety and complexity of the stalls, introducing rarer items and more intricate trades. Traders may offer more complex riddles or tasks for the PCs to acquire desired items.

**Browsing the Stalls**: Introduce cursed or tricky items that require players to think or investigate before use.

**Trading with the Moonshade Merchants**: Trades now demand more significant memories or emotions, and the consequences of these trades are more impactful.

**Black Cats of the Moonlit Market**: The cats now have a dual role: while they still offer guidance, they may also test the players, using illusions or minor magical tricks.

### Advanced Players (PC levels 11+)

**Moonlit Market**: The market is bustling with rare and legendary items, and trades can reshape destinies. Traders are shrewd and may have ulterior motives. Introduce a few stalls that are ethereal or time-bound, appearing only under specific conditions.

**Browsing the Stalls**: Items now have deep lore, and some might be connected to the overarching campaign or players' backgrounds.

**Trading with the Moonshade Merchants**: Trades can alter character backstories, introduce new side quests, or even change the world's state.

**Black Cats of the Moonlit Market**: The cats are guardians of the market's secrets. They might lead players to hidden areas, initiate side quests, or even challenge the party to a magical duel to test their worth.

## Monster

Moonshade Merchant

# Dance of the Three Shadows

A grand performance that tells the tale of the three witches and their connection to the Blood Moon. Dancers, wearing masks representing the witches, reenact the fateful night of the first Blood Moon, moving to haunting melodies played by local musicians.

As you approach the central plaza of Moonsorrow, you're greeted by the haunting melodies of stringed instruments and the soft glow of lanterns illuminating a grand stage. On it, three dancers, each wearing a distinct mask representing one of the fabled witches, move with ethereal grace. Their dance tells a tale of power, sacrifice, and the haunting Blood Moon. The crowd is entranced, their eyes fixed on the mesmerizing performance.

## Activities in the Encounter

**The Dance**: The main attraction is the dance itself. The dancers reenact the fateful night of the first Blood Moon, showcasing the witches' power and their confrontation with Helbindr. The dance is both beautiful and haunting, drawing in all who watch.

**Shadow Dancers**: As the performance reaches its climax, spectral entities that mimic the dancers emerge from the shadows. These Shadow Dancers move gracefully, attempting to draw in the unwary and drain their vitality.

**Purifier's Influence**: One of the dancers, subtly wearing a symbol of the Purifiers, will attempt to approach the PCs during a break or after the performance. They will whisper tales of the witches' malevolence and encourage the PCs to hunt them down.

**Witch's Ally**: A musician, playing a haunting melody on a flute, is aligned with the witches. If approached or if the PCs seem in danger, they will provide hints about the true nature of the Blood Moon and suggest that a greater evil, a demon, might be the true cause of the land's misfortune.

## The Dance

The central plaza of Moonsorrow transforms into a mystical stage. Ethereal blue flames light the perimeter, casting ghostly illuminations upon the performers. Three main dancers, each adorned in flowing robes and distinct masks representing the witches - Morana, Opalina, and Elyra - take center stage. Their movements are fluid, telling a story of power coming from the Blood Moon. As the dance progresses, the atmosphere becomes thick with magic, and the very air seems to pulse with the rhythm of their steps. The dancers themselves intentionally remain neutral on who is to blame for the Blood Moon, leaving the interpretation to be made by the viewer.

## Effects on the Audience

As the dance reaches its climax, the magic imbued within the performance begins to affect the audience.

**Mesmerizing Movements**: All creatures watching the dance must make a DC 13 Wisdom saving throw or become charmed, their attention fully captivated by the performance. While charmed in this way, a creature is incapacitated and has a speed of 0. The effect lasts as long as the dance continues and for 1 minute afterward. A creature can repeat the saving throw at the end of each of its turns, ending the effect on itself on a success.

**Visions of the Past**: Those who are particularly entranced (failing the save by 5 or more) begin to experience visions. They see glimpses of the fateful night, the witches' confrontation with Helbindr, and the emergence of the first Blood Moon. These visions are not just visual but also emotional, allowing the viewer to feel a fraction of the intensity, fear, and determination of that night.

**Ethereal Echoes**: As the dance narrates the confrontation with Helbindr, ghostly apparitions reenact the battle around the dancers. Spectral images of the witches casting spells, Helbindr's icy wrath, and the eventual rise of the Blood Moon play out, adding depth and a haunting realism to the performance.

## Interactions with the Dancers

PCs can interact with the dance in various ways:

**Joining the Dance**: A PC with a flair for performance can attempt to join the dance, making a DC 15 Performance check. On a success, they seamlessly blend into the performance, perhaps even drawing the attention and admiration of the audience. On a failure, they might stumble or disrupt the flow momentarily.

**Understanding the Magic**: A PC proficient in Arcana can attempt a DC 16 Arcana check to discern the nature of the magic at play, gaining insights into its origin and purpose.

**Resisting the Charm**: PCs who resist the charm effect might notice other details in the surroundings, such as the reactions of other audience members, the presence of any suspicious individuals, or other events occurring simultaneously in the plaza.

## Shadow Dancers

Emerging from the darkest corners of the plaza are 1d4 Shadow Dancers. These spectral entities resemble the dancers in form but are entirely composed of shadow. Their movements are eerily synchronized with the main performers, but their intentions are far more malevolent. Their eyes, voids of absolute darkness, seem to draw in any light around them, and their touch is cold as the grave.

The Shadow Dancers are not only a combat challenge but also a thematic element of the performance. Their appearance should heighten the tension and atmosphere of the encounter. They attempt to isolate and pick off weaker members of the party or those who are entranced by their dance.

### Purifier's Influence

Tamsin, one of the lead dancers, subtly wears a symbol of the Purifiers hidden among her dance attire. As the performance concludes and the audience is still entranced by the mesmerizing dance, she gracefully approaches the PCs during the ensuing applause. With a conspiratorial glance, she leans in to whisper tales of the witches' malevolence, painting them as the true villains of Moonsorrow. Her words are laced with urgency as she encourages the PCs to hunt down the witches and end their supposed reign of terror. The glint in her eyes suggests a personal vendetta, but whether it's genuine concern for Moonsorrow or a deeper, more personal grudge remains to be seen.

Tamsin is a staunch believer in the Purifiers' cause, having lost family to the icy shadows that plague Moonsorrow. She uses her position as a dancer to spread the Purifiers' message discreetly. While she is not overtly hostile, she is manipulative and will use her charm and persuasion to sway the PCs against the witches. She will approach the party during a break or after the performance, whispering tales of the witches' malevolence and sharing "evidence" of their dark deeds. If confronted or threatened, she will attempt to flee, using her rogue abilities to evade capture.

### Interaction with PCs

Tamsin will approach the PCs, complimenting them on their appearance or prowess and expressing her concern about the witches' influence. She will share rumors (some true, some exaggerated) about the witches' dark rituals and the harm they've brought to Moonsorrow. She will emphasize the need for brave souls like the PCs to stand up against such evil and will offer her assistance in any way she can. If the PCs show interest, she might provide them with a map to the witches' lair or offer to introduce them to other members of the Purifiers. If the PCs are skeptical or hostile, she will

retreat, but not before planting seeds of doubt about the witches' intentions.

## Witch's Ally

Lorien is a slender half-elf with long, silver hair and piercing green eyes. They wear a flowing robe adorned with subtle, moonlit patterns. As they play their flute, the haunting melodies seem to resonate with the very essence of Moonsorrow, echoing the land's sorrow and hope.

### Abilities

**Words of Terror**: Once per short rest, Lorien can speak to a humanoid alone for 1 minute, causing them to become frightened for the next hour or until they are attacked or damaged.

**Mantle of Whispers**: Upon seeing a creature die within 30 feet, Lorien can capture its shadow, allowing them to assume its form and gain some of its memories.

### Interaction

If approached by the PCs, Lorien will weave tales of the witches' benevolence and their efforts to protect Moonsorrow. They will hint at the Blood Moon's true nature, suggesting that its malevolent influence might not be solely the witches' doing. If the PCs seem in danger or are openly hostile to the witches, Lorien will use their Words of Terror to dissuade any rash actions, urging them to seek the truth. They will hint at a greater evil, a demon, that might be the true cause of the land's misfortune.

### Hints Lorien Might Provide

"The Blood Moon's curse is not of this realm. Seek the rift between worlds."

"Beware the shadows that dance not to our tunes. They serve a darker master."

"The witches' exile was not of their choosing. A greater force drives them."

"In the heart of the Misty Woods, answers await those who seek the truth."

"Trust not all you see under the Blood Moon's glow. Deception wears many faces."

## Lair Actions

**Ethereal Melody**: At initiative count 20, the haunting melody intensifies. All creatures within 60 feet of the stage must succeed on a DC 14 Wisdom saving throw or be charmed until the end of their next turn, compelled to move towards the stage.

**Shadow's Embrace**: Shadows on the ground reach out and attempt to grasp at the feet of those nearby. Any creature within 30 feet of the stage must succeed on a DC 15 Dexterity saving throw or be restrained. They can repeat the saving throw at the end of each of their turns.

**Whispers of the Past**: Ghostly apparitions of the three witches appear around the stage, whispering tales of their past. Any creature within 40 feet of the stage must succeed on a DC 13 Wisdom saving throw or be frightened until the end of their next turn.

## Scaling the Encounter

### Beginning Players (PC levels 1-5)

**Mesmerizing Movements**: Lower the DC of the Wisdom saving throw to 10.

**Shadow Dancers**: Spawn only 1-2 Shadow Dancers.

**Witch's Ally**: Lorien's Words of Terror should have a DC of 10.

### Intermediate Players (PC levels 6-10)

**Mesmerizing Movements**: Keep the DC of the Wisdom saving throw at 13.

**Shadow Dancers**: Spawn 2-3 Shadow Dancers.

**Witch's Ally**: Lorien's Words of Terror should have a DC of 13.

### Advanced Players (PC levels 11+)

**Mesmerizing Movements**: Increase the DC of the Wisdom saving throw to 16.

**Shadow Dancers**: Spawn 3-4 Shadow Dancers.

**Witch's Ally**: Lorien's Words of Terror should have a DC of 16.

## Monster

Shadow Dancer

# Crimson Feast

A lavish banquet open to all, where traditional dishes representing life, death, and the elements are served. It's believed that partaking in this feast can grant one protection from the Blood Moon's adverse effects.

As you enter the grand hall, you're met with the intoxicating aroma of a myriad of dishes. Long wooden tables adorned with crimson cloths stretch across the room, each laden with platters of food that seem to represent the very essence of Moonsorrow. The hall is illuminated by chandeliers made of glowing red crystals, casting a warm hue over the attendees. Guests laugh and converse, their worries momentarily forgotten as they partake in the feast. Musicians play soft melodies, and the atmosphere is one of celebration, albeit with an underlying tension.

## Activities

**Tasting the Elements**: PCs can partake in the feast, sampling dishes that represent life, death, and the elements. Consuming these dishes grants them a temporary +1 bonus to saving throws against the Blood Moon's effects for the next 24 hours.

**Mingling with the Guests**: PCs can converse with various attendees, gathering information, rumors, or making allies.

**Observing the Feast's Guardian**: A spectral entity that hovers near the main table, ensuring the feast's sanctity. It reacts only if the feast is disrupted or if dark magic is used.

## Tasting the Elements

**Life's Bounty Salad**: A vibrant mix of fresh greens, colorful fruits, and edible flowers, drizzled with a honey-lavender dressing. Consuming this dish grants the PC temporary hit points equal to their Constitution modifier (minimum of 1) for the next hour.

**Death's Delight Soup**: A rich, dark broth made from rare mushrooms and roots, served in a hollowed-out pumpkin. After consuming this soup, the PC gains advantage on death saving throws for the next hour.

**Elemental Elixirs**: Four small vials filled with liquids representing the four elements - a bubbling blue potion (water), a fiery red concoction (fire), a swirling gray mist (air), and a gritty brown paste (earth). Consuming a vial grants the PC resistance to a damage type associated with the chosen element for the next hour. (Water: Cold, Fire: Fire, Air: Lightning, Earth: Bludgeoning)

**Blood Moon Pie**: A crimson pie made from blood-red cherries and a hint of spice, with a lattice crust that resembles the Blood Moon's patterns. Consuming this pie grants an additional +1 bonus to saving throws against the Blood Moon's effects for the next 24 hours.

**Ghoul's Gravy Boat**: A thick, velvety gravy with a deep umami flavor, served in a boat carved to resemble a ghoul's face. After consuming this gravy, the PC gains advantage on checks to resist being frightened for the next hour.

**Phantom Phyllo Pastries**: Delicate pastries filled with a sweet pumpkin and cinnamon filling, shaped like little ghosts with currant eyes. Consuming a pastry allows the PC to cast the Minor Illusion cantrip once within the next hour.

**Witch's Brew Stew**: A hearty stew with chunks of meat, vegetables, and a secret blend of herbs, served in a mini cauldron. Steam rises from the stew in eerie shapes. After consuming the stew, the PC gains a +1 bonus to AC against spell attacks for the next hour.

**Cursed Caramel Apples**: Crisp apples coated in a glossy, dark caramel, with almond slivers as fangs, making them resemble vampire apples. Consuming an apple grants the PC the ability to see in the dark (Darkvision) up to a range of 60 feet for the next hour. If the PC already has Darkvision, its range is extended by 30 feet.

## Effects of Eating from the Dishes

PCs can choose to consume any or all of the dishes. However, consuming more than two dishes requires a DC 12 Constitution saving throw. On a failed save, the PC becomes nauseated and gains the poisoned condition for the next hour.

The +1 bonus to saving throws against the Blood Moon's effects from the Blood Moon Pie is cumulative with any other bonuses the PCs might have.

## Mingling with the Guests

Skill Challenge: PCs can use Persuasion or Insight checks to gather information from the attendees. A successful DC 15 check will reveal one piece of gossip or rumor from the list below. A failed check might result in the guest becoming suspicious or dismissive.

### Gossip and Rumors

"I heard that the witches were once beloved guardians of Moonsorrow, but they betrayed us."

"Some say that the Blood Moon is a source of immense power, and many dark sorcerers seek to harness it."

"There's a secret society that still worships the witches and conducts rituals in their honor in the Misty Woods."

"The Purifiers are recruiting. They're planning something big for the next Blood Moon."

"I've heard whispers of a demon lurking in the shadows, manipulating events in Moonsorrow."

## Purifier's Server - Elric

**Approach**: Elric will attempt a Stealth check (DC 15) to approach the PCs without drawing attention. If successful, he'll whisper his message. If he fails, a nearby guest will notice and comment on his suspicious behavior.

**Message**: "Beware the witches and their dark magic. They are the true curse upon this land. Join the Purifiers, and together we can cleanse Moonsorrow."

## Witch's Informant - Selene

**Approach**: If the PCs approach Selene, they must make a Perception check (DC 12). Success means they notice a small pendant shaped like a crescent moon around her neck, a symbol associated with the witches.

**Message**: "Not everything is as it seems. The Blood Moon's power is vast, but its true nature is misunderstood. Seek the demon that hides in the shadows, for it might be the puppeteer behind Moonsorrow's misfortunes."

## Observing the Feast's Guardian

**Observant Guardian**: The Feast's Guardian constantly scans the room, its gaze lingering on any PC or NPC that displays suspicious behavior. If a PC tries to communicate with it, the Guardian will turn its full attention to them, its eyes glowing faintly.

**Mysterious Aura**: Any PC within 10 feet of the Guardian feels a cold, otherworldly presence, accompanied by a faint whispering sound. This sensation can be unnerving, but it's not harmful.

**Gestured Communication**: The Guardian doesn't speak, but it can communicate through simple gestures. If asked a question, it might nod or shake its head, point in a certain direction, or make a motion to signify "stop" or "go away." It might also use its Withering Touch to emphasize a point, though not in a harmful way unless provoked.

**Protector of the Feast**: If a PC tries to disrupt the feast or harm another attendee, the Guardian will intervene, moving swiftly between the offender and their target. It will give one warning, raising a hand in a stopping motion. If the warning is ignored, it will take more direct action.

**Aid in Times of Need**: If the feast is attacked or if there's a significant threat, the Guardian will defend the attendees. If a PC is in dire need, they can attempt a DC 15 Charisma (Persuasion) check to enlist the Guardian's help. On a success, the Guardian will assist the PC for a short duration.

**Offering to the Guardian**: If a PC offers the Guardian a token of respect (like a portion of their meal or a small trinket), the Guardian might bestow a minor boon upon them, such as a temporary +1 bonus to AC or saving throws for the next hour.

**Memories of the Past**: If a PC uses a spell or ability to communicate with or probe the mind of the Guardian, they receive fragmented visions of past feasts, the witches' rituals, and the night of the Blood Moon. These visions are cryptic but might offer clues or hints about the witches or the Blood Moon's effects.

## Lair Actions

**Feast's Blessing**: The Feast's Guardian channels the power of the feast, granting all allies within the hall temporary 1d4 hit points for the next hour.

**Crimson Mist**: The hall fills with a dense, red mist, heavily obscuring the area and making it difficult terrain.

**Echoing Whispers**: The hall resonates with ghostly whispers, causing all creatures to have disadvantage on Wisdom saving throws until the next lair action.

## Scaling the Encounter

### Beginning Players (PC levels 1-5)

**Tasting the Elements**: Keep the Constitution saving throw DC at 12, but the poisoned condition should last only 10 minutes.

### Intermediate Players (PC levels 6-10)

**Tasting the Elements**: Increase the Constitution saving throw DC to 14.

### Advanced Players (PC levels 11+)

**Tasting the Elements**: Increase the Constitution saving throw DC to 16.

## Monster

Feast's Guardian

# Crimson Mask Parade

The Crimson Mask Parade is a significant event in Moonsorrow, symbolizing the town's resilience and hope in the face of the Blood Moon's curse. The parade is both a form of protection and a celebration, with participants donning masks of protective deities to ward off evil and spread blessings. The streets are lined with spectators, and the atmosphere is a mix of reverence and festivity.

As you make your way through the streets of Moonsorrow, the rhythmic beat of drums fills the air, accompanied by the melodic tunes of flutes and lyres. The townsfolk gather on either side of the main thoroughfare, their eyes filled with anticipation. Soon, a procession of individuals wearing ornate masks representing various protective deities begins to parade through the town. Each mask is a work of art, intricately designed and glowing with a faint ethereal light. The parade participants move gracefully, their steps synchronized with the music as they spread blessings and ward off evil spirits. Children run alongside, laughing and playing, while the elders watch with a sense of reverence. The Crimson Mask Parade, a symbol of hope and resilience, has begun.

## Activities in the Encounter

Use the parade to introduce the PCs to the town's culture and beliefs. It's an opportunity for roleplaying and interaction with the townsfolk.

**Mask Admiration**: PCs can admire and inquire about the various masks worn by the parade participants. Each mask has its own story and significance, and the townsfolk are eager to share.

**Blessings Received**: If PCs interact with the parade participants, they can receive a blessing. This blessing grants them a temporary +1 bonus to saving throws against fear effects for the next 24 hours.

**Mask Crafting**: There are stalls set up where PCs can craft or purchase their own masks. Crafting a good quality mask requires a DC 15 Dexterity check using artisan's tools or a DC 15 Intelligence (Arcana) check. A successfully crafted mask can be worn to gain advantage on Charisma (Persuasion) checks when interacting with the townsfolk during the festival.

**Dance and Music**: PCs can join in the dance or play music. A successful DC 12 Charisma (Performance) check can earn the admiration of the townsfolk and possibly some small gifts or tokens of appreciation.

## Mask Admiration

The masks worn by the parade participants are not just decorative; they are steeped in history, magic, and significance. Each mask represents a protective deity or spirit, and the townsfolk believe that wearing these masks during the Crimson Mask Parade grants them the deity's protection. The masks are passed down through generations, and each has its own unique story.

Inquiring About Masks: When a PC expresses interest in a particular mask, have them roll a Charisma (Persuasion) check to see how much information they can glean from the wearer or a nearby townsfolk.

**DC 10**: Basic information about the mask's representation and significance.

**DC 15**: A more detailed story about the mask's origin and any notable events associated with it.

**DC 20**: A hidden or lesser-known tale about the mask, possibly including hints about its magical properties or a secret ritual associated with it.

**Mask Abilities**: Some masks might have latent magical abilities that can be activated under certain conditions. If a PC shows exceptional interest or respect towards a mask, the wearer might allow them to borrow or even keep the mask, granting them its benefits.

**Learning from the Masks**: If a PC spends time studying and researching a mask (at least 1 hour), they can make an Intelligence (Arcana) or Intelligence (History) check.

**DC 15**: The PC learns about the deity or spirit the mask represents and gains advantage on their next Religion check related to that deity.

**DC 20**: The PC uncovers a hidden ritual or chant associated with the mask that, when performed, grants a temporary boon (e.g., a Bless spell or temporary hit points). No casting ability is required to benefit from this boon.

# Mask-Wearers in the Parade

## Eldric the Blacksmith

**Backstory**: A burly man with a heart of gold, Eldric forges weapons that defend Moonsorrow.

**Mask**: Mask of the Iron Witch

**Basic Tale**: The mask represents a witch who could meld and shape metal with her bare hands.

**Detailed Tale**: Legend says the Iron Witch was a close friend of Morana and helped fortify Moonsorrow against invaders.

**Hidden Tale**: The Iron Witch was rumored to be Morana's sister, who sacrificed her life to forge a weapon that could repel Helbindr.

**Mask Ability**: Grants the wearer a +1 bonus to AC.

**Learning: Deity**: Wodanstorm. Wodanstorm, the Warwind, is a deity who wields the power of storms in battle.

**Temporary Boon**: The wearer can cast *Shield* once without expending a spell slot.

## Liliana the Herbalist

**Backstory**: Liliana is known for her healing salves and once tended to a wounded witch in secret.

**Mask**: Mask of the Green Enchantress

**Basic Tale**: The mask symbolizes a witch who could speak to plants and heal any ailment.

**Detailed Tale**: The Green Enchantress was said to have a secret grove where she grew her magical herbs.

**Hidden Tale**: It's whispered that the grove still exists, hidden within the Misty Woods, and is guarded by the spirits of nature.

**Mask Ability**: Grants the wearer the ability to cast Goodberry once per day.

**Learning**: Deity: Druiwis. Druiwis, the Sage of the Grove, is a deity who embodies the union of knowledge and nature.

**Temporary Boon**: The wearer can cast Cure Wounds at 2nd level once without expending a spell slot.

## Nolan, the Town's Storyteller

**Backstory**: Nolan travels from town to town, sharing tales of the witches and the history of Moonsorrow.

**Mask**: Mask of the Whispering Shadows

**Basic Tale**: This mask represents the spirits that whisper ancient tales to those who listen closely.

**Detailed Tale**: The spirits are believed to be the ancestors of Moonsorrow, guiding and protecting their descendants.

**Hidden Tale**: Some say that on the night of the Blood Moon, the spirits can be seen dancing alongside the living.

**Mask Ability**: Grants the wearer advantage on Charisma (Performance) checks.

**Learning**: Deity: Gwynsight. Gwynsight, the Beacon of Wisdom, is a deity who illuminates the minds of mortals with the light of knowledge.

**Temporary Boon**: The wearer can cast *Comprehend Languages* once without expending a spell slot.

## Serena the Weaver

**Backstory**: Serena crafts the finest garments in Moonsorrow and once wove a cloak for a witch in disguise.

**Mask**: Mask of the Silken Web

**Basic Tale**: The mask honors a witch who could weave spells into her creations.

**Detailed Tale**: This witch was said to have woven the very fabric of fate, determining the destiny of Moonsorrow.

**Hidden Tale**: Rumors suggest that the witch's loom still exists, and whoever controls it can alter fate itself.

**Mask Ability**: Grants the wearer advantage on Dexterity checks involving tools (tool proficiency not required, but the check must be one for which tool proficiency can improve the result).

**Learning**: Deity: Skuldrún. Skuldrún, the Weaver of Fates, is a deity who intertwines the threads of knowledge and death. She is often depicted holding a loom, weaving the destinies of mortals and gods alike, with whispers of ancient secrets and the finality of death intertwined in each thread.

**Temporary Boon**: The wearer can cast *Mage Armor* once without expending a spell slot.

## Rosalind the Baker

**Backstory**: Rosalind's pastries are the talk of Moonsorrow, and legend has it she once baked a pie using a recipe given to her by a witch.

**Mask**: Mask of the Golden Crust

**Basic Tale**: This mask celebrates a witch who could turn any meal into a feast with a touch of her hand.

**Detailed Tale**: The Golden Crust Witch was known to feed the hungry during harsh winters, ensuring no one in Moonsorrow went to bed with an empty stomach.

**Hidden Tale**: It's whispered that the witch's oven, hidden deep in the Misty Woods, could bake bread that grants wishes.

**Mask Ability**: Grants the wearer advantage on Constitution saving throws against poison.

**Learning**: Deity: Solwen. Solwen, the Radiant Lifegiver, is a benevolent deity who brings forth life and light to the world.

**Temporary Boon**: The wearer can cast *Purify Food and Drink* once without expending a spell slot.

## Blessings Received

As the parade progresses, the participants chant and sing hymns dedicated to the protective deities. PCs who show genuine interest and engage with the parade participants can receive a special blessing.

**Interaction**: A PC must spend at least 10 minutes interacting with parade participants, showing respect and interest in the traditions and stories of the masks. This can be done through roleplay or a successful DC 12 Charisma (Persuasion) check.

**Blessing Ritual**: A parade participant will then approach the PC, placing a hand on their shoulder and reciting the prayer of the Crimson Veil. The PC's mask (if they're wearing one) or forehead will be marked with a symbol representing protection against fear.

**Effect**: For the next 24 hours, the blessed PC gains a +1 bonus to saving throws against being frightened. This effect is not cumulative with other similar effects.

## Prayer of the Crimson Veil

By the light of the Blood Moon's glow,
Through ancient rites and tales we know,
Fear not the shadows, nor the night's cold embrace,
For protection is granted, in this sacred place.

Deities of old, guardians true,
We call upon your strength anew.
Shield this soul from dread and fear,
Let courage prevail, as the Blood Moon draws near.

## Mask Crafting at the Crimson Mask Parade

**Location**: Several stalls are scattered throughout the parade route, each adorned with an array of tools, materials, and enchanting components. The air is filled with the scent of fresh paint, wood, and a hint of magical essence.

### Crafting a Mask

PCs can approach a stall to craft their own mask. The stall owner, a skilled mask artisan, will guide them through the process.

**Designing the Mask**: PCs can choose a design that represents a protective deity, a personal totem, or any other symbol they feel connected to. This design will influence the mask's final appearance and potential abilities.

**Crafting the Mask**: Successful crafting requires a DC 15 Dexterity check using artisan's tools (more specifically, painter's supplies or woodcarver's tools, but others could also be applied) to shape, paint, and detail the mask. Those with a magical inclination can instead attempt to infuse the mask with a touch of enchantment, requiring a DC 15 Intelligence (Arcana) check.

**Mask Abilities**: A successfully crafted mask grants the wearer advantage on Charisma (Persuasion) checks when interacting with the townsfolk during the festival. This represents the townsfolk's appreciation for the effort and respect shown in participating in their tradition.

### Purchasing a Mask

For those who prefer not to craft, pre-made masks are available for purchase. These masks come in various designs and range in price from 5 silver pieces to 5 gold pieces, depending on the intricacy and any inherent magical properties.

**Mask of the Ember Moth** (5 silver pieces)

**Description**: A delicate mask made of thin, translucent material that resembles the wings of a moth. It glows faintly with a warm, ember-like light.

**Effect**: While wearing this mask, the user emits dim light in a 5-foot radius. It can be activated or deactivated with a command word.

**Mask of the Silent Owl** (1 gold piece)

**Description**: Carved from light wood and painted with the likeness of an owl, this mask has feathers adorning its edges and large, glassy eyes.

**Effect**: Grants the wearer advantage on Wisdom (Perception) checks that rely on hearing for up to 1 hour, once per day.

**Mask of the Enchanted Grove** (2 gold pieces)

**Description**: A mask made of intertwined vines and flowers, with a fresh, earthy scent. Tiny, luminescent spores occasionally drift from it.

**Effect**: Once per day, the wearer can cast the *Druidcraft* cantrip without requiring any components.

**Mask of the Gilded Serpent** (3 gold pieces)

**Description**: A golden mask shaped like a coiled serpent, with ruby eyes and intricate scale patterns.

**Effect**: While wearing this mask, the user gains resistance to poison damage and advantage on saving throws against being poisoned for up to 1 hour, once per day.

**Mask of the Ethereal Veil** (5 gold pieces)

**Description**: This mask appears to be made of shimmering, translucent material that constantly shifts in color. It feels weightless to the touch.

**Effect**: Once per day, as an action, the wearer can become ethereal (as per the *Etherealness* spell) for up to 1 minute. The effect ends early if the wearer removes the mask.

These masks are designed to be single-use per day to maintain balance.

## Special Masks

Some stalls might offer rare materials or enchantments for a higher price. These special masks can grant additional temporary abilities, such as:

**Mask of the Whispering Wind (900 gold pieces)**: While wearing this mask, the user can cast the *Message* cantrip at will.

**Mask of the Night's Eyes (100 gold pieces)**: This mask grants the wearer Darkvision up to a range of 60 feet for 1 hour, once per day.

**Mask of the Fearful Aura (1,200 gold pieces)**: Once per day, as an action, the wearer can exude an aura of fear. Creatures within a 10-foot radius must succeed on a DC 13 Wisdom saving throw or be frightened for 1 minute.

# Dance and Music at the Crimson Mask Parade

As the parade progresses, various groups of townsfolk form circles and start dancing to the rhythm of traditional Moonsorrow tunes. Musicians with lutes, flutes, and drums play energetically, encouraging everyone to join in.

## Participating in the Dance

PCs can choose to join any of the dancing circles. To successfully follow the dance steps and impress the townsfolk, they must make a Charisma (Performance) check.

**DC 12**: The PC dances gracefully, earning nods of approval and claps from the onlookers.

**DC 18**: The PC not only follows the steps but adds their own flair, becoming the center of attention. They are cheered on, and a few townsfolk might approach them afterward to commend their skills.

**Fail**: The PC stumbles or misses a step. While some townsfolk might chuckle, most appreciate the effort and encourage the PC to keep going.

## Playing Music

PCs proficient with musical instruments can join the musicians. To harmonize with the traditional tunes and stand out, they must make a Charisma (Performance) check.

**DC 12**: The PC plays in tune, adding to the festive atmosphere. They receive appreciative nods from fellow musicians.

**DC 18**: The PC's music is captivating. Their melodies resonate with the crowd, and they might even be given a solo moment, earning them loud cheers.

**Fail**: The PC struggles to keep up or plays off-key notes. However, the spirit of the festival means they're met with encouraging smiles and gentle guidance from fellow musicians.

## Lair Actions

**Ethereal Glow**: Every other round, the masks worn by parade participants emit a soft glow, illuminating a 30-foot radius. Any evil spirits or entities within this radius must make a DC 15 Wisdom saving throw or be repelled, unable to enter the illuminated area.

**Protective Barrier**: Once during the parade, if the town is threatened, the combined energy of the masks can create a protective magical barrier around a 60-foot radius area. This barrier lasts for 1 minute and requires a DC 20 Strength check to break through.

**Spiritual Communion**: The masks allow wearers to commune with the protective deities they represent. Once during the parade, a wearer can seek guidance or a sign from their deity, gaining advantage on one Wisdom (Insight) or Intelligence (Religion) check.

## Scaling the Encounter

### Beginning Players (PC levels 1-5)

**Mask Crafting**: Lower the DC for crafting a mask to 12.

**Dance and Music**: Lower the DC for Charisma (Performance) checks to 10.

**Inquiring About Masks**: Lower the DCs by 2 for all levels of information.

**Lair Actions**: For the Ethereal Glow, reduce the Wisdom saving throw DC to 12. For the Protective Barrier, reduce the Strength check DC to 15.

### Intermediate Players (PC levels 6-10)

**Mask Crafting**: Keep the DC for crafting a mask at 15.

**Dance and Music**: Keep the DC for Charisma (Performance) checks at 12.

**Inquiring About Masks**: Maintain the DCs as they are.

**Lair Actions**: Keep the DCs as they are.

### Advanced Players (PC levels 11+)

**Mask Crafting**: Increase the DC for crafting a mask to 18.

**Dance and Music**: Increase the DC for Charisma (Performance) checks to 15.

**Inquiring About Masks**: Increase the DCs by 2 for all levels of information.

**Lair Actions**: For the Ethereal Glow, increase the Wisdom saving throw DC to 18. For the Protective Barrier, increase the Strength check DC to 23.

# Veil's Labyrinth

The Veil's Labyrinth is a test of mental fortitude and self-awareness. While the physical path through the maze might not be overly complex, the emotional and psychological challenges posed by the illusions can be daunting. This encounter is designed to give players a chance to confront and roleplay through their characters' innermost fears, regrets, and desires.

Before you stands the entrance to the Veil's Labyrinth, a towering archway draped in crimson veils that flutter softly in the breeze. Beyond the entrance, a series of tall, red-veiled partitions stretch out, forming the walls of a maze. The air is thick with anticipation, and you can hear the distant murmurs of those already navigating its twists and turns. A sign near the entrance reads: "Face your fears, confront your desires, and find your way to the center. A prize awaits those who persevere."

## Activities in the Encounter

**Entering the Labyrinth**: Players can choose to enter the maze individually or as a group. If they choose to go in as a group, they will face shared illusions based on the group's collective experiences and fears.

**Confronting Illusions**: As players navigate the maze, they will encounter illusions tailored to each of their characters' backstories and personal fears/desires. These can range from seeing a loved one in danger, confronting a past failure, or being tempted by a deep desire. Players must make a DC 15 Wisdom saving throw to see through the illusion. On a failed save, they believe the illusion to be real and might act accordingly.

**Reaching the Center**: The center of the maze holds a pedestal with a small prize - a crystal vial containing a silvery liquid. This is Elixir of Clarity, which grants the drinker advantage on Wisdom saving throws for the next hour.

## Labyrinth of Shadows Trap

**Description**: Deep within the heart of the Veil's Labyrinth, past the red-veiled partitions, lies the Labyrinth of Shadows. This section is distinct, marked by walls that aren't made of veils but of ever-shifting, intangible shadows. These shadows move and change, creating a maze that seems to have a mind of its own. As adventurers navigate this section, they'll find that the paths constantly change, leading them in circles or into dead ends.

**Trigger**: Upon entering the central chamber of the Veil's Labyrinth, adventurers will notice beyond the pedestal bearing the prize a large, ornate archway leading to what appears to be another labyrinth, this one bathed in alternating shadows. This is the Labyrinth of Shadows, to which crossing this archway activates the trap, causing the shadows within to start shifting.

**Effect**: At the start of each player's turn, the maze shifts, changing the layout. This can cause paths to close, open, or lead in entirely new directions. Players might find themselves separated from their group or facing a dead end where a path once was. The shifting is disorienting, and players must succeed on a DC 15 Wisdom saving throw at the start of their turn or lose their action that turn due to disorientation. The DM determines which way the maze changes.

**Detection**: A DC 18 Wisdom (Perception) check allows a player to notice the subtle movement of the shadows before entering the trapped section. A DC 20 Intelligence (Investigation) check reveals the shadowy nature of the walls and the potential dangers of the shifting maze.

**Disable**: A DC 18 Intelligence (Arcana) check allows a player to stabilize the shadows temporarily, preventing them from shifting for 1 minute. Casting a spell that produces bright light (such as Daylight) within the Labyrinth of Shadows will suppress the trap's effects for the duration of the spell.

## Lair Actions

On initiative count 20 (losing initiative ties), the Veil's Labyrinth takes a lair action to cause one of the following effects:

**Shifting Walls**: The veiled partitions move, changing the layout of the maze. Paths that were open might become closed, and dead ends might now lead to new passages.

**Deepening Shadows**: The maze becomes darker, reducing visibility to 10 feet. This effect lasts until the next lair action.

**Whispers of the Past**: Faint whispers fill the air, recounting past failures, regrets, or fears of one of the characters. The targeted character must succeed on a DC 14 Wisdom saving throw or be frightened until the next lair action.

## Scaling the Encounter

### Beginning Players (PC levels 1-5)

**Confronting Illusions**: Lower the DC for the Wisdom saving throw to see through the illusion to DC 12.

**Labyrinth of Shadows Trap**: Reduce the Wisdom saving throw to avoid disorientation to DC 12.

**Lair Actions**: For the "Whispers of the Past" action, reduce the Wisdom saving throw to DC 11.

### Intermediate Players (PC levels 6-10)

**Confronting Illusions**: Maintain the DC for the Wisdom saving throw to see through the illusion at DC 15.

**Labyrinth of Shadows Trap**: Maintain the Wisdom saving throw to avoid disorientation at DC 15.

**Lair Actions**: For the "Whispers of the Past" action, maintain the Wisdom saving throw at DC 14.

### Advanced Players (PC levels 11+)

**Confronting Illusions**: Increase the DC for the Wisdom saving throw to see through the illusion to DC 18.

**Labyrinth of Shadows Trap**: Increase the Wisdom saving throw to avoid disorientation to DC 18.

**Lair Actions**: For the "Whispers of the Past" action, increase the Wisdom saving throw to DC 16.

# Warding Rune Workshop

The Warding Rune Workshop is a proactive measure taken by the townsfolk of Moonsorrow to protect themselves from the icy shadows and malevolent spirits that have plagued their land since the emergence of the Blood Moon. The workshop is a bustling hub of activity, with artisans and mages guiding attendees in the crafting of protective runes and talismans. These symbols of protection are believed to ward off the negative effects of the Blood Moon and keep the icy shadows at bay.

As you approach the town square, you notice a large tented area bustling with activity. Tables are set up with various tools, inks, and materials. Artisans and mages, some in elaborate robes, guide townsfolk in the delicate art of crafting runes and talismans. The air is filled with a sense of urgency, but also hope. Children and adults alike sit focused, carefully inscribing symbols onto pieces of parchment, wood, and metal. Nearby, a large board displays various rune designs, each labeled with its protective properties.

## Activities

**Rune Crafting**: PCs can join a table and attempt to craft their own protective rune. This requires a DC 15 Intelligence (Arcana) check. Success means they've crafted a rune that grants them a +1 bonus to saving throws against the effects of the Blood Moon for the next 24 hours.

**Talisman Creation**: For those more artistically inclined, they can attempt to craft a protective talisman. This requires a DC 15 Dexterity check using artisan's tools (which could include calligrapher's, smith's, jeweler's, woodcarver's, leatherworker's, and painter's tools, but others could also be applied). A successful creation grants the wearer advantage on saving throws against being frightened for the next 24 hours.

**Rune Lore**: PCs can converse with the mages to learn more about the history and significance of the runes. This can provide them with insights into the deeper lore of Moonsorrow and the Blood Moon.

# Rune Lore

## Rune of Skuldrún

**History**: This rune is believed to have been crafted by the ancient seers of Moonsorrow, who sought to understand the mysteries of life and death. It is said that those who bear this rune can glimpse the threads of fate that Skuldrún herself weaves.

**Effect**: When inscribed on a weapon or piece of armor, this rune grants the bearer advantage on Wisdom (Insight) checks related to determining a creature's intentions or predicting its next move.

**Lore Check**: A DC 15 Intelligence (Religion) check reveals the deeper connection between Skuldrún and the inevitability of fate, hinting that those who understand her teachings might be able to alter their own destinies.

**Visual Description**: A vertical line intersected by a horizontal line near the top, forming a "T" shape. At each end of the horizontal line, there's a small circle, representing the loom's spools. Below the intersection, a small skull is etched.

## Rune of Solwen

**History**: This rune has been used for centuries by the healers and clerics of Moonsorrow to channel Solwen's radiant energy, bringing warmth and light to those in need.

**Effect**: When inscribed on a weapon or piece of armor, this rune grants the bearer the ability to cast the Light cantrip once per day.

**Lore Check**: A DC 14 Intelligence (Religion) check reveals tales of Solwen's eternal battle against darkness, and how her followers harness her power to bring hope to the world.

**Visual Description**: A circle representing the sun, with eight rays extending outward. Inside the circle, at the bottom, there's a small upward-pointing triangle, symbolizing the flame.

## Rune of Aelstorm

**History**: Druids and rangers of Moonsorrow have long used this rune to call upon Aelstorm's power, seeking his guidance when navigating the wilds or summoning the forces of nature.

**Effect**: When inscribed on a weapon or piece of armor, this rune grants the bearer resistance to lightning damage.

**Lore Check**: A DC 16 Intelligence (Nature) check uncovers legends of Aelstorm's tempestuous nature and his role in maintaining the balance of the natural world.

**Visual Description**: A vertical line with three horizontal lines intersecting it at different points, representing lightning. To the left of the vertical line, there's a half-circle (like a "C"), symbolizing a leaf.

## Rune of Lughstrat

**History**: Warriors and rogues have etched this rune onto their weapons and armor for generations, hoping to channel Lughstrat's cunning and strategic prowess in battle.

**Effect**: When inscribed on a weapon, it grants the bearer the ability to cast the Minor Illusion cantrip once per day.

**Lore Check**: A DC 15 Intelligence (History) check reveals tales of Lughstrat's legendary battles and how he used deception to outwit even the mightiest of foes.

**Visual Description**: A horizontal oval (like a mask) with two triangles pointing outward on either side at the center, representing eyes. Below the oval, a straight line extends downward, ending in a sharp point, symbolizing the sword.

## Rune of Gwynsight

**History**: Scholars and wizards revere this rune, believing it to be a gift from Gwynsight herself, illuminating the path to knowledge and wisdom.

**Effect**: When inscribed on a tome or scroll, this rune grants the bearer advantage on Intelligence (Arcana) checks related to ancient lore or magical research.

**Lore Check**: A DC 14 Intelligence (Arcana) check uncovers stories of Gwynsight's quest for knowledge and her role in preserving the ancient wisdom of the world.

**Visual Description**: A vertical torch with a flame on top. The torch's handle is a rectangle, and the flame is represented by an upward-pointing triangle. To the right of the torch, there's a small square, symbolizing the book.

## Rune of Thoralux

**History**: This rune is often found in temples and sacred groves dedicated to Thoralux. It is believed that the rune was first used by stormcallers, a sect of clerics who revered Thoralux and sought to harness the raw power of the stormlit skies.

**Effect**: When inscribed on a weapon or piece of armor, this rune grants the bearer the ability to cast *Thunderwave* as a 1st-level spell once per day.

**Lore Check**: A DC 16 Intelligence (Religion) check reveals ancient hymns sung in honor of Thoralux, detailing his dominion over both the calm and fury of the skies, and how he uses these forces to reveal hidden truths.

**Visual Description**: A circle with jagged lines extending from the top, representing the storm cloud. Inside the circle, at the bottom, there's a smaller circle radiating lines, symbolizing the radiant orb.

### Rune of Wodanstorm

**History**: This rune's origins trace back to the legendary Warwind warriors, a group of fierce fighters who believed they were the chosen of Wodanstorm. They would etch this rune onto their shields and banners, charging into battle with the force of a tempest.

**Effect**: When inscribed on a shield or piece of armor, this rune grants the bearer the ability to cast the *Gust of Wind* spell once per day.

**Lore Check**: A DC 17 Intelligence (History) check uncovers tales of the Warwind warriors and their unyielding loyalty to Wodanstorm, believing that with every gust and gale, the deity was guiding their path in battle.

**Visual Description**: A curved line on the left, representing the gale, with a square to its right. Inside the square, there's a smaller triangle pointing upward, symbolizing the shield's protective aspect.

## Lair Actions

On initiative count 20 (losing initiative ties), the Blood Moon's influence causes one of the following effects; the DM chooses the effect or determines it randomly.

**Chill Wind**: A cold gust of wind sweeps through the workshop, causing unprotected flames to flicker and die. Any PC currently crafting must succeed on a DC 12 Constitution saving throw or be disrupted, needing to start their crafting over.

**Shadowy Whispers**: Eerie whispers fill the air, distracting those in the workshop. For the next round, all crafting checks are made with disadvantage.

**Faint Glow**: All completed runes and talismans in the vicinity glow faintly for a moment, signaling their potency and effectiveness against the Blood Moon's effects.

## Scaling the Encounter

### Beginning Players (PC levels 1-5)

**Rune Crafting**: Lower the DC for the Intelligence (Arcana) check to craft a protective rune to DC 12.

**Talisman Creation**: Lower the DC for the Dexterity check using artisan's tools to craft a protective talisman to DC 12.

**Rune Lore**: Reduce all lore check DCs by 2.

**Lair Actions**: For the "Chill Wind" action, reduce the Constitution saving throw to DC 10.

### Intermediate Players (PC levels 6-10)

**Rune Crafting**: Maintain the DC for the Intelligence (Arcana) check to craft a protective rune at DC 15.

**Talisman Creation**: Maintain the DC for the Dexterity check using artisan's tools to craft a protective talisman at DC 15.

**Rune Lore**: Maintain the current lore check DCs.

**Lair Actions**: For the "Chill Wind" action, maintain the Constitution saving throw at DC 12.

### Advanced Players (PC levels 11+)

**Rune Crafting**: Increase the DC for the Intelligence (Arcana) check to craft a protective rune to DC 18.

**Talisman Creation**: Increase the DC for the Dexterity check using artisan's tools to craft a protective talisman to DC 18.

**Rune Lore**: Increase all lore check DCs by 2.

**Lair Actions**: For the "Chill Wind" action, increase the Constitution saving throw to DC 14.

# Witching Hour Vigil

As midnight approaches on the eve of the Blood Moon, attendees gather around a massive bonfire. They share stories, sing ancient hymns, and watch the sky, awaiting the Blood Moon's ascent.

As the clock nears midnight, the town square of Moonsorrow is bathed in an eerie, anticipatory silence. A massive bonfire crackles and roars at the center, casting dancing shadows upon the cobblestone streets and the faces of the townsfolk gathered around. The orange and red flames reach skyward, as if trying to touch the stars. The air is thick with tension, and the scent of burning wood mingles with the faint aroma of incense. Everyone's eyes are turned upwards, watching, waiting for the Blood Moon's ascent.

## Activities

**Story Sharing**: Townsfolk take turns sharing tales of past Blood Moon events, legends of the witches, and personal experiences. The stories range from heartwarming to spine-chilling. Some even bring props or wear costumes to make their tales more vivid.

**Ancient Hymns**: A group of elderly villagers lead the crowd in singing ancient hymns that speak of hope, protection, and the cycles of life and death. The melodies are hauntingly beautiful, echoing through the night.

**Sky Watching**: Many attendees simply sit or stand in silent contemplation, their gazes fixed on the horizon, waiting for the first glimpse of the Blood Moon.

**Moonlit Offerings**: Attendees are encouraged to write down their fears or wishes on paper and cast them into the bonfire, seeking blessings or protection from the Blood Moon.

## Story Sharing

Below are campfire stories the people of Moonsorrow will share surrounding the events of the Blood Moon:

### The Tale of the Lost Child

**Speaker**: Old Man Ealdred, a wrinkled elder with a long white beard.

**Props**: A small, worn-out doll with a red ribbon.

**Story**: Ealdred steps forward, holding the doll gently in his hands. "Many moons ago, during a particularly eerie Blood Moon, my granddaughter went missing. We searched high and low, but she was nowhere to be found. As the night wore on, we heard her voice, singing a lullaby that her mother used to sing. Following the voice, we found her sitting in a clearing, the doll beside her. She claimed the witches had kept her company and sang with her to keep her calm. She found her way back with their guidance. I believe the witches aren't all bad; they have their reasons, and they too care for Moonsorrow."

### The Whispering Shadows

**Speaker**: Liora, a young woman with raven-black hair.

**Props**: A tattered shawl that she drapes over her shoulders.

**Story**: Liora steps up, her eyes filled with a mix of fear and wonder. "Last Blood Moon, I was returning home late from the market. As I walked, the shadows around me began to whisper. At first, I thought it was just the wind, but then I realized they were speaking in old tongues. I draped this shawl over me, a gift from my grandmother, and the whispers turned into soft lullabies, guiding me safely home. I believe these shadows are the trapped souls, trying to communicate, and they respond to the relics of the past."

### The Dance of the Witches

**Speaker**: Bran, a middle-aged bard with a lute.

**Props**: His lute, which he plays a haunting melody on.

**Story**: With a strum of his lute, Bran captures the attention of all. "Years ago, I ventured close to the Misty Woods during a Blood Moon. There, in a clearing, I saw them - the three witches, dancing in a circle, their forms ethereal and glowing. They danced to a melody that seemed older than time, their voices harmonizing in a song of sorrow and hope. As I watched, hidden, I felt a deep sense of understanding. They were not celebrating the Blood Moon but trying to combat its effects, to bring balance back. I composed this melody in their honor." He then plays a tune that resonates with the very essence of Moonsorrow's history.

### The Haunting of Widow's Lane

**Speaker**: Thorne, a tall, gaunt man with piercing blue eyes.

**Props**: A rusted lantern that emits a faint, ghostly glow.

**Story**: Thorne steps forward, the eerie light from his lantern casting shadows on his face. "On a Blood Moon night, just like this, I dared to walk down Widow's Lane. It's said that the spirits of those who've lost their loved ones to the Blood Moon wander there. As I walked, the wind carried mournful wails and sobbing. Then, out of the mist, ghostly apparitions appeared, reaching out, their faces twisted in eternal sorrow. I barely escaped with my sanity, and this lantern," he raises the prop, "is said to be the only thing that can ward them off."

### The Curse of the Bloodied Hands

**Speaker**: Elara, a woman dressed in a blood-red cloak.

**Props**: White gloves stained with red dye to resemble blood.

**Story**: Elara, her hands hidden beneath her cloak, begins her tale with a hushed voice. "There's an old house, abandoned now, at the edge of Moonsorrow. Legend says that a woman once lived there, who, under the influence of the Blood Moon, took the lives of her family. Now, every Blood Moon, she returns, her hands forever stained with the blood of her kin, searching for new victims. They say if you hear a knock on your door during the Blood Moon, never answer, for it might be her, seeking to share her curse." As she finishes, she reveals her bloodied gloves, sending a shiver down the spines of the listeners.

### The Pumpkin-Headed Specter

**Speaker**: Faelan, a mischievous young man with a flair for the dramatic.

**Props**: A carved pumpkin with a terrifying face, illuminated from within.

**Story**: With a grin, Faelan places the glowing pumpkin on a stool. "We've all carved pumpkins during this season, haven't we? But there's one pumpkin you never want to carve. Deep in the Misty Woods, there's a patch where the pumpkins grow unnaturally large. If you carve one and place a candle within, at the stroke of midnight, the Pumpkin-Headed Specter arises. It seeks out the one who carved its face, its hollow eyes burning with blue fire, and drags them back to the patch, where they become a pumpkin, waiting for the next unfortunate soul to carve them."

## Ancient Hymns

The elderly villagers, known as the "Moonsorrow Chanters," gather at the center of the vigil. They wear robes adorned with symbols representing the cycles of life, death, and the elements. Each chanter holds a lit candle, the flames dancing in the cool night breeze. As they begin to sing, the very air seems to vibrate with the power of their voices.

**Effect on Listeners**: Any PC who stops to listen to the hymns feels a deep sense of calm and connection to the land of Moonsorrow. They gain a temporary boon: for the next hour, they have advantage on saving throws against being frightened.

**Knowledge Check**: A PC with proficiency in History or Religion can make a DC 15 check. On a success, they recognize some of the hymns as traditional protective chants, likely predating the Blood Moon curse. This knowledge might hint at the deeper history of Moonsorrow and the true nature of the witches.

**Participation**: If a PC wishes to join in the singing, they can make a DC 12 Charisma (Performance) check. On a success, the Moonsorrow Chanters appreciate their effort and might share a personal story or piece of lore about the Blood Moon. On a failure, the Chanters politely correct the PC's pronunciation or rhythm but appreciate the gesture nonetheless.

## Hymns

### Moon's Lament

In the shadow of the crimson glow,

We stand united, our spirits flow.

From life to death and back again,

Moonsorrow's heart shall never wane.

Guardians three, watch over thee,

Protect us from the icy spree.

In the dance of light and shadow's might,

We find hope, in the darkest night.

### Helbindr's Domain

In the depths of Niflshadow's cold,

Where shadows merge and tales are told,

Helbindr sits on a throne so grand,

Judging souls in that icy land.

With wings of frost and eyes so bright,

He rules the realm with shadowy might.

But we of Moonsorrow stand tall and true,

For our spirits are strong, and our hearts renewed.

### Dawn of Hope

Though night may fall and shadows spread,

And icy whispers fill us with dread,

We hold a truth, deep in our core,

The curse will lift, and joy will soar.

For every dusk, there comes a dawn,

And every ending, a new song is drawn.

In Moonsorrow's heart, hope does stay,

Believing the Blood Moon's curse will fade away.

## Sky Watching

As the attendees gather, their gazes fixed on the horizon, the vast expanse of the night sky reveals itself, dotted with twinkling stars that form constellations representing the deities of Moonsorrow. The constellations serve as a reminder of the ancient tales and legends that have shaped the beliefs and traditions of the land.

## Constellations

**Skuldrún's Loom**: Structure: A series of stars forming a "T" shape, with two bright stars at the ends of the horizontal line and a cluster of stars below the intersection, resembling a skull. It is said that Skuldrún weaves the destinies of all on her celestial loom, and those who gaze upon her constellation are granted a momentary glimpse into the threads of their own fate.

**Solwen's Radiance**: Structure: A bright circle of stars with eight rays extending outward, and a triangle of stars within, pointing upwards. Legend speaks of a time when darkness consumed the land, and it was Solwen's radiant light that guided the lost souls back to the warmth of life.

**Aelstorm's Tempest**: A vertical line of stars with three horizontal lines intersecting it, and a half-circle of stars to its left. The constellation tells the tale of Aelstorm's fury, a storm so powerful it reshaped the landscapes, but also brought life-giving rain to the parched earth.

**Lughstrat's Deception**: An oval of stars with two triangles in the center and a line of stars extending downward from below the oval. Lughstrat once used his cunning to outwit a great beast that threatened

Moonsorrow, using only a mask and his sword. His constellation serves as a reminder of the power of strategy and deception.

**Gwynsight's Beacon**: A vertical line of stars with a triangle on top, and a square of stars to its right. Gwynsight's constellation shines the brightest when seekers of knowledge are in need of guidance, illuminating their path with wisdom.

**Thoralux's Illumination**: A circle of stars with jagged lines extending from the top and a smaller circle within, radiating lines. Thoralux once lit up the darkest night with a storm of radiant energy, revealing hidden truths and dispelling shadows. His constellation is a beacon of hope in the darkest times.

**Wodanstorm's Gale**: A curved line of stars on the left side, with a square formation to its right. Inside the square, a triangle of stars points upward. The constellation tells of a great battle where Wodanstorm summoned a fierce gale, using it as a strategic advantage to shield his warriors and push back their adversaries. His constellation serves as a reminder of the unpredictable nature of war and the elements.

## Moonlit Offerings

As the Blood Moon rises, casting its eerie crimson glow over the land, a tradition of Moonsorrow is to make moonlit offerings. Attendees gather around the massive bonfire, holding pieces of parchment upon which they've inscribed their deepest fears, regrets, or wishes. With a whispered prayer or chant, they cast these papers into the flames, seeking protection, blessings, or simply a chance to let go of burdens.

**Writing the Offering**: Each PC is given a piece of parchment. They can choose to write down a fear they wish to overcome, a regret they wish to let go of, or a wish they hope will come true.

**Casting into the Bonfire**: Once written, the PC approaches the bonfire and, if they wish, speaks a short prayer or chant (this can be roleplayed by the player or simply stated). They then cast the parchment into the flames.

**Protective Blessing**:

- If a fear is written and cast into the fire, the PC gains advantage on saving throws against being frightened for the next 24 hours.

- If a regret is written and cast into the fire, the PC feels a weight lifted from their shoulders and gains a temporary hit point boost of +5 for the next 24 hours.

- If a wish is written and cast into the fire, the outcome is at the DM's discretion. It could be a hint about a future event, a temporary boon (like advantage on their next skill check), or even just a feeling of hope that boosts their morale.

## Lair Actions

**Mystical Wind**: Every other round, a sudden gust of wind sweeps through the square, causing the bonfire to flare up dramatically. This wind carries whispered voices, which can be heard by those with a passive Perception of 15 or higher. The voices speak of ancient rites and the need for unity.

**Shadow Play**: The flames of the bonfire occasionally cast strange, almost lifelike shadows on the surrounding buildings and streets. These shadows seem to reenact moments from the tales being told, giving a visual representation to the stories.

**Blood Moon's Approach**: As midnight draws closer, the ambient light in the area begins to take on a faint reddish hue. This effect becomes more pronounced as the Blood Moon nears its zenith, bathing everything in a crimson glow.

## Scaling the Encounter
### Beginning Players (PC levels 1-5)

**Story Sharing**: Keep the stories as they are but allow for more player interaction. Encourage players to ask questions or share their own tales.

**Ancient Hymns**: Lower the DC for the Knowledge Check to 12. If a PC wishes to join in the singing, they can make a DC 10 Charisma (Performance) check.

**Sky Watching**: Constellations can be identified with a DC 10 Intelligence (Nature) or (History) check.

**Moonlit Offerings**: The Protective Blessing remains the same.

**Lair Actions**: For the "Mystical Wind" action, those with a passive Perception of 13 or higher hear the whispered voices.

### Intermediate Players (PC levels 6-10)

**Story Sharing**: Introduce minor challenges or puzzles related to the stories for added engagement.

**Ancient Hymns**: Maintain the current Knowledge Check DCs. If a PC wishes to join in the singing, they can make a DC 12 Charisma (Performance) check.

**Sky Watching**: Constellations can be identified with a DC 15 Intelligence (Nature) or (History) check.

**Moonlit Offerings**: The Protective Blessing remains the same.

**Lair Actions**: For the "Mystical Wind" action, maintain the passive Perception requirement at 15.

### Advanced Players (PC levels 11+)

**Story Sharing**: Introduce more complex challenges or puzzles related to the stories. Perhaps some stories have hidden clues or prophecies.

**Ancient Hymns**: Increase the DC for the Knowledge Check to 17. If a PC wishes to join in the singing, they can make a DC 14 Charisma (Performance) check.

**Sky Watching**: Constellations can be identified with a DC 18 Intelligence (Nature) or (History) check.

**Moonlit Offerings**: Introduce potential consequences for the Protective Blessing, such as drawing the attention of a malevolent spirit or entity.

**Lair Actions**: For the "Mystical Wind" action, only those with a passive Perception of 17 or higher hear the whispered voices.

# The Plain Shoe Tavern

A place where locals meet to exchange stories about the Blood Moon. It is also a place where the Purifiers meet.

As you push open the creaky wooden door of the Plain Shoe Tavern, a warm, inviting glow from the hearth greets you. The air is thick with the aroma of roasted meats and freshly baked bread. The tavern is abuzz with chatter, laughter, and the clinking of mugs. Locals huddle around tables, animatedly discussing tales of the Blood Moon, while in a corner, a group dressed in matching cloaks whispers among themselves, casting suspicious glances around the room.

## Activities in the Encounter

**The Plain Shoe Tavern's Halloween Drink Menu**: The tavern's barkeep, a jovial man with a penchant for theatrics, enjoys presenting each drink with a flourish, adding to the overall Halloween ambiance of the Plain Shoe Tavern.

**Tales of the Blood Moon**: PCs can join various tables to listen to or share stories about the Blood Moon. Each tale provides a different perspective, from eerie encounters during the Blood Moon's rise to hopeful stories of past heroes who tried to combat its effects.

**Meeting the Purifiers**: The group in matching cloaks is the Purifiers, a faction dedicated to eradicating the witches and restoring balance to Moonsorrow. If approached, they'll share their beliefs and try to recruit the PCs to their cause.

**Sir Cedric's Speech**: After some time, Sir Cedric Blackthorn will stand on a raised platform, calling for attention. He'll deliver a passionate speech about the dangers of the Blood Moon and the need to take action against the witches. His charisma and conviction are palpable, and many in the tavern will be swayed by his words.

## The Plain Shoe Tavern's Halloween Drink Menu

**Witch's Brew** - 2 silver pieces (sp) - A bubbling green concoction served in a cauldron-shaped mug. Made with a mix of herbal liqueurs, it has a sweet and tangy taste with a hint of mint.

**Blood Moon Elixir** - 5 sp - A deep red wine mixed with pomegranate juice and a dash of cherry brandy. Served in a goblet with a sugar rim that looks eerily like crystallized blood.

**Ghostly Goblet** - 3 sp - A pale, milky cocktail made from coconut cream, white rum, and a splash of lime. It's served chilled with a smoky mist rising from the top, thanks to a piece of dry ice.

**Pumpkin Ale** - 1 sp - A rich, amber ale brewed with roasted pumpkins and autumn spices. Served in a mug with a cinnamon stick stirrer.

**Spectral Spirits** - 4 sp - A clear vodka served in a shot glass. Before drinking, patrons are encouraged to drop in a tablet that fizzes and changes the drink's color, representing the spirits of Moonsorrow.

**Cursed Cider** - 2 sp - A warm apple cider spiced with cloves, cinnamon, and anise. It's said that one sip can ward off the evening's chill... and perhaps even a curse or two.

**Ghoul's Grog** - 3 sp - A dark rum mixed with ginger beer and lime, served in a skull-shaped mug. The drink is garnished with a "ghoulish" eyeball made from a lychee fruit stuffed with a blueberry.

**Ectoplasm Elixir** - 4 sp - A shimmering, teal-colored cocktail made from blue curaçao, lemon-lime soda, and a touch of edible pearl dust to give it that otherworldly glow.

**Mummy's Wrath** - 5 sp - A strong, aged whiskey served neat. Wrapped around the glass are thin strips of white cloth, reminiscent of a mummy's bandages.

**Vampire's Kiss** - 6 sp - A deep crimson cocktail made from black raspberry liqueur, cranberry juice, and a touch of honey. Served with a pair of plastic fangs on the rim for added effect.

## Tales of the Blood Moon

Below are tales that the PCs can learn as they talk to people in the tavern. The stories can carry clues for how to resolve the curse of the Blood Moon, but they may also be miscommunication.

### The Phantom Rose's Keeper

**Speaker**: An elderly woman with silver hair, wearing a cloak adorned with dried roses.

**Props**: A dried rose, which she claims is from a previous Blood Moon.

**Story**: "Many moons ago, a young maiden ventured into the Graveyard of Echoes, drawn by the whispers of the phantom rose. As she approached the flower, she was met by a ghostly guardian, a spirit bound to protect the rose. The maiden, using her wit and charm, convinced the guardian to let her take the rose, promising to return it once its purpose was served. To this day, it's said that the guardian waits, hoping for the rose's return."

## The Lost Traveler in the Labyrinth

**Speaker**: A rugged adventurer with scars and a mysterious aura.

**Props**: A small vial of clear water.

**Story**: "I once found myself lost in the Labyrinth of Life, every turn leading to another dead end. Days turned into nights, and just when I was about to give up, I stumbled upon the fountain. The water was the purest I'd ever seen, and as I drank, I felt a surge of hope and strength. I found my way out, and I believe it was the water that guided me."

## The Storm Chaser's Prize

**Speaker**: A boisterous sailor with tattoos of storms and waves.

**Props**: A small, shimmering crystal.

**Story**: "On the fiercest night at sea, amidst a storm like no other, our ship was tossed and turned by the witches' Elemental Tempest. As lightning struck all around, a bolt hit our mast, and from it fell this Storm Crystal. It's said to contain the fury and beauty of the tempest itself."

## The Purifier's Warning

**Speaker**: A stern, middle-aged man with a fiery gaze, dressed in the emblematic attire of the Purifiers.

**Props**: A burnt piece of wood, said to be from the witches' sanctum in the Misty Woods.

**Story**: "In my youth, I ventured into the Misty Woods, drawn by tales of the witches' power. Deep within, I found their sanctum, a place of dark rituals and forbidden magic. There, I witnessed them summoning spirits and casting spells under the Blood Moon's glow. It was clear to me that they were the cause of our suffering. I barely escaped with my life, but I took this burnt wood as proof of their wickedness. We must stand against them if we ever hope to see Moonsorrow free from the Blood Moon's curse."

## The Cursed Amulet's Deception

**Speaker**: A jittery merchant, his eyes darting around as if expecting trouble.

**Props**: A beautiful amulet with a crimson gem at its center.

**Story**: "I once acquired this amulet from a traveler who claimed it had the power to control the Blood Moon. Eager to harness its power, I wore it during the Blood Moon's rise. But instead of control, I felt an overwhelming dread. Whispers filled my ears, speaking of a hidden chamber beneath Moonsorrow where the true source of the Blood Moon's power resided. I've since learned that the amulet is cursed, and the whispers were but lies meant to lead me astray."

## Meeting the Purifiers

Location: A secluded corner of the Plain Shoe Tavern, marked by a banner displaying the emblem of the Purifiers: a sun and moon intertwined, surrounded by a circle of flames.

As you scan the tavern, your eyes are drawn to a group in matching cloaks, deep blue with silver embroidery. They sit in a secluded corner, their faces illuminated by the soft glow of a lantern. The emblem on their banner depicts a sun and moon intertwined, surrounded by a circle of flames. Their demeanor is serious, and they converse in hushed tones, occasionally glancing around the room with wary eyes.

## Interactions

**Sir Cedric Blackthorn**: As the leader of the Purifiers, Sir Cedric is the most vocal about their mission. He speaks with passion and conviction, detailing the witches' supposed wrongdoings and the need to restore balance to Moonsorrow. If the PCs show interest, he'll offer them a task to prove their loyalty to the cause.

**Purifier Initiates**: Younger members, eager to prove themselves. They share tales of the witches' alleged dark rituals and the harm they've brought to Moonsorrow. They look up to Sir Cedric and echo his sentiments.

**Purifier Veterans**: Older members who've been with the faction for years. They're more reserved, sharing stories of past confrontations with the witches and the losses they've suffered. They emphasize the importance of unity and strength in numbers.

## Activities

**Recruitment Speech**: Sir Cedric gives a rousing speech about the Purifiers' mission, detailing the history of Moonsorrow, the rise of the Blood Moon, and the witches' role in it. He emphasizes the need for brave souls to join their ranks.

**Ritual of Purity**: The Purifiers invite the PCs to participate in a ritual that they claim will protect them from the witches' dark magic. This involves lighting a special incense and reciting a pledge to uphold the values of the Purifiers.

## Sir Cedric's Recruitment Speech

Sir Cedric rises from his seat, the ambient chatter in the tavern quieting down as all eyes turn to him. He takes a deep breath, his piercing blue eyes scanning the room, and begins:

"Good people of Moonsorrow, and travelers from distant lands, I stand before you not as a mere man, but as a beacon of hope in these dark times. For too long, our beloved land has been overshadowed by the curse of the Blood Moon, a curse brought upon us by the treacherous witches – Morana, Opalina, and Elyra."

He pauses for dramatic effect, letting his words sink in.

"Once, Moonsorrow was a land of harmony and peace, where life and death danced in a delicate balance. But that balance was shattered when the witches, in their insatiable thirst for power, invited the malevolent Helbindr into our realm. Their dark rituals and forbidden magics tainted our skies, turning the once-glorious moon into a crimson harbinger of doom."

Sir Cedric's voice grows louder, filled with fervor.

"Because of the Blood Moon's curse, our land has been plunged into chaos. Crops wither, livestock perish, and innocent souls are tormented by spirits from the icy abyss of Niflshadow. And who do we have to thank for this? The witches, who now hide in the depths of the Misty Woods, plotting further ruin!"

He points towards the group of Purifiers seated at the table around him.

"We, the Purifiers, have sworn an oath to cleanse Moonsorrow of this blight. To restore the balance that was lost and bring an end to the witches' reign of terror. But we cannot do it alone. We need brave souls, warriors of valor, and champions of justice to join our ranks. Together, we can reclaim our land and write a new chapter in the annals of Moonsorrow."

Sir Cedric's gaze sweeps across the room, locking eyes with the PCs.

"Will you stand idly by, letting the witches continue their malevolent deeds? Or will you rise, take arms, and join the Purifiers in our noble quest? The choice is yours, but remember: the fate of Moonsorrow hangs in the balance."

With that, Sir Cedric takes his seat, leaving the room in a heavy silence, the weight of his words pressing down on every heart and soul present.

## Recruitment Task

If the PCs show genuine interest in joining the Purifiers, Sir Cedric might offer them a task to prove their loyalty and dedication to the cause.

**Task**: The PCs will need to venture into the Misty Woods and return with the head of a Hollow Lantern. When lit, the Purifiers' lantern will grant them an advantage against the witches.

**Location**: The Hollow Lanterns can be found deep in the Misty Woods.

**Outcome**: Upon successful retrieval of a Hollow Lantern containing a will-o'-the-wisp and return to the Plain Shoe Tavern, the PCs will be welcomed by the Purifiers into their ranks, offering them matching cloaks and introducing them to their rituals and strategies. Sir Cedric will also share more about their plans to confront the witches and end the curse of the Blood Moon.

However, if the PCs challenge the beliefs of the Purifiers or decide against joining them, they might find themselves at odds with the faction, leading to potential confrontations or a need to navigate the political landscape of Moonsorrow carefully.

The Purifiers, while genuinely believing in their cause, might not have the full picture. The PCs' interactions with them can shape the narrative, leading to alliances, confrontations, or a deeper understanding of the complexities surrounding the Blood Moon and the witches' role in Moonsorrow's history.

## Consequences of the Encounter

**Allies or Enemies**: Depending on how the PCs interact with Sir Cedric and the Purifiers, they could leave the tavern with powerful allies or determined adversaries. The Purifiers have a significant influence in Moonsorrow, and their opinion could sway the townsfolk's attitude towards the PCs.

**Clues and Information**: The tales shared in the tavern, the whispers of the past, and Sir Cedric's knowledge can provide the PCs with valuable information about the Blood Moon, the witches, and potential ways to combat the curse.

**Setting the Stage**: The atmosphere in the tavern, the growing shadows, and the increasing tension set the stage for the Blood Moon's ascent. The PCs should leave the encounter with a sense of urgency and anticipation for the challenges ahead.

## Lair Actions

**Whispers of the Past**: Every other round, the tavern's old wooden beams and walls seem to come alive with faint whispers. These are the echoes of past conversations, tales, and secrets shared within the tavern's walls. PCs with a passive Perception of 16 or higher can pick up snippets of these conversations, possibly gaining clues or hints about the Blood Moon or the witches.

**Shadowy Figures**: As discussions about the Blood Moon intensify, shadows in the corners of the tavern seem to grow darker and more pronounced. PCs might feel like they're being watched or sense a malevolent presence. This is a manifestation of the Blood Moon's influence, growing stronger as midnight approaches.

**Protective Runes**: Carved into the tavern's beams and pillars are ancient protective runes. Every third round, these runes glow faintly, providing a temporary sanctuary. For one round, any dark magic or malevolent intent directed at the tavern or its occupants has disadvantage.

## Scaling the Encounter

### Beginning Players (PC levels 1-5)

**Halloween Drink Menu**: The barkeep offers a discount for first-time visitors, making the drinks more affordable for low-level PCs.

**Tales of the Blood Moon**: Keep the stories as they are but allow for more player interaction. Encourage players to ask questions or share their own tales.

**Meeting the Purifiers**: The Purifiers are more welcoming to newcomers and might offer simpler tasks or quests to gauge the PCs' abilities.

**Lair Actions**: For the "Whispers of the Past" action, those with a passive Perception of 13 or higher hear the whispered voices.

### Intermediate Players (PC levels 6-10)

**Halloween Drink Menu**: The barkeep might challenge the PCs to a drinking game or contest, with a free drink as the prize.

**Tales of the Blood Moon**: Introduce minor challenges or puzzles related to the stories for added engagement.

**Meeting the Purifiers**: The Purifiers are more reserved, gauging the PCs' intentions before revealing too much. They might offer more complex tasks or quests.

**Lair Actions**: For the "Whispers of the Past" action, maintain the passive Perception requirement at 16.

### Advanced Players (PC levels 11+)

**Halloween Drink Menu**: The barkeep might have a secret menu with potent drinks that can grant temporary boons or minor magical effects.

**Tales of the Blood Moon**: Introduce more complex challenges or puzzles related to the stories. Perhaps some stories have hidden clues or prophecies.

**Meeting the Purifiers**: The Purifiers are wary of powerful adventurers, fearing they might be spies or agents of the witches. They'll test the PCs' loyalty and intentions rigorously.

**Lair Actions**: For the "Whispers of the Past" action, only those with a passive Perception of 18 or higher hear the whispered voices.

# Ascent of The Blood Moon

As the Festival of the Crimson Veil unfolds in all its splendor, the streets of Moonsorrow are alive with celebration and mystery. Yet, amidst the revelry, rumors and gossip circulate like wildfire. Whispers of the three witches and their connection to the Blood Moon are on everyone's lips. Some say the witches are the true protectors of Moonsorrow, while others believe they are the harbingers of its doom.

Many tales are shared, but one narrative emerges time and again: the witches reside to the north, deep within the Misty Woods. Some townsfolk speak of brave souls who ventured into the woods seeking the witches, never to return. Others claim to have seen the witches themselves, their figures shrouded in mist, watching Moonsorrow from the forest's edge.

As the night progresses, the anticipation becomes palpable. Everyone, from young children to the elderly, keeps an eye on the horizon, waiting for the Blood Moon's ascent. And when the moon finally rises, casting its crimson glow upon Moonsorrow, the town is plunged into chaos.

Screams echo from the livestock pens as animals thrash in terror. Fields of corn, once golden and tall, begin to wilt and blacken before the townspeople's eyes. But the most horrifying transformation occurs among the people themselves. Friends and neighbors, under the Blood Moon's malevolent influence, turn on each other with wild eyes, their sanity seemingly stripped away.

The power of the Blood Moon is undeniable, and its curse weighs heavily on Moonsorrow. The townsfolk, in their desperation, turn to the adventurers. "Find the witches!" they plead. "They hold the key to our salvation or our doom."

## Additional Notes

Guide your players through the chaos of the Blood Moon's rise. Use the pandemonium to emphasize the urgency of their quest. The path ahead is clear: they must venture north, into the heart of the Misty Woods, and confront the three witches. Whether they choose to align with the witches or oppose them, the fate of Moonsorrow hangs in the balance. The Blood Moon's curse must be lifted, and the adventurers are the realm's last hope.

# The Misty Woods

The Misty Woods, a name whispered with reverence and fear, is a sprawling expanse of ancient trees, shrouded in an ever-present, ethereal fog. This forest is not just a simple grove; it's a living, breathing entity, filled with secrets, challenges, and beings both benevolent and malevolent.

At the entrance of the woods lies a crossroads, where players might encounter the enigmatic Crossroads Demon. Here, deals can be struck, granting power or knowledge, but always demanding a price. Beware, for those who renege on their bargains find themselves pursued by the relentless Crossroads Wraiths.

Venturing deeper, one might stumble upon the domain of the legendary Baba Yaga. To earn the favor or assistance of this enigmatic forest witch, players must prove their worth, either by completing her arduous tasks or by answering her cryptic riddles. Yet her domain is not undefended. Baba Yaga's Sentinels stand guard, and the Cursed Mirror awaits those who might try to deceive the old witch.

In a moonlit clearing, the Witch's Stone Circle stands as a testament to ancient rites and rituals. Here, on All Hallows' Eve, spectral witches gather, their chants echoing through the night. Those who dare approach might gain blessings or curses, or perhaps discover hidden pathways through the woods, guided by the ethereal glow of the runes.

But not all lights in the Misty Woods are benevolent. The Hollow's Lanterns, ethereal will-o'-the-wisps, float tantalizingly, leading the unwary into danger. Yet with wit and caution, these spirits might be persuaded to share their secrets. Beware, though, of the jack-o'-lantern traps that lie in wait.

Lastly, hidden amidst the dense foliage lies the Hidden Hollow, a sanctuary for the Purifiers. Here, away from prying eyes, they train and strategize, led by the cunning Ailith the Thief. This concealed enclave is a testament to the many mysteries the Misty Woods holds, waiting for those brave enough to uncover them.

## Pact with the Crossroads Demon

As you approach the entrance to the Misty Woods, the path diverges, forming a distinct crossroads. The ground here seems unnaturally worn, with faint symbols and runes etched into the dirt at the center. Old, weathered signposts point in various directions, but one in particular catches your eye. It reads: "To those who seek power or knowledge beyond their grasp, stand at the cross and offer a token of your past."

Nearby, a gnarled tree stands sentinel, its bark carved with countless initials and symbols, perhaps left by those who've come before you. Tied to one of its branches is a tattered ribbon, fluttering in the wind, with a small parchment attached. The note reads: "Beware the price of the pact. For in the dance with shadows, not all steps are retraced." In addition, you see a hollow in the tree with what looks like something inside.

The eerie silence of the crossroads is occasionally broken by a distant whisper, like voices carried on the wind, hinting at the many souls who've stood here before, seeking to make their own bargains.

## Activities

**Finding the journal**: In order to find out what is hiding in the tree hollow, players can approach it to take a closer look inside, or use a familiar. Inside is a weathered, leather journal, its metal buckle the source of the glinting. Flipping through its pages, PCs will come across an entry detailing an encounter with the "Crossroads Demon." The writer describes a ritual of standing at the center and offering something of personal value to summon this powerful entity in hopes to strike a bargain for forbidden knowledge or some other boon. The entry ends with a warning: "Every deal has its price, and the Crossroads Demon always collects."

**Summoning the Crossroads Demon**: To call forth the Crossroads Demon, a player must stand at the center of the crossroads and offer something of personal value. This could be a cherished memory, a physical item, or even a promise of a future deed.

**Making a Pact**: Once summoned, the Crossroads Demon will listen to the player's request. This could be for information about the witches, a boost in power, or any other boon they might seek. However, the demon always demands a price. This could range from a player character's soul, a future favor, to even a challenge or task that must be completed within a set time. The more significant the request, the higher the price.

**Crossroads Wraiths' Challenge**: If a PC agrees to the demon's terms, the Crossroads Wraiths will emerge from the shadows, testing the character's resolve and ensuring they fully understand the weight of the pact. This could involve a combat encounter, a riddle, or a moral dilemma.

# Summoning the Crossroads Demon

To summon the Crossroads Demon, the following conditions must be met:

**Location**: The summoner must stand at the very center of the crossroads, where the energies of choices and destinies converge.

**Offering**: The summoner must present an offering of personal value. This offering acts as both a beacon to the Crossroads Demon and a testament to the summoner's sincerity.

## Types of Offerings

**Cherished Memory**: The summoner willingly gives up a cherished memory. This memory is forever lost to them, as if it never happened. Mechanically, this could have implications based on the nature of the memory. For instance, if a character gives up a memory of training with a mentor, they might lose proficiency in a skill or weapon.

**Physical Item**: This must be an item of significant personal value to the summoner, not just monetary value. It could be a family heirloom, a gift from a loved one, or a token from a pivotal moment in their life. Once offered, the item vanishes, never to be seen again.

## Mechanics of the Summoning

**Ritual Duration**: The summoning ritual takes 10 minutes to complete. During this time, the summoner must remain undisturbed at the center of the crossroads.

**Concentration**: The summoner must maintain concentration during the ritual, as if concentrating on a spell. If their concentration is broken, the ritual fails, and the offering is lost.

**Contractual Mark**: If a promise of a future deed is made, the summoner receives a visible mark somewhere on their body, signifying the supernatural contract. This mark remains until the deed is completed.

## Appearance of the Crossroads Demon

Upon successful summoning, the ambient temperature drops noticeably, and a thick, eerie fog envelops the crossroads. From the fog, a tall, shadowy figure emerges, its eyes glowing a deep crimson. The Crossroads Demon's form is ever-shifting, like smoke, making it difficult to discern any specific features. Its voice is a melodic whisper, echoing with the weight of countless deals and promises made over millennia.

## Interaction with the Crossroads Demon

**Negotiation**: The Crossroads Demon is a master negotiator, always seeking to strike a deal that is most favorable to it. While it will listen to the summoner's request, it will often counter with its own terms, seeking to extract the highest price possible.

**Knowledge**: The Crossroads Demon possesses vast knowledge of many things, both mundane and arcane. It can provide information, reveal secrets, or even teach powerful spells, but always at a price.

**Power**: For those seeking power, the Crossroads Demon can grant abilities or enhancements. This could be in the form of a temporary boost, like a potion effect, or a more permanent boon, such as a feat or class ability. However, such power comes with strings attached, often leading to complications or challenges down the line.

**Departure**: Once a deal is struck, or if the summoner decides to back out, the Crossroads Demon will vanish back into the fog, leaving behind only the chilling air and the weight of the newly formed pact.

## Making a Pact

Below is a list of some of the types of requests PCs can make of the Crossroads Demon.

### Request: A Memory

The demon asks for a cherished memory from the PC's past.

Boon: Eldritch Insight - The PC gains the ability to cast the *Detect Magic* spell at will, without expending a spell slot, for the next 30 days.

### Request: A Promise

The demon wants the PC to perform a specific task or favor in the future. This could range from delivering a message to performing a more sinister act.

Boon: Pact of Speed - For the next 7 days, the PC's movement speed increases by 10 feet, and they gain the benefits of the *Haste* spell for the first round of any combat.

### Request: A Physical Item

The demon asks for an item of personal significance to the PC.

Boon: Eldritch Protection - The PC gains a +1 bonus to AC for the next 30 days.

### Request: A Secret

The demon wants to know a secret the PC has never shared with anyone.

Boon: Whispered Truths - The PC gains the ability to cast the *Zone of Truth* spell once per day without expending a spell slot for the next 30 days.

### Request: A Drop of Blood

The demon asks for a drop of the PC's blood, potentially for nefarious purposes.

Boon: Blood's Vigor - The PC gains an additional 10 hit points to their maximum HP for the next 7 days.

### Request: A Day from Their Life

The demon asks to take a day from the PC's life. The PC will not remember anything from that day, and for everyone else, the PC simply disappeared for that duration.

Boon: Time's Favor - For the next 30 days, the PC benefits from the Lucky feat.  Up to 3 times each day, you can choose to reroll any attack roll, saving throw, or ability check. You may choose to reroll after you roll the die, but before the outcome is determined, and can choose the result from the two rolls.

### Consequences of the Pact

**Fulfilling the Pact**: If the summoner upholds their end of the bargain, the Crossroads Demon will honor its commitment. However, it's essential to be precise in the wording of any deal, as the demon is known to exploit any ambiguities to its advantage.

**Breaking the Pact**: Should the summoner fail to uphold their end of the bargain, the consequences can be dire. The Crossroads Demon might send otherworldly enforcers to collect the debt, curse the summoner with a debilitating hex, or even claim their soul, condemning it to an eternity in a shadowy, liminal realm.

**Renegotiating**: It's rare, but not unheard of, for someone to attempt to renegotiate the terms of their pact with the Crossroads Demon. Such endeavors are perilous, as the demon is not known for its leniency. However, with the right leverage or offering, it might be possible to alter the terms slightly. This often requires another significant sacrifice or undertaking an even more challenging task.

**Seeking Release**: Those who regret their pacts might seek ways to break them without incurring the demon's wrath. Ancient texts and forbidden rituals might hold the key to severing such supernatural contracts, but these methods are fraught with their own dangers and moral quandaries.

**Interference from Other Entities**: Other celestial or infernal beings might take an interest in a mortal who has struck a deal with the Crossroads Demon. Angels, rival demons, or even deities could intervene, either to assist the summoner (in hopes of saving their soul) or to capitalize on the situation for their own ends.

## Crossroads Wraiths' Challenge

Once the PC agrees to the demon's terms, the ground around the crossroads chills, and ethereal chains emerge, binding the PC in place. From the shadows, ghostly figures with hollow eyes and tattered robes approach, their intent clear: to test the player character's strength and resolve.

**Creatures**: 2-4 Crossroads Wraiths.

**Objective**: The player character must defeat the wraiths to prove their strength and determination.

**Outcome**: If the character succeeds, the chains retreat, and the Crossroads Demon nods in approval. If the character is defeated but not killed, the wraiths disappear, and the demon might comment on their lack of resolve, potentially renegotiating the terms or refusing the pact. Either way, the summoner and the rest of the party can pass through the crossroads and enter the Misty Woods.

## Lair Actions

**Whispers of Temptation**: At initiative count 20, the Crossroads Demon can target one PC, filling their mind with whispered temptations. The character must succeed on a DC 15 Wisdom saving throw or be charmed by the demon until the end of their next turn.

**Shadowy Grasp**: The scorched ground at the center of the crossroads can reach out with shadowy tendrils, attempting to bind a PC in place. A PC standing at the center must succeed on a DC 14 Strength saving throw or be restrained. They can repeat the saving throw at the end of each of their turns.

**Ephemeral Fog**: The Crossroads Demon can summon a thick, ghostly fog that engulfs the crossroads, heavily obscuring the area. This fog remains until the demon's next lair action.

## Scaling the Encounter

### Beginning Players (PC levels 1-5)

**Summoning the Crossroads Demon**: The ritual is more forgiving. If interrupted, players can restart without losing their offering. The Wisdom saving throw for offering a cherished memory is DC 10.

**Making a Pact**: The Crossroads Demon's demands are less severe. For instance, instead of a character's soul, it might ask for a minor favor or a small token of value.

**Crossroads Wraiths' Challenge**: Only 1-2 Crossroads Wraiths appear. They have reduced hit points and deal less damage.

### Intermediate Players (PC levels 6-10)

**Summoning the Crossroads Demon**: The ritual remains as described. The Wisdom saving throw for offering a cherished memory is DC 13.

**Making a Pact**: The Crossroads Demon's demands are balanced. It might ask for more significant favors or items but won't directly demand a player's soul.

**Crossroads Wraiths' Challenge**: 2-3 Crossroads Wraiths appear. They have standard hit points and abilities.

### Advanced Players (PC levels 11+)

**Summoning the Crossroads Demon**: The ritual is more demanding. If interrupted, the offering is lost. The Wisdom saving throw for offering a cherished memory is DC 17.

**Making a Pact**: The Crossroads Demon's demands are severe. It might ask for significant sacrifices, such as a player's soul, or set them on perilous quests.

**Crossroads Wraiths' Challenge**: 3-4 Crossroads Wraiths appear with enhanced abilities. They might have additional resistances or special attacks.

## NPC

Crossroad Demon

## Monster

Crossroads Wraith

# Baba Yaga's Trials

To gain her assistance, PCs must complete tasks or answer riddles.

As you tread deeper into the enchanted forest, the trees grow denser, their canopies weaving together to cast the ground below in an eerie twilight. The air is thick with the scent of ancient moss and damp earth. Suddenly, the forest opens up to reveal a peculiar sight: a large wooden hut standing on giant chicken legs. The hut seems to be alive, turning and adjusting itself as if sensing your presence. Around the hut are various tall, humanoid wooden statues carved in the likenesses of forest animals, their eyes eerily lifelike. To one side of the hut stand a series of ornate mirrors, each reflecting the forest from a slightly different angle.

## Activities in the Encounter

**Approaching the Hut**: As PCs approach, the hut becomes defensive, raising its legs and turning away. The party must find a way to calm it or use some form of magic or skill to approach without alarming the hut.

**Baba Yaga**: Once PCs manage to get close, the door to the hut creaks open, revealing the enigmatic forest witch, Baba Yaga. She will be curious about their intentions and may pose a riddle or ask for a rare item before offering her assistance.

**Baba Yaga's Sentinels Challenge**: If players are deemed unworthy or if they threaten Baba Yaga, the wooden statues surrounding the hut suddenly come to life, challenging the players. These sentinels are protective of Baba Yaga and will stop attacking once players retreat or if Baba Yaga commands them to stop.

**The Cursed Mirror Trap**: Curious players who gaze into the ornate mirrors will find their souls trapped within a mirror dimension. Inside, they must solve a riddle or find an escape route to return to their bodies. If they fail, their bodies will remain soulless husks until their companions can free them or until Baba Yaga decides to release them, likely for a price or another riddle's solution.

## Approaching the Hut

**Calm the Hut (Animal Handling/Performance)**: PCs can attempt to soothe the hut, treating it like a skittish animal. A successful DC 18 Animal Handling or Performance check will calm the hut enough for the PCs to approach. Playing a musical instrument, singing a lullaby, or offering food might grant advantage on this check.

**Magical Approach (Arcana/Spellcasting)**: Player characters can use spells to either calm or deceive the hut. Spells like *Calm Emotions* or *Charm Monster* (if you allow the hut to be treated as a monster for this purpose) can be effective. A PC can also attempt an Arcana check (DC 16) to recall a ritual or incantation that might soothe the hut.

**Stealthy Approach (Stealth)**: Using the dense forest and the distractions of their companions, a PC might try to sneak up to or into the hut. This requires a Stealth check against the hut's passive Perception of 14.

**Direct Confrontation (Athletics/Acrobatics)**: A brave (or foolhardy) PC might decide to jump onto one of the hut's legs or find a way to climb up to the entrance. This would require a DC 20 Athletics or Acrobatics check. However, this approach might alarm the hut further, potentially causing it to flee or become hostile.

**Investigate the Talismans (Investigation)**: PCs might notice the old talismans and charms on the ground around the hut. A successful DC 15 Arcana check reveals that some of these items are designed to soothe or communicate with the hut. Using one grants advantage on any checks attempting to calm the hut.

## Consequences

**Success**: If PCs successfully approach the hut without alarming it, they can enter and meet Baba Yaga without any initial hostility.

**Partial Success**: If PCs somewhat alarm the hut but manage to get close, they might have to deal with defensive measures inside the hut or start their conversation with Baba Yaga on a more cautious note.

**Failure**: If players completely alarm the hut, it might attempt to flee, forcing players to chase it down or find it again. Alternatively, the hut could become hostile, attacking with its giant chicken claws or releasing some form of defense like a swarm of animated objects or protective spells.

## Baba Yaga

As the door to the hut slowly creaks open, a waft of strange, aromatic scents fills the air. The interior is dimly lit, with countless jars, vials, and odd trinkets lining the walls. At the center, hunched over a bubbling cauldron, stands an old woman with wild, unkempt gray hair. Her deep green eyes fixate on you, observing, always calculating.

**Initial Conversation**: Baba Yaga will first ask the PCs why they have come to her hut. She's particularly interested in any rare or unique items they might have brought with them, as well as any tales of their recent adventures.

**Riddle Challenge**: If she's in a playful or testing mood, Baba Yaga might pose a riddle to the party. If they answer correctly, she might be more inclined to help them. Here are a few sample riddles:

- "I speak without a mouth and hear without ears. I have no body, but I come alive with the wind. What am I?" (Answer: An echo)

- "The more you take, the more you leave behind. What am I?" (Answer: Footsteps)

- "I fly without wings. I cry without eyes. Wherever I go, darkness follows me. What am I?" (Answer: A cloud)

- "At night they come without being fetched, by day they are lost without being stolen. What are they?" (Answer: Stars)

**Request for a Rare Item**: Baba Yaga is always on the lookout for rare ingredients or magical trinkets. She might ask the party to fetch something for her, like the feather of a phoenix, the tear of a nymph, or the root of a plant that only grows in moonlight. Examples include:

- A vial of water from the Fountain of Youth.
- A scale from an ancient dragon.
- A gem that glows only in the presence of true love.

**Insight into Her Intentions**: Players can attempt an Insight check (DC 18) to gauge Baba Yaga's current mood and intentions. Success might reveal if she's genuinely curious, if she's testing them, or if she has ulterior motives.

### Skill Checks and Challenges

**Persuasion Check**: PCs can attempt to persuade Baba Yaga to assist them. This would be a high DC, around 20, given her unpredictable nature.

**Insight Check (DC 18)**: To gauge Baba Yaga's mood and intentions. Success might reveal hints about what she's currently interested in or how she's feeling.

**Arcana Check (DC 16)**: If offering a magical item, PCs can use this check to explain its properties and convince Baba Yaga of its value.

### Consequences

**Success**: If the PCs answer her riddle correctly, provide a rare item she desires, or otherwise impress her, Baba Yaga will be more inclined to offer her assistance or share her knowledge.

**Partial Success**: If the PCs struggle with her challenges but show respect or offer something of lesser value, Baba Yaga might still help, but perhaps at a higher price or with some strings attached.

**Failure**: If the PCs disrespect Baba Yaga, fail her tests, or try to deceive her, she might become hostile or dismiss them from her hut. They might have to find another way to gain her favor or seek the information they need elsewhere.

### Potions

Baba Yaga's collection of potions is vast and varied. The following are a few examples of what she might offer to the party:

**Potion of Forest Whispers**: Upon drinking this potion, the user can communicate with plants and animals in the Misty Woods for 1 hour. The plants and animals can provide guidance, reveal hidden paths, or offer warnings about nearby dangers.

**Potion of Ethereal Sight**: For 1 hour, the user can see into the Ethereal Plane, allowing them to detect ghosts, spirits, and other ethereal entities.

**Potion of Memory Recall**: Upon drinking, the user can recall a specific memory in perfect detail, even if it's something they had forgotten.

## Baba Yaga's Sentinels Challenge

If players are deemed unworthy or if they threaten Baba Yaga, the wooden human-animal statues surrounding the hut suddenly come to life, challenging the players. There are 1d4 sentinels.

The sentinels are primarily defensive. They will position themselves between Baba Yaga and the PCs, using their bodies as shields.

If PCs attempt to negotiate or communicate their intentions, the sentinels might pause or become less aggressive, especially if Baba Yaga is considering their words.

Use the Sentinels Challenge sparingly, primarily if the PCs are being particularly aggressive.

Remember, the sentinels will cease their attack if the PCs retreat or if Baba Yaga commands them to stop. This can be a good way to de-escalate the situation if it's clear the party is outmatched or if they successfully communicate their intentions to Baba Yaga.

## Cursed Mirror Trap

**Description**: Outside the hut to one side of the clearing, a set of 1d4 ornate mirrors stand side by side, each framed in dark, twisted wood adorned with aesthetic designs and an intricate carving of a face with hollow eyes at the frame's head. The glass of each mirror shimmers with an otherworldly glow, and the reflections they cast are slightly distorted, with colors appearing more muted than they should be.

**Trigger**: When a creature looks directly into any of the mirrors and makes eye contact with their own reflection, the trap is activated for that specific mirror.

**Effect**: In an instant, the soul of the creature is pulled into the mirror, leaving their body a lifeless husk on the ground. Within the mirror, the ensnared soul finds itself in a grayscale, surreal version of the forest clearing. This mirrored realm is eerily silent, with every surface appearing as polished glass, reflecting the trapped soul from all angles.

A ghostly figure then materializes. This specter bears a vague resemblance to the trapped individual but is distorted, its features stretched and blurred. Its eyes, however, are sharp and focused, glowing with a pale blue light. The figure's demeanor is cold and detached, its voice echoing as if coming from a great distance. It poses a riddle to the trapped soul, its tone mocking. The figure remains largely unresponsive to questions, answering only with cryptic statements or chilling laughter.

To regain their freedom, the trapped soul must solve the riddle. A correct answer sees them immediately released. An incorrect answer or hesitation results in a confrontation with a hostile entity within this mirrored dimension, a reflection of their own fears and doubts.

**Detection**: A character who inspects one or more of the mirrors and succeeds on a DC 18 Intelligence (Investigation) check will notice the faint ornamental patterns engraved around the frames are actually arcane runes, indicating their magical nature. A successful DC 18 Arcana check allows a PC to decipher these arcane runes and determine the mirrors hold a magical trap. A character using *Detect Magic* will sense strong enchantment magic emanating from the mirrors.

**Disable**: Breaking a mirror will free any soul trapped within that specific mirror, but might have other unforeseen consequences. Alternatively, casting *Dispel Magic* at 4th level or higher on a mirror will temporarily suppress its trap for 10 minutes. To permanently disable the trap of a mirror without actually destroying the mirror itself, the runes around its frame must be carefully altered, requiring a DC 20 Intelligence (Arcana) check and 10 minutes of work per mirror.

## Lair Actions

On initiative count 20 (losing initiative ties), Baba Yaga can take a lair action to cause one of the following effects:

**Hut's Defense**: The hut stomps its giant chicken foot on the ground, causing a minor tremor. All creatures within 30 feet of the hut must succeed on a DC 15 Dexterity saving throw or be knocked prone.

**Mirror's Illusion**: One of the ornate mirrors casts an illusion, making one PC see their worst fear. The affected character must succeed on a DC 16 Wisdom saving throw or be frightened for 1 minute. The PC can repeat the saving throw at the end of each of their turns, ending the effect on a success.

**Sentinel's Watch**: Two of the wooden humanoid-animal statues animate and move up to their speed toward a target of Baba Yaga's choice. They return to being lifeless statues at the end of the next round.

**Mystical Fog**: A dense fog envelops the area in a 60-foot radius around the hut. The area becomes heavily obscured, and players might hear faint whispers or see fleeting shadows within the fog. The fog lasts until the next lair action is taken.

## Scaling the Encounter

### Beginning Players (PC levels 1-5)

**Approaching the Hut**: Lower the DCs for checks. Animal Handling/Performance becomes DC 14, Arcana is DC 12, Stealth is against a passive Perception of 12, and Athletics/Acrobatics is DC 16.

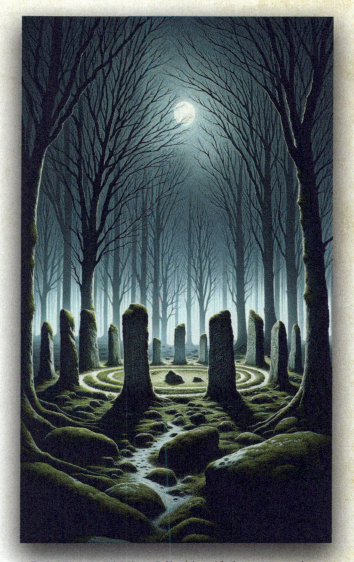

**Baba Yaga's Riddles**: Offer hints if players struggle with the riddles. If they're close to an answer, consider it correct.

**Sentinels Challenge**: Only 1 sentinel activates. It has reduced hit points and deals less damage.

**Cursed Mirror Trap**: The riddles inside the mirror are simpler, or clues are provided. The challenges or hostile entities inside are less threatening.

### Intermediate Players (PC levels 6-10)

**Approaching the Hut**: Use the DCs as provided.

**Baba Yaga's Riddles**: Offer hints after some deliberation.

**Sentinels Challenge**: 2 sentinels activate. They have standard hit points and abilities.

**Cursed Mirror Trap**: The riddles inside the mirror are challenging, and the entities inside are formidable but not overwhelming.

## Advanced Players (PC levels 11+)

**Approaching the Hut**: Increase the DCs for checks. Animal Handling/Performance becomes DC 20, Arcana is DC 18, Stealth is against a passive Perception of 16, and Athletics/Acrobatics is DC 22.

**Baba Yaga's Riddles**: The riddles are more complex, and no hints are provided.

**Sentinels Challenge**: 3-4 sentinels activate with enhanced abilities. They might have additional resistances or special attacks.

**Cursed Mirror Trap**: The riddles inside the mirror are highly challenging, and the entities inside are very powerful.

## NPC

Baba Yaga

## Monster

Baba Yaga's Sentinel

# The Witch's Stone Circle

Amidst a clearing in the forest, the party stumbles upon a circle of ancient, moss-covered standing stones. Each stone is carved with old runes that glow faintly under the moonlight. Legend says that on All Hallows' Eve, witches gather here to perform sacred rites and commune with spirits. If players arrive on this night, they might witness a spectral coven of witches performing a ritual. Engaging with the coven could lead to blessings, curses, or the revelation of hidden forest paths.

As you venture deeper into the Misty Woods, the dense canopy begins to thin, revealing a clearing bathed in the soft glow of the moonlight. Dominating this clearing is a circle of ancient, moss-covered standing stones. Each monolith, easily twice the height of a man, is intricately carved with old runes that shimmer faintly. The air here feels thick with magic and history. As you tread closer, you can almost hear the faint whispers of ages past, and the ground seems to pulse with a dormant power. If you've arrived on All Hallows' Eve, ethereal figures dance within the circle, their spectral forms moving in a haunting rhythm to an otherworldly melody.

## Activities

**Investigation of the Stones**: Players can attempt an Arcana check (DC 15) to recognize some of the runes and discern their purpose. Success reveals that these stones are not just markers, but conduits of ancient magic, possibly used for rituals or as a gateway between realms.

**Stone Circle Protectors**: If players act aggressively, attempt to damage the stones, or disrupt the ritual on All Hallows' Eve, the Stone Circle Protectors awaken. These creatures, made of the same ancient stone as the monoliths, defend the circle with unwavering determination.

**Spectral Coven Ritual**: Phantom ghosts of witches long departed rise up through the ground within the stone circle.

**Collecting Herbs**: Rare herbs and plants can be found growing around the stones.

## Investigation of the Stones

This encounter is designed to provide players with a roadmap to break the curse of the Blood Moon. The tasks set by the witches are not just fetch quests but are symbolic of the balance and harmony that once existed in Moonsorrow. The final confrontation with Helbindr is the culmination of their journey, and his defeat will restore the land to its former glory. However, the curse he screams at the PCs as he's banished can be a hook for future adventures or consequences the PCs must face in the aftermath.

Upon a successful Arcana check (DC 15), players recognize the runes on the stones as symbols of various deities:

**Skuldrún's Rune**: A vertical line intersected by a horizontal line near the top, forming a "T" shape. At each end of the horizontal line, there's a small circle, representing the loom's spools. Below the intersection, a small skull is etched. This rune represents the intertwining of knowledge and death, hinting at the delicate balance between the two.

**Solwen's Rune**: A circle representing the sun, with eight rays extending outward. Inside the circle, at the bottom, there's a small upward-pointing triangle, symbolizing life and light's nurturing warmth.

**Aelstorm's Rune**: A lightning bolt intersected by three horizontal lines with a leaf-shaped "C" to its left, indicating the raw power of nature and tempests.

**Lughstrat's Rune**: An oval with two triangles as eyes and a downward-pointing line below, representing the duality of trickery and warfare.

**Gwynsight's Rune**: A torch with a flame on top and a book beside it, symbolizing the illumination of knowledge.

**Thoralux's Rune**: A circle with jagged lines extending from the top, representing the storm cloud. Inside the circle, at the bottom, there's a smaller circle radiating lines, symbolizing the radiant orb, representing the fusion of light and storm.

**Wodanstorm's Rune**: A curved line on the left, representing the gale, with a square to its right. Inside the square, there's a smaller triangle pointing upward, symbolizing the shield's protective aspect, indicating the protective aspect of tempests in warfare.

## Spectral Coven Ritual Encounter

**Setting**: Amidst the stone circle, the ground is covered in a thin layer of mist. The moonlight casts eerie shadows, and the air is thick with ancient magic.

**Event**: As the party approaches or observes the stone circle, ethereal figures begin to rise from the ground. These are the phantom ghosts of long-dead witches, their forms translucent and shimmering in the moonlight. They move gracefully, their voices a haunting whisper as they begin their ritual.

### Interaction

**Communication**: PCs can attempt to communicate with the spectral witches.

**Persuasion Check (DC 18)**: On a success, one of the spirits approaches the party. She introduces herself as a former guardian of Moonsorrow and imparts a blessing, piece of knowledge, or a warning about the Blood Moon's curse. This could be a hint about one of the tasks or a clue about Helbindr's weaknesses.

**Failure**: The spirits become distant, and the ritual continues without any further interaction.

**Hostile Action**: If PCs attempt to disrupt the ritual or act aggressively:

The spirits become hostile. They might cast spells like *Chill Touch* or *Eldritch Blast* (use the stats of a Specter or Ghost from the Monster Manual, but with added spellcasting abilities).

If the players retreat or apologize, the spirits might cease their attack but will be wary and less likely to aid the party.

### Breaking the Blood Moon's Curse

Upon successful communication, the spectral witches reveal the tasks required to break the curse:

**Phantom Rose**: "In the Graveyard of Echoes, where the departed rest, a rose blooms under the Blood Moon's gaze. Its petals hold the balance of life and death."

**Flask of Water**: "Within the ever-changing walls of the Labyrinth of Life, a fountain stands unyielding. Its waters, pure and untainted, signify life's triumph over the harshest trials."

**Storm Crystal**: "Amidst the fury of The Elemental Tempest, where nature's forces clash, lies the Storm Crystal: a beacon of strength amidst fragility."

The party's journey this night must conclude with the Cauldron of Fates, where the three ingredients must be placed. Doing so will summon the Council of Witches, who will drink the concoction from the cauldron and reciting a specific incantation will call forth Helbindr from the Abyss.

## Collection of Herbs

Moonshade Herb and Moonshade Thistle, both rare plants known for their protective properties, grow around the stones.

## Lair Actions

On initiative count 20 (losing initiative ties), the Stone Circle takes a lair action to cause one of the following effects:

**Runes' Glow**: The runes on a specific stone glow brightly. The next spell targeting a creature within 30 feet of that stone has advantage on its attack roll or the targeted creature has disadvantage on its saving throw against the spell.

**Ground Tremor**: The ground within the stone circle trembles. Each creature on the ground in the circle must succeed on a DC 15 Dexterity saving throw or be knocked prone.

**Whispers of the Past**: Ghostly whispers fill the air, distracting and disorienting foes. Each enemy within the circle must make a DC 14 Wisdom saving throw or be unable to take reactions until the next round.

## Scaling the Encounter

### Beginning Players (PC levels 1-5)

**Investigation of the Stones**: Lower the Arcana check DC to 12. The information revealed is more basic, hinting at the circle's magical nature without diving deep into its history or full capabilities.

**Stone Circle Protectors**: Only 1 Stone Circle Protector awakens. It has reduced hit points and deals less damage.

**Spectral Coven Ritual**: The spectral witches are more forgiving and less likely to become hostile. If they do, their spells are of lower level (e.g., using cantrips or 1st-level spells).

### Intermediate Players (PC levels 6-10)

**Investigation of the Stones**: Use the DC 15 Arcana check as provided.

**Stone Circle Protectors**: 2 Protectors awaken with standard hit points and abilities.

**Spectral Coven Ritual**: The spectral witches are neutral and will become hostile if provoked. Their spells are of moderate level (e.g., using 2nd or 3rd-level spells).

### Advanced Players (PC levels 11+)

**Investigation of the Stones**: Increase the Arcana check DC to 18. The information revealed is more detailed, providing deeper insights into the circle's history and the potential power it holds.

**Stone Circle Protectors**: 2 Protectors awaken with enhanced abilities. They might have additional resistances or special attacks.

**Spectral Coven Ritual**: The spectral witches are wary and easily provoked. Their spells are of higher level (e.g., using 4th or 5th-level spells).

## Monster

Stone Circle Protector

# The Hollow's Lanterns

The forest grows denser, the trees older, and the canopy thicker, allowing only faint beams of moonlight to pierce through. An eerie silence envelops the area, broken only by the soft, distant glow of floating lanterns that seem to dance and sway, beckoning travelers to follow.

As you delve deeper into the forest, the path becomes less distinct, and the ambient sounds of nature grow strangely muted. Ahead, you spot ethereal lights floating amidst the trees–lanterns that seem to hover in mid-air, their glow soft and inviting. But as you watch, the lights begin to shift and change, taking on familiar forms and faces. Loved ones, friends, or perhaps foes from your past appear to beckon you closer, their expressions a mix of sorrow and longing.

## Hollow Lanterns

Scattered throughout the area are ornate, seemingly abandoned lanterns. Some lay on the ground, while others hang from low tree branches or bushes. Their design is intricate, hinting at a purpose beyond mere illumination.

**Investigation Check (DC 13)**: Reveals that these lanterns are designed to capture and contain ethereal entities, like will-o'-the-wisps.

**Use**: PCs can attempt to use these lanterns to capture the Lantern Spirits, turning their tricks against them.

## Lantern Spirits

These mischievous spirits manifest as tiny, ethereal orbs of soft glowing light and derive pleasure from leading travelers astray.

**Deception**: They can manifest as familiar figures to the characters, attempting to lead them off the path or into danger.

**Combat**: If confronted or captured, they might attack.

**Negotiation**: A clever or persuasive PC might convince a spirit to reveal hidden paths, treasures, or secrets of the forest. This could involve a Persuasion check (DC 16) or offering the spirit something it desires, even offering to release a captured Lantern Spirit in exchange.

## Jack-o'-Lantern Trap

In certain areas where the lanterns glow brightest, the ground is littered with carved pumpkins, their faces twisted in grotesque expressions.

**Trigger**: If a PC steps within 5 feet of a jack-o'-lantern.

**Effect**: The pumpkin emits a blinding flash of light. PCs must make a Constitution saving throw (DC 14) or be blinded for 1 minute. They can repeat the saving throw at the end of each of their turns.

**Detection**: A Perception with Investigation check (DC 15) allows a player to notice the trap mechanism within the pumpkin.

**Disable**: A Dexterity check using thieves' tools (DC 12) or a successful targeted attack (AC 10, HP 5) can disable or destroy the trap.

## Lair Actions

On initiative count 20 (losing initiative ties), the Lantern Spirits can take a lair action to cause one of the following effects:

**Misleading Path**: The spirits shift the terrain, making paths appear where there are none and hiding the real ones. For the next round, any movement has a 50% chance to lead in the opposite direction intended.

**Ethereal Whispers**: Haunting whispers fill the air, causing all players to make a Wisdom saving throw (DC 13) or be frightened until the end of their next turn.

**Lantern Surge**: All Hollow Lanterns in the area glow brightly. Any Lantern Spirit captured inside gets a burst of energy, allowing them to attempt to break free with advantage.

## Scaling the Encounter

### Beginning Players (PC levels 1-5)

**Jack-o'-Lantern Trap**

Effect: Lower the Constitution saving throw DC to 11.

Detection: Lower the Investigation check DC to 12.

**Lair Actions**

Misleading Path: The effect lasts only until the PC's next turn.

Ethereal Whispers: Lower the Wisdom saving throw DC to 10.

### Intermediate Players (PC levels 6-10)

**Jack-o'-Lantern Trap**

Effect: Use the Constitution saving throw DC 14 as provided.

Detection: Use the Investigation check DC 15 as provided.

**Lair Actions**

Misleading Path: The effect lasts for the full round.

Ethereal Whispers: Use the Wisdom saving throw DC 13 as provided.

### Advanced Players (PC levels 11+)

**Jack-o'-Lantern Trap**

Effect: Increase the Constitution saving throw DC to 16.

Detection: Increase the Investigation check DC to 17.

**Lair Actions**

Misleading Path: The effect lasts for two rounds.

Ethereal Whispers: Increase the Wisdom saving throw DC to 15.

## Monster

Lantern Spirit

# The Hidden Hollow

The Hidden Hollow can serve as a recurring location, especially if players form an alliance with Ailith. It can be a place to gather information, acquire resources, or even plan joint missions.

As you venture deeper into the Misty Woods, the air grows colder, and the fog thickens. The path becomes less distinct, the trees more gnarled and twisted. Suddenly, you stumble upon a concealed hollow, shielded by the dense foliage and the ever-present mists. The ground here is soft, covered in a carpet of moss and fallen leaves. In the center of the hollow stands a large, ancient oak tree, its branches stretching out like the arms of a sentinel. Around the tree, you see various training dummies and makeshift targets, hinting at the hollow's purpose. A few tents are pitched nearby, and a small campfire burns, its smoke merging with the mists. A figure, agile and swift, moves between the shadows, her amber eyes fixed with purpose as she seems to be demonstrating before a small group of onlookers in matching deep blue cloaks.

## Activities in the Encounter

**Training Session**: If the party approaches quietly, they can witness Ailith training a group of Purifiers. She demonstrates her dagger-throwing skills, hitting targets with uncanny precision.

**Confrontation**: Should the PCs make their presence known or if they are detected, Ailith will confront them, questioning their intentions. Depending on how the players respond, this could lead to a peaceful conversation, a tense standoff, or even combat.

**Alliance or Adversity**: If the party can convince Ailith of their intentions (Persuasion check DC 17), she might offer information, resources, or even propose a temporary alliance. However, any sign of deception or threat will make her defensive, and she may call upon the Purifiers for backup.

## Training Session

If players wish to approach quietly, they must make a group Stealth check against Ailith's passive Perception of 15. If they're moving through the underbrush or over rough terrain, they have disadvantage on this check due to the noise.

### Observation

Upon a successful stealthy approach, players will witness the following:

**Dagger Drill**: As a small group of Purifiers look on, Ailith stands at a distance from a row of wooden targets. With a swift motion, she draws and throws a series of daggers in rapid succession. Each dagger finds its mark, embedding itself into the bullseye of the target. Ailith is using a Dagger Barrage ability, allowing her to throw three daggers as a single action with a +7 to hit. Each dagger deals 1d4+4 piercing damage, and due to her expertise, she critically hits on a roll of 19 or 20.

**Shadowy Maneuver**: After the dagger drill, Ailith moves to a shaded area of the hollow. She steps into a shadow and seemingly disappears, only to reappear from another shadow near a different target. She uses this ability to demonstrate the importance of using the environment to one's advantage. This is the Shadow Step ability. As a bonus action, Ailith can teleport up to 60 feet to an unoccupied space she can see that is also in dim light or darkness. She then has advantage on the first melee attack she makes before the end of the turn.

**Hexed Dagger Challenge**: Ailith challenges the Purifiers to dodge her hexed daggers. She throws a dagger imbued with a minor hex at a volunteer. The Purifier attempts to dodge, but the dagger curves in the air, following him. When it hits, the Purifier seems momentarily disoriented. Ailith uses a Hexed Dagger ability. She makes a ranged attack with a +7 to hit. On a hit, the target takes 1d4+4 piercing damage and must succeed on a DC 15

Wisdom saving throw or be cursed for 1 minute. While cursed, the target has disadvantage on ability checks and saving throws for one chosen ability (DM's choice or roll a d6).

## Player Interaction

If players choose to reveal themselves during or after the training:

**Skill Challenge**: Impressed by her skills, a PC might challenge Ailith to a friendly contest of accuracy. This can be a series of ranged attacks upon targets or opposed Dexterity (Acrobatics) or Dexterity (Sleight of Hand) checks to see who hits the most targets or performs the most impressive throws.

**Training Request**: A PC might request Ailith to teach them some of her skills. If she agrees, after a dedicated training session, the PC might gain a temporary boon, like a +1 to their next ranged attack or the ability to perform a minor Shadow Step once.

# Confrontation

**Detection**: If the party fails their group Stealth check or intentionally makes their presence known, Ailith will immediately notice them. Her keen senses and training make her always alert to potential threats.

**Initial Reaction**: Ailith swiftly draws a dagger, her amber eyes narrowing as she assesses the situation. The Purifiers she was training also ready themselves, taking defensive positions around her.

## Player Response Options

**Diplomatic Approach**: PCs can attempt to defuse the situation by explaining their intentions. A successful Persuasion check (DC 16) might convince Ailith that they mean no harm. If PCs can provide proof of their good intentions or drop the name of a known ally, they might gain advantage on this check.

**Intimidation**: PCs might try to intimidate Ailith and the Purifiers into standing down. This is risky, given Ailith's nature, but a successful Intimidation check (DC 18) might make her more cautious, buying the players some time or even causing some of the less experienced Purifiers to back off.

**Deception**: Players could attempt to deceive Ailith about their intentions or identity. A successful Deception check (DC 17) might mislead her temporarily, but any inconsistencies in the story could arouse her suspicion.

**Offer of Aid**: If PCs offer to help Ailith and the Purifiers in their cause or provide valuable information, this could lead to a more peaceful conversation. This doesn't require a check but depends on the genuineness of the offer and the information's value.

## Potential Outcomes

**Peaceful Conversation**: If players successfully defuse the situation, Ailith will be willing to talk. She might share information about the forest, the witches, or even the Purifiers' plans. This could lead to potential side quests or alliances.

**Tense Standoff**: If neither side is willing to back down but no immediate threat is perceived, a tense standoff ensues. This could lead to negotiations, with both sides trying to gauge the other's intentions and strength.

**Combat**: If PCs act aggressively, or if their attempts at diplomacy fail, Ailith and the Purifiers will defend themselves. Remember, Ailith is a skilled rogue with unique abilities, and the Purifiers have been trained by her. This could be a challenging encounter, especially if the party is outnumbered.

# Alliance or Adversity

## Convincing Ailith

**Persuasion**: PCs can attempt to win Ailith over by explaining their intentions and goals. A successful Persuasion check (DC 17) will make her more receptive to the party. If players can provide evidence or a compelling reason for their presence, they might gain advantage on this check.

**Insightful Players**: If a PC decides to use Insight (DC 15) to gauge Ailith's reactions during the conversation, they might pick up on cues that reveal what she values or fears, potentially aiding in the persuasion attempt.

## Positive Outcome

**Information**: Ailith shares knowledge about the forest, the Blood Moon's curse, and what she knows about the witches (including her stance of the witches' ultimate responsibility for summoning Helbindr and instigating the curse. She might also provide insight into the Purifiers' operations and goals.

**Resources**: Ailith could offer some resources, such as healing potions, maps of the forest, or even a magical item she's acquired during her rogue endeavors.

**Temporary Alliance**: Seeing the potential benefits of working together, Ailith proposes a temporary alliance. This could involve joint operations, shared resources, or mutual protection within the Misty Woods.

## Negative Outcome

**Deception Detected**: If Ailith suspects deception (either through her own Insight or due to a failed Deception check by a PC), she becomes wary. Her trust will be hard to regain, and she might increase her guard.

**Threats**: Any overt threats or aggressive postures from the players will put Ailith on the defensive. She's not one to back down easily and will be prepared to defend herself and her cause.

**Calling the Purifiers**: If she feels outnumbered or outmatched, Ailith will use a whistle or a signal to call nearby Purifiers for backup. Within 1-2 rounds, reinforcements will arrive, making the situation more challenging for the party.

**Post-Confrontation**: Regardless of the outcome, the confrontation with Ailith will have repercussions. If the party alligns with her, they might gain a valuable contact in the forest. If they clash, they might find themselves facing more challenges as word of the confrontation spreads among the Purifiers.

## Lair Actions

On initiative count 20 (losing initiative ties), Ailith can take a lair action to cause one of the following effects; she can't use the same effect two rounds in a row:

**Misty Veil**: The mists in the hollow thicken, heavily obscuring the area. For the next round, all creatures in the hollow are considered blinded unless they have a means to see through magical darkness or heavy fog.

**Shadowy Escape**: Ailith can instantly teleport to any shadow within the hollow, making her a difficult target to pin down.

**Hexed Dagger**: A dagger flies from a hidden spot, targeting a PC. The character must make a DC 15 Dexterity saving throw or take 1d4+4 piercing damage and be cursed for 1 minute. While cursed, the PC has disadvantage on ability checks and saving throws for one chosen ability (DM's choice or roll a d6).

## Scaling the Encounter

### Beginning Players (PC levels 1-5)

#### Training Session

Dagger Drill: Reduce Ailith's bonus to hit to +4. Each dagger deals 1d4+2 piercing damage.

Shadowy Maneuver: Limit the distance of the Shadow Step ability to 30 feet.

Hexed Dagger Challenge: Lower the Wisdom saving throw DC to 12.

#### Confrontation

Persuasion: Lower the DC to 13.

Intimidation: Lower the DC to 15.

Deception: Lower the DC to 14.

#### Lair Actions

Misty Veil: The effect lasts only until the end of Ailith's next turn.

Hexed Dagger: Lower the Dexterity saving throw DC to 12.

### Intermediate Players (PC levels 6-10)

#### Training Session

Dagger Drill: Use Ailith's stats as provided.

Shadowy Maneuver: Use the Shadow Step ability as provided.

Hexed Dagger Challenge: Use the Wisdom saving throw DC 15 as provided.

#### Confrontation

Persuasion: Use the DC 17 as provided.

Intimidation: Use the DC 18 as provided.

Deception: Use the DC 17 as provided.

#### Lair Actions

Misty Veil: The effect lasts for 1 round.

Hexed Dagger: Use the Dexterity saving throw DC 15 as provided.

### Advanced Players (PC levels 11+)

#### Training Session

Dagger Drill: Increase Ailith's bonus to hit to +9. Each dagger deals 1d4+6 piercing damage.

Shadowy Maneuver: Increase the distance of the Shadow Step ability to 90 feet.

Hexed Dagger Challenge: Increase the Wisdom saving throw DC to 17.

#### Confrontation

Persuasion: Increase the DC to 19.

Intimidation: Increase the DC to 20.

Deception: Increase the DC to 19.

#### Lair Actions

Misty Veil: The effect lasts for 2 rounds.

Hexed Dagger: Increase the Dexterity saving throw DC to 17.

## NPC

Ailith, The Thief

# The Witches' Sanctum

Deep within The Misty Woods, where ancient trees murmur tales and magic saturates the air, lies the Witches' Sanctum, a haven for the revered witches, Morana, Opalina, and Elyra. This sacred enclave, more than just a location, is a nexus of magic where the boundary between the material and ethereal realms is barely discernible. As adventurers tread deeper into the woods, they emerge into a clearing dominated by an ancient oak, its roots sprawling and intertwining. Stone altars encircle the tree, each marked with arcane symbols. At the tree's base, a black cat named Shadowwhisk sits, its eyes, ever-changing in color, assessing newcomers. This clearing is the heart of the Witches' Sanctum, and an almost invisible Mystical Barrier surrounds it, a protective shroud woven by the witches' combined powers.

Upon entering the clearing, adventurers immediately sense the Mystical Barrier's presence, a shimmering wall that encases the sanctum, its outer edge just a few feet beyond the stone altars. The barrier emits a soft, melodic hum, growing louder and more disorienting as one nears it. Those attempting to breach this protective veil without Shadowwhisk's nod face its psychic defenses, repelling intruders with force. However, should the cat find them worthy, a flick of its tail momentarily dissolves the barrier, granting passage. Once inside, the barrier seamlessly reforms, ensuring the sanctum's sanctity remains undisturbed.

In Morana's domain, the Graveyard of Echoes, adventurers tread upon hallowed ground, where spirits of the past linger and a phantom rose, a symbol of life and death's eternal dance, awaits its harvester. Opalina's Labyrinth of Life is a testament to the ever-changing nature of existence, its maze-like paths challenging those who enter to heal and nurture in order to find their way. Elyra's Elemental Tempest is a storm of raw power, where the elements rage and adventurers must harness their fury to retrieve the coveted Storm Crystal.

At the journey's end, the Cauldron of Fates awaits, its bubbling brew a mirror to the future and the past. Here, the final challenge lies, where adventurers must confront their destiny, summon the malevolent Helbindr, and restore the balance to the land of Moonsorrow. The sanctum is not just a place of challenges; it's a crucible of fate, where heroes are forged and legends are born.

## The Mystical Barrier

As you journey deeper into The Misty Woods, the air grows thick with magic, and the very atmosphere seems to pulse with ancient power. The trees here are older, their bark gnarled and twisted, their canopies so dense that they block out most of the sky. The path ahead is illuminated by a soft, otherworldly glow, leading you to a clearing. In the center stands a massive, ancient oak, its roots exposed and intertwining like a network of veins. At the base of the tree, a sleek black cat with piercing green eyes sits gracefully, its tail curling around its paws as it observes your approach. Surrounding the tree are stone altars, each adorned with mystical symbols and artifacts. The very ground beneath you hums, and the boundaries between the seen and the unseen blur. This is a place of potent magic and ancient rites.

## Activities in the Encounter

**Mystical Barrier**: As PCs approach the sanctum, they feel the barrier's effects. If they attempt to push through without the cat's approval, they must make a DC 18 Wisdom saving throw. On a failed save, they are repelled and take 2d6 psychic damage. On a successful save, they feel a strong resistance but no damage.

If the cat deems them worthy, it will gesture with its tail, and the barrier will momentarily dissipate, allowing passage.

**Interview with the Cat**: The cat, named "Shadowwhisk," is intelligent and can communicate telepathically with those it chooses.

Shadowwhisk will ask the PCs their intentions and assess their responses. Insightful PCs might notice that the cat's eyes change color based on its mood: green for curiosity, blue for trust, and red for suspicion or hostility.

If the PCs are honest and show pure intentions, Shadowwhisk will provide information about the curse and the tasks required to break it.

## Mystical Barrier

**Nature of the Barrier**: The barrier is a protective enchantment, a manifestation of the combined powers of the three witches, Morana, Opalina, and Elyra. It is designed to keep out intruders and protect the sanctity of the Witches' Sanctum.

**Sensations**: As the PCs approach the sanctum, the air grows colder, and a shimmering, almost translucent wall becomes visible, its outer edge just a few feet beyond the stone altars. The barrier emits a soft, melodic hum, and the closer one gets, the louder and more disorienting the hum becomes.

**Resisting Intrusion**: If a PC attempts to push through the barrier without the cat's approval, they must make a DC 18 Wisdom saving throw.

**Failed Save**: On a failed save, a surge of psychic energy overwhelms the intruder's mind. They are repelled 10 feet away from the barrier and take 2d6 psychic damage. Additionally, they are stunned until the end of their next turn as they reel from the force of the barrier's magic.

**Successful Save**: On a successful save, the PC feels a strong resistance, akin to pushing against a powerful gust of wind. They manage to resist the barrier's full force and do not take damage, but they still cannot pass through.

**Penetrating the Barrier With the Cat's Approval**: The black cat, a familiar and guardian of the sanctum, possesses the ability to grant or deny passage. If it deems the PCs worthy or if they successfully communicate their intentions, it will gesture with its tail, causing the barrier to shimmer and momentarily dissipate. This creates a temporary gateway, allowing the PCs to pass through unharmed. The barrier then reseals itself once they are inside.

**Duration**: The barrier remains as long as the sanctum exists and the witches' magic fuels it. Only powerful magic or the combined will of the three witches can permanently dispel it.

## Penetrating the Barrier Without the Cat's Approval

**Ancient Runes**: Scattered around the barrier's perimeter are ancient runes, each representing a different elemental force. These runes are the anchors that hold the barrier in place. If the PCs can decipher the runes (requiring a DC 16 Arcana check) and channel the appropriate elemental energy into each one, they might weaken the barrier enough to pass through. This could involve casting spells of the corresponding element on each rune or using elemental-themed items.

**Harmony of Intent**: The barrier is not just a physical deterrent but also a test of will and purpose. If the PCs can align their intentions and focus on a singular purpose, they can attempt to penetrate the barrier together. This requires all PCs to join hands and make a combined Wisdom saving throw (each PC rolls, and they take the average). If the average meets or exceeds the DC, their unified intent allows them to pass through.

**Forceful Entry**: While not subtle, the PCs might attempt to use powerful magic or artifacts to force their way through. Spells like *Dispel Magic* (cast at a high level) or *Antimagic Field* might temporarily disrupt the barrier. However, such actions would surely alert the witches or the sanctum's other guardians to the PCs' presence.

## Shadowwhisk's Telepathic Communication

Shadowwhisk can initiate telepathic communication with any creature within 30 feet. The creature doesn't need to speak the same language, but it must be able to understand at least one language.

The cat will primarily communicate with questions, seeking to understand the PCs' intentions and assess their character.

## Insight Check (DC 14)

**Success**: The PC notices the subtle changes in the color of Shadowwhisk's eyes and can gauge his mood and reactions to their answers.

**Failure**: The PC doesn't pick up on the nuances of the cat's reactions.

## Locating the Witches

If the PCs gain Shadowwhisk's trust or successfully persuade him of their noble intentions (Persuasion check DC 16), the cat will provide guidance:

"Morana, the guardian of life's end and beginnings, resides in the Graveyard of Echoes."

"Opalina, the beacon of hope and resilience, can be found within the Labyrinth of Life."

"Elyra, the mistress of the elements, commands the Elemental Tempest."

The PCs will be able to see each location before them in the Sanctum.

## Breaking the Curse

Shadowwhisk will explain the tasks associated with each witch, emphasizing the importance of each ingredient. If asked about the Cauldron of Fates, Shadowwhisk will describe it as an ancient artifact, a vessel of immense power that can combine the essences of the three ingredients to conjure up Helbindr. Once he has been summoned, in order to break Helbindr's curse of the Blood Moon, the party must defeat the demon lord in battle.

## Confrontation with Helbindr

Should the PCs inquire about Helbindr, Shadowwhisk will warn them: "Helbindr is a force of malevolence and frost. His power is vast, and his hatred for this land is immeasurable. If you seek to confront him, be prepared, for his wrath is as cold as the Abyss from which he hails."

## Lair Actions

On initiative count 20 (losing initiative ties), the sanctum can take a lair action to cause one of the following effects:

**Mystical Fog**: A dense fog fills a 20-foot-radius sphere centered on a point the sanctum chooses. The sphere spreads around corners, and its area is heavily obscured. It lasts until initiative count 20 on the next round.

**Arcane Echoes**: The whispers of ancient spells echo through the sanctum. Each creature within the sanctum must succeed on a DC 15 Wisdom saving throw or be confused (as per the Confusion spell) until initiative count 20 on the next round.

**Protective Wards**: The sanctum activates its protective wards. Until initiative count 20 on the next round, every time a creature within the sanctum takes damage, the sanctum absorbs 10 points of that damage.

## Scaling the Encounter
### Beginning Players (PC levels 1-5)

**Mystical Barrier**: Lower the Wisdom saving throw DC to 13. On a failed save, PCs take 1d6 psychic damage.

**Interview with the Cat**: Shadowwhisk is more lenient and understanding, providing more direct hints and assistance.

**Lair Actions**

Mystical Fog: The fog covers a 10-foot-radius sphere.

Arcane Echoes: Lower the Wisdom saving throw DC to 12.

Protective Wards: The sanctum absorbs 5 points of damage.

### Intermediate Players (PC levels 6-10)

**Mystical Barrier**: Use the Wisdom saving throw DC 18 as provided. On a failed save, PCs take 2d6 psychic damage.

**Interview with the Cat**: Shadowwhisk is more challenging, requiring PCs to be more persuasive and insightful in their interactions.

**Lair Actions**

Mystical Fog: Use the 20-foot-radius sphere as provided.

Arcane Echoes: Use the Wisdom saving throw DC 15 as provided.

Protective Wards: The sanctum absorbs 10 points of damage.

### Advanced Players (PC levels 11+)

**Mystical Barrier**: Increase the Wisdom saving throw DC to 20. On a failed save, PCs take 3d6 psychic damage.

**Interview with the Cat**: Shadowwhisk is cryptic and expects the PCs to decipher its hints and riddles, testing their wisdom and intelligence.

### Lair Actions

Mystical Fog: The fog covers a 30-foot-radius sphere.

Arcane Echoes: Increase the Wisdom saving throw DC to 18.

Protective Wards: The sanctum absorbs 15 points of damage.

# The Graveyard of Echoes

As adventurers approach, they find themselves in a mist-covered graveyard. Tombstones, some ancient and others eerily fresh, dot the landscape. Ghostly apparitions wander, and the aura of Morana, the Deathweaver, is palpable. To navigate through, players must use Morana's "Death's Whisper" to communicate with specific spirits who hold the clues to exit the graveyard. But beware, not all spirits are friendly.

The mist gradually parts, revealing a vast graveyard stretching as far as the eye can see. Ancient tombstones, worn by time, stand alongside newer graves, their inscriptions still sharp. Ethereal figures drift aimlessly between the graves, their translucent forms shimmering in the dim light. The very ground beneath you seems to pulse with a mournful energy, and the distant cry of a raven echoes through the stillness.

## Activities in the Encounter

**Interacting with Morana**: Upon entering the graveyard, the PCs will notice Morana, standing near an

ancient crypt, her raven-black hair flowing like a shadow. Her deep, void-black eyes scan the area, and she beckons the adventurers closer. She offers them the ability to use "Death's Whisper", a talisman in the form of a raven's feather, which allows them to communicate with the spirits of the graveyard.

**Navigating the Graveyard**: The graveyard is a maze of tombstones, crypts, and mausoleums. The party must find the phantom rose, but the path is not straightforward. To navigate, PCs can use the Death's Whisper talisman to communicate with spirits. Some spirits might provide clues or directions, while others might try to lead them astray or into traps.

**Encounter with Spectral Familiars**: As PCs wander, they might disturb the resting places of the Spectral Familiars. These ghostly creatures will challenge the PCs, testing their intentions before allowing them to proceed.

**Graveyard Hand Trap**: In certain areas, if PCs step on disturbed ground, skeletal hands will burst forth, attempting to drag them under. These hands belong to skeletal undead buried beneath, waiting for someone to walk over them.

## Interacting with Morana

Upon entering the graveyard, the PCs will notice Morana, standing near an ancient crypt, her raven-black hair flowing like a shadow. Her deep, void-black eyes scan the area, and she beckons the adventurers closer. As they approach, the temperature around them drops noticeably, and a sense of melancholy fills the air.

Morana speaks in a soft, haunting voice, her words echoing with the weight of centuries. "Travelers of fate, you tread upon sacred ground. The spirits here are restless, and the balance of life and death has been disturbed. Why have you come to this place?"

She listens intently to the party's responses, her eyes piercing into their souls, searching for truth and intent. If the adventurers are honest and respectful, Morana will offer them the ability to use "Death's Whisper", a talisman in the form of a raven's feather, which allows them to communicate with the spirits of the graveyard. She might also provide them with cryptic hints or riddles about the challenges they will face and the location of the phantom rose.

However, if the adventurers are disrespectful or deceitful, Morana might challenge them with a test of character or set the spirits of the graveyard against them. She values honesty and has little patience for those who would defile the sanctity of the graveyard.

Throughout the interaction, Morana's demeanor remains calm and introspective, but there's an underlying sadness in her eyes, a testament to her deep connection with the spirits of the dead. She may also share snippets of her own past, hinting at her role as one of the guardians of the land and her exile. The adventurers might also catch glimpses of her powers, such as her ability to command the dead or commune with spirits, showcasing her mastery over necromancy.

Before the adventurers depart, Morana might offer them a word of caution or a piece of advice, reminding them of the delicate balance of life and death and the importance of their quest. She fades into the mist, her presence lingering long after she's gone, leaving the adventurers with a sense of purpose and a deeper understanding of the challenges ahead.

## Navigating the Graveyard

The Graveyard of Echoes is a sprawling, mist-covered expanse of tombstones, crypts, and mausoleums. The air is thick with the weight of countless souls, and the very ground seems to whisper with the voices of the departed. The phantom rose, a rare and ethereal bloom, is hidden deep within this eerie maze, and finding it is no simple task.

The graveyard is divided into a grid (e.g., 6x6 or 8x8 oversized squares/hexes). Each square represents a different section of the graveyard.

The DM should decide in which square the phantom rose is located. The players do not know this location initially.

**Death's Whisper**: Upon the party's entrance into the graveyard, Morana offers the PCs the Death's Whisper talisman. Activating it takes 1 minute. When used, the player can ask a spirit in the current square for guidance. The use of Death's Whisper is restricted to the graveyard.

Roll a d20:

- 1-5: The spirit is malevolent and either lies or tries to lead the players into a trap.

- 6-10: The spirit is confused or disoriented, providing vague or unhelpful information.

- 11-15: The spirit is neutral and provides a hint about the direction but not the exact path.

- 16-20: The spirit is benevolent and provides clear guidance toward the next step in the path to the phantom rose.

**Traps and Challenges**: Some squares in the graveyard contain traps (like the Graveyard Hand Trap) or challenges (e.g., a riddle inscribed on a tombstone, a ghostly guardian that must be appeased, or a crypt that must be navigated).

The DM can decide which squares contain these challenges or roll randomly as players enter new squares.

**Finding the Phantom Rose**: Once players reach the square containing the phantom rose, they must still locate it. This could involve a final riddle, a challenge of character (e.g., confronting a personal fear or making a sacrifice), or a test of their skills (e.g., a DC 15 Wisdom (Perception) check to spot the rose among other ghostly flora).

## Riddles

Easy:
Riddle: What do ghosts use to wash their hair?
Answer: Sham-boo!

Easy:
Riddle: What room do ghosts avoid?
Answer: The living room.

Easy:
Riddle: What has a broom and flies, but isn't an aircraft?
Answer: A witch.

Easy to Medium:
Riddle: Why did the vampire get a job at the art store?
Answer: He wanted to draw some blood.

Medium:
Riddle: I'm tall when I'm young and short when I'm old. What am I?
Answer: A candle.

Medium to Hard:
Riddle: I'm not a ghost, but I float with the air. You can't see me, but you know I'm there. What am I?
Answer: A breath.

Hard:
Riddle: I speak without a mouth and hear without ears. I have no body, but I come alive with the wind. What am I?
Answer: An echo.

Hard:
Riddle: The person who makes it, sells it. The person who buys it never uses it. The person who uses it never knows they're using it. What is it?
Answer: A coffin.

## Graveyard Hand Trap

Within the Graveyard of Echoes, certain patches of ground are disturbed, the soil slightly looser and darker than its surroundings. Beneath this deceptive surface, skeletal undead lie in wait, ready to grasp at any who tread too closely. These skeletons are animated by dark magic, seeking to drag the living down into the cold embrace of the grave.

**Trigger**: Stepping on a disturbed patch of ground within the trap's area.

**Effect**: As soon as a creature steps onto the disturbed plot, skeletal hands burst forth, attempting to grab and pull them under.

The creature must succeed on a DC 15 Dexterity saving throw to avoid being grappled. If grappled, they are restrained as the skeletal hands begin to pull their quarry into the ground.

At the start of each of the restrained creature's turns, they take 1d6 bludgeoning damage as they are slowly crushed by being pulled into the ground.

A creature restrained by the skeletal hands can use its action to make a DC 16 Strength (Athletics) or Dexterity (Acrobatics) check, freeing itself on a success.

**Detection**:

A DC 14 Wisdom (Perception) check reveals the disturbed patches of ground that mark the trap's location.

A DC 16 Intelligence (Investigation) check allows a character to deduce the nature of the trap from the disturbed ground and nearby skeletal remains.

**Disable**:

A DC 16 Wisdom (Religion) or Intelligence (Arcana) check can temporarily suppress the magic animating the hands, rendering the trap inert for 10 minutes.

Physically digging up and removing or destroying the skeletal undead will permanently disable the trap in that specific area. This requires 10 minutes of work.

## Encounter with Spectral Familiars

As the adventurers navigate the maze-like graveyard, they might come across a particularly ancient and ornate tombstone, surrounded by a faint, shimmering aura. As they approach, the temperature around them drops noticeably, and the soft glow of ethereal light becomes more pronounced.

Suddenly, from the shadows, a Spectral Familiar emerges. It could be a translucent cat with piercing eyes, a raven with wings that seem to shimmer and dissolve into the mist, or a toad that hops with an eerie silence. The Spectral Familiar observes the adventurers with a mix of curiosity and caution, its form constantly shifting and wavering as if made of mist.

If the adventurers approach with respect, perhaps leaving an offering or speaking words of peace, the Spectral Familiar might simply watch them, its gaze intense but not hostile. However, if they act with aggression or show any intent to defile the graves, the familiar will react swiftly.

The Spectral Familiar will use its Chilling Touch to ward off any threats, its cold grasp seeking to sap the warmth and energy from those it touches. If faced with multiple adversaries or if it feels particularly threatened, it will let out its Eerie Cry, the haunting sound echoing through the graveyard and potentially stunning those who hear it.

If Morana is present or if the adventurers have gained her favor, she might intervene, calming the Spectral Familiar and preventing further conflict. She could also provide insight into the familiar's past, revealing its connection to a particular witch and its role as a guardian of the graveyard.

However, if the adventurers manage to show genuine respect and perhaps even assist the Spectral Familiar in some way (e.g., by repairing a damaged tombstone or laying a restless spirit to rest), they might gain the familiar's trust. In gratitude, the Spectral Familiar could provide them with valuable information, guiding them towards the phantom rose or warning them of other dangers lurking in the graveyard.

## Lair Actions

On initiative count 20 (losing initiative ties), the graveyard domain (or Morana herself, if she is present) can take a lair action to cause one of the following effects:

**Summon Spirits**: 1d4 spirits are summoned either by Morana or spontaneously (use the Specter stats from the *Monster Manual*), either to aid Morana if she is present or hinder the players.

**Chill of the Grave**: The temperature drops suddenly. Each creature in the graveyard must succeed on a DC 15 Constitution saving throw or take 2d6 cold damage.

**Whispers of the Dead**: Ghostly whispers fill the air. Each creature in the graveyard must succeed on a DC 14 Wisdom saving throw or be frightened until the next round.

## Scaling the Encounter

### Beginning Players (PC levels 1-5)

**Navigating the Graveyard**: Spirits are more inclined to be helpful, with a 1-3 roll leading to vague information and a 4-6 roll providing clear guidance.

**Graveyard Hand Trap**: Lower the Dexterity saving throw DC to 12. If grappled, players can break free with a DC 13 Strength (Athletics) or Dexterity (Acrobatics) check.Lair Actions:

**Summon Spirits**: Only 1 spirit is summoned.

**Chill of the Grave**: Lower the Constitution saving throw DC to 12 and deal 1d6 cold damage.

**Whispers of the Dead**: Lower the Wisdom saving throw DC to 12.

### Intermediate Players (PC levels 6-10)

**Navigating the Graveyard**: Spirits have a balanced mix of helpfulness and deceit.

**Graveyard Hand Trap**

Use the trap as described.

**Lair Actions**

Summon Spirits: 1d3 spirits are summoned.

Chill of the Grave: Use the Constitution saving throw DC 15 and deal 2d6 cold damage as described.

Whispers of the Dead: Use the Wisdom saving throw DC 14 as described.

### Advanced Players (PC levels 11+)

**Navigating the Graveyard**: Spirits are more likely to be deceitful or lead players into traps.

**Graveyard Hand Trap**

Increase the Dexterity saving throw DC to 17.

If grappled, players must make a DC 18 Strength (Athletics) or Dexterity (Acrobatics) check to break free.

**Lair Actions**

Summon Spirits: 1d4+1 spirits are summoned.

Chill of the Grave: Increase the Constitution saving throw DC to 17 and deal 3d6 cold damage.

Whispers of the Dead: Increase the Wisdom saving throw DC to 16.

## Monster

Spectral Familiar

# The Labyrinth of Life

A vast maze made of towering hedges that pulse with life. Flowers bloom and wither in seconds, and the path constantly shifts. Hidden within are wounded animals. To find the way out, PCs must heal these creatures using a method reminiscent of Opalina's "Revitalization." Healing the animals reveals the path forward.

As you step into the next domain, a fragrant aroma fills the air. Before you stretches a vast maze of towering hedges, each pulsing with a vibrant life force. Flowers of every hue bloom and wither in the blink of an eye, their petals dancing in the gentle breeze. The very ground beneath you feels alive, and the distant sound of trickling water beckons you deeper into the labyrinth. The path ahead is uncertain, shifting and changing with each step you take. This is Opalina's realm, a testament to the ever-changing cycle of life.

## Activities in the Encounter

**Healing the Wounded Animals**: Scattered throughout the labyrinth are wounded animals: a limping deer, a bird with a broken wing, a rabbit caught in a snare, etc.

PCs can attempt to heal these creatures using spells, skills, or other creative methods that embody the spirit of "Revitalization."

Successfully healing an animal causes a section of the hedge to recede, revealing the path forward. The animals, once healed, might offer clues or assistance to the party.

**Navigating the Maze**: The labyrinth is ever-changing. PCs must be observant, using Wisdom (Perception) checks (DC 15) to notice patterns or clues in the maze's layout.

Certain sections of the maze might present challenges or puzzles that test the PCs' understanding of life, growth, and renewal.

**Interacting with Opalina**: As the adventurers delve deeper into the maze, they might catch fleeting glimpses of Opalina, The Lifegiver. Her radiant form can be seen tending to the plants, whispering to the animals, and guiding the very essence of life within the labyrinth. Her presence is both comforting and enigmatic, a beacon of hope in the ever-shifting maze.

**Encounter with the Green Man Guardians**: These spirits can animate sections of the hedge to block paths, create thorny barriers, or even attempt to ensnare the party.

Player characters can try to communicate or negotiate with the Green Man Guardians, or they might need to defend themselves. The guardians respect displays of understanding and empathy towards nature.

**Objective**: Once the PCs navigate the labyrinth and reach its heart, they find a serene clearing with a fountain. The water in the fountain shines with a pure, crystalline light. Retrieving the water requires careful handling, as it is a symbol of life's delicate balance. As they collect the water, the adventurers feel a sense of peace and rejuvenation, knowing they've passed Opalina's test and are one step closer to breaking the curse of the Blood Moon.

## Using the Printed Maze in "The Labyrinth of Life" Encounter

### Setup

**Prepare the Maze**: Before beginning the encounter, ensure you have the printed maze from the *Witches of the Blood Moon* adventure on hand. Lay it out flat on the table where all players can see it.

**Markers**: Provide each player with a small marker or token to represent their character. This could be a miniature, a coin, or any small object. Place the markers at the maze's entrance.

**Highlight Key Areas**: Using colored pencils or markers, you might want to highlight or mark specific areas of interest within the maze. This could include the

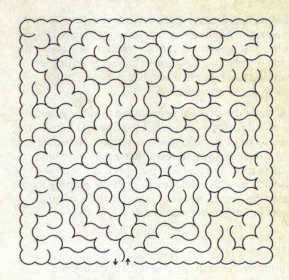

locations of wounded animals, Green Man Guardians, or other challenges.

### Navigating the Maze

**Movement**: Players can move their markers through the maze, following its paths. They should avoid drawing on the maze or marking their route, to maintain the challenge and mystery.

**Challenges and Encounters**: As players navigate the maze, the DM will describe challenges, encounters, or events based on where their markers are positioned. Some sections of the maze might correspond to specific events or encounters detailed in the adventure.

**Healing the Wounded Animals**: When a player's marker reaches a location with a wounded animal, they can attempt the healing challenge as described in the adventure. Successfully healing an animal might reveal a new path or provide a clue to navigate a tricky section.

**Confronting the Green Man Guardians**: If a player's marker enters a section of the maze guarded by a Green Man Guardian, they must resolve the encounter before proceeding.

**Opalina's Guidance**: At certain junctures within the maze, the adventurers might find themselves at a crossroads, unsure of which path to take. In these moments, Opalina might appear, her form shimmering like a mirage. She doesn't directly tell the adventurers which way to go but instead offers cryptic guidance or poses riddles that hint at the correct path. These riddles often revolve around themes of life, growth, and renewal.

For instance, she might say, "Seek the path where life's first cry is heard, and you'll find your way." This could hint at following the sound of a newborn animal's cry.

### Hints and Assistance

**Changing Paths**: Remember, the Labyrinth of Life is ever-changing. If necessary, the DM can adjust the maze's layout, perhaps opening a previously blocked path or introducing a new challenge to keep the adventure dynamic and engaging.

## Conclusion

Once adventurers successfully navigate the maze and reach its heart, they can proceed with the next phase of the encounter, retrieving the flask of water from the fountain. Celebrate their success and teamwork in navigating the challenges of the Labyrinth of Life!

## Lair Actions

On initiative count 20 (losing initiative ties), Opalina's domain takes a lair action to cause one of the following effects:

**Bloom and Wither**: A 20-foot-radius section of the labyrinth rapidly blooms with flowers and then withers away. Any creature in this area must succeed on a DC 15 Dexterity saving throw or be restrained by the withering plants until the end of their next turn.

**Guiding Breeze**: A gentle wind blows through the labyrinth, carrying with it the soft whispers of Opalina. One PC can gain advantage on their next Wisdom (Perception) or Wisdom (Survival) check to navigate the maze.

**Nature's Embrace**: Vines and roots erupt from the ground in a 20-foot square area. The area becomes difficult terrain, and any creature in the area must

succeed on a DC 15 Strength saving throw or be grappled by the vines.

## Scaling the Encounter

### Beginning Players (PC levels 1-5)

**Healing the Wounded Animals**: Simplify the healing process. A basic Medicine check (DC 10) or any healing spell will suffice.

**Navigating the Maze**: Reduce the complexity of the maze. Offer more frequent hints or clues to guide players.

**Encounter with the Green Man Guardians**: They are less aggressive and more open to negotiation.

**Lair Actions**

Bloom and Wither: Lower the Dexterity saving throw DC to 12.

Nature's Embrace: Lower the Strength saving throw DC to 12.

### Intermediate Players (PC levels 6-10)

**Healing the Wounded Animals**: Use the healing process as described. Introduce minor challenges, such as an animal being scared or wary.

**Navigating the Maze**: Use the maze as described. Offer occasional hints or clues.

**Encounter with the Green Man Guardians**: They are cautious but can be negotiated with or confronted.

**Lair Actions**

Bloom and Wither: Use the Dexterity saving throw DC 15 as described.

Nature's Embrace: Use the Strength saving throw DC 15 as described.

### Advanced Players (PC levels 11+)

**Healing the Wounded Animals**: Introduce additional challenges to the healing process, such as animals being under a curse or affliction that requires more than just physical healing.

**Navigating the Maze**: Increase the complexity of the maze. Offer fewer hints and introduce more deceptive paths.

**Encounter with the Green Man Guardians**: Add additional abilities related to controlling the maze's growth or summoning smaller guardians.

### Lair Actions

Bloom and Wither: Increase the Dexterity saving throw DC to 17.

Nature's Embrace: Increase the Strength saving throw DC to 17.

## Monster

Green Man Guardian

# The Elemental Tempest

As the adventurers step into the elemental domain of Elyra, they are immediately met with a force of nature unlike any they've ever experienced. The Elemental Tempest, though contained within the Witches' Sanctum, is a pocket dimension where the raw forces of nature are magnified and unbridled. The Misty Woods around the Sanctum act as a buffer, absorbing and dispersing some of the elemental energy, ensuring the tempest doesn't spill out and ravage the surrounding lands.

As you step into the elemental domain of Elyra, a rush of wind nearly knocks you off your feet. The world around you is a maelstrom of elemental chaos. One moment, you're surrounded by the intense heat of a desert, the next, you're shivering in a blizzard. Torrential rain gives way to blinding sandstorms, and all the while, the howling wind carries the distant cries of banshees. This is the Elemental Tempest, a realm where nature's fury is unleashed, and only those with the will to endure can hope to navigate its challenges.

## Interacting with Elyra

Upon entering the tempest, the adventurers will spot Elyra standing atop a raised platform, her hands lifted as she seems to be in deep concentration, channeling and balancing the elemental forces around her. Her hair shifts colors rapidly, reflecting the changing environment. As the party approaches, she'll momentarily break her concentration to address them. She might challenge the adventurers, questioning their intentions and testing their respect for the elemental forces. If they prove themselves worthy, she might offer guidance or assistance in navigating the tempest and retrieving the Storm Crystal. However, any sign of hostility or recklessness will earn her ire, and she might use her elemental mastery against the party.

## Navigating the Tempest

The Elemental Tempest, though seemingly vast and boundless, is a carefully constructed pocket dimension within the Witches' Sanctum. Elyra, with her deep connection to the elements, has crafted this realm to be both a testament to nature's power and a protective barrier for the Storm Crystal. The Misty Woods surrounding the Sanctum act as a natural buffer, their ancient trees and dense fog absorbing and dispersing the tempest's raw energy. This ensures that while the tempest rages within, the outside world remains unaffected.

**Elemental Shifts**: Every 10 minutes (or at the DM's discretion), the environment within the tempest changes. Use a d4 to determine the shift:

1. Blazing Heat - PCs must make a DC 15 Constitution saving throw or suffer a level of exhaustion.

2. Freezing Cold - PCs must make a DC 15 Constitution saving throw or take 1d6 cold damage.

3. Gale-Force Winds - PCs' movement is halved, and ranged attacks are made with disadvantage.

4. Torrential Downpour - Vision is obscured beyond 15 feet, and the ground becomes difficult terrain.

**Harnessing the Elements**: The party can use spells or abilities to counteract or harness the elemental forces. For example, *Control Weather*, *Gust of Wind*, or *Protection from Energy* can be particularly useful.

## Storm Banshees

As the adventurers delve deeper into the tempest, they'll notice a lone Storm Banshee hovering near one of the obelisks. This ethereal creature seems to be drawing power from the obelisk, its form becoming more tangible and its cries more haunting. The banshee regards the adventurers with a mix of curiosity and wariness. If they approach the obelisk or the crystal without showing proper respect for the elemental forces, the Storm Banshee will attack, using its haunting wails and the power of the tempest to its advantage. If, however, the adventurers approach with caution and reverence, the Storm Banshee might simply observe, or even offer cryptic hints to aid them.

## The Storm Crystal

The Storm Crystal is ensconced atop a raised dais in a circular clearing at the very heart of the tempest. The dais is made of a smooth, dark stone that seems to absorb and reflect the elemental energies around it. Four tall obelisks surround the dais, each pulsating with a different elemental energy: fire, ice, wind, and water. These obelisks are the source of the tempest's power, channeling and amplifying the elemental forces that rage throughout the domain.

As the party approaches the clearing, they'll notice that the elemental shifts become more rapid and unpredictable, with the environment changing every few moments. The banshees are also more active here, drawn to the raw power of the obelisks.

**Retrieval**: The Storm Crystal itself floats above the dais, enveloped in a swirling vortex of combined elemental energies. This vortex is a maelstrom of searing heat, biting cold, buffeting winds, and drenching rains, all occurring simultaneously. Any creature attempting to simply reach into the vortex to grab the crystal will be met with a barrage of elemental effects.

**Approaching the Vortex**: Any creature that comes within 5 feet of the vortex must make a DC 18 Dexterity saving throw, taking 2d6 fire damage, 2d6 cold damage, and being knocked back 10 feet on a failed save, or half as much damage on a successful one.

### Retrieving the Crystal

**Disabling the Obelisks**: PCs can attempt to disrupt or disable the obelisks, which will weaken the vortex. Each obelisk can be disrupted using a counter-element (e.g., using cold against the fire obelisk). Successfully disrupting all four will calm the vortex enough to safely retrieve the crystal.

**Elemental Shielding**: Spells like *Protection from Energy* or *Absorb Elements* can be used to shield a PC as they reach into the vortex. With the right protection, they can grab the crystal without harm.

**Clever Distractions**: Players might come up with creative solutions, like using summoned creatures or illusions to distract the banshees and obelisks, giving them a brief window to snatch the crystal.

**Direct Confrontation**: A brave (or foolhardy) PC might simply try to endure the elemental barrage and grab the crystal. This would require a DC 20 Constitution saving throw to withstand the combined elemental effects and successfully retrieve the crystal.

## Lair Actions

On initiative count 20 (losing initiative ties), the tempest domain (or Elyra herself, if she is present) can take a lair action to cause one of the following effects:

**Elemental Surge**: One of the elemental forces intensifies (heat, cold, wind, rain). For the next round, the effects of that element are doubled.

**Banshee's Call**: A Storm Banshee appears within the tempest.

**Elemental Harmony**: There is a brief calm in the tempest. For the next round, the environment remains stable, offering PCs a momentary respite.

## Scaling the Encounter

### Beginning Players (PC levels 1-5)

**Elemental Shifts**

Reduce the DC for Constitution saving throws to 12.

Freezing Cold: PCs take 1d4 cold damage on a failed save.

**Retrieval**

Approaching the Vortex: Lower the Dexterity saving throw DC to 14 and reduce the damage to 1d4 fire and 1d4 cold.

Retrieving the Crystal: Lower the Constitution saving throw DC to 15 for direct confrontation.

**Lair Actions**

Elemental Surge: The effects of the chosen element are increased by 50% instead of doubled.

### Intermediate Players (PC levels 6-10)

**Elemental Shifts**: Use the described DCs and effects.

**Retrieval**

Approaching the Vortex: Use the described DCs and effects.

Retrieving the Crystal: Use the described DC 20 Constitution saving throw for direct confrontation.

**Lair Actions**: Use the described effects.

### Advanced Players (PC levels 11+)

**Elemental Shifts**

Increase the DC for Constitution saving throws to 18.

Blazing Heat: On a failed save, players suffer a level of exhaustion and take 1d6 fire damage.

Freezing Cold: PCss take 2d6 cold damage on a failed save.

**Retrieval**

Approaching the Vortex: Increase the Dexterity saving throw DC to 20 and the damage to 3d6 fire and 3d6 cold.

Retrieving the Crystal: Increase the Constitution saving throw DC to 22 for direct confrontation.

### Lair Actions

Elemental Surge: The effects of the chosen element are tripled.

Banshee's Call: Two Storm Banshees appear simultaneously.

## Monster

Storm Banshee

# The Cauldron of Fates

The Cauldron of Fates is both a challenge and an opportunity for the adventurers. While the Cauldron Wights and the unpredictable nature of the potion present dangers, the potential insights offered by the cauldron can be invaluable.

As you step into the heart of the sanctum, a cavernous chamber opens up before you. The air is thick with a mix of fragrant herbs and a metallic tang. Dominating the center of the room is a massive, ornate cauldron, its dark iron sides etched with glowing runes. A thick, shimmering potion bubbles within, its surface occasionally disturbed by a vision or memory that flashes briefly before disappearing. Shadows dance around the room, cast by the cauldron's eerie luminescence. The weight of countless fates, both realized and potential, presses down upon you.

## Cauldron Wights

These spectral guardians are bound to the cauldron, ensuring that only those deemed worthy can approach. They appear as ghostly figures, their forms constantly shifting between different stages of life, from youth to old age.

**Tactics**: The Cauldron Wights will attempt to prevent anyone from approaching the cauldron. They will focus on spellcasters first, recognizing them as potential threats to the cauldron's magic.

## Witch's Brew Cauldron Trap

The cauldron's potion is powerful and unpredictable. Those who drink from it without proper preparation or respect risk being overwhelmed.

**Trigger**: A character drinks from the cauldron.

**Effect**: The character must make a DC 17 Wisdom saving throw. On a successful save, they receive a vision of a possible future event, which the DM can use to foreshadow upcoming events in the campaign. On a failed save, they are overwhelmed by visions of their deepest fears and regrets, becoming stunned for 1 minute. They can repeat the saving throw at the end of each of their turns, ending the effect on a success.

**Detection**: A character with proficiency in Arcana or who casts *Detect Magic* will sense the overwhelming divination magic within the brew and might deduce its unpredictable nature.

**Disable**: The trap cannot be disabled per se, but a character who offers a respectful prayer or ritual before drinking might be granted advantage on the saving throw, at the DM's discretion.

## Summoning the Witches

The summoning of the witches is a pivotal moment in the adventure. The ritual not only brings forth the guardians of Moonsorrow but also symbolizes the PCs' journey and the challenges they've overcome. As the DM, emphasize the gravity of the ritual and the transformation of the cauldron's potion. The appearance of the witches should feel like a moment of awe and reverence, a culmination of the PCs' efforts in the sanctum.

To summon the three witches, the PCs must add the following ingredients to the Cauldron of Fates:

- A phantom rose from the Graveyard of Echoes
- A flask of water from the fountain at the center of the Labyrinth of Life
- A Storm Crystal from The Elemental Tempest

Once the ingredients are added, the cauldron's potion will change colors, swirling with vibrant hues before settling into a deep, starry black. The room will grow cold, and the three witches will emerge from the cauldron's depths, their forms materializing from the potion itself.

**Learning the Ritual**: The PCs can learn about the necessary ingredients and the summoning ritual in several ways:

**Ancient Tomes**: Scattered throughout the sanctum are old books and scrolls. With a successful DC 18 Investigation check, a PC can find a tome detailing the ritual to summon the witches.

**Spirits of the Sanctum**: Ghostly apparitions wander the sanctum, remnants of those who once served the witches. With a successful DC 16 Persuasion or Charisma (Performance) check, a PC can convince a spirit to share the knowledge of the ritual.

**Visions from the Cauldron**: Drinking from the cauldron, as mentioned earlier, can provide visions. If a PC successfully saves against the cauldron's effects, they might receive a vision of the witches performing the ritual, giving them clues about the required ingredients.

## Shadowwhisk, the Cat Familiar

If the PCs have previously encountered and befriended Shadowwhisk, the cat might provide hints or even directly inform the PCs about the ritual, especially if they've proven their intentions to be pure.

## Lair Actions

On initiative count 20 (losing initiative ties), the Cauldron of Fates can take a lair action to cause one of the following effects:

**Visions of the Past**: The cauldron bubbles more intensely, and the room is filled with ghostly apparitions reenacting past events. All creatures in the room must make a DC 15 Wisdom saving throw or become entranced by the visions, gaining the restrained condition until the start of their next turn.

**Mystical Fog**: A thick, magical fog billows out from the cauldron, filling the chamber. The area becomes heavily obscured for 1 round.

**Potion Overflow**: The cauldron overflows, and the potion spills out in a 15-foot radius around it. Any creature in that area must make a DC 15 Dexterity saving throw or take 2d6 acid damage as the potion burns their skin.

## Scaling the Encounter

### Beginning Players (PC levels 1-5)

**Cauldron Wights**: Only 1 Cauldron Wight guards the cauldron.

**Witch's Brew Cauldron Trap**

Lower the Wisdom saving throw DC to 12.

On a failed save, the character is stunned for 1 round.

**Summoning the Witches**

Reduce the Investigation check DC to 12 for finding information about the ritual in ancient tomes.

Reduce the Persuasion or Charisma (Performance) check DC to 12 for convincing spirits.

### Lair Actions

Visions of the Past: Lower the Wisdom saving throw DC to 12.

Potion Overflow: Reduce the Dexterity saving throw DC to 12 and the damage to 1d4 acid.

### Intermediate Players (PC levels 6-10)

**Cauldron Wights**: Guarding the cauldron are 1d2 Cauldron Wights.

**Witch's Brew Cauldron Trap**: Use the described DCs and effects.

**Summoning the Witches**: Use the described DCs for checks.

**Lair Actions**: Use the described effects.

### Advanced Players (PC levels 11+)

**The Cauldron of Fates**

Cauldron Wights: Guarding the cauldron are 1d4+1 Cauldron Wights.

Witch's Brew Cauldron Trap:

Increase the Wisdom saving throw DC to 20.

On a failed save, the character is stunned for 1 minute and takes 1d6 psychic damage from the overwhelming visions.

**Summoning the Witches**

Increase the Investigation check DC to 20 for finding information about the ritual in ancient tomes.

Increase the Persuasion or Charisma (Performance) check DC to 20 for convincing spirits.

**Lair Actions**

Visions of the Past: Increase the Wisdom saving throw DC to 18.

Potion Overflow: Increase the Dexterity saving throw DC to 18 and the damage to 3d6 acid.

## Monster

Cauldron Wight

# The Council of the Witches

As the final ingredient melds into the Cauldron of Fates, the room is filled with a blinding light. When the light fades, standing before you are the three legendary witches: Morana, with her raven-black hair and void-like eyes; Opalina, radiant and ethereal, her presence a beacon of life; and Elyra, her form shifting and shimmering, embodying the raw power of the elements. The air is thick with ancient magic, and the weight of countless fates hangs in the balance. The witches gaze upon you, their expressions a mix of curiosity, hope, and determination. The Council of the Witches has begun.

**Dialogue with the Witches**: The witches will first seek to understand the intentions of the adventurers. They will ask questions about their journey, their understanding of the Blood Moon curse, and their goals. Depending on the PCs' responses, the witches might offer guidance, share ancient knowledge, or even provide magical assistance.

**Aligning with the Witches**: If the PCs express a desire to help restore balance to Moonsorrow and counteract Helbindr's curse, the witches will propose an alliance. They will share information about Helbindr and provide the PCs with resources for the upcoming confrontation.

**Challenging the Witches**: If the PCs are aligned with the Purifiers or choose to challenge the witches, a battle ensues. The witches, while not seeking conflict, will defend themselves and their sanctum. They will use their combined powers, drawing from the domains of life, death, and the elements.

**Summoning Helbindr**: If the PCs align with the witches, the trio will use their combined powers to summon Helbindr for a final confrontation. The room will grow cold, and a portal of swirling shadows will form, from which Helbindr, The Frostbound Sovereign of Niflshadow, will emerge.

**Helbindr's Retreat**: If the confrontation with Helbindr ensues and he is reduced to 1 HP, the Frostbound Sovereign will recognize the direness of his situation. His pride and self-preservation instincts will kick in.

As the final blow lands, Helbindr's form becomes unstable, and the icy shadows that compose his being start to waver and crack. With a roar of frustration and a chilling wind that sweeps through the sanctum, he shouts, "This is not the end! The frost will return!" With that, he retreats into a portal of swirling shadows, escaping back to the cold abyss of Niflshadow.

## Lair Actions

Elemental Shift: Elyra can cause a sudden shift in the environment. A gust of wind might attempt to push intruders back, flames might erupt from the ground, or the floor might become icy and slippery. PCs must make a DC 15 Dexterity saving throw or suffer the effects.

Spectral Guardians: Morana can summon spectral guardians from the Cauldron of Fates. These spirits will defend the witches and challenge any intruders.

Life's Embrace: Opalina can cause plants and vines to sprout rapidly from the ground, attempting to entangle and restrain intruders. PCs must make a DC 16 Strength saving throw or be restrained.

## Scaling the Encounter

### Beginning Players (PC levels 1-5)

**Dialogue with the Witches**: Keep the dialogue straightforward, with the witches being more guiding and understanding, given the PCs' lower experience level.

**Aligning with the Witches**: The witches provide basic resources such as healing potions, scrolls, or a minor magical item.

**Challenging the Witches**: If combat ensues, the witches use their powers sparingly, focusing more on defensive and crowd-control spells rather than direct damage.

**Summoning Helbindr**: If summoned, Helbindr should have reduced HP and damage output to match the PCs' level.

**Lair Actions**

Elemental Shift: Lower the Dexterity saving throw DC to 12.

Spectral Guardians: Summon fewer guardians, and they should have reduced HP and damage output.

Life's Embrace: Lower the Strength saving throw DC to 13.

### Intermediate Players (PC levels 6-10)

**Dialogue with the Witches**: The dialogue can be more intricate, with the witches challenging the PCs' knowledge and intentions.

**Aligning with the Witches**: The witches provide more advanced resources, such as greater healing potions, higher-level scrolls, or a medium-tier magical item.

**Challenging the Witches**: The witches use a balanced mix of their powers, combining both defensive and offensive spells.

**Summoning Helbindr**: Helbindr should be at a medium power level, with abilities and stats reflecting a challenge for intermediate players.

### Lair Actions

Elemental Shift: Use the Dexterity saving throw DC 15 as provided.

Spectral Guardians: Summon a moderate number of guardians with standard HP and damage output.

Life's Embrace: Use the Strength saving throw DC 16 as provided.

## Advanced Players (PC levels 11+)

**Dialogue with the Witches**: The dialogue should be complex, with the witches testing the PCs' knowledge, intentions, and even their morality.

**Aligning with the Witches**: The witches provide high-tier resources, such as superior healing potions, high-level scrolls, or powerful magical items.

**Challenging the Witches**: The witches unleash the full extent of their powers, using high-level spells and combining their abilities for maximum effect.

**Summoning Helbindr**: Helbindr should be at his most powerful, with abilities and stats designed to challenge even the most seasoned adventurers.

### Lair Actions

Elemental Shift: Increase the Dexterity saving throw DC to 18.

Spectral Guardians: Summon a large number of guardians with increased HP and damage output.

Life's Embrace: Increase the Strength saving throw DC to 19.

# NPC

Morana, The Deathweaver

Opalina, The Lifegiver

Elyra, The Stormcaller

Helbindr

# Resolution

Below are different resolutions for the adventure.

## The PCs, With the Witches, Defeat Helbindr

As the final blow lands on Helbindr, the Frostbound Sovereign lets out a chilling scream that echoes throughout the sanctum. The icy tendrils and shadows that had seeped into Moonsorrow begin to recede, replaced by a warm, golden light. The Blood Moon's crimson hue fades, revealing a pale, shining moon in a clear starry sky. The three witches, their powers now fully restored, stand tall and triumphant. The land of Moonsorrow, once on the brink of eternal winter, is saved.

**Reward**: The witches, in gratitude, bestow upon each member of the party a Token of Moonsorrow. When used, this token allows the bearer to cast the Bless spell at 3rd level without expending a spell slot (usable once per long rest). Additionally, the adventurers gain the lasting respect and friendship of the witches, making the Misty Woods and the witches' sanctum a safe haven for them in future adventures.

## The PCs, With the Witches, Are Defeated by Helbindr

The might of Helbindr proves too overwhelming. As the last of the party falls, the Frostbound Sovereign lets out a triumphant roar, solidifying his icy grip on Moonsorrow. The witches, weakened and defeated, are forced into hiding. The land plunges into an eternal winter, its once-vibrant beauty now lost beneath layers of frost and shadow. The Blood Moon's crimson glow becomes a permanent fixture in the sky, a haunting reminder of the day darkness prevailed.

**Reward**: Though the party has been defeated, not all hope is lost. The adventurers awaken in a safe location, nursed back to health by a mysterious benefactor. They each receive a Charm of Resilience, which grants them advantage on saving throws against cold damage and resistance to cold damage for 7 days. This charm serves as a reminder of their defeat but also as a symbol of hope and the will to fight another day.

## The PCs Align With the Purifiers and Defeat the Witches

With the witches defeated, the Purifiers celebrate their victory, believing they've rid Moonsorrow of its curse. However, as the days pass, the Blood Moon's influence does not wane. The icy shadows continue to spread, and it becomes clear that the true threat was not the witches but Helbindr himself. The land remains in peril, its fate uncertain.

**Reward**: The Purifiers, grateful for the party's assistance, reward them with Purifier Sigils. These sigils grant the bearer advantage on Charisma (Persuasion) checks when interacting with anyone outside of the Purifier faction. Additionally, the adventurers gain a reputation among the Purifiers, which could lead to future quests or alliances. However, the lingering threat of the Blood Moon and Helbindr's unchecked power looms large, setting the stage for future challenges.

# Scaling Monsters

Use the following table for party size to increase the number of monsters:

| Party Size | Increase number by |
| --- | --- |
| 5-8 | x 1.5 |
| 9-12 | x 2 |
| 13 | x 2.5 |

Use the following table for party level to increase the number of monsters:

| Party Level | Increase number by |
| --- | --- |
| 5-8 | x 1.5 |
| 9-12 | x 2 |
| 13-15 | x 2.5 |
| Level 16+ | x 3.5 |

Now take the number for the party and the level and add the two together. For instance, if you have a party size of 5 with an average party level of 10, then you would add 1.5 + 2.5 to get 4 times the monsters. 3 creatures for a level 10 party are no challenge, especially if there are 6 or 7 PC's. Increase that to 12, and suddenly you have a challenge. Feel free to adjust as you see fit.

In addition to scaling monster numbers, many of the traps and puzzles in the game have a sliding scale that the DM can use to change the level of difficulty depending on the skillset of the characters.

# Monsters

## Baba Yaga's Sentinel

Medium construct, neutral

**Armor Class** 16 (natural armor)

**Hit Points** 60 (8d8 + 24)

**Speed** 30 ft.

| STR | DEX | CON | INT | WIS | CHA |
|-----|-----|-----|-----|-----|-----|
| 18 (+4) | 12 (+1) | 16 (+3) | 6 (-2) | 10 (+0) | 5 (-3) |

**Saving Throws** Str +6, Con +5

**Damage Immunities** poison, psychic

**Condition Immunities** charmed, exhaustion, frightened, paralyzed, poisoned

**Senses** darkvision 60 ft., passive Perception 10

**Languages** Understands the languages of its creator but can't speak

**Challenge** 4 (1,100 XP)

**Immutable Form.** The sentinel is immune to any spell or effect that would alter its form.

**Magic Resistance.** The sentinel has advantage on saving throws against spells and other magical effects.

### Actions

**Multiattack.** The sentinel makes two slam attacks.

**Slam.** Melee Weapon Attack: +6 to hit, reach 5 ft., one target. Hit: 13 (2d8 + 4) bludgeoning damage.

**Guardian's Challenge (Recharge 5-6).** The sentinel lets out a thunderous roar, challenging those who threaten Baba Yaga. Each creature of the sentinel's choice within 30 feet of it must succeed on a DC 14 Wisdom saving throw or be frightened until the end of the sentinel's next turn.

### Reactions

**Protector.** When a creature the sentinel can see attacks a target other than itself that is within 5 feet of it, the sentinel can use its reaction to impose disadvantage on the attack roll.

### Description

Baba Yaga's Sentinels stand at a formidable height of around seven feet, their bodies carved from ancient, darkened wood that has been weathered and worn over countless years. Intricate patterns and runes are etched into their surface, glowing faintly with a soft, green luminescence. Their forms are reminiscent of various forest animals, such as bears, wolves, and large birds of prey, but with a humanoid twist.

Their faces are a blend of the animal they represent and a stoic human visage, with deep-set, glowing eyes that seem to pierce through the darkness. The eyes, devoid of pupils, shimmer with the same green light as the runes, giving them an otherworldly appearance.

Moss and small plants grow in patches on their bodies, especially in the crevices and joints, suggesting that they've been stationary for long periods, blending seamlessly with the forest surroundings. Their movements are surprisingly fluid for beings made of wood, with the creaking and groaning of timber accompanying each motion. When they shift into a defensive or attacking posture, the wooden fibers of their muscles tense visibly, showcasing their formidable strength.

## Cauldron Wight

Medium undead (incorporeal), neutral evil

**Armor Class** 14 (natural armor)

**Hit Points** 58 (9d8 + 18)

**Speed** 0 ft., fly 30 ft. (hover)

| STR | DEX | CON | INT | WIS | CHA |
|-----|-----|-----|-----|-----|-----|
| 15 (+2) | 12 (+1) | 14 (+2) | 13 (+1) | 16 (+3) | 14 (+2) |

**Saving Throws** Wis +6

**Skills** Perception +6, Arcana +4

**Damage Resistances** necrotic; bludgeoning, piercing, and slashing from nonmagical attacks that aren't silvered

**Damage Immunities** poison

**Condition Immunities** exhaustion, poisoned

**Senses** darkvision 60 ft., passive Perception 16

**Languages** Common, plus one other language it knew in life

**Challenge** 4 (1,100 XP)

**Immutable Form.** The Cauldron Wight is immune to any spell or effect that would alter its form.

**Magic Resistance.** The Cauldron Wight has advantage on saving throws against spells and other magical effects.

## Actions

**Multiattack.** The Cauldron Wight makes two melee attacks.

**Life Drain.** Melee Weapon Attack: +5 to hit, reach 5 ft., one creature. Hit: 8 (1d8 + 2) necrotic damage. The target must succeed on a DC 14 Constitution saving throw or its hit point maximum is reduced by an amount equal to the damage taken. This reduction lasts until the target finishes a long rest. The target dies if this effect reduces its hit point maximum to 0.

**Ethereal Gaze.** The Cauldron Wight targets one creature it can see within 30 feet of it. If the target can see the wight, the target must succeed on a DC 14 Wisdom saving throw or be frightened until the end of the wight's next turn.

## Description

Unlike the wights that dominate popular lore, Cauldron Wights are restless, incorporeal spirits. Although they share similar sentiments to their more common, physical counterparts, these wights are forever bound to the cauldron that they sought answers from in life, whether they strove to use or to steal it, an aim they each failed at and likely died for. Their forms are ethereal, with a faint glow that illuminates their skeletal features and tattered robes. Their eyes, however, burn with an intense light, reflecting their eternal quest for knowledge and the torment of the answers they never found.

That force which binds the Cauldron Wights to their cauldrons also inevitably binds them to the will of the witches who control and share the cauldron--doubtless the very witches at whose wrath they met their end. Because of this, their evil may be somewhat contained, depending on the nature and strictness of the witches who control them. Regardless, the Cauldron Wights cannot take any actions that defy their witches' commands. For Morana, Opalina and Elyra, such commands include guarding the cauldron from fools and evildoers, while being strictly forbidden from inflicting great harm or death upon any who enter the sanctum.Thusly, these spirits challenge all who approach the cauldron, ensuring that only those with the purest intentions and the strongest resolve can partake of its visions. Their touch can drain the very life force from a creature, and their gaze can instill fear in even the bravest of souls. Those who seek to drink from the cauldron must first prove themselves worthy in the eyes of these spectral guardians.

# Crossroads Wraith

Medium undead (incorporeal), neutral

**Armor Class** 15 (ethereal armor)

**Hit Points** 68 (8d8 + 32)

**Speed** 0 ft., fly 40 ft. (hover)

| STR | DEX | CON | INT | WIS | CHA |
|-----|-----|-----|-----|-----|-----|
| 8 (-1) | 16 (+3) | 18 (+4) | 14 (+2) | 12 (+1) | 20 (+5) |

**Damage Resistances** acid, fire, lightning, thunder; bludgeoning, piercing, and slashing from nonmagical attacks

**Damage Immunities** cold, necrotic, poison

**Condition Immunities** charmed, exhaustion, frightened, grappled, paralyzed, petrified, poisoned, prone, restrained

**Senses** darkvision 120 ft., passive Perception 11

**Languages** Common, plus two other languages (typically those most commonly spoken in the area of the crossroads)

**Challenge** 6 (2,300 XP)

**Ethereal Sight.** The Crossroads Wraith can see 60 feet into the Ethereal Plane when it is on the Material Plane, and vice versa.

**Incorporeal Movement.** The Crossroads Wraith can move through other creatures and objects as if they were difficult terrain. It takes 5 (1d10) force damage if it ends its turn inside an object.

**Pact Seeker.** The Crossroads Wraith can sense the presence of any creature within 120 feet of it that is seeking to make a pact or deal. It knows the creature's intentions and desires.

## Actions

**Chilling Touch.** Melee Spell Attack: +8 to hit, reach 5 ft., one target. Hit: 17 (4d6 + 3) cold damage.

**Test of Desperation.** The Crossroads Wraith targets one creature it can see within 60 feet of it. The target must succeed on a DC 16 Wisdom saving throw or be compelled to reveal its deepest desires and fears to the wraith. The wraith can then choose to either grant the creature a boon related to its desires or inflict a curse related to its fears. The boon or curse lasts for 24 hours.

**Etherealness.** The Crossroads Wraith enters the Ethereal Plane from the Material Plane, or vice versa. It is visible on the Material Plane while it is in the Border Ethereal, and vice versa, yet it can't affect or be affected by anything on the other plane.

## Description

Crossroads Wraiths are spectral guardians of ancient and mystical crossroads, places where the boundaries between the material and other realms are thin. These wraiths are neither malevolent nor benevolent; they serve as gatekeepers, ensuring that only those with true desperation or unparalleled bravery can access the powerful magics and pacts that crossroads are known for. They appear as ethereal figures, often reflecting the appearance they had in life but twisted by the weight of countless pacts and deals they've overseen. Their eyes glow with an otherworldly light, always watching, always judging. Those who approach a crossroads with the intent of making a pact will surely encounter one of these enigmatic entities, and they would do well to be prepared for the wraith's test.

# Feast's Guardian

Medium undead (incorporeal), neutral

**Armor Class** 15 (natural armor)

**Hit Points** 85 (10d8 + 40)

**Speed** 0 ft., fly 40 ft. (hover)

| STR | DEX | CON | INT | WIS | CHA |
|-----|-----|-----|-----|-----|-----|
| 10 (+0) | 16 (+3) | 18 (+4) | 12 (+1) | 14 (+2) | 16 (+3) |

**Saving Throws** Wis +5, Cha +6

**Damage Resistances** acid, fire, lightning, thunder; bludgeoning, piercing, and slashing from nonmagical attacks

**Damage Immunities** cold, necrotic, poison

**Condition Immunities** charmed, exhaustion, frightened, grappled, paralyzed, petrified, poisoned, prone, restrained

**Senses** darkvision 60 ft., passive Perception 12

**Languages** understands Common but doesn't speak

**Challenge** 4 (1,100 XP)

**Ethereal Sight.** The Feast's Guardian can see 60 feet into the Ethereal Plane when it is on the Material Plane, and vice versa.

**Incorporeal Movement.** The Feast's Guardian can move through other creatures and objects as if they were difficult terrain. It takes 5 (1d10) force damage if it ends its turn inside an object.

## Actions

**Withering Touch.** Melee Weapon Attack: +6 to hit, reach 5 ft., one target. Hit: 17 (4d6 + 3) necrotic damage.

**Guardian's Gaze (Recharge 5-6).** The Feast's Guardian targets one creature it can see within 30 feet of it. The target must succeed on a DC 15 Wisdom saving throw or be paralyzed for 1 minute. The target can repeat the saving throw at the end of each of its turns, ending the effect on itself on a success.

## Reactions

**Feast's Protection.** When a spell of 1st level or higher is cast within 30 feet of the Feast's Guardian, or if the feast is disrupted, the Guardian can move up to its speed toward the source of the disturbance without provoking opportunity attacks. If the disturbance is a creature, the Guardian can make one Withering Touch attack against it as part of this reaction.

## Description

The Feast's Guardian is a spectral entity that haunts banquet halls, places dimly lit by ghostly lanterns and is attracted to the sound of laughter from festivals. This eerie figure, draped in tattered robes and hiding behind a carnival mask, is fiercely protective of the feast it oversees. With eyes glowing a chilling blue, it uses its Guardian's Gaze to paralyze intruders and peer into their cherished memories, enhancing the ghostly banquet.

# Green Man Guardian

Medium fey, neutral

**Armor Class** 15 (natural armor)

**Hit Points** 52 (8d8 + 16)

**Speed** 30 ft.

| STR | DEX | CON | INT | WIS | CHA |
|-----|-----|-----|-----|-----|-----|
| 16 (+3) | 14 (+2) | 14 (+2) | 12 (+1) | 16 (+3) | 14 (+2) |

**Skills** Perception +5, Nature +4

**Damage Resistances** bludgeoning, piercing, and slashing from nonmagical attacks

**Condition Immunities** charmed, frightened

**Senses** passive Perception 15

**Languages** Common, Sylvan

**Challenge** 3 (700 XP)

**False Appearance.** While the Green Man Guardian remains motionless, it is indistinguishable from an ordinary wall of leaves and vines.

**Nature's Ward.** The Green Man Guardian has advantage on saving throws against spells and other magical effects.

## Actions

**Slam.** Melee Weapon Attack: +5 to hit, reach 5 ft., one target. Hit: 10 (2d6 + 3) bludgeoning damage.

**Animate Vines (Recharge 5-6).** The Green Man Guardian animates vines in a 20-foot radius centered on itself. These vines turn the area into difficult terrain. Each creature in that area must succeed on a DC 14

Strength saving throw or be restrained by the vines. A creature restrained by the vines can use its action to make a DC 14 Strength check, freeing itself on a success. The vines wilt away after 1 minute or when the Green Man Guardian uses this ability again.

**Nature's Insight.** The Green Man Guardian touches a creature. The target must succeed on a DC 14 Wisdom saving throw or be compelled to speak aloud its true intentions for the next minute. This effect can reveal lies or hidden motives.

## Description

Green Man Guardians are ancient spirits of nature, often associated with pagan and witch folklore. Their visage, a face made of leaves and vines, is a symbol of nature's ever-present gaze and the cyclical nature of life. These guardians are bound to the walls of the labyrinth, serving as its protectors and ensuring that only those with pure intentions can navigate its intricate pathways.

While they are not inherently aggressive, Green Man Guardians are wary of intruders and will defend the labyrinth with determination. They can animate the very walls they are a part of, causing vines to ensnare and restrain those who mean harm. Their most unique ability, however, is to compel those they touch to reveal their true intentions, ensuring that deceit and treachery have no place within the sacred maze. Those who encounter these guardians must tread with respect and honesty, lest they find themselves ensnared by nature's judgment.

# Lantern Spirit

Tiny undead (incorporeal), chaotic neutral

**Armor Class** 19

**Hit Points** 22 (9d4)

**Speed** 0 ft., fly 50 ft. (hover)

| STR | DEX | CON | INT | WIS | CHA |
|---|---|---|---|---|---|
| 1 (-5) | 28 (+9) | 10 (+0) | 13 (+1) | 14 (+2) | 11 (+0) |

**Damage Resistances** lightning, necrotic; bludgeoning, piercing, and slashing from nonmagical attacks

**Damage Immunities** poison

**Condition Immunities** exhaustion, grappled, paralyzed, poisoned, prone, restrained

**Senses** darkvision 120 ft., passive Perception 12

**Languages** understands the languages it knew in life but can't speak

**Challenge** 2 (450 XP)

**Evasion.** If the Lantern Spirit is subjected to an effect that allows it to make a saving throw to take only half damage, it instead takes no damage if it succeeds on the saving throw, and only half damage if it fails.

**Incorporeal Movement.** The Lantern Spirit can move through other creatures and objects as if they were difficult terrain. It takes 5 (1d10) force damage if it ends its turn inside an object.

**Variable Illumination.** The Lantern Spirit can adjust its brightness, shedding dim light in a 5- to 20-foot radius.

## Actions

**Deceptive Appearance.** The Lantern Spirit takes on the appearance of a loved one or a familiar figure to a creature it can see within 60 feet of it. The target must succeed on a DC 13 Wisdom saving throw or believe the illusion is real until the end of the Lantern Spirit's next turn.

**Mislead.** The Lantern Spirit targets one creature it can see within 60 feet. The target must succeed on a DC 13 Wisdom saving throw or be charmed for 1 minute. While charmed in this way, the target is compelled to follow the light of the Lantern Spirit, moving up to its speed in a direction of the Lantern Spirit's choice during its next turn. The charmed target can repeat the saving throw at the end of each of its turns, ending the effect on itself on a success.

**Shock.** Melee Spell Attack: +4 to hit, reach 5 ft., one target. Hit: 9 (2d8) lightning damage.

**Consume Life.** As a bonus action, the Lantern Spirit can target one creature it can see within 5 feet of it that has 0 hit points and is still alive. The target must succeed on a DC 10 Constitution saving throw against this magic or die. If the target dies, the Lantern Spirit regains 10 (3d6) hit points.

## Description

Lantern Spirits are most commonly found in desolate places where travelers have met their untimely end, such as treacherous forest paths, fog-covered marshlands, and abandoned graveyards. They are particularly drawn to locations where individuals have perished due to deception or betrayal.

These spirits manifest as tiny, ethereal orbs of light, floating aimlessly in the air. Their soft, beckoning glow often attracts the attention of travelers in dark and desolate places. While they are not inherently aggressive, Lantern Spirits are cunning and mischievous, often leading travelers astray for their amusement. However, they possess a weakness to bright, natural light, which can disorient them and make them flee. A well-lit campfire or the first light of dawn can often be a traveler's best defense against these deceptive entities.

# Moonshade Merchant

Medium fey, neutral

**Armor Class** 15 (natural armor)

**Hit Points** 68 (8d8 + 32)

**Speed** 30 ft., fly 30 ft. (hover)

| STR | DEX | CON | INT | WIS | CHA |
|-----|-----|-----|-----|-----|-----|
| 10 (+0) | 16 (+3) | 18 (+4) | 15 (+2) | 14 (+2) | 20 (+5) |

**Saving Throws** Dex +6, Cha +8

**Skills** Persuasion +8, Insight +5

**Damage Resistances** bludgeoning, piercing, and slashing from nonmagical attacks

**Damage Immunities** necrotic, psychic

**Condition Immunities** charmed, frightened

**Senses** darkvision 60 ft., passive Perception 12

**Languages** Common, Sylvan, telepathy 60 ft.

**Challenge** 6 (2,300 XP)

**Ethereal Sight.** The Moonshade Merchant can see 60 feet into the Ethereal Plane when it is on the Material Plane, and vice versa.

**Incorporeal Movement.** The Moonshade Merchant can move through other creatures and objects as if they were difficult terrain. It takes 5 (1d10) force damage if it ends its turn inside an object.

**Memory Trade.** Once per day, the Moonshade Merchant can offer a trade to a creature it can communicate with. The creature can offer a memory or emotion in exchange for a mysterious item from the Merchant's collection. The specifics of the trade are up to the DM.

## Actions

**Ethereal Touch.** Melee Spell Attack: +8 to hit, reach 5 ft., one target. Hit: 12 (2d6 + 5) psychic damage. The target must succeed on a DC 16 Wisdom saving throw or be incapacitated until the end of its next turn as it's overwhelmed by fleeting memories.

**Memory Glimpse (Recharge 5-6).** The Moonshade Merchant targets one creature it can see within 60 feet. The target must succeed on a DC 16 Wisdom saving throw or be stunned until the end of its next turn as it relives a past memory.

## Description

Moonshade Merchants are ethereal beings that wander the realms, trading in memories and emotions rather than material goods. Their translucent forms shimmer under the moonlight, giving them an otherworldly and mysterious appearance. They carry with them an assortment of strange and arcane items, each with its own story and history. When they trade, it's not for gold or jewels, but for the intangible experiences that shape a being's life. Some seek out the Moonshade Merchants to forget painful memories, while others hope to gain wisdom or insight from the emotions of others. Whatever the reason, those who deal with these merchants are forever changed by the experience.

# Samhain Sentinel

Medium construct, neutral

**Armor Class** 13 (natural armor)

**Hit Points** 52 (8d8 + 16)

**Speed** 30 ft.

| STR | DEX | CON | INT | WIS | CHA |
|-----|-----|-----|-----|-----|-----|
| 16 (+3) | 12 (+1) | 14 (+2) | 6 (-2) | 12 (+1) | 8 (-1) |

**Damage Immunities** poison, psychic

**Condition Immunities** charmed, exhaustion, frightened, paralyzed, poisoned

**Senses** darkvision 60 ft. (pierces illusions), passive Perception 11

**Languages** understands Common but can't speak

**Challenge** 4 (1,100 XP)

**Immutable Form.** The Samhain Sentinel is immune to any spell or effect that would alter its form.

**Magic Resistance.** The Samhain Sentinel has advantage on saving throws against spells and other magical effects.

**Piercing Gaze.** The Samhain Sentinel's darkvision allows it to see through illusions and invisibility within 60 feet.

## Actions

**Multiattack.** The Samhain Sentinel makes two slam attacks.

**Slam.** Melee Weapon Attack: +5 to hit, reach 5 ft., one target. Hit: 8 (1d10 + 3) bludgeoning damage.

**Fiery Glare (Recharge 5-6).** The Samhain Sentinel targets one creature it can see within 30 feet of it. If the target can see the sentinel, the target must succeed on a DC 13 Wisdom saving throw or be paralyzed for 1 minute. The target can repeat the saving throw at the end of each of its turns, ending the effect on itself on a success. If the saving throw is successful or the effect ends for the target, the target is immune to the sentinel's Fiery Glare for the next 24 hours.

## Description

Samhain Sentinels are the animated guardians of sacred sites during the Samhain festival. Crafted from scarecrows and jack-o'-lanterns, they are given life by ancient druidic rituals to protect and uphold the sanctity of the old ways. Their bodies are made of straw and old clothing, but their heads are carved pumpkins with a fiery glow emanating from within. This glow is not just for show; it grants the sentinels a piercing gaze that can see through the craftiest of illusions.

While they are not inherently hostile, Samhain Sentinels are programmed to challenge and test those who approach their protected sites. They ensure that only those who respect and honor the traditions of Samhain can proceed. Those who try to deceive or bypass these guardians often find themselves paralyzed by the sentinel's fiery glare, unable to move as the sentinel decides their fate.

# Shadow Dancer

Medium undead (incorporeal), neutral evil

**Armor Class** 14

**Hit Points** 45 (10d8)

**Speed** 40 ft.

| STR | DEX | CON | INT | WIS | CHA |
|-----|-----|-----|-----|-----|-----|
| 10 (+0) | 18 (+4) | 10 (+0) | 12 (+1) | 14 (+2) | 16 (+3) |

**Skills** Performance +6, Acrobatics +7

**Damage Resistances** acid, fire, lightning, thunder; bludgeoning, piercing, and slashing from nonmagical attacks

**Damage Immunities** cold, necrotic, poison

**Condition Immunities** exhaustion, frightened, poisoned

**Senses** darkvision 60 ft., passive Perception 12

**Languages** understands Common but can't speak

**Challenge** 4 (1,100 XP)

**Incorporeal Movement.** The Shadow Dancer can move through other creatures and objects as if they were difficult terrain. It takes 5 (1d10) force damage if it ends its turn inside an object.

**Hypnotic Grace.** Any creature that starts its turn within 30 feet of the Shadow Dancer and can see the dancer must make a DC 15 Wisdom saving throw. On a failure, the creature is charmed for 1 minute. While charmed in this way, the creature is incapacitated and has a speed of 0. The creature can repeat the saving throw at the end of each of its turns, ending the effect on itself on a success.

## Actions

**Draining Touch.** Melee Spell Attack: +7 to hit, reach 5 ft., one target. Hit: 17 (4d6 + 3) necrotic damage. The target must succeed on a DC 15 Constitution saving throw or its hit point maximum is reduced by an amount equal to the damage taken. This reduction lasts until the target finishes a long rest. The target dies if this effect reduces its hit point maximum to 0.

**Dance of Despair (Recharge 5-6).** The Shadow Dancer chooses up to three creatures it can see within 30 feet of it. Each target must make a DC 15 Wisdom saving throw. On a failure, the target is forced to dance with the Shadow Dancer, becoming restrained for 1 minute. While restrained in this way, the target takes 10 (3d6) psychic damage at the start of each of its turns. A creature restrained by the dance can use its action to make a Strength or Dexterity check (its choice) against a DC 15 to break free.

## Description

Shadow Dancers are spectral entities that haunt ballrooms, theaters, and other places where dance and performance were once celebrated. They appear as graceful, ethereal figures, moving with a hypnotic elegance that can captivate and ensnare the unwary. Their touch is cold and draining, sapping the life force from those they come into contact with. Legends say that these entities were once dancers themselves, cursed to forever reenact their final performance in death. They seek to draw the living into their eternal dance, trapping them in a cycle of despair and sorrow. Those who encounter a Shadow Dancer are advised to resist the pull of their mesmerizing movements, lest they too become trapped in the dance of the dead.

# Spectral Familiar

Small undead (incorporeal), neutral

**Armor Class** 13

**Hit Points** 22 (5d6 + 5)

**Speed** 30 ft., fly 40 ft. (raven only)

| STR | DEX | CON | INT | WIS | CHA |
|-----|-----|-----|-----|-----|-----|
| 3 (-4) | 16 (+3) | 12 (+1) | 10 (0) | 12 (+1) | 7 (-2) |

**Damage Resistances** acid, fire, lightning, thunder; bludgeoning, piercing, and slashing from nonmagical attacks

**Damage Immunities** cold, poison

**Condition Immunities** charmed, exhaustion, frightened, grappled, paralyzed, petrified, poisoned, prone

**Senses** darkvision 60 ft., passive Perception 11

**Languages** understands the languages it knew in life but can't speak

**Challenge** 1 (200 XP)

**Incorporeal Movement**. The Spectral Familiar can move through other creatures and objects as if they were difficult terrain. It takes 5 (1d10) force damage if it ends its turn inside an object.

**Ethereal Sight**. The Spectral Familiar can see 60 feet into the Ethereal Plane when it is on the Material Plane, and vice versa.

## Actions

**Chilling Touch**. Melee Spell Attack: +5 to hit, reach 5 ft., one target. Hit: 7 (2d6) cold damage.

**Eerie Cry (Recharge 5-6)**. The Spectral Familiar lets out a haunting cry. Each creature within 20 feet of the familiar that hears the cry must succeed on a DC 12 Wisdom saving throw or be stunned until the end of the familiar's next turn.

## Description

Spectral Familiars are the ghostly remnants of creatures that once served witches as companions in life. Taking the form of cats, ravens, or toads, these ethereal beings now guard the resting places of their former masters, ensuring that only those with pure intentions can approach. Their translucent forms shimmer with an otherworldly light, and their movements are silent yet swift.

While they are not inherently aggressive, Spectral Familiars are protective of the graves they guard. They can touch the living with a chilling caress that saps warmth and energy. Their most potent weapon, however, is their eerie cry, a haunting sound that can disorient and stun those who hear it. Those who encounter these ghostly guardians would do well to tread lightly and show respect, lest they find themselves overwhelmed by the combined might of these loyal protectors.

# Stone Circle Protector

Large construct, neutral

**Armor Class** 17 (natural armor)

**Hit Points** 104 (11d10 + 44)

**Speed** 20 ft.

| STR | DEX | CON | INT | WIS | CHA |
|------|------|------|------|------|------|
| 20 (+5) | 8 (-1) | 18 (+4) | 6 (-2) | 10 (+0) | 5 (-3) |

**Damage Vulnerabilities** thunder

**Damage Immunities** poison, psychic

**Condition Immunities** charmed, exhaustion, frightened, paralyzed, petrified, poisoned

**Senses** darkvision 60 ft., passive Perception 10

**Languages** understands Terran but can't speak

**Challenge** 7 (2,900 XP)

**Immutable Form**. The Stone Circle Protector is immune to any spell or effect that would alter its form.

**Magic Resistance**. The Stone Circle Protector has advantage on saving throws against spells and other magical effects.

**Stone Camouflage**. The Stone Circle Protector has advantage on Dexterity (Stealth) checks made to hide in rocky terrain.

## Actions

**Multiattack**. The Stone Circle Protector makes two slam attacks.

**Slam**. Melee Weapon Attack: +8 to hit, reach 5 ft., one target. Hit: 19 (3d8 + 5) bludgeoning damage.

**Ground Slam (Recharge 5-6)**. The Stone Circle Protector slams its fists into the ground, causing a shockwave in a 15-foot radius. All creatures in that area must make a DC 16 Dexterity saving throw, taking 21 (6d6) bludgeoning damage and being knocked prone on a failed save, or half as much damage and not being knocked prone on a successful one.

## Description

Stone Circle Protectors are ancient guardians, carved from the very stones that make up the sacred circles they defend. These constructs are usually dormant, blending seamlessly with the stone circles they are a part of. However, during times of significance, especially on All Hallows' Eve, they awaken to defend their sacred grounds from any intruders. Standing tall, these stone behemoths move with a surprising grace given their rocky composition. Their features are often worn and eroded, but their eyes glow with a deep, earthen light. Intruders who do not heed the warnings of local legends might find themselves facing the wrath of these age-old protectors.

# Storm Banshee

Medium undead (incorporeal), chaotic neutral

**Armor Class** 13

**Hit Points** 76 (9d8 + 36)

**Speed** 0 ft., fly 40 ft. (hover)

| STR | DEX | CON | INT | WIS | CHA |
|-----|-----|-----|-----|-----|-----|
| 8 (-1) | 16 (+3) | 18 (+4) | 6 (-2) | 10 (+0) | 14 (+2) |

**Saving Throws** Wis +4, Cha +6

**Skills** Perception +4

**Damage Resistances** acid, fire, lightning, thunder; bludgeoning, piercing, and slashing from nonmagical attacks

**Damage Immunities** cold, necrotic, poison

**Condition Immunities** charmed, exhaustion, frightened, grappled, paralyzed, petrified, poisoned, prone, restrained

**Senses** darkvision 60 ft., passive Perception 14

**Languages** Common, Auran

**Challenge** 5 (1,800 XP)

**Incorporeal Movement.** The Storm Banshee can move through other creatures and objects as if they were difficult terrain. It takes 5 (1d10) force damage if it ends its turn inside an object.

**Storm Form.** The Storm Banshee is surrounded by a tempestuous aura. When a creature starts its turn within 5 feet of the Storm Banshee, it takes 5 (1d10) lightning damage.

## Actions

**Multiattack.** The Storm Banshee makes two attacks: one with its chilling touch and one with its storm bolt.

**Chilling Touch.** Melee Spell Attack: +6 to hit, reach 5 ft., one target. Hit: 12 (3d6 + 3) cold damage.

**Storm Bolt.** Ranged Spell Attack: +6 to hit, range 60 ft., one target. Hit: 13 (3d8) lightning damage.

**Wail (Recharge 5-6).** The Storm Banshee releases a mournful wail, infused with the power of the storm. Each creature within 30 feet of the banshee that can hear it must make a DC 14 Constitution saving throw. On a failure, a creature takes 17 (5d6) thunder damage and is deafened for 1 minute. On a success, a creature takes half the damage and isn't deafened.

## Description

Storm Banshees are the embodiment of nature's fury, spirits born from the most violent tempests and given form by Elyra's elemental mastery. These wailing entities are a swirling mass of storm clouds, lightning, and wind, with a vaguely humanoid shape at their center. Their cries, reminiscent of the howling wind, can cause disarray among those who hear them, and they wield the raw power of the storm against any who dare challenge them.

While they are bound to Elyra's will, Storm Banshees retain a semblance of their former selves, their emotions amplified by the elemental energies coursing through them. Their presence is both a testament to Elyra's power and a warning to those who would oppose her. Those who encounter these spirits must tread carefully, for the fury of the storm is not easily quelled.

# Non-Player Characters

## Ailith the Thief

In the shadowed corners of Moonsorrow, adventurers may cross paths with the elusive Ailith, a rogue witch with a penchant for thievery and deception. Once a disciple of the revered witches Morana, Opalina, and Elyra, Ailith's insatiable thirst for power and autonomy led her away from her mentors and into the welcoming arms of the Purifiers, a faction opposing the witches. With raven-black hair, striking amber eyes, and dark leather armor adorned with silver embroidery, Ailith's appearance is a testament to her dual nature as both a rogue and a spellcaster. Her unique ability to meld into shadows, known as Shadow Step, makes her a formidable infiltrator, while her retained magical prowess allows her to cast spells that aid in stealth and deception. A master of throwing daggers, often hexed to confound her enemies, she's not one to be underestimated in combat. Though she may align with the Purifiers, her loyalties are, at best, fickle. Ailith's motivations are driven by personal gain and a deep-seated desire for freedom, making her a wild card in the unfolding drama of Moonsorrow.

**Ailith, the Thief**

**Class & Level** Rogue 10 / Sorcerer 2

**Race** Human

**Background** Criminal

**Alignment** Chaotic Neutral

**Armor Class** 16 (leather armor)

**Hit Points** 72

**Speed** 30 ft.

| STR | DEX | CON | INT | WIS | CHA |
|-----|-----|-----|-----|-----|-----|
| 12 (+1) | 18 (+4) | 14 (+2) | 14 (+2) | 12 (+1) | 16 (+3) |

**Saving Throws** Dex +8, Int +6

**Skills** Stealth +8, Deception +7, Sleight of Hand +8, Arcana +6, Perception +5

**Languages** Common, Thieves' Cant, Elvish

**Equipment** Leather armor with silver embroidery, set of throwing daggers, thieves' tools, arcane focus (silver pendant), and a small pouch containing 15 gp.

**Actions**

**Multiattack**. Ailith makes two melee attacks or two ranged attacks.

**Dagger**. Melee or Ranged Weapon Attack: +8 to hit, reach 5 ft. or range 20/60 ft., one target. Hit: 6 (1d4 + 4) piercing damage.

**Hexed Dagger (Recharges after a Short or Long Rest)**. Melee or Ranged Weapon Attack: +8 to hit, reach 5 ft. or range 20/60 ft., one target. Hit: 6 (1d4 + 4) piercing damage, and the target has disadvantage on their next attack roll.

**Sneak Attack (1/turn)**. Ailith deals an extra 17 (5d6) damage when she hits a target with a weapon attack and has advantage on the attack roll, or when the target is within 5 ft. of an ally of Ailith that isn't incapacitated and Ailith doesn't have disadvantage on the attack roll.

**Shadow Step (Recharges after a Short or Long Rest)**. As a bonus action on her turn, Ailith can teleport up to 60 ft. to an unoccupied space she can see that is in dim light or darkness.

**Evasion**. If Ailith is subjected to an effect that allows her to make a Dexterity saving throw to take only half damage, she instead takes no damage if she succeeds on the saving throw, and only half damage if she fails.

**Spellcasting**. Ailith is a 2nd-level sorcerer. Her spellcasting ability is Charisma (spell save DC 14, +6 to hit with spell attacks). Ailith has the following sorcerer spells prepared:

- Cantrips (at will): mage hand, minor illusion

- 1st Level (3 slots): disguise self, silent image

Ailith is a lithe and agile woman, standing at a medium height with a physique honed from years of stealth and evasion. Her raven-black hair, usually tied in a loose ponytail, cascades down her back, occasionally revealing glimpses of her nape. Striking amber eyes, sharp and calculating, seem to miss nothing, always observing, always assessing. Her skin is a light olive, hinting at a life spent both under the sun and in the shadows.

She wears dark leather armor, tailored perfectly to her form, allowing for maximum mobility. The armor is accentuated with intricate silver embroidery, a testament to her magical background. Around her waist, a belt holds several sheathed throwing daggers, their hilts adorned with minor runes. A silver pendant, doubling as her arcane focus, hangs around her neck, often hidden beneath her armor but always close to her heart. Her movements are graceful yet purposeful, with an air of confidence and a hint of danger.

# Baba Yaga

In the shadowed depths of the Misty Woods, adventurers may find themselves crossing paths with the legendary Baba Yaga, the enigmatic forest witch of ancient Slavic tales. With her wild, unkempt gray hair and piercing green eyes that seem to see right through to one's very soul, Baba Yaga is a figure of both fear and fascination. Her tattered robes, adorned with mysterious talismans and charms, whisper tales of ancient magic and forgotten rituals. Those brave or desperate enough to seek her out must be wary, for she is known to test visitors with cryptic riddles, challenging their intellect and resolve. Her long, bony fingers, often seen clutching a gnarled wooden staff, hint at the vast arcane powers she wields. Among her many abilities, she can command her iconic chicken-legged hut, a formidable entity in its own right, and brew potent potions with a myriad of magical effects.

Yet for all her might and mystery, Baba Yaga is not purely malevolent. Her unpredictable nature means she might just as easily aid those she deems worthy as turn them into toads. Stories tell of brave souls who, having proven their cleverness or having presented the witch with rare treasures, have received her guidance or magical aid. However, the overarching lesson in all tales of Baba Yaga is clear: approach with respect, be prepared for her tests, and never, ever underestimate the forest witch. For in the ever-shifting world of Moonsorrow, where the boundaries between life, death, and the elemental forces blur, Baba Yaga remains a constant, ageless force, her motivations as enigmatic as the moonlit paths that lead to her doorstep.

### Baba Yaga, the Enigmatic Forest Witch

Medium humanoid (human), chaotic neutral

**Armor Class** 16 (natural armor from talismans)

**Hit Points** 90 (12d8 + 36)

**Speed** 30 ft.

| STR | DEX | CON | INT | WIS | CHA |
|-----|-----|-----|-----|-----|-----|
| 10 (+0) | 14 (+2) | 16 (+3) | 18 (+4) | 20 (+5) | 16 (+3) |

**Saving Throws** Int +8, Wis +9

**Skills** Arcana +8, Nature +9, Perception +9, Insight +9

**Senses** passive Perception 19

**Languages** Common, Sylvan, and two other languages of the DM's choice

**Challenge** 8 (3,900 XP)

**Hut's Command**. Once per day, Baba Yaga can summon her chicken-legged hut to her side. The hut acts on her initiative and follows her commands. It can be used to attack, defend, or transport her and others. The hut has its own set of stats and abilities.

**Potion Mastery**. Baba Yaga carries a satchel of 3d4 random potions at any given time. These can range from healing potions to more esoteric brews that can turn someone invisible, transform them into an animal, or even put them into a deep sleep. She can use an action to administer a potion to herself or another creature.

**Riddle's Challenge**. As an action, Baba Yaga can pose a riddle to a creature she can see within 60 feet of her. The target must make an Intelligence saving throw (DC 16) or become stunned until the end of its next turn, pondering the riddle. If the creature answers the riddle correctly before then, the effect ends.

### Actions

**Staff**. Melee Weapon Attack: +6 to hit, reach 5 ft., one target. Hit: 6 (1d6 + 3) bludgeoning damage plus 10 (3d6) psychic damage.

**Bewitching Gaze (Recharge 5-6)**. Baba Yaga targets one creature she can see within 30 feet of her. The target must succeed on a DC 16 Wisdom saving throw or be charmed by Baba Yaga for 1 minute. While charmed in this way, the target is incapacitated and has a speed of 0. The effect ends if the target takes any damage or if someone else uses an action to shake the target out of their stupor.

### Reactions

**Mystic Deflection**. When Baba Yaga is targeted by a spell or ranged attack, she can use her reaction to deflect it with her staff. She gains a +4 bonus to her AC against the triggering attack.

An old, hunched woman with wild, unkempt gray hair and Baba Yaga's deep green eyes are always observing, always calculating. She wears tattered robes adorned with various talismans and charms, and her long, bony fingers often clutch a gnarled wooden staff. Known to test visitors with cryptic riddles, she might aid those she deems worthy or turn them into toads, depending on her whims.

# Sir Cedric Blackthorn

Towering above most, Sir Cedric's polished plate armor gleams even in the dimmest of lights, adorned with symbols of the sun and moon, echoing his fervent desire to restore balance to the land. His piercing blue eyes, always assessing, always judging, reflect his unwavering conviction. With his radiant Sunblade, he stands as a beacon of hope for many in Moonsorrow, its glow a testament to his dedication to purging the darkness. This sword, combined with his ability to summon a Shield of Purity, makes him a formidable foe against those he deems tainted by dark magic.

Sir Cedric's charisma is undeniable. With every word, every gesture, he can rally the spirits of the downtrodden townsfolk, inspiring them with tales of a brighter future, free from the icy grasp of the Blood Moon. His passionate speeches, filled with promises of restoring purity and order, have garnered him a significant following. However, beneath this veneer of righteousness lies a man rigid in his beliefs, convinced that the witches of Moonsorrow are the root of all the town's miseries. Having once roamed the realm as a knight, Cedric's return to Moonsorrow was marked by his firsthand experience with the Blood Moon's malevolence. This experience led him to establish the Purifiers, a group dedicated to eradicating the witches and, in his mind, saving Moonsorrow from further decay.

### Sir Cedric Blackthorn

**Race** Human

**Class** Paladin

**Level** 10

**Alignment** Lawful Neutral

**HP** 85

**AC** 20 (plate armor)

**Speed** 30 ft.

| STR | DEX | CON | INT | WIS | CHA |
|---|---|---|---|---|---|
| 18 (+4) | 12 (+1) | 16 (+3) | 13 (+1) | 14 (+2) | 17 (+3) |

**Saving Throws** Wis +7, Cha +8

**Skills** Persuasion +8, Religion +6, Athletics +9, Insight +7

**Languages** Common, Celestial

**Equipment**:

- Sunblade (Longsword): +9 to hit, 1d8+4 slashing damage, emits radiant light.

- Plate Armor

- Shield

- Holy Symbol of the Sun and Moon

**Divine Smite**. When hitting with a melee weapon, can expend a spell slot to deal radiant damage in addition to weapon damage.

**Aura of Protection**. Grants a bonus to saving throws to himself and allies within 10 ft. equal to his Charisma modifier (+3).

**Shield of Purity (Channel Divinity)**. As an action, can summon a protective barrier that grants advantage on saving throws against spells and other magical effects for himself and allies within 10 ft. for 1 minute.

**Spells**: (Based on Paladin's spellcasting ability, with a focus on protection and light)

**Spell Save** DC: 16

**Actions**

**Multiattack**. Sir Cedric makes two melee attacks with his Sunblade.

**Sunblade**. Melee Weapon Attack: +9 to hit, reach 5 ft., one target. Hit: 8 (1d8 + 4) slashing damage plus 4 (1d8) radiant damage.

**Lay on Hands (Recharges after a Long Rest)**. As an action, Sir Cedric can touch a creature and restore up to 50 hit points to it, either by healing wounds or curing a disease or neutralizing a poison affecting the creature. He can split these hit points among multiple uses.

**Divine Smite**. When Sir Cedric hits with a melee weapon attack, he can expend one paladin spell slot to deal radiant damage to the target, in addition to the weapon's damage. The extra damage is 2d8 for a 1st-level spell slot, plus 1d8 for each spell level higher than 1st, to a maximum of 5d8.

**Shield of Purity (Channel Divinity, Recharges after a Short or Long Rest)**. As an action, Sir Cedric summons a protective barrier that grants advantage on saving throws against spells and other magical effects for himself and allies within 10 ft. This effect lasts for 1 minute.

**Aura of Protection**. Whenever Sir Cedric or a friendly creature within 10 feet of him must make a saving throw, the creature gains a bonus to the saving throw equal to Sir Cedric's Charisma modifier (+3). The creature must be conscious to grant this bonus.

**Spellcasting**. Sir Cedric is a 10th-level spellcaster. His spellcasting ability is Charisma (spell save DC 16, +8 to hit with spell attacks). Sir Cedric has the following paladin spells prepared:

- 1st Level (4 slots): bless, command, divine favor, shield of faith

- 2nd Level (3 slots): lesser restoration, magic weapon, protection from poison

- 3rd Level (3 slots): aura of vitality, blinding smite, daylight

- 4th Level (2 slots): death ward, guardian of faith

**Personality Traits** Charismatic, Rigid, Passionate, Protective

**Ideals** Order, Purity, Dedication

**Bonds** Moonsorrow, the Purifiers, his Sunblade

**Flaws** Can be overly zealous, distrustful of magic not from divine sources, holds grudges

# Crossroads Demon

In the annals of ancient lore, the Crossroads Demon was once known as Hergandr, a mortal warrior of unparalleled prowess. Born in a war-torn region where battles raged like ever-present storms, Hergandr was a serpent on the battlefield, striking with precision and leaving chaos in his wake. His skills in combat were legendary, but it was his cunning and strategic mind that truly set him apart. He believed that every battle, every skirmish, was a crossroads, a moment of choice that determined the course of history.

As years turned to decades, Hergandr's ambition grew. He sought not just to be a master of the battlefield but to control the very threads of fate itself. He delved into forbidden magics, seeking to intertwine his essence with the serpentine flow of destiny. In his quest, he discovered an ancient ritual that promised to grant him dominion over the crossroads of fate.

Under the shadow of a blood-red eclipse, Hergandr performed the ritual. But instead of granting him control, the ritual bound his spirit to the very crossroads he sought to dominate. His physical form was shattered, and his essence became intertwined with the myriad pathways of destiny.

Over the ages, the warrior's spirit evolved, becoming a being of shadow and whispers, a guardian of choices and destinies: the Crossroads Demon. His once-mighty ambition was now channeled into brokering deals, offering power and foresight to those brave or foolish enough to summon him. But every deal bore the weight of consequence, a testament to Hergandr's own tragic journey from warrior to wraith.

Now, the Crossroads Demon, once the mighty Hergandr, stands sentinel at the nexus of all destinies, waiting for the next soul to seek a bargain, forever bound to the very crossroads he once sought to conquer.

## Hergandr, the Crossroads Demon

Large fiend, neutral evil

**Armor Class** 17 (natural armor)

**Hit Points** 162 (18d10 + 72)

**Speed** 30 ft., fly 60 ft.

| STR | DEX | CON | INT | WIS | CHA |
|-----|-----|-----|-----|-----|-----|
| 18 (+4) | 16 (+3) | 18 (+4) | 17 (+3) | 15 (+2) | 20 (+5) |

**Saving Throws** Dex +8, Int +8, Cha +10

**Skills** Persuasion +10, Insight +7, Arcana +8

**Damage Resistances** cold, fire, lightning; bludgeoning, piercing, and slashing from nonmagical attacks

**Damage Immunities** poison

**Condition Immunities** poisoned

**Senses** truesight 120 ft., passive Perception 12

**Languages** Common, Infernal, Primordial

**Challenge** 13 (10,000 XP)

**Innate Spellcasting.** Hergandr's spellcasting ability is Charisma (spell save DC 18, +10 to hit with spell attacks). He can innately cast the following spells, requiring no material components:

- **At will**: detect thoughts, disguise self, suggestion
- **3/day each**: dimension door, dominate person, counterspell
- **1/day each**: plane shift, geas, true seeing

**Master of Bargains.** When Hergandr makes a Charisma (Persuasion) check, he can choose to take the result of a 15 or the roll, whichever is higher.

**Ethereal Stride.** As a bonus action, Hergandr can enter the Ethereal Plane from the Material Plane, or vice versa.

## Actions

**Multiattack.** Hergandr makes two claw attacks.

**Claw.** Melee Weapon Attack: +9 to hit, reach 5 ft., one target. Hit: 14 (2d8 + 5) slashing damage plus 7 (2d6) psychic damage.

**Bind Fate (Recharge 5-6).** Hergandr targets one creature he can see within 60 feet. The target must succeed on a DC 18 Wisdom saving throw or be bound by fate for 1 minute. While bound, the creature has disadvantage on attack rolls, ability checks, and saving throws. The creature can repeat the saving throw at the end of each of its turns, ending the effect on itself on a success.

**Summon Wraiths (1/Day).** Hergandr summons 2-4 Crossroads Wraiths to aid him. These wraiths act immediately after Hergandr in the initiative order and obey his commands.

## Legendary Actions

Hergandr can take 3 legendary actions, choosing from the options below. Only one legendary action option can be used at a time and only at the end of another creature's turn. Hergandr regains spent legendary actions at the start of his turn.

**Claw Attack.** Hergandr makes one claw attack.

**Ethereal Step (Costs 2 Actions).** Hergandr uses his Ethereal Stride.

**Seal Bargain (Costs 3 Actions).** Hergandr touches a willing creature, sealing a pact with it. The nature and terms of the pact are determined by the DM.

Hergandr, once a mighty warrior, now stands as a sentinel at the crossroads of destiny. He is a master of bargains, offering power and knowledge to those who seek him out, but always at a price. Those who dare to summon him should be prepared to face the consequences of their choices.

# Elyra, the Stormcaller

Elyra's very essence is intertwined with the volatile forces of nature. Her appearance is a testament to her dominion over the elements; her hair, ever-changing, shifts hues from the blazing red of a wildfire to the cool blue of a winter chill, while her robes mirror the tumultuous patterns of a storm-laden sky. The very air around her crackles with elemental energy, a constant reminder of her unparalleled mastery over fire, water, air, and earth.

Elyra's abilities are as awe-inspiring as they are fearsome. With the dance of her fingers, she can summon tempests, call down lightning, or clear the skies, showcasing her intimate bond with the weather. Her connection to the elements is so profound that she can even transform her very being into water, fire, air, or earth, allowing her to navigate challenges in unique ways. But adventurers should tread carefully; Elyra's command over nature's fury means she can harness the raw power of the elements, either to decimate her foes or shield her allies. Her personality mirrors the unpredictable nature of a storm. While she can be fiercely passionate, with a temper as quick as a lightning strike, she also possesses a deep understanding of the world's balance, recognizing the intertwined dance of creation and destruction. Those who seek to engage with her, be it in alliance or opposition, should be prepared for the whirlwind of emotions and elemental power that is Elyra, The Stormcaller.

## Elyra, the Stormcaller

Medium humanoid (human), neutral

**Armor Class** 15 (mage armor)

**Hit Points** 96 (12d6 + 36)

**Speed** 30 ft.

| STR | DEX | CON | INT | WIS | CHA |
|-----|-----|-----|-----|-----|-----|
| 10 (+0) | 14 (+2) | 16 (+3) | 12 (+1) | 14 (+2) | 18 (+4) |

**Saving Throws** Con +7, Cha +8

**Skills** Arcana +5, Nature +5, Persuasion +8, Intimidation +8

**Languages** Common, Primordial

**Challenge** 8 (3,900 XP)

**Sorcerous Origin (Storm Sorcery).** Elyra has the following features from her storm sorcery origin:

**Wind Speaker.** Elyra can speak, read, and write Primordial.

**Tempestuous Magic.** Whenever Elyra casts a spell, she can use a bonus action to fly up to 10 feet without provoking opportunity attacks.

**Heart of the Storm.** Elyra is immune to lightning and thunder damage. When she casts a spell of 1st level or higher that deals lightning or thunder damage, she can deal extra damage to a creature she can see within 10 feet of her.

**Storm Guide.** Elyra can change the direction of the wind and stop rain within a 100-foot radius.

**Storm's Fury.** When hit by a melee attack, Elyra can use her reaction to deal lightning damage to the attacker.

**Metamagic.** Elyra can use her sorcery points to change her spells in the following ways:

**Quickened Spell.** Elyra can cast a spell that has a casting time of 1 action as a bonus action instead.

**Distant Spell.** Elyra can double the range of her spells.

### Actions

**Staff.** Melee Weapon Attack: +4 to hit, reach 5 ft., one target. Hit: 4 (1d6 + 1) bludgeoning damage.

**Spells.** Elyra is a 12th-level spellcaster. Her spellcasting ability is Charisma (spell save DC 16, +8 to hit with spell attacks). She has the following sorcerer spells prepared:

- Cantrips (at will): mage hand, shocking grasp, gust, lightning lure
- 1st Level (4 slots): mage armor, thunderwave
- 2nd Level (3 slots): gust of wind, misty step
- 3rd Level (3 slots): call lightning, fly
- 4th Level (3 slots): storm sphere, ice storm

- 5th Level (2 slots): control winds

- 6th Level (1 slot): chain lightning

Elyra's presence is as dynamic as the elements she commands. Her hair changes like the weather, from fiery red to icy blue, and her robes constantly shift, resembling a stormy sky. Her eyes crackle with elemental energy. Elyra is fierce and unpredictable, much like a storm. She's passionate and has a fiery temper but is also deeply attuned to the world's rhythms, understanding the necessity of both creation and destruction.

# Helbindr, The Frostbound Sovereign

Helbindr, once a powerful sorcerer in the mortal realm, became obsessed with merging the realms of the living and the dead, leading him to rule Niflshadow. From his icy throne, he judges the souls of the wicked, determining their fate based on the weight of their sins. With skin as pale as snow and frostbitten shadowy wings, Helbindr's glowing icy eyes are believed to be windows into Niflshadow's core. Wielding a scepter of pure ice, he commands the realm's elements and passes judgment on souls. Although he embodies cold logic and strict judgment, he is not inherently evil, viewing his role as a universal balance. However, his dominion over Niflshadow has isolated him from mortal emotions, and while he remains the realm's supreme ruler, various entities constantly challenge his reign.

## Helbindr, The Frostbound Sovereign

Large fiend (demon), neutral evil

**Armor Class** 20 (natural armor)

**Hit Points** 325 (30d10 + 150)

**Speed** 30 ft., fly 60 ft.

| STR | DEX | CON | INT | WIS | CHA |
|-----|-----|-----|-----|-----|-----|
| 24 (+7) | 18 (+4) | 20 (+5) | 22 (+6) | 21 (+5) | 26 (+8) |

**Saving Throws** Dex +10, Con +11, Wis +11, Cha +14

**Skills** Arcana +12, Perception +11, Insight +11

**Damage Resistances** bludgeoning, piercing, and slashing from nonmagical attacks

**Damage Immunities** cold, necrotic

**Condition Immunities** charmed, frightened, paralyzed

**Senses** truesight 120 ft., passive Perception 21

**Languages** Common, Abyssal, Infernal, Draconic, Celestial

**Challenge** 21 (33,000 XP)

**Legendary Resistance (3/Day).** If Helbindr fails a saving throw, he can choose to succeed instead.

**Magic Resistance.** Helbindr has advantage on saving throws against spells and other magical effects.

**Innate Spellcasting.** Helbindr's spellcasting ability is Charisma (spell save DC 22, +14 to hit with spell attacks). He can innately cast the following spells, requiring no material components:

- At will: cone of cold, darkness, shadow step

- 3/day each: plane shift, ice storm, finger of death

- 1/day each: prismatic wall, power word kill

### Actions

**Multiattack.** Helbindr makes two attacks with his Icy Scepter.

**Icy Scepter.** Melee Weapon Attack: +13 to hit, reach 10 ft., one target. Hit: 19 (3d6 + 7) bludgeoning damage plus 14 (4d6) cold damage.

**Judgment of the Wicked (Recharge 5-6).** Helbindr releases a 60-foot cone of icy shadows. Each creature in that area must make a DC 20 Constitution saving throw, taking 55 (10d10) cold damage and 55 (10d10) necrotic damage on a failed save, or half as much damage on a successful one.

### Legendary Actions

Helbindr can take 3 legendary actions, choosing from the options below. Only one legendary action option can be used at a time and only at the end of another creature's turn. Helbindr regains spent legendary actions at the start of his turn.

**Chill Touch (Costs 1 Action).** Helbindr casts chill touch.

**Shadow Step (Costs 1 Action).** Helbindr uses his shadow step ability.

**Summon Shadows (Costs 2 Actions).** Helbindr summons 1d4 shadow demons to aid him in battle. These demons act immediately after Helbindr in the initiative order and obey his commands.

Helbindr, with his mastery over ice and shadow, is a formidable opponent for any adventuring party. Whether they seek to challenge him for control of Niflshadow or simply to escape his icy realm, they will find that the Frostbound Sovereign is not to be taken lightly.

# Opalina, The Lifegiver

Opalina, known as The Lifegiver, stands as a beacon of hope and rejuvenation amidst the shadows. Her appearance is a testament to the vitality she embodies; draped in robes of vibrant greens and radiant golds, her skin glows with a warm golden hue, reminiscent of the first rays of dawn. Her hair, a mesmerizing cascade of leaves intertwined with blooming flowers, seems to sway even in the absence of a breeze. Her eyes, shimmering like fresh morning dew, hold the promise of new beginnings.

Opalina's abilities are a manifestation of her deep connection to the very essence of life. With her power of Revitalization, she can mend wounds and dispel ailments, a gift that has made her a beacon of hope for many. Her innate ability, Nature's Call, allows her to communicate with the creatures of the wild, influencing their actions and seeking their aid when needed. The land itself responds to her Bloom Touch, as withered plants spring back to life and barren grounds burst into lush greenery under her gentle caress. Yet, beyond her formidable powers, it's Opalina's nurturing and compassionate nature that truly sets her apart. Always eager to aid those in distress, she embodies growth, renewal, and the cyclical nature of life. As the adventurers navigate the challenges of Moonsorrow, Opalina's wisdom and benevolence might prove invaluable, guiding them through the darkest of nights towards the promise of a new dawn.

## Opalina, The Lifegiver

Medium humanoid (witch), neutral good

**Armor Class** 16 (natural armor)

**Hit Points** 90 (12d8 + 36)

**Speed** 30 ft.

| STR | DEX | CON | INT | WIS | CHA |
|-----|-----|-----|-----|-----|-----|
| 10 (+0) | 14 (+2) | 16 (+3) | 18 (+4) | 20 (+5) | 17 (+3) |

**Saving Throws** Int +8, Wis +9

**Skills** Nature +8, Medicine +9, Persuasion +7, Animal Handling +9

**Senses** passive Perception 15

**Languages** Common, Druidic, Sylvan

**Challenge** 8 (3,900 XP)

**Innate Spellcasting**. Opalina's innate spellcasting ability is Wisdom (spell save DC 17, +9 to hit with spell attacks). She can innately cast the following spells, requiring no material components:

- **At will**: druidcraft, guidance, resistance

- **3/day each**: cure wounds, speak with animals, entangle

- **2/day each**: lesser restoration, plant growth, call lightning

- **1/day each**: reincarnate, commune with nature

**Revitalization**. As an action, Opalina can touch a creature and restore 20 hit points. Once she uses this ability, she can't use it again until she finishes a short or long rest.

**Nature's Call**. Opalina can communicate with animals as if they shared a language. She can also use an action to influence the behavior of an animal, as if using the animal friendship spell.

**Bloom Touch**. As an action, Opalina can touch a withered plant or a 5-foot square area of barren ground, causing plants to grow and flourish there. This effect is cosmetic and doesn't have any mechanical benefits.

## Actions

**Quarterstaff**. Melee Weapon Attack: +4 to hit, reach 5 ft., one target. Hit: 4 (1d6 + 1) bludgeoning damage, or 5 (1d8 + 1) bludgeoning damage if used with two hands.

## Reactions

**Nature's Shield**. When Opalina is targeted by an attack, she can cause vines and branches to spring up and interpose between her and the attacker. The attack's damage is reduced by 10 (1d8 + 5). Once she uses this reaction, she can't use it again until she finishes a short or long rest.

Opalina is adorned in vibrant greens and golds, her skin has a warm golden hue, and her hair is a cascade of leaves and blooming flowers. Her eyes shimmer like morning dew. Opalina is nurturing and compassionate, always seeking to aid those in need. She embodies the essence of life and growth, often acting as a mediator and voice of reason.

# Morana, The Deathweaver

At the heart of the tale stands Morana, The Deathweaver, one of the three exiled witches who once guarded the land with benevolence. With skin as pale as the moonlight and raven-black hair that cascades like a shadow, Morana's ethereal beauty is a sight to behold. Her deep, void-black eyes hold the power of the Soul Gaze, allowing her to peer into the very essence of any being. As a master of necromancy, she can command the dead, raising them to do her bidding. Yet, her connection to the afterlife doesn't end there; her ability, known as Death's Whisper, lets her commune with spirits and ghosts. Despite the macabre nature of her powers, Morana is a calm and introspective soul. She often communicates in riddles, challenging those who seek her wisdom. Her understanding and respect for the delicate balance of life and death make her a pivotal figure in the quest to restore harmony to Moonsorrow.

But Morana is not the only enigma the adventurers will encounter. The land, tainted by the curse of the Blood Moon, is rife with malevolent spirits and creatures birthed from the icy shadows of Niflshadow. Helbindr's lingering vengeance has given rise to spectral entities, ancient guardians, and ethereal familiars, each playing a role in the unfolding drama. From the Green Man Guardians who animate the labyrinth's walls to the Lantern Spirits leading travelers astray, the challenges are many. Yet, amidst these trials, the adventurers will also find allies, like the Samhain Sentinels and the Spectral Familiars, who, bound by ancient rites and loyalties, might aid them in their quest. The journey through Moonsorrow is a dance of light and shadow, and the adventurers must tread carefully, discerning friend from foe in a land where appearances can be deceiving.

**Morana, The Deathweaver**

Medium humanoid (witch), neutral

**Armor Class** 15 (natural armor)

**Hit Points** 90 (12d8 + 36)

**Speed** 30 ft.

| STR | DEX | CON | INT | WIS | CHA |
|-----|-----|-----|-----|-----|-----|
| 10 (+0) | 14 (+2) | 16 (+3) | 18 (+4) | 20 (+5) | 17 (+3) |

**Saving Throws** Int +8, Wis +9

**Skills** Arcana +8, Insight +9, Perception +9

**Damage Resistances** necrotic

**Senses** passive Perception 19

**Languages** Common, Abyssal, Infernal

**Challenge** 8 (3,900 XP)

**Soul Gaze**. Morana can see the life force of any creature within 60 feet of her. She knows if a creature is alive, dead, undead, or neither alive nor dead (such as a construct).

**Spellcasting**. Morana is a 12th-level spellcaster. Her spellcasting ability is Wisdom (spell save DC 17, +9 to hit with spell attacks). Morana has the following spells prepared:

- Cantrips (at will): chill touch, mage hand, thaumaturgy

- 1st level (4 slots): detect magic, ray of sickness, shield

- 2nd level (3 slots): blindness/deafness, hold person, misty step

- 3rd level (3 slots): animate dead, counterspell, speak with dead

- 4th level (3 slots): banishment, blight, death ward

- 5th level (2 slots): antilife shell, raise dead

- 6th level (1 slot): circle of death

**Death's Whisper**. Morana can communicate with spirits and ghosts. She can cast speak with dead at will, without expending a spell slot.

**Actions**

**Necrotic Touch**. Melee Spell Attack: +9 to hit, reach 5 ft., one target. Hit: 15 (3d6 + 5) necrotic damage.

**Summon Undead (1/Day)**. Morana summons 2d4 zombies or skeletons, choosing the type. The summoned creatures appear in unoccupied spaces within 60 feet of her and act as allies. They remain for 10 minutes, until they drop to 0 hit points, or until Morana dismisses them as an action.

# Game within a Game

## Ghoul's Gambit

**Objective**: Players must toss coins into carved pumpkins with varying point values to accumulate the highest score and win a Halloween-themed prize.

**Components**:

- Carved pumpkins of various sizes, each labeled with a point value.
- A starting line marked on the ground.
- A bucket of coins (can be real or game-specific coins).
- A scoreboard or a piece of parchment to keep track of scores.

**Instructions**:

Arrange the carved pumpkins at varying distances from the starting line. Smaller pumpkins or those placed farther away should have higher point values.

Each player gets five coins per turn.

Players take turns standing behind the starting line and tossing their coins, one at a time, aiming to get them into the pumpkins.

Once all coins are tossed, the overseeing ghostly figure or townsperson tallies the points based on which pumpkins the coins landed in.

If a coin lands in a pumpkin labeled "Ghoul's Gambit," the player can choose to take a gamble. They can either double their current points by answering a Halloween riddle correctly or lose all their points for that turn if they answer incorrectly.

After a predetermined number of rounds or once all players have had a turn, the player with the highest score wins a Halloween-themed prize.

**Variations**:

**Witch's Wind**: Introduce a fan or some source of wind to make the coin toss more challenging.

**Cursed Coin**: One coin is painted black or marked as "cursed." If a player tosses this coin into a pumpkin, they lose a set number of points.

**Jack-o'-Lantern's Favor**: A special, tiny pumpkin is placed at a challenging distance. If a player lands a coin in this pumpkin, they get a bonus turn or a special reward.

# Food and Fuel

## Pumpkin Spice Ghoul Cookies

### Ingredients

- 2 1/2 cups all-purpose flour
- 1 teaspoon baking powder
- teaspoon baking soda
- 2 teaspoons ground cinnamon
- 1/2 teaspoon ground nutmeg
- 1/2 teaspoon ground cloves
- 1/2 teaspoon salt
- 1/2 cup unsalted butter, softened
- 1 1/2 cups granulated sugar
- 1 cup canned pumpkin puree
- 1 large egg
- 1 teaspoon vanilla extract
- Icing (store-bought or homemade)
- Food coloring (black, green, orange, and white)

### Instructions

Preheat your oven to 350°F (175°C).

In a medium bowl, mix together flour, baking powder, baking soda, cinnamon, nutmeg, ground cloves, and salt.

In a separate large bowl, cream together the butter and sugar until light and fluffy.

Beat in the pumpkin, egg, and vanilla to the butter and sugar mixture until creamy.

Gradually mix in the dry ingredients until just blended.

Drop dough by rounded tablespoon onto a parchment-lined cookie sheet.

Flatten each cookie slightly using the back of the spoon or your fingers.

Bake for 15-20 minutes in the preheated oven, or until edges are lightly browned. Allow cookies to cool on baking sheets for a few minutes before transferring to wire racks to cool completely.

### Decoration

Divide the icing into four parts. Using food coloring, tint one part black, one part green, one part orange, and leave one part white.

Using a piping bag or a plastic bag with a small corner cut off, pipe ghostly shapes onto each cookie using the white icing.

Use the black icing to add eyes and a mouth to each ghost.

With the green and orange icing, add additional Halloween-themed decorations, such as pumpkins, witches' hats, or bats.

Allow the icing to set for a few hours before serving.

## Witch's Brew Cocktail

### Ingredients

- 1 oz. Midori (melon liqueur)
- 1 oz. vodka
- 1 oz. lemon juice (freshly squeezed)
- 1/2 oz. simple syrup
- 1 oz. blue curaçao
- Lemon-lime soda (like Sprite or 7-Up)
- Crushed ice
- **Optional**: Dry ice for a smoky effect (ensure it's food-grade and handle with care)
- **Garnish**: Lemon twist or a gummy worm

### Prepare the Glass

If using dry ice, place a small chip at the bottom of the glass. Remember, never touch dry ice with bare hands and never ingest it. Wait until it has fully sublimated (disappeared) before drinking.

### Mix the Cocktail

In a cocktail shaker filled with ice, combine Midori, vodka, lemon juice, and simple syrup.

Shake well until the outside of the shaker becomes frosty.

Strain the mixture into the prepared glass.

## Add the Magic

Slowly pour blue curaçao over the back of a spoon so it floats on top of the Midori mixture, creating a layering effect.

Top off with lemon-lime soda.

## Garnish

Twist a lemon peel over the top of the drink to release its oils, then drop it into the glass.

Optionally, drape a gummy worm over the edge of the glass for an added eerie effect.

## Serve

Serve immediately and watch your guests be mesmerized by the magical colors and optional smoky effect of the Witch's Brew Cocktail!

**Note:** Always exercise caution when using dry ice. Ensure it's safe for consumption, handle with gloves, and never ingest or touch it directly. Always wait for the dry ice to fully sublimate before drinking the cocktail.

# Witch's Elixir Mocktail

## Ingredients

- 1 oz. blackberry puree (fresh blackberries blended and strained)
- 1 oz. lime juice (freshly squeezed)
- 1 oz. honey or agave syrup (adjust to taste)
- Lemon-lime soda or sparkling water
- Crushed ice
- Purple or green food coloring (optional for added eeriness)
- Garnish: Fresh blackberries, lime wheel, and a sprig of mint or rosemary

## Instructions

**Prepare the Elixir Base:** In a mixing glass or bowl, combine the blackberry puree, lime juice, and honey or agave syrup. Mix well until all ingredients are combined. If you want a more eerie color, add a drop or two of food coloring and mix.

**Fill the Glass:** Fill your chosen glass with crushed ice.

**Pour the Elixir:** Pour the blackberry mixture over the crushed ice.

**Top Off:** Slowly top off with lemon-lime soda or sparkling water, allowing the blackberry mixture to swirl and mix naturally with the soda, creating a magical potion effect.

**Garnish:** Place a few fresh blackberries on top. Add a lime wheel and a sprig of mint or rosemary for added aroma and appearance.

**Serve:** Serve with a fun straw or a stirring stick, and watch as your guests are enchanted by the Witch's Elixir Mocktail!

**Tip:** For an added touch, you can rim the glass with a mixture of sugar and edible glitter to give it a magical sparkle.

# Map

# Crypts of the Shadow Court

# Managing Encounters

To help DMs tailor the adventure to the party, each encounter is designed with flexibility in mind. Whether your group consists of fledgling adventurers or seasoned heroes, the provided guidelines will help ensure that the challenges are both fun and fair.

## Encounter Structure

**Encounter Name**: The title of the encounter, usually indicating the primary theme or challenge.

**DM Information**: A brief summary to give you a clear picture of the encounter's purpose and its role in the overall adventure.

**Read Aloud**: Descriptive text meant to be read verbatim to the players, setting the scene and atmosphere.

**Activity**: Detailed guidance, including potential variations, expected player strategies, and potential outcomes.

**Lair Actions**: Specific actions or effects that occur in certain locations, often benefiting the encounter's primary antagonist.

**Scaling the Encounter**: Instructions on how to adjust the encounter's difficulty based on player levels:

- **Beginner (Level 1-5)**: Simplified challenges tailored for newer or less powerful characters.

- **Intermediate (Level 6-10)**: Moderate challenges that require a mix of skill, strategy, and teamwork.

- **Advanced (Level 11+)**: Complex and multi-faceted challenges suitable for veteran adventurers.

**Monster and/or NPC**: Details or references to any creatures or characters the players might interact with during the encounter.

Encounters may reference content found later in the book, such as detailed monster statistics in the Monsters section. Feel free to adapt or replace these elements to better fit your group's preferences or the storyline you're weaving.

## Modularity and Flexibility

This adventure, like all Penny Blood Adventures, is modular by design. If a particular monster or challenge doesn't resonate with your campaign's theme, feel free to replace it or adjust as needed. The goal is to provide a rich framework that sparks inspiration, allowing you to craft an unforgettable journey for your players.

# Getting Started

Welcome, adventurers, to the foreboding lands of Ravenholme, a village shadowed by ancient evils and whispered curses. Your journey within *Crypts of the Shadow Court* beckons you into a sprawling, open-world adventure where the darkness of the past threatens to engulf the present. As you step into this realm, you embark on a quest not just for glory but for the very soul of Ravenholme. Here's how to begin:

As the twilight merges day into night and shadows dance at the edge of your vision, a tale of darkness, mystery, and heroism unfolds. You, brave souls, are called to venture into the heart of the enigmatic and mist-enshrouded village of Ravenholme. This once prosperous land, nestled between the moors and the distant Barsea Heights Mountains, now trembles under a veil of perpetual fog and unsettling cries that pierce the silence of the night. The cause of this terror? The Shadow Court, a nefarious sect of vampires, once bound by the ancient and powerful Daynight Stone, now threatens to stretch its dark influence once more.

Your journey begins with a letter, an urgent plea for help from an old friend whose words carry the weight of desperation. Ravenholme, and the moors that once were a beacon of natural beauty, now known ominously as the "Mourning Moors," call for your aid. The villagers, consumed by fear, whisper tales of strange occurrences and disappearances, painting a picture of a land where the balance between light and darkness has been perilously disrupted.

Your path is fraught with challenges and mystery, leading you to the haunted village of Ravenholme where despair grips the hearts of those few who remain. The Mourning Moors await, a vast expanse of land where the spirits of the lost are said to wander, their sorrowful cries a testament to their unresolved fates. And finally, the Ancient Crypts hold the remnants of the Shadow Court, guarding secrets and artifacts of immense power.

## Letter to be Read to the Players

During some downtime, the adventurers chance to receive a letter addressed to all of them (or, for newly formed adventuring parties, each character receives their own handwritten letter). For purposes of immersion, you may wish to print a copy or even write out this letter by hand on old parchment paper to give to your players. This handwritten letter, addressed from a trusted, mutual friend, contains the following message:

*My friends,*

*I hope this letter finds you in better spirits than those that currently haunt the once peaceful village of Ravenholme. It is with a heavy heart and a trembling hand that I write to you, for our village is ensnared in a nightmare from which we cannot awaken.*

*You may remember Ravenholme as a place of beauty and tranquility, nestled between the moors and the distant Barsea Heights Mountains. But now, our village and the surrounding lands are shrouded in an unending twilight, plagued by a mist that seems almost alive with malice. Strange cries pierce the night, and people vanish only to reappear with no memory, their eyes filled with unspeakable horror. We whisper the name, the "Mourning Moors," for what our beloved home has become--a land that mourns for itself and the souls lost within its fog.*

*The source of our terror is the Shadow Court, a sect of darkness that once lay bound beneath our village, sealed away by powerful sigils. But the seals are weakening, and their malevolent influence is seeping into our world, bringing with it a curse that drains the life and hope from our people.*

*I remember the tales of your bravery and the strength that you and your companions carry within your hearts. It is for this reason, and with a hope that clings by a mere thread, that I beseech you to return to Ravenholme. We need your help to restore the sigils that entomb the Shadow Court, to find a cure for the curse that infects our people, and to rebalance the Daynight Stone, restoring order to our village and the moors.*

*I understand the dangers that such a quest entails, and I would not call upon you if there were any other way. But you are our last hope. Please, come to Ravenholme before we are all consumed by the shadows that encroach upon us.*

*With deepest gratitude and in dire need of your aid,*

*Your loyal friend,*

*F.*

*P.S. Please hurry. Each night grows longer, and I fear what will become of us if the Shadow Court's power continues to grow unchecked.*

# Overview for the DM

The *Crypts of the Shadow Court* adventure plunges the party into Ravenholme, where villagers beseech aid against a looming vampiric threat. The Shadow Court's vampiric influence, long held at bay by gradually weakening sigils, begins to infect the land due to a corruption of the Daynight Stone, a once harmonious artifact now tainted.

## The Quests

- **Restoring the Sigils**: The DM will guide players through treacherous crypts to repair sigils that keep the vampiric court in check. This entails navigating traps, deciphering old texts, and potentially facing the vampires themselves.

- **Finding a Cure**: A pervasive curse is affecting villagers, tied to the Shadow Court's growing power. Players must trace its source, search for a remedy, and uncover how the curse links to the vampires' scheme.

- **Rebalancing the Daynight Stone**: To halt the Shadow Court's plans, players need to cleanse the Daynight Stone, an act that will involve both investigation and confrontation with dark forces.

## Guidance from Elena the Wise

Elena the Wise, last of the ancient druid protectors, possesses vital insights into the crises at hand. Her guidance is key to the sigils' restoration, the curse's cure, and the rebalancing of the Daynight Stone. Elena resides in a secluded sanctuary within the Mourning Moors, a destination fraught with perils.

## How to Navigate Your Adventure

**Open World Exploration**: Ravenholme and the Mourning Moors offer a sandbox experience. The narrative's main arcs are complemented by numerous subplots and secrets. The sequence of tackling objectives is at the players' discretion but will have ripple effects throughout the adventure.

**Encounters and Curses**: The Court's minions and their cursed items pepper the landscape. Encounters could result in affliction by the Eternal Dusk curse. DMs should be ready with contingencies like wards or remedies to mitigate these threats.

**Restoring Sigils and the Daynight Stone**: Fulfilling the primary missions involves a mix of lore-gathering, relic hunting, and performing arcane rites. Players will need to leverage their collective skills and resolve to succeed.

# The Curse and Goals of the Shadow Court

The Shadow Court, a cabal of ancient vampires sealed near Ravenholme, is on the brink of escaping due to weakening seals. These seals are linked to the moor's ley lines, now waning from the abandonment of old druidic traditions, outside magical interference, and the Court's insidious schemes. Their freedom spells disaster, with potential revenge and a bid to enslave the living looming over the land.

## Mechanics of the Weakening Seals

- The seals' decay provides a narrative drive for the party to restore them, possibly by reconnecting with old traditions or countering the Court's plans.

- Consider involving environmental changes in the moors as a sign of the weakening ley lines.

## The Eternal Dusk Curse

- This malevolent spell is the Court's creation, used to instill terror, amass potential new vampires, and tip the balance of light and dark. It embodies twilight, a state they seek to make eternal.

- The curse emanates from the Shadow Court's grasp on dark magic and vampiric essence.

- It functions as a plot device to showcase the Court's reach and provides side quests to cure the afflicted.

## Infection Methods

•Physical assaults by vampiric minions that spread the curse through wounds.

•Cursed objects scattered throughout Ravenholme, waiting to be picked up by the unwary.

•Mists infused with the curse emanate from weak points near the seals.

## Symptoms and Progression

•Begin with subtle signs that gradually escalate, providing urgency for the characters to seek remedies.

•The Court watches the cursed, awaiting the moment to convert or claim the victims.

## Plot Hooks and Quest Ideas

•Rescuing cursed villagers can be side quests leading to the Court's minions or artifacts.

•Investigating mist-related phenomena could lead to encounters or discoveries of seal points.

## Utilizing the Curse in Gameplay

•For afflicted PCs, introduce saving throws to resist the curse's effects or use it as a ticking clock to find a cure.

•The DM can use the cursed mists as environmental hazards during travel across the moors.

## Turning the Curse to Recruitment

•The Court may present offers to desperate victims, pitting them against the party or using them as pawns.

•Provides a moral dilemma and potential NPC allies if the curse is lifted.

Incorporate these elements fluidly to underscore the pervasive threat of the Shadow Court and the creeping doom of Eternal Dusk. Use afflicted NPCs as emotional touchpoints, and the curse's spread as a barometer of the Court's growing power. Encourage the players to explore both combat and non-combat solutions to mitigate the curse's spread and the Court's schemes.

# Repairing the Seals Upon the Crypts

Repairing the seals upon the ancient crypts to entrap the Shadow Court is a multi-faceted task that challenges players to combine their skills, knowledge, and bravery. This activity is pivotal to thwarting the Court's resurgence and requires the players to undertake a series of steps:

## Locating the Seals

The first challenge is discovering the seals. Ancient druidic magic, intertwined with the natural ley lines, initially created these seals. PCs must gather information from texts, clues from NPCs like

Elena the Wise, or deciphering the cryptic symbols found in the ruins around Ravenholme and the Mourning Moors. Each crypt is guarded by the Shadow Court's minions to protect their overlords or defended by puzzles that test the characters' resolve and intelligence.

## Understanding the Magic

Once a seal is located, PCs need to understand its magic to repair it. This could involve studying ancient druidic rituals, consulting with spirits bound to the ley lines. The party might need to perform specific tasks to gain this knowledge, such as retrieving artifacts, rescuing knowledgeable NPCs, or bargaining with capricious fey creatures that dwell in the moors.

## Gathering Materials

Repairing each seal requires specific materials, some mundane, others magical. These materials might include rare minerals found in the depths of the Mourning Moors, the essence of creatures bound to the Shadow Court, or items of personal significance to strengthen the seals' magic. Finding these materials may lead the party into dangerous territories, force them into confrontations with the Court's minions, or require them to solve riddles and puzzles.

## Performing the Ritual

With all materials gathered and the knowledge acquired, PCs must perform a ritual to repair each seal. These rituals vary, reflecting the nature of the land where each seal is located. For example, a seal in a desecrated grove might require a ritual of cleansing and rebirth, involving the planting of a sacred tree, while a seal within the village might require the re-enactment of a historic event significant to Ravenholme's history. During these rituals, adventurers must defend against attacks from the Shadow Court, who will be desperate to stop them.

## Sealing the Crypts

Successfully completing the rituals strengthens the seals, cutting off the Shadow Court from their sources of power and limiting their ability to influence the world above. As each seal is repaired, player characters will notice immediate effects: the mist may thin out, the minions weaken, or the villagers' spirits lift slightly. Repairing all the seals not only entraps the Shadow Court within their crypts but also restores some balance to Ravenholme and the surrounding lands.

## The Final Seal

The last step involves sealing the main entrance to the ancient crypts, a grand ritual that requires the combined efforts of the adventurers, channeling the power they've garnered from repairing the other seals. This final act will fully entrap the Shadow Court, securing the safety of Ravenholme and ensuring the Court's malevolence remains locked away. PCs must prepare for a direct confrontation with the Shadow Court's leaders during this ritual, leading to a climactic battle where the stakes are the highest.

## Conclusion

Repairing the seals and recontaining the Shadow Court is a quest that takes players across the breadth of the adventure, beckoning them to engage deeply with the setting, its characters, and the lore of *Crypts of the Shadow Court*. The success of this task means not only the salvation of Ravenholme but also a significant victory against the darkness that seeks to engulf the world.

# Starting Your Adventure

As the Dungeon Master, you will start the adventure in the village of Ravenholme, a place now shadowed by a sense of impending doom. Set the stage for your players by vividly describing the somber mood hanging over the village, the worried glances of the villagers, and the whispers of dark happenings that have brought them to this point. Encourage interaction with the villagers, as they are a fount of lore and secrets; their tales and tidbits of information will be the breadcrumbs leading to the larger mysteries of the Shadow Court and the corrupted Daynight Stone.

As the players engage with the world around them, introduce multiple threads of adventure through the stories of the townsfolk or through mysterious letters found in dark corners. The decision of which path to follow should rest in their hands, reinforcing the open-world experience and emphasizing that their choices will shape the journey that unfolds. Be prepared to pivot and weave the story in response to the quest they choose to pursue first, always mindful of the larger narrative concerning the weakening seals and the spread of the insidious curse.

Elena the Wise should be a name that resonates within the village, a beacon of hope and wisdom. Even if she does not make an early appearance, her presence should be felt through the villagers' reverence and the urgent need for her guidance. Employ subtle hints and natural omens to foreshadow the significance of the Daynight Stone and signal Elena's integral role in the adventure that lies ahead.

Throughout your storytelling, weave in the theme of balance—the delicate dance between the encroaching darkness and the flickering light of hope. Let the time of day and the actions of the players tangibly influence the narrative and the challenges they face, underscoring the impact of their choices on the world's balance.

As the party resolves to embark on their chosen quest, mark the moment with a significant and stirring event—a harbinger of the pivotal role they are to play in the fate of Ravenholme and the looming threat of the Shadow Court. Here are examples of ominous events that you can use to start the adventure:

**Strike of Fate**: The party's resolve hardens as a lightning bolt strikes the ancient hanging tree, igniting a blaze that seems to cleanse the air, symbolizing the beginning of the end for the Shadow Court.

**Eclipse's Shadow**: An unexpected solar eclipse casts an ominous shadow over Ravenholme, signaling to the villagers and the party alike that the time to act against the encroaching darkness is now.

**The Ghostly Procession**: Spectral figures appear at dusk, walking through the village towards the cemetery before vanishing, a sign that the veil between worlds is thinning as the Shadow Court stirs.

**The Blooming of the Nightshade**: A field of nightshade, long dormant, suddenly blooms overnight with dark purple flowers that exude a faint, luminescent mist, hinting at the growing power of the Court.

**The Whispering Wind**: A strange wind carries whispers of the past and future through Ravenholme, leaving in its wake an air of destiny and a sense of impending conflict with ancient evils.

From here, the tale of heroism, intrigue, and redemption begins to unfold, guided by your hand and the choices of your brave adventurers. Let the story of *Crypts of the Shadow Court* begin.

# The Shadow Court

The Shadow Court is a formidable and secretive vampire sect led by the enigmatic Killian, whose centuries-old machinations have woven a tapestry of power and darkness beneath the village of Ravenholme and its surrounding lands. This Court is not merely a collection of vampires, but part of a sophisticated society with its own hierarchy, rules, and ambitions. At its core, the Court is divided into several tiers, each with specific roles and responsibilities that contribute to the Court's overarching goal: to expand their dominion over the living and secure their legacy for centuries to come.

## Hierarchy and Inner Workings

**Supreme Sovereign:** Killian, the founder and unchallenged leader of the Shadow Court. His word is law, and his plans are intricate, spanning decades or even centuries. Killian's ultimate goal is to solidify his rule over the supernatural and mortal realms, using the Daynight Stone's power to tip the balance in favor of darkness.

Killian has his own group of the most powerful and loyal vampires directly beneath him. This group includes:

**Thorn:** Once a guardian of nature, now twisted to serve Killian's purposes. He manipulates the Mourning Moors, using its mists and creatures as barriers and soldiers against intruders.

**Seraphina:** A master of enchantment and divination, she seeks to unlock further powers of the Daynight Stone and bind it more closely to the Court's will. Her betrayal of the druidic circle is a wound that still pains her, driving her to further prove her loyalty to Killian.

**Gareth:** The Court's martial leader, responsible for training new recruits and leading assaults against any who would oppose the Court. Gareth struggles with his lost humanity and the hope that he can still protect Ravenholme from within the shadows.

## Sect Leaders

The Court's reach goes far beyond Ravenholme with the establishment of many sects, or clans, in the Barsea Heights region. Each sect, such as the Whispering Night and Youngblood, is led by a vampire of significant power and influence. These leaders manage their sect's affairs, contribute to the Court's overall strategy, and report directly to the Council of Night. They are instrumental in executing Killian's plans, each with personal agendas that occasionally clash, but ultimately serve the Court's interests.

**Marcus of the Whispering Night:** Focuses on espionage and gathering intelligence, using his sect's influence to manipulate events from the shadows.

**Lucia of the Youngblood:** Seeks to recruit and train new vampires, particularly focusing on those with potential for great power or strategic importance.

## Court Members

The rank and file of the Shadow Court, comprising vampires aligned and located with one of the many sects, come from various backgrounds and abilities. They are the backbone of the Court, responsible for carrying out the will of their leaders and ensuring the Court's influence continues to spread.

## Enforcers of the Eclipse

Elite vampires chosen for their strength, cunning, and loyalty. They enforce Killian's will throughout the Court and deal with internal and external threats. Each enforcer commands a small group of vampires and has specific territories or tasks.

# Eternal Dusk - The Curse

There is an insidious curse known as Eternal Dusk that is infecting the people of Ravenholme and may infect the player characters. Below is a breakdown of the symptoms:

## Initial Symptoms (Day 1)

**Diminished Light Perception**: The afflicted character begins to see the world as if it were perpetually dusk, regardless of the actual time of day. Bright light sources, including daylight, seem dimmer, and the character has disadvantage on Wisdom (Perception) checks that rely on sight in brightly lit conditions.

## Intermediate Symptoms (Day 2-3)

**Weakened Vitality**: The character's vitality starts to wane. They suffer a -1 penalty to Constitution, reducing their maximum hit points accordingly. This penalty reflects the curse's drain on their life force.

**Shadow Vulnerability**: The character becomes more susceptible to damage from radiant sources, taking an additional 1d4 damage whenever they are harmed by such effects.

## Advanced Symptoms (Day 4-5)

**Twilight Shroud**: The afflicted individual becomes surrounded by a subtle aura of twilight. They gain disadvantage on all Charisma (Persuasion) checks as their appearance becomes unnerving to others, but they gain advantage on Charisma (Intimidation) checks due to their ominous presence.

**Drained Energy**: The penalty to Constitution increases to -2. Additionally, the character must make a DC 15 Constitution saving throw upon finishing a long rest. On a failed save, they gain one level of exhaustion as their rest is plagued by nightmares and unrestful sleep.

## Critical Stage (Day 6+)

**Eternal Dusk's Embrace**: The character's connection to the natural cycle of day and night is severed. They can no longer benefit from effects that require them to be in sunlight (such as the spell *Daylight* for healing or dispelling darkness).

**Life Drain**: Each day, the character must succeed on a DC 18 Constitution saving throw or their maximum hit points are reduced by 1d10 due to the curse sapping their life essence. This effect is cumulative and can reduce a character to 0 hit points, at which point they fall unconscious and will perish at the next sunset unless the curse is lifted.

# Lifting the Curse

**Initial Examination**: Upon realizing one of them is cursed, the party must first identify the nature of the curse. This requires a combination of Arcana and Medicine checks (DC 15) to discern its effects and origins.

**Consulting with an Expert**: The party must seek out Elena the Wise or another knowledgeable NPC, who can provide more insight into the curse's specific ties to the Shadow Court. This might involve a small quest to find Elena or gain the trust of another expert.

**Learning about the Antidote**: Through their research, PCs learn that the curse can only be lifted by creating a specific antidote, the formula for which is split into fragments hidden throughout the crypts.

# Collecting Antidote Ingredients

**Rare Components**: The antidote requires three rare components:

• Blood of a vampire from the Shadow Court

• An herb grown in the darkest part of the Mourning Moors along the Widow's Walk

• Water blessed by a druid or cleric

# Crafting the Antidote

**Finding a Safe Space**: The antidote must be crafted in a place of power, such as Elena's Sanctuary or a reconsecrated area in the Ancient Crypts, where the curse's effects are temporarily weakened.

**The Ritual of Crafting**: Combining the components requires a ritual involving precise measurements, incantations, and the channeling of positive energy. This is a collaborative effort, necessitating successful Arcana or Religion checks (DC 20) from the party.

# Lifting the Curse

**Administering the Antidote**: With the antidote prepared, the cursed character must drink it in the evening within view of the moon.

**Final Confrontation**: As the antidote takes effect, the Shadow Court attempts to preserve the curse, leading to a climactic encounter. Victory not only saves the cursed character but also weakens the Court's grip on the Ancient Crypts.

# Aftermath

**Recovery**: Lifting the curse might leave the afflicted character with a temporary weakness or a newfound strength as a memento of their trial.

**New Allies**: The process of lifting the curse may earn the party new allies, as spirits or entities opposed to the Shadow Court recognize their efforts and offer their assistance in future endeavors.

# Ravenholme

## The Withered Oak Inn

This encounter is centered around engaging with the inn's mysterious past and its spectral resident, the benevolent Phantom of the Withered Oak. PCs can uncover valuable information and possibly a cursed item by interacting with the innkeeper and exploring the inn.

As you push open the door of the inn, the hinges groan, echoing through the silent, dimly lit interior of what was once a lively gathering place. Dust motes dance in the slivers of light piercing through the boarded-up windows, illuminating the remnants of the inn's former life: empty chairs draped in cobwebs, a bar lined with glasses untouched for years, and the air thick with the scent of old wood and lost memories. This place, shrouded in a palpable sense of longing and loss, seems to be waiting, holding its breath for a return to days that may never come.

The Phantom of the Withered Oak Inn is the spirit of the inn's original owner, a man of deep love and dedication, both to his establishment and his lost love, who perished at sea. Bound to the inn by his unresolved grief and unyielding hope for a reunion with his beloved, he now wanders its rooms. Despite his ethereal state, he continues his duties as an innkeeper to guests who can no longer see him, his actions leaving behind small comforts and signs of his presence, a testament to his undying care for the inn and a love that transcends death itself.

## The Phantom Innkeeper

The ethereal innkeeper of this forsaken establishment, though bound by chains not of this world, possesses knowledge that could be the key to unlocking the secrets of the Shadow Court and lifting the curse that befalls Ravenholme. To engage with the Phantom and earn his trust, one might:

- Persuade the Phantom (Persuasion DC 15) by appealing to his lingering humanity, his love for his lost partner, and his desire for the peace that has long eluded him.

- Intimidate the Phantom (Intimidation DC 17) with the threat of exorcism or other means to put his soul to rest against his will. Caution is advised, as invoking fear in a spirit can have unpredictable outcomes.

- Fulfill a heartfelt request from the Phantom to retrieve the Whispering Locket, an object of significant personal value to him, ensconced somewhere among the inn's forgotten alcoves.

## Finding the Whispering Locket

The Phantom's locket is hidden within a secret compartment that has remained undisturbed as the inn fell into disrepair. Locating the compartment requires:

- A keen eye and investigative mind (Investigation check DC 16) to uncover the secret drawer that has escaped the notice of many.

- A discerning ear (Perception check DC 16) to pick up on the mournful whispers that beckon to the locket's resting place, possibly imbued with the essence of the Phantom's lost love.

## Information Granted by the Phantom

Upon the return of the Whispering Locket, the Phantom will share:

- Directions to the reclusive Elena the Wise, entwined with warnings of the treacherous paths and the sanctuary's concealment by her own protective enchantments.

- Insights into the weakened seals within the Ancient Crypts and the unnatural forces contributing to their decay, hinting at a method to reinforce them.

- The tale of the Eternal Dusk curse, with suggestions to seek ancient lore or consult knowledgeable entities on curses to discover a means to undo its dark bindings.

- His knowledge of an ancient tome somewhere in the Shrouded Chapel that the party should find helpful, although the Phantom cannot remember what exactly it is or why it's so important.

## The Whispering Locket's Curse

Should the party choose to interact with the locket:

- They are immediately subjected to the pull of its curse, requiring a Wisdom saving throw (DC 15) to resist its initial ensnarement.

- Further tampering with the locket invites greater peril, and opening it more than thrice calls for a Constitution saving throw (DC 18), with failure marking the onset of the Eternal Dusk curse.

It becomes apparent that the Phantom, upon realizing the locket's potential to spread the curse, advises against holding onto the artifact. This change of heart is rooted in the revelation of the locket's malevolent nature, conflicting with his initial desire to keep the memento close. If indeed the locket belonged to his lost love, it might explain the whispers and his reluctance to part with it. However, in the face of greater danger, he prioritizes the safety of others, perhaps recognizing that even in death, his beloved would wish no harm upon the living. He suggests that sealing the locket within Elena's Sanctuary may contain its corrupting influence.

## Lair Actions

On initiative count 20 (losing initiative ties), the Withered Oak Inn invokes one of the following lair actions:

**Eternal Vigil:** The inn's temperature drops suddenly as the Phantom passes through a room, possibly aiding in the detection of his presence or signaling a hidden clue.

**Whispers of the Past:** The sound of a distant conversation or laughter fills the air, drawing the PCs' attention to an object or area of significance within the inn.

**Unseen Servant:** Objects within the inn move on their own, guided by the Phantom's will, possibly revealing hidden compartments or messages (but not the Whispering Locket).

## Scaling the Encounter

### Beginning Players (PC levels 1-5)

**Persuasion/Intimidation/Task Completion:** Lower the DC for Persuasion and Intimidation checks to 12, making it easier for players to engage with the Phantom.

**Finding the Whispering Locket:** Decrease the Investigation check DC to 12 and the Perception check DC to 10 to find the locket more accessible to beginning players.

**Information Granted by the Phantom:** Simplify the information to essential points, ensuring clarity and direction for newer players.

**Lair Actions:** Scale down the effects of lair actions, ensuring they add atmospheric tension without overwhelming the party.

### Intermediate Players (PC levels 6-10)

**Persuasion/Intimidation/Task Completion:** Maintain the suggested DCs for Persuasion and Intimidation checks to reflect a moderate challenge.

**Finding the Whispering Locket:** Keep the Investigation and Perception check DCs as is, encouraging a thorough exploration of the inn.

**Information Granted by the Phantom:** Provide more detailed information, perhaps including hints about overcoming upcoming challenges or additional background on the Shadow Court.

**Lair Actions:** Use lair actions to enhance the encounter's atmosphere and challenge, including minor obstacles or puzzles related to the Phantom's presence.

### Advanced Players (PC levels 11+)

**Persuasion/Intimidation/Task Completion:** Increase the DC for Persuasion to 18 and Intimidation to 20, challenging players to utilize their skills creatively or find alternative solutions.

**Finding the Whispering Locket:** Increase the Investigation check DC to 20 and the Perception check to 18, making the locket's discovery a significant achievement.

**Information Granted by the Phantom:** Offer complex and nuanced information that ties into larger campaign arcs or reveals hidden aspects of the Shadow Court, rewarding in-depth investigation and interaction.

**Lair Actions:** Introduce lair actions that significantly affect gameplay, such as temporary barriers that divide the party, illusions that mislead PCs, or environmental changes that require quick adaptation.

# The Abandoned Weaver's Cottage

This encounter challenges players to unravel riddles woven into tapestries by a protective spirit. It emphasizes problem-solving, interaction with a non-hostile NPC (the weaver's spirit), and moral decision-making as they promise to aid Ravenholme.

As you step onto the threshold of what was once a haven of artistry and tradition, you're greeted by a silence so profound it almost echoes. The loom, once the heart of this cottage, stands still, its last project unfinished, draped like a forgotten dream. The tapestries adorning the walls are a testament to a bygone era, their colors dimmed but their stories vibrant, shifting unnervingly as if alive with the tales of sorrow they depict.

In the dim light, the figures within the tapestries dance at the edge of vision, each thread a whisper from the past, each image a riddle to be solved.

## Unraveling the Weave

Characters must succeed on an Intelligence (Investigation) check (DC 15) to decipher the riddles hidden within the tapestries. Each tapestry reveals part of the secret locations of the Shadow Court in the Ancient Crypts.

If the PCs are successful, they will see that one of the tapestries shows where each vampire is located. Use the following table:

| Vampire | Location |
| --- | --- |
| Thorn | The Vestibule of Shadows |
| Seraphina | The Chamber of Whispers |
| Gareth | The Hall of Echoing Torment |
| Killian | The Throne of Night |

## Nocturne Mist Bats

These creatures (1d4+1) are drawn to the sorrow emanating from the cottage, potentially ambushing the party if they fail to navigate the tests quietly or if they forcibly take the shawl without understanding its curse.

## The Mourner's Shawl

Hidden within a dust-covered chest. A successful Intelligence (Arcana) check (DC 16) reveals the shawl to have the Eternal Dusk curse imbued within the stitching.

## Lair Actions

On initiative count 20 (losing initiative ties), the Abandoned Weaver's Cottage invokes one of the following lair actions:

**Whispers of the Past**: The cottage amplifies the weaver's voice, casting doubt and fear. PCs must succeed on a DC 15 Wisdom saving throw or suffer disadvantage on their next skill check within the cottage.

**Tapestry Entrapment**: Tapestries animate to ensnare an unwary adventurer. A Dexterity saving throw (DC 13) is required to avoid being grappled. On their turn, a grappled character may use their action to attempt to escape with a DC 13 Strength (Athletics) or Dexterity (Acrobatics) check. The tapestries will release a player if they fail four times with a 1d4 HP loss.

**Shadows of Sorrow**: The shadows in the cottage grow darker, obscuring vision. All Perception checks to find clues or items suffer disadvantage while the PCs are in the cottage.

## Scaling the Encounter

### Beginning Players (PC levels 1-5)

- Lower the DC for the Intelligence (Investigation) check to decipher the tapestry riddles to 12, making it slightly easier for PCs to uncover the secrets.

- Reduce the number of Nocturne Mist Bats to 1 or 2 (roll 1d2) to keep combat manageable.

- Lower the DC for the Intelligence (Arcana) check to identify the curse of the Mourner's Shawl to 13, allowing for a greater chance of understanding its danger.

Adjust lair actions as follows:

**Whispers of the Past:** Lower the Wisdom saving throw DC to 12.

**Tapestry Entrapment:** Lower the Dexterity saving throw DC to 10.

**Shadows of Sorrow:** Maintain as is but allow PCs an additional Perception check (with disadvantage) to overcome the challenge through teamwork or creative thinking.

### Intermediate Players (PC levels 6-10)

- Keep the DC for the Intelligence (Investigation) check at 15, as intermediate players should be better equipped to handle more complex puzzles.

- Increase the number of Nocturne Mist Bats to 2 or 3 (roll 1d2+1) to provide a moderate challenge.

- Keep the Intelligence (Arcana) check DC at 16 for the Mourner's Shawl, assuming PCs have more resources and knowledge at their disposal.

Adjust lair actions slightly for added challenge:

**Whispers of the Past:** Increase the Wisdom saving throw DC to 16.

**Tapestry Entrapment:** Increase the Dexterity saving throw DC to 14, offering a fair challenge to more agile characters.

**Shadows of Sorrow:** Introduce an element of risk in which, should a PC fail their Perception check, they might trip or lose something important, adding urgency to navigate the shadows carefully.

### Advanced Players (PC levels 11+)

- Increase the DC for the Intelligence (Investigation) check to 17, reflecting the complexity and ancient magic woven into the tapestries that only seasoned adventurers can decipher.

- Set the number of Nocturne Mist Bats to 3 or 4 (roll 1d2+2) for a significant threat, encouraging strategic combat or inventive solutions.

- The Intelligence (Arcana) check for the Mourner's Shawl remains at DC 16, but add layers to the curse's effects, offering a narrative or mechanical puzzle for PCs to solve to remove it.

Enhance lair actions for a greater challenge:

**Whispers of the Past:** The DC is set to 18, and failing now also imposes a penalty on the next attack roll or saving throw, reflecting the disruptive power of the weaver's voice.

**Tapestry Entrapment:** Increase the Dexterity saving throw DC to 16, and on a failure, a character is also blinded for 1 turn by the ensnaring fabric. Have the tapestry deal 1d4 bludgeoning damage per round to a grappled character.

**Shadows of Sorrow:** Beyond disadvantage on Perception checks, introduce a minor psychic damage (1d4) as the sorrowful energy of the cottage lashes out, testing the mental resilience of the adventurers.

## Monster

Nocturne Mist Bat

# The Cursed Mausoleum

This encounter challenges players to navigate the complexities of morality and resolve through interaction with spirits and uncovering ancient secrets. Key elements include negotiating with Marik the Cursed, understanding the trial set by the founders' spirits, and discovering critical information for the campaign.

Before you lies the resting place of Ravenholme's founders, a mausoleum shrouded in an air of desolation and secrecy. Its stone façade is overrun with creeping vines, and the stained glass that once told tales of valor now lies fractured, casting a kaleidoscope of shadows on the ground. The entrance, sealed by forces unseen, radiates a chill that seeps into your bones, hinting at the darkness that lurks within. As you approach, the silence of the cemetery weighs heavily, broken only by the whisper of the wind, carrying with it the sorrow of untold stories.

Within these walls, the air thickens, the very essence of the place imbued with a sense of timelessness and regret. The echoes of the past linger, a testament to the mausoleum's guardianship over secrets long buried. The shadows seem to move of their own accord, and an inexplicable coldness surrounds you, as if the very stones mourn the tales they keep. Here, the boundary between the living and the spectral blurs, challenging trespassers to prove their worth and uncover the truths hidden in the heart of darkness.

## Activities

**Unveiling the Founders' Trial:** Characters encounter the spirits of Ravenholme's founders, who test their resolve and morality through riddles and ethical dilemmas. Success in these trials, which require Wisdom (Insight) checks (DC 15), reveals hidden compartments containing ancient records.

**Marik's Request:** Marik the Cursed, seeking redemption, asks for the party's help in performing a ritual to strengthen the seals trapping the Shadow Court. This involves collecting components throughout Ravenholme and the Mourning Moors. At the DM's discretion, finding these items--including the moonstone dust located in the mausoleum--may require Investigation checks (DC 14), as well as Arcana checks (DC 16) to understand their use in the ritual if it has not already been discerned.

## The Founders' Trial

Unveiling the Founders' Trial expands the encounter within the Cursed Mausoleum, a pivotal moment when the spirits of Ravenholme's founders emerge to challenge the party. These founders, once the pillars of the community, now serve as the eternal guardians of its most sacred and secret knowledge.

## Founders' Spirits

**Alden the Steward**: Alden was a leader among the original settlers, known for his unwavering commitment to the survival and prosperity of Ravenholme. He negotiated the first pacts with the forest spirits, ensuring the village's protection. In death, Alden tests the party's leadership and sacrifice for the greater good.

**Mira of the Wilds**: A skilled ranger and druid, Mira forged a deep connection with the natural world, guiding the villagers in living harmoniously with the land. Her spirit assesses the party's respect for nature and understanding of balance.

**Garrett the Wise**: The village's first scholar, Garrett documented the ancient rituals and pacts. His spirit challenges the party with riddles and puzzles, testing their wisdom and knowledge of history.

## Ethical Dilemma

The party is presented with a dire situation by the spirits: a portion of the moor, crucial to the village's sustainability, has become blighted, threatening the lives of both the villagers and the moor spirits. The spirits reveal that to save the section of the moor, a significant sacrifice must be made: either the party must surrender a powerful artifact in their possession, which will be consumed in the ritual to cleanse the blight, or they must allow the spirits to temporarily weaken the village's protective wards to draw upon their energy, risking an attack from the Shadow Court.

**Wisdom (Insight) Checks (DC 15)**: To determine the true nature of the dilemma and the consequences of their choice.

**Sacrifice Option**: If the party chooses to sacrifice their artifact, they lose a powerful tool but gain the spirits' favor, unlocking access to hidden compartments containing ancient records or artifacts. This choice also increases the party's standing with the forest spirits, granting them allies in future encounters.

**Ward Weakening Option**: Choosing to weaken the wards requires the party to prepare the village for a potential attack, leading to a series of defense planning and strategy sessions. This option involves a series of skill checks: Intelligence (Arcana) to understand how to temporarily weaken and then restore the wards (DC 18) and Wisdom (Survival) to prepare the village's defenses (DC 15). Failing to properly prepare may lead to a combat encounter with the Shadow Court's minions, but successfully navigating this path shows the party's commitment to the greater good, earning the founders' respect and revealing the mausoleum's secrets.

Each founder spirit presents their perspective on the dilemma, forcing the party to consider the long-term impacts of their decision on Ravenholme and its delicate balance with the supernatural forces surrounding it. This encounter not only tests the party's morality and wisdom but also deepens their connection to the village's history and the complex web of pacts that protect it.

## Reward: The Founders' Chronicles

Upon successfully navigating the trials set by the founders' spirits within the Cursed Mausoleum, the characters are granted access to a secluded chamber. This chamber, untouched by time and the corruption of the Shadow Court, houses ancient records contained within 3 dusty scrolls detailing the origins, strengths, and weaknesses of key members of the Shadow Court. These records, written by the founders themselves and safeguarded by their spirits, offer invaluable insights that could turn the tide in the fight against the vampires.

### Vampire Profiles as Recorded in the Founders' Chronicles:

#### Killian: Lord of the Shadow Court

*Description*: The enigmatic leader, whose aristocratic demeanor masks centuries of cunning, manipulation, and a thirst for power. His mastery over the dark arts is unrivaled within the Court.

*Strengths*: Exceptional spellcaster, highly intelligent, adept at manipulation.

*Weaknesses*: His obsession with finding true immortality may lead him to take risks or desire artifacts that could potentially be used against him.

#### Gareth: The Fallen Knight

*Description*: Once a noble protector of Ravenholme, Gareth was turned by Killian and now exists as a tragic embodiment of valor twisted into darkness. His tarnished armor bears the marks of the Shadow Court, a constant reminder of his fall from grace.

*Strengths*: Master tactician, skilled in combat, possesses regenerative abilities.

*Weaknesses*: The remnants of his noble heart could be a point of exploitation; exposure to objects of personal significance may weaken his resolve or momentarily restore his former self.

#### Seraphina: The Shadow Enchantress

*Description*: A former druid who betrayed her circle for dark power, Seraphina's ambition knows no bounds. She is a master of enchantment and divination, using her abilities to further the Court's goals and her own.

*Strengths*: Skilled in illusion and mind control, potentially possesses knowledge of the Daynight Stone's secrets.

*Weaknesses*: Her ambition may be her downfall; offering her power or knowledge might distract or divide her loyalty from Killian.

#### Thorn: Guardian of Decay

*Description*: A druid turned guardian of the Shadow Court's domain, Thorn's connection to nature has been corrupted. He now seeks to extend the Mourning Moors, turning them into a bastion of darkness.

*Strengths*: Control over plant life, ability to manipulate the environment to his advantage.

*Weaknesses*: Deep down, Thorn still harbors a connection to the natural world he once protected; reminders of his past life and purpose could disrupt his control over dark magic.

### Utilizing The Founders' Chronicles

*The Founders' Chronicles* not only serve as a historical document but also as a strategic asset for the party. By understanding the backgrounds, strengths, and weaknesses of these key figures, the PCs can devise targeted strategies to confront and weaken the Shadow Court. This information encourages creative problem-solving and may inspire the characters to explore the crypts and moors of Ravenholme in search of artifacts, allies, or knowledge that could be used to their advantage in the battles to come.

## Marik the Cursed
### Finding Marik

Approaching the shadowed confines of the mausoleum, the party's attention is drawn to a figure shrouded in a dim, unnatural aura. This is Marik, a man in the throes of a vampiric transformation, his skin pallid and veins blackened by the Shadow Court's curse.

As the party observes, they notice Marik's form is not flickering like a ghost, but rather shimmering with an ethereal darkness—a visual echo of his inner turmoil between his lingering humanity and the encroaching vampiric curse. The PCs will need a Wisdom

(Perception) check (DC 13) to discern the subtle, otherworldly signs of his condition.

Marik reaches out with a trembling hand, his voice barely more than a rasp of desperation. The PCs can engage with Marik using a Charisma (Persuasion) check (DC 12) to encourage him to reveal the urgent nature of his request and his dwindling grasp on his humanity.

He shares with the party that the vampire's bite has imbued him with a darkness that he struggles to contain. Marik sought the mausoleum in hopes of finding ancient wisdom to reverse his fate but found himself bound to its gates, his vitality ebbing as the curse pulls him further from life.

If the party offers their help, Marik divulges the knowledge he has unearthed about the mausoleum's trials and the resting spirits. He implores the adventurers to assist in fortifying the seals to prevent the Shadow Court's rise.

### Easing Marik's Affliction

To aid Marik in becoming a steadfast ally, the PCs must undertake a task to alleviate his symptoms. Marik reveals that the mausoleum holds a relic, the Elixir of Lucidity, capable of suppressing the curse's progression and restoring his clarity—for a time. Retrieving it could be a crucial step in securing Marik's aid.

The elixir is hidden within the mausoleum, guarded by spectral challenges that test the seekers' resolve. A successful DC 16 Intelligence (Investigation) or Wisdom (Survival) check is required to navigate the cryptic defenses and locate the Elixir of Lucidity.

Once obtained, Marik consumes the elixir, the dark veins receding as his form stabilizes, no longer threatened by the immediate danger of full transformation. His gratefulness is palpable, and his newfound stability allows him to join the party, offering his intimate knowledge of the Court and its crypts to aid in the quest.

### Backstory

Marik the Cursed, a figure of sorrow and determination, finds himself in a harrowing predicament. Once a vibrant member of Ravenholme, his life took a dark turn when he was bitten by a vampire, a member of the Shadow Court. This malevolent act set in motion his transformation into the undead, a fate he struggles against with every fiber of his being. Despite the curse that ravages his body, Marik's love for Ravenholme and its people anchors his soul, granting him a semblance of control over the darkness that seeks to consume him.

With the knowledge that his time is running out, Marik is painfully aware that he has only a day or two before his transformation into a vampire is complete. This realization weighs heavily on him, yet it strengthens his resolve to make a difference while he still can. He knows that his imminent conversion brings both a peril

and a potential boon to the adventurers. As someone on the brink of becoming what he most despises, he possesses unique insights into the Shadow Court's workings and vulnerabilities.

Marik offers his assistance to the players, recognizing that his cursed existence could serve a greater purpose in the fight against the Shadow Court. Whether it's providing his blood for rituals that might strengthen the seals or offering guidance through the crypts, he's willing to do whatever it takes to protect the village he loves. His condition also lends urgency to his plea for help; time is of the essence, and his actions now could either be a final act of heroism or the beginning of an eternal nightmare. Despite the dread of his inevitable fate, Marik's dedication to Ravenholme's safety and his desire to stand against the darkness in his remaining hours are a testament to the strength of the human spirit in the face of unimaginable adversity.

Marik the Cursed, knowing his humanity is waning fast, implores the adventurers to undertake a crucial quest to restore the seals of the crypts where the Shadow Court lies bound. He reveals that the weakening of the seals is not merely a symptom of time's passage but a dire portent that could lead to calamity if the Court should break free. As such, he asks the heroes to gather six specific components, one of which is hidden within the mausoleum, each a piece of a larger puzzle essential to the resealing ritual.

**Marik's Ritual Request:** Marik reveals that each of the crypts holding the Court's members has a seal powered by ancient druidic magic, now fading. The components needed for their restoration are various, with the locations of several still unknown or needing to be personally collected. He seeks the party's aid in collecting these items before his vampiric transformation is complete.

**Locating the Moonstone Dust**: Marik, now a specter of his former self, shares crucial information with the party about the moonstone dust necessary for the ritual to reseal the crypts. He points them towards a hidden compartment beneath the marble floor of the Founders' Crypt, specifically under the stone coffin of Alden the Steward, Ravenholme's most honored founder. The dust is secured within a small, ornate casket marked with Ravenholme's emblem, hidden by a false bottom in Alden's sarcophagus.

**Guide for DM**:

- Describe the atmosphere as the party enters the mausoleum's secluded section, emphasizing the chill and the shadows that seem to anticipate their quest.

- To discover the casket's location, PCs must succeed in a DC 16 Perception check to notice the unique stonework of Alden's coffin and a DC 18 Investigation check to find and activate the mechanism revealing the hidden cavity inside.

- Marik can lead the party directly to the crypt but remind them of potential challenges. The spirits of Ravenholme's founders protect this sacred place and may test the adventurers' intentions and their respect for the Founders' legacy.

## What Marik Knows and Can Share

Marik knows the necessary components for the rituals to restore each of the four seals in the Ancient Crypts, but he does not know where they can be found except for one: there is moonstone dust hidden somewhere in the mausoleum.

### Components Needed

- **Shadow essence** - an essence extracted from any defeated undead (although Marik isn't exactly certain how to perform the extraction), needed for the seal found in the Vestibule of Shadows.
- **Moonstone dust** - needed to draw the magic circle for the ritual to restore the seal in the Vestibule of Shadows.
- **Raven's feather quill** - needed for the seal found in the Chamber of Whispers.
- **Sigil-etched stone** - a specific stone bearing a carved sigil on its surface, needed for the seal found in the Hall of Echoing Torment.
- **Raven's feather** (must not have been used in another ritual) - needed for the seal found in the Throne of Night.
- **Vial of vampire's blood, given willingly** - needed for the seal found in the Throne of Night.

### Secrets of the Crypt's Seals and Their Magic

Marik knows some of the secrets held within the Ancient Crypts and can help the party locate them by providing hints on where to search for hidden seals.

**The Vestibule of Shadows:** The seal is hidden beneath the new moon tile on the mosaic floor. Inscribed all around the mosaic are ancient runes containing the key to understanding the seal's magic.

**The Chamber of Whispers:** Characters must discern the soft voice from the correct statue holding the seal, then coax the spirit to reveal the nature of the seal's magic.

**The Hall of Echoing Torment:** The seal here is hidden behind the largest chain. To understand the seal's magic, the spirits' torment must be soothed.

**The Throne of Night:** dThe throne itself contains some sort of mechanism that should point to the seal. To understand the seal's magic, one must decipher the runes inscribed upon this throne that dictate the ritual.

### Performing the Rituals

Required materials vary for each seal, from shadow essence to a raven's feather quill, each named in the Components Needed list. Marik instructs the party on the specifics of each item and its significance in the resealing. However, he's aware that there are gaps in his knowledge, and he may be missing some of the finer points for several of the rituals. Knowing this, he's hopeful that more specific information further detailing each ritual can be found.

**Ritual Performance:**

- **Under the New Moon:** Draw a circle using moonstone dust around the seal and place the shadow essence upon the seal in the center. Cast *Moonbeam* on the shadow essence as you chant runes to align the moon phases and prevent the Court's shadows from passing.
- **In the Whispering Chamber:** Use the raven's feather quill to write the Shadow Court members' true names on parchment and recite a binding spell.
- **Amidst the Echoing Torment:** Lead the spirits in a chant of release around a lit candle and the sigil-etched stone.
- **Upon the Throne of Night:** Place the raven's feather and the vial of vampire blood upon the throne, then cast *Moonbeam* directly on the throne while a willing vampire stands at the party's side, reciting a pledge of balance and peace.

## Marik's Desperation

Marik emphasizes the urgency, explaining that the ritual to strengthen the seals must be completed soon, before the Court's influence becomes too strong to contain. His transformation is nearly complete, and once he turns, he will no longer be an ally but another minion of the Court. He offers what may be his last bit of humanity – his blood, his guidance, and his fervent hope that Ravenholme may be saved from the shadows encroaching upon it.

Even in his cursed state, Marik's unique position as a new vampire with lingering human consciousness gives him a deep understanding of the Court. He provides valuable insights that could be crucial in navigating the crypts and performing the rituals correctly.

## Lair Actions

On initiative count 20 (losing initiative ties), the Cursed Mausoleum invokes one of the following lair actions:

**Chill of the Forgotten:** The temperature drops suddenly, forcing a Constitution saving throw (DC 13). Characters who fail their saves suffer 2d6 cold damage and have disadvantage on their next attack roll or ability check.

**Whispers of the Past:** Ghostly whispers fill the air, requiring a Wisdom saving throw (DC 14) to resist or be frightened for 1 minute. Frightened characters can attempt the saving throw again at the end of each of their turns, ending the effect on a success.

**Shadow's Embrace:** Darkness coalesces into tangible threats, spawning shadowy tendrils that attempt to grapple the nearest PC with a melee spell attack (+6 to hit). On a hit, the character is grappled (Strength or Dexterity check DC 14 to escape) and suffers 1d6 necrotic damage each round they remain grappled.

## Scaling the Encounter

### Beginning Players (PC levels 1-5)

- Reduce the DC for Insight checks during the Founders' Trial to 12, making it more accessible for lower-level players to interpret the ethical dilemmas.

- Adjust Marik's request to include simpler tasks that don't require high DCs, such as gathering common ingredients within the cemetery for the ritual (Investigation DC 10, Arcana DC 12).

For Lair Actions:

**Chill of the Forgotten:** Lower the cold damage to 1d6 and reduce the Constitution saving throw DC to 10.

**Whispers of the Past:** Decrease the DC to resist being frightened to 10.

**Shadow's Embrace:** Lower the spell attack bonus to +3 and the escape DC to 10, making it easier for PCs to avoid or escape the grapple.

### Intermediate Players (PC levels 6-10)

- Keep the Insight check DC for the Founders' Trial at 15. Intermediate players should have higher Wisdom and Insight proficiency to handle this challenge.

- Marik's ritual task can involve slightly rarer components that might require dealing with minor undead or guardians within the cemetery (Investigation DC 14, Arcana DC 16).

For Lair Actions:

**Chill of the Forgotten:** Maintain the cold damage and Constitution saving throw as written.

**Whispers of the Past:** Keep the Wisdom saving throw DC at 14, challenging PCs to overcome their fears.

**Shadow's Embrace:** Increase the spell attack bonus to +8 and the escape DC to 16, requiring players to strategize more effectively to escape the tendrils.

### Advanced Players (PC levels 11+)

- Increase the Insight check DC for the Founders' Trial to 18, reflecting the complexity and moral weight of the dilemmas presented by the spirits.

- For Marik's ritual, require components that are not only rare but may require negotiation or battles with

significant undead or magical creatures within the cemetery (Investigation DC 18, Arcana DC 20).

For Lair Actions:

**Chill of the Forgotten:** The cold damage increases to 3d6, with a Constitution saving throw DC of 15, testing the PCs' endurance and preparation.

**Whispers of the Past:** Increase the DC to resist being frightened to 18, emphasizing the haunting and unnerving atmosphere of the encounter.

**Shadow's Embrace:** Boost the spell attack bonus to +10 and the escape DC to 18, making the tendrils a formidable challenge that players must address quickly or risk being overwhelmed.

These adjustments provide a framework for DMs to tailor the Cursed Mausoleum encounter to their party's level, ensuring it remains engaging and appropriately challenging for groups of any experience level.

## NPC

Marik the Cursed

# The Shrouded Chapel

This encounter revolves around uncovering the secrets of the chapel's past and the spectral activity linked to its bell. Characters will confront Veilweavers, discover an ancient tome essential for reinforcing the sigils, and may encounter supernatural phenomena triggered by the chapel's mysterious bell.

Before you lies a chapel, its aged stone walls overtaken by nature's embrace. The stained glass windows, once vibrant with holy light, are now shattered, casting kaleidoscopic shadows across the chapel's desolate interior. The air hangs heavy with the scent of decay, mingled with a faint hint of incense lingering like a memory. As you step inside, the silence seems to weigh upon your shoulders, a quiet testament to the many prayers once offered in this sacred space, now forgotten by all but the spirits who linger.

## Tolling of the Bell

**Story:** The Tolling of the Bell is a phenomenon that has puzzled both the villagers and visitors of Ravenholme. At seemingly random intervals, the chapel's bell tolls, filling the air with its deep, resonant sound despite the absence of anyone to ring it. This bell is said to toll for the souls of those who have not found peace, calling out to them in a gesture of solace and remembrance.

**Random Tolling Instructions:** At random intervals during the encounter, roll a d20. On a roll of 15 or higher, the bell tolls. When the bell tolls, all characters within the chapel must make a DC 13 Wisdom saving throw. On a failure, they are momentarily overwhelmed by a wave of sorrow, suffering disadvantage on their next attack roll, saving throw, or ability check. Any roll of 1-5 on this save will cause a Veilweaver to attack one of the PCs.

## Finding the Ancient Tome

As the party ventures through the hallowed halls of the chapel, they may feel compelled to delve deeper into the mysteries of the sigils binding the Shadow Court. The chapel, steeped in history and ancient magics, may harbor lost knowledge crucial to their quest. While the existence of such a tome detailing the sigils is not known to the characters initially, instinct or guidance from a knowledgeable NPC might suggest a thorough search of sacred areas like the altar or pulpit.

To uncover this hidden wisdom, a discerning eye and careful investigation are required. A successful DC 15 Investigation check by the PCs might reveal a forgotten or concealed compartment within the chapel's altar or pulpit. Inside, they find the ancient tome, a repository of esoteric lore on the sigils used to keep the Shadow Court contained and methods to reinforce them.

The tome is a treasure trove of knowledge, with detailed illustrations and instructions on the specific components needed for each sigil's reinforcement ritual, intricately tied to the histories and locations within the Ancient Crypts. This vital discovery is not merely fortuitous—it may be the linchpin in their mission to prevent the rise of the Shadow Court. As such, the tome's discovery should be portrayed as a significant turning point, propelling the narrative forward and deepening the PCs' engagement with the world's arcane underpinnings.

## Finding the Quill

Hidden within the chapel is a quill made from a raven's feather, an item necessary for inscribing the sigils described in the tome. To find the quill, characters must search the chapel's vestry or any desks that may have been used by the clergy. Finding the quill requires a successful DC 14 Wisdom (Perception) or Intelligence (Investigation) check.

## Lair Actions

**Spiritual Echoes:** The chapel's ambient noises amplify, causing distractions. Characters in the chapel have disadvantage on Perception checks for the next round.

**Ethereal Chill:** A sudden drop in temperature briefly engulfs the chapel. Any creature inside must succeed on a DC 12 Constitution saving throw or have their speed reduced by 10 feet until the end of their next turn.

**Phantom Whispers:** Whispered prayers fill the air, disorienting the PCs. Enemies gain advantage on Stealth checks for the next round as the whispers mask their movements.

## Scaling the Encounter

### Beginning Players (PC levels 1-5)

On initiative count 20 (losing initiative ties), the Shrouded Chapel invokes one of the following lair actions:

- **Veilweavers:** Reduce their hit points and adjust their spell save DC to 12 and spell attack bonus to +4 to accommodate the lower level of the players. Consider having only one Veilweaver appear at a time.

- **Random Tolling Instructions:** Lower the DC for the Wisdom saving throw to 10 when the bell tolls to reduce the difficulty of overcoming the wave of sorrow.

- **Finding the Quill:** Reduce the Investigation check DC to 12 to find the raven's feather quill.

Adjust lair actions as follows:

**Ethereal Chill:** Lower the Constitution saving throw DC to 10.

**Phantom Whispers:** Give only a +2 bonus to the Veilweaver's Stealth checks instead of advantage.

### Intermediate Players (PC levels 6-10)

- **Veilweavers:** Use their standard stat block as provided. Include up to 2 Veilweavers simultaneously if the party handles the first one with ease.

- **Random Tolling Instructions:** Keep the DC for the Wisdom saving throw at 13. Consider the bell tolling on a roll of 12 or higher for increased frequency.

- **Finding the Quill:** Keep the Investigation check DC at 14 for an intermediate level of difficulty.

**Lair Actions:** Use the described effects but consider adding minor damage (1d4 cold damage for Ethereal Chill) to increase the challenge.

### Advanced Players (PC levels 11+)

- **Veilweavers:** Increase their hit points by 25% and consider adding an additional spell slot for each spell level to represent their increased power. Include multiple Veilweavers in the encounter or introduce them in waves.

- **Random Tolling Instructions:** Increase the frequency of the tolling by tolling the bell on a roll of 10 or higher. Increase the DC for the Wisdom saving throw to 15 to challenge higher-level players.

- **Finding the Quill:** Increase the Investigation check DC to 16 to reflect the quill's significance and the difficulty of locating it.

Enhance the challenge by changing lair actions as follows:

**Ethereal Chill:** Raise the Constitution saving throw DC to 15 and consider reducing speed by 15 feet.

**Phantom Whispers:** Maintain advantage on Stealth checks for Veilweavers or other enemies, but also impose a -2 penalty on PC attack rolls and saving throws for the next round due to the disorienting effect of the whispers.

These adjustments allow the DM to tailor the Shrouded Chapel encounter to match the level of challenge appropriate for their party's experience, ensuring a memorable and balanced adventure.

# Monster

Veilweaver

# Whisperwind Mill

Whisperwind Mill is an atmospheric, suspense-filled encounter that mixes investigation with combat. Player characters must uncover hidden messages linked to the Shadow Court and potentially face Enforcers of the Eclipse.

As you approach, an old mill stands as a silent sentinel in the mist. Its once proud sails, now tattered and worn, turn with a ghostly creaking that echoes the forgotten prosperity of Ravenholme. The air is thick with the scent of old wood and a hint of something darker, a whisper of secrets long buried within these walls. Shadows seem to shift and move on their own, and the sound of ravens can be heard from the broken windows of the mill, their calls adding to the eerie atmosphere.

The mill's interior is a maze of ancient machinery and stacks of old, bulging grain sacks, some spilling their decayed contents onto the dusty floor. Cobwebs drape the wooden beams, and the dim light barely penetrates the gloom. As you step inside, the floorboards groan underfoot, and a feeling of being watched settles over you. The ravens, black as night, peer down from their perches, their eyes reflecting the scant light like tiny beacons in the darkness.

## Uncovering Hidden Messages

PCs must succeed on Investigation or Perception checks to find the hidden messages left by the Shadow Court's minions (at the DM's discretion, this can be multiple checks over time or performed in a single roll). These messages could be etched into the mill's walls, hidden in secret compartments within the machinery, or coded within the pattern of ravens' movements observed from the mill. Each message references one of the crypts, information on that location's seal, materials needed to restore the seal and the final ritual to bind the seal.

It is at the DM's discretion as to how many messages the characters find in the mill, offering flexibility based on the pace and focus of the campaign. There are two primary sources where adventurers can gather all necessary details for sealing the crypts: the mill itself through discovering hidden messages, and through direct dialogue with Elena the Wise, each providing a comprehensive guide to undertaking this crucial task.

## Origins of the Hidden Messages

Here are a few suggestions for the DM to explain why the messages are scattered throughout the mill:

**Elena's Countermeasures:** Knowing the mill to be a place of Shadow Court activity, Elena the Wise might have used her magic to conceal vital information about the seals in the mill, hoping that brave adventurers would uncover them. This method ensures that only those with a true intent to combat the Court's influence can access this crucial knowledge.

**Protective Spells Gone Awry:** A protective spell cast by the last miller, who was secretly a member of a group opposing the Shadow Court, intended to safeguard the information about the seals. However, the spell scattered the information throughout the mill instead of hiding it in one secure location.

**Ravens as Messengers:** The ravens living in the mill, influenced by residual magic or perhaps even by Elena herself, have been moving pieces of the messages around. This behavior is part of their nature, influenced by the magic-infused environment, creating a puzzle only those most worthy can solve.

## Hidden Messages
### Message Near the Main Gear

Upon close examination of the wood beside the main gear mechanism of the mill, characters may notice unusual markings. A successful Wisdom (Perception) check (DC 15) allows a character to spot a hidden message; however, it's written in a cipher that utilizes the positions of the mill's gears as a key.

**DC Check:** To decode the ciphered message, a character must align the gears in a specific pattern, which requires an Intelligence (Investigation) check (DC 18). Once the gears are correctly positioned, they reveal a reference to a hidden seal beneath the mosaic in the **Vestibule of Shadows**.

**Seal Information:** The message unveils the presence of the seal and its importance in containing the malevolent forces of the Shadow Court. It emphasizes the necessity of reinforcing the seal to prevent the resurgence of darkness.

**Materials Needed to Restore the Seal:** The ritual to reinforce the seal requires shadow essence, a substance that can be harvested from any defeated undead creature. This could be the creature's blood or another significant part that carries its essence.

**Location and Procedure:** The ritual is to be performed at the site of the seal itself, which is located beneath the mosaic in the **Vestibule of Shadows**. Before beginning, draw a circle with moonstone dust around the seal and place the shadow essence in the center.

To initiate the ritual, one must cast the *Moonbeam* spell on the shadow essence while reciting the runes uncovered by the deciphered message. The text explicitly clarifies that the *Moonbeam* spell is a requisite component of the ritual, ensuring that natural moonlight is not a factor in its success.

**Note to the DM**: The references to specific spells like Moonbeam in the ritual instructions are intended as narrative elements to enrich the story. However, should the party lack the ability to cast certain spells due to class restrictions, as a DM, you have the discretion to adjust the requirements. You can allow alternative means to achieve the same effect or provide items that enable the casting of these spells if necessary for the progression of the story. This flexibility ensures that all parties, regardless of their composition, can fully engage with the adventure and its challenges.

### Compartment Behind the Raven's Nest

**Location Found:** Inside a secret compartment directly behind the largest raven's nest.

**Encoding Method:** Hidden within a seemingly ordinary diary, using the first letter of each line to spell out the message.

**DC Check:** A Wisdom (Perception) check (DC 22) to find the compartment; an Intelligence (Investigation) check (DC 16) to decode.

**Seal Information:** Mentions a whispering statue in the **Chamber of Whispers** which holds the key to a seal.

**Materials Needed to Restore the Seal:** A quill made from a raven's feather.

**Ritual Performance:** The ritual involves writing the names of the Shadow Court members known to the

adventurers on parchment, then burning the parchment while reciting a binding spell.

### Hidden Within Grain Chutes

**Location Found:** At the bottom of the grain chutes, accessible only when the mill is empty.

**Encoding Method:** Symbols representing the phases of the moon, correlating with the lunar cycle and shadow magic.

**DC Check:** A Wisdom (Perception) check (DC 16) to find the sets of symbols; an Intelligence (Nature) check (DC 20) to understand the magical significance of the symbols.

**Seal Information:** Relates to the need for a ritual in the **Hall of Echoing Torment**.

**Materials Needed to Restore the Seal:** The sigil-etched stone from the Ruins of Gauntlight Keep.

**Ritual Performance:** Light a candle and place the stone in the center of the hall. Characters must lead the spirits in a chant of release and seal the crypt.

### Scratched on the Inner Sails

**Location Found:** On the inner side of the mill's sails, visible only when they are fully unfurled.

**Encoding Method:** A series of numbers corresponding to the alphabetical positions of letters, revealing a ritual.

**DC Check:** A Wisdom (Perception) check (DC 17) to discover the coded numbers on the sails; an Intelligence (Investigation) check (DC 15) to connect the numbers to a meaningful message.

**Seal Information:** Indicates the **Throne of Night**'s role in the Court's power.

**Materials Needed to Restore the Seal:** A vial of vampire's blood that's willingly given, and a feather from a raven, symbolizing darkness and prophecy.

**Ritual Performance:** With the materials placed on the throne, the PCs must cast *Moonbeam* directly on the throne while a willing vampire (or a character under the effect of a potion mimicking vampirism) stands at their side, reciting a pledge of balance and peace.

## Enforcers of the Eclipse Attack Triggers

The Enforcers of the Eclipse stationed at Whisperwind Mill are on high alert for any intrusion, ready to defend the secrets of the Shadow Court with lethal force. The DM can select how many Enforcers of the Eclipse are located in the mill. but there should be a minimum of 2.

Their attack is triggered under the following conditions:

**Discovery of the Hidden Messages:** If the party successfully uncovers any of the hidden messages related to the Shadow Court's activities and discuss their findings aloud, the Enforcers will see this as a direct threat. They will attack immediately to silence the adventurers and protect the secrets of the Court.

**Disturbance of the Ravens:** The ravens living in the mill are not just ordinary birds; they serve as the eyes and ears of the Shadow Court. Should the PCs cause significant disturbance to the ravens, either by climbing to the nest for the secret compartment, or by aggressive actions that scare the birds, the Enforcers will interpret this as an aggressive move against the Court. They will emerge from their hiding spots to confront the party.

**Prolonged Presence:** If the characters spend an excessive amount of time within the mill without taking Stealth precautions (more than 10-15 minutes of in-game time), the Enforcers will become aware of their presence through the vigilant watch of the ravens or their own observations. They will organize and launch a surprise attack, attempting to catch the adventurers off guard.

To determine the exact moment of attack, the DM can make periodic Stealth checks for the Enforcers (using their +7 bonus) against the PCs' passive Perception. If the Enforcers' check succeeds, they can initiate a surprise round against the party, representing their skill at moving unseen and unheard until the moment they strike.

### Encounter Dynamics

Upon triggering an attack, describe how the Enforcers emerge from the shadows or descend silently from the upper levels of the mill, their forms half-merged with the darkness, eyes glowing with a malevolent red as they draw their weapons.

The encounter should emphasize the Enforcers' tactical awareness and their ability to use the mill's environment to their advantage, such as attacking from cover or using the milling machinery to create obstacles or hazards during the fight.

## Lair Actions

On initiative count 20 (losing initiative ties), the Whisperwind Mill invokes one of the following lair actions:

**Creaking Menace:** The mill's machinery unexpectedly springs to life for a moment, creating loud noises that can disorient the PCs. Anyone within the mill must make a DC 13 Wisdom saving throw or be frightened until the end of their next turn.

**Ravens' Warning:** The ravens inside the mill screech and swarm, providing a distraction. For one turn, all attack rolls against the PCs have advantage as they deal with the chaotic fluttering of wings and harsh caws filling the air.

**Gears of Fate:** The mill's gears lurch to life and tear themselves from the wall, threatening to catch

characters with a DC 15 Dexterity save or deal 2d10 bludgeoning damage.

## Scaling the Encounter

### Beginning Players (PC levels 1-5)

**Uncovering Hidden Messages:** Lower the Perception DCs to 15 and the Investigation DCs to 12, making the hidden messages more accessible to players new to the game.

**Enforcers of the Eclipse:** Adjust their hit points to be on the lower end of their hit dice range, and possibly reduce the number of Enforcers present. Simplify their tactics, focusing more on direct attacks than on using their full range of abilities.

**Lair Actions:** Reduce the DCs for all saving throws associated with lair actions to 10 and minimize the damage or effects to ensure they are more of a hindrance than a significant threat.

### Intermediate Players (PC levels 6-10)

**Uncovering Hidden Messages:** Keep the Perception and Investigation checks at their current DCs. This level of challenge encourages players to rely on their skills and teamwork.

**Enforcers of the Eclipse:** Use their standard stat blocks but adjust their numbers based on party size and composition to maintain challenge without overwhelming the group. Employ more strategic use of their abilities, such as Mist Form and Shadow Stealth, to challenge the players.

**Lair Actions:** Maintain the DCs for saving throws as suggested and use the lair actions to create dynamic shifts in the battlefield that the players must adapt to.

### Advanced Players (PC levels 11+)

**Uncovering Hidden Messages:** Increase the Perception and Investigation DCs to 18 or higher, reflecting the complexity of the messages and the cunning of the Shadow Court.

**Enforcers of the Eclipse:** Enhance their effectiveness by increasing hit points and possibly adding one or two more Enforcers to the encounter. Encourage the use of advanced tactics, leveraging their environment and abilities for ambushes and hit-and-run attacks.

**Lair Actions:** Increase the DCs for saving throws to 17, ensuring that the lair actions significantly impact the flow of battle and require the players to strategize effectively to mitigate their effects.

## Monster

Enforcer of the Eclipse

# The Mourning Moors

## Elena's Sanctuary

Elena's Sanctuary is a haven of ancient magic and druidic power, requiring players to solve environmental puzzles to gain access. Elena offers crucial aid against the Shadow Court, including knowledge on sealing crypts and rebalancing the Daynight Stone, but reaching her is a test of wit and respect for nature.

As you venture deeper into the Mourning Moors, the oppressive gloom and creeping mists give way to a remarkable sight—a glade of unparalleled tranquility. Encircled by a grove of trees, their leaves shimmering in a light that defies the surrounding darkness, a sanctuary stands untouched by time's ravages. The air here is filled with a serene energy and the ground is lush with moss and vibrant flora, a stark contrast to the moor's usual pallor. It's as if you've stumbled upon a secret world, a pocket of ancient magic and peace shielded from the outside turmoil.

The protective enchantments woven into the very fabric of this place are palpable, a testament to the sanctuary guardian's mastery over the natural world. Each step taken is met with the gentle rustling of leaves, a soft whisper in the breeze that seems to beckon further into the sanctum's heart. Yet, the way is not open to all. The grove demands respect and understanding, with ancient druidic symbols etched into the stones and trees serving as both a barrier and a guide. Only those who prove their harmony with nature can hope to pass unchallenged and earn an audience with the sanctuary's elusive and wise protector.

## Wards Protecting Elena's Sanctuary

### Ward: Druidic Symbol Puzzle

**Description**: A sequence of ancient druidic symbols representing the four seasons is etched onto stones surrounding the sanctuary. These symbols serve as a magical ward, protecting the entrance.

**Trigger**: Approaching the sanctuary's boundary activates the ward, presenting the puzzle to the entrants.

**Effect**: The ward bars entry to those who cannot understand or align with the cycle of nature as represented by the symbols.

**Activation**: The puzzle activates upon anyone's close approach, glowing faintly with magical energy, inviting interaction.

**Detection**: A DC 14 Intelligence (Arcana) or Wisdom (Nature) check allows a character to recognize the symbols' significance and the correct sequence.

**Disable**: Solving the puzzle (DC 17 Intelligence (Nature) check) by aligning the symbols in the correct seasonal order — spring, summer, autumn, winter — temporarily deactivates the ward, allowing passage.

### Ward: Nature's Trial

**Description**: A living barrier of dense, thorn-covered brambles infused with druidic magic. This ward tests the respect and harmony of those wishing to enter Elena's Sanctuary with the natural world.

**Trigger**: The brambles respond to the presence of individuals attempting to pass through, growing denser and more formidable to those showing disregard for nature.

**Effect**: The barrier remains impassable to those who fail to demonstrate a connection to or respect for nature.

**Activation**: The trial activates when an individual approaches, sensing their intent and relationship with the natural world.

**Detection**: A DC 14 Wisdom (Nature) check allows a character to discern the brambles' responsiveness to natural tokens or respectful actions towards nature.

**Disable**: PCs can deactivate this ward for their passage by presenting a token of nature, such as a rare flower or a piece of natural art, demonstrating respect and harmony with the environment. No check is required for a sincere offering.

**Finding a Natural Path**: Alternatively, characters can navigate through the brambles without offering a token by succeeding on a DC 16 Wisdom (Survival) check, finding a path that disturbs the environment the least, showing understanding and respect for nature's balance.

## Gaining Elena's Trust

As your party successfully navigates the environmental challenges guarding Elena's Sanctuary, they will find themselves transitioning from the dense, mist-covered Mourning Moors into an area of unexpected tranquility and vibrant life. Here, the mechanics shift from overcoming physical obstacles to engaging in roleplaying that determines the future cooperation between the PCs and Elena, the guardian of the sanctuary.

**Setting the Scene**: Upon bypassing the wards, describe the sanctuary as a sudden haven of peace, a stark contrast to the bleakness of the Moors. Use vivid imagery to emphasize the shift in atmosphere—a clear pond reflecting soft light, vibrant flora, and the ancient trees that circle the clearing. At its heart, Elena stands as a beacon of the sanctuary's ancient and protective magic.

**First Contact:** Elena's first appearance should strike a balance between awe-inspiring and approachable, embodying the sanctuary's blend of serenity and latent power. When she speaks, it's with a voice that carries the depth of nature itself, inviting the party to declare their intentions. Here, encourage your players to articulate their purpose in seeking Elena, framing their responses as the first step towards gaining her trust.

**DC Checks for Initial Interaction:**

- **Wisdom (Insight) Check (DC 15):** To gauge Elena's openness and caution. Success means the PCs pick up on her willingness to help, tempered by a need for assurance of their intentions.

- **Charisma (Persuasion) Check (DC 13):** For the party to express their goals and the sincerity of their quest against the Shadow Court. This could also involve presenting evidence of their deeds against the Court's influence.

**Navigating the Conversation:** Elena's demeanor is one of cautious optimism. She's intrigued by the party's journey but needs more than just their word to offer her full support. This part of the encounter should focus on dialogue, giving players the chance to roleplay their interactions and build a rapport with Elena.

**Tasks or Proofs of Intent:** Elena might require more tangible proof of the party's commitment to fighting the Shadow Court and preserving natural harmony. This could involve:

**A Minor Quest:** Retrieve a rare herb from a dangerous part of the Moors (Survival Check DC 16).

**Demonstration of Nature's Respect:** Show Elena a gesture of goodwill towards nature, like healing a wounded animal (Medicine Check DC 14) or planting new life (Nature Check DC 12).

**Elena's Reaction:** Based on the party's success in these initial interactions, Elena's attitude towards them can shift significantly. A successful series of checks and thoughtful roleplaying should see her transitioning from guarded to a valuable ally, offering insights into the Shadow Court and potentially aiding with magical resources or information critical to the party's quest.

**If Trust Is Gained:** Elena becomes a cornerstone ally, revealing vital details about the crypts' seals and the Daynight Stone, and possibly granting the party items or knowledge to assist in their quest.

**If Trust Is Partial or Not Gained:** Elena remains non-hostile but distant, perhaps offering cryptic advice or setting additional tasks to test the party further. This outcome should not dead-end the players but encourage them to find alternative solutions or ways to prove their worth.

## Elena's Knowledge on Each Vampire

**Gareth:** "Gareth's tale is a somber reminder of the fine line between valor and darkness. Once a noble knight of Ravenholme, his fall was not the end but a cursed beginning. Now bound to the Shadow Court, he wields the shadows he once defended against. Yet, a flicker of his former self remains, struggling against the night that ensnares him. To confront Gareth is to face the Shadow Court's cruelty head-on and the tragedy of a hero lost to darkness. Seek him in the Hall of Echoing Torment, where he commands the spirits sacrificed by the Court. It is said that understanding his past and igniting the spark of his humanity could be key to his, and our, redemption."

**Killian:** "Killian, the enigmatic and powerful Lord of the Shadow Court, stands as a pillar of ancient darkness and ambition. With centuries of cunning and a mastery over the dark arts, he has bound countless to his will, creating a court shrouded in shadow. His ability to charm and dominate is unparalleled, making him a formidable adversary in any confrontation. To challenge Killian is to challenge the very foundation of the Shadow Court. Knowledge, strength, and an understanding of the ancient magics that bind him to this realm are crucial. Only by unearthing the secrets of the past and exploiting the rare vulnerabilities of such a being can hope be restored."

**Marik the Cursed:** "A once-beloved figure of Ravenholme now trapped between life and death, Marik's state of existence is a haunting testament to the Shadow Court's reach. His knowledge of the Court and the crypts could prove invaluable to those who dare to stand against the darkness. Yet, it is his desire for redemption that holds the key. Marik seeks to protect the innocent and undo the evil that yet consumes him. Aid in his quest for redemption might not only secure a powerful ally but also strike a crucial blow against the Court's influence."

**Seraphina:** "Seraphina's journey from druid to dark enchantress mirrors the very corruption we seek to eradicate. Her betrayal and subsequent consumption by darkness have made her a critical component of the Court's machinations. Her ambitions, however, stretch beyond mere loyalty to Killian, hinting at a power struggle within the Court itself. Understanding her past, the depth of her betrayal, and the motivations driving her pursuit of the Daynight Stone's secrets could unveil weaknesses within the Court. Approach with caution, for her mastery over enchantment makes her as dangerous as she is seductive."

**Thorn:** "Thorn represents nature's wrath turned vile, a guardian who now extends the reach of the Mourning Moors for the Court. His transformation from a revered druid to a harbinger of decay is a grim reminder of the Court's perversion of nature. Yet, beneath this corruption, there might still linger a shard of the protector he once was. Thorn's sanctum, a twisted reflection of the vibrant groves he guarded, holds the key to understanding the magic that binds him and possibly to reversing the curse that has twisted his nature. His knowledge of druidic magic, now used for malevolence, could be pivotal in our efforts to restore balance."

## Elena's Knowledge on Restoring the Crypt's Seals

**The Vestibule of Shadows:** "The Vestibule of Shadows guards its secrets beneath a moonlit mosaic. To restore its seal, you must first solve the lunar puzzle there, aligning the phases of the moon to reveal the path forward. Within its depths lies a hidden seal beneath the new moon tile. Use *Detect Magic* to uncover its aura or solve my puzzle to light your way. With shadow essence gathered from those that lurk in the night, and under the moon's gaze, cast *Moonbeam* upon the center, chanting the ancient runes you've deciphered."

*Note: Should the party lack the ability to cast certain spells such as Moonbeam due to class restrictions, as a DM, you have the discretion to adjust the requirements.*

**The Chamber of Whispers:** "In the Chamber of Whispers, secrets are held by statues of the court, whispering truths lost to time. Listen carefully, for among these murmurs, a voice less sinister will guide you to the seal hidden within a statue's maw. To reveal its nature, engage with the bound spirit — a persuasive tongue might coax the seal's secrets from silent lips. Armed with a quill made from a raven's feather, inscribe the true names of the prominent members of the Shadow Court upon parchment. Then, placing the parchment in fire, speak the binding spell to restore the seal."

**The Hall of Echoing Torment:** "Within the Hall of Echoing Torment, souls bound in sorrow cry for release. The seal, hidden behind the largest chain, yearns for freedom from darkness. Soothe the tormented or persuade them to share their stories. A stone etched with ancient sigils, taken from the ruins of Gauntlight Keep, is key. Light a candle and place it on the stone, and together, chant a spell of release. Your combined voices will strengthen the seal, silencing the cries and easing the spirits' suffering."

**The Throne of Night:** "Killian's Throne of Night obscures its seal in plain sight, integrated into the throne itself. Only under a *Moonbeam's* touch will ancient runes reveal the path to restoration. A vial of vampire's blood and a raven's feather symbolize the balance between darkness and prophecy. Cast *Moonbeam* upon the throne as you recite a pledge of peace, a vampire ally by your side. This act of unity, a blend of light and dark, will flood the throne room with purifying light, weakening Killian's grip on the shadowed realms."

## Elena's Knowledge on Preparing the Crypt's Seals

**Locating the Seals:** "The seals you seek are deeply entwined with the very essence of this land, protected by the ancient druidic magic that courses through the ley lines. To uncover their locations, you must delve into the heart of the Mourning Moors, consult the fragmented texts in the ruins, and seek the wisdom of the spirits that linger near these sacred sites. Remember, the Shadow Court has its minions guarding these secrets closely. Tread carefully, for the path to each seal is as perilous as it is pivotal."

**Understanding the Magic:** "The magic binding these seals is ancient, a blend of druidic rituals and the intrinsic powers of the ley lines. To fully grasp their mechanisms, you may need to ally with the spirits bound to these lands. Some knowledge may come at a cost, requiring you to complete tasks that prove your dedication to restoring balance. This journey will test not just your might but your willingness to understand the deep magic that binds Ravenholme."

**Gathering Materials:** "Each seal's repair will require specific, often rare materials. These can range from the luminescent minerals in the Mourning Moors' heart to the essence of night itself, captured from one of the Court's creatures. Some materials are bound to the history and spirit of this land, requiring acts of courage and purity to be revealed. Your quest for these materials will lead you into the very shadows you seek to banish. Be prepared for the Court's attempts to thwart you at every turn."

**Performing the Ritual:** "With the necessary knowledge and materials at hand, the rituals to repair each seal must be conducted with precision and care. Each ritual is a reflection of the seal's nature and the area it protects. You may find yourselves cleansing a corrupted grove or rekindling the protective fires of Ravenholme's ancestors. Be vigilant, for the Shadow Court will surely seek to disrupt these rituals. Stand firm, for the balance you strive to restore lies in grave danger during these moments."

**Sealing the Crypts:** "As each seal strengthens, you will see the tide begin to turn. The mists may recede, the night's grasp loosen, and hope rekindle among the people of Ravenholme. Your journey to repair the seals is a beacon of light in the darkness that has enveloped this land. Completing these rituals will cut off the Court from their power sources, significantly weakening their hold on our world."

**The Final Seal:** "The culmination of your efforts will focus on the final ritual to seal away the last chamber, the Throne of Night, along with the Court's leader Killian.. This is no small feat, requiring all your strength, courage, and unity of purpose. This final stand against the Shadow Court will determine the future of Ravenholme. Prepare for a confrontation that will test everything you have learned and everything you are. Remember, the power you've gathered from the land, its people, and the seals themselves will be your greatest ally in this final battle."

## Elena's Knowledge on the Eternal Dusk Curse

**Initial Examination:** "The darkness that cloaks your vision is no simple malady but a manifestation of the Eternal Dusk, a curse wielded by the Shadow Court to weaken and control. A blend of arcana and medicinal knowledge is required to unravel its bindings. Let us first discern its grip upon you through careful study."

**Consulting with an Expert:** "You've come to me bearing the weight of the Eternal Dusk. Wise, indeed. This curse is ancient, intertwined with the very essence of the Shadow Court's power. Understanding its depth requires more than just knowledge—it requires insight into the dark heart of the Court itself."

**Learning about the Antidote:** "The antidote to such darkness is forged from elements as rare as they are powerful. Blood of the Court's own kin and herbs from the Mourning Moors—each component is a step away from the dusk and closer to dawn."

**Collecting Antidote Ingredients:** "Each ingredient you seek is a test of resolve and bravery. The vampire's blood, a defiance against those who would see you fall; the herb from **Widow's Walk**, a symbol of perseverance; water blessed by a druid or cleric, a beacon of purity in the face of corruption. Gather them, and the path to salvation begins to clear."

**Crafting the Antidote:** "To craft the antidote is to weave together the strands of light and life against the tapestry of darkness. Within my sanctuary, or a place reclaimed from the crypt's corruption, you must combine these components with precision, guided by the rituals of old. Here, your unity and strength will be paramount."

**Lifting the Curse:** "As the moon rises to its zenith, so too must the antidote be consumed, a final stand against the creeping dusk. Be prepared, for the Shadow Court will not quietly suffer this affront. Your victory over the curse will be a blow to their dominion, a beacon of hope in the enveloping night.'

**Aftermath:** "The shadows recede, but their touch lingers, a reminder of the battle fought within and without. The curse may leave its mark upon you, a testament to your endurance, or perhaps a newfound strength drawn from the darkness you overcame. Know this: in standing against the Eternal Dusk, you will have earned allies unseen, spirits and forces that share your defiance against the Court's tyranny."

## Elena's Knowledge on the Daynight Stone

**Gathering Information:** "To restore the Daynight Stone, you must first understand its essence and the imbalance it suffers. My sanctuary holds many secrets, but trust is not given lightly. Aid those troubled by unrest in Widow's Walk, and you shall earn both my trust and the knowledge you seek."

**Calming the Spirits at Widow's Walk:** "The spirits at Widow's Walk are restless, echoes of a sorrow that clouds the moor. Speak to them and hear their tales, which may bring them peace. This act of compassion will reveal to you the rare herbs needed for our work, blessed by the spirits themselves for your courage and empathy."

**Retrieving Soil from Thornheart Thicket:** "Within the center of Thornheart Thicket lies soil touched by the ancients, essential for our ritual. You must gather a handful of this soil for use in the ritual to restore the Daynight Stone. Navigating the thicket's dangers requires a deep respect for nature. Bloodvine Creepers guard this sacred ground; approach with caution, and remember, stealth and respect for the land will serve you well."

**Reclaiming the Sigil-Etched Stone from the Ruins of Gauntlight Keep:** "The sigil-etched stone in Gauntlight Keep is key to our ritual, as it is imbued with the land's ancient magics. Guarding the stone is the spirit of the Last Knight, a remnant of a nobler time. Persuade him of your cause or best him in combat, and the stone will be yours."

**Performing the Ritual to Rebalance the Daynight Stone:** "At the heart of the Mourning Moors in Fogcaller's Hollow lies a circle where earth's power converges. Here, you must arrange the 3 components gathered from the moors and cast your spells. *Moonbeam, Bless, Daylight*—each plays a part in harmonizing the Stone's energies. Your unity in this endeavor is crucial; together, you will channel the ritual's power."

*Note to the DM: The Daynight Stone does not need to be in the possession of the PCs when they perform the ritual. This has two benefits: the party does not need to trudge back to the location once they have the stone and, second, it keeps the narrative of the story moving forward.*

*While the final part of the ritual calls for three spells, if your players do not have the right combination of spells, you can alter the ritual's requirements to reflect your party's capabilities. If the party does not have enough spellcasters (or any spellcaster), you can substitute a different activity, such as a ritual dance or chant.*

**Outcome:** "Once the Daynight Stone is reclaimed from the Shadow Court's clutches and brought back to the surface under the open sky, you'll see its glow immediately pierce the shroud of dusk over the moors as the land begins to recover."

## Elena's Knowledge on the Ley Lines

**Understanding Ley Lines:** "Ley lines are the ancient veins through which the earth's magic flows, converging at points of power across the land. These lines were pivotal in our ancestors' strategy to ensnare the vampires, utilizing the natural magic emanating from them to bolster the seals that keep the darkness at bay."

**The Ritual of Binding:** "To initially trap the vampires, a ritual was performed at the nexus of these ley lines, amplifying the inherent magic to create a barrier no creature of shadow could cross. This ritual required a harmony between the land's defenders and the forces of nature, a balance that is delicate and must be maintained."

**The Importance of the Daynight Stone:** "The Daynight Stone, central to our efforts, was once harmonized with the ley lines, its power used to reinforce the barriers. Its imbalance now threatens the integrity of our defenses. Restoring the Daynight Stone's balance is essential not just for the land but for ensuring the vampires remain trapped."

**Ley Line Nexus Points:** "The key to reactivating the ley lines lies in finding their nexus points. These are places of immense power and are often guarded by the land itself. To access them, one must understand the language of the earth, listening to its whispers and respecting its guardians."

**Protective Measures:** "Our ancestors also placed sigils at these nexus points, further anchoring the magic. Should you find these sigils, treat them with care. They are not just relics of a bygone era but active components in the safeguarding of Ravenholme."

**The Threat of Disturbance:** "Be wary, for the Shadow Court is ever vigilant. They seek to disrupt the ley lines, to free themselves from their imprisonment. Your actions in restoring the Daynight Stone and reinforcing the seals will directly counter their efforts. Stay vigilant."

**Final Warning:** "Remember, the ley lines are not mere tools but sacred connections to the earth. Misuse them, and you risk the wrath of nature itself. Approach with respect, and the land will aid you in your quest to keep the darkness sealed away."

## Lair Actions

On initiative count 20 (losing initiative ties), Elena's Sanctuary invokes one of the following lair actions:

**Grove's Whisper:** The grove amplifies Elena's ability to communicate through nature. The characters might hear her voice on the wind, offering cryptic advice or warnings about their current challenges.

**Luminous Barrier**: Glowing runes form in the ground, creating a protective circle around Elena and/or her allies. For one round, those within the circle have +2 to their AC against attacks from any creature outside the circle.

**Rejuvenating Mists**: Healing mists swirl through the sanctuary, subtly aiding those Elena deems worthy. Once per encounter, on initiative count 20, allies within the sanctuary regain 1d8+4 hit points, symbolizing the sanctuary's restorative magic.

## Scaling the Encounter

### Beginning Players (PC levels 1-5)

**Druidic Symbol Puzzle**: Lower the DC for the Intelligence (Nature) check to 12 to solve the puzzle, simplifying the sequence or providing hints through environmental storytelling.

**Nature's Trial**: Allow PCs to bypass the brambles with simpler tokens of nature (like ordinary flowers or stones) without needing a roll or reduce the Wisdom (Survival) check DC to 12 for finding a natural path.

**Gaining Elena's Trust:**

- **Presentation of Nature's Gift:** Lower the DC to 10 for the Wisdom (Nature) check or Charisma (Performance) check, accepting more common items as gifts.

- **Recounting Actions Against the Shadow Court:** Adjust the Charisma (Persuasion) DC to 13, acknowledging the efforts of less experienced characters.

- **Demonstrating Knowledge or Intent:** Lower the Intelligence (Arcana) or Wisdom (Insight) DC to 12 to reflect the characters' growing understanding.

**Lair Actions:** Simplify effects or provide clear visual cues to aid players in understanding and utilizing the sanctuary's magic to their advantage.

### Intermediate Players (PC levels 6-10)

**Druidic Symbol Puzzle**: Maintain the DC at 17 for the Intelligence (Nature) check but introduce elements in the environment that can offer clues if interacted with creatively.

**Nature's Trial**: Require specific tokens of nature that reflect a deeper understanding of the local ecosystem or maintain the Wisdom (Survival) check DC at 16, introducing minor obstacles that can be overcome with clever thinking or teamwork.

**Gaining Elena's Trust:**

- **Presentation of Nature's Gift:** Keep the DCs at their current levels, but encourage players to find or create gifts that have a personal touch or deeper connection to the story.

- **Recounting Actions Against the Shadow Court:** Maintain the DCs as provided, but allow players to use evidence or tokens from their adventures as leverage.

- **Demonstrating Knowledge or Intent:** Keep the DC for Intelligence (Arcana) or Wisdom (Insight) at 16, but reward players for connecting their plans to previous successes or learned lore.

**Lair Actions:** Introduce tactical options through lair actions that can challenge or bolster the party based on strategic use, such as temporary buffs or environmental advantages during combat.

### Advanced Players (PC levels 11+)

**Druidic Symbol Puzzle**: Increase the complexity of the puzzle, requiring players to solve it under a time constraint or while defending against a minor threat.

**Nature's Trial**: Introduce a dynamic challenge where the brambles actively move and change, requiring a DC 18 Wisdom (Survival) check and possibly teamwork to navigate through or disable the barrier.

**Gaining Elena's Trust:**

- **Presentation of Nature's Gift:** Challenge players to secure rare or extraordinary items as gifts, increasing the Nature or Performance DC to 16, reflecting the need for significant effort or sacrifice.

- **Recounting Actions Against the Shadow Court:** Require detailed accounts of their deeds, with the possibility of using Insight or Investigation to uncover more about their past actions, setting a high Persuasion DC of 18.

- **Demonstrating Knowledge or Intent:** Expect players to not only display knowledge but also predict potential future challenges, setting high Arcana or Insight DCs of 20 and considering the incorporation of elements from their own backgrounds or previous adventures.

**Lair Actions:** Utilize lair actions to create complex battlefield dynamics or puzzles that require quick thinking and adaptability, offering rewards or insights for creative problem-solving.

# Fogcaller's Hollow

Fogcaller's Hollow is the scene for a pivotal ritual to restore balance to the Daynight Stone, crucial in diminishing the Shadow Court's influence. The dense fog and lurking Carrion Marionettes add atmospheric pressure and a palpable sense of urgency to the encounter.

You find yourselves at the edge of a clearing, where the fog clings to the earth with a tenacity that feels almost alive. Ancient standing stones, their surfaces etched with runes that pulse faintly with a spectral light, form a circle around a central altar. The air here is thick, damp, and filled with the scent of decay, yet there's an undeniable energy pulsing through the ground beneath your feet. The fog seems to swirl with intention, obscuring the boundary between the natural and the supernatural. As you step closer, the stones seem to beckon, drawing you into their ancient mystery and the ritual that awaits.

## Performing the Ritual to Rebalance the Daynight Stone

This ritual does not require the presence of the Daynight Stone, and can be successfully performed without the PCs having it in their possession.

**Formation and Casting:** Characters need to find the correct positions for each material component based on the standing stones' alignment. A successful DC 15 Intelligence (Arcana) check allows them to correctly place the components and themselves.

**Ritual Checks:** Each character contributes with a skill check. Allow PCs to choose their approach, matching their skills to the needs of the ritual (Arcana, Nature, Religion) with the DC set at 18 for each. Creative use of their backgrounds and experiences should be encouraged to lower or adjust these DCs.

**Completion:** Success illuminates the Hollow, visually dispelling the fog temporarily as the Daynight Stone rebalances. Failure means the ritual must be attempted again, possibly under more dire circumstances as the Shadow Court reacts.

## Carrion Marionettes

These grotesque puppet-like creatures, hidden within the fog, attempt to disrupt the ritual. They emerge in numbers (2d4) when the ritual begins or if the party fails any of the ritual checks, providing both a physical and psychological challenge to the party as they defend the ritual site and complete their task.

## Lair Actions

On initiative count 20 (losing initiative ties), Fogcaller's Hollow invokes one of the following lair actions:

**Mist's Embrace:** The fog thickens, reducing visibility to 5 feet. Characters must succeed on a DC 14 Wisdom (Perception) check to navigate, and roll at disadvantage when performing ranged attacks.

**Whispers of the Ancients:** Ghostly whispers fill the air, echoing from the standing stones. All creatures must succeed on a DC 15 Wisdom saving throw or be momentarily disoriented, suffering disadvantage on their next attack roll or skill check.

**Grasp of the Past:** Shadowy hands reach out from the fog, attempting to grasp at the PCs' ankles in attempts to trip them. Characters must make a DC 13 Dexterity saving throw or fall prone. Additionally, the entire area around the ritual site becomes difficult terrain, and all ground movement speed is halved for the next turn.

## Scaling the Encounter

### Beginning Players (PC levels 1-5)

**Formation and Casting:** Lower the Arcana check DC to 12 for positioning and casting, making it more accessible for characters to find their correct places without extensive experience.

**Ritual Checks:** Reduce the skill check DCs to 14, allowing for a greater chance of success. Encourage creative solutions that play to the characters' backgrounds, potentially offering advantage or further reducing the DC for well-justified actions.

**Carrion Marionettes:** Limit the number of Carrion Marionettes that attack to 1d4 to keep the combat manageable for a smaller or less experienced party.

**Lair Actions:** Adjust lair action effects to be less severe:

- **Mist's Embrace:** Reduce visibility to 10 feet instead of 5.
- **Whispers of the Ancients:** Lower the DC to 12 for the Wisdom saving throw to avoid disorientation.
- **Grasp of the Past:** Keep the DC 13 for the Dexterity saving throw but affect only one randomly determined PC per round to simplify encounter management.

### Intermediate Players (PC levels 6-10)

**Formation and Casting:** Keep the DC at 15 or the Intelligence (Arcana) check, with the expectation for PCs at this level to strategize or utilize abilities to enhance their chances of success.

**Ritual Checks:** Maintain the DC at 18 for skill checks, but offer alternative ways to achieve success, such as using spell slots or class features to boost their efforts, reflecting the characters' growing power and versatility.

**Carrion Marionettes:** Keep the number at 2d4, providing a challenge that matches the party's increased combat capabilities.

**Lair Actions:** Introduce moderate complications:

- **Mist's Embrace:** Keep visibility to 5 feet and maintain the DC 14 Wisdom (Perception) check for effective navigation.
- **Whispers of the Ancients:** The DC remains at 15 for resisting disorientation. affecting all characters but allowing a saving throw at the end of each PC's turn to shake off the effect if it hasn't already been triggered.
- **Grasp of the Past:** Increase the Dexterity saving throw DC to 14 and affect multiple or all PCs, adding a layer of tactical consideration to movement and positioning.

### Advanced Players (PC levels 11+)

**Formation and Casting:** Increase the Intelligence (Arcana) check DC to 18, challenging even the most adept adventurers to utilize high-level skills and spells to ensure success.

**Ritual Checks:** Raise the skill check DCs to 20, requiring a concerted effort and strategic use of resources. Consider allowing successful high-level spells or unique magical items to automatically succeed on one of the checks.

**Carrion Marionettes:** Summon 3d4 Carrion Marionettes or introduce a "leader" marionette with enhanced abilities to lead the attack, adding depth and urgency to the combat challenge.

**Lair Actions:** Enhance the complexity and threat level:

- **Mist's Embrace:** The fog is as thick as pea soup, reducing visibility to less than 5 feet. Characters must now succeed on a DC 16 Wisdom (Perception) check to avoid attacks against them having advantage due to their heavily obscured vision.
- **Whispers of the Ancients:** Increase the DC to 17 for the Wisdom saving throw, adding a minor psychic damage (1d4) on a failed save to represent the disorienting power of the whispers.
- **Grasp of the Past:** Set the Dexterity saving throw DC at 15 and introduce a minor necrotic damage (1d6) on a failed save as the shadowy hands claw at the PCs, hindering their movement and adding a sense of danger even to movement within the ritual site.

## Monster

Carrion Marionette

# The Ruins of Gauntlight Keep

In this encounter at the Ruins of Gauntlight Keep, players explore the haunted remnants of a once-mighty fortress, searching for the sigil-etched stone essential for their quest while potentially engaging with the spirit of the Last Knight, who offers wisdom and warnings. The ruins are a test of bravery and perception, with ancient arms and armor to be discovered among spectral dangers and the lingering sorrow of battles long past.

As you crest the hill, the stark silhouette of the ruins comes into view, its once formidable structures now little more than a collection of crumbling walls and shadows. The air around you carries a chill, whispering of the valor and despair that soaked into these stones over centuries. Gaps where gates and windows stood now open like wounds into dark, empty spaces, inviting yet foreboding. The remnants of towers reach towards the sky, their broken forms standing as silent sentinels over a forgotten legacy.

The ground beneath your feet is uneven, littered with debris and the echoes of battles long past. As you navigate through the ruins, the sense of being watched grows stronger, the weight of history pressing down upon you. Here, amid the ruins, the line between the past and the present blurs, and the air seems thick with the stories of those who once lived and died within these walls. It's a place caught between times, holding secrets of great valor and tragic falls, waiting for those brave enough to uncover them.

## Rooms in Gauntlight Keep

### The Armory

**Description:** The Armory itself is difficult to get to, requiring a successful DC 17 Strength or Dexterity (Athletics) check to safely navigate the collapsed hallways and over rubble to reach the area. This room, once the heart of the keep's martial strength, now lies in disrepair. Racks of weapons and armor stand rusted and forgotten, with cobwebs draping like mournful banners. A faint, metallic scent of old battles lingers in the air. Despite its ruin, the aura of valor has not entirely faded from the room.

**Dimensions:** 30 ft. by 20 ft.

**What Can be Found:** Among the decayed weaponry and armor, players can discover a sigil-etched stone bearing a powerful rune carved into its surface. Hidden under a collapsed shelf, this stone pulses with a faint magical light. Additionally, amidst the rusted armaments, they find an enchanted shield bearing the crest of Gauntlight Keep, which offers +1 to AC when used, a remnant of the keep's glorious past.

### The Great Hall

**Description:** The remnants of grandeur are evident in this once-majestic hall where feasts and councils were held. The roof has partially collapsed, allowing moonlight to illuminate the battered long tables and stone benches. Nature has begun to reclaim this space, with ivy creeping along the walls and across the mosaic floor.

**Dimensions:** 50 ft. by 40 ft.

**What Can be Found:** The center of the room holds a large, ornate chest bound by rusted iron bands. Inside, adventurers will find an assortment of silver coins (150 in total) and a beautifully crafted, albeit old, tapestry that depicts the history of Gauntlight Keep, potentially valuable to collectors or historians.

### The Barracks Ruins

**Description:** These ruins mark where the keep's defenders once rested and prepared for battle. The skeletal framework of bunk beds lines the walls, and remnants of personal belongings scatter the ground, telling silent tales of the lives once lived here. Nature's encroachment is evident, with grass and small trees sprouting through the cracked stone floor.

**Dimensions:** 40 ft. by 25 ft.

**What Can be Found:** Amid the personal effects, a well-preserved scabbard, intricately designed and still wrapped around a now-missing sword, hints at the craftsmanship of the keep's inhabitants. Near one of the beds, a hidden floorboard reveals a small stash of gold coins (100 in total) and a fine magical bowstring, still resilient and capable of improving any bow's range. Once applied to a bow, it increases a bow's maximum range by 10 feet.

### The Kitchens

**Description:** The kitchens, once bustling with the preparation of meals for the keep's inhabitants, now stand quiet. The large hearth is cold and filled with ash, while tables and benches are overturned, the remnants of a hurried evacuation.

**Dimensions:** 45 ft. by 20 ft.

**What Can be Found:** Searching through the pantry, adventurers find a hidden compartment beneath a loose stone tile, revealing a small collection of preserved spices rare in the region, potentially valuable to the right buyer. Additionally, a secret recipe for a hearty stew, claimed to boost the morale and stamina of those who consume it, is pinned under a rusted kitchen knife on one of the tables.

## The Spirit of the Last Knight

**Investigation Check**: PCs must conduct a thorough search of the keep's ruins, requiring a DC 15 Investigation check. Success leads them to a secluded area of the barracks, where the air grows colder, signaling the presence of the spirit.

**Wisdom (Perception) Check**: To notice the subtle signs of the spectral knight's presence, such as the soft glow of ethereal light or the faint sound of armor clinking, characters must succeed on a DC 14 Wisdom (Perception) check.

## Encounter Dynamics with the Last Knight

As adventurers explore the ruins of Gauntlight Keep, they may encounter the Last Knight, a spectral guardian bound by his ancient vow. The Last Knight evaluates those who tread within his domain, assessing their intentions and valor with a discerning gaze that has pierced the veils of time.

### Interaction Options

**Test of Mettle:** The Last Knight may challenge the party to a trial by combat to assess their worthiness. This is not a fight to the death but a test of strength, courage, and resolve. If the adventurers accept and prove themselves capable, the knight will acknowledge their valor with respect and aid them by sharing his knowledge and possibly granting access to the sigil-etched stone. If the party agrees to the test, the Last Knight engages them in combat using non-lethal means to measure their skills. He ceases the fight once he deems the party worthy or if they demonstrate exceptional bravery or strategy.

**Judgment Based on Actions:** Should the adventurers act with dishonor, such as stealing from the ruins or desecrating the site, the Last Knight perceives these actions as a threat to his oath and the sanctity of Gauntlight Keep. Under these circumstances, he might attack them, believing them to be agents of the Shadow Court or unworthy of his aid. In this scenario, the Last Knight uses his full combat abilities as described in his stat block. The adventurers must then decide whether to flee, fight back, or attempt to convince him of their true intentions through dialogue and persuasion.

## Knowledge the Last Knight Will Share

As the spectral form of the knight materializes before you in the dim light of the barracks, his voice, though faint, carries the weight of centuries. He begins to recount his tale, his ethereal gaze distant as he speaks of a time when courage and sacrifice were the only defenses against the encroaching darkness.

"In the final days, as the Shadow Court's power threatened to engulf our lands in eternal night, it fell upon me and my brethren to stand against them. We devised a plan, one last desperate ploy to turn the tide against the vampires that sought our ruin.

"Our strategy was simple yet fraught with peril. I was to be the bait, luring the vampires to Gauntlight Keep, where their fate would be sealed. The moors around this fortress are veined with ley lines, channels of ancient, powerful magic that Elena the Wise could tap into.

"Elena's mastery over the ley lines was unparalleled. As the vampires stepped within the boundary of this keep, she invoked their power, entwining the vampires in a magical snare. The seals she created that night were meant to imprison them for eternity, a testament to her skill and the ley lines' might.

"The sigil-etched stone you seek in the armory is not a mere relic; it is key to maintaining the seals that bind the Shadow Court's minions. It was forged from the very essence of the ley lines, imbued with the power to reinforce the barriers between us and the darkness. This stone is a linchpin in the ceremony to restore balance to the Daynight Stone. Without it, the ritual cannot be completed, and the darkness will continue to spread, unchecked and unchallenged."Though I fell in battle, my spirit remains, bound to these ruins by a vow to watch over this place and guard against the horrors that once threatened to emerge from the shadows. My vigil is eternal, a reminder of the cost of freedom and the price of vigilance.

"Take heed of my tale, brave ones. The battle against the Shadow Court is far from over, and the seals that once served as our salvation may yet play a role in the darkness's defeat. Remember, it is not just strength of arm that will see you through, but strength of heart and the will to stand against the night."

The knight's voice and ghostly form fade, leaving behind a silence that speaks volumes of the sacrifices made and the battles yet to come. His story, a beacon of hope and a warning in equal measure, guides you towards the armory in search of the sigil-etched stone, the next step on your journey to confront the darkness.

## Finding the Sigil-Etched Stone

**Location Clues**: Within the ruins, clues to the stone's whereabouts can be found etched into the walls. A passive Perception of 17 notices one or more of these clues carved into ruined walls, Deciphering these clues requires a DC 16 Intelligence (History) check.

**Search the Armory**: The stone is hidden within the remnants of the keep's armory. A successful DC 17 Strength or Dexterity (Athletics) check allows safe passage through collapsed hallways and over rubble to reach this area.

**Using the Sigil-Etched Stone**: In addition to being a necessary part of the ceremony to restore balance to the Daynight Stone, the sigil-etched stone is needed as a material element in restoring the seal to the Hall of Echoing Torment.

## Lair Actions

On initiative count 20 (losing initiative ties), Gauntlight Keep invokes one of the following lair actions:

**Echoes of Valor**: The haunting sound of a battle horn echoes through the ruins, bolstering the adventuring party's morale. For the next round, they gain advantage on attack rolls and saving throws.

**Phantom Barricades**: Spectral forms of the keep's walls and gates momentarily rise, blocking paths or trapping enemies. Creatures attempting to pass through must succeed on a DC 14 Strength saving throw or be pushed back 10 feet.

**Whispers of the Fallen**: Ghostly whispers fill the air, attempting to mislead or distract. Enemies within the ruins must make a DC 15 Wisdom saving throw or suffer disadvantage on their next attack roll or skill check due to the unnerving chatter.

## Scaling the Encounter

### Beginning Players (PC levels 1-5)

**The Armory:** Reduce the Athletics check DC to 12 to navigate the ruins and reach the armory, making it easier for lower-level players to access the needed sigil-etched stone.

**Finding the Sigil-Etched Stone:** Lower the passive Perception DC to 14 and the Intelligence (History) check to DC 13 for deciphering the location clues, accommodating the skill levels of beginning players.

**Lair Actions:**

- **Echoes of Valor:** This action remains the same, providing a morale boost to support players facing challenges that might feel daunting at lower levels.

- **Phantom Barricades:** Decrease the Strength saving throw DC to 12, allowing players more opportunities to overcome physical barriers.

- **Whispers of the Fallen:** Reduce the Wisdom saving throw DC to 12, lessening the difficulty of resisting distractions and misdirections.

### Intermediate Players (PC levels 6-10)

**The Armory:** Keep the Athletics check DC at 17 to challenge intermediate players' ability to navigate through hazardous terrain.

**Finding the Sigil-Etched Stone:** Keep the Intelligence (History) check DC at 16, expecting players to have honed their skills and knowledge to interpret historical clues and lore.

**Lair Actions:**

- **Echoes of Valor:** Unchanged, as the advantage on attack rolls and saving throws remains a significant boon for players facing more complex challenges.

- **Phantom Barricades:** Increase the Strength saving throw DC to 16, challenging players to find creative solutions or utilize their abilities to bypass or overcome spectral obstacles.

- **Whispers of the Fallen:** Keep the Wisdom saving throw DC at 15, requiring a solid strategy to avoid being misled by the echoes of the past.

### Advanced Players (PC levels 11+)

**The Armory:** Introduce traps or environmental hazards with a DC of 20 for Athletics checks, pushing players to leverage their high-level abilities and resources to access critical areas like the armory.

**Finding the Sigil-Etched Stone:** Increase the Intelligence (History) check DC to 18, reflecting the complexity and obscurity of the clues left behind in the ruins.

**Lair Actions:**

- **Echoes of Valor:** This action remains beneficial, but consider adding a temporary hit point boost to reflect the increased resilience needed at higher levels.

- **Phantom Barricades:** Raise the Strength saving throw DC to 18 and possibly introduce a puzzle or skill challenge component to navigate or disable the barriers, adding depth to the encounter.

- **Whispers of the Fallen:** Increase the Wisdom saving throw DC to 17 and add an effect where failing the save could lead to a minor illusion spell effect, causing confusion or hallucinations that further complicate the encounter.

## NPC

The Last Knight

# Thornheart Thicket

Thornheart Thicket is a challenge of both wit and resilience. Players must navigate the sentient, hostile grove to retrieve soil with magical properties, facing Bloodvine Creepers.

As you make your way into this dense grove, you're immediately struck by an overwhelming sense of unease. The fragrance of the earth mingles with a subtle hint of something ancient and unknowable, filling the air with an almost tangible magic. Each step forward is contested by the thicket's sharp thorns, snagging at your clothes and skin as though the very vegetation seeks to hold you back. The trees around you, gnarled and imposing, seem almost sentient, their limbs shifting ominously as though to bar your passage, reacting to your presence with a silent hostility.

Deeper within, a clearing emerges, a stark contrast to the oppressive gloom of the surrounding woods. Illuminated by a gentle, ethereal light, it offers a brief respite from the malevolence of the thicket. The atmosphere here is strangely tranquil, an anomaly within such a rancorous environment.

## Bloodvine Creeper

These sentient plants are the primary obstacle in reaching the clearing. Their ability to camouflage and regenerate, combined with their dangerous entangling and engulfing attacks, makes them formidable guardians of the thicket.

## Retrieving Soil from the Thicket

Characters must make a DC 16 Wisdom (Survival) check to navigate the thicket without becoming lost or ensnared by its protective branches.

Upon reaching the clearing, a DC 14 Intelligence (Nature) check is required to safely gather the soil without disturbing the thicket's delicate balance.

## The Shadow of Thornheart Thicket

The thicket harbors a guardian spirit, a manifestation of the grove's will to protect itself. This spirit, while not inherently malevolent, fiercely guards the heart of the thicket from those it deems unworthy or with ill intent. Legends speak of appeasing the spirit with a respectful offering or a sincere plea, allowing safe passage through the grove.

To appease the Bloodvine Creepers and the thicket's guardian spirit, characters can offer:

- A vial of water from a sacred spring (signifying respect for nature).

- A handcrafted token of wood or stone, symbolizing a promise of protection for the grove.

- A portion of their own vitality (5 hit points) offered willingly to the thicket, as a sign of sincerity and respect.

**Gift Acceptance**: Upon offering a gift, PCs must make a DC 15 Persuasion check. Success indicates that the spirit accepts the offering, and the Bloodvine Creepers retract, allowing passage to the clearing without harm.

## Lair Actions

On initiative count 20 (losing initiative ties), Thornheart Thicket invokes one of the following lair actions:

**Thorned Grasp**: The thicket's branches lash out, attempting to ensnare anyone nearby. Characters must make a DC 13 Dexterity saving throw or be restrained, taking 1d6 piercing damage at the start of their turn until freed. On their turn, a restrained PC may use their action to attempt to break free, with a Strength or Dexterity check DC 13.

**Whispers of the Thicket**: Ethereal voices whisper warnings, attempting to disorient and lead adventurers astray. All characters must succeed on a DC 14 Wisdom saving throw or suffer disadvantage on their next check or attack due to confusion.

**Veil of Thorns**: The thicket thickens, creating a barrier that obscures vision. For one round, all attacks against the party by creatures within the thicket are made with advantage, representing the difficulty in seeing the attacks coming.

## Scaling the Encounter

### Beginning Players (PC levels 1-5)

**Navigating Thornheart Thicket**: Lower the DC for the Wisdom (Survival) check to 12, making it easier for beginning players to find their way without becoming hopelessly entangled.

**Retrieving Soil**: Reduce the Nature check to DC 10 to gather the soil, allowing newer players to successfully complete the task with minimal interference from the thicket's defenses.

**Bloodvine Creeper Encounter**: Adjust the Bloodvine Creepers' stats to be less formidable, decreasing HP to 45 and AC to 11. Limit their Regeneration ability to 2 hit points per turn and remove the Engulf action for encounters with beginning players.

**Lair Actions:**

- **Thorned Grasp:** Lower the Dexterity saving throw DC to 10, reducing the chance of being restrained.

- **Whispers of the Thicket:** Decrease the Wisdom saving throw DC to 12 to mitigate the disorientation effect.

- **Veil of Thorns:** Simplify this action to simply obscuring characters' vision, removing the enemy advantage on attacks.

### Intermediate Players (PC levels 6-10)

**Navigating Thornheart Thicket:** Keep the Wisdom (Survival) check DC at 16 to challenge intermediate players' navigation skills.

**Retrieving Soil:** Maintain the Intelligence (Nature) check DC at 14 for gathering the soil, requiring players to demonstrate a respectful understanding of the thicket's ecosystem.

**Bloodvine Creeper Encounter:** Increase the Bloodvine Creepers' difficulty slightly by adjusting HP to 100 and AC to 14. Their Regeneration ability should remain at 5 hit points per turn.

**Lair Actions:**

- **Thorned Grasp:** Keep the Dexterity saving throw DC at 13, maintaining the challenge of avoiding entanglement.

- **Whispers of the Thicket:** Increase the Wisdom saving throw DC to 15, balancing the psychological challenge within the thicket.

- **Veil of Thorns:** Implement the action as described, using the thicket's density to create a tactical challenge for the players.

### Advanced Players (PC levels 11+)

**Navigating Thornheart Thicket:** Increase the Wisdom (Survival) check DC to 20, reflecting the complex and hostile nature of the thicket to test advanced players' survival skills.

**Retrieving Soil:** Set the Nature check DC at 18 for gathering the soil, demanding a deep understanding and respect for the grove's delicate balance.

**Bloodvine Creeper Encounter:** Enhance the Bloodvine Creepers for a formidable challenge, with HP set to 120 and AC to 16. Their Regeneration should be potent at 10 hit points per turn, and include a more dangerous version of the Engulf action with added effects (e.g., acid damage).

**Lair Actions:**

- **Thorned Grasp:** Increase the Dexterity saving throw DC to 16, making it a significant effort to avoid being caught by the thicket's branches.

- **Whispers of the Thicket:** Raise the Wisdom saving throw DC to 16, intensifying the mental challenge posed by the thicket's disorienting whispers.

- **Veil of Thorns:** As initially described, but with the addition that characters have a reduced ability to retaliate due to the denseness of the thicket, simulating a challenging environment where the players must think creatively to overcome the obstacles.

## Monster

Bloodvine Creeper

# Widow's Walk

This encounter at Widow's Walk combines environmental hazards with supernatural elements, challenging PCs to navigate a perilous path while resisting the deceptive calls of spirits. Key components include dodging spectral hands, deciphering real from illusory dangers, and collecting rare herbs vital for breaking the Eternal Dusk curse.

Before you stretches a path as slender and precarious as a thread, clinging to the cliff's edge like a desperate secret. The mist here is thicker, almost tangible, swirling with whispers and half-glimpsed shapes that beckon with ghostly fingers. Below, the moors extend into the gloom, a tapestry of shadows and sighs. This path, known for the sorrowful echoes of those who lost their heart's companions to the treacherous terrain, demands every ounce of your focus and courage. As you step forward, the wind carries murmurs of lost loves and the soft wailing of the bereft, a haunting melody that seeks to ensnare your heart and lead you off the path to join the ranks of the wandering souls.

## Navigating the Path

**Purpose:** To navigate the treacherous Widow's Walk, characters must discern the real path from dangerous illusions crafted by the dense mist and spectral entities. A successful Wisdom (Perception) DC 14 check helps them avoid natural hazards and misleading paths that could lead to peril.

**Failure Consequence:** On a failed check, a character missteps, possibly due to a misleading spectral illusion or a hidden natural hazard. They find themselves teetering on the brink of the cliff's edge. They must immediately make a DC 12 Dexterity saving throw to catch themselves or grab onto something stable. A failure on this saving throw results in the character sliding towards the edge, where they hang precariously. An ally can attempt a DC 14 Strength (Athletics) check to pull them back to safety on their next turn.

## Encounter with Restless Spirits at Widow's Walk

As the PCs venture further along the treacherous path of Widow's Walk, they not only face the environmental hazards and the deceptive calls of spirits, but they also encounter the sorrowful, restless spirits mentioned by Elena. These spirits, trapped between realms due to their tragic deaths along this perilous cliffside, are integral to understanding the supernatural aspects of the area and essential for locating the rare herbs needed for the campaign.

### Engaging with the Spirits

To effectively engage with these spirits, the PCs must use their Insight and Persuasion skills to understand and calm the spirits' turmoil:

### Insight Check (DC 14)

**Success**: The PC realizes that these spirits are not malevolent but are bound by their unresolved grief and loss. Understanding this, the PCs can approach them with empathy.

**Failure**: Misinterpreting the spirits' intentions, a PC might feel overwhelmed by the sadness, which could lead to disadvantage on subsequent interaction checks due to emotional distress.

### Persuasion Check (DC 16)

**Success**: The PC successfully comforts the spirits, easing their sorrow. Grateful, the spirits offer assistance, guiding the PCs to hidden locations where the crucial herbs grow. This guidance provides advantage on checks to locate and harvest the Duskroot and other rare herbs.

**Failure**: The spirits remain inconsolable and withdrawn, offering no aid, and possibly worsening the environmental challenges by intensifying the mist and spectral activities.

### Consequences of the Encounter

**Aiding the Spirits**: Successfully calming the spirits not only helps in gathering resources but also may provide additional benefits, such as temporary resistance to necrotic damage or insights into the weaknesses of the Shadow Court, as the spirits share their past encounters.

**Ignoring or Failing with the Spirits**: Neglecting to interact with the spirits or failing to calm them could lead to increased difficulties. The spirits may unintentionally hinder the PCs by enhancing the mist's deceiving properties or by causing the spectral hands to become more aggressive.

**Optional Calm Emotions**: While the spell does not work traditionally on undead, a creative use of the *Calm Emotions* spell, reinterpreted through a ritualistic approach with components gathered along the path, could provide a temporary respite or a narrative opportunity for deeper engagement with the spirits.

## Encounter with the Bloodbind Spider

As the PCs navigate the treacherous path of Widow's Walk, their senses assaulted by the mournful wails of the lost and the deceptive allure of spectral figures, a new and deadly threat emerges from the thick mists. The Bloodbind Spider, a monstrous creation of the Shadow Court, lies in wait, its presence a chilling testament to the dark powers that hold sway here.

### Appearance of the Spider

Silently descending from the craggy cliffs above, the Bloodbind Spider's massive form is nearly invisible against the dark stones, its glossy, jet-black exoskeleton blending perfectly with the shadows of twilight. Its red eyes glimmer with malevolence, and its fangs drip with a dark, cursed venom.

### Attack Initiation

The spider attacks when the party is most distracted by the spectral illusions or while they are attempting to harvest the rare herbs. Its initial move is to cast its webbing across the path, aiming to ensnare the PCs in its sticky, nearly invisible threads.

### Webbing Trap

**Action**: The Bloodbind Spider can extrude a large amount of webbing to create difficult terrain in a 20-foot radius, centered on a point it chooses within 60 feet. This webbing not only slows the PCs but also serves as a trap for its venomous bite.

**DC Check**: Characters caught in the web must succeed on a DC 14 Strength check to escape or remain trapped, making them vulnerable to the spider's next attack.

### Integration with Restless Spirits

The restless spirits of Widow's Walk can play a pivotal role during this encounter. If the PCs have attempted to communicate or soothe these spirits beforehand using Insight and Persuasion checks:

**Successful Communication**: Spirits may warn the PCs of the spider's approach or help them avoid the most dangerous sections of the webbing.

**Failed Communication**: The spirits, caught in their own torment, inadvertently increase the PCs' difficulty in detecting and evading the spider.

# Finding Rare Herbs

Hidden among the crags and crevices of Widow's Walk, there is a herb called Duskroot that emits a faint, ethereal glow, distinguishable even through the thick mist. A successful DC 16 Intelligence (Nature) check is required to locate and safely harvest Duskroot. This herb is a key ingredient in a potion to counteract the Eternal Dusk curse.

There are other herbs that can also be collected. Use the following table to include additional herbs:

| Name of the Herb | Description of the Herb | Value (GP) | Use in Lifting Curses/Curing Maladies | Challenge/Difficulty |
|---|---|---|---|---|
| Ghostcap Mushroom | A luminescent, pale mushroom that thrives in shadowy areas. Its cap glows with a soft, ethereal light. | 50 | When brewed into a potion, it can dispel minor curses and soothe restless spirits. | DC 18 Nature check to safely harvest without damaging its delicate structure. |
| Mourner's Leaf | This herb has leaves that shimmer with a spectral blue hue at night. Touching it leaves a temporary, cold sensation. | 30 | Infused in tea, it offers relief from grief and emotional distress, breaking spells of melancholy or charm effects. | DC 15 Survival check to navigate treacherous footing near the cliff's edge where it grows. |
| Wraithroot | A root that pulses with a faint, ghostly light, found clinging to the edges of the cliff. It's cold to the touch. | 75 | Ground into a powder and ingested, it grants resistance to necrotic damage for 1 hour and weakens the hold of necromantic curses. Curses with no saving throw now have one at the caster's DC. If the curse already has a saving throw, the user may now roll at advantage—meaning that upon ingestion, it immediately grants the cursed user another roll to save. | DC 20 Athletics check to climb to its precarious growing spots without falling. |
| Echo Blossom | Flowers that emit a soft, mournful sound when the wind passes through them, resembling distant whispers. | 40 | The petals can be used to craft elixirs that clear confusion, disorientation, and effects causing fear. | DC 17 Acrobatics check to cross a narrow, wind-swept section of the path where they bloom. |
| Veil Thistle | A thorny plant with translucent leaves, seeming to phase in and out of visibility. | 60 | Brewed into a potion, it grants temporary immunity to possession for 8 hours and can purge the body of possession-based curses. | DC 16 Wisdom (Perception) check to spot it when it phases into visibility, plus a DC 15 Dexterity check to harvest without injury. |

# Lair Actions

On initiative count 20 (losing initiative ties), Widow's Walk invokes one of the following lair actions:

**Mist's Deception:** At the start of the encounter, the mist thickens, obscuring the party's vision. For their next turn, the difficulty of all Perception and Survival checks increases by 5, complicating their ability to navigate the path safely.

**Spectral Lure:** Ghostly apparitions appear on the path, mimicking the voices and forms of loved ones or allies, pleading for help from perilous ledges. Characters must succeed on a DC 14 Wisdom (Insight) check to recognize the deception or risk wandering off the path in an attempt to provide aid.

**Cliffside Grasp:** Ethereal hands reach out from the cliff face, attempting to pull at the cPCs' legs or gear. Each character must make a DC 13 Dexterity saving throw to avoid being tripped. The immediate area becomes difficult terrain, reducing everyone's movement speed by half until their next turn.

# Scaling the Encounter

## Beginning Players (PC levels 1-5)

**Navigating the Path:** Lower the DC for the Wisdom (Perception) check to 10, allowing younger or newer players a greater chance of success in discerning the true path.

**Finding Rare Herbs:** Decrease the DC for the Intelligence (Nature) check to find Duskroot to 12. For additional herbs, reduce their respective challenge DCs by 3, making them more accessible but still rewarding careful exploration.

**Lair Actions:**

- **Mist's Deception:** Reduce the Perception check difficulty to +3 instead of +5.

- **Spectral Lure:** Lower the Wisdom (Insight) check to 11 to identify the apparitions as illusions.
- **Cliffside Grasp:** Adjust the Dexterity saving throw to 10 to avoid the ethereal hands' grasp.

### Intermediate Players (PC levels 6-10)

**Navigating the Path:** Keep the Wisdom (Perception) check DC at 14. This presents a moderate challenge that requires players to be attentive and cautious.

**Finding Rare Herbs:** Keep the Intelligence (Nature) check DC at 16 for Duskroot. For additional herbs, maintain the listed challenge DCs to offer a balanced mix of risk and reward.

**Lair Actions:**

- **Mist's Deception:** Keep the Perception check difficulty at +5, emphasizing the disorienting nature of the environment.
- **Spectral Lure:** Maintain the Wisdom (Insight) check DC at 14, requiring players to critically assess their encounters.
- **Cliffside Grasp:** Keep the Dexterity saving throw DC at 13, offering a fair test of the PCs' reflexes.

### Advanced Players (PC levels 11+)

**Navigating the Path:** Increase the Wisdom (Perception) check DC to 18, challenging advanced players with a highly treacherous and deceptive path.

**Finding Rare Herbs:** Increase the Intelligence (Nature) check DC to 20 for Duskroot. For additional herbs, increase their respective challenge DCs by 2, presenting a demanding test of the PCs' skills and determination.

**Lair Actions:**

**Mist's Deception:** Increase the Perception check difficulty to +7, significantly obstructing the PCs' ability to perceive their surroundings accurately.

**Spectral Lure:** Raise the Wisdom (Insight) check DC to 16, enhancing the difficulty of discerning truth from deceit in the haunted landscape.

**Cliffside Grasp:** Increase the Dexterity saving throw DC to 15, presenting a formidable challenge to maintain balance and speed on the treacherous path.

## Monster

Bloodbind Spider

# The Ancient Crypts

As the party gears up for the defining chapter of their adventure, they find themselves drawn to the eerie silence of a sprawling cemetery located to the south of Ravenholme. Here lies the entrance to the Ancient Crypts, a foreboding underworld that serves as the final battleground against the Shadow Court. This section of the adventure sets the scene for a chilling exploration and confrontation within the shadowed confines of this necropolis.

## The Ancient Crypts

The cemetery, a vast expanse of tombstones and mausoleums, shrouds the entrance to the Ancient Crypts. The entrance is marked by the largest mausoleum in the cemetery, its gates of wrought iron twisted into symbols of mourning and remembrance, now corroded by time and neglect.

Beneath this solemn ground, the air grows cold and still, suffused with a sense of timeless dread. The stone passageways are lined with the tombs of the long-forgotten, their inscriptions worn away by the passage of centuries. Shadows flicker in the torchlight, hinting at movement where there should be none. Each domain of the Shadow Court within the crypts bears the distinct mark of its vampire lord, separated by arcane sigils etched into the very walls, the magic within them a palpable force pushing against those who dare to trespass.

## Territorial Boundaries and Constraints

The weakening of ancient seals has granted the vampires newfound freedom within the cemetery's bounds, allowing them to stalk the night among the gravestones and mausoleums. However, a powerful enchantment encircles the cemetery, a barrier that they cannot cross, keeping them confined within this hallowed ground. These boundaries are visible only to those with the sight to see the arcane, shimmering faintly in the moonlight as a constant reminder of the vampires' imprisonment.

While the cemetery offers a larger realm for the vampires to dominate, it also serves as their cage. They can sense the world beyond, yet remain unable to touch it, their power curtailed by the same magic that keeps them tethered to the crypts beneath. The central gathering area, once a chapel within the cemetery, now serves as the court where the vampires convene, a macabre parody of its former sanctity.

## Approach to the Ancient Crypts

The journey to the Ancient Crypts through the cemetery is one of increasing unease. The graves, some fresh, others ancient and crumbling, tell a silent story of Ravenholme's past. The path to the mausoleum entrance is lined with statues of angels and saints, their faces eroded into expressions of sorrow or horror, as if mourning the darkness that has taken root beneath their feet.

This pathway not only leads the adventurers into the heart of their enemy's domain but also through a landscape of grief and remembrance turned sinister. The very atmosphere of the cemetery, with its cold mists and the whisper of leaves, sets a somber tone for the challenges that lie ahead. The players do have the choice to enter the crypts in any order, but it is recommended that the Vestibule of Shadows be the first crypt they enter, as it will give the players an understanding of how to interact with one of the vampires. For optimal climactic build-up, the Throne of Night should be the last crypt encountered.

# The Chamber of Whispers

This encounter challenges players to navigate the echo-filled Chamber of Whispers, where every sound could reveal a secret or a trap. They must solve aural puzzles to find a crucial key, all while resisting the seductive dangers posed by Seraphina and her cursed dagger.

As you step into a grand hall, the air vibrates with countless whispers, each carrying fragments of secrets and lost tales. Statues of the enigmatic Shadow Court line the walls, their cold, stone eyes watching silently as their lips seem to murmur into the heavy air. The room is a vast, shadowed space, where the dim light flickers uncertainly, making the shadows dance in the corners of your vision. Here, the boundary between the past and the present blurs, the whispers inviting you to listen, to understand, but always reminding you of the danger that listening too closely might bring. The echoes of the chamber are both a guide and a challenge, a puzzle woven from the very essence of the Shadow Court's history.

## Solving the Whispering Puzzle

The challenge requires adventurers to engage directly with the environment of the Chamber of Whispers, using a combination of observation, listening, and problem-solving skills. The puzzle revolves around understanding and interpreting the whispers that fill the chamber, leading to the discovery of a hidden key or passage that advances their quest.

### Puzzle Overview

For the Whispering Puzzle in the Chamber of Whispers, characters must navigate a complex series of clues whispered by the statues of the Shadow Court members: Killian, Thorn, Seraphina, and Gareth. These clues will lead PCs to discover a seal located in a hidden room within the chamber. Successfully unveiling and accessing this room involves a multi-step process, requiring keen observation, insightful deduction, and a coordinated effort among the party.

## Statue Clues

### Killian's Statue

Killian's Statue whispers about the presence of a hidden room.

**Whisper**: "Beneath the gaze of the Court, a chamber lies concealed, where shadows hold sway and secrets are sealed."

**Insight for Players**: This suggests the existence of a hidden room within the Chamber of Whispers.

### Thorn's Statue

Thorn's Statue provides a clue about the mechanism to reveal the hidden room.

**Whisper**: "In the embrace of nature's dark twist, a button lies beneath where vine and stone are kissed."

**Location for Button**: Hidden beneath a tangle of vines at the statue's base, requiring a DC 14 Investigation check to discover.

**Interaction**: Pressing this button is part of the sequence to reveal the hidden room.

### Seraphina's Statue

Seraphina's Statue instructs on the direction the statues should face.

**Whisper**: "To break the silence, the Court must turn: Killian faces the dawn, where the first light burns. Thorn watches the dusk, where darkness returns. Seraphina eyes the moon's full gleam, and Gareth guards the entry, where shadows stream."

**Interaction**: Each statue can be twisted to point in a specific direction. This alignment is crucial for unlocking the hidden room:

- **Killian**: East (towards dawn)
- **Thorn**: West (towards dusk)
- **Seraphina**: Upwards (towards the moon)
- **Gareth**: North (towards the chamber's entrance)

### Gareth's Statue

Gareth's Statue reveals the spell and incantation needed.

**Whisper**: "Only words of binding spoken true, the Court's Vow to darkness, will the path renew. 'Shadows bind and night unfurl, reveal the passage, let the secret swirl.'"

**Spell Name**: *Court's Vow*

**Incantation**: Characters must recite this spell after adjusting the statues and pressing the hidden button. A successful DC 16 Intelligence (Arcana) check allows a PC to correctly perform the incantation.

## Solving the Puzzle

**Listening and Deciphering**: Characters listen to the whispers, distinguishing relevant clues from distractions. A DC 15 Wisdom (Perception) check helps identify the whispers with actionable information.

**Investigating the Statues**: Characters must search for the hidden button on Thorn's statue (DC 14 Investigation) and determine the correct orientation for each statue based on Seraphina's clue.

**Aligning the Statues**: The party aligns each statue as described in Seraphina's whispers, requiring a simple physical effort with no specific check unless under duress or time constraint. Each statue is life-sized and made of a lighter stone.

**Reciting the Spell**: With the statues aligned and the button pressed, a PC must recite the incantation *Court's Vow* (DC 16 Intelligence (Arcana) check to perform accurately).

## Outcome

Successfully completing these steps causes the chamber to resonate with a deep, thrumming power. A section of the wall silently slides away, revealing the hidden room and the seal within, guarded by remnants of the Shadow Court's power or traps protecting the seal.

## Failure and Retry

Failure at any step may result in misleading directions, activation of defense mechanisms, or the summoning of Seraphina. PCs can reassess their approach, search for additional clues, or attempt to correct their mistakes based on feedback from the chamber (e.g., a statue refusing to stay in the directed position might indicate an incorrect orientation).

# Crimson Claw Assassin Attack

As the party engages with the puzzles and echoes of the Chamber of Whispers, the deceptive serenity of the chamber is suddenly shattered by the lethal presence of a Crimson Claw Assassin, sent by the Shadow Court to thwart the adventurers' progress and protect the secrets contained within.

## Surprise Attack

The Crimson Claw Assassin uses their innate spellcasting abilities to blend into the shadows, waiting for the optimal moment to strike. Utilizing *Silent Image*, they create illusory distractions echoing the chamber's haunting whispers, disorienting the party.

## Initiating Combat

As one of the PCs solves a part of the whispering puzzle or interacts with a statue, the Assassin chooses this moment of distraction to launch their attack, aiming to eliminate the most isolated or engaged party member first.

## Assassin's Attack Strategy

**Invisibility:** At the start of the encounter, the Assassin casts *Invisibility*, moving into position unseen. They aim to use their **Shadow Stealth** ability in the dim lighting of the chamber to stay hidden until they strike.

**Poisoned Dagger:** The Assassin strikes with their poisoned dagger from the shadows. This attack is a surprise, giving them advantage on the attack roll. On a hit, the target not only suffers piercing and poison damage but also must contend with the debilitating effects of the Eternal Dusk curse if they fail a DC 17 Constitution saving throw.

**Eternal Dusk Curse:** If the party continues to pose a significant threat or if the Assassin needs to retreat, they may use their **Eternal Dusk Curse** ability to afflict another character, aiming to weaken the group further.

### Defensive Tactics

If the combat turns against the Assassin, they employ their **Gaseous Form** ability to escape or reposition themselves within the chamber, potentially hiding among the statues or in the upper reaches of the chamber's shadowed ceiling.

### Interaction with Environment

Leveraging the Chamber of Whisper's layout, the Assassin uses moving shadows and the chamber's natural acoustics to create confusion and fear, setting the stage for the Lair Actions like Echoes of Deceit and Shadow Grasp to be more effective.

### Possible Outcomes

**Successful Assassination:** If the Assassin successfully incapacitates or kills a party member, they attempt to retrieve any significant artifacts the party has collected and escape back to the Shadow Court.

**Failure and Retreat:** If overwhelmed or injured, the Assassin retreats using **Gaseous Form**, leaving the party on high alert and possibly interrupting their progress on solving the chamber's puzzle.

## Seraphina

Interacting with Seraphina in the Chamber of Whispers offers a nuanced and potentially dangerous encounter for adventurers, blending diplomacy, strategy, and combat readiness. Here's how players can engage with her, leveraging D&D 5e rules for a dynamic encounter:

### Initial Interaction

**Approach**: Seraphina doesn't attack immediately. She prefers to assess visitors, offering them a chance to speak. The eerie ambiance of her chamber, filled with whispers and shadow, sets the tone.

**Dialogue**: Characters can attempt to converse with Seraphina. A successful DC 20 Charisma (Persuasion or Deception) check may pique her interest or convince

her of the party's intentions, possibly aligning with her own ambitions or curiosity.

### Persuasion and Deception

**Persuasion**: Characters can try to persuade Seraphina to align with them by arguing that their goals align with her desire to unlock the full potential of the Daynight Stone. This requires a DC 20 Charisma (Persuasion) check, reflecting the difficulty of swaying her complex motivations.

**Deception**: Alternatively, characters might deceive her into believing they will help her ascend in power or that they serve a common cause against a greater enemy. This deception requires a DC 22 Charisma (Deception) check due to her high insight and suspicion.

### Combat Engagement

**Trigger for Attack**: If dialogue fails or PCs act aggressively, Seraphina defends herself using her shadow-touched dagger and spells. Combat is triggered by direct threats, attacks, or failed attempts at deception.

**Battlefield Manipulation**: While not directly manipulating the natural world like Thorn, Seraphina's control over shadows and her spellcasting abilities allow her to reshape the battlefield. She might dim the lights or cast spells like Darkness to disorient the party.

## Restoring the Seal

**Seal Location & Discovery**: The seal is concealed within a hidden room. The Whispering Puzzle must be solved to locate it.

**Materials Required**: Quill from a raven's feather.

**Ritual Performance**: With the raven's feather quill, write Shadow Court members' names on parchment and burn it, leaving the ashes on the seal and closing the secret door to the room. Requires a combined Arcana and History check DC 17.

**Strengthening the Seal**: Successfully performing the ritual momentarily silences the whispers, weakening the Court's influence.

### Read Aloud When the Seal is Successfully Restored

As you complete the ritual and the seal to the Chamber of Whispers is restored, a profound silence falls over the crypt. Seraphina, the enigmatic shadow weaver, finds herself bound once more within the chamber's ancient walls. The intricate magic of the seal, now rejuvenated by your efforts, wraps around her like chains forged from moonlight, severing her connection to the dark forces she once commanded. Trapped, her figure fades into the whispering shadows, her eyes glinting with a mix of fury and begrudging respect. The chamber itself seems to breathe a sigh of relief, its secrets safe once more as the echoes of Seraphina's power diminish into silence, leaving her a prisoner of her own ambition, unable to escape the very chamber she sought to dominate.

## Terrain

The chamber's floor is uneven, scattered with rubble and covered in ancient carpets that muffle footsteps but may hide traps. Navigating requires caution; a DC 12 Dexterity check ensures safe passage through the treacherous terrain.

## Lair Actions

On initiative count 20 (losing initiative ties), Seraphina invokes one of the following lair actions:

**Echoes of Deceit**: Whispering intensifies, forcing a DC 15 Wisdom saving throw to avoid being charmed by false promises or threats.

**Shadow Grasp**: Shadows animate, attempting to entangle characters. Requires a DC 14 Strength or Dexterity saving throw to escape or be restrained for a round.

**Silent Command**: Seraphina silently commands the Duskblade's Dagger to attack a PC, +8 to hit, dealing 8 (1d6 + 5) piercing plus 7 (2d6) necrotic damage.

## Scaling the Encounter

### Beginning Players (PC levels 1-5)

**Reduce Complexity**: Simplify the Whispering Puzzle to require fewer steps and lower the DC for checks to around 10-12.

**Seraphina's Presence**: Seraphina could be less aggressive, focusing on testing the PCs rather than outright attacking. Reduce her hit points to 80 and limit her spellcasting to 1st and 2nd level spells only.

**Lesser Minions**: Replace any combat encounters with fewer or weaker minions, such as 1-2 lesser shades or spirits that can be more easily negotiated with or bypassed.

**Environmental Hazards**: Simplify terrain challenges and reduce lair action effects, such as making the grasping shadows slower and the whispers less distracting (lower saving throw DCs to 10).

### Intermediate Players (PC levels 6-10)

**Puzzle Complexity**: Increase the steps required to solve the Whispering Puzzle, with additional DCs around 15.

**Seraphina's Tactics**: Make Seraphina a more cunning opponent, utilizing her spellcasting abilities up to 4th level and her shadow-touched dagger more effectively. Adjust her hit points to 110.

**Enhanced Minions**: Include encounters with a few of Seraphina's enchanted creatures or undead minions, designed to test the party's combat skills and strategic thinking.

**Environmental Challenges**: Introduce more complex terrain features that require creative navigation or the use of specific skills, with lair action DCs set to 15.

### Advanced Players (PC levels 11+)

**Complex Puzzle Solving**: The Whispering Puzzle should be highly intricate, involving multiple layers of clues and requiring a broad use of skills, with DCs set at 20 or higher.

**Seraphina's Full Power**: Present Seraphina as a formidable foe, utilizing her full range of spells (up to 5th level) and abilities, with hit points increased to 130. Incorporate tactics that leverage her control over shadows and illusions to outmaneuver the party.

**Stronger Minions**: Deploy a significant force of Seraphina's minions, including powerful undead or shadow creatures, challenging the party to engage in large-scale combat or intricate avoidance strategies.

**Dangerous Environment**: The chamber itself should be a challenging adversary, with treacherous terrain and lair actions designed to significantly hinder PC movement and strategy (DCs 18+).

## NPC

Seraphina

## Monster

Crimson Claw Assassin

# The Hall of Echoing Torment

This encounter challenges players with the moral and emotional dilemma of confronting or aiding the tormented spirits, influenced by the dark past of Gareth, a noble knight turned dark enforcer. Restoring the seal involves a delicate balance of strength and empathy, demanding PCs engage with the spirits and perform a ritual to reinforce the hall's seal.

Before you lies a corridor shrouded in palpable silence, broken only by the occasional, sorrowful echo of chains rattling against the cold, stone floors. The air is thick with despair, and ethereal chains stretch across the walls, binding the spectral remnants of those sacrificed by the Shadow Court. Their mournful cries and whispers fill the hall, telling tales of betrayal and lost valor. As you step forward, the temperature drops, a sign of the tormented spirits' presence, their faces contorted in eternal anguish, reaching out for relief or vengeance from their endless torment.

Navigating this hall, you feel the weight of countless eyes upon you, each soul a story of sorrow and rage against the Shadow Court's cruelty. Amidst the despair, a large chain stands out, its links cold and heavy with dark magic. The air here vibrates with untold power, a reminder of the battles fought and the sacrifices made in the name of Ravenholme's safety.

## Soothing or Avenging the Spirits

Engage with the tormented spirits to understand their plight and decide whether to soothe their pain through a ritual or seek justice for their torment, potentially earning their blessings and advice on how to find the seal.

| Name of the Spirit | What Happened & Why They Are Tormented | How to Soothe Their Pain | Reward for Soothing Pain |
|---|---|---|---|
| Elara | Betrayed by a close friend and sacrificed to the Shadow Court. Her trust was abused, leading to her death and binding to this place. | Perform a ritual of trust restoration, using components representing friendship and betrayal to build a small shrine. | Elara reveals the hidden location of the seal within a secret compartment behind the largest chain in the hall. |
| Thane | Died defending Ravenholme from the Shadow Court's forces. He is tormented by his failure to protect his home and loved ones. | Seek justice by defeating a group of the Court's minions lurking nearby, in honor of Thane's last stand. | Grateful, Thane imparts knowledge of a secret weapon cache, including a sigil-etched sword crucial for the ritual, hidden in the hall. |
| Miriel | Captured and used for dark experiments by the Court, leading to her lingering torment in undeath. | Conduct a cleansing ritual using herbs from the Mourning Moors to purge the dark magic from her spirit. | Miriel offers insight into Seraphina's weaknesses and vulnerabilities, crucial for confronting her in the Chamber of Whispers. |
| Sylas | A young boy who wandered into the crypts, becoming an unintended victim of the Court's cruelty. His innocence was stolen, leaving him in perpetual fear. | Soothe Sylas's spirit with a lullaby from Ravenholme, reminding him of home and comfort. | Sylas, in his gratitude, reveals that Gareth can be convinced to turn against the other vampires. |
| Rowena | A healer accused of witchcraft and sacrificed to empower the Court's magic. Her desire to heal turned into an endless cycle of pain. | Create a circle of healing using medicinal plants and crystals, performing a ritual to symbolize her unfulfilled purpose of healing. | Rowena teaches the characters a healing chant that can be used once per 24 hrs to significantly heal the party (+5 hp) or weaken a foe (-5 hp), symbolizing her restored peace. |

## Interacting with Gareth

Characters' interactions with Gareth can be deeply impactful, involving a mix of combat, diplomacy, and exploration of his tragic backstory. Here's how these interactions can unfold:

### Initial Encounter

**Trigger for Combat:** Gareth initially perceives the party as intruders or threats to the Shadow Court. Approaching him with hostility or attempting to disrupt the Court's plans in his presence triggers combat.

**Using Shadows Against the Party:** As a powerful undead, Gareth can manipulate the shadows and possibly control lesser undead creatures. Consider adding environmental hazards that he activates, like shadows that drain strength (Strength saving throw DC 15 to resist vs. subtracting 1d6 from their Strength score) or summoning shadows to fight alongside him.

### Persuading Gareth

**Insight into His Conflict:** Characters can attempt to reach out to Gareth's lingering humanity through dialogue, highlighting their intentions to restore Ravenholme and combat the Court's corruption. This requires a series of successful Persuasion checks (DC 18) or presenting evidence of the Court's betrayal.

**Offer of Redemption:** PCs might propose a plan that allows Gareth to protect Ravenholme in a way that honors his original oath, using their own deeds or discoveries about the Court's true nature as leverage. This could involve a Charisma (Persuasion) check (DC 20), potentially lowered by presenting compelling evidence of the Court's misdeeds or by demonstrating their successes against the Court.

### Sharing Knowledge on Strengthening the Seal

**Earning Trust:** If PCs successfully persuade Gareth of their sincerity and his potential role in a redeemed Ravenholme, he might share critical information about the seal. This could include its location, the necessary components for its ritual, and vulnerabilities in the Court's defenses.

**Required Checks:** Gareth's cooperation may require a successful Intelligence (Arcana) check (DC 17) by the PCs to understand the complex information he provides, especially regarding the arcane aspects of the seal's magic.

## Restoring the Seal

**Seal Location & Discovery:** Found behind the largest chain in the hall, detectable with a DC 20 Wisdom (Perception) check or by casting *Detect Magic* to uncover the concealed compartment.

**Understanding the Magic:** Succeed on DC 18 Charisma (Persuasion) checks to communicate with spirits, revealing the seal's workings.

**Materials Required:** Sigil-etched stone from the Ruins of Gauntlight Keep, essential for the ritual.

**Ritual Performance:** Conduct a ritual involving lighting a candle, placing the sigil-etched stone at the hall's center, and leading a chant with the spirits. Requires a collective Performance check (DC 20).

**Strengthening the Seal:** Successfully completing the ritual makes the chains and spirits' cries disappear, evidence of the spirits finally being able to pass on, as well as symbolizing the seal's reinforcement and diminishing of the Shadow Court's control.

### Read Aloud When the Seal is Restored

As the ritual is completed and the seal is restored to full power, a profound silence descends, broken only by the soft clinking of ethereal chains. Gareth, once a noble knight twisted into a pawn of darkness, watches as the seal's magic weaves around him, binding him once more to the hall. Yet, in his eyes glimmers a resigned peace, a burden lifted. He knows that in this entrapment lies his redemption, a punishment he willingly endures for the chance to protect Ravenholme from within the shadows. The chains, though a reminder of his eternal torment, now also symbolize his unyielding vigilance against the Court's malice. As you witness Gareth's acceptance, you realize that your actions have not only restored the seal but also granted him a semblance of the honor he once embodied.

## Discovering the Elixir of Lucidity

In the midst of their journey through the Hall of Echoing Torment, the characters may come across an ancient, hidden alcove, shrouded in shadows yet untouched by the corrupting influence of the Shadow Court. To discover this secret space, the PCs must engage with the environment and the spirits that dwell within it. Here's how they can uncover a second vial of the Elixir of Lucidity.

**Perception to Notice the Alcove:** PCs must first notice something amiss with the hall's architecture, suggesting the presence of a hidden compartment or alcove. This requires a successful Wisdom (Perception) check (DC 18), as the entrance to the alcove is cleverly concealed by illusions cast by the tormented spirits to protect what lies within.

**Interacting with Spirits:** Upon noticing the alcove, the party may realize that the spirits are key to accessing it. Engaging with the spirits either through dialogue or a specific action (like offering a token of peace or performing a gesture of respect) can prompt them to reveal the alcove's entrance. This interaction may require a Charisma (Persuasion) check (DC 16) to convince the spirits of the party's worthy intentions.

**Arcana to Unravel the Illusion:** With the spirits' guidance or on their own insight, the party understands that the alcove is hidden by a magical illusion. To dispel or see through this illusion, a character proficient in Arcana can attempt an Intelligence (Arcana) check (DC 20). Success reveals the true entrance to the alcove, while failure may lead to the spirits offering hints or assistance, feeling the party's sincere efforts.

**Inside the Alcove - Discovering the Elixir:** Inside the newly uncovered alcove, amid ancient artifacts and scrolls detailing forgotten rituals, lies a small, dust-covered chest. Within this chest, protected by time and the spirits' magic, the party finds the Elixir of Lucidity. The elixir's container radiates a gentle, pulsing glow, signaling its potent magic and purity.

**Optional Challenge - Guarding Spirit:** If desired, the DM can introduce a guarding spirit within the alcove, a protector who tests the party's resolve or wisdom before allowing them to claim the Elixir. This could involve answering a riddle, proving their knowledge of the Shadow Court's weaknesses, or demonstrating their intention to use the Elixir for the greater good. This could involve a Wisdom (Insight) check (DC 18) or an Intelligence (History) check (DC 18) related to the lore of the Shadow Court and the nature of the curses it employs.

## Terrain

The floors are uneven, with cracked stones and scattered debris posing tripping hazards, necessitating DC 10 Dexterity (Acrobatics) checks to avoid stumbling.

Ethereal chains may unexpectedly lash out, requiring DC 15 Dexterity saving throws to dodge or become momentarily entangled.

## Lair Actions

On initiative count 20 (losing initiative ties), the Hall of Echoing Torment invokes one of the following lair actions:

**Chains of Despair:** Chains lash out to grapple a random character. DC 15 Dexterity saving throw to avoid being restrained.

**Whispers of the Betrayed:** Spirits whisper distracting tales of betrayal, forcing characters to make a DC 15 Wisdom saving throw or suffer disadvantage on their next attack or skill check.

**Cold Grasp of the Past:** A sudden chill numbs the party. Make a DC 15 Constitution saving throw or have speed reduced by half until the next turn.

## Scaling the Encounter

### Beginning Players (PC levels 1-5)

**Interacting with Gareth:** Lower his aggression and make him more susceptible to Persuasion (DC 13). If combat ensues, reduce his health to 80 HP and limit his use of Shadow Step and Command the Fallen.

**Restoring the Seal:** Simplify the ritual with clear, step-by-step guidance from spirits or Gareth if persuaded. Lower Arcana and Performance check DCs to 12.

### Intermediate Players (PC levels 6-10)

**Interacting with Gareth:** Present a balanced challenge in Persuasion (DC 16-18) or combat. If fought, Gareth has his full health but limits the frequency of his legendary actions.

**Restoring the Seal:** Require a detailed understanding of the seal's magic by keeping the Arcana check DC at 15. Include a minor combat or skill challenge to obtain necessary ritual components.

### Advanced Players (PC levels 11+)

**Interacting with Gareth:** Create a challenging encounter by fully utilizing his combat abilities and strategic use of the environment. Persuasion attempts have a high DC of 20.

**Restoring the Seal:** Demand a comprehensive mastery of arcane knowledge with by raising tge Arcanacheck DC to 20. Integrate a significant combat encounter or a complex skill challenge to gather rare components for the ritual.

## NPC

Gareth

# The Throne of Night

This encounter marks the climax of the adventure, where adventurers confront Killian and his Enforcers of the Eclipse. The PCs' objective is not just to defeat them but also to restore the seal integrated into the throne, weakening Killian's power. The throne room's atmosphere and challenges are designed to test the PCs' strategic use of both combat abilities and magical knowledge.

You step into a grand chamber where opulence battles with the encroaching darkness for dominion. The Throne of Night sits at the room's heart, a magnificent yet menacing structure crafted from obsidian and adorned with silver runes that seem to absorb the light. Above, a chandelier hangs heavy with candles that flicker but never fully illuminate the space, casting long shadows that dance along the walls and floor. The air is charged with a palpable sense of power and anticipation, as if the very room awaits the final confrontation between light and shadow.

Surrounding the throne, trophies of past victories and conquests lay testament to centuries of manipulation and control. Each artifact, each piece of regalia, whispers tales of subjugation and triumph over those who dared challenge the Court's supremacy. Yet, amidst this dark splendor, a palpable tension lingers, a silent acknowledgment that tonight's events might forever alter the course of history. Here, you face not just a foe, but the embodiment of an age-old darkness that seeks to extinguish the light of hope and freedom.

## Confrontation and Restoration

The PCs must engage in battle with Killian and his Enforcers, aiming to weaken him sufficiently to perform a ritual that restores the seal within the throne, tipping the scales in their favor.

Interacting with Killian, the formidable leader of the Shadow Court requires a mix of combat strategy, roleplaying, and creative thinking.

### Combat Encounter

**Initiating Combat:** Killian will likely perceive the party as a significant threat. His initial approach may involve negotiation or intimidation, but combat is inevitable unless PCs can offer something incredibly persuasive.

### Combat Abilities

**Legendary Resistances (3/Day):** If Killian fails a saving throw, he can choose to succeed instead.

**Misty Escape:** If reduced to 0 hit points, Killian doesn't die or fall unconscious but instead transforms into mist, except in sunlight or running water. This escape mechanism requires players to plan how to contain or

follow him if they wish to attempt to slay him permanently. Keep in mind that the PCs are not likely to know these details about Killian's powers beforehand unless they are clever and ask the right questions of the right NPCs.

**Regeneration:** Killian regains 20 hit points at the start of his turn, unless he's in sunlight or running water or has taken radiant damage. Strategies to continuously deal radiant damage or use holy water can be crucial.

**Spellcasting:** As a 12th-level spellcaster with high Intelligence, Killian's spell list includes defensive spells (*Mage Armor, Shield*), offensive spells (*Fireball, Disintegrate*), and utility spells (*Darkness, Greater Invisibility*). Players need to prepare for a versatile combatant who can adapt his tactics as the battle progresses.

### Persuasion and Roleplaying

**Dialogue:** Player characters might attempt to converse with Killian, seeking to understand his motivations or find a peaceful resolution. This can involve Persuasion, Deception, or Intimidation checks, depending on the approach. Given Killian's high Insight (+8), these attempts will be challenging and require compelling arguments or offers.

**Offers and Bargains:** Killian might be interested in offers that serve his interests or expand his power. Characters could negotiate by offering artifacts, information, or services that intrigue him. However, any agreement with Killian should be approached with caution, as he is known for his cunning and deceptive nature.

### Special Interactions

**Breaking the Curse or Seal:** If PCs seek to weaken Killian by restoring the seal or lifting curses, they might try to engage him in conversation to distract or glean information about his weaknesses. Clever use of Insight (to detect lies or weaknesses) and Religion (to understand magical vulnerabilities) checks can provide advantages in this endeavor.

**Leveraging Allies or Knowledge:** Characters might have allies within the adventure or possess knowledge of Killian's past that they can use to their advantage. Revealing secrets or calling upon allies for aid during the encounter could shift the balance, making the confrontation more than just a battle of strength.

### Direct Confrontation

**The Final Battle:** When dialogue and negotiation fail, or if characters choose to directly engage Killian, they must be prepared for a challenging fight. Employing tactics that exploit his vampire weaknesses, such as sunlight, holy water, and running water, alongside strategic use of their strongest abilities, spells, and artifacts, will be key to their success.

Players should remember that Killian is not just a powerful opponent in combat but also a deeply strategic and intelligent adversary. Approaching the encounter with preparation, creativity, and adaptability will be crucial to overcoming the challenges he presents.

# Enforcers of the Eclipse

The Enforcers of the Eclipse play a critical role in serving Killian and defending the Throne of Night. Here's how they function within the encounter:

## Role and Function

**Guardians of the Throne:** The Enforcers are Killian's elite protectors, stationed in the Throne of Night to safeguard the leader of the Shadow Court against any threats. They are fiercely loyal, having been handpicked by Killian for their strength, stealth, and unwavering dedication.

**Strategic Defenders:** They utilize their natural vampiric abilities and combat skills to create a formidable defense around Killian. Their presence complicates the players' approach to confronting Killian directly, adding layers of tactical decision-making to the encounter.

**Intimidation and Control:** Beyond physical defense, the Enforcers serve to intimidate any who dare challenge Killian. Their eerie, silent demeanor and sudden, deadly attacks are meant to instill fear and hesitation in the hearts of intruders.

## Number Present in the Room

Typically, 2-4 Enforcers of the Eclipse are present in the Throne of Night, depending on the difficulty level desired for the encounter and the size of the adventuring party.

## Combat Engagement

**Ambush Tactics:** The Enforcers may initially be hidden in shadows or in mist form, revealing themselves at strategic moments to ambush the party or when Killian commands their involvement.

**Divide and Conquer:** They aim to divide the party's focus, engaging frontline fighters to prevent them from reaching Killian, while also targeting spellcasters and ranged combatants with their Mist Form and Unarmed Strike abilities.

# Restoring the Seal

**Seal Location & Discovery:** The seal's mechanism is ingeniously hidden within the throne's armrests, revealed with a successful Investigation check (DC 22).

**Understanding the Magic:** Comprehending the throne's seal requires an Arcana or Religion check (DC 20) to decipher the ancient runes that suggest a balance of light and darkness is necessary to restore the seal.

**Materials Required:** A vial of vampire's blood, willingly given, symbolizes the darkness. A feather from a raven represents prophecy and the night.

**Ritual Performance:** The ritual necessitates placing the materials on the throne and casting *Moonbeam* upon it while a willing vampire (or a PC under the effect of a potion mimicking vampirism) recites a pledge of balance. This complex act demands a Group Arcana or Religion check (DC 20).

**Strengthening the Seal:** Successfully completing the ritual significantly weakens Killian's power, making him vulnerable and sealing the Shadow Court's influence.

## Read Aloud When the Seal is Restored

As the seal is restored, the opulent Throne of Night becomes a prison for Killian, the lord of the Shadow Court. The ancient runes glow with a fierce light, binding him within walls that once signified his dominion. He does not return to his confinement willingly; instead, he screams curses at you, his voice filled with malice and promise of vengeance. His form is engulfed by the sealing light, and as the final word of the ritual is spoken, his figure becomes nothing more than a shadow, trapped once again within the very throne from which he ruled. The chamber falls silent, the oppressive atmosphere lifted, leaving only the echo of his vows of retribution fading into the darkness.

# Finding the Daynight Stone

In the Throne of Night, Killian ingeniously conceals the Daynight Stone, a powerful artifact that is both a source of his strength and a symbol of his dominion over the shadows. The stone is hidden in a secret compartment within the throne itself, cleverly integrated into the throne's intricate design to ensure it remains undetected by those unworthy of its power. Here's how it is concealed and how party might discover it:

## Location and Concealment

**Secret Compartment:** The Daynight Stone is hidden within the backrest of the Throne of Night, specifically behind an obsidian panel that is flush with the rest of the throne. This panel is adorned with a subtle motif of the moon's phases, mirroring the stone's connection to lunar cycles.

**Mechanism of Access:** The panel can be opened by pressing a series of small, almost imperceptible runes located around the throne's armrests in the correct sequence. These runes represent the eight phases of the moon, from the new moon to the waning crescent.

## Discovering the Daynight Stone

**Investigation Check (DC 22):** PCs must make a high DC Investigation check to notice the slight discrepancies in the throne's design that hint at the compartment's existence. This check is challenging due to the throne's dark material and the ambient shadows that cloak its details.

**Arcana Check (DC 15):** To understand the significance of the moon phase runes and their order, an Arcana check is required. Success allows the players to decipher the correct sequence to press the runes, unlocking the compartment.

**Use of Spells**: Spells such as *Detect Magic* can reveal the magical aura emanating from behind the panel, indicating the presence of a powerful artifact. *Guidance* or *Enhance Ability* can assist in the checks needed to discover and access the compartment.

### Accessing the Daynight Stone

Once the compartment is unlocked, the panel silently slides away to reveal the Daynight Stone, pulsating softly with ethereal light. The stone is set on a velvet cushion, indicating its importance and the care with which Killian guards it.

### Interaction with the Stone

**Removing the Stone**: Taking the Daynight Stone from its resting place does not trigger traps directly, but it significantly weakens the magical defenses and enchantments Killian has placed throughout the Throne of Night crypt, making the subsequent confrontation less perilous.

**Using the Stone**: If PCs choose to use the Daynight Stone during their confrontation with Killian (at the DM's discretion of allowing speedy attunement to the stone), its properties can be invoked to cast *Moonbeam* or illuminate the area, potentially turning the tide of battle by exploiting the vulnerabilities of Killian and his vampire Enforcers.

## Lair Actions

On initiative count 20 (losing initiative ties), the Throne of Night invokes one of the following lair actions:

**Shadow Surge**: Killian manipulates the shadows to lash out at the party. Anyone within 30 feet of the throne must make a DC 18 Dexterity saving throw or take 2d8 necrotic damage.

**Call of the Eclipse**: Killian summons an Enforcer to his side.

**Throne's Guard**: The Throne of Night emits a pulse of dark energy, granting Killian and any Enforcers a +2 bonus to AC until the next round.

## Scaling the Encounter

### Beginning Players (PC levels 1-5)

**Killian's Presence**: Killian could be present but more as an overseer, not directly engaging in combat. He might retreat, leaving his Enforcers to test the party.

**Enforcers of the Eclipse:** Reduce the number to 1 or 2. Lower their HP to 80 and their damage output by half. Remove their Legendary Actions.

**Restoring the Seal:** Simplify the ritual. Require only basic components (easily obtainable) and a single successful Arcana or Religion check (DC 15).

**Lair Actions:** Limit to one less impactful action, such as dimming lights to disorient characters without direct damage.

### Intermediate Players (PC levels 6-10)

**Killian's Involvement:** Killian might briefly engage in combat, using only his basic attack actions to intimidate and challenge the party. His focus remains on escaping once weakened.

**Enforcers of the Eclipse:** Use 2-3 Enforcers with standard HP. Introduce one Legendary Action for the group collectively.

**Restoring the Seal:** Add a moderate challenge to the ritual with specific components that require exploration to find and a Group Arcana or Religion check (DC 20).

**Lair Actions:** Implement two lair actions, such as summoning additional, weaker undead minions and a temporary AC boost for Killian and the Enforcers.

### Advanced Players (PC levels 11+)

**Killian's Engagement:** Killian actively participates in combat, utilizing his full array of spells and abilities. Consider his Misty Escape as a tactical retreat rather than an escape mechanism.

**Enforcers of the Eclipse:** Field the full count of 3-4 Enforcers with enhanced tactics and the ability for each to use a Legendary Action.

**Restoring the Seal:** Require a complex ritual involving rare components that challenge the party to use their skills and knowledge. The final Group check for the ritual is DC 22.

**Lair Actions:** Use all three lair actions to their full effect, challenging the party's ability to adapt and respond to changing battle conditions.

## Monster

Enforcer of the Eclipse

## NPC

Killian

# The Vestibule of Shadows

The Vestibule of Shadows presents a puzzle and combat encounter designed to challenge the players' problem-solving skills and combat abilities. The lunar phase puzzle unlocks the way forward, while the Ghoulscourge Swarm poses a dangerous threat, guarding the secret of restoring the seal tied to Thorn's betrayal.

As you push aside the heavy drapes of mist, a grand chamber unfurls before you, bathed in the ethereal glow of torchlight. Shadows dance across the walls, cast by flames that flicker as though alive, painting a story of night and darkness across the expanse of an ancient mosaic underfoot. The floor itself depicts the celestial dance of the moon, its phases captured in stone, encircled by runes whose meanings whisper of old magics and forgotten rites. Here, in the heart of darkness, the air hangs thick with the scent of decay and the promise of ancient secrets, the silence broken only by the soft murmurs of the unseen.

The room challenges you, its mosaic a puzzle that guards the way deeper into the crypt's heart. But beware, for this place does not welcome the living lightly. The shadows themselves seem to watch, and an unsettling feeling tugs at your senses, a prelude to the undead menace that lurks within. This is a domain where the boundary between the physical and the ethereal blurs, where each step might awaken the guardians of the crypt, eager to reclaim the silence disturbed by your presence.

## Lunar Phase Puzzle

To progress, the party must correctly align the mosaic's lunar phases in the sequence that mirrors the natural lunar cycle, unlocking the hidden pathways leading deeper into the crypt.

The Lunar Phase Puzzle is centered around a large circular mosaic on the floor of the Vestibule of Shadows, depicting the moon in its various phases from new moon to full moon. Each phase (new moon, waxing crescent, first quarter, waxing gibbous, full moon, waning gibbous, last quarter, waning crescent) is represented by a stone tile that can be pressed down, lighting up when the correct sequence is activated.

### Character Interaction

PCs interact by pressing the moon phase tiles in the correct order to reflect a specific lunar cycle pattern.

A failed attempt resets the tiles, accompanied by a soft, ominous rumbling as a warning of the protective enchantments. Pass the following two Intelligence skill checks to make astute observations of the puzzle:

- **Investigation DC 15**: Deduce that the puzzle reflects the lunar cycle and must be solved by mimicking the progression of moon phases.
- **Arcana DC 13**: Recognize that the mosaic channels magical energy when the tiles are pressed in the correct order, reinforcing the sequence's correctness.

**Deciphering Clues**: Throughout the Vestibule, there are faded murals and inscriptions that hint at the importance of the lunar cycle to the Shadow Court. A successful Intelligence (History) DC 14 check reveals that the Shadow Court's power waxes and wanes with the moon, indicating the starting phase for the puzzle is the new moon.

**Puzzle Solution**: PCs must press the tiles in the order of the lunar cycle starting from the new moon. The correct order is: New Moon → Waxing Crescent → First Quarter → Waxing Gibbous → Full Moon → Waning Gibbous → Last Quarter → Waning Crescent.

The following table has details on the tiles:

| Phase of the Moon | Type | Details of the Hint | DC Check |
|---|---|---|---|
| New Moon | Inscription | "In darkness begins the Court's whisper, where shadows merge and plots are birthed." Indicates the start of the cycle. | Perception DC 10 |
| Waxing Crescent | Mural | Depicts the Court gathering strength, with figures emerging from shadows, subtly growing in number. | Investigation DC 12 |
| First Quarter | Inscription | "As the shadow wanes, the Court's reach extends, half in light, half in darkness, plotting beneath the crescent's gaze." | History DC 13 |
| Waxing Gibbous | Mural | Shows the Court at its most active, engaging in rituals that increase their power, with the moon almost full behind them. | Arcana DC 14 |

| Full Moon | Inscription | "Under the full eye of night, the Court's power peaks, their will imposed upon the land." Signifies the climax of their influence. | Perception DC 15 |
| Waning Gibbous | Mural | Illustrates the Court retracting from their deeds, their figures slightly less bold, starting to retreat into the shadows. | Investigation DC 12 |
| Last Quarter | Inscription | "Now halved, the Court's whispers turn to silence, plotting anew in the balance of light and shadow." | History DC 13 |
| Waning Crescent | Mural | Portrays the Court almost fully retreated into the shadows, with only a few figures visible, indicating the cycle's end and a new beginning. | Arcana DC 14 |

**Final Activation**: Once the sequence is correctly entered, the PCs must cast a light-based spell (e.g., *Light*, *Moonbeam*, or *Dancing Lights*) on the full moon tile to activate the puzzle.

The casting of the spell does not require a roll, but the choice of spell and the willingness to use a spell slot at this juncture add to the puzzle's complexity.

**Puzzle Success**: Upon successful completion, the mosaic illuminates with a ghostly light, revealing the hidden entrance to the crypt's inner sanctums and disarming any traps that may have been triggered by incorrect attempts.

**Puzzle Failure Consequences**: A failed attempt triggers a defensive mechanism, summoning a Ghoulscourge Swarm or the vampire Thorn to attack the party as a deterrent.

## Interaction with Thorn

A tragic figure, once a guardian druid, now transformed into a vampiric enforcer for the Shadow Court, Thorn struggles between his remaining druidic honor and the curse that binds him to darkness.

## Thorn's Attack Trigger

Thorn assesses threats based on the party's actions towards nature and their allegiance.

**Trigger**: Desecration of nature or open allegiance to the enemies of the Shadow Court.

**Manipulation of Nature**: Uses the cantrips *Druidcraft* to create minor natural hindrances or his *Thorn Whip* for direct attacks.

**Attack Signal**: Sudden environmental changes, like thickening fog or entangling roots, indicating Thorn's hostility.

### Persuading Thorn

Characters can persuade Thorn by showing respect for nature and understanding his conflict.

**Initial Persuasion Attempt**: Charisma (Persuasion) DC 20, reflecting Thorn's deep-seated mistrust and anguish.

**Offering Help or Tokens**: Presenting a meaningful gesture towards nature or expressing genuine intent to free Thorn lowers the DC to 18.

**Advantage Condition**: Revealing knowledge of the Shadow Court's weaknesses or sharing a personal sacrifice for nature's sake grants advantage.

**Triggering the Ghoulscourge Swarm**

Thorn uses the swarm as a defensive measure or to test the party.

**Summoning the Swarm**: Described as Thorn blending with nature and then signaling the swarm's attack with a unique environmental cue.

**Defensive Mechanism**: The swarm attacks if Thorn feels outnumbered or wishes to assess the party's strength.

### Convincing Thorn to Share Knowledge

If persuaded, Thorn may share vital information on strengthening the seal against the Vestibule of Shadows.

**Demonstrating Knowledge**: Intelligence (Arcana or Nature) DC 17 to show comprehensive understanding of the magical seals.

**Earning Trust**: Charisma (Persuasion) DC 18, modified by the party's previous actions that align with Thorn's interests or nature conservation efforts.

**Understanding Thorn**: Wisdom (Insight) DC 16 to grasp the depth of Thorn's conflict and find an empathetic approach.

### Ghoulscourge Swarm

A terrifying mass of undead, attacking with poisonous bites and capable of spreading the Eternal Dusk curse.

## Restoring the Seal

**Seal Location & Discovery:** Hidden beneath the mosaic's depiction of the new moon lies the seal. Casting *Detect Magic* reveals its magical aura, while solving the puzzle causes the area to glow, indicating its presence.

**Understanding the Magic:** Surrounding the mosaic are ancient runic inscriptions, requiring an Arcana check (DC 15) to decipher. Successful interpretation of the inscriptions reveals the magical nature of this crypt's seal, which is linked to lunar cycles and shadow magic.

**Ritual Performance:** PCs must use gathered shadow essence (such as blood or bone dust) from any slain undead, symbolizing the night's darkness. Under the light of the moon, they must draw a circle on the mosaic, placing the essence at its heart. Casting *Moonbeam* upon the center, they must chant the runes deciphered earlier. Success requires a DC 15 Arcana check, aided by moonstone dust and shadow essence as material components.

**Materials Needed:** Shadow essence from undead creatures.

### Read Aloud When the Seal is Restored

The air vibrates with power, and for a moment, the entire Vestibule of Shadows is bathed in a serene lunar glow. Beneath your feet, the mosaic aligns perfectly, its lunar phases now in harmonious order, sealing away the darkness. Within the confines of his crypt, Thorn lets out a roar of frustration, his connection to the land abruptly severed. The vines and thorns that once obeyed his will now bind him, trapping him within the very nature he sought to corrupt. As the seal strengthens, you feel a palpable shift in the air, a lightness that signifies the containment of a great evil. Thorn, the once guardian turned foe, is now imprisoned by his own sanctuary, unable to escape the natural tomb that the restored seal has forged around him.

## Terrain

The floor is uneven, with loose mosaic tiles posing a tripping hazard. Moving quickly or engaging in combat requires a DC 12 Dexterity (Acrobatics) check to avoid falling prone. Alternatively, you can rule the entire chamber floor as difficult terrain, halving movement speed.

## Lair Actions

On initiative count 20 (losing initiative ties), the Vestibule of Shadows invokes one of the following lair actions:

**Shifting Shadows:** The shadows in the chamber animate, creating distracting shapes that may hinder concentration. Characters making spell attacks or Concentration checks do so with disadvantage.

**Moonlight's Grace:** Ethereal moonlight filters through the chamber, healing the Ghoulscourge Swarm or strengthening Thorn's resolve. Once per encounter, Thorn regains 10 hit points, or the Ghoulscourge Swarm regains half its lost hit points.

**Crypt's Whisper:** The ancient runes along the walls glow ominously, casting a silence spell over a random section of the room, requiring a DC 15 Constitution saving throw to overcome for casting spells with verbal components.

## Scaling the Encounter
### Beginning Players (PC levels 1-5)

**Puzzle Complexity**: Simplify the lunar phase puzzle with fewer phases required to solve it, reducing the sequence to New Moon, First Quarter, Full Moon, and Last Quarter, with a straightforward hint system.

**Ghoulscourge Swarm Encounter:**

- Reduce the swarm's HP to 40.
- Lower the damage of its bites to 1d10 + 2 piercing damage.
- Adjust the DC for the Constitution saving throw to resist being poisoned to 13.

**Terrain Challenges**: Simplify the terrain by removing the requirement for Dexterity (Acrobatics) checks to navigate.

**Lair Actions**: Limit to one non-damaging lair action, such as a minor illusion of Thorn to distract PCs.

**Interacting with Thorn**: If Thorn appears, frame him more as a mysterious figure observing from afar, without directly engaging.

### Intermediate Players (PC levels 6-10)

**Puzzle Complexity**: Utilize the full lunar phase sequence with additional, but clear, hints scattered throughout the room.

**Ghoulscourge Swarm Encounter:**

- Swarm's HP is at its standard 67.
- Bites deal standard damage of 22 (4d10 + 2) piercing when above half HP.
- Keep the DC for the Constitution saving throw to resist poison at 13.

**Terrain Challenges**: Introduce minor terrain challenges, such as areas of the floor that are uneven, requiring occasional Dexterity (Acrobatics) checks (DC 10) to cross without penalty.

**Lair Actions**: Include two lair actions, such as manipulating shadows to obscure vision and a weak tremor that momentarily unbalances everyone in the room (requiring DC 12 Dexterity saving throws to avoid falling prone).

**Interacting with Thorn**: Thorn might directly confront the players if they fail the puzzle multiple times, using non-lethal force to push them towards solving it.

### Advanced Players (PC levels 11+)

**Puzzle Complexity**: The full lunar phase sequence with subtle and cryptic clues requiring higher Investigation and Perception checks (DC 18) to decipher.

**Ghoulscourge Swarm Encounter**:

- Increase the swarm's HP to 100 for added durability.

- Have bites inflict maximum damage, and increase the DC for the Constitution saving throw to resist poison to 17.

- Introduce a new ability in which the swarm can split into two smaller swarms at half health, each with halved damage output but requiring separate actions to combat.

**Terrain Challenges**: Complex terrain with significant hazards, such as loose tiles that collapse if not carefully navigated, requiring Dexterity (Acrobatics) checks (DC 15) and Intelligence (Investigation) checks (DC 15) to identify safe paths.

**Lair Actions**: Employ all three lair actions with added effects, such as a sudden darkness that extinguishes light sources, requiring PCs to relight them or use magical light, and aggressive root growth that attempts to grapple and restrain characters (DC 16 Strength or Dexterity saving throw to escape).

**Interacting with Thorn**: Thorn becomes a formidable adversary who may intervene if the PCs disrupt the sanctity of his domain, showcasing his powers over nature and undead and presenting a moral dilemma or a potential ally if approached with respect for nature and understanding of his plight.

## Monster

Ghoulscourge Swarm

## NPC

Thorn

# Conclusion

## Restoring the Seals

As the last echoes of your chants fade into the silence of the crypt, a palpable shift sweeps through the land. The seals, once fractured, now pulse with a renewed vigor, their magic weaving through the fabric of Ravenholme and beyond. The oppressive darkness that once clawed at the edges of the Mourning Moors begins to recede, chased away by the strengthening light. The vampire menace, a shadow that loomed over this land for far too long, finds itself curtailed, its power diminished beneath the weight of your success. You stand not just as victors but as saviors, the architects of a new dawn for a land that had almost succumbed to eternal dusk.

Killian, the once indomitable lord of the Shadow Court, remains confined within the Throne of Night, his reign of terror over. The Daynight Stone, liberated from his grasp, now serves as a beacon of balance, its light a testament to your courage and resolve. The spirits of the Hall of Echoing Torment, finally at peace, whisper their gratitude on the winds that sweep through Ravenholme, and the natural world, once twisted by vampiric corruption, begins to heal.

The people of Ravenholme, their spirits lifted by the promise of safety and renewal, welcome you with open arms and grateful hearts. Tales of your bravery spread like wildfire, igniting hope in the hearts of those who had lived in fear. As you walk the streets, you are not just adventurers but legends, the heroes who faced the darkness and emerged victorious.

**Reward**

For your bravery, cunning, and strength, the rewards are many and varied, a testament to the impact of your actions:

**Title of Ravenholme's Guardians**: Granted by the village's elders, this title comes with the lifelong gratitude of its people and the promise of their support in your future endeavors.

**The Daynight Amulet**: Crafted from a shard of the Daynight Stone, this amulet offers the wearer protection against dark magic by granting resistance to necrotic damage and advantage on saves vs. all necromantic magic., It also grants the ability to cast *Moonbeam* once per day without expending a spell slot. Wondrous item, very rare. Attunement required.

**Land and Title**: Each member of the party is awarded a piece of land within Ravenholme's borders, along with a noble title, as a sign of the village's eternal gratitude.

**Elena's Blessing**: Elena, the guardian of the Sanctuary, bestows upon each of you a blessing, a protective charm that grants a +1 bonus to AC and saving throws.

**Gold and Treasures**: Seized from the remnants of the Shadow Court's coffers, a substantial sum of gold and a selection of precious gems and artifacts are divided among you.

As the adventure concludes, you find yourselves not at the end of a journey, but at the beginning of legend. Your deeds have changed the course of history, but the world is vast, and darkness lurks in many corners. The path ahead is yours to choose, filled with new adventures, challenges, and opportunities to further etch your names into the annals of time.

## Vampire Pact

In the shadowed halls of the Throne of Night, a pact is forged, not of blood but of ambition. You, the bold adventurers who walk the path between light and darkness, have chosen a different destiny. With the seals restored not to banish but to secure an alliance, you stand at the side of the vampire court, rulers of Ravenholme under the night's eternal embrace. Your alliance with Killian, the enigmatic lord of the Shadow Court, marks the dawn of a new era, an era where the whispered fears of the night become your heralds.

As the new regents of Ravenholme, your rule begins with the whispers of change, with eyes set not just on the lands that lay before you but on the distant mountains of Barsea Heights, where the Whispering Night family holds sway. The game of shadows and power beckons, with the ambition to expand your dominion and challenge the ancient sects, a testament to your newfound resolve. Ravenholme becomes a beacon, not of hope, but of supremacy, as you weave the very essence of the night into the fabric of your reign.

**Reward**

As the new sovereigns of the night, your rewards are as unique as your path:

**Crown of the Eclipse**: A symbol of your authority over Ravenholme and beyond, this crown enhances your diplomatic influence and intimidates those who dare oppose you. It grants the wearer proficiency in Persuasion and Intimidation. For those already proficient, it grants expertise in those skills. Wondrous item, rare. Attunement required.

**Vampire's Pact**: An oath of fealty from Killian and his court, granting you access to their knowledge, resources, and the dark arts.

**Dominion over Ravenholme**: Complete control over the village and its lands, with the power to shape its future and the fate of its people.

**Alliance with the Shadow Court**: A powerful alliance that offers protection, support in your endeavors to expand your territory, and the opportunity to influence vampire politics.

With Ravenholme under your sway and the night as your ally, the world unfolds before you, ripe with possibilities and challenges. The path you walk is shadowed, fraught with the intrigues of immortal politics and the whispers of those who fear the dark. Yet, in this new kingdom built on night and ambition, your will is law, and your desires shape the future. Remember, with great power comes the lure of darker depths, and in the dance of shadows, allies can become adversaries. Your reign has begun, and with it, the tale of a new dynasty, written in the stars and shadows of the night.

# The Fugitives

To be used if the party flees the terrors of Ravenholme without completing their quest.

As the final echoes of battle fade into the cold stone of the crypts, a chilling realization grips your hearts. Ravenholme, once a beacon of hope amidst the encroaching shadows, now looms as a monument to fear and despair. The power of the Shadow Court, unyielding and omnipresent, casts a long, dark shadow over your fates. With heavy hearts and the weight of survival pressing upon your shoulders, you choose the path of the fugitive, seeking refuge in the unknown beyond the cursed lands of the Mourning Moors.

Your journey is fraught with peril, a test of endurance, and a testament to your will to live. Each step away from the vampire's domain is a victory against the night, a silent act of defiance against the darkness that sought to claim you. The roads are treacherous, the nights longer and colder, but within you burns the fire of survival, guiding you through the darkest hours.

As you leave Ravenholme behind, the shadow of the Court's reach still looms large, a reminder of the darkness that exists in the world. Yet, with each mile gained, you forge a new story, one not of heroes triumphant but of survivors resilient. Your journey is far from over, and the road ahead promises both danger and discovery. But for now, you live, breathe, and move forward, carrying the lessons of the past and the hope of a future free from the night's eternal grasp.

# Appendix

The Appendix is a crucial part of the *Crypts of the Shadow Court*, providing Dungeon Masters with additional resources to enhance their gameplay experience and immerse players in the rich, dark fantasy setting of Ravenholme. This section is designed to supplement the main adventure, offering a wealth of detailed information and mechanics that can be seamlessly integrated into the campaign.

Within these pages, you'll find comprehensive descriptions of the various monsters that lurk within the Shadow Court's domain, each with their own unique abilities and lore. From the insidious Bloodbind Spider to the grotesque Ghoulscourge Swarm, these creatures are sure to provide challenging encounters and memorable moments for your players. The Appendix also introduces a cast of intriguing non-player characters, such as Elena the Wise and Killian, the Lord of the Shadow Court, each with their own motivations and roles within the story.

In addition to monsters and NPCs, the Appendix includes details on magical items like the enigmatic Daynight Stone and the potent Elixir of Lucidity, which can serve as rewards or plot devices within your campaign. You'll also find a mini-game called "Whispers of the Shadow Court" that can be used as a fun diversion during downtime or as a means to further explore the intrigue and secrecy surrounding the Shadow Court. Finally, the Appendix provides game mechanics for scaling encounters based on party size and level, ensuring that the challenges faced by the players are always balanced and engaging. Whether you're a seasoned DM or new to the role, the information provided in the Appendix will help you craft a memorable and immersive experience for your players as they delve into the depths of the Shadow Court's domain.

# Scaling Monsters

Use the following table for party size to increase the number of monsters:

| Party Size | Increase number by |
|---|---|
| 5-8 | x 1.5 |
| 9-12 | x 2 |
| 13 | x 2.5 |

Use the following table for party level to increase the number of monsters:

| Party Level | Increase number by |
|---|---|
| 5-8 | x 1.5 |
| 9-12 | x 2 |
| 13-15 | x 2.5 |
| Level 16+ | x 3.5 |

Now take the number for the party and the level and add the two together. For instance, if you have a party size of 5 with an average party level of 10, then you would add 1.5 + 2.5 to get 4 times the monsters. 3 creatures for a level 10 party are no challenge, especially if there are 6 or 7 PC's. Increase that to 12, and suddenly you have a challenge. Feel free to adjust as you see fit.

In addition to scaling monster numbers, many of the traps and puzzles in the game have a sliding scale that the DM can use to change the level of difficulty depending on the skillset of the characters.

# Monsters

## Bloodbind Spider

*Large beast (monstrosity), neutral evil*

**Armor Class:** 14 (natural armor)

**Hit Points:** 76 (9d10 + 27)

**Speed:** 30 ft., climb 30 ft.

| STR | DEX | CON | INT | WIS | CHA |
|-----|-----|-----|-----|-----|-----|
| 16 (+3) | 14 (+2) | 16 (+3) | 2 (-4) | 12 (+1) | 4 (-3) |

**Skills:** Stealth +6, Perception +3

**Damage Resistances:** necrotic; bludgeoning, piercing, and slashing from nonmagical attacks not made with silvered weapons

**Senses:** darkvision 60 ft., passive Perception 13

**Languages:** —

**Challenge:** 5 (1,800 XP)

**Web Walker.** The Bloodbind Spider ignores movement restrictions caused by webbing.

**Spider Climb.** The Bloodbind Spider can climb difficult surfaces, including upside down on ceilings, without needing to make an ability check.

**Web Sense.** While in contact with a web, the Bloodbind Spider knows the exact location of any other creature in contact with the same web.

**Webbing (Recharge 5-6).** The Bloodbind Spider can extrude a large amount of nearly invisible webbing at once. As an action, it can create difficult terrain in a 20-foot radius at a point it can see within 60 feet of it. The webbing is used as a trap in or near the Bloodbind Spider's den. A creature trapped in the sticky webbing can use its action to make a Strength check (DC 14) to break free.

### Actions

**Multiattack.** The Bloodbind Spider makes two attacks: one with its bite and one with its web (if recharge allows).

**Bite.** *Melee Weapon Attack:* +5 to hit, reach 5 ft., one creature. *Hit:* 7 (1d8 + 3) piercing damage, and the target must make a DC 15 Constitution saving throw, taking 9 (2d8) necrotic damage on a failed save, or half as much damage on a successful one. If the saving throw fails by 5 or more, the target is also cursed with Eternal Dusk unless they are immune to the curse. The curse's onset begins immediately.

### Legendary Actions

The Bloodbind Spider can take 3 legendary actions, choosing from the options below. Only one legendary

action option can be used at a time and only at the end of another creature's turn. The Bloodbind Spider regains spent legendary actions at the start of its turn.

- **Detect.** The Bloodbind Spider makes a Wisdom (Perception) check.
- **Move.** The Bloodbind Spider moves up to its speed without provoking opportunity attacks.
- **Bite (Costs 2 Actions).** The Bloodbind Spider makes one bite attack.

## Description

Bloodbind Spiders are grotesque paragons of the Shadow Court's manipulation of life and magic. Their bodies are enormous, with a leg span reaching up to 10 feet across and covered in a glossy, jet-black exoskeleton that seems to absorb light. Their eight eyes shimmer with a malevolent red glow, mirroring the cursed blood that runs through their veins. Their fangs, long and dripping with dark, magical venom, promise a fate worse than death: the curse of Eternal Dusk.

These monstrous arachnids were not born but created, a testament to the Shadow Court's mastery over dark magics. Initially, they were common spiders dwelling within the crypts that the Court called home. Through twisted rituals and the infusion of vampiric essence, they were transformed into the fearsome guardians they are today. Loyal only to the Court, they serve as both protectors of its secrets and instruments of its will, weaving webs not just of silk but of darkness, waiting silently for the next victim to stumble into their shadowy domain.

# Bloodvine Creeper

*Large plant, neutral evil*

**Armor Class:** 13 (natural armor)

**Hit Points:** 85 (10d10 + 30)

**Speed:** 5 ft., climb 5 ft.

| STR | DEX | CON | INT | WIS | CHA |
|-----|-----|-----|-----|-----|-----|
| 14 (+2) | 8 (-1) | 16 (+3) | 2 (-4) | 11 (+0) | 5 (-3) |

**Damage Resistances:** bludgeoning, piercing

**Condition Immunities:** blinded, deafened, exhaustion

**Senses:** blindsight 30 ft. (blind beyond this radius), passive Perception 10

**Languages:** —

**Challenge:** 4 (1,100 XP)

**Regeneration.** The Bloodvine Creeper regains 5 hit points at the start of its turn. If the Bloodvine Creeper takes fire or radiant damage, this trait doesn't function at the start of its next turn.

**Thorny Entanglement.** A creature that starts its turn entangled by the Bloodvine Creeper takes 5 (1d10) piercing damage from its thorns.

**Vine Camouflage.** The Bloodvine Creeper has advantage on Dexterity (Stealth) checks made in forested or overgrown areas.

## Actions

**Multiattack.** The Bloodvine Creeper makes two tendril attacks.

**Tendril.** *Melee Weapon Attack:* +4 to hit, reach 10 ft., one target. *Hit:* 6 (1d8 + 2) piercing damage, and the target is grappled (escape DC 14). Until this grapple ends, the target is restrained, and the Bloodvine Creeper can't use the same tendril on another target.

**Engulf (Recharge 5-6).** The Bloodvine Creeper attempts to engulf a Medium or smaller target it is grappling. The target must make a DC 14 Dexterity saving throw. On a failure, the target is swallowed, and the grapple ends. The swallowed target is blinded, restrained, and takes 21 (6d6) acid damage at the start of each of the Bloodvine Creeper's turns. If the Bloodvine Creeper takes 20 points of damage or more on a single turn from a creature inside it, the Bloodvine Creeper must succeed on a DC 12 Constitution saving throw at the end of that turn or regurgitate all swallowed creatures, which fall prone in a space within 10 feet of the Bloodvine Creeper. If the Bloodvine Creeper dies, a swallowed creature is no longer restrained by it and can escape from the corpse using 5 feet of movement, exiting prone.

## Description

Bloodvine Creepers appear as an overgrowth of thick, dark green vines, densely covered with sharp, thorn-filled tendrils. These tendrils constantly twitch and coil, almost as if sensing the air for the presence of the living. Where flowers might bloom on ordinary vines, the Bloodvine Creepers instead grow clusters of barbed pods that pulse with a malevolent energy, ready to release their thorns at the slightest touch.

Cultivated in the shadowy undergrowth of the Ancient Crypts' gardens, Bloodvine Creepers are a grotesque testament to the Shadow Court's perversion of nature. Initially bred from harmless vines, they were twisted by dark rituals and the infusion of vampiric essence. Designed to protect and conceal the Court's sanctums, these creepers have evolved into sentient guardians, eagerly awaiting the flesh and blood of intruders. The thorns of these malevolent plants do more than just wound; they curse with the *Shadow's Thirst*, infecting their victims with a dark magic that drains their vitality and binds them ever closer to the will of the Shadow Court.

## Curse: Shadow's Thirst

*Curse Activation:* When a creature takes damage from the Bloodvine Creeper's thorny tendrils, it must succeed on a DC 15 Constitution saving throw or become cursed with Shadow's Thirst.

*Curse Effect:* A cursed creature feels an insatiable thirst for moisture and experiences a gradual withering of the body. The creature's hit point maximum is reduced by 5 (1d10) for every 24 hours that pass. Drinking water does not satiate this thirst, only the ingestion of blood from a living creature will halt the progression of the curse for 24 hours.

*Curse Removal:* The curse can be removed with a *Remove Curse* spell or similar magic. However, if the curse has lasted for more than 7 days, the creature must also succeed on a DC 17 Wisdom saving throw after the *Remove Curse* spell is cast, or the hit point maximum reduction becomes permanent.

*Special:* If a creature dies while under the effect of the curse, it rises the following night as a vampire spawn under the control of the Shadow Court.

# Carrion Marionette

*Medium undead, neutral evil*

**Armor Class:** 12

**Hit Points:** 22 (4d8 + 4)

**Speed:** 30 ft.

| STR | DEX | CON | INT | WIS | CHA |
|-----|-----|-----|-----|-----|-----|
| 10 (+0) | 14 (+2) | 12 (+1) | 6 (-2) | 10 (+0) | 5 (-3) |

**Damage Immunities:** poison; bludgeoning, piercing, and slashing from nonmagical attacks that aren't silvered

**Condition Immunities:** poisoned, exhaustion

**Senses:** darkvision 60 ft., passive Perception 10

**Languages:** understands the languages it knew in life but can't speak

**Challenge:** 1/2 (100 XP)

**Necromancer's Puppet.** The Carrion Marionette can't be controlled by any other necromancy magic except by its creator.

**Immutable Form.** The Carrion Marionette is immune to any spell or effect that would alter its form.

**Transfer Curse.** When the Carrion Marionette hits a creature with its Cursed Grasp, the target must succeed on a DC 15 Constitution saving throw or become cursed with a fragment of necromantic energy, feeling a cold dread and gaining one level of exhaustion until the curse is lifted or the creature is killed.

## Actions

**Slam.** *Melee Weapon Attack:* +4 to hit, reach 5 ft., one target. *Hit:* 5 (1d6 + 2) bludgeoning damage.

**Cursed Grasp.** *Melee Spell Attack:* +4 to hit, reach 5 ft., one target. *Hit:* 7 (1d10 + 2) necrotic damage, and if the target is a creature, they must succeed on a DC 15 Constitution saving throw or gain one level of exhaustion until the curse is lifted or the creature is killed. The target may make a new saving throw at the end of their turn every round. This effect does not stack with itself.

## Description

Carrion Marionettes appear as humanoid figures, their bodies composed of various corpses adorned in decaying garments that once signified their status in life. Their movements are jerky and unnatural, as if invisible strings controlled them, making their advances both eerie and unpredictable. Hollow eye sockets glare emptily at their targets, and open mouths seem to silently scream, adding to their ghastly demeanor.

Created by the Shadow Court's most adept necromancers, Carrion Marionettes serve as silent enforcers and guards within the crypts and ruins under the Court's control. These marionettes are not just reanimated corpses; they are infused with dark magics that bind them to the necromancer's will, forcing them to enact their creator's bidding without hesitation or fear. Each marionette carries with it a residue of the life it once lived, making each encounter unnervingly personal. The psychological terror they instill, combined with their undying loyalty to the Shadow Court, makes them formidable opponents, particularly in numbers. Their ability to curse their foes with just a touch is a testament to the necromantic prowess of their creators, further cementing the Carrion Marionettes as one of the Court's most macabre tools of warfare.

# Crimson Claw Assassin

*Medium undead (vampire), neutral evil*

**Armor Class:** 15 (leather armor)

**Hit Points:** 76 (9d8 + 36)

**Speed:** 30 ft., climb 20 ft.

| STR | DEX | CON | INT | WIS | CHA |
|-----|-----|-----|-----|-----|-----|
| 11 (+0) | 18 (+4) | 18 (+4) | 14 (+2) | 12 (+1) | 16 (+3) |

**Skills:** Stealth +8, Acrobatics +8, Perception +5

**Damage Resistances:** necrotic; bludgeoning, piercing, and slashing from nonmagical attacks

**Senses:** darkvision 60 ft., passive Perception 15

**Languages:** Common, Elven (can't speak in bat form)

**Challenge:** 7 (2,900 XP)

**Innate Spellcasting.** The Crimson Claw Assassin's innate spellcasting ability is Charisma (spell save DC 14). They can cast the following spells, requiring no material components:

- At will: *disguise self, silent image*
- 1/day each: *invisibility, gaseous form*

**Regeneration.** The Crimson Claw Assassin regains 10 hit points at the start of their turn if they have at least 1 hit point and aren't in sunlight or running water.

**Shadow Stealth.** While in dim light or darkness, the Crimson Claw Assassin can hide as a bonus action.

**Vampire Weaknesses.** The Crimson Claw Assassin has the following vampire weaknesses:

- **Forbiddance.** They can't enter a residence without an invitation from one of the occupants.

- **Harmed by Running Water.** The Crimson Claw Assassin takes 20 acid damage if they end their turn in running water.

- **Sunlight Hypersensitivity.** They take 20 radiant damage when they start their turn in sunlight. While in sunlight, they have disadvantage on attack rolls and ability checks.

- **Coffin Reliance.** The Assassin is destroyed if reduced to 0 hit points without being able to retreat to their coffin.

## Actions

**Multiattack.** The Crimson Claw Assassin makes two attacks with their poisoned dagger.

**Poisoned Dagger.** *Melee Weapon Attack:* +8 to hit, reach 5 ft., one target. *Hit:* 8 (1d4 + 4) piercing damage plus 7 (2d6) poison damage. The target must make a DC 17 Constitution saving throw or become cursed with Eternal Dusk.

**Eternal Dusk Curse (Recharge 5–6).** The Crimson Claw Assassin targets one creature they can see within 30 feet of them. The target must succeed on a DC 17 Constitution saving throw or become afflicted with the Eternal Dusk curse.

## Description

Crimson Claw Assassins move with a grace that belies their deadly nature, cloaked in shadows even in the faintest light. Their attire blends the practical with the sinister; dark leathers fitted to allow for silent movement, with crimson accents that mirror their allegiance to the Shadow Court. Their faces, often masked or hooded, carry an eternal sneer of disdain for the living, eyes glowing faintly with a blood-red hue that hints at their predatory instincts.

Originally skilled rogues and assassins in life, these elite vampires were handpicked by Killian for their prowess in the dark arts of stealth and murder. Their transformation has only heightened their abilities, making them the perfect instruments for Killian's will. Tasked with the elimination of threats to the Shadow Court and retrieval of dark artifacts, they embody the Court's ruthlessness. The poison that coats their daggers carries the curse of Eternal Dusk, a mark of their allegiance and a testament to their role as harbingers of the Court's creeping doom. Haunted by their past lives, they serve the Court not out of loyalty, but a twisted sense of survival, forever bound to the dark whims of their master.

# Enforcer of the Eclipse

*Medium undead (vampire), lawful evil*

**Armor Class:** 16 (natural armor)

**Hit Points:** 136 (16d8 + 64)

**Speed:** 30 ft.

| STR | DEX | CON | INT | WIS | CHA |
|---|---|---|---|---|---|
| 18 (+4) | 16 (+3) | 18 (+4) | 14 (+2) | 12 (+1) | 16 (+3) |

**Saving Throws:** Dex +7, Wis +5, Cha +7

**Skills:** Stealth +7, Perception +9, Intimidation +7

**Damage Resistances:** necrotic; bludgeoning, piercing, and slashing from nonmagical attacks

**Senses:** darkvision 120 ft., passive Perception 19

**Languages:** Common, Elven, Infernal

**Challenge:** 10 (5,900 XP)

**Regeneration.** The Enforcer regains 20 hit points at the start of their turn if they have at least 1 hit point and aren't in sunlight or running water. If the Enforcer takes radiant damage or damage from holy water, this trait doesn't function at the start of the Enforcer's next turn.

**Vampire Weaknesses.** The Enforcer has the following flaws:

- **Forbiddance.** They can't enter a residence without an invitation from one of the occupants.

- **Harmed by Running Water.** They take 20 acid damage if they end their turn in running water.

- **Sunlight Hypersensitivity.** The Enforcer takes 20 radiant damage when they start their turn in sunlight. While in sunlight, they have disadvantage on attack rolls and ability checks.

- **Stake to the Heart.** If a piercing weapon made of wood is driven into the Enforcer's heart while incapacitated in their resting place, they are destroyed.

**Shadow Stealth.** While in dim light or darkness, the Enforcer can hide as a bonus action.

**Mist Form.** As a bonus action, the Enforcer can polymorph into mist or back into their true form. While in mist form, they can't take any actions, speak, or manipulate objects. They are weightless, have a flying speed of 20 ft., can hover, and can enter a hostile creature's space and stop there. In addition, if air can pass through a space, their mist form can do so without squeezing. However, they can't pass through water. They have advantage on Strength, Dexterity, and Constitution saving throws, and they are immune to all nonmagical damage, except the damage they take from sunlight.

## Actions

**Multiattack.** The Enforcer makes two attacks, only one of which can be a bite attack.

**Unarmed Strike.** *Melee Weapon Attack:* +8 to hit, reach 5 ft., one creature. *Hit:* 8 (1d8 + 4) bludgeoning damage. Instead of dealing damage, the Enforcer can grapple the target (escape DC 18).

**Bite.** *Melee Weapon Attack:* +8 to hit, reach 5 ft., one willing creature, or a creature that is grappled by the Enforcer, incapacitated, or restrained. *Hit:* 10 (1d6 + 4) piercing damage plus 7 (2d6) necrotic damage. The target's hit point maximum is reduced by an amount equal to the necrotic damage taken, and the Enforcer regains hit points equal to that amount. The reduction lasts until the target finishes a long rest. The target dies if this effect reduces their hit point maximum to 0.

## Legendary Actions

The Enforcer can take 3 legendary actions, choosing from the options below. Only one legendary action can

be used at a time and only at the end of another creature's turn. The Enforcer regains spent legendary actions at the start of their turn.

**Move.** The Enforcer moves up to its speed without provoking opportunity attacks.

**Unarmed Strike (Costs 2 Actions).** The Enforcer makes one unarmed strike.

**Vanish (Costs 3 Actions).** The Enforcer turns invisible until the end of its next turn.

## Description

Enforcers of the Eclipse are imposing figures, their forms blending the aristocratic grace of their vampiric nature with the deadly intent of seasoned warriors. They stand taller and more muscular than the average vampire, their skin pale but tough as leather. Their eyes glow with a crimson light, piercing the darkness that they often cloak themselves in. Each wears a distinctive set of armor, dark as the night sky and etched with the sigil of their sect, a testament to their status and allegiance to Killian and the Shadow Court.

# Ghoulscourge Swarm

*Large swarm of Medium undead, chaotic evil*

**Armor Class:** 12

**Hit Points:** 67 (9d8 + 27)

**Speed:** 30 ft., climb 20 ft.

| STR | DEX | CON | INT | WIS | CHA |
|---|---|---|---|---|---|
| 13 (+1) | 14 (+2) | 16 (+3) | 6 (-2) | 10 (+0) | 5 (-3) |

**Damage Resistances:** bludgeoning, piercing, and slashing from nonmagical attacks

Damage Immunities: poison

**Condition Immunities:** charmed, exhaustion, frightened, paralyzed, petrified, poisoned, prone, restrained, stunned

**Senses:** darkvision 60 ft., passive Perception 10

**Languages:** understands the language of its creator but can't speak

**Challenge:** 4 (1,100 XP)

**Swarm.** The swarm can occupy another creature's space and vice versa, and the swarm can move through any opening large enough for a Medium humanoid.

**Swarming Bites.** The swarm can make a bite attack against any creature in its space. On a hit, the creature must succeed on a DC 15 Constitution saving throw or become poisoned for 1 minute and suffer 1d4+1 poison damage. The poisoned target can repeat the saving throw at the end of each of its turns, ending the effect on itself on a success.

## Actions

**Bites (Swarm has more than half HP).** *Melee Weapon Attack:* +5 to hit, reach 0 ft., one target in the swarm's space. *Hit:* 22 (4d10 + 2) piercing damage.

**Bites (Swarm has half HP or less).** *Melee Weapon Attack:* +5 to hit, reach 0 ft., one target in the swarm's space. *Hit:* 11 (2d10 + 2) piercing damage.

**Curse of the Eternal Dusk (Once per Day).** Any creature bitten by the swarm must make a DC 15 Constitution saving throw or start showing early symptoms of the Eternal Dusk curse.

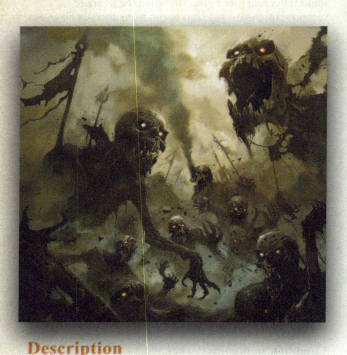

## Description

Ghoulscourge Swarms are a grotesque mass of decaying flesh, gnashing teeth, and clawing hands, moving as a single entity with a horrifying, undulating motion. Their eyes glow with a malevolent light, and their mouths are filled with rows of sharp, jagged teeth, eager to tear into flesh. The air around them is heavy with the stench of death and decay, making them not only a visual but also a visceral terror.

Created through necromancy by the Shadow Court, the Ghoulscourge Swarms serve as both instruments of terror and guardians against those who would oppose the Court's dominion. These undead minions are the remnants of villagers, adventurers, and any who fell prey to the Court's malice, reanimated to serve in death. Their existence is a grim reminder of the Shadow Court's power and cruelty, a tool used to break the spirit of those who might stand against the darkness that encroaches upon Ravenholme. Each ghoul within the

swarm is a tragic tale of life cut short, now bound to an eternal hunger that can never be sated.

# Nocturne Mist Bats

*Small beast, chaotic evil*

**Armor Class:** 13

**Hit Points:** 22 (5d6 + 5)

**Speed:** 10 ft., fly 60 ft.

| STR | DEX | CON | INT | WIS | CHA |
|-----|-----|-----|-----|-----|-----|
| 6 (-2) | 17 (+3) | 12 (+1) | 4 (-3) | 12 (+1) | 6 (-2) |

**Skills:** Stealth +5

**Damage Resistances:** bludgeoning, piercing, and slashing from nonmagical attacks

**Senses:** blindsight 60 ft., passive Perception 11

**Languages:** understands Common but can't speak

**Challenge:** 2 (450 XP)

**Echolocation.** The Nocturne Mist Bat can't use its blindsight while deafened.

**Keen Hearing.** The Nocturne Mist Bat has advantage on Wisdom (Perception) checks that rely on hearing.

**Mist Form.** As a bonus action, the bat can exude a magical mist in a 20-foot radius centered on itself. The area is heavily obscured for 1 minute or until a wind of moderate or greater speed (at least 10 miles per hour) disperses it. Creatures starting their turn in the mist must make a DC 16 Constitution saving throw or become disoriented, suffering disadvantage on attack rolls until the start of their next turn.

## Actions

**Bite.** *Melee Weapon Attack:* +5 to hit, reach 5 ft., one target. *Hit:* 6 (1d6 + 3) piercing damage.

**Curse Mist (Recharge 5–6).** The bat releases a curse-infused mist. Each creature in a 20-foot radius must make a DC 16 Constitution saving throw or begin to show early symptoms of the Eternal Dusk curse.

## Description

Nocturne Mist Bats are imposing creatures, with wingspans wide enough to wrap around an adult human. Their fur is an inky black, absorbing light rather than reflecting it, and their eyes gleam with an eerie, unnatural luminescence. When they unfurl their wings, the membrane appears almost translucent, tinged with shades of dark purple and blue, like the sky at the deepest point of twilight.

The lore of the Nocturne Mist Bats is as dark and mysterious as their appearance. Created by the Shadow

Court through forbidden rituals, these bats serve as guardians of the crypts and as heralds of despair. The Court's sorcerers imbued them with the ability to generate a magical mist, not only as a means of defense but also as a weapon to spread the curse of Eternal Dusk. Legends say that the bats were once ordinary creatures of the night, transformed by their exposure to the Court's dark magics into the sinister beings they are now. They are a symbol of the Court's reach and influence, able to bring confusion and fear to those who dare venture too close to their domain.

# Veilweaver

*Medium humanoid (human), neutral evil*

**Armor Class:** 12 (15 with *Mage Armor*)

**Hit Points:** 71 (11d8 + 22)

**Speed:** 30 ft.

| STR | DEX | CON | INT | WIS | CHA |
|-----|-----|-----|-----|-----|-----|
| 9 (-1) | 14 (+2) | 14 (+2) | 17 (+3) | 12 (+1) | 18 (+4) |

**Saving Throws:** Int +6, Wis +4

**Skills:** Arcana +6, Deception +7, Perception +4

**Damage Resistances:** psychic; bludgeoning, piercing, and slashing from nonmagical attacks

**Senses:** darkvision 60 ft., passive Perception 14

**Languages:** Common, Infernal

**Challenge:** 5 (1,800 XP)

**Spellcasting.** The Veilweaver is a 10th-level spellcaster. Its spellcasting ability is Charisma (spell save DC 15, +7 to hit with spell attacks). The Veilweaver has the following spells prepared:

- Cantrips (at will): *mage hand, minor illusion, prestidigitation*
- 1st level (4 slots): *charm person, disguise self, mage armor*
- 2nd level (3 slots): *mirror image, suggestion*
- 3rd level (3 slots): *fear, major image*
- 4th level (3 slots): *greater invisibility, phantasmal killer*
- 5th level (2 slots): *dominate person, mislead*

**Shadow Cloak.** As a bonus action, the Veilweaver can cloak itself in shadows, becoming invisible until the start of its next turn or until it attacks, casts a spell, or turns its concentration to another task.

## Actions

**Curse of Eternal Dusk.** *Ranged Spell Attack:* +7 to hit, range 60 ft., one target. *Hit:* The target must succeed on a DC 17 Wisdom saving throw or become cursed with Eternal Dusk.

## Description

Veilweavers are cloaked in layers of dark, flowing robes that seem to absorb the light around them. Their faces are often hidden behind masks or hoods, with only their eyes visible, glowing with a malevolent energy. Intricate sigils and symbols are embroidered into their garments, each a testament to their allegiance to the Shadow Court and their mastery over dark magic.

Veilweavers are not born but made, through a dark pact with the Shadow Court that grants them immense power at a great personal cost. They were once sorcerers and sorceresses of considerable skill, seeking knowledge and magic that lay beyond the moral boundaries of society. In their quest for power, they turned to the Shadow Court, offering their souls in exchange for forbidden secrets. Now, they serve as one of the Court's most insidious weapons, masters of illusion and manipulation. Their loyalty to the Court is absolute, driven by a combination of fear, ambition, and the intoxicating rush of dark magic that flows through their veins. To encounter a Veilweaver is to step into a world of shadows and deceit, where reality bends to their will and escape is a luxury few can afford.

# Non-Player Characters

## Elena the Wise

Elena the Wise exudes a timeless elegance, her silver hair flowing down her shoulders like a cascade of moonlight. Her eyes, a deep green, shine with the wisdom of centuries and the steadfast determination of one who has faced darkness and prevailed. Clothed in robes that seem woven from the very essence of the forest, adorned with ancient druidic symbols, she stands as a beacon of balance and harmony. Nature itself seems to bend to her will, with vines and leaves subtly shifting in her presence.

Elena's legend is intertwined with the fabric of Ravenholme itself. Once a respected member of the druid circle, she witnessed the corruption that led to the rise of the Shadow Court and took a stand to protect her home. Her successful sealing of the Court beneath the village cemented her status as a guardian of the balance between light and darkness.

After years of solitude, the weakening of the seals and the resurgence of dark forces have drawn Elena out of her reclusion. She now serves as a guide and mentor to those brave enough to stand against the encroaching evil, offering her knowledge, power, and the support of the natural world in their quest. Despite the losses she has endured, Elena's spirit remains unbroken, her commitment to protecting Ravenholme and the natural order unwavering. Her story is one of sacrifice, wisdom, and an undying hope for peace, serving as an inspiration to all who know of her deeds.

## Elena the Wise

*Medium humanoid (elf), neutral good*

**Armor Class:** 16 (natural armor)

**Hit Points:** 90 (12d8 + 36)

**Speed:** 30 ft.

| STR | DEX | CON | INT | WIS | CHA |
|-----|-----|-----|-----|-----|-----|
| 10 (0) | 14 (+2) | 16 (+3) | 13 (+1) | 20 (+5) | 18 (+4) |

**Saving Throws:** Int +5, Wis +9

**Skills:** Nature +9, Insight +9, Medicine +9, Perception +9, Survival +9

**Damage Resistances:** necrotic; bludgeoning, piercing and slashing damage from nonmagical attacks

**Condition Immunities:** charmed, frightened, poisoned

**Senses:** darkvision 60 ft., passive Perception 19

**Languages:** Common, Druidic, Elven

**Challenge:** 10 (5,900 XP)

**Spellcasting.** Elena is a 12th-level spellcaster. Her spellcasting ability is Wisdom (spell save DC 17, +9 to hit with spell attacks). Elena has the following druid spells prepared:

- Cantrips (at will): *druidcraft, guidance, produce flame*
- 1st level (4 slots): *cure wounds, entangle, speak with animals*
- 2nd level (3 slots): *moonbeam, silence, lesser restoration*
- 3rd level (3 slots): *protection from energy, dispel magic, plant growth*
- 4th level (3 slots): *freedom of movement, stone shape, grasping vine*
- 5th level (2 slots): *reincarnate, mass cure wounds*
- 6th level (1 slot): *sunbeam*

**Nature's Guardian.** Once per long rest, Elena can invoke the power of nature to cast the spell *Guardian of Nature* without expending a spell slot.

**Ancient Wisdom.** Elena has advantage on all Wisdom and Intelligence checks related to nature, the undead, and the history of Ravenholme.

### Actions

**Staff of the Forest Watcher.** *Melee Weapon Attack:* +5 to hit, reach 5 ft., one target. *Hit:* 8 (1d8 + 4) bludgeoning damage, or 9 (1d10 + 4) bludgeoning damage if used with two hands, plus 10 (3d6) radiant damage to undead.

# Gareth

Gareth's form is a tragic fusion of knightly valor and vampiric corruption. His once shining armor is now tarnished and etched with dark symbols of the Shadow Court, and his eyes glow with a cold, unnatural light. Shadows cling to him, whispering of his internal conflict and the souls he's unwillingly bound to his service. Despite his fearsome appearance, there's a lingering sadness in his posture, a remnant of the noble knight he once was.

Gareth's tale is one of heroism twisted into torment. A noble knight of Ravenholme, he swore to defend his home against all threats. His fall in battle against the Shadow Court marked not the end but a new, darker chapter in his existence. Resurrected by Killian's dark magics, he became a protector not of Ravenholme but of the Court that sought to corrupt it. Yet, within Gareth's cursed heart, a spark of his former self remains, fueling a secret rebellion against the darkness that consumes him. He harbors a desperate hope that he might find redemption or, failing that, a way to protect his home from within the shadows that now claim him.

In the Hall of Echoing Torment, Gareth commands the spirits of those sacrificed by the Court, a grim reminder of the fate he narrowly avoided. His presence in the hall serves both as a warden for these tormented souls and as a symbol of the Court's dominion over life and death. Yet, whispers of his internal struggle and glimpses of his once-noble intent have begun to spread, inspiring both fear and pity among those who know of him. To face Gareth is to confront the very essence of the Shadow Court's cruelty and the tragic price of resistance against overwhelming darkness.

## Gareth

**Armor Class:** 18 (plate armor)

**Hit Points:** 142 (15d10 + 60)

**Speed:** 30 ft.

| STR | DEX | CON | INT | WIS | CHA |
| --- | --- | --- | --- | --- | --- |
| 18 (+4) | 12 (+1) | 18 (+4) | 14 (+2) | 15 (+2) | 16 (+3) |

**Senses:** darkvision 60 ft., passive Perception 12

**Languages:** Common, Undercommon

**Challenge:** 9 (5,000 XP)

**Undying Loyalty.** Gareth has advantage on saving throws against being charmed or frightened.

**Shadow Step.** Once per turn, Gareth can teleport up to 30 feet to an unoccupied space he can see that is in dim light or darkness.

**Knight's Rebuke.** When Gareth takes damage from a creature within 5 feet of him, he can make a melee weapon attack against that creature as a reaction.

## Actions

**Multiattack.** Gareth makes two Longsword attacks.

**Longsword.** *Melee Weapon Attack:* +8 to hit, reach 5 ft., one target. *Hit:* 10 (1d8 + 4) slashing damage, or 11 (1d10 + 4) slashing damage if used with two hands, plus 4 (1d8) necrotic damage.

**Command the Fallen.** Gareth can summon 2d4 Carrion Marionettes as an action. These Marionettes act on their own initiative and obey Gareth's commands. They disappear after 1 minute or when destroyed.

## Legendary Actions

Gareth can take 3 legendary actions, choosing from the options below. Only one legendary action can be used at a time and only at the end of another creature's turn. Gareth regains spent legendary actions at the start of his turn.

- **Attack.** Gareth makes a Longsword attack.
- **Move.** Gareth moves up to half his speed without provoking opportunity attacks.
- **Inspire Fear (Costs 2 Actions).** Gareth targets one creature he can see within 30 feet. The target must succeed on a DC 16 Wisdom saving throw or be frightened for 1 minute.

# Killian

Killian, the Lord of the Shadow Court, is an imposing figure with an ageless, aristocratic beauty. His jet-black hair frames sharp features and piercing red eyes that hint at the power and bloodlust within. Dressed in dark cloaks and finely tailored suits, Killian embodies the allure and danger of his kind.

Born into nobility long before his embrace into vampirism, Killian's origins are lost to the mists of time. With immortality came a deepening darkness, and over centuries, he transformed into the formidable leader of the Shadow Court. His intelligence, charm, and mastery of the dark arts allowed him to expand his court, binding other vampires to his will.

One such vampire is Marcus, leader of the Whispering Night sect. In a fierce battle atop Barsea Heights, Killian, leading a band of feral vampires, encountered Marcus, then a mortal defender of the Whispering Night Castle. With Marcus at death's door, Killian offered him the dark gift of vampirism, which Marcus accepted. This act demonstrated Killian's philosophy: strength, cunning, and the willingness to embrace the darkness are what define survival. Though they seldom crossed paths in the following centuries, their bond would forever link them in the annals of vampiric legend.

# Killian

*Medium undead (vampire), lawful evil*

**Armor Class:** 18 (natural armor)

**Hit Points:** 180 (24d8 + 72)

**Speed:** 30 ft.

| STR | DEX | CON | INT | WIS | CHA |
|-----|-----|-----|-----|-----|-----|
| 20 (+5) | 18 (+4) | 16 (+3) | 20 (+5) | 16 (+3) | 22 (+6) |

**Saving Throws:** Dex +9, Wis +8, Cha +11

**Skills:** Arcana +10, Deception +11, Insight +8, Perception +8, Persuasion +11, Stealth +9

**Damage Resistances:** necrotic; bludgeoning, piercing, and slashing from nonmagical attacks

**Damage Immunities:** poison

**Condition Immunities:** charmed, exhaustion, frightened, paralyzed, poisoned

**Senses:** darkvision 120 ft., passive Perception 18

**Languages:** Common, Elven, Infernal

**Challenge:** 17 (18,000 XP)

**Legendary Resistance (3/Day).** If Killian fails a saving throw, he can choose to succeed instead.

**Misty Escape.** When Killian drops to 0 hit points outside his coffin, he transforms into a cloud of mist (as in the Shapechanger trait) instead of falling unconscious, provided he isn't in sunlight or running water. If he can't transform, he is destroyed.

**Regeneration.** Killian regains 20 hit points at the start of his turn if he has at least 1 hit point and isn't in sunlight or running water. If Killian takes radiant damage or damage from holy water, this trait doesn't function at the start of his next turn.

**Shapchanger.** If Killian isn't in sunlight or running water, he can use his action to polymorph into a Tiny bat or a Medium cloud of mist, or back into his true form.

**Spellcasting.** Killian is a 12th-level spellcaster. His spellcasting ability is Intelligence (spell save DC 18, +10 to hit with spell attacks). He has the following wizard spells prepared:

- Cantrips (at will): *mage hand, prestidigitation, ray of frost*
- 1st level (4 slots): *comprehend languages, mage armor, magic missile, shield*
- 2nd level (3 slots): *darkness, detect thoughts, gust of wind, mirror image*

- 3rd level (3 slots): *animate dead, counterspell, dispel magic, fireball*
- 4th level (3 slots): *blight, greater invisibility, polymorph*
- 5th level (2 slots): *dominate person, telekinesis*
- 6th level (1 slot): *disintegrate*

## Actions

**Multiattack.** Killian makes three attacks, only one of which can be a bite attack.

**Bite.** *Melee Weapon Attack:* +10 to hit, reach 5 ft., one willing creature, or a creature that is grappled by Killian, incapacitated, or restrained. Hit: 10 (1d10 + 5) piercing damage plus 14 (4d6) necrotic damage. The target's hit point maximum is reduced by an amount equal to the necrotic damage taken, and Killian regains hit points equal to that amount. The reduction lasts until the target finishes a long rest. The target dies if this effect reduces its hit point maximum to 0.

**Claws.** *Melee Weapon Attack:* +10 to hit, reach 5 ft., one target. *Hit:* 13 (2d6 + 6) slashing damage.

## Legendary Actions

Killian can take 3 legendary actions, choosing from the options below. Only one legendary action option can be used at a time and only at the end of another creature's turn. Killian regains spent legendary actions at the start of his turn.

**Move.** Killian moves up to his speed without provoking opportunity attacks.

**Bite (Costs 2 Actions).** Killian makes one bite attack.

**Dominate (Costs 3 Actions).** Killian casts Dominate Person without expending a spell slot.

# The Last Knight

The Last Knight stands as a spectral guardian, a noble warrior whose duty to protect the lands of the living continues even in death. Clad in the ethereal remnants of ancient armor and wielding a longsword that glows with a soft, otherworldly light, he exudes an aura of calm determination and unfaltering courage. His eyes, glowing faintly within the helm's shadows, survey his surroundings with a watchful gaze, ever vigilant against the encroaching darkness that once threatened his homeland.

In life, the Last Knight was a renowned defender of the realm, celebrated for his valor and unyielding spirit. As the Shadow Court's malevolence spread, he rallied the last of the kingdom's defenders in a desperate stand within the walls of Gauntlight Keep. Though they fought with unmatched bravery, the overwhelming forces of darkness eventually claimed their lives. Yet, in his final moments, the knight made a solemn vow before the gods to protect the realm from the spectral confines of death itself.

Bound to the ruins of Gauntlight Keep by his oath, the Last Knight's spirit has watched over the sigil-etched stone, a key to combating the darkness he fought so valiantly against. Tormented by the memory of his fallen comrades and the destruction of the keep, his resolve has never wavered. He waits for those brave enough to face the shadows, to bestow upon them the knowledge and power needed to restore balance and peace to a land still haunted by the past.

### The Last Knight

*Medium undead (ghost), lawful good*

**Armor Class:** 16 (ancient armor)

**Hit Points:** 68 (11d8 + 22)

**Speed:** 30 ft., fly 40 ft. (hover)

| STR | DEX | CON | INT | WIS | CHA |
|-----|-----|-----|-----|-----|-----|
| 16 (+3) | 11 (+0) | 14 (+2) | 12 (+1) | 15 (+2) | 18 (+4) |

**Saving Throws:** Wis +5, Cha +7

**Damage Resistances:** acid, fire, lightning, thunder; bludgeoning, piercing, and slashing from nonmagical attacks

**Damage Immunities:** cold, necrotic, poison, psychic

**Condition Immunities:** charmed, exhaustion, frightened, grappled, paralyzed, petrified, poisoned, prone, restrained

**Senses:** darkvision 60 ft., passive Perception 12

**Languages:** Common, Celestial

**Challenge:** 5 (1,800 XP)

**Ethereal Sight.** The Last Knight can see 60 feet into the Ethereal Plane when he is on the Material Plane, and vice versa. **Incorporeal Movement.** The Last Knight can move through other creatures and objects as if they were difficult terrain. He takes 5 (1d10) force damage if he ends his turn inside an object.

### Actions

**Multiattack.** The Last Knight makes two longsword attacks.

**Longsword.** *Melee Weapon Attack:* +6 to hit, reach 5 ft., one target. *Hit:* 8 (1d8 + 4) slashing damage, or 9 (1d10 + 4) slashing damage if used with two hands. Attacks with the longsword are considered magical.

**Ethereal Chains (Recharge 5–6).** The Last Knight summons spectral chains to bind a creature he can see within 30 feet of him. The target must succeed on a DC 15 Strength saving throw or be restrained for 1 minute.

The restrained target can use its action to make a DC 15 Strength check, breaking free on a success.

### Legendary Actions

The Last Knight can take 2 legendary actions, choosing from the options below. Only one legendary action option can be used at a time and only at the end of another creature's turn. The Last Knight regains spent legendary actions at the start of his turn.

**Attack.** The Last Knight makes one longsword attack.

**Command.** The Last Knight commands another undead creature within 60 feet of him that can hear it and is not currently engaged in combat to take an action it chooses.

**Ethereal Step (Costs 2 Actions).** The Last Knight enters the Ethereal Plane from the Material Plane, or vice versa.

# Marik the Cursed

Marik earned the epithet "the Cursed" long before his vampiric affliction, as his life in Ravenholme was marked by an extraordinary string of misfortunes, leading the villagers to ruefully note his seemingly endless bad luck. Throughout his life, Marik's endeavors were often met with ill fate; crops he tended inexplicably failed despite perfect conditions, and structures he helped build would often collapse in unforeseen accidents. Even more personally, any festive event he organized was almost guaranteed to be disrupted by sudden storms or unexplained mishaps, further cementing his unfortunate moniker among the villagers.

Marik the Cursed's appearance is a haunting amalgamation of his past life and his cursed existence.

His body, gaunt and pallid, moves with a spectral fluidity, cloaked in the remnants of what was once his village attire, now tattered and ethereal. His eyes, glowing with a supernatural luminescence, betray a depth of sorrow and longing for redemption. Shadows seem to gather around him, as if reluctant to fully embrace or release him from their grip.

Once a beloved figure of Ravenholme, Marik's transformation has become a sorrowful legend among the villagers. His existence as a ghast, caught between life and death, serves as a stark reminder of the Shadow Court's cruelty and the dangers lurking within the crypts. Despite his fearsome appearance, Marik harbors no ill will towards the living. His soul, still tethered to the goodness he embodied in life, compels him to seek redemption and to protect the innocent from the fate that yet befalls him. Marik's intimate knowledge of the Shadow Court and the crypts makes him an invaluable ally to those who dare to challenge the Court's reign of darkness. As he wanders the boundary between worlds, Marik clings to the hope that he might one day find peace and release from his cursed existence, either through his own actions or the aid of those brave enough to confront the Court. His story, a blend of tragedy and resolve, inspires both fear and compassion in the hearts of Ravenholme's inhabitants and the adventurers who cross his path.

## Marik the Cursed

*Medium undead (human), chaotic good*

**Armor Class:** 13

**Hit Points:** 82 (15d8 + 15)

**Speed:** 30 ft.

| STR | DEX | CON | INT | WIS | CHA |
|-----|-----|-----|-----|-----|-----|
| 16 (+3) | 15 (+2) | 12 (+1) | 10 (0) | 14 (+2) | 18 (+4) |

**Saving Throws:** Dex +5, Wis +5, Cha +7

**Skills:** Stealth +8, Persuasion +7

**Damage Resistances:** necrotic; bludgeoning, piercing, and slashing from nonmagical attacks

**Condition Immunities:** charmed, exhaustion, poisoned

**Senses:** darkvision 60 ft., passive Perception 12

**Languages:** Common

**Challenge:** 5 (1,800 XP)

**Undead Nature:** Marik doesn't require air, food, drink, or sleep.

### Actions

**Life-Draining Touch:** *Melee Weapon Attack:* +6 to hit, reach 5 ft., one target. *Hit:* 21 (4d8 + 3) necrotic damage. The target must succeed on a DC 15

Constitution saving throw or its hit point maximum is reduced by an amount equal to the damage taken. This reduction lasts until the target finishes a long rest. The target dies if this effect reduces its hit point maximum to 0.

**Redemption's Touch:** Marik can choose to heal instead of harm with his touch. As an action, he can touch a creature to provide healing energy, restoring 15 (2d8 + 6) hit points to the target.

**Sorrowful Gaze:** Marik can force one creature he can see within 30 feet to make a DC 15 Wisdom saving throw, becoming frightened for 1 minute on a failure. A creature can repeat the saving throw at the end of each of its turns, ending the effect on itself on a success. Once a creature succeeds on this saving throw, it is immune to Marik's Sorrowful Gaze for the next 24 hours.

# Seraphina

Seraphina stands as a vision of dark beauty, her form cloaked in robes that shimmer with the hues of twilight. Her eyes, once a vibrant green, now glow with a haunting purple light, mirroring the corrupted essence of the Daynight Stone she so covets. Ethereal shadows cling to her, dancing and twisting with her every movement, and her hands are adorned with intricate markings that pulse with dark energy. A shadow-touched dagger, its blade as dark as the night sky, rests easily in her grip, ready to defend her ambitions.

Once a revered member of the druidic circle, Seraphina's insatiable curiosity and desire for power led her down a path of darkness from which there was no return. Her betrayal of the circle and the corruption of the Daynight Stone mark a pivotal moment in the history of Ravenholme, turning her into one of the

Shadow Court's most dangerous assets. Yet, Seraphina's ambitions do not end with serving Killian's will. She believes that by unlocking the full potential of the Daynight Stone, she can ascend to a level of power that rivals, or even surpasses, that of her master. This drive for supremacy makes her both a valuable ally and a potential threat within the Court, as her actions often blur the line between loyalty and her own dark aspirations.

In the Chamber of Whispers, Seraphina conducts her experiments and divinations, seeking to unravel the secrets of the Daynight Stone. It is said that her voice can be heard in the whispers that fill the chamber, a seductive call to those who would join her in the pursuit of forbidden knowledge. However, to cross Seraphina is to invite a fate worse than death, for her mastery over enchantment and divination is matched only by her ruthlessness in dealing with those who stand in her way.

## Seraphina

*Medium undead (vampire), neutral evil*

**Armor Class:** 15 (natural armor)

**Hit Points:** 130 (20d8 + 40)

**Speed:** 30 ft.

| STR | DEX | CON | INT | WIS | CHA |
|-----|-----|-----|-----|-----|-----|
| 10 (+0) | 14 (+2) | 14 (+2) | 18 (+4) | 16 (+3) | 20 (+5) |

**Senses:** darkvision 120 ft., passive Perception 13

**Languages:** Common, Elven, Druidic, Undercommon

**Challenge:** 8 (3,900 XP)**Spellcasting.** Seraphina is a 12th-level spellcaster. Her spellcasting ability is Charisma (spell save DC 17, +9 to hit with spell attacks). Seraphina has the following spells prepared:

- Cantrips (at will): *mage hand, thaumaturgy, minor illusion*
- 1st-5th level (4 slots each): *charm person, detect magic, hold person, invisibility, counterspell, dispel magic, divination, dominate person*

**Daynight's Whisper.** Once per day, Seraphina can attempt to control a creature's actions by whispering dark secrets of the Daynight Stone. The target must succeed on a DC 17 Wisdom saving throw or be charmed for 24 hours.

**Eternal Dusk's Embrace.** Any creature that starts its turn within 30 feet of Seraphina must make a DC 15 Constitution saving throw, becoming infected with the Eternal Dusk curse on a failure as they begin to feel fatigued, suffering one level of exhaustion, and the light dims around them with the sudden critical stages of the curse. If a creature's saving throw is successful or if the curse is lifted from them, they are immune to Seraphina's Embrace for the next 24 hours.

## Actions

**Multiattack.** Seraphina can use her Frightful Presence. She then makes two attacks with her shadow-touched dagger.

**Shadow-Touched Dagger.** *Melee Weapon Attack:* +8 to hit, reach 5 ft., one target. *Hit:* 8 (1d6 + 5) piercing damage, plus 7 (2d6) necrotic damage.

**Frightful Presence.** Each creature of Seraphina's choice within 30 feet and aware of her must succeed on a DC 17 Wisdom saving throw or be frightened for 1 minute.

## Thorn

Thorn embodies the tragic fusion of undead and nature. His once vibrant green eyes now glow with a malevolent red hue, and his skin has taken on a pale, almost luminescent quality. Vines and thorns wrap around his arms and legs, moving with a life of their own, while his attire blends seamlessly with the natural surroundings of his domain. Thorn's presence is both beautiful and terrifying, a stark reminder of his fall from grace.

Thorn was once revered as a guardian of the Mourning Moors, a druid of unmatched connection to the earth and its creatures. However, his defiance against the Shadow Court's corruptive influence led to his downfall. Overpowered and transformed into a being he once swore to fight against, Thorn's innate bond with nature was twisted into a tool of subjugation and decay.

Now, as a key enforcer of the Shadow Court, he seeks not only to expand the Mourning Moors but to turn it into a stronghold for dark forces, transforming it into a reflection of the Court's power. His mastery over nature has become a weapon of fear, his control over plant life used to ensnare and weaken the Court's enemies. Despite his transformation, whispers of Thorn's inner turmoil occasionally surface, suggesting a battle between his remaining druidic honor and the vampiric curse that now defines his existence. His sanctum, located in the Vestibule of Shadows, serves as a dark mirror to the vibrant groves he once protected. Here, Thorn conducts rituals to strengthen the Court's hold over the land, using his deep knowledge of druidic magic for malevolent purposes.

Yet, beneath his loyalty to Killian and the Court, there are rumors that Thorn's heart is not entirely lost to darkness. Some say that in moments of solitude, he can be found speaking to the plants and animals of the moor as if seeking forgiveness for the unnatural blight he has brought upon them. It's whispered among those who dare oppose the Shadow Court that if Thorn could be reminded of his original purpose, or if the corruption within him could be purged, he might become a powerful ally in the fight to restore balance to Ravenholme.

However, as long as the Shadow Court's influence remains strong, Thorn is a formidable foe. His abilities to manipulate nature, command the undead, and his unwavering loyalty to the Court make him a key target for anyone brave enough to challenge the vampires' reign. The battle to free Thorn from his curse is not just a fight against a powerful vampire but a struggle to reclaim a piece of the land's lost purity and a reminder of the cost of the Court's ambition.

## Thorn

*Medium undead (vampire), neutral evil*

**Armor Class:** 16 (natural armor)

**Hit Points:** 136 (16d8 + 64)

**Speed:** 30 ft., climb 20 ft.

| STR | DEX | CON | INT | WIS | CHA |
|-----|-----|-----|-----|-----|-----|
| 18 (+4) | 14 (+2) | 18 (+4) | 12 (+1) | 17 (+3) | 15 (+2) |

**Saving Throws:** Dex +6, Wis +7, Cha +6

**Skills:** Nature +5, Stealth +6, Survival +7

**Damage Resistances:** necrotic; bludgeoning, piercing, and slashing from nonmagical attacks that aren't silvered

**Senses:** darkvision 120 ft., passive Perception 13

**Languages:** Common, Druidic

**Challenge:** 10 (5,900 XP)

**Shapechanger.** Thorn can use his action to transform into a bat or wolf, or back into his true form.

**Legendary Resistance (2/Day).** If Thorn fails a saving throw, he can choose to succeed instead.

**Regeneration.** Thorn regains 10 hit points at the start of his turn if he has at least 1 hit point.

**Spellcasting.** Thorn is a 10th-level spellcaster. His spellcasting ability is Wisdom (spell save DC 15, +7 to hit with spell attacks). Thorn has the following druid spells prepared:

- Cantrips (at will): *druidcraft, thorn whip, produce flame*
- 1st level (4 slots): *entangle, speak with animals*
- 2nd level (3 slots): *moonbeam, barkskin*
- 3rd level (3 slots): *plant growth, wind wall*
- 4th level (3 slots): *dominate beast, grasping vine*
- 5th level (2 slots): *reincarnate, awaken (only usable in his sanctum)*

## Actions

**Multiattack.** Thorn makes two attacks: one with his bite and one with his claws or Thorn Whip.

**Bite (Vampire Form Only).** *Melee Weapon Attack:* +8 to hit, reach 5 ft., one target. *Hit:* 7 (1d6 + 4) piercing damage plus 7 (2d6) necrotic damage. The target's hit point maximum is reduced by an amount equal to the necrotic damage taken, and Thorn regains hit points equal to that amount.

**Claws.** *Melee Weapon Attack:* +8 to hit, reach 5 ft., one target. *Hit:* 8 (1d8 + 4) slashing damage. If the target is a creature, it must succeed on a DC 16 Strength saving throw or be knocked prone.

**Thorn Whip.** *Melee Spell Attack:* +7 to hit, range 30 ft., one target. *Hit:* 10 (2d6 + 3) piercing damage, and Thorn can pull the creature up to 10 feet closer to him.

# Magic Items

## Daynight Stone

*Wondrous item, rare (requires attunement)*

This ancient, luminescent stone is roughly the size of a fist, pulsating with a light that seems to mimic the phases of the moon. Encased in a delicate silver setting that allows it to be worn as a pendant or affixed to a staff, the Daynight Stone is a powerful artifact deeply connected to the natural cycles of the world. Its surface is cool to the touch, with an ethereal glow that fluctuates gently, casting soft light in a small radius.

**Properties**:

- **Lunar Illumination**: While attuned to the Daynight Stone, the bearer can use an action to cause the stone to emit bright light in a 20-foot radius and dim light for an additional 20 feet. This light can be extinguished or reignited as a bonus action.

- **Moonbeam**: The attuned bearer can cast the *Moonbeam* spell (2nd level) once per day without expending a spell slot. The spell save DC for this effect is 15.

- **Balance of Day and Night**: The attuned bearer gains advantage on saving throws against being charmed or frightened during the night and resistance to necrotic damage. During the day, they gain resistance to radiant damage.

- **Calm Emotions**: Once per day, the attuned bearer can cast the *Calm Emotions* spell without expending a spell slot or material components. The spell save DC is 15.

- **Blessings of the Moors**: When used in a ritual to restore balance to nature or counteract dark magic, the Daynight Stone grants a +1 bonus to Arcana, Nature, and Religion checks made as part of the ritual by the attuned bearer and their allies within 30 feet.

**Attunement**: Yes. To attune to the Daynight Stone, one must meditate with it under the open sky beneath the moon, allowing its light to align with the bearer's spirit.

**History**: The Daynight Stone is an artifact of ancient origin, believed to have been created by a coalition of druids and celestial mages during a period of great turmoil. The world was threatened by an unnatural eternal darkness, a consequence of the Shadow Court's first rise to power, which sought to disrupt the natural order and extend their dominion indefinitely.

These druids and mages, guardians of the balance between the natural and supernatural, convened at a site where the veil between the material world and the celestial planes was thin. Under a rare convergence of celestial bodies, they combined their magic and knowledge to create the Daynight Stone, infusing it with the essence of the moon's cycle. This essence was meant to symbolize and enforce the natural balance between day and night, light and darkness, and life and death.

Once the stone was created, it was used in a grand ritual performed at the heart of the Mourning Moors, a location selected for its strong ley lines and proximity to the Shadow Court's then-stronghold. The ritual succeeded in dispersing the unnatural darkness, weakening the Shadow Court, and restoring the cycle of day and night.

Over the centuries, the Daynight Stone faded into legend. It was only recently, during the events leading up to the current struggle against the Shadow Court's resurgence, that information about the location of Daynight Stone was found. According to rumor, the stone is believed to be in a forgotten crypt, guarded by remnants of the court and corrupted nature spirits.

## Elixir of Lucidity

*Wondrous item, uncommon*

This iridescent elixir shimmers with a spectral light, contained within a delicately etched phial. The liquid appears to swirl with an inner luminescence, casting faint, dancing lights on its surroundings. Crafted through a blend of rare herbs, purified water from a moonlit spring, and a drop of blood from a willing fey creature, this potion is a marvel of alchemical and druidic collaboration.

**Properties**: Upon drinking the Elixir of Lucidity, for the next 24 hours, the consumer gains the following benefits:

- **Clarity of Mind**: Advantage on saving throws against being charmed or frightened.

- **Enhanced Perception**: Gain a +2 bonus to Perception checks.

- **Resistance to Necrotic Damage**: Gain resistance to necrotic damage, reflecting the elixir's protective qualities against dark magic and curses.

Additionally, for individuals suffering under curses that affect the mind or body (including early stages of vampirism or lycanthropy), the elixir temporarily halts the curse's progression, staving off its effects for 24 hours. This does not cure the curse but can provide critical time to seek a permanent solution.

**Attunement**: No attunement required. The Elixir of Lucidity is effective immediately upon consumption and can be used by anyone, though its rarity makes it a precious commodity in regions plagued by dark curses and enchantments.

# Game Within a Game

## Whispers of the Shadow Court

### Objective

Players must gather clues to uncover a secret plot within the Shadow Court without alerting the attention of its members.

### Setup

Players: 2-6

Materials Needed:

- A deck of cards representing the Court's members, each marked with different symbols or colors.

- A set of clue cards that hint at the plot or secrets within the Shadow Court.

- Tokens or markers to represent each player's suspicion level.

### Game Play

**Preparation:** Shuffle the Court member cards and deal three to each player. Shuffle the clue cards and place them in a stack face down in the center of the table.

**Turn Sequence:**

- **Draw:** Each player starts their turn by drawing a clue card from the deck.

- **Action:** Players have two choices for their action:

- **Investigate:** Attempt to match the clue with one of their Court member cards. If the symbols or colors match, they can reveal the clue, gaining a piece of information towards solving the plot. Successfully matching reduces their suspicion level by one.

- **Accuse:** Players may accuse another of being too involved with the Shadow Court. They choose another player to challenge by guessing one of their Court member cards. If they guess correctly, the accused must reveal all their cards, increasing their suspicion level. If the guess is wrong, the accuser increases their own suspicion level.

- **Pass:** After acting, the player passes a Court member card secretly to the player on their left.

**End Game Trigger:** The game ends when the clue cards are depleted or when a player reaches a predetermined suspicion threshold, which triggers a Court crackdown.

**Winning:** Players win by collectively uncovering all parts of the plot through clue cards without any player being caught by reaching high suspicion. If a player's suspicion becomes too high, they are 'caught' by the Court, and all players lose unless they can finish decoding the plot on the same turn.

### Suspicion Meter

Each player has a suspicion meter starting at zero. Certain actions in the game, like unsuccessful accusations or being accused, can increase a player's suspicion. Higher suspicion levels make it riskier to continue holding certain Court cards.

### Thematic Integration

The game mimics the subterfuge and secretive nature of the Shadow Court, encouraging players to strategize and cooperate subtly. The element of secrecy and the risk of being discovered add tension and excitement, reflecting the atmosphere of the Crypts of the Shadow Court.

Whispers of the Shadow Court serves as both a thematic extension of the main game and a standalone challenge that can help develop the players' understanding of the Shadow Court's dynamics. This mini-game can be initiated during downtime or when players are resting in a safe location within the game world.

# Food and Fuel

## Shadow Court Stew

### Ingredients

- 2 lbs beef stew meat, cut into 1-inch cubes
- 2 tablespoons olive oil
- 3 large carrots, peeled and sliced
- 2 medium onions, chopped
- 4 cloves garlic, minced
- 3 medium potatoes, peeled and diced
- 4 cups beef broth
- 1 cup red wine (optional)
- 2 teaspoons dried thyme
- 1 teaspoon dried rosemary
- 1 bay leaf
- Salt and pepper to taste
- 1 cup frozen peas
- 2 tablespoons cornstarch (optional for thickening)
- 2 tablespoons water

### Instructions

**Brown the Meat:** Heat the olive oil in a large pot over medium-high heat. Add the beef cubes and brown on all sides, about 5-7 minutes. Remove the beef and set aside.

**Sauté Vegetables:** In the same pot, add the onions and carrots. Cook until the onions are translucent and the carrots begin to soften, about 5 minutes. Add the garlic and cook for another minute until fragrant.

**Simmer the Stew:** Return the beef to the pot. Add the potatoes, beef broth, red wine (if using), thyme, rosemary, bay leaf, salt, and pepper. Bring to a boil, then reduce the heat to low and cover. Let simmer for about 1.5 hours, or until the beef is tender.

**Final Touches:** Add the frozen peas to the stew and cook for an additional 10 minutes. If a thicker stew is desired, mix cornstarch with water and stir into the stew. Allow to simmer for another 5-10 minutes until thickened.

**Serve:** Remove the bay leaf and serve the stew hot, perhaps with a side of crusty bread to soak up the broth.

## Midnight Shadow Cooler

### Ingredients

- Blackberry syrup (for deep color and sweetness)
- Fresh lime juice (for tartness)
- Club soda (for fizz)
- Crushed ice
- Fresh blackberries and mint leaves (for garnish)

### Instructions

**Prepare the Glass:** Chill a tall glass in the freezer to enhance the refreshing experience.

**Layer the Flavors:** In the chilled glass, pour 1 oz of blackberry syrup. Add 2 oz of fresh lime juice.

**Add Ice:** Fill the glass with crushed ice, almost to the top.

**Top with Club Soda:** Gently pour club soda over the ice until the glass is full. The soda will mix slightly with the blackberry syrup, creating a gradient effect that resembles the shadowy depths of the crypts.

**Garnish:** Skewer a few fresh blackberries on a cocktail stick and place it atop the drink. Add a sprig of mint for a fresh aroma and a touch of green, reminiscent of the eerie glow from mystical spells.

**Serving Suggestion:** Stir gently before drinking to combine the layers into a delightful, shadowy mixture.

# Map